Beyond Enkription

The Burlington Files

Bill Fairclough

Legal Notices

All characters in this publication are fictional or fictitious and any similarity or resemblance to real persons, living or dead is purely coincidental, not intended and should not be inferred. While as in all fiction, the literary perceptions and insights are loosely based on experience, all names, characters, places, situations and incidents are either products of the author's imagination or are used fictitiously.

Copyright © 2014 The Burlington Files Limited
All rights reserved.

ISBN: 1497314186
ISBN 13: 9781497314184
Library of Congress Control Number: 2014906166
CreateSpace Independent Publishing Platform
North Charleston, South Carolina

Introduction, The Author & The Series

Bill Fairclough is the author of this book and The Burlington Files series. He was born in England in 1950. In the early seventies Bill qualified as a Chartered Accountant. By 1978 he founded a niche global intelligence agency known as "Faire Sans Dire". Since then that organisation has operated under many guises, as has the author.

In 2012 Faire Sans Dire published its first ever press release to its clients which outlined the cyber-issues at the heart of the Edward Snowden spy saga. Over a year later the world's media latched on to Edward Snowden's flight to "freedom" or escape from justice depending upon your point of view. Since then those cyber-issues have been debated around the world and many laws and practices have been or will be changed.

Apart from running Faire Sans Dire for well over thirty years, Bill has also worked as a bean counter in both practice and industry. During his career he has been a director and executive of several well known international businesses. He's trod on the tails of many a fat cat and despatched some household name villains over the decades.

This book and indeed the series are loosely based on some of Bill's and his former associates' experiences while involved with the Burlington family for many years. Notwithstanding that, please refer to our legal notices.

Beyond Enkription is the first tome Bill has written in the series, The Burlington Files. The series is about the Burlington family and their ubiquitous relationships with state backed intelligence agencies over many decades. The series covers events involving the Burlington family ranging from the First World War to 9/11 and the related Nisha incidents and beyond.

Our story starts in 1974 and is loosely based on authentic events and characters some of which rocked and shocked the contemporary establishment. There is no way we could make this stuff up unless we were on weed or worse! You can sigh with relief though. There won't be one book published for each year since 1974.

The discerning landed gentry might call this book a novel. Connoisseurs might call it an old fashioned journal. The less polite hoi polloi might conjure up more disrespectful descriptions. If pushed, we might irreverently describe it as a "novelog", a novel and weblog wrapped as one, rather like a diary about a fish and chip takeaway but without too much salt and vinegar to keep it all tasteful.

You may find it is a tad like reading a TV series about a dynastic family such as the feuding Ewings in Dallas. There are two differences though. This book is about intrigue and duplicity in the world of espionage and primarily based on actual diaries of real people and newspaper clippings. Being based on diaries and newspaper articles the book is a trifle episodic but that's life.

Of course, we could have padded it inside out, like Dallas or Sherlock Holmes, with family reunions, birthday parties, weddings and funerals as well as the mandatory resurrection of characters long presumed dead. We didn't. It would have become repetitious like the lives of some of us whose main purpose in reading is to escape such quotidian boredom.

The book includes obtuse information already in the public domain and secrets exhumed from underneath long forgotten tombstones. In their prime, a few members of the Burlingtons were household names in Anglo-American and opposing intelligence agency circles. Other family members spent most of their lives hiding behind a parliament of pseudonyms, spurning any form of recognition, honours or medals.

The first book should be illuminating for most readers as we have all shared life in the ordinary world the Burlingtons inhabited. It's just that we may have missed the sinister world in the floors below and above the one we live on. In any event, you will be served up an intriguing insight into the truly tortuous goings on inside intelligence agencies.

That insight remains relevant today. There will always be traitors, double agents, informants and whistle blowers. Just think of Edward Snowden in 2013. Most of those descriptions, and worse besides, have been attributed to him after his revelations about modern day espionage. Maybe the most telling open secrets about Mr Snowden are that despite being a US citizen working on NSA secrets he did a runner to China then Russia of all places and accepted honours in Russia, Germany and elsewhere. Determining his motivation may not be quite as simple as he would have you believe. Maybe he is the real thing: tinker, traitor, thief and spy. After all, he's admitted to the first three!

For all we know you may look upon the likes of Snowden as heroes or traitors. So be it. This book and the rest of the series show how hard it is to distinguish between good and evil, rapscallions and traitors. It is a grey world with too many shades to tot up.

More Information

For more information about the author, The Burlington Files or Beyond Enkription please visit FaireSansDire.Org and TheBurlingtonFiles.Org. We can only apologise if the websites have been closed down by the authorities. They were up and running when we went to print.

Preface

Before we kick off, a smidgeon of background information might be helpful. Realistic espionage novels, intriguing ones in particular, have much written in between the lines. Like Agatha Christie novels you can kick yourself once you realise you should have spotted the villain several chapters earlier. Beyond Enkription is no exception.

While on the subject of exceptions, when you are reading Beyond Enkription and you think this is unbelievable clap trap then that's when in truth it was almost certainly based on real events. You can even Google some of the events but do bear in mind all our legal warnings and caveats. What you may find via the web, hearsay or some other source may contradict what is written in this novel which is fiction: It is not true, it is imaginary.

It's also worth keeping an eye out on what's going on between the lines. The real story may be a diversionary tactic to distract you, mere disinformation, and just like the spelling of Enkription, we didn't get it wrong!

For those who don't know their MI5s from their MI6s, and even for those of you who believe you do, our brief prologue is mandatory reading. You'll avoid misunderstandings or missing points that might lead to disappointment later. Once you've read that it should be plain sailing, although we do recommend you wear a bullet proof life jacket at all times.

Also, as we do in real life, follow our ABC code when reading this and the other books in the series and you won't go astray.

Assume nothing.
Believe nobody.
Check everything.

The ABC code originated from the Flying Squad but others, MI5 included, appear to claim it was their concept as do many authors.

In a series spread over several decades a seemingly insignificant event could have a butterfly effect. A trivial incident might deter an atrocity worse than 9/11 a decade later. A new born baby might turn into a terrorist or vigilante within twenty or so years. Or a boring young man lurking in the shadows might save hundreds of thousands of lives and yet remain an unsung hero.

On the subject of unsung heroes, Edward Burlington takes centre stage in the series. It goes without saying that other characters may therefore appear to spend too much time focusing on what Edward does. Instead they might have done better to focus on what is missing, what they don't know he is up to, but the obvious can be deceptive and in this series often is. Also, watch how, when and why they are focusing and remember, self-interest and survival are natural human penchants.

Most of those Edward associates with are perfidious, scheming and crafty manipulators. Some are even double-crossing double agents. So get someone to watch your back when reading this. Few who associate with Edward are as generous or altruistic as him by many a long mile.

Our diarised saga, a year in the life of the Burlington family, kicks off on 5th March 1974. Harold Wilson has been Prime Minister for only twenty four hours and Alvin Stardust's "Jealous mind" is number one in the UK singles hit parade. President Nixon is still in office, but Watergate is looming and Terry Jacks' "Seasons in the sun" is topping the US billboard. It's no coincidence that 5th March was one of the Burlington's birthdays but for the sake of identity theft minimisation we won't say more.

Now, if you're too young to remember 1974, Abba didn't have a number one hit until 6th April when they won the Eurovision Song Contest with "Waterloo". The timing had nothing to do with UK tax planning as they lived in Sweden. If you are too young to have heard of Abba email your history teacher and demand a refund. Even James Bond films hadn't debuted on TV by then. Some might say thank heavens!

In 1974 today's electronically integrated world was only just evolving. Computers were not household items, the internet was many years away from creation, handheld cell phones weighed nearly three pounds and few cars apart from upmarket taxis had telephones installed.

Later that year India will become a nuclear power. Lynden Pindling will enjoy his first anniversary as Prime Minister of the Bahamas despite having failed to sell off all the islands by then. West Germany will beat Holland to win the World Cup. For those English supporters reading, handkerchiefs may be necessary as England didn't even qualify but Haiti and Scotland did.

The Rumble in the Jungle will take place in Kinshasa and Muhammad Ali will knock out George Foreman. Luckner Cambronne, the vampire of the Caribbean, will sell tens of thousands of body parts to hospitals and universities in the USA. On a lighter note in the USA, ignoring Ronald DeFeo's atrocities in Amityville on Long Island, former Beatle John Lennon will join Elton John for a rare Thanksgiving performance in Madison Square Garden.

However, for those who populated the grey world in which the Burlingtons lived, their hushed headlines were to be dominated by less glamorous events in 1974. Unpublicised diplomatic and political scandals, obloquy in the public domain such as Watergate and terrorism featured. As the Libyan backed Irish Independent

Preface

Republican Army, the IRA, stepped up their bombing campaign on mainland Britain fears of nuclear proliferation and global terrorism increased.

Now let's move onward to the prologue. If you plan on understanding this book then reading the prologue is a must but we won't ask you to sit an exam afterwards. If part way through the book you find this saga episodic fear not. This novelog is not exclusively based on diaries. We have had to reconstruct quite a lot of what presumably took place where access to records, newspaper archives and diaries proved impossible for understandable reasons. However, much has been taken from diaries and pretending to be good journalists we wanted to stick to the basics rather than sex up what the Burlingtons did.

The problem with diaries is they are intervallic by nature and often contain contradictions even if reporting the same incident. By way of simple illustration, one man's gain is another's loss. Seemingly disconnected events may be easily connected later in time. It goes without saying the truth can often become barely discernible once several diaries and newspaper cuttings are scrutinised simultaneously.

Nevertheless we have tried to faithfully adhere to the Burlingtons' diaries throughout 1974, rather than re-arrange events to sensationalise the saga. Thus you can label this book any which way you choose: fiction or nonfiction, novel or family biography, history or diary, chronicle or novelog. We don't mind one iota. As the literary critic you'll be right whatever you choose. We just call it a family saga.

If you want to return to an earlier chapter in the saga to revisit a diarised episode you mistakenly thought you understood we've made it easy peasy lemon squeezy for you. There's a detailed list of the contents to help guide you through this tortuous maze of this particular year in the lives of the Burlington family.

So, bear with the seeming monotony and simplicity of the location descriptions in the index. It's intentional. You can watch them flick by on our website, as if sitting aboard a train, if it hasn't been derailed by the CIA or GCHQ or a counter-espionage agency in some faraway place. Anyway, there's no need to study or even bother reading the index now so you can skip it. You won't gain an edge or be able to guess the plots by scrutinising it.

Do pace yourself for your journey through the book though. We don't want you to be derailed too or become part of a slow motion train wreck and have to return to the beginning. Mind you, if you're fascinated by it or like it so much, you may want to read it more than once. We have tried to make every word count including the little ones!

Contents

Prologue · 1

Chapter 1 - Tuesday 5th March · 13
Wimpole Street Marylebone, London England · 13

Chapter 2 - Tuesday 5th March · 20
Harley Street Marylebone, London England · 20

Chapter 3 - Tuesday 5th March · 28
Harley Street Marylebone, London England · 28
George Street Marylebone, London England · 35
Westminster Bridge Road Lambeth, London England · 37

Chapter 4 - Wednesday 6th March · 39
Scotland Yard Victoria, London England · 39
Church Hill Carshalton, Surrey England · 42
Scotland Yard Victoria, London England · 43
Caledonian Road Islington, London England · 45
Lingwala, Kinshasa Congo · 45
Scotland Yard Victoria, London England · 47

Chapter 5 - Thursday 11th April · 51
London England, Kinshasa Congo & Antwerp Belgium · 51
De Wallen, Amsterdam Holland · 52
North Shields & Newcastle, Tyne & Wear England · 53
Jesmond Newcastle, Tyne and Wear England · 55
Whitley Bay, Tyne and Wear England · 60

Chapter 6 - Friday 12ᵗʰ April · 61
The West End, London England · 61
The North of England & Ijmuiden Holland · 65

Chapter 7 - Friday 12ᵗʰ April · 66
The Downs Epsom, Surrey England · 66

Chapter 8 - Friday 12ᵗʰ April · 77
Montagu Square Marylebone, London England · 77
St Paul's Church Yard, The City of London England · · · · · · · · · · · · · · · · · · · 79
Abingdon Street Westminster, London England · 84

Chapter 9 - Friday 12ᵗʰ April · 88
Abingdon Street Westminster, London England · 88

Chapter 10 - Friday 12ᵗʰ April · 102
St Paul's Church Yard, The City of London England · · · · · · · · · · · · · · · · · · 102
Montagu Square Marylebone, London England · 103
Rupert Street Soho, London England · 109
Montagu Square Marylebone, London England · 114

Chapter 11 - Friday 3ʳᵈ May · 117
Duke Street St James's, London England · 117
Montagu Square Marylebone, London England · 119
Duke Street St James's, London England · 119
St Paul's Church Yard, The City of London England · · · · · · · · · · · · · · · · · · 120
Duke Street St James's, London England · 121

Chapter 12 - Friday 3ʳᵈ May · 125
Duke Street St James's & The West End, London England · · · · · · · · · · · · · 125
St Paul's Church Yard, The City of London England · · · · · · · · · · · · · · · · · · 128
Westminster Bridge Road Lambeth, London England · · · · · · · · · · · · · · · · 128
Heathrow Airport Hillingdon, London England · 134

Chapter 13 - Saturday 4ᵗʰ May · 138
Praed Street Paddington, London England · 138
Abingdon Street Westminster, London England · 141
Montagu Square Marylebone, London England · 142
Westminster Bridge Road Lambeth, London England · · · · · · · · · · · · · · · · 145

Contents

Chapter 14 - Monday 20th May ··········· 150
Westminster Bridge Road Lambeth, London England ··········· 150
The Strand Westminster, London England ··········· 154

Chapter 15 - Saturday 8th June ··········· 165
Montagu Square Marylebone, London England ··········· 165
Magdala Avenue Islington, London England ··········· 168

Chapter 16 - Monday 10th June ··········· 177
De Wallen, Amsterdam Holland ··········· 177
Montagu Square Marylebone, London England ··········· 181
Lambeth Palace Road Lambeth, London England ··········· 184
Westminster Bridge Road Lambeth, London England ··········· 186

Chapter 17 - Monday 17th June ··········· 189
Abingdon Street Westminster, London England ··········· 189
La Gare du Nord, Paris France ··········· 189
Jamaica Road Bermondsey, London England ··········· 190
Magdala Avenue Islington, London England ··········· 195

Chapter 18 - Thursday 20th & Friday 21st June ··········· 201
Kings Cross Camden & Albany Street Regents Park, London England ··········· 201
Magdala Avenue Islington, London England ··········· 204
Montagu Square Marylebone, London England ··········· 206

Chapter 19 - Friday 21st June ··········· 210
Magdala Avenue Islington, London England ··········· 210

Chapter 20 - Friday 21st to Sunday 30th June ··········· 222
Albany Street Regents Park, London England ··········· 222
Beachy Head, East Sussex England ··········· 223
The Downs Epsom, Surrey England ··········· 224
Jamaica Road Bermondsey, London England ··········· 227
Westminster Bridge Road Lambeth, London England ··········· 228
Heathrow Airport Hillingdon, London England ··········· 229

Chapter 21 - Sunday 30th June to Monday 1st July ··········· 232
West Bay Street Nassau, New Providence Island Bahamas ··········· 232
Bay Street Nassau, New Providence Island Bahamas ··········· 233

Chapter 22 - Monday 1ˢᵗ to Wednesday 17ᵗʰ July · 242
Delancey Street Nassau, New Providence Island Bahamas · · · · · · · · · · · · · · · · · · · 242
New Providence & Paradise Islands Bahamas · 243
Central Park Manhattan, New York USA · 247
West Bay Street Nassau, New Providence Island Bahamas · · · · · · · · · · · · · · · · · · 249

Chapter 23 - Wednesday 17ᵗʰ July · 251
The Burlington Bunker Corsham, Wiltshire England · 251
Parliament Street Westminster, London England · 256

Chapter 24 - Friday 19ᵗʰ to Saturday 27ᵗʰ July · 261
Copacabana Beach, Rio de Janeiro Brazil · 261
New Providence & Paradise Islands Bahamas · 270

Chapter 25 - Sunday 28ᵗʰ July to Thursday 1ˢᵗ August · 275
Oakville, Toronto Canada · 275
Niagara Falls, Canada & USA · 276
The South Side & Downtown Chicago, Illinois USA · 277
West Bay Street Nassau, New Providence Island Bahamas · · · · · · · · · · · · · · · · · · 279

Chapter 26 - Thursday 1ˢᵗ August to Monday 23ʳᵈ September · · · · · · · · · · · · · · · · 281
Bay Street Nassau, New Providence Island Bahamas · 281

Chapter 27 - Wednesday 25ᵗʰ September · 287
London Road Royal Tunbridge Wells, Kent England · 287

Chapter 28 - Thursday 3ʳᵈ October to Monday 4ᵗʰ November · · · · · · · · · · · · · · · · 297
Bay Street Nassau, New Providence Island Bahamas · 297
Las Olas Fort Lauderdale, Florida USA · 299
Bay Street Nassau, New Providence Island Bahamas · 300
Lyford Cay, New Providence Island Bahamas · 301
Bay Street Area Nassau, New Providence Island Bahamas · · · · · · · · · · · · · · · · · · 303
West Bay Street Nassau, New Providence Island Bahamas · · · · · · · · · · · · · · · · · · 307

Chapter 29 - Thursday 7ᵗʰ to Tuesday 12ᵗʰ November · 310
Westminster Bridge Road Lambeth, London England · 310

Contents

Chapter 30 - Wednesday 13th to Saturday 16th November · · · · · · · · · · · · · · · · · · 318
Charing Cross Road Westminster & The West End, London · · · · · · · · · · · · · 318
Ngaliema, Kinshasa Congo · 319
Cabinda Airport, Cabinda Congo · 320
Lingwala & Centre Ville, Kinshasa Congo · 321
Westminster Bridge Road Lambeth, London England · · · · · · · · · · · · · · · · · · 330

Chapter 31 - Monday 18th to Friday 22nd November · 333
Shirley Street Nassau, New Providence Island Bahamas · · · · · · · · · · · · · · · · · 333
Grand Turk, Turks & Caicos Islands · 336
Arcahaie, Ouest Haiti · 339
Menetas, Ouest Haiti · 340

Chapter 32 - Friday 22nd November to Wednesday 11th December · · · · · · · · · · · 341
Rue de Chilli Saint Gerard, Port-au-Prince Haiti · 341
Avenue Lamartiniere Nazon, Port-au-Prince Haiti · 345
Rue de Chilli Saint Gerard, Port-au-Prince Haiti · 347

Chapter 33 - Thursday 12th & Friday 13th December · 350
Rue de Chilli Saint Gerard, Port-au-Prince Haiti · 350
Rue Sans Fil Bel Air, Port-au-Prince Haiti · 351
Route Soleil Cite Soleil & Downtown, Port-au-Prince Haiti · · · · · · · · · · · · · · 353
Duvalier International Airport Delmas, Port-au-Prince Haiti · · · · · · · · · · · · · 356
The Civic Center Miami, Florida USA · 361

Chapter 34 - Saturday 14th December · 362
Miami International Airport Miami, Florida USA · 362

Chapter 35 - Saturday 14th to Monday 16th December · 370
The Civic Center Miami, Florida USA · 370
The Strand Westminster, London England · 372

Chapter 36 - Tuesday 17th to Friday 20th December · 377
De Wallen, Amsterdam Holland · 377
Rosslyn Hill Camden, London England · 378
The City of London & The West End, London England · · · · · · · · · · · · · · · · · 379

Chapter 36 - Tuesday 17ᵗʰ to Friday 20ᵗʰ December (Continued) · · · · · · · · · 380
The Downs Epsom, Surrey England · 380
Nassau, New Providence Island Bahamas · 381

Chapter 37 - Saturday 21ˢᵗ December · 383
Bermuda International Airport, Hamilton Bermuda · · · · · · · · · · · · · · · 383
Charing Cross Road & George Street Westminster, London · · · · · · · · · · 385

Epilogue · 388

Prologue

Since the Middle Ages, and no doubt for centuries before then, young men, whether university students or not took sides, went on crusades and enjoined in raucous rebellions. Nowadays though, we often see both adolescent men and women crusade or jihad or whatever. They can proudly boast they feature on Facebook or can be seen on TV footage or YouTube ... in riots or at terrorist training camps. Maybe throughout history they were taught with intent or by mistake to rebel by their elders? Or perchance it is just a normal stage of adolescence.

Apart from their incumbents and graduates most people look upon Oxford and Cambridge universities as equals. Few know or dare reveal that Cambridge was a child of Oxford, spawned as a result of a dispute between the locals and the students at Oxford in 1209. Many of the Oxford Dons fled from the local mafia and established a university at Cambridge.

In the mid to late nineteen thirties the hot topics at both universities were not jihads or crusades but the rights and wrongs of communism and fascism. By then both universities were the breeding grounds for MI5 and MI6 officers. Many students and academics lent leeward towards communism often because they were led to believe it to be anti-fascist. Others inclined to starboard because they were persuaded communism was fascism.

Many from Oxbridge volunteered to fight in the Spanish Civil War. They joined either the far right Nationalists under Franco or the Republicans who lost. Franco was supported by Adolf Hitler and Benito Mussolini. The three year war culminated in Generalissimo Francisco Franco being recognised as Spain's leader. Irony had it he was crowned on April Fools' Day in 1939. The Second World War started five months later on 1st September.

During the thirties Cambridge spawned Kim Philby OBE (codename Stanley). He was the notorious spy who allegedly commanded a spy ring christened the Cambridge Five. No spy novel is complete unless the Famous Five are mentioned even if irrelevant but, like the Profumo affair, they are relevant to The Burlington Files so we are going to mention them but only en passant. Philby's communist leanings culminated in his defection to Russia in 1963 after decades as a successful double agent. He was bang in the heart of British intelligence.

His co-traitors were Donald Maclean (codename Homer), Guy Burgess (codename Flicks) and Sir Anthony Blunt KVCO (codename Johnson). There was one other who was never definitively named and shamed. So why not label them the Cambridge Four?

The fifth man was believed to be John Cairncross (codename Liszt) but that was debatable. We have overheard unsubstantiated and scurrilous rumours that the fifth man went to Oxford but we don't believe them. Indeed, the rumours smell fishy given the rivalry betwixt the universities but then fiction is often spot on in contrast to the status quo historians accept as gospel.

Whatever, all four and Cairncross went to Trinity College, Cambridge apart from Maclean who attended Trinity Hall in Cambridge University. Philby was in charge although Blunt who was the eldest, claimed to have recruited them and is believed to have tipped Philby off before he fled Beirut, Moscow bound.

Credible theories suggest there were many more than five in the spy ring. There were. Most of those who defected were hailed as heroes in the USSR. However, Philby was such a convincing double agent that he spent years under virtual house arrest after his defection. The KGB quite literally didn't trust him. Can you blame them? He was a double agent after all and arguably the most effective in the combined history of Russia and Great Britain.

Anyway, all of them were eventually given honours or titles in the USSR though poor Philby only collected his posthumously. The honours and titles they collected in the UK were stripped away as opposed to handed back. Mind you, even Churchill refused a title he was once offered: Sir Winston would have gone down in history as the Duke of London.

Much has been written about the Cambridge Five including Philby's autobiography, My Silent War. Philby even featured as the Tailor or Bill Haydon, the double agent, in John Le Carré's Tinker Tailor Soldier Spy. Even Rory Gallagher and Simple Minds refer to Kim Philby in songs they wrote and records they produced. However, little has ever been chronicled in the annals of history about the Oxford Triumvirate. Who were they? Would you believe a paranoid cripple with a homemade walking stick, a narcissist who carried a comb and mirror with him at all times and a chemist who never perspired in public? It sounds inconceivable but it's true.

What have the Cambridge Five or the Oxford Triumvirate to do with this saga or even the Burlingtons apart from all often being referred to as the irreligious Oxbridge Eight? The first point is that reality can be stranger than fiction. If you were reading a nonfiction historical book entitled the Cambridge Five you might be miffed to discover there were only four of them. No one dared name and shame the fifth man ... or maybe first woman. Who cares? All that matters is five was the wrong number.

Prologue

It just goes to show what MI5 and MI6 are like when seen at their best in real life. Incapable of resolving the most damaging spy scandal they ever faced. Utterly incompetent too: the espionage went on for decades and some of the double agents were about as high as you could get in the intelligence services pecking order.

What's more, as many including the Oxford Triumvirate noted in hindsight, the treachery was all so obvious. No wonder MI5 and MI6 spent many of the ensuing paranoid lustra squabbling like children and blaming one another instead of clearing up the foul mess. They even lied to the CIA to pretend it all ended in 1949 before Philby was posted to Washington. So, who else has yet to be exposed?

In 1974 the powers that be including the Oxford Triumvirate knew Blunt was working for the KGB. Blunt wasn't exposed until 1979. One way or another the Oxford Triumvirate about whom little has been written and nothing sung were party to sorting out the Cambridge Five. They also sorted out a few other spy scandals before 1974 including the Vassal and Profumo affairs. Incidentally, on a confidential note the Profumo scandal nearly engulfed Roger Burlington in its flames but we will hear more on that later.

The paranoia created by the Cambridge Five mattered. It remained all pervasive, ever present in the mindset of British intelligence for many quinquennia way beyond 1974. After the demolition of the Cambridge Five and the incarceration of Profumo the British intelligence services suffered from paranoia and deranged inquisitions. Many in the CIA argued they deserved what they got.

The Oxford Triumvirate had much in common. In 1933 each of them obtained scholarships to Keble College in Oxford while only nineteen years old. Just like the Cambridge Five they hated fascism but despite many of their friends taking sides in the Spanish Civil War not one of the Oxbridge Eight participated. The Triumvirate later worked together in the Second World War, some with members of the Cambridge Four. The Oxford trio were all patriotic British Empire minded right wing Tories; not communists, Russian sympathisers like their Cambridge comrades. The Triumvirate had all been JIC members from time to time after the war but 1974 was the first time they were all serving members simultaneously.

For those of you unfamiliar with the purported controls exercised over the UK's intelligence services, the JIC was a part of the British Cabinet Office. It provided advice to the government on issues of security, defence and foreign affairs. The JIC oversaw the three intelligence and security agencies: the Secret Intelligence Service (in short, SIS to old farts or MI6 to modernists), the Security Service (MI5) and GCHQ (communications or eavesdroppers). There were other bits too such as the defence intelligence section of the Ministry of Defence (MoD) and splinter groups of anarchists representing the armed forces.

The JIC usually held weekly meetings which were attended by the Chiefs of MI6, MI5 and GCHQ. Normally the head of the CIA's London Station sat in on the meetings. Mind you it was hardly necessary because by 1974 the CIA had bugged everything that moved and anybody who could blow wind down the corridors of Whitehall whether janitors or Joint Intelligence Committee members.

So as not to get you as confused as some paranoid JIC old boys became on occasion, we'll simplify matters. More often than not, from now on we'll refer to this hotchpotch of governmental departments as the intelligence services. That should suffice although these departments bred like horseshoe crabs in times of crises. The "MI" brethren were a notorious breed in this respect. No matter where you trod you probably brushed past them or stood on them by mistake.

Even Winnie the Pooh was recruited indirectly. Well, his author, Alan Alexander Milne was, but to MI7b would you believe, not five or six? MI7b was devoted to military propaganda in the Great War just as MI3 was focused on gun control in the early seventies. The numbers just kept on multiplying as did their work force which needs an explanation too.

All these intelligence services' workforces all over the world were structured without exception on an upstairs downstairs basis. If you thought the fires of slavery were snuffed by Wilberforce please return to school and if you can't remember the way ask for the bike sheds: there's no fire without smoke.

Everybody who was recruited and worked for intelligence services fell into one of two kettle pots. Upstairs were what they liked to call the officers, the patricians. They were the permanent upper crust employees on their payrolls, not the proletariat such as temps or consultants. The patricians forged their careers inside the intelligence services which employed them. They might have been chiefs, commanders or plain operatives but they were all officers.

Downstairs was a different kettle full of common hermit crabs. These were the plebs recruited to scurry about doing most of the dirty work. They weren't your archetypal officers or employees educated at Eton and Oxbridge. These were commoners, riff raff, and known as the officers' agents, as in "secret agents".

These secret agents were often referred to as mere objects and usually called assets or on occasion adjuncts, not exactly intimate terms. Sometimes they were paid in pittances of peppercorn. More often they simply did what they were recruited for because of their moral, religious or political persuasions or convictions: often otherwise called blackmail, extortion or coercion.

Officers called case officers sometimes acted as agents but by 1974 it was uncommon. There was a chasm between being an officer and an agent. Why? If an agent fell into the chasm his or her demise was quietly forgotten or clandestinely covered up. The agent's existence and ties to the intelligence services would be denied. Plausible deniability was the order of the twentieth century and still is today.

Agents, whether pebbles or boulders, were disposable and deniable in the eyes of the intelligence services; some were even set up with pre-planned obsolescence built

Prologue

in. No wonder they were called assets or adjuncts but no matter what agents were called, unlike officers they could be abandoned. However, officers had to be salvaged from the chasm if they fell in, unless of course they were traitors.

Anyway, the Triumvirate did not fall into the chasm and comprised Roger Burlington CBE (nickname Twister), Sir Douglas Castle (TeaLeaves) and Sir Peter Stafford (TrumPeter or the Peacock behind his back). Despite all the similarities and shared experiences they were distinctly different characters. As you'll understand later, they were sometimes lethal adversaries and at other times allies by default.

In the shifting grit of time amidst the secrets they often shared they could be acting in unison at breakfast. By lunchtime TeaLeaves Castle and TrumPeter Stafford could have sided against Twister Burlington and then TeaLeaves would side with Twister against the Peacock for supper. Yet as Big Ben chimed on the last stroke of midnight they'd all be back on the same side.

It was as if their motto was three's company, two's a crowd. The only time you could tell something was amiss was when one of them called TrumPeter Peacock. They were responsible for their own nicknames, at Oxford in 1934 after ordering three teas on a rare abstemious visit to the Randolph Hotel.

Unlike Stafford and Burlington, Castle was from humble stock and born and bred as an only child north of Watford Gap. He was educated at Manchester Grammar. His parents ran a men's barber shop in Oldham near Manchester and, yes, they did sell rubber Johnnies and, no, he wasn't a mistake.

He was the only one in the Triumvirate to be recruited for the British intelligence services when at university. Maybe that helped account for his never having married. Back then he was a fine figure of a man, dashing and debonair. In 1945 he momentarily lost interest in everything, including his career, after the love of his life walked out on him. Despite that he persevered in MI6 and using his intelligence wisely, steadily rose through the ranks.

Now he limped round the corridors of Whitehall wearing a cardigan, like some ageing librarian. He leant on a thick homemade stick, to support a leg shattered during the war. It wasn't splintered on the brave beaches of Normandy or anything intrepid like that but in a stampede out of the flooded bomb shelter at Balham Station. People who didn't know him would never have guessed he was so high up in the ranks of MI6 and not infrequently chaired the weekly JIC meetings.

Regardless of his senior position he was the weak link in the Triumvirate and knew it. His dumpling silhouette said it all. In contrast to Peter's dapper Savile Row or Italian suits and Roger's forever immaculate but grey and boringly correct attire Castle looked a total tramp, balding head to scuffed shoes. At five foot six he always looked diminutive next to the other two who were both over six feet tall.

Nevertheless, in brain power he sometimes outshone Peter but rarely Roger. Like Peter albeit for different reasons, by 1974 he was a loner. Sir Douglas Castle was an unusual contradiction of an overall loser who'd won in so many respects. On a superficial glance, most people would have judged him as having enjoyed a highly successful career. However, for Castle the cup was now constantly half empty. Increasingly consumed with failure he became a depressed shadow of his younger self. All that did was make him more susceptible to bouts of paranoia which was exacerbated by his never having a holiday from MI6 in almost forty years.

Once the Second World War started Peter Stafford, who was by then a Chartered Accountant, left the City of London. Along with many of his Etonian dormitory mates of old he followed Castle into the intelligence services. Peter was the antithesis of Castle. A silky slick hustler if ever there was one, lubricated with diplomatic skills equal to Disraeli's or Kissinger's.

There was no doubting he was a brilliant public speaker and a showman who spent more time looking in the mirror than a catwalk model. He pretended to be intellectual by collecting rare books but never opened them. The Peacock was surprisingly bourgeois given his classical and expensive education. Yet he was a dazzling salesman and would have made an immaculate Foreign Secretary.

His nicknames, unlike those of Castle and Roger Burlington, were self-explanatory. They reflected the essence of the man. Despite his forever rumoured AC-DC tendencies he rose to the top echelons of MI5. In that era such leanings were not openly acceptable or legal in most supposedly civilised countries. He indulged in one other questionable habit. When agitated or excited, he chain smoked large fat Brazilian cigars.

Peter married once, just after leaving Oxford, but was divorced within a year. Callous rumours spread about the true reason for the annulment of his marriage. The worst was that Mr Stafford could not stand sharing the bathroom mirror with anyone. Maybe if he'd spent less on Brylcreem he could have afforded two mirrors.

There were rabbit warrens full of Staffords all over southern England. They didn't have much time for his egocentric addiction, sexual leanings or chimney stack smoking habits. After his discordant divorce he was disinherited. Not that he needed the dosh.

Once the war ended in Japan he continued as a Chartered Accountant in the City of London and used that and working for a few years as a finance director in industry as his cover while in MI5. By 1974 Sir Peter had laid to rest most of his intelligence activities other than remaining on the JIC and by 1970 was loaded. Now he was a senior partner in one of the largest international accountancy firms in the world.

The Burlingtons were reasonably affluent but they didn't own the Burlington Arcade. Sir Peter Stafford could have bought it on a whim. The Burlington ancestry could be traced back to the Duke of Devonshire but only in a circuitous way. In reality their background was far less grandiose than the name implied. Not that Roger

Prologue

Burlington staked any claims in that regard. He was too modest, retiring and shy to do so.

Born on the banks of the Thames in Putney, he went to the local grammar school where his Dad just so happened to be a dreadfully strict headmaster. After leaving Oxford Roger started work at a company called Imperial Chemical Industries, better known as ICI.

By the time the Second World War began Roger was a clinical cutting-edge scientist. Only a few months passed before his expertise was tapped to determine what ingredients would create ever more devastating bombs to help annihilate the Nazis' industrial power base. First he was sent to Billingham in County Durham to conduct his experiments but the enemy learnt what their northern factories were for and started trying to blitz them so his research base was moved.

Later in the war Roger formally joined the intelligence services. While there he spent an increasing amount of time down south in Porton Down in Wiltshire, normally out of range of returning enemy bombers. His research work was extended to help Churchill's dirty tricks brigade, the SOE or Special Operations Executive. Roger was an old fashioned humourless Q of the Fleming variety and Bond notoriety. Except what he dreamt up was for real and his products were as potent as mass lethal injections.

His reputation spread and he was promoted to handle more daunting tasks. By then all the Triumvirate were reunited one way or another. Roger's contribution to the war effort became on a need to know only basis to help his US counterparts with Project Manhattan, trying to create an atomic bomb. The project was top secret: so secret Roger didn't know its name or real purpose. He thought it was about heavy water which excited the Nazis more than watching the tide come and go on the beaches at St Tropez. Roger was a man of many secrets. His wife Sara did not share them all but none were of a sexual nature. The couple met during the war courtesy of her attachment to Douglas Castle but more on that fetid fiasco later.

The east and west became more entrenched in what Orwell christened the cold war. Scientists with Roger's knowledge and experience were in short supply. In 1960 he was coincidentally seconded from ICI again to run much of Porton Down, the government's secret scientific research centre.

The science park was a seven thousand acre complex that conducted experiments into chemical and biological weapons. Established in 1916 during the Great War the centre was originally used to develop mustard, chlorine and phosgene gases. The Germans used them first in 1915 and they cost the British dearly in the early part of the Great War.

Given the paranoia about a potential nuclear nightmare in the sixties, Roger soon became a regular visitor to JIC meetings to explain nuclear developments and to calm nerves. Later, once in charge of Porton Down, he became a full member of the JIC.

Roger was good at explaining multifarious tortuous topics courtesy of his analytic mind and his upbringing as the eldest son of an exacting headmaster. Within five short minutes armed only with chalk and blackboard he could unravel the complexities of nuclear physics. After that even a child could understand how it all worked let alone some of the old codgers still sitting on the JIC in 1974. His becalming style and comforting mannerisms reassured the fearful majority on edge during the Cuban missile crisis.

Roger was a demure man and in an unspoken way as cool as a stalagmite and as deadly as a stalactite. His colleagues aptly likened him at times to a mild mannered Clark Kent. You'd never see him break into a sweat no matter what the heat or pressure. Sara's falling for him was hardly unpredictable. By 1974, his hair was more silver than black and he still wore his heavy, black-rimmed spectacles. He could have passed for Kim Philby in the fog of war on a moonless night. Like Philby, he could smoke sixty cigarettes a day. For non-smokers, sitting in a room with Peter Stafford and Roger Burlington was akin to a Guy Fawkes' night inside a concentration camp. It was lethal.

There were other sides to Roger though apart from mentoring the JIC and fulfilling his role as an ICI director in the seventies. He wasn't a colourful character. On close inspection he was a multicoloured one. It was just that the many colours were unpretentious, restrained and sometimes barely discernible. There was his secret side and his public persona. He was a Machiavellian political manipulator having been a staunch Tory supporter and close collaborator of both Harold Macmillan and Alec Douglas-Home. That much was public knowledge but the topics they discussed were absolutely off anybody else's radar.

Roger never socialised with Ted Heath though despite or because of the close relationship between Sir Peter Stafford and Heath. Above all else Roger Burlington tried not that successfully to be a family man. Quietly he did his best for his wife Sara and his two sons, Hugh and Edward. Hugh was the elder by eighteen months. However, Sara did the heavy lifting when it came to family matters and he loved her for that and forgave her for her main weakness: applying her strengths too dramatically, forever over strenuously.

Sara was a ruthless security expert. She served in both MI6 and MI5 in the Second World War. By 1974 she may have been a tad rusty but hadn't forgotten anything she'd learnt since 1939. That was when she volunteered to go anywhere so that she could skin and chop up Nazis. She said she could do it just like her Mum used to prepare rabbits for Sunday lunches during the Great Depression. Someone took her word for it and she was handed a job in MI6 on a dinner plate. She never looked back after that other than the odd glance over her shoulder.

Her operating behind enemy lines became so legendary that she was ordered to cease for her own safety. The Nazis displayed photos of her everywhere and offered a substantial reward for her capture. Rumours were that there were more photos of her in occupied Europe than of Ginger Rogers in the USA.

Instead of killing Nazis she was promoted to help plug leaks in the intelligence services. Later she trained anyone who came within shouting distance how to kill, interrogate or torture. The Nazi publicity still didn't stop her joining in on some risky weekend jaunts across occupied Europe after D-Day. She continued to work in intelligence dealing with internal affairs and training almost until the day Hugh was born.

By 1974 she only looked after her family. There was no debate that sometimes she was overly melodramatic but always oblivious to political niceties. She also became a schemer extraordinaire. Sara even taught Dr Beeching, the notorious railway sidings cutter, the meaning of cuts. What's more her address book read like a redacted version of Who's Who. It listed every prima donna in the British intelligence services and the Cabinet Office since Super Mac became Prime Minister in 1957.

More about Sara later but suffice it to say she guarded Roger's back better than a highly trained Rottweiler. Woe betides anyone if she scented them approaching him or his sons from the wrong direction. You'll either love her or loathe her but you won't be able to ignore her. She is far more intelligent than you might at first think so be wary.

After bearing two sons Sara decided they should follow in their parents' footsteps and enter the intelligence services. First they needed to go to Oxford as their father had to garnish the requisite credentials to succeed in the corridors of Whitehall. Hugh was more like his Dad than his Mum but Edward showed a more cavalier side to his nature from an early age. His parents were constantly distracted by matters of state and found it difficult to steer either of their little horrors in their chosen direction.

Hugh wanted to pursue a more academic life. His younger brother picked up scholarships and awards effortlessly but he was refused entry to Oxford. The refusal was in euphemistic terms what one might generously describe as a misunderstanding. It was a fuck up, a right bleeding disaster, and it put paid to any fast track career for him within the intelligence services. Hugh was an Oxford educated free-thinker who turned into a bookseller or so it appeared in 1974. Edward was a firecracker who after refusal at the pearly gates of Oxford and his release from prison, yes prison, continued to burn at both ends.

From 1969 Edward was as an offbeat accountant by day and an undercover agent by night. He was a child prodigy with a photographic memory. Not to mention a sixth sense, bordering on telepathy which he shared with Hugh. His aptitudes frequently made him look eccentric or act bizarrely. Hence he could be a bagful of contradictions at times.

After graduating and collecting a PhD in oriental languages, Hugh went to work in Blackwell's, which at the time was Oxford's premier bookshop. Meanwhile Sara was forever concerned that Roger's days at ICI might come to a premature end far sooner than expected. Jobs for life were becoming a fad of good old yesterdays. So, with pro bono help courtesy of Sir Peter Stafford's business acumen, Sara and Hugh persuaded Roger to buy premises in London's Charing Cross Road and establish an antiquarian bookshop.

It killed three birds with one Frisbee. Hugh was experienced enough to run the shop after working in Blackwell's. It represented a welcome challenge which he embraced sufficiently to make it a success. Second, it saved Sara from having to socialise with an eye out for a quango job for Roger. No fears lingered that Roger might end up on a train in a siding with no driver. Finally Roger was genuinely interested in antique books. He had been a serious collector for years and would relish working alongside Hugh.

The fact that the premises had once been a brothel and were on occasion used by MI6 was immaterial. By 1974 Hugh was running the family bookshop and making profits, just. The value of the premises was up despite the ongoing recession. So, ceteris paribus, the business would still be around to keep Roger busy in his retirement and Hugh in gainful employment for many decades to come.

Paradoxically that assured expectancy of longevity was not something the youngest Burlington shared. Before even attending school he was branded as a mischievous rascal with ten lives and, as tails follow cats, matters deteriorated. In his mid to late teens he was lured by the bright lights and glamour of discos, nightclubs and casinos. It wasn't as if he was a natural born criminal. As he grew up in the sixties he simply embraced the good times. Sometimes it just so happened to be illegal such as going to gigs and discos before he reached the age to drink and crash an automobile.

Apart from being a frequent under age visitor of casinos and nightclubs, once he learnt life existed south of Watford he wasn't averse to sharing an occasional marijuana joint with seductive southerners. They needed to look like Diana Rigg or somehow measure up to his contemporary vision of a goddess. Consequently, in his teens he sped through life by aeroplane, in express trains or in the fast lane in fast cars oblivious to potholes and sleeping policemen.

Well, that is until some malicious buggers framed him for murder. They were aided by some distinctly obnoxious bent coppers. So, instead of freaking out on a scholarly life at university he ended up in prison. His parents had no alternative but to use their influence anyhow they could to extract him from the quagmire into which he'd been so unjustly dumped. They turned him. At first he was press ganged into what at best could be described as being a police informant. There was no alternative. It was self survival, a one way ticket through the prison gates.

Prologue

So he helped the proper police infiltrate and bring to justice those who framed him and murdered his closest friend. The young man proved rather accomplished at that so his role was extended with great effect. He infiltrated corruption not only linked to the bright lights and glamour that originally led him astray. His targets became more sinister.

TrumPeter Stafford, his parents and Hugh then persuaded him to take the seemingly righteous path of qualifying as a Chartered Accountant. That was difficult. On being pressurised into choosing a career path, Edward set his sights on becoming a professional footballer. It took Hugh all his persuasive powers to make it clear that Edward was about the only person who thought he possessed the potential to be a great goalkeeper.

As Hugh tried to explain to his brother, anyone checking Edward's sporting résumé would have placed him on the reserve team or the substitutes' bench if he was lucky. They would have soon discovered that the hat-tricks he referred to were own goals and that his well intentioned diving tactics rarely stopped balls from going in the net!

Indeed, given the number of car and boat crashes Edward caused, any manager worth his salt would realise Edward would have difficulty in stopping anything including smoking. Eventually Edward agreed to let Brian Clough decide after his mother intervened and sprung a trap. Brian grew up next door to Sara and the families were still in regular contact even though Clough moved from the north east to manage Derby's football team.

The brothers drove down to the midlands. Edward started questioning his own abilities after one of Clough's Derby centre forwards chosen from the under sixteen squad hit ten penalties past him. Edward dived the wrong way on each penalty. Reluctantly he accepted his career path lay elsewhere.

His being a top team's or even England's goalkeeper was a cherished dream of his and was hard to discard. Needless to say that didn't stop him from playing as a hobby and dreaming of fame at Old Trafford or St James's Park. Sara was overjoyed that her plans with Sir Peter and Brian worked out as expected.

She persuaded the Triumvirate to keep Edward busy. Consequently, long before his twenty first birthday Edward was manipulated into becoming both an articled clerk destined to be a fully fledged accountant and an undercover agent. However, his manipulators overlooked Edward was his own man, a contrarian and a persuasive young man as well.

Edward's being an intelligence officer rather than an asset was not an alternative given his past even though he was proven completely innocent of murder. Those responsible all received life sentences by 1972. Although his failure to become an officer initially saddened Sara, by 1973 she wasn't that bothered about the distinction. Up until then there was no real reason that she knew of for concern. She reckoned given time the past would be forgiven or forgotten and not long from then he'd be an officer and just conceivably a gentleman.

Given his parents' backgrounds and spheres of influence it was no fluke that Edward evolved into the nearest thing to an intelligence officer. In 1974 he was in his early twenties and an expendable asset. Nevertheless, while still naive and carefree, he was becoming experienced. By now he knew how to infiltrate dangerous organisations and understand criminal psyches.

Since going down that alleyway his life was being repeatedly pushed to the edge. His mother wasn't kept informed. Roger only received brief and occasionally misleading accounts of what he was doing. That was up until 1974. By then his parents were reassessing the risks that never even bothered Edward. Yes, they had successfully pulled him from the brink of being wrongfully imprisoned for life. Yet by February 1974 his parents' scheme to steer him in their footsteps was beginning to look as if it might backfire.

Any life was a good life when compared with being slung in prison for a murder you hadn't committed. That was how Sara and Roger justified the manipulative and underhand ways they stage-managed Edward's parallel careers. Was Edward his own man? Not yet. He'd been liberated from prison only to be caged up in so many other ways. The sheer extent of his manipulation limited his choices, his being himself and free.

Yet keeping him in line had been a problem since he was a child and 1974 was no different. Anyway, those that kept him in line thought what they did was for his own good. Deep down they knew he would break free one day. As 1974 unfolded his parents were already asking why they extracted their son from the jaws of hell only to watch him drift down the River Styx.

As our story begins, his life has become much more dangerous than when he was another species of excitement addict. His zest for driving fast cars, drinking too much, gaming in casinos, going on the pickup in discos and nightclubs and mixing with the wrong sorts were benign in comparison. Now instead of naively mucking in with ne'er do wells by mistake he was introduced to even worse sorts to help the intelligence services find ways of silencing them. Yet in 1974 Edward was still naive and attracted to those bright lights of old.

Now you can relax as we move to the heart of our story. We start with only about nine months of 1974 left to go. Whatever you do, don't expect Edward to mature overnight. Also, don't sit up waiting for Hugh to find his perfect match, marry her and sire sextuplets by Christmas. More to the point though, don't forget your ABCs now Sara's antennae have been reactivated.

Figuratively speaking Edward is being kicked or passed around like a football. That's what being an asset means. You have little control over what direction you move in and when or how you get there. If you are an agent or asset you rarely know the truth about why you're going where, what for and when. Expendable and deniable agents are never in control of their own destiny as Edward is about to discover.

Chapter 1
Tuesday 5th March

Wimpole Street Marylebone, London England

Wimpole Street runs parallel to and just west of Harley Street. It has always been a step or two behind its more illustrious neighbour despite its being a cluster of medical excellence. In 1974 that neighbourhood was the last place in London you would expect trouble. Your chances of being mugged there were zero and even the IRA wouldn't strike anywhere a nurse or hospital patient could be harmed. It would not be good propaganda to damage a neighbourhood crammed full of do-gooders. Wimpole and Harley Street were like ants' nests choc a block with overpriced prima donna doctors and dentists.

Yet evil lay behind the veneer of the shining teeth implants, the platinum hip replacements and the false boobs with golden tassels that kept the private medical profession rich. Beneath the glowing opulent surface, there lay a sinister segment few could have imagined.

As tears streamed down the cheeks of Li, a young Chinese mother, she was asking her twin sister Ling why it had come to this as they undressed in a modest million pound terraced house in Wimpole Street. Yes, she broke the law in Beijing by giving birth to twins, a boy and girl, but that was three years ago now. Since then her devoted husband Jun had shepherded them from one haven to another. After a week's deprivation at Antwerp they finally reached safety in the posh end of London. They could rest there now and start afresh. The only problem was they hadn't seen the infant twins since boarding a freighter at Antwerp destined for Woolwich docks.

Two days ago the three adults, still in their late teens, had been locked in a flat for their own safety: well that's what they were told. To make sure UK immigration officers or the police didn't find them. The only sustenance they had since arriving in Antwerp was cold rice and water. The meat balls the trio were offered everyday tasted so peculiar Jun told them to flush them down the toilet. Not one of them had eaten human flesh before so just as well they followed his instincts.

They had no idea Li's innocent twins had been abducted in Belgium for onward sale to a paedophile ring. They were told the twins would follow separately. It was too dangerous to travel together as a family. Never having studied European history, images of human cattle trains heading to concentration camps never crossed the tracks of their minds. The twin sisters sobbed as they did what the doctor told them: undress then take a shower. Ominous was an understatement.

Li was forced to witness her husband's gruesome mutilation. Jun, also in his late teens, had only been given mild local anaesthetics ahead of the major surgical procedure. Butchery might have been a better description. His wife was strapped to a chair to watch. The surgeon took him apart piece by piece to preserve his kidneys and liver. Vital body organs were worth a lot on the black market. So was the film of his wife watching the surgeon carry out this butchery and so too would be the film of what was just about to happen.

Jun's discarded remnants were bagged. Li, his wife, had been forced to put them in the bin-liners. The bags were ready for disposal and the surgeon dumped them on the landing. Ling was locked away upstairs during the operation but they were now reunited in a plush bedroom suite and sobbing as they did what the middle aged overweight surgeon told them. He left them to undress and locked the door.

The effeminate cameraman, wearing a weird multicoloured speckled suit, looked more like a clown than a photographer. He went for a piss, returning with his flies undone and shared a bottle of champagne with the surgeon as they tidied up in the surgery. The champagne and iced glasses came from the industrial refrigeration unit where the kidneys and liver were being frozen. There were other body parts in the walk in freezer. Together the men moved the camera equipment upstairs into the luxury penthouse suite on the floor above the makeshift surgery. Li and Ling had showered and were starting to dress as they entered. The surgeon was not pleased.

'Who the fuck said you could get dressed. Take those bloody rags off you stupid bitches. You're going to be fucked first.'

The clown showed them what he meant by taking his own trousers off and pointing at their clothes. Petrified, the girls started to undress.

They sat huddled together naked on the red satin duvet on a king sized four poster bed. A small kitchen axe handle was protruding out of one of the bedside table drawers. The surgeon started hurriedly undressing, aroused at the thought of what was to come next. The cameraman was readying his equipment. Both men's testosterone levels were rising rapidly by now. The surgeon was salivating in anticipation of raping each twin in front of the other before he axed one of them to death. The cameraman would decide who lived depending upon their performances.

It didn't matter a jot which of the twins was the winner: she had already been sold. Olga, the receptionist, would be taking her to her new home in Essex but not before her East European husband pleasured himself and the surviving twin had tidied up and bin-bagged the hacked torso of her sister.

Chapter 1 - Tuesday 5th March

Downstairs Olga was reading a magazine with her feet up on the reception desk. She was a big woman, over six feet tall and that helped her get her rotten rocks off when at her favourite fetish parties, bondage and brutality, B&B soirees. Olga married the surgeon after meeting him at a B&B party. They had much in common.

The doorbell rang. From the look of the van outside it was for the weekly delivery of medicines and medical supplies. The interruption irritated her. She pushed the buzzer to open the front door without bothering to move. A scruffily dressed tall man stumbled in and dumped a large box on the reception table. He pulled a crumpled delivery sheet from his pocket.

'Sign here please luv.'

His Geordie accent was heavy.

'Don't "luv" me young man. You're new here, what's your name?'

He thought up the first name that came to his mind.

'Adam luv.'

'Well Adam, don't put that dirty box on my clean table.'

The young man looked at his watch. With more urgency than before he picked up the box and placed it on the reception desk where she propped up her feet.

'Don't put it on my desk either. Where did they dig you up? This is Wimpole Street not Newcastle docks. Take it upstairs to the first floor. Second door on the left and wipe your filthy shoes on the mat before you go.'

She signed the delivery note. He picked it up quickly and put it in his overalls' pocket. After obligingly wiping his feet he moved the box off the reception table and headed for the staircase. Olga resumed her reading.

The front door bell rang again. She could see two men and two women but couldn't understand what they said. Olga pushed the buzzer underneath her desk and the door sprung open again while she opened the drawer to her desk and reached inside it. They rushed at her. Olga tried to pull a handgun from the drawer.

She was too slow. Adam kicked the drawer shut. You could hear her wrist bone snap and he whacked the back of her head with a hard rubber cosh. One of his accomplices lashed out at her too. Olga's teeth followed the path of the antique truncheon that swiped across her mouth showering Adam in blood. Olga the snob passed out as her screams stopped the very second they started.

Adam was already silently racing up the stairs followed by Chong and Dao. The girls were gagging Olga and roping her to her chair. They too were Chinese. Chong had grabbed Olga's gun. They had all arrived there together but been held up in traffic courtesy of an IRA bomb scare which meant they were half an hour late. Edward was aware that the consequences could be devastating as the black bin bags lay silent witness to on the third floor landing.

The surgeon was by now naked, yet so fat he couldn't have seen his own hard on beneath the layers of flab protruding like waves of rubber rings around his invisible navel. He handed the twins a paper written in Chinese explaining the rules of the game. This was not the first time he and the cameraman had played this game out but it would be the last. Li was still sobbing so the surgeon grabbed Ling.

He splayed her legs and forced himself inside her. Her struggling and screaming were to no avail. The fat surgeon raped her while trying to show his best side to the camera. He was bobbing up and down on top of her like some grotesque beanbag. Li had turned away. She couldn't watch any more. Through her tears she saw the axe handle sticking out of the bedside table drawer.

Adam burst into the bedroom unwittingly bashing the cameraman's head against the door in his rush. The surgeon turned to see what was happening. As he did Li grabbed the moment, seized the axe and sank it as hard as she could into his shoulder. Before Li could rip it out and thrash at him again Adam yanked the surgeon off Ling by his hair and slammed his head against one of the bed posts. The post cracked.

Adam turned back to deal with the cameraman. With a single blow from his cosh he transformed his pretty face into what looked like a hotchpotch of mashed potato with ketchup. The blood pouring from the cameraman's mouth added to the pot pourri of his colourful clothing.

Both the Chinese men arrived and started gagging the perverts and roping them together. The gagging was hardly necessary as neither could talk.

'You look for others. Shout if you want help and we come. Here, take the gun. We tie up these pricks real tight for you.'

Maylin, Dao's wife, soothingly and reassuringly helped the distraught girls to dress; to retain what little was left of their dignity. They were both covered in the butcher's blood. Adam came back into the bedroom after checking the rest of the flat. He couldn't understand the torrents of Chinese chatter. His friends were explaining to the twins what had happened to them and where they were to go now to be safe.

'All clear guys. How are they?'

'They are ok Mister Edward. We were too late for Jun in the bin-bag.'

'Who was he?'

'Jun married to Li here.'

'Tell Li I am so sorry I was too late for him.'

'She understood Mister Edward.'

'Tell her we have rescued her children and she will be with them in an hour.'

'I have said it to them. She says you are wonderman Mister Edward.'

'We fucking failed them Chong, we were too bloody late. How many more will go through this shit? Why did a shithead in the IRA make a call? Why? We should have saved them all. That was the plan. We fucking failed.'

'Don't be cross with yourself Mister Edward. It was traffic's fault not your's.'

'That's a lame excuse Chong. Are these dirty pigs tied up?'

Chapter 1 - Tuesday 5th March

'There is no escape for them or fat woman below.'

'Good man. Dao can make a call from downstairs.'

Edward Burlington looked in disgust at the beanbag of a surgeon, just one of the butchers in that upper crust neighbourhood he'd singled out to face rough justice. He was still unconscious but the cameraman was writhing but to no effect. His naked groin was swollen thanks to Chong's occasional kicks as opposed to any perverse sexual arousal. Burlington spoke in his Geordie accent.

'You are the fucking scum of the planet mate. When you're put away for life we'll make sure you and that fat pervert pray you never wake up again. You're in for brutal buggery on fried bread and ketchup every day for life. Don't forget to send us a holiday snap if you're still alive at Xmas.'

Edward nonchalantly kicked the cameraman in the groin. It looked nonchalant but it was a hard professional kick followed by another to the chin. You could hear his head crack against the surgeon's. Both were out cold now.

'Have the girls any bags or clothes?'

Li answered him by shaking her head. Edward checked there were no problems before they all left. Olga was still unconscious and no doubt on awakening would relish the bondage. She might even enjoy it in prison. That would be a shame but then she was such a posh old cow it was unlikely. As one might not have expected of Wimpole Street there was blood and teeth all over the thick pile of the luxurious carpet as they calmly walked to the awaiting van.

While the others left Dao made a 999 call. The police held many recordings of this vigilante hero's voice from earlier emergency calls but were clueless as to who he was. As an illegal immigrant, he didn't exist officially. Chong, Dao and their wives were the first illegals Edward saved earlier in the year and they had agreed to help him rescue others from similar horrors to those they once faced.

Yet no one in the British police or the intelligence services linked Edward to the many crime scenes an anonymous Chinese caller kept bringing to their attention. Young Burlington didn't want to take the credit anyway. If he had his handlers in Special Branch would have gone apoplectic. His involvement would have jeopardised the success of Operation Standpipe where he was at the cutting-edge. A few dozen more lives were inconsequential to Her Majesty's Government when contrasted with bringing that operation to a satisfactory closure. Edward fully understood but didn't share that point of view which is why raids like today's had become commonplace since late January.

Edward and his Chinese disciples were quite a team by now having rescued dozens from the grisly jaws of unspeakably depraved deaths. This was Edward's first failure and he was furious with himself. If only he'd known about the damn traffic snarl up he could have missed lunch, played less with the children or just woken up earlier. Indeed he could have taken so many alternative paths and Li's children would still have a loving and devoted father.

Chong moved the van further away from the flat. They waited patiently for the police to arrive and then left, helping each other remove their facial disguises. Shu and Maylin, the wives of Chong and Dao, had both been involved in amateur drama and pantomimes since they were youngsters and could change each of the team's appearances in a few minutes. First port of call was to drop Li and Ling off at a basement flat beneath an upmarket antique bookshop in Charing Cross Road. All the girls disembarked there. The new arrivals would stay at the flat for a week to recuperate and learn enough English or Scottish to get by before a proper home was found for them and they were given new identities.

An elderly Scottish nurse was waiting for them inside with the children. She was a trauma specialist and would look after them for a week or more, indeed as long as she thought necessary. She was given misleading and limited information as to where her patients came from but Edward reckoned she would have helped without the pay, she was that devout.

All the costs were ostensibly met by some no nonsense Triads from China Town or so it was rumoured. Maybe they just claimed the credit for it or acted as a front for someone else or a charitable organisation. Who knew? They certainly helped in other ways because they would not see their own kind being mutilated or abducted. No matter what, it was all well organised and seemed to be funded by someone with access to ample reserves. Edward organised that side of it but it only took up an hour of his time once a week. Of equal importance was that he maintained the thin red line to stop any gratuitous revenge murders. Woe betides anyone who stood in Chong's way on one of Edward's rescue missions.

The three year olds were so lucky to have been rescued. Had Edward not been instructed to organise their abduction they would have been lost forever. Shu, Maylin and he had played hide and seek with them while preparing for the raid on Wimpole Street. It was a good way to take your mind off what was to come. It could have easily turned into a bloodbath for some of those cornered inhuman rats who resisted the rescue squad's assaults. If it had it would not have been the first time.

Chong then set off for Montagu Square. The girls had already tried wiping Edward down but his clothes and hair were still stained with the blood of those animals he was forced to manhandle. The three men sat in silence until they arrived near the block of flats where he lived. Dao broke the silence.

'We do not know how to say enough thank you Mister Edward. Will this be the last of the rides?'

'I'll know by tomorrow Dao. I can't tell you more than that now. You make sure the kids and girls are alright and I will see you all on Thursday if I am still alive. I have a strange sensation that tonight is going to be tough, tougher than all we've done together. If I can't see you for some reason …'

Chapter 1 - Tuesday 5th March

'Don't say that Mister Edward. We want you living for meal on Thursday we promise you.'

'I'll be there. Don't worry. Now go tidy yourselves up. Anyone would think you'd been in a fight looking the way you both do.'

They clasped hands and said their goodbyes. Edward hopped out. He needed to make it back again to more ordinary work at the office before four that afternoon and then a quick five-a-side practice match. A long day and night still lay ahead of him and it was getting colder as a northerly wind gathered pace.

Dao took over driving from Chong and they returned the van to China Town where its number plates were changed again after it was repainted. So far as the police were concerned the vigilantes had hearts of molten gold compared to the pigs they were handing over to the police but they all knew the very act of handing them over was de facto murder.

Once inside they would meet real rough justice. Perverts never lasted long in prison. Edward used that argument to restrain the four of them on earlier raids. There were enough Chinese in British prisons along with some of Edward's connections to make those they left awaiting incarceration after Dao's 999 calls wish they had been murdered.

As noted in Edward's diary this had been a sickening day with one more premature guest earmarked for the mortuary.

Chapter 2
Tuesday 5th March

Harley Street Marylebone, London England

Mac was on his way to war, the theatre of war being in Harley Street. With luck tonight should see the end of Operation Standpipe. For the last few months he never thought he would hear those words: the end of Operation Standpipe. Now it was so near provided young Burlington did everything right. Mac was in a positive mood for once, invigorated and ready to go. He hoped young Edward was in a similar frame of mind. They were due to meet shortly. He'd just received confirmation Burlington was on his way from the City and would be on time.

Edward believed that the team he met last week were police because Mac was Special Branch and told him they were. What this Special Branch man didn't tell him was that the team were MI5 and SAS counter terrorist specialists and when they came in they came in shooting. The duplicity ran deeper than that. Mac was MI6, not Special Branch.

He was currently in the back of a surveillance vehicle camouflaged under the guise of a London black cab that was moving into the Harley Street area. Exactly according to plan the phantom cab headed to the rendezvous point. It was almost nine in the evening. He took a slug from his hipflask that contained about a quarter bottle of neat, single malt scotch. Mac watched the windscreen wipers swipe the sleet away, back and forth, back and forth, again and again.

Most of his squad would soon be moving into position. There would be one last briefing and then it would be green for go. The driver was now aimlessly circling around the target area. Mac ordered him to head for the rendezvous, the Dover Castle, a pub close by the target as Edward's black cab, also driven by an MI5 specialist, passed Euston Station not far away. Both Mac and Edward were thinking about the tracks they had travelled down to reach tonight. It had been a long arduous journey.

Mac's hands hadn't been dirtied at the coal face for years. These days, he was more accustomed to luncheon meetings in a suit and tie than wearing a pair of overalls on top of a bulletproof vest. He was exhilarated being back on ops. For a change

Chapter 2 - Tuesday 5th March

Mac was far away from the bosses and the philosophers and this particular op was far too high profile to trust to the rank and file.

Sir Douglas Castle himself was involved at the top end because of the diplomatic connections, which was as rare as a nun in a bikini. Standpipe was the name Castle gave the operation. The government might be rationing petrol through standpipes in the streets if there was a cock-up and any oil producing state took offence. Mac reckoned a good result might even be worth an MBE or more, which could prove useful when he retired from the intelligence services. So he didn't want any cock-ups now they were so tantalisingly close to hauling the rats in to face justice, and they were the filthiest rodents he'd ever seen.

Young Edward Burlington became involved with Standpipe through Mac and one Miss Tessa Hislop, Mac's new PA. At the time Mac and Tessa were on secondment to MI5 but she told Edward she worked as a PA for some high ranking cop and wanted to supplement her pay. He liked her best of all those who answered his advert in the Standard. She said she knew Mac after she had cunningly prompted Edward to mention his name so Tessa said if he wanted a reference Mac would give one. Edward thought there was nothing odd with a copper's secretary moonlighting so did just that.

Anyway, Mac and Edward had already worked together in the past and trusted each other. Mac spoke highly of Tessa so she was given the job of helping out a couple of nights a week with his freelancing as an accountant in the music business. Mac said it would work out well as she could act as a kind of liaison officer between them if either of them were busy. That suited Edward too as his diary was rarely empty.

Edward had no idea the response to his advert was fixed by MI5 but who gave a shit: he had acquired a damn good secretary. He called her his PA and she called herself his handler at work in Century House and all were happy, particularly Mac. Her new sideline allowed her to be where Mac wanted her, as close to Edward as anybody was at that time.

MI5's first opportunity to infiltrate this politico-crime syndicate came when word on the street had it they were looking for a load of television sets. Tessa located a crook called Johnny Johnson, known as JJ for short. JJ looked like a Madame Tussaud replica of Edward Burlington. It was that simple and in real life JJ would have been just what the syndicate wanted. He was on parole after a stretch in Brixton Prison. All MI5 needed to do next was swap Edward for him.

To clinch Edward's involvement Mac said Special Branch needed him to infiltrate a crime syndicate that was abducting and sexually abusing illegals, possibly children. The mob concerned was seeking a Man Friday to run about for them no questions asked. As expected he didn't need any more persuasion having worked under cover with Mac before, when he was exposing corrupt local politicians from the Tyne to the Tees and in far off lands. Nevertheless, he still didn't realise he was mixed up with the intelligence services and Mac wanted it kept that way.

JJ did a deal and was sent to Canada with a new identity but only after young Burlington studied the man's every little idiosyncrasy for a few weeks. Once Edward mastered the art of being JJ without arousing suspicion off JJ went. They were so physically alike it was uncanny. Just as well though as the background checks undertaken by the crime syndicate were thorough. They went so far as to enrol a prison mate of JJ's to watch Edward arrive at Harley Street and confirm he was indeed the genuine JJ. He did.

Mac was shocked at just how tough minded Edward had become since they first met around 1969. After having spent weeks in JJ's company he'd smiled when he told Mac to his face he would not take part in Operation Standpipe. Young Burlington selflessly wanted JJ treated better than originally contemplated. He even had the nerve to negotiate JJ's deal for him. That alone cost the taxpayer £12,000 more than budgeted, which was roughly half what Tessa earned in a year but there was so much more than a peanut butter sarnie at stake that Mac went along with it.

Edward's first tester for the crime syndicate was to steal a thousand brand new television sets. Special Branch made it happen without a hitch. Mac promised him protection from the start and told him he'd be pulled out at the first sign of trouble. It was a lie. That wasn't the way it went and trouble almost inevitably lay ahead tonight, hence an ambulance was part of the backup squad.

Young Burlington was unusually good at infiltration and undercover work and he knew how to use his wits to stay alive. As an accountant he also attained a head for commerce. Much to Mac's amazement he returned a tidy profit for MI6 from selling the TV sets which more than made up for the cost of JJ's windfall. Edward recognised they had rarity value and negotiated accordingly. They had genuine serial numbers, were still under guarantee and if checked there was no record of their having been stolen. That was just what the syndicate wanted and found out to their satisfaction when they checked too. Of course, MI5 had only paid "cost" which was a third of their retail value at the time.

After the television sets the gang trusted him as the man who could get them whatever they wanted fast. Mac's JJ was soon on the inside after the background checks but their boss, a Mr Cyrus Burton, was born with a suspicious mind that never ceased questioning anything out of place or untoward. Only when the syndicate started paying him was there a problem. Edward didn't want the tainted money. Tessa told him being paid and acting interested in making dosh as JJ would have done was the only way to keep his cover so he was forced to act it out. So Edward collected his pay once a fortnight and handed it over to Mac.

Despite a colourful life since being refused entry to Oxford University, Edward was a natural altruist. He didn't like to see the poor and underprivileged being beaten

Chapter 2 - Tuesday 5th March

around by the rich and the reprobate. That wasn't to say he was a holier-than-thou do-gooder, he just liked to even up the odds now and then when the innocent and the vulnerable were being abused. Like with the Manunta Mob up north and now what Edward nicknamed the Magnificent Seven down south.

By day he was an auditor with a prestigious accountancy firm called Porter Williams. By night he was an MI6 asset, even though he didn't know he was working for MI6. Edward wasn't a pseudo superhero who wore his underpants out over his trousers or anything daft like that. He was more of an anti-hero who did what he did because it seemed right to him.

He just liked doing what he was tasked to do because the assignments were more like diversions than work and luckily he was far better at delivering results than he was in goal. Helping others gave him a sense of pride, an inner calm and contentment. There was a quasi-religious air to it all, no rationale you could measure, no cash to put in the bank but he was not religious, not a believer in any gods that mankind could define.

Mac already knew all this from their profiling work and his closeness to young Burlington over the years. As Edward never asked for money, being a true Scot Mac never offered any. Obviously Mac paid any costs Edward incurred but in all respects he was a bargain for MI6. Mind you, officially he was meant to be paid £1 a month for legal reasons so that he was technically a government employee. The miserly sods didn't even pay him that although Edward didn't see them as scrooges.

Edward faced danger and took risks, not because he was exceptionally brave or courageous. He liked living dangerously but not in a suicidal mode. Half the time he didn't realise what he was getting into and, by the time he did, it was usually too late to back out. His reward was the satisfaction of knowing he had done some good in the shitty world we all have to share.

While on the subject of shit, he was right in it now and he was reminded of that earlier this afternoon in Wimpole Street but he didn't even have a fleeting thought about going absent on leave. He couldn't let Tessa, Mac or Chad Cooper's team down, that wasn't his style.

Edward sarcastically called the syndicate the Magnificent Seven because their board comprised that number, five men and two women. Between them, they controlled an international organisation that catered for the hardcore sexual habits of a growing network of depraved and perverted diplomats, which spanned out from London across the globe. The syndicate made millions from their trade and their most profitable operations were extortion, blackmail and fraud. They even used their diplomatic clients to facilitate much of their sordid activity. A cool business model in anyone's book: the clients who paid the most did most of the work.

It had been the diplomatic connections that first attracted the interest of MI6. Those connections made the whole operation tricky. If anyone put a foot wrong, the

UK and its allies could find themselves at the wrong end of an oil embargo. That was the last thing the government wanted in the middle of a recession.

For Edward the job wasn't too risky at the beginning. That was before he found out that Cyrus Burton was in charge and the syndicate was more of a front than a decision making board of directors. Burton was a depraved psycho who contaminated the air around him. Edward found it nauseating to be in the same room with the man so he was as relieved as Mac that this undercover operation was coming to a close. If all went well tonight Burton would be consigned to the cage that was waiting for him.

That may have been wishful thinking because rats are at their most dangerous when cornered. Calling the odds on whether Edward might walk out unscathed tonight was far from straightforward. What he didn't know was what happened when plans went wrong, His asset status meant MI6 would make sure nobody would ever know what happened to him despite his camaraderie with Mac. For a start, no one could get close enough to question them, except maybe his mother.

As an undercover agent Edward had to swim in the same sewer Burton and the syndicate crapped in. While there he discovered Burton was trafficking men, women and children sometimes only for their vital organs. Diplomats in Burton's address book and organised crime gangs supplied the raw material from the slum streets of third world countries. The raw material was fodder for sadistic and brutal snuff films. Many of those who survived were sold off to pimps, perverts and pleasure houses. Others were used for medical experiments or as unwilling organ donors.

When Edward first found out what he was mixed up in, he was physically sick after seeing a collection of body parts for the first time. He met Mac and asked if he could speed up the destruction of the whole putrefied rats' nest. Mac tried to put any such thoughts out of his mind. Edward was told in no uncertain terms he could only rid the world of this plague by sticking to the plan. Edward being Edward though decided he'd do it his way, not in Mac's regimental way. While playing Mac's ball game he also started his own with Chong, Dao and their women whom he had covertly freed moments before they were all to be circumcised on film in a debauched sex scene before being slaughtered.

From Mac's perspective if they went in shooting they'd be doubtless charged with some crime or other. The legal eagles involved with the gang and their diplomatic clientele would get the bastards off and they'd just start up again elsewhere. There needed to be enough proof to outweigh the diplomacy factor and put all the scum involved behind bars for good. Failing that, they needed to force them onto planes back home. With any luck many would face worse than a British prison as a home coming welcome. If justice took its course some might even be executed or stoned to death.

Chapter 2 - Tuesday 5th March

From Edward's perspective Mac was right but he wasn't going to stand by and let them get away with any shit in the meantime. So at every opportunity either side of the North Sea he, Chong, Dao and their wives helped anyone they could to escape. Where possible they would make sure the bastards involved were apprehended by the police if incriminating evidence such as human body parts was littered about the premises. Of course, MI6 knew of what the police labelled the Vigilante Chink but never thought the Vigilante Chink was cover for Edward.

Mac thought Edward's involvement was limited to following his instructions to get evidence. That was dangerous enough as assignments go because the gang, being diplomats, were truly lawless.

Once accepted, the new JJ had to gain access to Burton's computer files and other documents as specified by Mac. Typically they sought financial records which he collected in dribs and drabs. On one visit he'd managed to print out a copy of Burton's address book. He put the pages destined for Mac in the false bottom of his biggest briefcase.

What Edward thought far more important than the address book was a large stack of shipping manifests he saw. They were too much to copy then so the next day he went back and copied the lot along with some guest lists he'd found for one of Burton's parties. He was taking a huge risk.

He'd been left alone for the evening. Well he thought he had until Black Rod, one of the syndicate, clambered aboard the lift. Burlington had to use his largest briefcase again and an outsized Harrods' shopping bag he took from a waste paper basket to carry the damn stuff home as there was that much of it. Anyway, he made it past the dozy sentry who didn't even question why Edward was carrying so much paper. Rod was so observant that a herd of elephants could have trumpeted their way past him and he would have reported all was quiet in the jungle.

As Edward had collected a ton of documents, once safely home he proudly called Tessa and told her about the manifests, address book and contact lists he had copied. She came over in a flash. Edward emptied the contents of his briefcase and the Harrods' shopping bag onto his dining room table. Tessa was overwhelmed by the sheer volume of useful data. She took it back to Century House to examine it in depth. She assumed the guest lists were what Edward referred to as the address book.

In actuality, they weren't quite the same but that didn't matter. Tessa had lots of diplomats' names and addresses and the manifests. The copy of the address book was still in Edward's larger briefcase. That was the one he normally only used when travelling overseas. In the excitement he'd forgotten to flip the hidden catch so the false bottom stayed shut. It didn't matter though; they had more than enough names and contact details.

Only in late February did Edward accidentally find out even more atrocities were occurring. Burton referred to these as the sardine tin contingencies. That happened when he'd been trying to get more data Mac asked for to do with the ships and cargoes they claimed to have lost.

If a ship carrying unwitting immigrants came under even the slightest suspicion the vessel was scuttled out at sea. It went under with its illegal passengers still on board, always confined and usually in containers. The syndicate claimed insurance for some fictitious lost cargo as well as the vessel. The manifests were not just part of an insurance fraud but a cover for mass murder. They were important evidence but by themselves not enough to secure any convictions. Most importantly, they didn't incriminate the diplomats involved.

Inhuman was the term Edward used for Burton's carnage. An even more intense revulsion for Cyrus Burton grew inside him. Yet despite risking his life to gain this evidence, the proof he gathered was never enough for Mac. Given the diplomatic clientele and their immunity to prosecution MI6 wanted the Magnificent Seven on tape. MI6 wanted them openly admitting to their crimes and exposing everyone involved from ambassadors to their underlings. That was Edward's task tonight and it was a big bloody ask.

They met as planned in a reserved room at the back of the Dover Castle in Weymouth Mews. Mac handed Edward a gun for the first time. He showed him how the safety catch worked but deliberately forgot to tell him the bullets in it were blanks. The two of them were huddled in the corner with Mac's right hand man, Chad Cooper. Only Edward wasn't eating anything. Mac was trying to be as casual as possible but even his experience couldn't repress his intense excitement.

'You know Edward I've never seen you drink orange juice in a pub. I gather you were collected from a pub in the City. Have you been on the booze?'

'I can honestly report only half lagers and not that many my lord. Anyway I can hardly turn up sober as a saint. They'll get suspicious. I know what I'm meant to do tonight and I'll fucking get it done. You want Burton finished just as much as I do. Let's just hope the shit doesn't slip out of your clutches once I'm through. I'll do my bit if you do your's, soberly. My life depends on it.'

In contrast to Mac's officers Edward didn't have to play the "yes sir no sir" charade with him. Mac tried to make light of the unexpectedly pugnacious tone of the reply. Probably nerves and that wasn't surprising. This op was nearing its finale. The last thing he wanted was to even slightly upset the camaraderie and morale they'd built up.

'I wanted to make sure your breath smelt like JJ's would. That's all.'

Mac knew everyone including himself sometimes drank before ops. For some months now Edward had been on what they called a cold blooded mission, a job for a singleton. Unlike in the traditional theatre of war, when you looked around for reinforcements or reassurances, there were usually none. Anyway, this time was different

Chapter 2 - Tuesday 5th March

because there was backup. What's more, as Edward rightly said, those he was meeting would be suspicious if they couldn't sense he'd been down the pub.

Yet Mac wasn't at home with being answered back or questioned by anyone so young but he was used to young Burlington by now and got the gist of Edward's comments. Mac wasn't the tip of the rapier tonight, young Edward was. Mac reverted to his dour Scottish humour to take the heat away emphasising his gravelly rasping Glaswegian dialect.

'Aye, as I know how much you love Dana noo are your flies zipped up and only your safety catch hard on mon laddie?'

Edward grinned, nodding his head as he gulped down more of his juice.

'Tonight let's use "I want a piss" again as the call sign for immediate help. Did you get that Chad?'

'I want a piss sir.'

'Good. Now any questions either of you?'

'Are my wires working?'

'We'll test them outside again before you go. Anything else?'

'Any policemen want to finish off my triple vodka and orange?'

They laughed uneasily. Edward misread Mac and thought he was bordering on being unfair and hypocritical. After all, he always drank so much scotch starting before noon that he was probably over the limit all day.

After visiting the gents, they were all soon outside in the shadows, away from the pub where no street lights shone directly. They tested their equipment for the last time. Edward set off on foot to wait in the cold at the northern most end of Harley Street. Chad nudged him just before he left.

'Chin up you scoundrel and I'll buy you a couple afterwards.'

Edward winked back, now primed and ready to go into what in his diary he'd later call the shadows of the valley of death.

Chapter 3
Tuesday 5th March

Harley Street Marylebone, London England
A bitter wind blew down from Regents Park and whistled round the corner of Harley Street and Marylebone Road. Edward Burlington hunched into his upturned collar outside a large terraced house that morphed into an upmarket medical centre inside the mansion.

He was packing a Glock automatic and wired from his balls to the back of his neck. Why? Mac wanted to hear every syllable of what was going to be said or even whispered. Edward couldn't see the two large sham post office vans parked out of sight in Ulster Place and York Terrace but he knew they were there although he didn't know about the ambulance. Nor could he hear the men inside those vehicles but they could hear him. He reported in to Mac.

'I'm in position, all looks normal.'

There was no point in saying "over and out" as he was on a one way channel but talking to Mac gave him some sense of reassurance, but not much. None of them were wearing uniforms. Edward wondered why that was. Come to think of it, he hadn't seen anyone in uniform so far on this operation. Edward put the doubts out of his head. It was pointless second guessing about stuff like uniforms now. Mac must have had his reasons for wearing mufti and the time to tango had arrived.

It was like that with Edward, things came to mind that he should've thought about earlier, should've concerned him earlier. That was him in a cameo, always had been, jump first and worry if he wasn't wearing a parachute later.

Edward shivered in the Harley Street cold until Mac's cab pulled up on the opposite side of the street. Chad Cooper signalled to Mac that he and four of his SAS team were in position in the courtyard at the back of the house. The cab lights dipped once to let Edward know he was on stage next. Now was the time for him to perform. As Mac's phantom cab sped off into the night Burlington descended the rusted spiral steps to the unlit basement and rang the bell. Mac relayed the news.

'We have made entry. Stand by now. Over and out.'

Chapter 3 - Tuesday 5th March

The solid oak door was opened with caution, almost ominously as Edward ignored the camera above his head. Rick Borges let him in and slammed and bolted shut the door behind him. It reminded Edward of the first time his prison cell door was shut. Borges was a wiry man with a pale complexion. He looked like a heroin addict but Edward knew his only poison was ketamine. Borges took it in hefty doses to blot out his mind. He hated the sight of blood or thinking too much about the atrocities and obscenities he was helping to perpetrate in pursuit of a bigger bank balance.

'Follow me JJ. How are you anyway? I haven't seen you for a week.'

'Still at it Rick.'

Edward followed Borges down along three lengthy corridors to a large room. An eclectic mix of leather sofas and chairs faced the French windows that overlooked a small courtyard. The heavy curtains were almost completely drawn, so nobody could see in, or out.

Edward looked round the room. He knew everybody, except for one stranger. A tall, handsome, blonde man, wearing mirrored sunglasses who looked like he'd just stepped out of a swimwear ad in Dansk Magazine. The man took a quick but quizzical look at Edward, to make sure he'd recognise him if he saw him again. Then he slipped away into the peripheral shadows as his footsteps faded into the awkward silence he left behind.

Rick's wife, Patricia, patted the sofa beside her as Dana her sister moved to make room.

'Sit down between us my darling boy.'

Edward sat down between the two sisters. Neither said another word. It was odd, most odd. Normally they never stopped prattling.

The sisters and Rick were dentists even if they didn't spend much time in their clinics. The women appeared to be twins but weren't. Their horn-rimmed spectacles made them look like irksome schoolteachers rather than demure dental practitioners. They had a definite east-west look about them. Their family could trace its ancestry to the Indonesian island of Sumatra.

Cyrus Burton was bordering on being drunk and in a typically aggressive mood. Burton was a well built man and could pass for a pugnacious Oliver Reed on a bad night. Black Rod, known as Dr Mobutu in professional circles, was lying on a sofa set apart from the others. He was reading a magazine with naked white teenagers on the cover and seemed to be interfering with himself. Rod was from the Congo and was blacker and fatter than any man Edward had ever seen in his life. He certainly didn't look like your archetypal Harley Street doctor, more like a witch doctor!

The group was completed by the Bashir twins, Atif and Hamid, a pair of Pakistani accountants who were always tactile and together, forever touching one another. Edward assumed there might be some breed of incestuous shenanigans going on but he didn't try to find out because he wasn't interested.

That was the syndicate he christened the Magnificent Seven. A motley crew of unlikely international criminals and not what you'd see in the movies. Even so Edward knew better than to underestimate them. They may have seemed ridiculous, comical and caricature at times. In reality they were a bunch of savages, to Mac akin to a pack of rats that should be poisoned. To Edward they were like an intrusion of cockroaches that needed stamping out.

Only the clunking of the elevator shattered the stillness and silence in the room. A silence so thick you could pick up dollops of it with a spoon. Edward was uncomfortable, worried. Something was wrong. Was his cover blown? The elevator thumped onto its landing slot on the basement floor, the doors creaking as they opened. Several seconds later Rick came back into the room and thrust an envelope towards Edward.

'Your fortnight's pay JJ.'

'Ta. I need that.'

JJ took it and stuffed it awkwardly into his trouser pocket not bothering to count the money. He'd pass it on unopened as usual to Tessa for Scotland Yard to check for prints and forgeries when they next met. At least they were still giving him brown envelopes, so it couldn't be his cover that had blown. There was another ominous silence until Burton opened his foul mouth.

'Rod, if you don't stop playing with yourself, you'll be wearing your balls for a bloody bowtie.'

He turned to Edward.

'I want you to pick up a cargo JJ. Use the transit.'

'Croft does the pickups doesn't he?'

'Not anymore.'

Croft was Burton's driver. Edward needed to draw this out, get something on the tape for Mac. If he didn't do it tonight, he'd have to come back to this rats' nest again. He decided to push his luck.

'How come?'

'I cut his fucking throat didn't I JJ. Do you want to know why?'

Edward nodded. This was the stuff Special Branch wanted.

'He was moonlighting on me. I paid him well and he was fucking about behind my back for the Bozgüney brothers.'

The Bozgüneys were a Turkish outfit that Burton sometimes passed what was left of his immigrants on to when he was finished with them. The big man was dribbling with rage now but Edward needed more.

'What's the cargo?'

He had already guessed but he needed Burton to confirm it for Mac.

'What the fuck d'you think? Choir boys my dear, little Bulgarians with tight little arses and innocent open round mouths with angelic lips. All under eleven, for a party next week. Virgins, just how my ever fucking diplomatic clients like them. You got a problem with that JJ?'

'Not if you don't. Where's the pickup point?'

'Woolwich, pier seven, near the fucking ferry. The Iphigenia.'

'When?'

'Now if you don't bloody mind my dear boy.'

Edward knew he'd have to leave. There could be no stalling once Burton gave him a direct order but he doubted Mac had enough for the bust.

Dana smiled at Edward as he tried to lift himself up from the sofa. Her smile was one of those leering smiles, like a snake has after it's swallowed a mongoose.

'Does the talk about little choir boys turn you on JJ?'

'Not into that stuff thank you Dana.'

'You sure?'

She ran her hand across his crotch. Edward didn't react fast enough as he tried to stand up, failing to push her hand away and slipping backwards onto the sofa. He realised the bloody gun had slid across the front of his trousers when he put the money in his pocket. Now Dana was staring at what looked like half a hard on of all things.

The next Edward knew, Dana's hand was inside his jeans. She yanked out the gun and along with it came some of the wiring Edward had taped to him. He was for once at a loss what to do next. Before he could react Patricia grabbed him by the hair and Dana shoved the gun barrel into his half open mouth trying to pull the trigger. The only sound was that made by a tooth falling out of Edward's mouth. It landed on the table. Blood dripped down the gun and onto Dana's wrist. Her expression was of bewilderment and excitement and her eyes glistened with unrequited anticipation. Burton laughed mockingly.

'The safety catch is still on you dumb bitch.'

The big man approached menacingly hauling Edward up, as Rick tied Edward's hands behind his back with a length of flex he'd ripped off a table lamp.

'What the fuck's this JJ?'

'I never trusted him Cyrus.'

'Who asked you? Get that bloody gun out of his bleeding mouth, you stupid fucking whore.'

Dana withdrew the bloody gun and Burton grabbed it from her hand.

Chad Cooper heard every word as he peered through a gap in the heavy velvet curtains covering the French windows. Time to party, he thought.

'Real trouble. Team One. What are your orders? Over …'

'Wait for my signal. Over and out.'

Mac wanted more. The phantom cab came to an abrupt halt outside the medical centre and his umbrella rolled onto the floor. He slid back the safety catch from the submachine gun strapped to the back of the driver's seat. His adrenalin was flowing again for the first time in ages. He took another slug from the hip flask.

'Ambulance to Team One now. Stand by for further orders. Over and out.'

Edward Burlington was in deep trouble. From Mac's viewpoint though, the operation was more important than any one man's life, especially the life of an asset even if he was Sara Burlington's son. It would take years to set this up again. It was a judgement call Mac was prepared to make.

Chad and his team stood by ready to make an entry.

Patricia ripped open Edward's shirt and tore the audio equipment from his body. Burton took it from her and looked at it quizzically, as a gorilla might some foreign yet vaguely familiar object.

'You didn't answer my bloody question you fucker.'

'What bloody question?'

'This.'

Burton shook the wiring in front of Edwards's face and threw it against the wall. Black Rod had by now heaved himself out of his sofa and started stamping on the stuff, assuming it wouldn't continue working. It did. Mac kept listening and recording as Chad and his team overheard the lot. They watched and they waited.

'Insurance.'

'Insurance? What for? Haven't I paid you enough?'

Edward was thinking on his feet.

'I needed something, in case you decided to eliminate me, like you did Croft.'

'Croft was a fool. I thought you were smarter. Who the fuck are you working with?'

'Some mates and they're outside waiting.'

'Are they now? I don't believe you. Mind you, if they are bloody there, they're just as dumb as you. We'll sort out these fucking goons.'

'I know about the Helios, yes and all the other boats.'

'What the fuck do you know JJ?'

JJ was now desperately trying to buy time. Where the hell were Chad and the backup team? Should he use the code words now? Burton would shoot him as quick as look at him or stab him or gouge his eyes out or ...

'How you blew them out of the water, along with the poor sods in them just for the insurance.'

Burton laughed. Spit came from his drunken mouth and spattered Edward's face. The others laughed with him like hyenas.

'So, we scuttled a few ships for insurance money. Doesn't everyone?'

'Not with over fifty people in crates in the hold.'

'People? They weren't people. They were scum, the shit on the sole of my shoe, just like you now I think of it. Who's going to miss them? We did the world a favour drowning that crap.'

Chapter 3 - Tuesday 5th March

Burton turned to the others.

'Didn't we?'

A chorus of affirmation echoed round the room and was picked up by the microphones lying on the ground against the wall. Edward kept stalling.

'I know about the TV sets.'

'The TV sets you stole?'

'I know they went into the hospitals where you sold people for experiments.'

'If we sold them to the hospitals, as least we provided them with some fucking entertainment.'

Burton roared with laughter for what seemed an eternity. Then his expression turned to a repulsive grimace.

'I've had enough of this bollocks.'

He held out a hand to Rick.

'Knife, scalpel now you prick!'

Edward decided he must call time.

'You know I've always wanted to tell you this to your ugly face. You're a fucking shit Burton, do you know that? Anyway I want a piss.'

'Piss in your pants if you want. It'll be your last time and you ain't going to have a last fucking cigarette.'

Even with the ketamine Rick only had the stomach for blood on a screen or from a sedated patient. He didn't want to see and hear the real thing.

'He'll bleed Cyrus.'

Burton's fury was turning his face purple. He screamed at Rick.

'A fucking syringe then. This fucking Glock will wake up the bleeding street. Hurry up you prick head. Then we'll deal with his fucking fictional friends.'

Rick went to the elevator and Edward could just hear it creaking its way upstairs. He didn't have long left. Where was Mac? The wire they tied his wrists with was tightening the more he tried to break free and cutting into his flesh. He was hauled across the room by Black Rod who pinned Edward's arms back in a vice like grip.

Black Rod, with his back to the curtains, was by now lifting his prisoner in the air as Edward repeated again and again.

'I want a piss. Give me a fucking fag.'

It was as if his life depended on it and it did. The words were repeated in an ever increasing frenzy as each second passed like an hour at a time. Burton responded to each plea with the same words.

'Shut the fuck up.'

He slapped Edward hard on the side of his face time after time. Death was waiting for Burlington. Burton was pointing the gun at his forehead and the sisters were hovering round him like a pair of slobbering vultures. Rick came back quickly with a syringe in one hand and a small bottle of clear liquid in the other. Burton glared at Rick.

'Give me that.'

Rick Borges didn't. The Bashir brothers held each other's hands and stood with their backs to the curtains. They were the first to take delivery of the impact as the French window caved in to the ear-shattering sound of multiple explosions.

Cooper came through first and whacked Black Rod's neck with the butt of his Uzi. Burton pulled the trigger and the flash and blast of expanding air from the blank almost knocked Edward unconscious. He slumped to the floor as Black Rod thudded to the ground.

Team One followed Chad through the disintegrated window. They were all in filthy oil stained blue boiler suits and carrying sawn off shotguns. Cooper fired a burst of bullets into the ceiling. Chad's team looked as intended, complete amateurs, more like garage mechanics than SAS.

'Everybody on the bloody floor. Now!'

Burton was the last to lie on the carpet. His face was defiant and made it clear he considered these goons to be a crew of small time operators. Chad grabbed the syringe and bottle from Rick while Team One were cuffing the others. Chad looked into Rick Borges' frightened eyes.

'Roll up your fucking sleeve.'

'No. You'll kill me.'

'That's the idea you shit. Then we'll give the others a shot.'

Rick screamed and Chad put one punch on his chin knocking him clean out. The others squirmed on the floor. All except Burton: he lay motionless next to Black Rod's lifeless body. Cooper spat a squirt of saliva onto the carpet. He threw the syringe and bottle on the floor, stamped on them and continued in his best Cockney accent.

'Think yourselves lucky we're not murdering bastards like you lot. If you ever come after JJ we are coming back and then we will bloody well kill you. Got that? We will fucking kill you. Tie them up lads and let's get out of here.'

He fired another burst into the ceiling. As two of Chad's men cuffed the gang on the floor tying them together, the others ransacked the room. They took the pictures, a chunky table fag lighter, anything that looked valuable. Chad swiftly and stealthily stuck two pin microphones into the back of the sofa where Black Rod had been masturbating. No one was watching him as the others finished their allotted tasks.

'Let's get JJ to a pub. Once his face is cleaned up and his hair combed he'll be right. Did I hear you wanted a piss?'

Edward was helped into the waiting ambulance. Team One mopped up any traces that might link the intelligence services to the raid. They then withdrew from what was about to become a crime scene. Edward regained his full faculties as a doctor

Chapter 3 - Tuesday 5th March

wiped his face and head clear of blood to assess the damage. A nurse took his pulse and blood pressure. The doctor smiled ruefully.

'Not too much damage. Nothing a dentist, a good haircut and a drink or two wouldn't fix, that's what I'd say.'

The doctor was right. That was all Edward needed despite another painful close shave with death. He was given a couple of painkillers.

Mac was listening inside the cab. Someone with a Scandinavian accent was talking to Burton.

'They were not police.'

'I fucking know that.'

'They were armed with sawn off shotguns, not your normal police weapons of choice.'

'They were fucking nerds. I'll find them and kill them all, especially that JJ fucker. Who does he think he is, Joan of fucking Arc?'

As the others tried to get each others' cuffs off they gabbled on about what evidence would need to be destroyed, just in case JJ and his crew tried to blackmail them. They might as well have been signing confessions in front of a high court judge. They were even naming some of the high ranking diplomats involved, while the tape recorders whirred on and all the proof Mac prayed for kept on coming.

Mac sat and listened almost in disbelief as the unintended confessionals continued and then, snapping out of his daydream, he called the real head of Special Branch.

'It's your turn now George.'

George Street Marylebone, London England

Edward was whisked away by cab. He never attended official debriefings, only the piss-ups afterwards, if invited. Instead of going straight home as any sensible person would have done he dropped into his local, the Aristocrat in George Street not far from Selfridges. The pub had quite a reputation with the in crowd.

'Hello Edward my love, forget to open the door when you came in did you? Pint top of Carling is it?'

He nodded but smiling was awkward. The jolliness of his welcoming reception said it all. Edward picked up his drink and tried to swig it back but more of it dribbled down his neck and onto the carpet than went down the intended plug hole.

'You'd better use a straw darling or all of that will be on the carpet. Here, have one of these.'

He took the black straw and sat upstairs in a corner with his back to the wall. He thought about tonight. Only an hour or so before the Harley Street operation he had been drinking with half a dozen of his workmates in the basement of Ye Olde London in Ludgate Hill. Even one of Edward's audit team managers, good old Raj, couldn't miss out on that occasion. He and others joined Edward and Hugh after the five-a-side football match. Edward's day was not without variety.

The mini piss-up was to celebrate Scamp's first birthday: seven and a half weeks in dog years. Any excuse would do. Scamp was the brothers' beloved Labrador. Although finally house trained by Edward, Scamp was still a puppy and loved to bits by both brothers.

As usual, the banter revolved around football and taking the piss out of the firm's partners. Edward was habitually the master of ceremonies on such occasions until his goalkeeping skills were subjected to close scrutiny. The five-a-side and rarer full team football matches and these sporadic booze-ups that followed them were the only fun part of working for Porter Williams for many attendees.

Hugh was well known to Edward's contemporaries as a referee at serious outdoor football games with other City accountancy firms. He knew all the partners who played. That way he enjoined in taking the piss out of the bosses. The butt of most of the jokes was Edward though when reminded of his more stunning goalkeeping performances. Even Hugh joined in the piss taking today.

'Ed, when you tie up your boot laces, ever thought of facing the opposition rather than your own goal posts. That way, instead of picking up the ball from the back of the net you might collect a back pass.'

There was much laughter. No one at work knew of where Edward had been earlier that afternoon or where he was scheduled to be later that night.

Edward didn't drink to calm his nerves. His problem was nothing scared him. He knew he hadn't been drinking to gain courage. In fact the opposite was true. He'd resorted to halves to make sure he was just right for tonight and it had worked. Normally he was imbued with a reckless disregard for his own safety and took risks that would be called unnecessary by more cautious men.

In hindsight he hadn't needed any Dutch courage but would've preferred a bulletproof vest to another drink. Mind you, Burton had tried to shoot him in the face so that would not have been much good. All Edward was thinking was thank God they had cocked up and put blanks in his gun by mistake. Little did he know that was not why he was still alive. As the saying goes, even if he was being backed up by a rapid response team, no matter how rapid they were, they couldn't move faster than a flying bullet.

Edward's mind ceased its ramblings. All he could think of was that Burton was now history. Well, he hoped so. He decided to try and be sociable and went down to stand at the bar sipping his lager through the black straw he'd been given. Some of his local drinking mates were soon asking questions and, like Annie behind the bar were taking the piss.

'So Edward is it true that you tried to save a penalty in your mouth this evening?'

Chapter 3 - Tuesday 5th March

This banter went on and on but Edward was finding it harder to answer back in similar style and laughing was hard too. The painkillers he'd been given earlier enjoined with the lager into a slumber land cocktail as he sucked away at his second pint. His numbed lips couldn't even tell where the tip was when he put a cigarette in his mouth.

He should have gone straight home after the Harley Street operation. Instead he left half way through his third pint. As was Edward's wont, he had jumped at the thought of a drink but should have thought through the consequences of making an impromptu stop before going home. Yet once he was there nothing was going to stop him weathering out the squall.

Edward should have realised that drinking anything would be difficult without a straw; smoking would be like having an anaesthetic and talking at the same time well nigh impossible. Never mind. He had survived Harley Street and this unscheduled stop.

Westminster Bridge Road Lambeth, London England

Not long after ten o'clock Mac headed back to Century House for a quick debriefing. It had been easier and quicker than he thought. The op hadn't been perfect. Nothing was, but it had gone well. Young Burlington had kept his cool and once again proved his weight in gold as an asset. Mac grinned to himself. It may have taken a month or so longer than he expected but he'd the evidence he had sought in his pocket so to speak and maybe a knighthood to boot. This would certainly go down as the foremost diplomatic incident in British history outside wartime.

Edward had entrapped Burton and that should be a lesson not even that rat would forget in haste.

Yet Mac, of all people, had got it all so wrong. Given his experience he should have known nothing was that simple, never would be. He had passed the baton to Special Branch and should have realised from that moment he would have no idea of what was happening. If he had that smirk would have been wiped off his face faster than a crocodile can snap its jaws shut.

The spiders' webs of fate were drawing disparate people together as the butterfly effects of time chaotically dragged them inescapably closer. The first assignment accomplished by Edward Burlington in 1974 was but the start of a long journey as midnight struck on that 5th March and the first train symbolically heaved itself away from the station.

As the clock kept on relentlessly ticking there would be many more bodies jettisoned from that train. And as one diary showed there were many other trains already queuing up for equally ghoulish rides elsewhere. So far there was only Black Rod's body in a black bag by the side of the track.

While on the subject of that "one diary", it was Mac's. His diaries resembled British Rail timetables. They were all written in incomprehensible terminology referring to stations, tracks, lines, trains, coaches and passengers as if they were part of the ops he worked on. We have fastidiously tried to decode them and use his metaphors to reflect the gist of his thinking where we can. You'll soon understand why Mac thought along tram lines!

Chapter 4
Wednesday 6th March

Scotland Yard Victoria, London England
At three in the morning George Simpson was still being briefed by his officers. The briefings were by now sporadic. Those syndicate members found in Harley Street were detained without putting up any resistance.

The Bashirs were found huddled together in a cupboard under the rear staircase by the cranky lift. The Borges fled upstairs to their apartments but the fragile doors were no match for Special Branch's battering rams. Black Rod's body was taken away for an autopsy.

The Bashirs and Borges were now kicking their chair legs while sat in interview rooms. They decided to keep quiet after delivering their well rehearsed lines. In police speak the Bashirs hinted that they would sing but wouldn't venture much further until they were reunited. Each volunteered to do a deal but only on various conditions. One was that they would hand over what they had in terms of addresses for Burton.

The three Borges refused to speak until their diplomatic immunity was acknowledged so they just waited in separate rooms silently chain smoking. It was obvious each syndicate member had jointly and separately planned for this day. Special Branch had too.

Somehow the Congolese Ambassador had been informed of Black Rod's murder and armed with three heavy duty lawyers was waiting impatiently in a visitors' lounge in Scotland Yard. The ambassador refused to say how he knew of Rod's death other than that he heard it on the diplomatic grapevine just like jungle drums beating. Their government wanted the villains who did it extradited to the Congo to face rough justice. What's more the ambassador was awaiting instructions from the President no less on what was to happen next but declined to say any more.

At first George thought the ambassador was bluffing or was off his diplomatic trolley. However, the Congolese legal team came up with a barrage of arguments that sounded convincing. They quoted various sections of British Acts of Parliament as to why extradition was appropriate. George was left with no alternative but to call in the Foreign Office experts. They were on standby anyway. Two had already spent nearly three hours hanging on the end of their home phones in a stop start conference call. Two others who lived in the West End came in to Scotland Yard.

A seemingly peculiar element of the Congolese claims was that the mansion in Harley Street was an extension to their embassy and therefore Congolese territory. Soon after being presented with that unexpected claim George discovered the Congolese Ambassador had been accidentally overheard calling his people. The ambassador should have known better. He had used a special phone in the visitors' lounge. One of his staff reported that their President had ordered the embassy to prepare to sever diplomatic relations with the UK. George expected diplomatic mayhem but he had not anticipated it at this speed, vitriol or level.

Soon the Congolese Ambassador wasn't the only ambassador to have crawled out of bed or been dragged from a casino and assembled a cackle of lawyers to accompany him to Scotland Yard. The Syrian, Libyan and Egyptian Ambassadors were queuing up and none of them were used to being kept waiting by anyone especially in the middle of the night. To make matters worse and more confusing the Foreign Office reported there were hostile movements afoot overseas. The British Ambassadors in all those countries plus Sudan, Somalia and Pakistan had been summoned to emergency meetings irrespective of what the time was. They had been given no explanations and were now uncontactable.

Back in Scotland Yard the lawyers representing the abused diplomats were totting up every minute they sat waiting, prowling around the room like scavenging hyenas. They showed no genuine concern for their clients. The longer they were kept waiting the better as their meters ticked over at their highest inconceivable charge out rates. When their eyes blinked with tiredness you could see fifty pound notes flashing by in the slots where their eyes should have been. What's more they were all singing from the same hymn sheet. They all claimed the Harley Street property as their territory and diplomatic immunity for their citizens. Someone had put their ducks in a diplomatic procession for them.

The Congolese Ambassador demanded the Foreign Secretary attend. Also there had been a call from the British Ambassador's secretary in the Congo to the Foreign Office saying he had been summarily called to see the President with no explanation. There was so much going on so quickly that no one had a grip on what was happening. Political hornets' nests were ablaze across an exponentially increasing area of Africa and the Middle East after the lawyers became involved. Operation Standpipe had landed in a thorny diplomatic bouncy castle which was not good news for Special Branch.

George was first told of the ambassadors and their hyenas for hire starting to arrive downstairs after midnight. They had each been asked in turn why they had come in and then left to stew for a while. Rather than risk claims of inhuman treatment

Chapter 4 - Wednesday 6th March

within under an hour of each arrival he responded. Officers were despatched to take each ambassador and his lawyers to a separate interview room. Once there they had to formally ascertain in minute detail precisely what they wanted and if possible find out how they found out about the incident.

Everything was becoming much more convoluted than at first thought. All of the syndicate members were British citizens which complicated matters. The Bashir brothers, while Pakistani diplomats turned out to be Syrian diplomats too. As for the three Borges, while Indonesian diplomats, they were both Libyan and Egyptian diplomats as well. Naturally they all claimed diplomatic immunity despite the police's cynicism as to their true diplomatic statuses. The complex charade was intended to obfuscate issues and confuse the police plus provide freedom passes to the five live syndicate board members detained.

The briefing continued on and off as more news arrived. Mac was furious but had kept his anger well hidden so far while listening in on the conference call from Century House. Two more Foreign Office lawyers enjoined the conference from their homes. Mac, like them and the ambassadors, had been woken up. At least he had two hours' kip. For Mac sleep was like fuel. Even a small top up would keep him going for hours at his chosen pace.

Mac could not believe it. Barely three minutes passed twixt cup and lip between his teams pulling out and George's men going in yet there was not a trace of Burton. Similarly that man with a Scandinavian accent evaporated despite the police having cordoned off the area surrounding the Harley Street mansion. George was told the police were still searching the mansion and its surrounds with police dogs but so far to no avail. That was only part of the bad news.

Simpson and all the lawyers advising him had agreed unanimously on one issue. Chad Cooper must be arrested on suspicion of murder. That was why they asked Mac to join in the call. Mac argued his case but to no purpose. He was told the Foreign Office would almost certainly get the charges dropped but to avert an international incident the arrest had to be made. There would be no mention of Chad's true colours but the law was now being used against the police with some ferocity.

The MI5 theatre of Cooper and co acting as Brixton gangsters may have momentarily fooled Burton as stun grenades flashed and bullets riddled the Borges' basement ceiling. It hadn't fooled the lawyers though once juxtaposed with the near simultaneous arrest of their clients.

There was even more bad news. No documents of significance and no computers had yet been found in the Harley Street mansion which housed the Borges' medical centre and their apartments. The searches were still in their early days though. Other teams were now at the Bashirs' offices and flat in Mayfair. Searches of Black Rod's premises in Hampstead were underway. Each of the syndicate's other known residences and cars were also being searched or tracked down across the UK. As for Burton, they still didn't have a UK address for him despite years of detective work.

Church Hill Carshalton, Surrey England

Chad and his wife Joanna were woken by hammering on their front door at about the same time as Mac was trying to defend him on the conference call. They could see the blue lights silently flashing from upstairs. Chad looked at her almost with embarrassment and with apologies written all over his face. They didn't need to say anything as their well rehearsed plan swung into action. They'd gone through this before, four times.

Joanna gingerly opened the solid oak door: three heavy duty chain latches were secured to it. Chad stood motionless watching the police on a TV screen wired up to his home CCTV system. Every other second it flickered round from one side of their house to the next. As he watched he clutched his Uzi. The gun was to have been handed back to stores later that morning.

'Can I have some ID please?'

The uniformed inspector presented her with his ID card. She inspected it with care.

'Inspector Martins, you do understand that because of my husband's job we must check first.'

'Yes madam, but if we hear anything odd we will have to force entry.'

She called Scotland Yard from a phone in the hallway in sight of the police inspector who was peering through the gap between the wall and the entrance door. Martins could just see some bleary eyed children taking up their perches at the top of the staircase. That's all we need now he thought.

Joanna replaced the phone onto its wall mounting.

'It's an all clear darling.'

She unchained the door and Chad appeared submissively holding the Uzi by its barrel as the police inspector entered their home.

'Presumably you want this and me?'

'Yes sir.'

He gave Martins the gun and put his hands out in a gesture to show he was ready to be cuffed. Meanwhile Joanna was shooing the kids back to bed.

'There will be no need for that sir. You can get dressed before we go but one of my men will accompany you.'

Chad nodded. Inspector Martins then read Mr Cooper his rights and charged him. He was allowed to make a call and tried ringing Mac but was told he was engaged and said he was not to be disturbed. Chad called no one else and went upstairs. He kissed his children good night and then dressed, brushed his teeth and shaved: he always tried to sparkle in the morning, even mornings like this.

Chapter 4 - Wednesday 6th March

There were two police vans and an unmarked car parked outside the Cooper's house in Church Hill. Several officers who had gone to the adjoining back gardens returned. They left with the others apart from Martins and two plainclothes sergeants from Special Branch who stayed to bring in Chad.

Once Chad was dressed, after a private farewell to Joanna he was whisked away in the unmarked car which headed for Scotland Yard. Martins hadn't met Chad Cooper before but knew of his reputation. Respect was the order of the day. Mind you if he had misbehaved they were ready for him. Well over a dozen of their bulkiest officers were present. They would normally be seen with balaclavas on bulldozing drug barons' front doors or in the front line of a riot squad.

Scotland Yard Victoria, London England

George Simpson had just broken off from the conference call he was hosting and gone to take two more urgent operational calls on his secretary's phone outside his office. He returned to join in the call and his face was a canvas of mixed emotions.

'I bloody well told you so Mac. If only you'd let us handle the whole thing Burton would have been in custody by now.'

'Rubbish George. You couldn't have controlled JJ ...'

'Look Mac, forget all that nonsense. We've been over that chestnut enough already. By splitting control of the operation it wasn't seamless. You bloody well called us in two minutes too late. Were you day dreaming of a knighthood or what?'

'No I damn well wasn't.'

'If that's the case then how come we arrived in less than a minute and Burton escaped.'

Mac instinctively knew Simpson had something up his sleeve so rather than put his foot in any more of his own shit he let him continue. Simpson was a cunning bugger though. How else could he have guessed what Mac had been thinking?

'I've just been told how he escaped with that Scandinavian you overheard. They used a tunnel from the basement that led to an old communal bomb shelter and exited via Park Square West the other side of Marylebone Road. Yes you've guessed it. Just outside where our cordon was about nearly three hours ago. They could be in France by now for all we know.'

'Shit. Are you sure?'

'Do two pairs of fresh footprints sound convincing enough?'

'Ok but we've still busted the damn syndicate and their diplomatic front.'

'Don't hold your breath. We've rooms full of their lawyers. Based on the advice you and I have been listening to for the last two hours this is not going to be a walkover.'

Mac had gone to bed a happy man an hour or so ago and was now getting despondent. Simpson continued.

'... and I am genuinely sorry to say we have now arrested your Mr Cooper and charged him with murder.'

'Holy shit. Was that necessary?'

'Mac, have you been asleep during this conference call? All the lawyers said we had no option under the circumstances. Your Mr Cooper's on his way here. He may even be in the cells downstairs by now. There was no bother when we collected him. We'll interview him properly later. I suggest you get some kip and head over here by say ten this morning. By then we'll know where we are with these bloody legal vultures. We'll also have spoken to the Foreign Secretary about this damn mess. It'll make a good wake up call for the new guy, what's his name again?'

The younger of the lawyers present interjected.

'James Callaghan'.

Mac agreed to turn up at Scotland Yard at ten and hung up his phone. He didn't want to get in the way. George was a fair and frank man and he would be stretched to the limit dealing with this situation. Mac knew everything was damn complicated legally; he'd been told so by some of the UK's best lawyers. They all knew following the textbook was crucial now. All the proper procedures had to be gone through even if purely for show.

Chad would have to be suspended, pending trial or in reality so he thought until the bloody Congolese dropped charges in exchange for what? Well that was up to the Foreign Office. At least he would be out on bail but then he couldn't work. What with the damn IRA and all this, the intelligence services, particularly MI5, needed all the help they could get which was why he and many others from MI6 had been seconded there in the first place.

Anything could happen in the next day or so. Mac decided not even to think about it. He'd sleep at Century House rather than go home. His family weren't expecting him back now anyway. The powers that be would smooth it all out one day. As he tried to doze off Mac asked himself if he should have acted sooner.

How much more violence would have been permissible if it had been a police or MI5 operative under cover in that house, and not just an asset like Burlington? Would there have been more corpses? Had he been right to insist he handled the first part of the operation last night? He still believed so but could he have called in George's team sooner than he did? Definitely yes.

No matter what, he knew he had been ball watching as Burlington was wont to say. He'd sat too long just listening to the proof pouring along his wires. Ok, Burton had escaped yet he had the evidence to cull the diplomatic abuses. Maybe by being overly cautious he was responsible for Chad having to move in so heavily but then that had always been Chad's style. As he was already nearing his fortieth birthday with grey hairs creeping through his broad head of wiry hair one might have thought he would have learnt by now.

Chapter 4 - Wednesday 6th March

Caledonian Road Islington, London England

Burton and the Scandinavian were holed up in one of London's many brothels north of Kings Cross Station in the infamous Cally Road. The whorehouse was less than a mile or so from Harley Street but in all other respects its bricks and mortars were in a different world. That was a world Burton thrived in and he owned this one amongst many other plusher bordellos spread across the globe.

They had seen all the police and their vehicles when they emerged on the north side of Marylebone Road. His Scandinavian minder, Jordan, had been quick to get a passing cab which was out of the police's line of sight before heading towards Kings Cross. Finally they made it to temporary safety. They had no idea whether the large police presence was connected with them but Jordan took no chances with Cyrus Burton. He meant too much to him for that.

Jordan didn't dismiss the heavy policing as a coincidence; he was too experienced and shrewd to rule out the obvious. He even noted the vans were parked facing the wrong way on the south side of Marylebone Road. They were of course all within two hundred yards of the Harley Street mansion they had just escaped from.

Lingwala, Kinshasa Congo

The first task Burton dealt with once indoors was to get hold of Sadiq Solomon's number and call him. Sadiq was a key contact of his in Africa and a high ranking civil servant living in Kinshasa, formerly called Léopoldville. Solomon possessed the political skills of Machiavelli as he had been in situ in the Congo or Zaire for some twenty years or more.

As Mobutu's right hand man he was one of the few senior public officials to survive Mobutu's ruthless coups in the sixties. His being the only one still alive nearly ten years later said it in one. He was de facto the vice president in more ways than one and a very shrewd one at that. He had managed to place most of his family in powerful positions to watch his back and guard his front.

By the way, El Presidente Generalissimo Joseph-Desiré Mobutu had an annoying habit of changing names. He changed the name of his country and the names of many other places under his dictatorial command. He even changed his own name so we'll just refer to him as Mobutu and the Congo as the Congo.

Cyrus Burton told Sadiq his version of what happened and that Black Rod, Mobutu's brother, was dead. Mobutu having been awoken by Sadiq called Burton back. He was incandescent with fury and out for revenge. Sadiq had to translate what Mobutu said every now and again as he was so crazed. They offered Burton sanctuary in their London Embassy but Jordan advised against it. The British authorities would have found out sooner or later and he'd then have been trapped. For the moment anyway Jordan reckoned the route they always used for emergency exits from the UK looked a far better bet.

Burton suggested Solomon together with Mobutu call some of their friends in the Middle East and Africa. He recommended including Syria, Libya, Egypt, Sudan and Somalia on the never ending list. Solomon actually asked if he had a world map with him at one point! The general idea was to ferment hostility towards Her Majesty's Government.

Mobutu agreed to call as many friends in high places as he could. His friends represented the world's most debauched tyrants and dictators and included Uganda's Idi Amin, Libya's Gaddafi and other equally charming yet persuasive heads of state. However, he had more important allies in NATO: in particular in Belgium, France, the UK and the USA. The West had backed Mobutu's rise to power in the sixties and continued to look upon his country, his Congo, as an ally in the heartland of Africa. The diplomatic world was a small one and Burton lay in its heartland knowing just how powerful a world it was.

Despite being the bearer of such terrible news Burton was thanked before the line went dead. Mobutu didn't give a damn what the time was in those countries he called. Sadiq Solomon was tasked with handling calls into the UK to establish the facts and started by calling the new Prime Minister, Harold Wilson, as they didn't know who the new bloody Foreign Secretary was. That call got him nowhere apart from being transferred to the Foreign Office but he couldn't get through to the Foreign Secretary let alone a switchboard operator: no one even bothered to answer the damn phone.

By now Solomon was as frustrated and furious as his boss. His out of date contact list of influential British civil servants extended to a dozen or so people he'd had dealings with in MI6 over the years so he decided he would try to get them out of bed too. Like the diplomatic world, in many respects the intelligence community also lived in a small world: often they overlapped. He got through to the switchboard this time and demanded to speak with Sir Douglas Castle.

Castle wasn't available so Solomon asked to speak to each of his contacts whose rank and influence diminished until he reached the bottom of his list. Most no longer worked there, not that he was told that, and he was that desperate he even asked for the likes of George Francis and Giles Cartwright but alas they too no longer toured around Africa on MI6's behalf as fake arms dealers. They weren't much higher in rank than Tessa anyway.

Of those who still worked at MI6, they like the rest of the good and great in Great Britain were asleep behind not to be disturbed notices. Given the time in London the switchboard operators said they would pass on the messages to those he had tried to speak to. They did but via Mac who only got the messages at about seven in the morning because, other than in respect of standard emergency procedures, he too had said he was not to be disturbed unless George Simpson rang.

Once Mobutu called Gaddafi it became clear that the diplomats had been subjected to a brutal and unlawful attack by the British government. The Libyan Embassy

Chapter 4 - Wednesday 6th March

in London had already been told so by the Borges' lawyers. It took minutes on discovering this for Mobutu and Solomon to send in their ambassador armed with lawyers. The other tyrants directly involved did likewise in London. Many others ordered the resident British Ambassadors out of bed for pre-breakfast grillings as happened in Kinshasa.

Mobutu, Solomon and Gaddafi knew dozens of diplomats apart from their own might be facing absolute disgrace. Their warning calls had been well received particularly in those countries whose diplomats were already detained: Syria, Libya, Pakistan and Egypt. Mobutu and Solomon reminded everyone they called of the depravities of the sexual shenanigans and other more macabre misdemeanours of their so called diplomats. If these were ever publicised they might lose the support of whichever of the big two, the USA and USSR, they had a cosy relationship with. The mere mention of that spurred most into action for fear of losing the backing of whichever super power supported them.

Burton's general idea was to cause as much brouhaha as conceivably possible in the ensuing twenty four hours so that he could exit the UK without difficulty. Luckily Jordan was with him and he knew precisely how to arrange matters including bribing the right officials.

Sadiq called them back when the opportunity arose. He explained what Mobutu and he had picked up from the Libyans and others about the Bashirs and Borges having been taken into custody. Jordan, forever cautious, changed his plans yet again once he had confirmation of his suspicions. His guess was every normal departure point from the UK would be watching for Cyrus Burton and possibly even someone with a Scandinavian accent. He was absolutely spot on as usual.

Scotland Yard Victoria, London England

Mac arrived early at just before nine o'clock. He went to console Chad in his cell until Joanna turned up having left her parents in charge of getting the kids to school. She brought spare clothes and what else Chad forgot or hadn't been able to take with him. Mac reassured her he would be out by the weekend. Then having thought about it more said he meant the one beginning the 16th March not the 9th March. Joanna just stared at him. Chad pretended to pass it off with an insipid joke but no one was laughing with him.

Mac promised to call Edward at Chad's behest to postpone the piss-up planned for tonight. He then bowed out as benevolently as he could, promising to keep them both abreast of the rapidly changing picture. Between their furrowed brows he could see that they were worried, expecting him to do better and sort it out quicker.

By ten o'clock, when Mac joined George Simpson, he was introduced to some new faces. It soon became obvious that George and those he'd been in conference with earlier hadn't slept a twinkle. There had been many overnight developments but progress was being hampered by the new Foreign Secretary.

Mac reported that the Congolese government had tried to contact Sir Douglas Castle and several others earlier in the morning but MI6 had not responded yet. One of the lawyers said the calls should be returned out of courtesy and all past or future calls relating to Dr Mobutu should be referred to him. Mac agreed and slipped out of the room to call Tessa to make the necessary calls and arrangements.

Jim Callaghan had a jolly full diary already for Foreign Office guided tours and photo shoots not even taking into account his first full Cabinet meeting and celebratory dinner that evening. So the Civil Service were told to keep him apprised of any major developments but otherwise handle the crisis "as he would have". As they had only just been introduced that was a cunning "you'll never be able to blame me if things go wrong" instruction. Obviously Callaghan was learning fast. After all, as Sir Douglas had told Mac, if Operation Standpipe wasn't carefully handled petrol stations would run out of fuel in days. Stockpiles would be held aside for the emergency services and governmental use and riots would ensue.

There was clarity on some legal fronts. Each floor of the Harley Street property had been leased to different countries including Syria, Libya, Egypt and the Congo. All of them sub-let their parts back to a trust in the British Virgin Islands. As no one knew or would say who the beneficiaries of the trust were the Congolese claims for Chad's extradition fell away. In addition, the other niceties of the Congolese demands for his rendition proved groundless. Chad was bailed on Friday 16th March once the spectre of his visiting the Congo faded into fantasy but he still faced murder charges.

The three Borges's claims to diplomatic immunity were quashed on technicalities so far as Libya and Egypt went but they were validated as Indonesian diplomats. Nonetheless the Indonesian Ambassador was summoned to the Foreign Office and despite his protestations his three diplomatic staff were summarily expelled. They were forced to go at once. There were no pleasantries like a change of clothes or picking up any personal possessions or prescription drugs on the way from Scotland Yard to Heathrow and onward to Jakarta.

The Bashirs were quite canny. Their Syrian diplomatic status was confirmed but they wished to remain in London. They did a deal under threat of being returned to Pakistan where the ISI, Pakistan's equivalent to MI6, had a few expensive questions they wanted to put to them. The raids on their Mayfair flat and offices unexpectedly yielded no information of any value, yet.

As promised the police were given many addresses for Burton but after a lot of research and a few raids they might as well have been randomly plucked out of telephone directories for the Greater London area. Maybe they had been but the Bashirs thought they were genuine and had every reason to shaft Burton now if they could do it behind closed doors. As with any raids, where possible future benefits might be

Chapter 4 - Wednesday 6th March

obtained, MI6 always bugged where they searched. In the Bashirs' case every room in their offices and home was wired including the roof garden above their flat in Hallam Street.

So in exchange for their continued residence in the UK they swapped selected safety deposit keys which were held in safe custody at the Syrian Embassy. The boxes collected from the Mayfair bank contained the syndicate's accounts. They fastidiously detailed with flawless accuracy and clarity every penny ever received and paid out by the syndicate. More importantly they recorded what each transaction related to and who, including their contact details, was involved. The whole scenario was playing out as if the twins knew one day their records would be used. Perverts they might have been but not stupid ones. Together with Mac's tapes taken on the night of the incursion they constituted explosive evidence.

However, they didn't include any details of Cyrus Burton's whereabouts or even his name. There were dozens of entries for various people just referred to as Smith whose addresses were all GCHQ, MI5 or MI6 premises. The addresses included Century House but there were no other contact details. Someone rather clever knew one day the Bashirs would have to play their trump card. This was one way of raising two fingers to the British law enforcement authorities.

There was clear evidence of many dozens of diplomats based in London being involved one way or another in appalling crimes. Jim Callaghan finally put his feet under his desk and reviewed the files along with the joint testimony submitted by MI6 and Special Branch. The expulsions began within days.

The official report into Standpipe made light of Burton's escape. In Appendix P Section 17 Paragraph 32 (c) (IV) reference was made to improving liaison and coordination between factions of law enforcement authorities involved in time sensitive raids. Otherwise the document read like a congratulations card and a request for recognition in the New Year's honours list.

However, if anyone thought that was the last they'd seen of Cyrus Burton and Jordan, let alone their corrupt diplomatic clientele, they would be sadly mistaken. Drums would be beaten loud and hard in the Congo more than once in 1974 and many of those already close to Edward would assemble to hear the drumbeats for different reasons.

As the Burlingtons' diaries revealed, Operation Standpipe was far from over and the next stop wasn't even in spitting distance. The Bashir brothers weren't finished in their dealings with Burton. Burton was far from finished with JJ. MI6, the piggy in the middle, was still snoring in the guards' van as spiders spun cobwebs of intrigue around them.

George Simpson, as if the station master, waived his flag and the coaches lumbered and lurched into the dark leaving him forlornly behind: a gloomy silhouette ...

just discernible through the fading platform lights, now transformed into memories of past Christmas illuminations.

In hindsight the train's passengers were oblivious as the express thundered through another station bypassing the Foreign Office who were too busy celebrating "their" successes in the first class waiting room like it was Hogmanay.

☙❧

Chapter 5
Thursday 11th April

London England, Kinshasa Congo & Antwerp Belgium

In the aftermath of Operation Standpipe, more than two hundred and forty diplomats, including several ambassadors, were clandestinely expelled by the Foreign Office. That was more in any single year than in any decade in peacetime in the history of the UK.

Many of these people were rather more active in the Burton crime syndicate than simply playing diplomacy as most normal people would know it but being official envoys all were immune from prosecution. As they were involved one way or another in extortion, blackmail, paedophilia, hard core porn, human trafficking, murder or slavery none of their governments protested that much. Soon everything just settled down like sand in the wake of a sudden and short lived squall.

Mobutu calmed down once Sadiq explained the consequences of rocking any boats on the Congo River. The river was a symbolic snaking line in the jungle for many Congolese as it separated Kinshasa from Brazzaville. Mobutu succumbed to Solomon's wisdom. The last thing he wanted was to upset the USA who along with Belgium had backed his coups. Of course, unbeknownst to the diplomatic reprobates their involvement with Burton was now known to the CIA who were privy to the JIC's chronicles. The CIA and FBI asked many questions about Operation Standpipe once its success was broadcast to all JIC members.

Mobutu's brother Black Rod was given a state funeral. The Congo was rewarded with a good deal on a few obsolete jets from the Royal Air Force at peppercorn cost. The strengthened ties between the two countries were referred to by the Foreign Office in press releases.

Purely coincidentally, as they say, the USA unexpectedly threw its economic clout into the ring. For some reason it supported the ludicrous notion of an internationally recognised heavyweight boxing match between two US citizens later in 1974 being held in Kinshasa of all places. Would any sane person have taken a bet on that? The fight was to be known as the rumble in the jungle, between Muhammad Ali and George Foreman. It was destined to be one of the most celebrated and historic matches ever.

Beneath the radar all charges were formally dropped against Chad Cooper in the first week of April. On 8th April he was recalled to work after a fortnight's holiday mountain climbing in the Highlands. The Congolese Embassy, under threat from the Foreign Office to expose all of their diplomats' true activities, wisely decided to drop every accusation it concocted.

Edward had his tooth replaced and his face healed quickly. He was told to be careful in case Burton tried to take revenge. Thankfully he wasn't damaged goods and it hadn't interfered with his football schedule. That was a top priority by now as the season was nearing its end.

Where Burton had gone after his escape remained a mystery. Mac was convinced the syndicate boss would lay low and no doubt undergo plastic surgery to change his rugged features. That way he'd only be recognisable by the sound of his voice. Intelligence sources placed Burton somewhere between Bangkok and Hong Kong. If they were right Edward was relatively safe for now because if in the Far East Burton would be concentrating on fresh fields. Nobody knew who the Scandinavian was, or where he went after the SAS burst into the mansion in Harley Street.

The JIC didn't know everything, even if every so often its members believed it did. The intelligence sources that put Cyrus Burton in some exotic far eastern location were wrong. Burton was in the last place anyone would think of looking for him. He was back in the heart of De Wallen, Amsterdam's red light district, right next door to the epicentre of one of his old empires in Antwerp.

Mac was correct about one matter. Burton underwent extensive plastic surgery within days of his escape. The surgeon who performed the procedure died in a tragic accident in the outskirts of Antwerp shortly afterwards. The surgeon and his team burned to death in a fire at his clinic and all their records went up in smoke. Not that much of a tragedy in reality. The surgeon was another one of Burton's special surgeons like the beanbag in Wimpole Street.

Facially, Burton was no longer recognisable as his old self. He also grew a beard which he kept well groomed and changed his name to Carl Hanson. The man now looked ten years younger than the one on Interpol's wanted posters.

Burton and Hanson would have been on Sara Burlington's most wanted list too but for her husband not yet sharing what he learnt about his son's role in Standpipe. Therefore Sara as yet was blissfully unaware of not only Operation Standpipe but also the extent of her youngest son's involvement in it. She had no idea of the danger he'd been placed in even though she knew he was working undercover for MI6. If she had been, there would have been blood on the carpets of the JIC meeting rooms by now.

De Wallen, Amsterdam Holland

At one minute past the stroke of midnight on 11th April Hanson decided to test his parvenu features and matching passport. Despite Jordan's protests they had planned a modest trip back to the UK. He studied his new naked self in a full length mirror. Jordan, blonde haired all over, entered the room. He too was undressed and smiled when he saw Carl's naked body.

'Nice and hard everywhere.'

Hanson didn't turn around, just continued to stare at himself in the mirror.

'Thank you Jordan. Are we ready?'

'We will be. Once we get dressed, but first things first ...'

Not long after having sex together on the bedroom floor they left the penthouse apartment over Hanson's prestigious nightclub heading for a boat.

North Shields & Newcastle, Tyne & Wear England

Hanson consumed nearly half a litre of duty free vodka on the ferry crossing from Ijmuiden to the UK. Still relatively sober though, he and Jordan glided through passport control and customs without a problem. The journey had been a long one with delay after delay and Jordan was tired. They wanted to fly instead of take to the seas but they didn't fancy pushing Hanson's luck with airport security. As Hanson had put it so candidly, airport security was tighter than a lamb's arse. Indeed security had heightened at all entry and exit points across the UK as the IRA escalated the insurgency phase of their campaign against Britain.

'You didn't have to come too Cyrus.'

'Carl, I'm fucking Carl now!'

'Sorry Carl. I could have come alone.'

'What? You don't know how to masturbate! You mean I was to miss all the fun. Take a fucking break.'

They were picked up by an inconspicuous Ford Transit van on the quayside, which was driven by a heavily tattooed man. The van headed towards the Jesmond area of Newcastle. Burton and Jordan checked the Colt 45s, complete with silencers and ammunition the driver took out from the glove compartment and handed to them. After a twenty minute drive through the light, late morning traffic, the van pulled up round the corner from a large town house in Osborne Road. The building was owned by a bent solicitor if anyone had tried to trace the ownership but they hadn't. Even if they had they'd never have tracked it back to Burton let alone Hanson.

Jordan walked past the sprawling house. The curtains upstairs were closed. When he turned round and came back again, they were open. The tattooed man slipped out of the van and unlocked the front door. Hanson went inside his house. As soon as his boss was out of sight, Jordan told the man with the patchwork tattoos to carry on to Newcastle Central Station. Once there they waited for the mid-day train from London.

Jordan watched as the Bashir brothers walked along the arrivals platform towards the ticket gates. He knew they'd done a deal with the police otherwise they wouldn't be strolling around like little Napoleons. They looked like a couple of doting penguins in the Antarctic. Carl said doing a deal was alright, he'd have done the same. The diplomats they shopped were no loss and dumping them in the shit was partie du jeu. The higher-ups nearly all managed to avoid incarceration so they could be used again at a later date. Extortion had no statute of limitations.

Hanson and Jordan also knew that they had especially carefully deceived the Bashirs. The twins didn't have enough information about their old master, Cyrus Burton, to do him any serious damage. They didn't even have a telephone number for him: calls were always one way instructions. What Jordan didn't know, and wanted to find out was, if they were being tailed. The blonde man knew all about surveillance from his younger years in Swedish military intelligence.

The Bashirs held hands and carried no briefcases, as they came through into the main station concourse. They let go of each others' hands. Their friends advised them that behaving like that was not the done thing up north. As they glanced around, expecting to be met, the twins kept looking at one another for comfort. Jordan continued his surveillance until all the other passengers had gone through and they were standing alone. The brothers looked forlorn. Jordan signalled to a member of his team dawdling around the taxi queue, who walked towards the Bashirs. The old toothless woman scared them as a gargoyle might children as she slipped a piece of paper into Atif's hand and blurred into those queuing for tickets at the station entrance.

Jordan kept up his observation as the brothers joined the arriving passengers queuing up at the taxi rank. The van followed the Bashirs' cab to an address in the Byker area of Newcastle. Byker was a police prohibited precinct of Newcastle and as rough as a badger's rectum. Any suspicious to-ing and fro-ing wouldn't be given a second glance, unless it was by the police. Look outs surrounded their intended destination.

The taxi drove off after depositing the Bashirs outside a seedy house with its upper windows decoratively boarded up with corrugated iron. The brothers were now holding hands again and looked afraid. Jordan waited a few minutes, to see if any unexpected vehicles went past or parked nearby or if the look outs signalled trouble. The street was as quiet as a neglected cemetery. The accountants hadn't been followed.

That meant they were bugged.

The tattooed transit driver approached the twins, signalled with a finger to his lips for them to stay silent, and took them inside the house. As the accountants were taking off their clothing and changing into overalls Jordan entered. The Swede pointed to their rings and watches and they discarded them as well.

Both the brothers neatly folded their clothes and placed them on two chairs in the centre of the front room. Jordan liked the symmetry of the twins' naked bodies but said nothing. He wanted to shag them together but again didn't have time. Hanson

Chapter 5 - Thursday 11th April

was waiting. Both twins now wearing clothes more suited to Byker than Bond Street were bundled into the back of the van. That was the last time they saw daylight until the back doors were opened again inside a garage at Hanson's town house in the posher part of Newcastle.

Jesmond Newcastle, Tyne and Wear England

Jordan led them through to a large office where Hanson was waiting, a half empty bottle of vodka on the desk in front of him. The brothers didn't recognise him, until he spoke.

'Atif, Hamid I'm so glad you came.'

'Cyrus ... is it you?'

'It is indeed.'

'My God, you look so young and different, so new and interesting.'

'Thank you my dears.'

'We didn't tell them anything important Cyrus.'

'Who?'

'The police.'

'Of course you didn't.'

'It's all JJ's doing.'

'His day will fucking well come.'

MI5 ordered that there should be no surveillance of the accountants as long as the tracker devices covertly planted on them were operational. Why risk being spotted and blow any chance of moving closer to Burton, when technology could do the job just as well, if not better. GCHQ at Cheltenham monitored the accountants' trip, all the way from London to the house in Byker.

The law enforcement agencies didn't believe Cyrus Burton would be at the other end of the Bashirs' rendezvous, seeing as reports still placed him in within five hundred miles of Hong Kong or Bangkok. The bugs in the Bashirs' flat had revealed they were going up north to meet a Pakistani in the restaurant business. So it seemed worthwhile checking if the Bashir brothers' unusual journey to Newcastle led them anywhere of interest. Whoever they were meeting might also prove to be interesting.

Someone at GCHQ was in contact with MI5 in London and the Chief Constable of the Tyne and Wear police.

'They're at number 176 Crawhall Road, Byker.'

'Are they still on the move?'

'No sir. They seem to be stationary at the moment.'

'It's a dangerous area. We should enter that house now.'

'No. Let's just keep tabs on them for the moment.'

The local police boss wasn't happy. He didn't trust technology and favoured good old fashioned kick the door down tactics but was overruled. Neither MI5 nor GCHQ trusted the Tyne and Wear cops to do the job right, so the collaboration between north and south was tense, volatile and even nit-picking.

'We don't know what these two are doing. They could be up to anything.'

'We should wait.'

'No, we should enter.'

There was a breath hissing pause at the London end of the communications triangle.

'Alright then, send in some ground surveillance but do it carefully.'

'We'll move in ...'

'No you won't move in one inch. Just watch and report back. We can't go at this half-cocked.'

'Have it your way then.'

'We'll let you know when the transmitters move again.'

The three way exchange continued, with voices being raised and then raised again.

'That's not my way.'

'It's common sense. Just get on with it.'

'Bloody southerners.'

'Still no movement.'

'Just check the house and let me know who goes in and out.'

'What did you say?'

The southerners heard the sound of a door slamming as the Chief Constable left the room.

Three hours later, GCHQ were reporting that the Bashir brothers were still stationary. The Chief Constable had people pushing prams and bicycles past the door and mending motors in the street. The Crawhall Road residents knew the surveillance team weren't Byker locals and were giving them the evil eye. Anyone local peering through a window of any house nearby number 176 would've quickly known something was amiss.

Nobody did though.

MI5 confirmed the tenant at Crawhall Road didn't exist and there was no telephone inside the house under surveillance. A gas leak sprung up from nowhere and the Newcastle cops entered under the guise of workmen who arrived in a borrowed British Gas van. They discovered two neatly stacked piles of expensive clothes on two chairs, with Italian leather shoes underneath and solid gold Rolex watches and Cartier rings on top.

They asked what GCHQ wanted done with the transmitters they found in the buttons. MI5 said the accountants would be back for their clothes, so they bugged and camera'd the whole house. An unmarked van listened to the silence and watched the stillness in the house from a few hundred yards away on City Road.

Chapter 5 - Thursday 11th April

Listened and watched. Listened and watched.

On the more affluent side of Newcastle, the accountants were beginning a serious vodka drinking session with their playmate of old, Cyrus Burton. They didn't know he was now Carl Hanson and nobody told them. The twins were temptingly and salaciously showing off their new overalls over their trim naked bodies.

They were celebrating the end of the era of illegal immigrants and scuttling ships and the dawn of their leader's new enterprise. The twins had been paying platinum members of Burton's previous sex freaks' club, along with about five thousand others but few could afford platinum status. He and Jordan had footage of a good percentage of them performing unnatural and illicit acts and their intention now was to blackmail them into couriering Class A narcotics. They would operate some porn clubs in Amsterdam, Manila and Bangkok, just to keep everybody sweet.

'The big money is in drugs these days.'

'What if they won't comply?'

'They won't know it's us doing the blackmailing. They might even pay us to trace the fucking blackmailers for them. Beautiful, eh?'

The twins smiled, believing they were going to carry on as accountants in this new drug empire, just as they had in the old, hardcore porn and body parts businesses. Burton beamed back at them. Evil was an apt description of the way his lips parted when he spoke.

'If they don't know who's blackmailing them, they'll be too scared not to fucking comply. These pleasant little bodily contact sports they like carry death penalties in some bloody countries ... and not by lethal injection either.'

Burton's smile was like that of a vampire, drawing lips back over its fangs.

'They can courier the drugs in their bleeding diplomatic pouches for all I care. These fucking kangaroos will jump at my command and go anywhere we choose.'

Jordan spoke, having been silent up to now and keeping off the booze.

'The raw material will come from Bogota and Kabul. We have already negotiated deals. Buying at source is so cheap.'

'Where will we place the money?'

Atif spoke as if it was a given the twins were in on this new caper. Burton poured more vodka.

'We'll keep it in the Caribbean. That's better than Pakistan, don't you think? Before then, I have an arousing video you must see. You'll both love this.'

Jordan produced a tape and inserted it into a video player. The Bashirs sat back together on the couch in anticipation, by now half naked.

A map of Pakistan appeared at the start of the film and then the camera zoomed in to a bank, where an ageing banker was inspecting some cheques. The film was being fast forwarded. There was a close up focusing on two cheques. A London map appeared next followed by pictures taken inside an office. Atif Bashir stood up in a whiter shade of skin than on his arrival in Jesmond and asked for the toilet. All the sexual stirrings in his mind had vanished in a flash. Burton pointed the Colt 45 at him.

'Let's wait until the end, shall we my dear?'

There were two people in the office on the film: Atif and Hamid Bashir. They were speaking in Urdu but the tape came complete with English subtitles.

'You think they won't notice five million?'

'They are in the far east with other things on their minds. Cyrus wouldn't miss ten million. That interfering nobody, Jordan, would spot any more than that.'

'Ten million it is then.'

'We can put the cheque through the Habib Karachi Bank.'

'Uncle Zamir of course.'

Jordan stopped the video. The Bashir brothers sat sheepishly staring at the paused images of themselves salivating avariciously on the screen. They held each other's hands. Atif was shaking with trepidation. Hamid had wet himself. Jordan looked menacing. Reference to him as an interfering nobody did not augur well for the Bashir brothers.

'How ...?'

'Did I find out? You forget I have friends in the ISI.'

'We needed a short term loan Cyrus. We didn't know where you were or we would have told, sorry, asked you. I mean said what we'd done. We were only joking about Jordan. You must have seen the joke, didn't you?'

'Very funny wasn't it Jordan. It's alright, don't worry. We have been in touch with your kind old Uncle Zamir.'

Burton clapped his hands together, as if he'd just concluded a profitable deal.

'Your good uncle's agreed to help me get my money back: what's left of it. All you have to do is sign and fingerprint these forms.'

Jordan shoved two bank transfer authorisations, an ink pad and pen in front of the twins.

'Oh I forgot to add that I promise not to tell the ISI.'

Suspicious money transfers into Pakistan were scrutinised by their Inter-Services Intelligence agency, the ISI. The ISI expected a substantial commission on anything that couldn't be explained properly and backed up with apposite paperwork. The Bashirs hadn't paid, so they could expect no sympathy from Karachi.

After the brothers signed and finger printed the forms, Jordan handcuffed them together: right hand to left hand and left hand to right hand. The twins were left looking into each other's panicky faces. Jordan and Burton just laughed at the felicitousness of this. After that they all just stood around and waited.

Within an hour, a telex came through certifying receipt of just under £8.5 million in a British Virgin Islands' bank account. Then another telex rattled through carrying the tragic news that uncle Zamir had committed suicide. It stated he'd tragically taken

Chapter 5 - Thursday 11th April

an overdose of heroin and his body had just been discovered at the Habib Karachi Bank by an ISI operative. What the spy was doing at the bank was not divulged.

Burton commiserated with the twins but his faux sympathy soon turned to anger.

'As you can see from all this shit, you've spent a million and a half of my money. A million and a half in less than a fucking fortnight. Where did it go?'

'Our family.'

'We have many relatives.'

'Who can consume a million and a half in days?'

'We're sorry.'

'Sorry is not enough, I'm afraid.'

'We'll pay you back Cyrus.'

'I'm afraid that's not enough either my dear boys.'

Burton's lack of expletives signified he was playing games with the twins much to his depraved self gratification. He nodded to Jordan, who dragged the Bashirs down an endless corridor after their erstwhile boss, Atif taking backward steps and Hamid shuffling forward. Burton continued to explain their predicament.

'You see my dears, if I let this go, everybody will think I'm a soft touch, like velvet toilet paper. People from Hong Kong to Houston and back will be queuing up to relieve me of my hard earned cash and wipe their arses with the bigger bank notes.'

They soon arrived in what was once a small ballroom which had been converted into an indoor swimming pool. A video camera overlooked the pool and a trestle table and chair had been set up close to the edge. There was a portable TV and a bottle of vodka on the table. Burton sat down and poured himself a full glass.

Jordan pulled a switchblade from his pocket and cut the brothers' overalls from their bodies, then dragged them, naked, to the crazy paving around the deep end. They were still cuffed together, about to die together just as they had fought with one another to escape from their mother's womb. Burton switched on the TV and an image of the far end of the pool appeared on the screen. He swallowed a large mouthful of vodka and muttered to himself "Allah Akbar" as Jordan shoved the twins into the pool.

The Bashirs thrashed around in the water, trying to gasp in air as they sank and surfaced then sank and surfaced, again and again. They each pushed the other down in their attempts to get their heads above water. Instead of holding hands as was their way, they were now drowning each other trying to keep their heads bobbing above water in turns.

Their dying pleas became less audible and the bobbing up and down more infrequent. With a creepy smile spreading across his usually expressionless face Jordan gradually increased the volume of Chopin's second Piano Concerto, the Funeral March, until the twins floated lifelessly as if in each others' arms. After some ten minutes or so Jordan stopped the recording and turned off the sombre music. He rewound the video and settled down on the couch close to Carl to share a large joint and watch the film repeatedly. All went well and to plan. Now Hanson could satisfy his warped curiosity. He had bet Jordan a grand that when the twins drowned, they would both die with hard ons.

Whitley Bay, Tyne and Wear England

Once darkness fell, the bodies were fished out of the pool and Jordan carved the word Trash on each of their backs with his switchblade. They were then bagged and thrown into the back of the Ford Transit. From Jesmond the corpses were taken to a deserted stretch of coast not far from the bay and dumped over a cliff into the sea. Hanson was sending a message in a bottle to the world. When news of the Bashirs' demise rippled through the underworld everyone would think twice about doing deals with the authorities in future. The videotape would be made widely available to illustrate this in graphic detail.

All the peripheral evidence, such as overalls, bags and handcuffs, was thrown into a container of sulphuric acid. The residue would be disposed of later. They melted away just as Burton had but the difference was Burton was back as Hanson now. He was that rotten rubber ball you threw away but it always bounced around and rolled back towards you.

JJ had agreed to the rules of the ball game but he'd broken the pirates' code. That turncoat JJ was now high up on Hanson's list of priorities. He had been filed in Hanson's venomous mind under V for vendetta or vengeance.

As the Bashirs set out on their final journey more passengers, Edward Burlington included, were queuing up to board the ghost train pulling in at platform one. As the apocryphal locomotive hauled its carriages through the night the slumbering travellers had no idea who was in which coach or why or even where they were heading.

While on the subject of ignorance, no one on board connected to MI6 had any idea that two passengers had been slung overboard as the train hurtled onwards. Maybe the train was to split and go in different directions? As the diaries for that day showed, no one on board knew or even had a clue.

Chapter 6
Friday 12ᵗʰ April

The West End, London England

The time was after one in the morning when Edward Burlington arrived at the Golden Palace Casino off Shaftesbury Avenue. This casino wasn't a regular haunt of his so he didn't know the staff as intimately as he did in some of the other Mayfair and West End clubs and casinos.

His eye was on a croupier who'd attracted his attention on a previous visit. Her name was Suzie, an Algerian with gorgeous skin the colour of a quadroon. He hoped to take her home tonight, at least for a drink, and win on her roulette table and possibly let her experience the springs on his bed.

He'd already been coerced by his workmates to join them for one of their birthday binges earlier. Hugh and of course Scamp attended. It had been for a good cause as they'd played darts. Edward started the betting. They raised a few hundred quid for foreign orphans living in a hostel in Islington. No one bar Edward knew how they had been deprived of their parents.

To top it up Edward bet three quid to everyone in the pub he could muster to place a bet. All they did was watch and see if an inebriated Hugh could hit triple twenty or the centre ring on the dartboard three times given ten shots. Bulls-eye Hugh did it after Edward insisted Hugh give his glasses a thorough cleaning. Much to Edward's relief it worked as he was running out of cash. The landlord, an old Oxford drinking buddy of Hugh's, made sure the charity received the proceeds.

Edward then hit a casino near Coco's in Cromwell Road before ending up at the Palace. He had won over a grand in Kensington before picking up a few hundred quid on zero at Suzie's table. A few spins with some of his winnings went passed to see if zero came up again. It didn't. After leaving the croupier a generous tip and an invitation to join him for a drink he cashed in his coloured chips and strolled over to the private bar. He downed a pint while he was waiting. She turned up after changing her low-cut croupier outfit for a sleek and seductive dress which revealed much more than her uniform.

'Hi.'

'Hi.'

'I'm Suzie.'

'I know. It said so on your name clip.'

'So, what else do you know about me?'

'Nothing apart from the pleasure you must get looking at yourself in the mirror.'

Edward realised just how cheesy that might have sounded and immediately wished he could withdraw it. He couldn't. As was his habit when in a tight spot he nervously rubbed his hand over a faded childhood scar on his left eyebrow. It was as if he was trying to draw her attention away from his naff comment towards a less important flaw. He prayed it left the right impression. It did. She smiled back bashfully. Edward liked her, although he didn't know why.

Anyone with any sense would not have expected someone who was so entwined with the intelligence services to risk hooking up with this seductive woman. However, Edward wasn't working with them or so he'd been told so it never featured in his innermost thoughts. What's more he didn't fear risk. He did what he wanted and took home women on occasion without having a clue if they were KGB plants, just good fun or both. Suzie wasn't like the others though. She had an aura about her many tube stops apart from the others he'd met in London's West End.

Mostly his liaisons didn't last long but this woman seemed different, more mysterious, which was what fascinated him about her in the first place. Most female croupiers were worldly and knew more about men than the men knew about them. Some were money grabbers and others were rich husband hunters but there was something else about Suzie, something behind her eyes, a melancholy that attracted him.

Edward was a romantic and a humanist. He preferred women with some substance to them, some esprit de la vie. Women who lived outside life's ordinary rail tracks and knew what life meant and he could tell by looking at them if they had it or not.

'You usually drink with women you flatter and know nothing about?'

'Not every day. Why don't you tell me a story?'

'Tell you a story?'

'Yes. About yourself. Then I'll begin to know you.'

She spoke with a slight French accent and, when she smiled, her perfect white teeth glinted behind her crimson sexual lips.

'I was an orphan.'

'Was?'

'When I was young.'

'So what are you now?'

'Now, I'm a woman, an Algerian woman too.'

Chapter 6 - Friday 12th April

Suzie sounded so triumphantly childlike that paradoxically it made her more of a woman. Edward smiled back at her. His instinct was right again. After lighting two cigarettes at once he handed one to her. She looked straight at him, with a fake frown.

'Of all the smoky gin joints in all the towns in ...'

He laughed. She laughed with him. They sipped away a couple more drinks and enjoyed many more laughs. Suzie's boss then sent them over cocktails courtesy of the house.

'What's this?'

'It's from Hakeem.'

'Who?'

'Hakeem Gola, my boss.'

Edward raised his glass to Hakeem. Once they'd downed their drinks, he cashed in his few rectangular chips and they left together in a black cab. After all the booze and the woman's intoxicating effect, Edward never thought about Greeks bearing gifts. He had been under surveillance since stepping through the doors of the casino a few hours earlier. Unusually he hadn't noticed anything untoward.

The time was late, or early, and it drizzled when they arrived at his flat in Montagu Square. Their conversation en route had been light and serious at the same time, the way it is with some women. The banter had been flirtatious and daring, semi-sophisticated. Above all, it had been stimulating, interesting.

Edward didn't even notice they were followed all the way back home. No surprise there. Suzie had placed her hand gently on his thigh to steady herself as the cab sped off to his flat. Back at the Golden Palace Casino, Hakeem Gola picked up the phone, dialled a number from memory and only said a couple of words.

'She's in.'

The flat was spacious. A small, bright reception area gave way to a more discreetly lit sprawling studio, his living room. The layout was appealing, with a darkly polished wooden floor chaotically strewn with bulky brown and white simulated fur rugs. In contrast framed prints of pictures by Balthazar Nebot, John Constable and the Cuyps hung tidily, perfectly horizontally on deep coloured walls. The kitchen was neatly separated from the lounge by a dumbwaiter and there was a small dining room come study full of family portraits. A crisp varnished wooden spiral staircase led up past the study to the three bedrooms, two bathrooms and roof garden.

It was Edward's second pad in Montagu Square. His first flat had been shared with two other aspiring young graduates of life but he'd moved out after a year or so, at first to nearby Quebec Mews to be with two rather naughty ladies, and then, after winning a bundle at roulette he had easily enough for a large deposit for his own place and the furniture to boot.

Edward's flat was his castle and no matter where else he went, this was the place he called home. A small oasis set in a fanatical world. He could be himself and forget about what everyone else wanted him to be and the cages they'd built around him. Those cages were tangible in a psychic way but he could not yet see them for what they were. In here, he was back in the womb, floating.

His pad was his sanctuary and as long as he was able to afford the mortgage that was what he wanted it to remain. If push came to dole queues he could let the other bedrooms and pay the mortgage but he liked being alone now, especially after his spell in prison. It may have appeared to be a paradox but when alone he was free, especially when alone with a woman like Suzie.

The studio was warm and they lounged on the floor, in front of an artificial log fire. They leant their backs against the sofa and watched the flames dance. He sensed her breath on his neck and face. She brought a scent of jasmine into the room with her. It was as if he could almost touch the fragrance of her, the woman she was, the essence of her in the flickering ambience. He kissed her breasts and her stomach, opening her black dress as he delved lower. She undid the buttons of his shirt. Her tongue flicked at his ear and then down his body as she gently removed his clothing until he could hold back no longer.

He was overwhelmed by the insularity of the woman. Even as they made love he could touch her loneliness, like his own. They were two of the same breed in their isolation, in their need for someone to share even a small part of their time without fear. Only a day, a fleeting hour or so, yet it would be forever memorable.

The life of a croupier could be as unnerving and dichotomous as being a spy. Someone was always watching you, always observing, waiting for you to make a mistake and, if you did it could be fatal. That's what they had in common, there on the floor in front of the fire. Or maybe all they shared was the bliss of sexual togetherness. She held him and he held her; they held onto each other.

Suzie lit a joint she took from her hand bag. They lay together in the flickering faux firelight and the aura of tenderness was all consuming. They relaxed and slipped into a twilight state of pleasure and passion. Edward forgot about everything else. When she spoke, her voice sounded distant, far away, echoing down some corridor of contentment.

'You ok?'

'I'm fine and you?'

'I'm lovely.'

'Yes, yes you are.'

She didn't ask him any other question. She knew he didn't want her to ask any. The stuff she had been sent to steal could wait. Wait until the serenity and the enchanting ambience of the early morning grew bright with a new day. Not long passed before the warmth and the weed lowered Edward's eyelids and he fell into a deep and satisfied sleep.

Chapter 6 - Friday 12th April

The North of England & Ijmuiden Holland

At five in the morning Hanson and Jordan set sail back from England to Ijmuiden with no problems at passport control or customs. There were no problems because they hadn't gone through them. They'd taken the same route that they used when escaping from London over a month ago via Newcastle docks. Police corruption and bribery in the seventies wasn't just limited to third world countries as your county councillors or Members of Parliament would have you believe!

The boss was back but not as Cyrus Burton. Now he had a new, secret identity and nobody knew when or where he'd make his next stage entrance or exit.

The bodies of the Bashir brothers were washed ashore late on Saturday 13th April, two days after they'd drowned. Only when they'd been identified did the Tyne and Wear police call off their surveillance of the silent house in Crawhall Road. The surveillance hadn't gone unnoticed by most locals. Others who traversed the area noted it too. They included a tattooed man who regularly drove a Ford Transit van through the Byker area of Newcastle back and forth from Jesmond to the docks.

The Bashir episode was eventually reported to Mac. It was yet another thorn in the catalogue of failures to bring Cyrus Burton to justice. Mac made his report to his boss. Sir Douglas Castle knew he was guilty in leaving the Bashir brothers out there as decoys to draw Burton back into the open. They'd helped shop hundreds of sick and twisted diplomats. Yet they'd still become disposable objects to MI6, just like the youngest Burlington save that he was alive; just the same as all the others who were expendable in the greater scheme of national security. He'd set himself up as the judge and jury they should have faced and now he was responsible for their execution.

The autopsies disclosed one peculiarity. There was no salt water in their lungs, just freshwater with traces of chlorine. This was kept under wraps and the coroner's verdict was death by misadventure.

The Newcastle Evening Chronicle reported their demise as a tragic boating accident off Whitley Bay. They commented that the wreck of the small pleasure cruiser they'd hired was never recovered. There was no way the authorities were going to give Cyrus Burton, the Beast, the satisfaction of telling the world he'd outsmarted them again. The word Trash carved into the Bashirs' backs and the piles of tidily stacked clothes in Byker weren't mentioned in the newspaper article.

Of course, none of them knew about the poolside video awaiting its world premiere so no one in MI6 had the release date diarised. According to Mac's diary MI6 were still searching London stations for Burton!

Chapter 7
Friday 12th April

The Downs Epsom, Surrey England

Alarms were ringing simultaneously at six o'clock in the Burlington home, near Epsom deep in the chalk downlands of Surrey. On one side of the bed, Roger knocked his Keighley mechanical spring driven clock to the floor as he fumbled for it without his glasses. On the other side, the automatic telephone alarm call was answered by Sara.

'Thank you.'

She put the phone down and athletically vaulted out of the bed, still fighting fit for a woman of fifty two with hardly a wrinkle in sight.

'Why do you always say thank you to that machine?'

Roger found his glasses and lit up an untipped Players Navy Cut cigarette. Sara didn't answer his question, just headed straight for the kitchen to make the coffee while Roger conjectured about the series of meetings he had scheduled in London. Both Sara's parents had been heavy smokers. Unlike most who worked with her in the intelligence services Sara had rarely smoked but Roger's habit didn't bother her.

Roger had been a member of the JIC for over ten years now even though he was no longer in charge at Porton Down. His continuing presence was much to the consternation of the current boss. Yet most in the know still looked upon Roger as the leading authority in the UK on weapons of mass destruction. Of course, he was himself a ground breaking architect of such during the Second World War and later during the nuclear development and proliferation years.

There were two related issues of a scientific nature on the JIC's agenda today. Roger was due to report on the uses of different types of plutonium, in addition to the dangers they posed to the public. The current head of Porton Down would be there too, droning on about the Euratom Treaty and the hazards of moving radioactive material. Both topics would guarantee a big yawn as far as Roger was concerned. The military top brass were bound to have questions they'd want answered in simple Anglo-Saxon words of one syllable. That was Roger's territory too, answering complex questions in plain English.

Chapter 7 - Friday 12th April

Afterwards, there was a private lunch arranged with the other Triumvirate members. The purpose of this luncheon was to talk about Roger's youngest son. Roger then planned to go to ICI's headquarters for his routine monthly planning meeting. Its location was just a short step across the road from the House of Lords' annex where the JIC meeting and lunch with Castle and Peter were scheduled. Roger was more a non-executive director at ICI nowadays. His role was rather more ambassadorial than operational. As a result, even though he was technically full time he didn't spend too much time in his office these days.

ICI was undoubtedly the largest global conglomerates in its field and Roger started there after he left Oxford with PhDs in chemistry and physics. He had never worked anywhere else, apart from for His or Her Majesty's Government. Back in those days he was a brilliant young scientist.

Roger and Sara both survived the blitz in the capital and elsewhere. Roger survived it by spending half his time up north in ICI's factories building ever increasingly devastating bombs to drop on the Nazi war machine. Sara survived it by spending half her time in occupied France. She'd even been brazen enough to pop into Germany itself for the occasional weekend.

They were ideologically and physically drawn together from the first time they met in Zone Q of the ministry's main building in Whitehall in June 1942. She was leaving as he was entering a meeting room to wait for Castle in the MoD's basement. She dropped a file she was carrying and he helped her pick up the scattered papers. Their first meeting was as corny as that.

'I can manage.'

'It's ok.'

'I said I can manage!'

'Sorry, I only meant to help.'

'What's your name?'

'Roger.'

'Well, Roger, I suppose I had better buy you lunch.'

He was too surprised and shy to reply. Roger wasn't accustomed to women being as frank and forward as Sara. What's more he was bowled over by her presence. She had presence alright and legs that went on forever. He had never met an image of Ginger Rogers including her bluish eyes although there were some noticeable differences. Sara was taller and her Teesside accent lacked the seductive American tone of screen and stage but then she never needed layers of Hollywood make-up to hide her attractive light facial freckles or a can of paint to cover all her well manicured talons.

As for dress sense, being brought up in the back streets of Middlesbrough was hardly a freedom pass to being a catwalk starlet but with what little she earned she tried her best. It was her friend and mentor, Alice Bailey, who later showed her how to make the most of her dashing looks and literally dress to kill. Alice also discovered Sara couldn't dance for toffee until she taught her how but Roger didn't care; his dancing skills were more akin to the goose step than the fox trot.

Anyway, it was not far off wartime love at first sight and on their first encounter Sara took Roger's silence as an affirmative and they shared one banger with their mash and gravy together in the MoD's austere canteen at noon later the same day. Sara insisted she pay for her own which she did much to Roger's embarrassment. They continued to keep in contact now and then, though not in any physical way.

When Sara went back to Middlesbrough to visit her parents she'd meet up with Roger if he was working in ICI's factories in Billingham. She usually checked surreptitiously to see if he would be there before fixing her home returns. Roger was always left speechless by Sara particularly as no matter what pub they visited up north she seemed to know most of the establishment by name.

On more than one occasion Douglas Castle found an excuse to accompany her and they'd all go out together. To say they were a naturally happy and relaxed threesome even in those days would have been debatable. These days it would have been a blatant fib. Roger later found out she had started a relationship with Castle which she openly admitted to when asked. She made no secret of it.

As the war dragged on and on they saw less of each other until early 1945. That was a while after Roger was posted to the top secret research unit at Porton Down. His task was to investigate the uses of heavy water and why the Nazis were so interested in it; Project Manhattan and all that. Roger was visiting London more frequently by then, not just on that project but on Special Operations Executive business. The SOE escapades often involved both Tealeaves and TrumPeter; sometimes Sara would join the Triumvirate for dinner.

In 1945 Project Manhattan assumed much greater importance and Sara's responsibilities encompassed making sure the British end of it remained top secret. Roger always hoped that one day there would be something between them ever since that day when he helped her to pick up her papers. Sara said she and Douglas Castle were no longer an item and that was it. Roger and she were engaged not long afterwards. That didn't stop Castle trying to win her back. On his last attempt he thought he nearly succeeded but it proved to be the gravest mistake of his life.

Roger learnt of Sara's heroism behind enemy lines after the war and what heroism it was too. He couldn't have done what she did for her country, nor could Castle and that was supposedly his command, his job. Castle had none of that instinctive if not impulsive raw courage, nor did Roger. Edward obviously inherited it from his mother.

Sara was a sexy and seductive woman back then. Even now she still had her figure and her flaming red hair and temper to match. She compensated for her absence of formal education by subtle use of her looks to rise through the ranks of the intelligence

Chapter 7 - Friday 12th April

services. What is more, she never once crossed any moral lines apart from her final morbid fling with Castle, after her engagement to Roger.

In most respects, she was a ruthless and determined woman driven by emotion and instinct unlike her more reasoning and prosaic husband. She knew how to cut someone's throat without flinching. Mind you if she and others like her hadn't they would have been murdered by the Nazis anyway. Someone had to do it for king and country.

Indeed without those SOE and SIS murderers the freedoms many take for granted in Europe today might not exist. She was good to have on your team, essential if your ship was in peril. In team Burlington, she was the one who made the major decisions in their lives. Once she set her mind to something, there was nothing she'd allow to get in her way.

Sara never liked Roger's nickname, the Twister, even though he could wrap her around his little finger playing with her words and she knew it. She associated the word more with Castle whose final fling had ultimately sickened her. Castle's actions were a blatant abuse of power and trickery, as Sara put it treachery which led to forced sex.

Roger's nickname arose from a strange Triumvirate meeting in Oxford. If he was asked to comment on something which had just been said he would repeat it word for word but with a totally different meaning. Roger wasn't even aware that on occasion such wit was in the neighbourhood of mockery. Sometimes his wordplay was deemed pugnacious and provocative by those on the receiving end. To him there was nothing wrong in it, just his scientist's nature to approach things from an analytical stance and without undue evocation.

Just after the war in Europe ended, Roger was sent on a secret mission to Dortmund in Germany. His job was to find out how close the Nazis were to developing bombs based on atomic science. These atomic bombs were later dropped on Hiroshima and Nagasaki by the Americans and brought that final phase of the war with Japan to a close.

Sara went with him to handle security and they decided to get married. Roger wasn't entirely sure her affair with his supposed friend Castle was over after Sara's admission. She'd told him in tears of having been compromised or ordered by Castle into having one humiliating last night of sterile sex with him. Roger forgave her but not him. She played dead as Castle had all but raped her. Years later she even accused Castle of necrophilia. Her choice of words wasn't the best but he knew what she meant.

Once the Second World War and Douglas became memories the biggest challenge Sara and Roger had to face up to was Edward's mischievous and rebellious nature. His rebellion culminated in his wrongful arrest and imprisonment for the murder of his closest friend, a one armed bandit king called Sam White.

It all happened so quickly after the disappointment of his being denied an Oxford scholarship. Edward went wild after being suspended from school. His ebullience was hardly startling since he'd been gated at public school, sent to barracks, for almost four years. He ended up mixing with the seedy side of life and rubbing shoulders with the wrong types just as he did at school. As Sara had said repeatedly they may have been characters but they were appalling characters. Little did she know?

He started life in London staying at a five star opulent hotel in the sumptuous Strand and soon thereafter Edward was arrested trying to leave the gents' toilets in Euston Station along with some other "guests". At the time it was London's best value for money hotel at two pence a night.

A losing streak at Soho casinos led him to that deluxe well-appointed haven where once the toilets were cleaned at two in the morning uninterrupted sleep behind a locked door was guaranteed after you grew accustomed to the tannoy announcements. Edward usually had too much to drink to notice that the three o'clock Birmingham New Street arrival was late or the four o'clock departure for Manchester Piccadilly had been cancelled. The toilet hotels were very popular and usually full by three in the morning. You couldn't hear the trains so that was alright.

The clientele were more like Edward, far better clad for the next day than beggars or street sleepers. Nearby in Bloomsbury were many hotels with long corridors and those who dossed down in the luxury of Euston station were often seen scavenging in the hotel corridors which were full of trays of barely eaten lukewarm breakfasts.

Edward lived out of a suitcase kept in a station lock up and preferred to bathe in the hotels than have to tube it to Bayswater for a five pence bath in the public baths. The tubes weren't cheap either! He was skint but trying to save up to hit back at the casinos that in his eyes had robbed him.

No matter what, once Edward was arrested more by chance as it happened, his mother had to intervene. His arrest was initially for clogging up the toilets as a vagrant but as soon as he was checked out he was charged with the murder of Sam White. She and Roger were staying up north at the time, in the serene calm of a beautiful village, Middleton One Row. The village was under thirty minutes drive from ICI's main factories in Billingham but a long way from London. They drove down at once to see Edward in Pentonville Prison of all places.

It took the application of Sara's undisputed interrogation techniques less than five minutes to satisfy her as to his innocence. Roger analysed every minute of what happened on the day of Sam's murder. With some providence on his side Hugh came up with a few key pieces of the jigsaw puzzle. The links between the bent rozzers and the club land mafia involved were then established.

Rather than have Edward wait for an unfair trial Roger and Sara pulled every string at their disposal to prove Edward's innocence. They harangued Castle and Sir Peter to enjoin them for justice. As a quid pro quo Edward was bailed and used as bait to infiltrate and catch those who'd dunnit. He spent just short of three months inside for no reason, long enough for him to learn a few new survival tricks.

The fact that he had been imprisoned meant the boy had many police files on his activities by now, albeit no criminal records per se. In spite of that, they would have been enough to unjustly limit his career and unfairly prevent him from taking on many jobs. It hadn't been his fault he could never be a lawyer or a Chartered Accountant. He had been professionally framed by some of the most corrupt police in the history of the UK.

However, on the basis that there are no smouldering remnants without a fire, completely ignoring Edward's innocence, much to Sara's disgust the powers that be had spoken. They ruled out his being recruited as an officer by the intelligence services as his parents planned. There was also the manner of his rejection from Oxford, which had been his intended route in, and there was no denying his culpability for that. All of that meant he couldn't be recruited through normal channels and instead became a deniable and disposable asset at the whim of the MI5 machine.

Edward proved to be a big success for MI5 and Castle in particular who, albeit in MI6, somewhat hypocritically claimed much of the credit for spotting him. While on bail Edward initially helped expose widespread police corruption and bribery in the north of England to clear his name. He later helped prove who murdered Sam White and others and the murder charges against him were formally withdrawn.

The falsified police records and bogus charges that had landed him in the shit were expunged. A long slate of other fictitious misdemeanours that had been added later to make him look a proper villain were also erased. The bent cops thought the catalogue of crime they created would make the conviction for murder easier to clinch. Any which way, it's worth remembering that the very act of expunging anything always leaves a trace.

In his terrier like manner Edward wouldn't let go. As he delved ever deeper into corruption he was egged on not just by Special Branch but also by the intelligence services. His infiltration of criminal organisations both UK based and overseas culminated in the Poulson corruption scandal and the resignation of the Home Secretary, Reginald Maudling in 1972.

Mac had been involved in some of this prior to 1972. That was the year Edward became his asset once his work was officially extended to infiltrating gangs from overseas. Put another way, by the summer of 1972 he had permanently migrated down south for his own protection. That meant working for MI6 although he still believed all those he worked with were Special Branch. Hence his pivotal role in Operation Standpipe because Mac reckoned he was the best asset he had.

What Roger learnt in the last week or so and Sara didn't know yet, was the full extent of the danger Edward had been placed in during the Poulson and Standpipe operations. That was why the Triumvirate was meeting for lunch. As far as Sara was concerned Roger was just going to make sure Edward was being afforded security fit for an officer.

If she had known what Roger now knew, her aspirations would have become her nightmares. She would have wished her son was walking the mean streets with the good-for-nothings and bad characters he befriended. Now though her suspicions were already aroused and it was inconsequential whether you put it down to intuition or experience. Sara was back on the warpath.

Roger was already on his fourth cigarette, while he sat waiting in the kitchen for his car. He was anxious to get away because he could see the signs. Sara stamped her foot on an ant heading into the house via the kitchen door. She finally squashed the unfortunate mite. No debate, she was edging towards one of her confrontational moods and they both knew it. Roger could tell she was instinctively aware there was more about his lunch meeting with Castle and Sir Peter than he'd disclosed. They were both Edward's bosses and Sara had a hunch that much was amiss.

'You've been out of the services since 1966. It's all changed now.'

'I should hope so too.'

'You'll always have the puppet masters, the likes of Castle and Peter and, I suppose, myself to some extent.'

'Which one of you is the tinker and which the tailor? None of you are soldiers and all three of you are spies.'

Sara smiled at her reference to the le Carré novel. Roger didn't.

'We're no longer responsible for what happens in the field.'

'Who is?'

'God may know but I am unsure. The military or police in practical terms, the politicians ultimately I suppose.'

'So who's safekeeping Edward?'

Roger knew the conversation would get round to their youngest son. Normally he tried to tell Sara only what she needed to know but she had a knack of extracting information from him without him being aware of it.

'The lower ranks I guess.'

'Who does he answer to?'

'One of Peter's underlings for normal accounting work, and one of Castle's gofers in MI6, maybe the government, ultimately, I suppose.'

'Not you?'

'Certainly not me.'

Sara was retired now, so she didn't have her finger on the pulse any more. That didn't mean she couldn't sense danger. She definitely didn't trust Castle and had good cause to be mistrustful. As for Sir Peter Stafford she wasn't that sure of which way he'd turn in a crisis. He wasn't rumoured to be AC-DC for nothing and his ego was probably the only thing that mattered to him anymore. So in Sara's reckoning in terms of trust he was a train wreck waiting to happen but at least he wasn't already a wreck like that Douglas bloody Castle.

What she wanted to know was who his handler was. From there she could soon find out the assignments selected for her son and what their classifications were. She doubted Roger would know that detail but he could help her find out.

'When I was in theatre there was a real war going on, not this phoney cold stuff. I went behind enemy lines. We trained spies in unarmed combat and survival skills. I know what it's like out there, so don't bullshit me. We both know you know more than you're saying.'

'I don't.'

'What on earth do you mean by "I don't"? Is Edward in danger or what?'

'There's always a certain amount of risk, you know that. I'm sure Castle keeps it to a minimum.'

Sara cunningly mimicked the Twister she knew better than anyone. Her mimicry was laced with sarcasm.

'What did you say again? "I'm sure Castle keeps it to a minimum." You don't mean maximum to increase his pension do you? That shit never gave a damn about his agents as you well know. I smell danger and if I'm not mistaken that fag you have just lit is your fifth today so Edward is in trouble. He must have a handler, and I bet he doesn't even know who that is.'

'She's called Tessa Hislop.'

'Why only tell me now? Only dogs should have handlers, not people? Why haven't you told me her name before? I'm going to do some gardening today. Do you get that?'

Roger got it alright. He sighed and looked at his watch. He'd fallen right into her trap and given her the name she needed. If Sara started digging trouble was bound to ensue as sure as shit follows a vindaloo. Why on earth had he been dumb enough to give away Hislop's name? Sara had won again and would be on the phone the moment he left. Where the hell was his taxi? Time to get going, before she started shattering the crockery, physically and metaphorically.

'They tell him nothing, so if something goes wrong, they can leave him down the mineshaft so he can't identify who they are or where they work.'

'They won't leave Edward in a hole while I'm on the JIC.'

'The last train from Paris to Calais always left empty in the war. I'm sure they don't tell you everything either.'

'Maybe not but don't forget you insisted that we encouraged, or rather, manipulated Edward's career after Oxford and those damn false charges. Why on earth did he get mixed up with those bastards? If he hadn't screwed up at Oxford he could have been the handler by now, instead of the asset.'

'Maybe we pushed too hard. Maybe I asked too much of him.'

Sara became momentarily conciliatory. She knew her husband was right. She just hadn't let go until they'd taken Edward back under their control after getting him out of prison. Well, they thought he was under their control.

Luckily he was tough enough not to have been buggered about in prison. After all, he had only just turned eighteen. Now she wasn't sure if she'd done the right thing putting him on a dual career path. Her vain hope had been that one day all would be whitewashed and MI6 would welcome him into their ranks. Yet there was nothing she could do about it at present, except to warn the Triumvirate not to let anything happen to her boy. Otherwise who knew what might happen?

'It's not like in a Fleming novel. Nowadays they mostly use mercenaries or freelancers or whatever you call them for the dirty work.'

'I know Castle has left people out there to swing in the wind.'

'Not anymore.'

'Are you sure? How do you know? Can you damn well prove it?'

A car horn beeped outside on the driveway.

'There's my taxi.'

'It can wait.'

'I have to go.'

Roger put on his coat and made for the door. Sara followed him out to the car.

'If anything happens to Edward, God help Sir Douglas bloody Castle. You tell him that. You tell him and that Hislop woman I'm on the case now.'

'I will.'

'If you don't, I'll get on the train to Waterloo and do it myself.'

Roger was already in the car and signalling for the driver to drive away fast. Never mind Castle or Tessa Hislop, God help Roger Burlington if anything happened to Edward. The last crisis he needed now was another Waterloo.

Sara waited until the cab was out of sight, then went back into the house and poured herself another cup of coffee. It was her work she missed most, being part of it. She had a few years off when she had the boys but couldn't stay away. As soon as they were old enough to go to school and stop harassing the neighbours by pretending to be snipers hidden in their bushes, she returned. She was slyly shunted sideways from security and training into a siding far from the main line and full of administrative duties and paper pushing which she loathed. So she left for good in 1966.

From then on she devoted her time to socialising and making sure Roger didn't get stabbed in the back at ICI or the JIC. She knew the government in crowd and was the woman everyone had to invite to cocktails or coffee mornings. She made all the right connections and was even more powerful outside the intelligence services than she had been when working in them.

Sara knew full well what was expected of MI6 assets despite Roger's assurances. She also knew what happened if their covers were blown. They were usually left

Chapter 7 - Friday 12th April

to fend for themselves and could prove no formal ties to the intelligence services. They went down the coal mines MI6 wanted explored. If there was an accident in the shaft, only rarely was it one of their gentlemanly officers or anyone they had to account for that was killed.

She could imagine Edward's handler saying "if you get tortured, please die quietly and don't tell anyone you work for MI6 or my career could be ruined". Everything was different in wartime, then there was nothing to deny. You were proud to be a sacrificial lamb or even a kamikaze pilot to make sure the right side won. These days if you sneezed near a beam holding up a diplomatic mineshaft, the fallout was disproportionate. It could result in all sorts of quasi-legal and political claptrap, embargos, international situations and standoffs.

She'd seen the bruises on her son's face after he was handcuffed and beaten by those pigs, the corrupt rozzers as Hugh christened them. The bent cops who'd fixed Edward up in Pentonville. She had wiped away his teenage tears in prison when he knew not who to turn to for solace. She knew, the more successful he was, the more dangerous the assignments would become. Any damn assignment that ended in the departure of a Home Secretary had to be hazardous, had to be in barracuda infested waters.

There was no point in blaming anyone else. She insisted they bring him on board even when they didn't want to after the Oxford fiasco. What else could she do? Leave him out on the streets to be killed by some crazed drug lord or schizophrenic villain? It didn't matter; nothing she said to herself mattered. Call it mother's intuition or whatever, she knew all she had done was replace one nightmare for another.

When she was in the intelligence services, officers knew the names of their agents in the field. They were real people, not just assets like today. Now, if Castle wanted something done, he just passed it down the line and they gave the dirty work to someone like her son. Castle wouldn't even know Edward was in danger until he was dead and then it would be too late.

She smashed her coffee cup into the sink.

Sara was losing it and that wasn't good. She must control her temper otherwise she'd have another attack of arrhythmia. The doctor would have to be called and she'd be given tranquilisers, banned from driving and put under virtual house arrest. After a few minutes her rage subsided. She wiped a tear from her left eye and picked up the phone.

Her face hardened as she took out her address book.

Meanwhile her husband was trying to read his papers ahead of the meetings scheduled later that day. He couldn't concentrate as his cab circled the Tolworth roundabout to join the London bound A3 dual carriageway. For some reason he kept thinking of Macmillan's "You've never had it so good" speech in 1957, not that it was strictly relevant to his reflections.

Relatively few intelligence officers across the world, MI6, KGB, CIA and the rest of them, had been obliterated since the Second World War ended. Certainly far less than in any single month of that war. Sara was habitually right often for obscure reasons. An intelligence officer's job had never been as dangerous as that of their agents. As long as the status quo of acronyms remained intact there was little doubt it would ever change.

Roger's cab neared Putney Bridge soon to be stuck in the inevitable traffic jam. Others using cheaper public transport to get to the JIC meeting were either just about to start out or on their way. The unquestionably rich ones attending, like Rear Admiral Putnam, were just waking up as they could afford to walk there at no cost. Even the equivalent of alarm bells were sounding in his youngest son's pad just behind Selfridges in Oxford Street as the sun shone through the early morning mist in Montagu Square.

For some unknown reason Sara started to keep a note of her concerns in a diary. Her's wasn't full of cryptic metaphors about trains passing through the night. It was full of fury and torment with opaque references to her obtuse plans to protect those closest to her through the downfall of those who threatened their very existence.

Chapter 8
Friday 12th April

Montagu Square Marylebone, London England

Edward woke to the sound of "Coming down again" from the Rolling Stones Goat's Head Soup album playing on the high-tech tape recorder Tessa lent him. He'd wired it up as an alarm clock. By nearly eight o'clock he'd only slept three hours.

Suzie was sprawled on his big bed, her arm across his chest. Edward couldn't remember getting into the bed. The last thing he recalled was making love on the floor. He kissed her sleepy forehead and slid out of bed so as not to disturb her. After a quick shower he dressed for work and scribbled a note for her. He pulled the duvet up over her stunningly beautiful body, kissed her on the lips and left for work.

Outside, he flagged down a passing black cab and headed for Porter Williams. More often than not he walked a mile or so of the way to work to keep fit, hopping on and off buses travelling to work. Today he was knackered and in a hurry. In addition, Peter Stafford wanted to see him and that was unusual as it was not a normal audit completion meeting.

Edward rarely went by tube from Marble Arch to St Pauls. He had heard enough of the IRA's bombs at night from his home and already put up with enough evacuations from tube stations. An added experience of being trapped in a London Underground ready-made coffin overloaded with toothpaste tubes full of passengers was best avoided.

If Tessa had been aware he'd left his flat to someone he'd known for less than a few hours she'd have given him an earful. He would have faced the reproach innocently rubbing his hand over a barely visible childhood scar in his left eyebrow as if to say enough was enough, he'd try not to do worse next time. That was Edward all over: naively trusting just when he shouldn't have been. Yet despite that weakness he'd survived: apart from his false imprisonment he'd never suffered from the errors of his ways.

Edward was a lean, muscular man of about twenty four and six feet tall, a few noticeable inches taller than Hugh. If a forensic artist was to sketch a mug shot of Edward, it would've looked like a composite of Lennon and McCartney whereas his brother looked slightly more Ringo like with heavy glasses. Edward's hair was too long for your typical 1974 accountant but at least it was tidy; Hugh's was shorter but on closer inspection the ragged edges showed who had cut it! Edward had John Lennon's nose and chin and his aquatic blue-green eyes were reminiscent of McCartney's little boy lost look that the ladies loved so much. Like Hugh, his accent normally followed his dress sense. If in an Austin Reed suit he sounded right royal or BBC neutral unless drunk. When drunk or with mere mortals like fellow Geordies he could mix and match it with the Eric Burdons of the world and preferred jeans and t-shirts to more formal garb.

His only other distinguishing features were a broken eyebrow and a faint abdominal scar where his appendix was removed in Austria. At the age of twelve while on a scout trip, he'd been left alone in Innsbruck to be chopped up like a rabbit on the operating table. That's how he described it when rescued by his mother. The slight scar above his eye was a reminder of his footballing heroics at prep school after being head-butted by a motionless goal post.

Most of Edward's girlfriends were nowadays first met at parties or occasionally in nightclubs. Courtesy of his private clients in the music business he seemed to have a never ending supply of back stage passes to gigs all over London. As one of the in crowd he was invited to many of the not to be missed parties after pop concerts or private gigs. By 1974 those clients earned him more than his Porter Williams package.

Those women who were close enough sometimes saw Edward as a loner but primarily as a high-roller, a young man who favoured the fast lane, a playboy with cash and a sharp car to match his swift lifestyle. He was a child of his times, a youngster who cut his teenage teeth in the swinging sixties. All in all he was a good catch, which was more than could be said of his goalkeeping skills.

Most of his women didn't last longer than a month or two at most. Sometimes they left his world because he quite literally ran out of time for them. His holding down three jobs at once one of which he never talked about didn't help. Nevertheless, while they were with him, he was as chivalrous as your traditional prince and didn't swan off with other girls. He was a one woman man, a trusting one at a time white knight.

Edward didn't do hard drugs or even drink spirits, just a lot of lager and occasionally marijuana. No matter what though, he was always ready for what the next day would bring, even if he could never predict what that might be. For Edward mornings were fresh opportunities to be grasped, looked forward to and, just like today, they were rarely accompanied by a hangover.

Even when he was in prison he woke knowing he was one day nearer release. His cup was never half empty despite his incarceration when he had every reason to be depressed and negative. When you've been set up and framed by pros, arrested and

Chapter 8 - Friday 12th April

slung in prison for a murder you hadn't done, survival is not that easy without a good dollop of hope, faith and courage.

Suzie Laurent knew none of this and was awakening as the drizzle cleared away and the day began as one of those dazzling crisp mornings when London was at its best. It was precisely nine o'clock when she opened the door to the roof garden and embraced the new day wearing one of Edward's white hotel souvenir dressing gowns. She basked in the sunshine for a few seconds, shivered and went back inside the flat.

At about the same time Edward was arriving in the offices of Porter Williams and heading for the elevator to take him to the eighth floor, Suzie read the note he left her. She should help herself to a shower and breakfast and he would try to be back at five that afternoon. If she wanted to stay she could or leave and meet him outside the flat then.

She had already noted there were security cameras on the roof garden and then realised they were inside too. They were everywhere apart from in his bedroom suite. She guessed the place was probably bugged to the buttresses as well but had no idea why. After a shower she made herself coffee and tried not to look suspicious to anyone who might be watching her.

She was accustomed to being watched on camera at work but then that was normal. This was not. She wondered if their love making was on camera but dismissed any concerns. Edward wasn't a pervert and surly he would have switched the ones in the lounge off somehow wouldn't he? She played back some of the records Edward left on the sofa but they sounded less compelling without him sharing them. It made her feel uneasy sharing the music with the silent cameras, so she got dressed and left. Outside, she found a nearby payphone and called Hakeem.

'I'm back in this afternoon but it might take longer. Cameras are hidden everywhere. Who knows what for? Je ne sais quoi. Do you have any idea why there are cameras everywhere?'

'Not a clue. Kinky sex probably. You have six weeks. That should be enough time.'

'I hope it is.'

'Don't fuck it up Suzie and don't call me again or talk about it at work until you've found it.'

St Paul's Church Yard, The City of London England

Raj Gupta Khan arrived at the office a few minutes after Edward, puffing and panting. Mr Khan was a slightly overweight man of about thirty, a jovial chap in a gentlemanly way who originally came from Goa.

Raj was a practical joker but was also meticulously thorough as an accountant and a popular character in the office. He loved his work. Raj was married to the job. Nothing else seemed to matter to him apart from food: large curries, usually phaal for dinner or vindaloo for lunch. The love of his life was none other than Porter Williams, a firm of Chartered Accountants in which Sir Peter Stafford was now a senior partner.

When TrumPeter Stafford had been a former finance director of ICI, over dinner one night at the Burlington's, he persuaded Edward to become a Chartered Accountant. Edward's arm had already been twisted but Peter put the final touches to the plan. The plan was hatched by Roger, at the instigation of Sara, to manipulate Edward's career path after he'd been released from gaol.

Once Peter's silken tones convinced Edward accountancy was his true calling, all was plain sailing. Sir Peter made TeaLeaves Castle fix Edward's police records so that when the Institute of Chartered Accountants checked Edward out, he was pristine. TrumPeter Stafford then made sure Edward was hired. Courtesy of not being a graduate his recruitment needed sponsorship by a senior partner. Edward had to put up with four years of being an articled clerk, as opposed to the normal three years for graduates. Anyhow, much of that was on training courses and absences from lectures weren't monitored that well at all.

That suited Edward's double moonlighting. The dark arts of accountancy were learnt by day and applied on his music business clientele while sorting out corruption at night. He was being manipulated and covertly controlled from every pillar to every post as his life progressed. Ironically, he didn't see his position like that and had no real idea of the extent of his manipulation, his enslavement, at least not yet.

Of course, Edward like everyone else in Porter Williams didn't know Sir Peter was from the intelligence services or still an active JIC member. Edward believed the man was doing him a favour after prison. He believed Peter helped him apply for a job at Porter Williams on account of his long friendship with his father and his disgust at Edward's wrongful imprisonment.

By virtue of being a JIC member, Peter knew when Edward was on assignment, so nothing was said in the office about Edward's absenteeism on the few occasions it was unavoidable. If questions were asked Peter's secretary, who had a soft spot for Edward, invented an alibi. She was blissfully unaware that either he or her boss had intelligence services connections. It couldn't be better. Edward was never told who was pulling his strings behind the scenes and everybody was happy. Everybody that is, apart from Sara.

Sir Peter joined Porter Williams from ICI where he had been their Finance Director. Now his time spent on JIC affairs was all charged to ICI, one of Porter Williams' clients of which he was the audit partner. That way he kept abreast of those issues that might concern the JIC such as work undertaken by ICI's consultancy division which provided technical advice to the key players in the international plutonium market. Naturally Roger was the boss of that division.

Chapter 8 - Friday 12th April

Sir Peter was stubbing out his second cigar of the morning when Edward appeared at his office door bang on time. As Edward entered Peter's silhouette was visible through the fog of smoke as he moved to open a window.

That was one positive for young Burlington, always punctual. The negative was when he wasn't, because that was more often than not the harbinger of bad news to come. Apart from bumping into Edward in lifts or in the corridor at work, Sir Peter would normally see him once a month at audit completion meetings. They also met, but infrequently, when he had time to pop his head round the door of the auditors' room on those rare and expensive occasions he bothered to visit clients. Today's meeting was therefore a rarity.

'You wanted to see me Peter?'

'Come in and close the door.'

Sir Peter shuffled some papers on his desk and picked up a report Edward wrote for him over six weeks ago, about Mines & Minerals International Plc. The client was known affectionately to Porter Williams' audit staff as MAMI, a South African mining conglomerate with many operating subsidiaries in the UK.

'Good work on the plutonium market report.'

Stafford smiled. Edward looked bemused. This wasn't why he'd been called into the office. The report was history. Edward hoped Peter had called the meeting by mistake but kept schtum; Peter didn't make mistakes like that. His ultimate boss was known to be slightly scatterbrained and even lacking in grey cells some mornings but was it a front. Well, sometimes it was.

Once, he and Raj enjoyed a hilarious session teaching him how to follow complex leasing transactions, with multicoloured pens to simplify the transaction flow. Edward mused to himself that double entry bookkeeping wasn't Peter's forte in spite of his alleged AC-DC tendencies. Nonetheless Edward never sensed any awkwardness in his presence even when in the back of a cab at night together.

Sir Peter was playing his accountant's hand and being deliberately abstruse. He hummed and hawed for another few minutes about historical trends of pricing matrices and currency conversions. After lighting another bulging Brazilian cigar the third time with his third matchstick he homed in on the point so fast that had it been a penalty Edward would have asked for a replay.

'How would you like to go to the Bahamas?'

'Sorry?'

'How would you like to go to the Bahamas?'

'On holiday?'

'To work, on a full time basis of course.'

'Wow! That sounds great. What's the catch?'

'None. As you know, Porter Williams have offices in both Miami and Nassau and elsewhere round the Caribbean and in most of Central America now. The financial services work out there in the Bahamas would suit you and you'd get to travel around the Americas I expect. It's only a small office when compared with here, obviously small.'

That sounded a downer to Edward.

'Is it something to do with my work here?'

'Oh no, on the contrary. They're laid back out there and we think a young get up and go chap like you could shake them up, improve their efficiency. Would you believe they don't even use our audit programmes? So you could put them on the right track, keep them on the straight and narrow, from a technical perspective only of course. It'll also mean you'll expand your experience of man management on the road to partnership one day. You can teach them to let the client do the work; they'll appreciate that out there.'

Sir Peter smiled, waiting for an answer, as he inhaled a ring of cigar smoke hovering above his mouth. He thought he knew what Edward was thinking. That he'd have to check with the handler he only knew as a police secretary. Then through her, with Mac and Special Branch even though he'd be checking with MI6. It amused him to have this power, this double identity, this ability to know everything and reveal nothing. He almost joked that by being based in Nassau Edward's moonlighting business might get an unexpected boost but to have said so would have given too many secrets away.

The only point was Sir Peter couldn't have been further from the truth. He didn't control Edward's mind which was conjuring up all the carnival beauties he'd seen in parades on TV in places like Rio and Jamaica. Edward was concentrating on pictures of bikini clad bombshells on sunbathed beaches not obtaining informal clearances.

'Of course, you don't have to decide now. You'll want to talk about it with your parents, I'm sure.'

'No, but I will tell them. Take it as signed, sealed delivered. I'm going.'

Edward emphasised "tell them" in the same way he would emphasise points at previous meetings and Sir Peter knew what that meant. Edward decided what would happen no matter what he or anyone else said. Sir Peter hadn't even discussed his damn salary yet or a myriad of what he considered potentially deal breaking issues.

After sowing the idea in this young man's mind Peter abruptly realised he had lost all his bargaining power. Edward might even go to Nassau with a competitor if he didn't deliver a good package soon. The last thing he had wanted was a decision now but he was dealing with young Burlington for whom making big decisions spontaneously was normal. When Peter initially thought it all through he decided it would look best to report that he had effectively almost clinched a deal subject to the senior Burlingtons say so. That way he was blameless if matters went awry later and it acknowledged that Roger and Sara were still in command after a fashion.

Chapter 8 - Friday 12th April

'Alright then, shall we say two days?'

'What for?'

'To decide. Say let me know after the weekend?'

'That will be more than enough. Take it as read I'm game for this. I mean I'll go. I've tons of questions. When will I start and for how long, what will the ...'

'All in good time Edward. It'll be soon. Let's say a month or two and for two years. All other details like salary, managerial position and so on will be decided in the fullness of time. It'll be a good deal for you because the package you'll get is tax free.'

Edward hadn't even thought of that but he knew just by looking at Sir Peter's body language now that the deal would be good. If the deal was crap he could back out; well, he hoped he could. Young Burlington would have gone this weekend if he could have. In hindsight it would have been far better if he had boarded any train or plane going anywhere out of London there and then.

'Sounds great.'

'Good man.'

Peter rose to his feet, put his cigar in his left hand and shook Edward's hand. The meeting ended, the deal was all but dusted. Castle and he had discussed the possibility of an overseas posting in principle after Standpipe. Castle could tell from deep down in his gut that Sara would find out about the dangers Edward unavoidably faced after 1969. If he were seen to be part of a scheme to move Edward into shelter, Sara would be a few more yards away from his back.

Castle suggested St Helena or the Ascension Islands to begin with as a clever diversionary tactic and then talked about offshore financial centres of substance in the Caribbean like the Bahamas. Peter hadn't realised Castle was jesting at first solely to steer him towards the Bahamas. Peter's only observation at the time was that it wasn't economical to have offices in isolated old ports like St Helena. He had said he got the gist though and would start by looking at sending Edward to Nassau.

Castle knew that Peter possessed the power to choose any office in the Porter Williams' empire and that Nassau was where Edward would end up working. That way if Peter started with the Bahamas he wouldn't need to look any further than Nassau. Peter knew Castle would want him in Nassau in preference to Miami. It would be easier for MI6 to keep him under surveillance there if he were used. What's more he wouldn't mix with any interfering Americans of CIA origin or so he thought.

As Peter had already squared Edward's transfer with Sir Douglas Castle in principle, he knew what the eventual result would be. All that was needed now was Roger and Sara fully on side, not that they could have stopped Edward but Peter could have found a good excuse to call it all off if they disapproved. Roger wasn't going to be the problem. Sara might be a different case altogether. That was unless she could be persuaded the move was for her son's security after Operation Standpipe and the escape of Cyrus Burton.

Roger would have to tell her more about the dangers Edward faced if he hadn't already done so. Little did he know what was happening in that regard as he was just about to find out.

Sir Peter guessed that Edward wasn't just being sent to the Bahamas to shake up Porter Williams' operation there. He had already surmised that the proposed secondment wasn't just for his personal security. Castle wasn't a generous man and would never have sown the seeds in his mind for that alone or would he?

Peter reckoned Edward was being despatched there to do more of MI6's dirty work. If as was his wont bloody TeaLeaves Castle was looking that far into the future to compromise Peter himself that was another matter. Peter was not going to be the scapegoat if Edward was framed or nearly murdered again. If TeaLeaves had that in mind then one day Peter would have his crystal balls for garters. He would poison his next cup of green tea so that he died before he could read the damn tea leaves telling him about it.

Edward went back to his office, while Stafford prepared for the JIC meeting. He took his brolly out, combing his hair in front of the full length mirror he'd attached to the inside of his coat cupboard door. He smiled knowingly at his sharp looks. Once fit for purpose he was whisked away in the firm's car, a black cab, to an annex at the House of Lords. His goal was to convince Roger and, more importantly, get Roger to persuade his wife, to not stand in the way of their son going to Nassau.

The more he thought about it as his cab made its way to Westminster, the more lingering doubts he had about Castle's motivation. He would keep quiet about his qualms and only divulge these developments over lunch at a moment of his choosing.

Abingdon Street Westminster, London England

Sir Douglas Castle had been at the House of Lords since half seven. They had used the annex as a contingency venue on earlier occasions. There was yet another series of bomb alerts at Century House. Douglas was advised to convene all meetings that week away from headquarters while new security measures were put in place.

He wasn't looking forward to chatting about the youngest Burlington with Roger. Despite their supposed friendship, their relationship had been strained to breaking point ever since the war days when both of them were after Sara.

Although the winning of Sara was ultimately a fait accompli to Roger, it still rankled with Castle. He saw it as a race, and love didn't feature in it at all. It appeared to him there was always an air of "the best man won" about Roger whenever the two of them met. To Castle it had always been a question of who would win Sara. Nor had he considered trivia like would they live happily forever after or anything soppy like that.

His concern wasn't so much that Sara had chosen Roger over him. More to the point was that he viewed her as a schemer who'd used him to get where she wanted

Chapter 8 - Friday 12th April

to go, then dumped him for the scientist. It was almost as if it had always been her intention. That's why he'd engineered the final fling. That's how he saw it then and now. Castle's hands were as always squeaky clean, it was all her doing.

His final fling must have been a bitter pill for Roger to gulp down but it served Sara bloody well right so far as Castle was concerned. At least he could say to himself he'd outwitted Britain's Mata Hari. His using sex as a tool for revenge wasn't going to look good in the Sir Douglas Castle memoirs though so he ditched his plans on publishing any. They wouldn't show him in a good light particularly if other matters capable of misinterpretation were taken into account including his treatment of her youngest son.

From Castle's perspective there was no doubt that Edward was good at what he did but he was Sara's and Roger's, not his son. In most ways that was a relief to Castle except that he mused too much on what might have been. That's when life started to become awkward for him. Back in the mid to late sixties he was honorary head of admissions at Keble College Oxford. Castle remembered the Burlington boy back then.

In fact he could recall him as a boy having seen him often enough since he was a baby. They also met at various regular Burlington bashes on Xmas Days or New Year Days and other times notably when Roger was stuck in Moscow. By the way, Castle never held any parties; it wasn't his style. He preferred to save up for retirement rather than squander his hard earned cash on such frivolities as partying or children. Anyway, Sara asked him if he'd make sure Edward made it into Keble. He said he'd do what he could.

After all, the boy achieved brilliant results in the entrance exams and his older brother was already there. So, it seemed a foregone conclusion that he'd become a scholar like his father was. Castle inanely thought it might at least earn him some brownie points with Sara. In truth a paranoid creep who abused and betrayed her would be the last person Sara was likely to favour. Even so it didn't stop his romantic imaginings on Cloud Douglas.

Edward came up to Oxford the night before the entrance interview and went to a party with Hugh and some of his mates. The lad was staying in Hugh's rooms in Keble College. He drank too much and shared a joint or two too many. So he lost his way back and was locked out. Edward then climbed over the wall from St. John's College next door and, being disorientated, was unable to find his way to his brother's rooms. He tried a few doors on the way and one of them opened. In his inebriated state, he somehow believed the bedroom he found himself in to be Hugh's.

So without any lights on he staggered towards what he thought was the bathroom, tripped up looking for the loo and threw up all over the bed. Unfortunately, the bed was occupied by an Oxford don who was on the interview panel the next morning.

Needless to say, Edward didn't get accepted. After giving her his word, Sara unfairly blamed Castle for her son being refused entry to Oxford and there was nothing he could say to persuade her otherwise. As Sara put it, Douglas should have made sure he got up to no hanky-panky by taking him out to dinner on the night of his arrival. She wasn't asking that much and, as she explained, it was obvious he would go out on the town having been gated at school all that term and more besides that. It was only one meal, a few hours at most. She even offered to pay.

Once her son had been told to pack his bags and never come back, Edward went missing. Sara thought he went back to his boarding school but he was found by police hanging around in Soho a few days later and expelled for the rest of the term. That was another thing Sara blamed Castle for, as a result of the Oxford eviction.

That was the beginning of the boy's real rebellion, as if he hadn't been rebellious enough already. The upshot of not getting into Oxford resulted in everything imaginable being Castle's fault. In the bold italic print of Sara's law there was causation. He had by omission pulled the detonator that started the landslide that wrecked the car which meant the appellant had to get on the train instead and it crashed into a cow crossing the track so he was responsible for the shortage of milk in the local grocery store next day. Well, you get the point!

Consequently, when Castle was asked, rather ordered by Sara, to help Roger, Peter and her get Edward out of prison he obeyed. One event led to another. Castle then unceremoniously dumped Edward onto what was akin to Sara's preferred career path. Even then that caused quarrels but Edward just made it, as an MI6 asset at the lowest level. Castle never put it in his equations of rights and wrongs but he could hardly refuse given his guilt about his treatment of Sara and others during the Second World War.

The telephone startled him out of his reminiscing. To his astonishment his nightmare became real in a split moment. It was Sara.

'I know Roger won't tell you what I said, so I'm going to let you know myself.'

'How the hell did you get this number?'

'My business. Now, listen here.'

Douglas grimaced and looked round, as if he expected her to be standing behind him, garrotte in hands.

'You realise this call will be recorded?'

'I don't bloody well care.'

'Sara, please.'

'It's about Edward.'

Castle swallowed audibly. He took a mouthful of water from the glass on his desk.

'A resourceful young man.'

'Yes and I want him to stay that way.'

'Why shouldn't he?'

Chapter 8 - Friday 12th April

'Don't give me your bullshit Douglas. You of all people know the dangers he's escaped. I've touched base with a few gardening friends. Let's leave it at that. I just want to make one point loud and clear. I don't like what I've heard. If you don't want to read about yourself and your war crimes in the News of the World, you make sure nothing happens to him. Do you hear me?'

She slammed down the phone before he could open his mouth.

Sir Douglas stared at the receiver in his hand, as if he expected Sara's arm to stretch out of the phone and clutch him by the throat. He dropped it back onto the cradle like a steaming infected turd. He breathed in and out deeply to control his exasperation but that was pointless.

Despite all the havoc and hassles Sara brought about, Castle owed plenty to Edward and he knew it. Castle had selfishly taken credit while Edward took the risks and there were no qualms of conscience over having done so. As for Sara, she should be paying him off for all the damage she'd caused by dumping him, not the other way round of course. At least, that's the way MI6 honcho Sir Douglas Castle saw it.

No surprise he was a bitter, lonely man. Still, surprises galore with no pussy attached had already started queuing up for him and Sara was the first in the queue, the captain on the bridge, the engine driver.

Little did Sir Douglas Castle know he was already on board a train wreck in slow motion dragging distances of time in phantom carriages behind it. What's more Sara was on board diarising it. Had he known she was he would have probably died of a heart attack before reaching the next scheduled stop.

ॐ

Chapter 9
Friday 12th April

Abingdon Street Westminster, London England

The JIC meeting recessed for lunch. They were running half an hour behind, due to Sir Peter Stafford's unpunctuality, for which he seemed unapologetic, almost adversarial. Even so, Sir Douglas Castle called an early recess to let people calm down and get the agenda back on course for the afternoon session. He was given the impression from Peter's demeanour that Porter Williams may have made progress on the Caribbean front with the youngest Burlington. Unfortunately for Castle, Peter hadn't been able to answer his question as Roger rejoined them at precisely the wrong time.

Roger Burlington took up most of the morning. The military wanted simple answers to highly complicated questions about plutonium, bauxite and cobalt. Castle thought about Sara's phone call and, after Roger was finished, asked for a formal minuting of the corruption case up north. He read out his draft. "The Poulson trial was now effectively over thanks in part to Edward Burlington's great service to his country by covertly assisting the authorities."

'My son did more than just assist. We'd never have ousted Maudling or concluded Standpipe the way we did if he hadn't used his own initiative.'

Sir Peter Stafford frowned.

'It's not a good idea to name someone who's merely an asset, Douglas, with all due respect Roger.'

Castle remembered Sara's threat.

'I think it is merited.'

'Edward has no idea what he's done or what the real risks were. Let's leave it at that.'

Castle looked towards Roger. Roger nodded. Rear Admiral Putnam, who represented the Navy, wanted to know why an asset was even on the agenda.

'As for this agent or asset this is about the third time this year he's cropped up in our papers. Why can't my son be knighted too? At least he has a rank. In my day using your own initiative meant acting against orders and most often in a dastardly cowardly fashion.'

Chapter 9 - Friday 12th April

The last comment sparked the normally becalmed Roger into a state of fury and he was not letting this one go.

'My son may be an asset as you so humanely say but he's still a human being and deserves to be treated as such, rank or no bloody rank. As for dastardly cowardly I've never heard such crap in all my life. Haven't you even bothered to read the bloody reports? Or did your monocle cloud over on recalling memories of your frigate's premature retreat from Tobruk when you reached the page where his courage was applauded?'

Castle looked daggers at Peter Stafford who took the point instantly. He realised Castle needed Roger on his side to convince Sara that Nassau was the best place for Edward right now. Sir Peter changed tack and almost apologetically interceded.

'Of course Roger, I'm sorry.'

The Admiralty man sneered.

'Maybe we should review the eligibility criteria for joining the intelligence services? Maybe we should allow criminals who walk off scot-free from murder charges in too, eh?'

This was a direct reference to Edward's record. Roger stood up, cigarette ash flying everywhere. He was fuming with incandescence.

'Maybe we should review the eligibility criteria for joining the intelligence services?'

The Twister had dealt Putnam a blow below the belt by repeating him word for word and producing the opposite meaning but Roger didn't hold back.

'We need streetwise, lateral thinkers who know how to fix a motorbike, not the rules of polo or where the best bars in Henley are. We could do with more people who speak foreign languages and less who only know the language of privilege.'

Peter was sitting beside Roger and he pulled at the flap of the scientist's jacket pocket, trying to make him get back in his chair.

'Not the time Roger.'

Roger almost told Peter to piss off but thought better of it. He realised it was Castle not Peter who was up to no good. Castle would never stand up for Edward other than to avoid the guillotine. Roger wouldn't sit down. It wasn't like him to be rocking the boat. He was a scientist, not a politician, but he was going to have his say now that he'd been provoked and he was quite enjoying it!

'As for treating assets as disposable deniable objects, that is as inhuman and morally repugnant as taking evidence by torture or murdering prisoners of war. Such despicable misconduct is a clear breach of the Geneva Convention.'

Castle squirmed in his seat at the mention of Geneva let alone the Geneva Convention. The Rear Admiral was even more disgruntled now that this low-grade asset seemed to have hijacked the whole meeting and he had been intellectually floored. His peers in the army and airforce looked just as peeved. Roger kept going.

'When we put someone on what we've classified as a dangerous mission, the law says we have a duty of care to protect that person. The law does not draw any distinction between an MI6 officer, agent, asset or adjunct.'

The Admiralty man laughed irreverently. He went for the jugular.

'Is the SIS now a meritocracy or just one big unhappy family? Or a collegiate affair, an Oxford equivalent of those Cambridge traitors? A Triumvirate?'

Sir Douglas Castle was the next one to go ballistic. He warned Putnam that his innuendo was bordering on being libellous. Sir Peter Stafford wasn't as polite as he joined in the deadly jousting match.

'If we're talking about incestuous and treacherous affairs, may I remind the Admiral of a soar point he may have below his waistline? I recall both he and his son, despite being an extremely petty officer, attended orgies, sorry receptions, with Christine Keeler and Mandy Rice Davies. If you want me to go into detail I will and I'll explain the John Vassall connection with your son. Wasn't it the Naval Intelligence Division you ran at the time Rear Admiral or were your brains still attached to your navel or up your arsehole then?'

The Triumvirate weighed in as only they knew how, each for his own reason, but pulling as a team. Roger to protect his youngest son. Castle to demolish suggestions he was a traitor. Peter to remind Putnam he had wrongly accused him many years ago of having an affair with Vassall, a notorious homosexual spy in British naval intelligence blackmailed by the Soviets and later sentenced for eighteen years.

Putnam and co were being bombarded from bow to stern and port to starboard as the Triumvirate tacked around them in ever decreasing circles probing then mocking, taunting then scoffing. The meeting then deteriorated further if that was possible into something akin to Prime Minister's question time in the House of Commons. That was why Sir Douglas Castle had to call an early lunchtime recess to allow tempers to cool. Putnam had been mortally wounded in the process and didn't make the afternoon session.

Luckily Roger wasn't involved in the afternoon session. He'd said his piece and was proud to have stood up for his son, even if he hadn't done so unreservedly earlier. He rang Sara from a public telephone. She didn't mention she had been digging around to find out about her son's activities.

'I told them.'

'Who?'

'Castle and the rest of them.'

'What exactly did you tell them Roger?'

He recounted the meeting ad verbatim with only minor embellishment of his own contribution.

'Do you think it'll have any positive results?'

'I hope so. I'm having lunch with Castle soon and Peter will be there so we'll see.'

Chapter 9 - Friday 12th April

'Good. Give me a call when you're finished.'

The lunch was switched to a safe-house nearby because of another security alert and a car took the Triumvirate round there. Every time a coded call came in from the IRA, Whitehall missed a heartbeat. To make matters worse, the weather took a similar turn to the meeting and the heavens were now chucking any hail available around Westminster. The Triumvirate hadn't an umbrella between them.

Castle sat inside a magnificent oak panelled dining room with marble angels cavorting all over the ceiling. Roger sat opposite him and Sir Peter sat at the head of the short table as if presiding between them. An aperitif of Amontillado had already been served but none of the men had tasted it yet. Castle was the first to speak.

'Roger, we've been friends for forty years now give or take, have we not?'

'Hmm, I think ...'

Peter was about to define "friends" but Roger saved him the trouble.

'I guess you could say so Douglas.'

Castle failed to spot the ambiguity and carried on.

'Did you know Sara called me this morning?'

'God no. How did she get the number?'

'Who knows? She threatened me with the News of the World.'

Both Roger and Peter remained silent. They both knew what that was all about and that Sara was capable of doing anything she threatened. Castle took a sip of his sherry and turned to look Roger in the eye.

'There's no doubt she now somehow knows the dangers your youngest son faced since being recruited as an agent. I won't conjecture how.'

'Don't look at me. She's been gardening, digging. You've a bloody cheek to accuse me of telling her details about Standpipe in particular.'

'I'm not accusing you Roger. She told me she had been digging too. Knowing her as I do she must have only just found out as she went berserk and got it off her chest, figuratively speaking.'

Roger bristled at the probable intentional jibes within the juxtaposition of "knowing her as I do" and the reference to Sara's chest but let him continue. He could fire a broadside up Castle's backside any time of his choosing.

Roger glanced at Peter having noticed Castle looking at him for help. Were they in cahoots? Had TrumPeter Stafford been preening his Peacock feathers with TeaLeaves in private while deciding his son's fate?

Peter just sat there gawkily twiddling a spoon between his fingers as if the meeting were at the Randolph Hotel in Oxford forty years ago. He was working out when to play his trump card neither of the others knew for sure he held. His soup spoon fell silently on to the carpet so he used his desert spoon instead. His face flushed momentarily. Castle ignored the Peacock's attention seeking and carried on but the tempo of his delivery was speeding up, getting more punchy, emphatic and truculent.

'You both know the history. Sara asked me to get Edward into Oxford so he could be recruited in the normal way. However, he threw up in the face of one of my Dons in the middle of the night and that was the end of that. That's when he made some errors of judgement in his choice of friends and ended up in prison. Admittedly the latter wasn't his fault. We all know who orchestrated his dual existence after that. Along with your good wife, Roger, we all had a hand in steering him to where he is today.'

'We know the history thank you.'

'You'll have to excuse me for reiterating, Roger, but the facts seem to have been forgotten. I am now getting the blame for everything that's happened to Edward since he slipped out of the womb.'

'That's not the point.'

'What is the point?'

'He has to be better protected. My son has been within a whisker or two from death too many times what with the northern police, the Manunta Mob, Maudling and now that psychopath Cyrus Burton.'

'You know I can't give him the same level of security as an official MI6 officer. He has a police record longer than War and Peace, for God's sake. I am aware his record was proven to be totally false but we've just witnessed that once JIC members see smoke they assume there's an inferno raging. If it ever hit the press that MI6 was using criminals even though deniable, untrue and wholly misguided can you imagine the fallout?'

'I sympathise with you Douglas, I genuinely do. Let's not exaggerate. Let's stop playing silly buggers. It only makes matters worse. My son is more honest than any one of us because he hasn't lived long enough to be half as devious.

He has no true criminal record full stop. I take the point about the ludicrous reactions of Putnam and his galoots. Yet if the intelligence services are only there to fret about smoke instead of engage in fire we might as well all go home. It's not as though he's bedded a double agent in wartime and then paid for her exit ticket is it now?'

Roger was furious and becoming facetious. Castle didn't appreciate his sarcasm or the implications one iota.

'Don't assume that seraphic attitude with me Roger. We're all manipulators here. That's what we do: manipulate, twist people's lives, whether they're friend or foe. As for your analogy with the war all I can say is Dei Gratia.'

Roger ignored the jibe about his family motto and refrained from cracking a contemptuous joke about TeaLeaves. He detected more than a hint of jaundice in Castle's voice and he speculated the ghastly remnants of the man might be thinking about Sara again when he said that. He lit another cigarette and wafted the smoke Castle's way to annoy him. An uneasy silence lay on top of the smoke now coming from Stafford's first cigar of the afternoon.

Chapter 9 - Friday 12th April

They served Chianti with the soup. Sir Peter didn't consider the wine ideal but made no comment as he stubbed out the cigar he had just lit. The quiet was strident, ear shattering. Peter intentionally said little up to now. His cigar butt was still smouldering as he dipped his spoon into the tempting bowl of Jerusalem artichoke and had a taste. It was delicious.

Sir Peter looked at Castle who was obviously waiting for his interjection. He knew Nassau might feature on the luncheon menu but Peter only hinted to Castle by way of an earlier gesture there might be any news on that front. Castle wanted it now more than his soup. After a short pause Sir Peter broke the icy silence following Roger's broadsides and Douglas' barrages.

'May I suggest a solution to this?'

The other two men were just lifting the soup spoons to their mouths. Now the silverware hovered in mid-air.

'A position has become vacant at the Porter Williams office in the Bahamas.'

The eyes of the other Triumvirate members opened a touch wider and their soup spoons proceeded to their mouths. Stafford took this to be a good sign, so he pressed on with his initiative.

'Security wise, this would be a good move. As I understand it, there may be dangers loitering about in the aftermath of Operation Standpipe. Also, for all I know, after the other stuff he's helped us with Edward may have other skeletons waiting to jump out of his wardrobe.'

'Cupboard.'

'What Douglas?'

'Out of his cupboard not wardrobe.'

'Whatever. Anyway, a break from London might be just the ticket for him right now, if you'll pardon the unintentional pun. Is it a pun? Well, what the hell.'

Roger looked at Sir Douglas Castle less aggressively. Castle raised his eyebrows and turned his head slightly sideways in an affirmative gesture. He'd hoped Peter might come up with something after they'd talked about it. It would help diminish his exposure to Sara. If any problem arose in the Caribbean, so far as he was concerned she could go and chase the Peacock instead of him.

'Have you mentioned this to Edward?'

'I have Roger.'

'So? Did he like the idea?'

'He seems conducive. I told him to check in with you and Sara first, before confirming.'

'Operations?'

'None as I understand it, just straightforward accounting and auditing. Probably be boring for the boy but the lifestyle is easygoing out there and he'll soon settle into it.'

All around the table knew Stafford was lying but even Roger turned a blind eye. Stafford had said it and Castle hadn't contradicted him. They all knew there would be no stopping Edward from carrying on his dual existence but at least this way there would be a break. It would give him a choice and although Edward didn't know it, he hadn't had many since getting out of Pentonville Prison. Roger pretended to be reluctant.

'I'll have to talk to Sara.'

Douglas knew the despondent tenor of Roger's statement disguised his excitement and soon found his own appetite again. He rapidly polished off his soup and called for the main course of peppered venison, which they served with Bordeaux. Stafford thought the wine thoroughly inappropriate but again said nothing. Sir Douglas stuffed his face and much to everyone's disgust spoke with his mouth full.

'We'll get Mac to make the necessary arrangements for Edward to be accommodated in a safe-house, with us on his doorstep, just in case. Edward needn't know about the arrangements.'

Sir Peter pre-empted him, making him look even more diminutive than he was. After all, Mac reported to Castle.

'Mac's outside in the corridor. I thought it might be useful to have him here. Shall I have him called in?'

Castle was always worried if he was surplus to requirements with these two around and today justified his fears. Even though he had placed the acorn of an overseas posting in Peter's brain they were the ones who had both delivered in so many ways since 1939 yet he had not.

Alan McKenzie, better known as Mac, sat on a red velvet chair in the hallway of the safe-house. He was in his late forties but having always looked boyish still seemed as ageless as a botox built movie star who never needed to shave. Being half way twixt five and six feet helped prop up his youthful facade. His emerald eyes sparkled above his rosy cheeks and no matter what he ate he remained always within a whisker of eight stone. Nevertheless, beneath that get up and go happy ever after youthful persona lurked quite a few demons. No debate, Mac constituted more contradictions than you could cram on board a commuter train from Surbiton to Waterloo.

He wasn't often called to this plush part of town and was looking rather dapper in a bowtie and Italian handmade suit. Along with his only other suit, it always carried a slim quarter bottle of scotch in its well lined bespoke inside pocket. That was his only real link with Scotland these days: scotch. His family lived near Surbiton now, not the Gorbals or overlooking the banks of the River Clyde. Mind you, he stayed overnight at Century House much of the week: he had to deal with Castle's progressively chronic crises which were becoming more frequent than those commuter trains full of confused conundrums.

Chapter 9 - Friday 12th April

Mac was also sensible and carrying his umbrella but the umbrella wasn't just for keeping the hail off his flash suits. The brolly was a recording device, a transmitter and a miniature gun that was capable of firing fifteen bullets. If he had been seconded to the Sahara his umbrella would have gone with him.

Even though it had been an opportunity to get his hands dirty again, he was glad Standpipe was finished. It took up time that could have been devoted to the IRA. MI5 had already picked up human intelligence that the IRA were planning some major trophy bombings for the summer. As usual, however, the intelligence services had no idea precisely where or when this escalation was to take place. Everyone was edgy. The IRA had already blown up a military barracks in Yorkshire and the M62 motorway. It was only a matter of time before they hit the big cities.

Assets had been used to infiltrate their terrorist cells and, on more than one occasion, the JIC was aware of planned IRA attacks in Northern Ireland and mainland Britain. They'd allowed some of the IRA's actions to go ahead. Not to safeguard their agents but to prevent the IRA from knowing they'd been infiltrated in the hope those assets might lead them to bigger and better coups. Such actions had precedents.

Winston Churchill didn't evacuate Coventry when the code breakers at Bletchley Park told him the town was to be heavily bombed in February 1940. There was within reason no human cost high enough to allow the Nazis to discover their communication signals had been decrypted. Conversely, agents had routinely been abandoned, resulting in their abduction, torture and murder. Denied meant lied and this was now a breach of the Geneva Convention and a potential war crime. After all, assets were human beings despite being labelled as objects so as to diminish any heartache when they were in peril or lost.

All this was going through Mac's mind while he sat waiting on an increasingly becalming red velvet chair. He thought it funny that the theme of war crimes should come into his head as soon as he stepped behind the secret walls of one of his own safe-houses. Of course, he was part of it all, a complicit part. He was an officer and gentleman for queen and country and the nation's security and all that bunkum.

Yet as he rebelliously reflected on the status quo as he was wont to more often than he should, from his perspective the whole system was geared to protecting the elite and their interests. They had no genuine allegiance to any national flag. Even the British monarchy came from all over Europe. If the UK went down the plughole in the morning, a good slug of the rich and famous would be the first off their Titanics. They'd soon set up in St Helena or Singapore. So why did he do it?

His route into the intelligence services was through the other door, the army. How he made it through that door was another story but allegations of wearing disguised high heels to prop up his height to over the minimum required and putting boot polish where his sideburns should have been were rife at the time. Mind you, he was barely sixteen at the time and since his salad days proved himself a man of valour time and again with distinction. At least he had a job, didn't he? Better than being a bloody security guard on a minimum wage or a doorman in a monkey suit outside some snobby hotel.

Yet he was as bad as the Triumvirate eating their quails' eggs or whatever they were dining on today. Mac would have pole vaulted over or abseiled down Mount Everest for a knighthood. Yes, when the chips were on the plate he envied them because they made it where they were today by being cleverer than he could ever be. At least he had no illusions about what he was doing and he was good at it.

As regards young Burlington he had people everywhere day and night: Tessa Hislop and even an insider in Porter Williams. All was in hand if you thought having only two people to monitor young Burlington was sufficient?

A heavy weight class of waiter came to the door and called him into the dining room. Mac was purposefully told to leave his umbrella in the brolly stand having been reassured it wouldn't be going anywhere without him. The Oxford Triumvirate was tucking into the peppered venison and he hoped they might offer him a plate, he'd had nothing to eat since breakfast and he was starving. They didn't. He was told to sit opposite Sir Peter, at the foot of the small rectangular table.

'Thanks for coming, Alan.'

Castle invariably called him Mac but Stafford only used nicknames for his equals and insisted on calling him Alan. Roger called him whatever suited him at the time. Castle tried to establish his authority and the direction the briefing was to take.

'Now Mac, you know why we've called you?'

'Security for young Burlington sir.'

Castle wiped his mouth and pushed the plate away. He took a sip of wine before replying. He had established control.

'Some concerns have been raised regarding his safety. I hope you can reassure us, Mac?'

'You want me to outline the current or future arrangements sir?'

Mac was under the impression he'd been brought here to talk about Nassau. He waited for an answer. There was none from Castle. He looked at Sir Peter, who stared blankly back at him. Roger unexpectedly interceded.

'Both please Mac.'

'Ok. At present young Burlington can call me at any hour of the day or night and has all my direct private numbers. We also have a man in Porter Williams with whom he works closely and, between him and Sir Peter, that side of things is well covered unless Peter has anything he wants to add.'

Peter didn't reply. Castle was farting about as usual waving at the waiter and returned to the fray.

'Get on with it Mac. We're not worried about his day job. I mean, what on earth could happen to him in an accountant's office good Lord only knows.'

Chapter 9 - Friday 12th April

'Yes sir. You are right of course. It's when he's not working that we have difficulty keeping tabs on young Burlington.

His seventh sense tells him when he's being followed and he regularly gives our people the slip. He sees it as a game even though I've told him more than once it is for his own good. Above all else, he likes to do what he wants, to be free. We may all delude ourselves into thinking we have him controlled but in reality that's not quite correct.

He'll go to a casino we've never heard of and find we can't enter without becoming members. By the time we've registered he'll have left by an exit next door but one so there's not much we can do about it.'

Roger found that irrational.

'How on earth can my son always be in a position to distinguish between one of your hoods and a genuine threat?'

'Fair point but as you'll all know from personal experience, ways exist of distinguishing between them. As I was saying, there's Tessa, of course. She works for him in a private capacity and he trusts her. She even has a set of keys to his flat and goes round there twice a week, maybe more.'

'Does he know who she is?'

'No. He believes I'm Special Branch and Tessa is from the police. He knows we are connected, somehow. My other observer is in Porter Williams but to Edward he is just another accountant who happens to have trainloads of diplomatic contacts. However, one thing Tessa can't keep tabs on is young Burlington's Achilles heel.'

'Which is?'

'Women.'

Mac explained that, setting aside work, his brother Hugh and his private clients, Edward rarely met the same people on a regular pattern. It proved to be a real headache for Tessa to process all the lovers in his life, and they were limited to the ones she had met or found out about.

'Does anyone live with him now?'

'I wish there was a steady girlfriend. It would save us train loads of time and unease. His bedding average is about a fortnight to six weeks, so I suppose he sleeps with at least a couple of different women a month. It may be less because he has to find them or them him in the first place.'

'Did I hear right? Bedding average? You make my son sound like a gardener. Does he sleep with prostitutes, escorts, those types?'

'He doesn't need to.'

'Where do all these women come from then?'

'He usually meets them at parties after, er musical concerts. They call them gigs nowadays. Or at La Valbonne, that's a club off Regent Street or the Speakeasy. He also frequents Dingwalls, Coco's, the Revolution or Ronnie Scotts but not Annabel's. He was chucked out of there with Hugh.'

'Hmm, we can see the picture, Alan.'

'He's also been a member of the Victoria Sporting Club, the Golden Palace and the Palm Beach. I could add the Mazurka, the Mandrake, the Barracuda but not Les Ambassadeurs anymore. He and Hugh were banned from there too.'

'My Lord, we've seen the picture thank you Mac.'

Roger lit up a Players Navy Cut cigarette. He'd been trying not to smoke during the main course. Mac's frankness about his son's nocturnal habits made the craving for a cigarette just too much to bear any longer.

'Apart from his social life, what other risks does my son face here in London?'

No one in the intelligence services or the police yet knew beyond doubt that Cyrus Burton had been back in the UK or left it in the first place let alone changed his name and appearance. Similarly nobody knew at that point in time that the Bashir brothers were bobbing up and down in the North Sea waiting to be washed ashore. Mac gave his assessment.

'Cyrus Burton is still at large. He is on every wanted list in the world, so we believe he's gone to ground in the orient.'

'How reliable is that intelligence?'

'As accurate as the length of any rope you care to choose. Burton's not called the Beast and the Reaper for nothing. The man is dangerous and unpredictable and shouldn't be underestimated.'

Castle was still hungry, now that he reckoned he'd gotten Sara off his back. He smiled round the table, not paying particular attention to what Mac was saying.

'Anyone for pudding?'

Both Roger and Peter shook their heads.

'Mac, surely you'll have something?'

'No thank you sir. I've already eaten.'

Mac lied, but if they weren't going to offer him a plate of venison, he didn't want their desert either.

'Well, I am hungry so I'll start.'

Castle chose apple strudel and whipped cream, ordering coffee and a selection of British cheeses for everyone else. Mac continued.

'Burton has access to at least fifty million in sterling. You can be sure he will have had plastic surgery.'

'So, what you're saying Mac is that Edward isn't completely safe?'

'None of us are ever that sir, but there's the issue of his past and those he put away not just for White's murder and the Poulson affair. There were other out of the ordinary jobs he's done for us. Who knows what unfinished business could be floating about out there?'

Chapter 9 - Friday 12th April

'For instance?'

'Bent coppers, gangsters, casino and club impresarios or if they're inside courtesy of your son, any of their mates not in prison. You name it, the list just goes on and on once you analyse it.'

Roger lit another cigarette, having barely finished the last.

'What can we do about that?'

'Not much. We've removed your son's police records in case anyone starts nosing into his history. They've been replaced with canny dummies and if anyone accesses them, we get to know at once.'

'A fairly basic measure, if I may say so Mac.'

Mac shrugged his shoulders. What did they want from him? He couldn't babysit one lad twenty four hours a day; he had Gaddafi and the bloody IRA to handle.

Peter looked at his watch. Time was getting on and he wanted to get to the point and wrap things up here.

'We can say that London poses a number of health risks to Edward, no matter how hard we try to protect him. Would that be a fair summation, Alan?'

'Yes Sir Peter.'

'What about Nassau then?'

'Much safer provided nobody knows he's there.'

'Yes but people will have to know.'

'Us, here in this room, Tessa, his mother, his brother and that's about it.'

Roger knew Sara would sanction Edward's move to the Bahamas, once the security situation was explained to her. After that it would be just a matter of when their son could go.

'When do you see this move taking place, Peter?'

'As soon as we can process the paperwork, work permits, etcetera.'

Roger turned his attention back to Mac.

'Until then Mac?'

'I'll increase the surveillance of his flat in Montagu Square. Tessa might be able to persuade him to wear a tag but I doubt it. Not much more I can do.'

'Thank you Alan.'

They didn't wave Mac away with a hand gesture or anything as crude as that but Mac knew his presence was no longer required. He stood up and left, simply nodding at the Triumvirate.

Mac's mind turned to more important matters as he left. If only they knew his secret? Before returning to Century House he slipped off the radar and headed for an off the record rendezvous in Regent Street. He slid through the entrance way as if entering the Lubyanka on an undercover operation. He left as anonymously with a look of self-satisfaction that only a connoisseur such as he could explain.

At Hamleys Mac collected his order without a red light getting in the way: the equivalent of fifty miles of OO gauge rail track, new station buildings and three new trains and carriages to boot. All being well his weekend would be a hectic one laying the new track and testing the new trains. He could now extend his network to Gatwick: another OO gauge replica airport liberated from bomb threats.

No one but his wife knew what his loft was really used for and Mac wanted it to stay that way. Even his daughters were banished from and ignorant of his kingdom in the sky. He had suffered enough jokes about his young at heart looks to know when enough was enough. The loft was heavily fortified and even separately alarmed from the rest of his home: it was that precious to him. Entrance could only be gained through two automatically locking doors: it was like boarding an air tight sealed nuclear submarine.

This hobby was serious though and he could never have enough to satisfy his love affair with railways which started with Robert Stephenson's Rocket in 1829 and was now everlasting. He even campaigned against the Beeching cuts and told Roger Burlington in no beating about the Tory grouse filled scrublands that the Conservative Party was making a terrible mistake axing off the rural railway network.

The sun was setting as the Triumvirate's meeting slithered to a halt and Mac daydreamed about his burgeoning travel network in the back of a cab on the way to Century House. Sir Douglas Castle returned with more atypical zest than anxiety in his hobble to the afternoon session of the JIC meeting. Roger confidently called Sara from his office to report how well he had done. Peter smiled inwardly as he was driven back to Porter Williams; it had been a productive day for all in terms of impressing others.

Back at the office Raj and Edward were trying to hurry the rest of the day away as the weekend loomed large. Edward would be on his way to the Bahamas within the next six weeks or so, all being well. In the meantime he and Raj were still having a laugh together coining in the profits for Porter Williams' partners.

Raj had no idea Edward was going to live in Nassau and Edward hadn't a clue Raj was working for Mac. Raj Gupta Khan, the innocuous jovial plump audit manager, was Mac's insider in Porter Williams. However, to the best of Mac's knowledge Raj had no idea that Sir Peter was ex-MI5 and a current JIC member? This convoluted co-existence had to unravel one day. The question was, how?

Exactly why Raj was trying to hurry the day away was a mystery as he would no doubt spend much of the weekend working anyway or eating anyhow. Raj was literally a ball of fun: his constant currying had rounded him off so at just over five feet he was just over fourteen stone.

Raj was a spitting image of the young Indian politician Bhimrao Ramji Ambedkar who helped establish India as a democracy and establish modern Buddhism in India. They had identical chubby faces when clean shaven and both thought it attractive to

Chapter 9 - Friday 12th April

accompany their cherubic looks with round monocular style spectacles on chains. Raj even joked he would become a Buddhist and change his name to Bhimrao Ramji Ambedkar so as everyone would have difficulty spelling it.

Well, only until Edward said he could end up being nicknamed the Bra or even worse! Ambedkar may have been brilliant but when a young man he resembled an Indian version of Billy Bunter. He was even nicknamed Babasaheb. Thus it was between Edward and Raj: forever poking fun at one another or having an affable wordy sparring match at every opportunity.

Meanwhile the saga continued to be diarised, with Sir Douglas' and Sir Peter's recollections respectively being economic with the truth or chock-a-block with self-adulation. Understandable really: at one time or another they had both planned publishing autobiographies albeit Castle had by now all but given up on his. That was not the case with the train spotter: Mac's memoirs were for self protection.

On reading all the accounts of this day it might have appeared as if the Burlington's train was in the sunshine having exited an underpass but it was to be a fleeting moment. The phantom express train was soon to disappear into a long dark tunnel.

༄༅

Chapter 10
Friday 12ᵗʰ April

St Paul's Church Yard, The City of London England

Raj and Edward had just returned to Porter Williams after a quick pub lunch. Ed had insisted on a speedy thirty minutes at the circular steak bar at Ye Olde London rather than another curry which might have taken well over an hour.

When Edward made his mind up at work even his managers and partners usually didn't argue. It wasn't that Edward threw tantrums or did anything daft. If he had he would have been sacked by now. He just possessed that natural ability to influence others in a fait accompli manner, a small fragment of son being like father.

The phone rang in Raj's office and Edward cheekily beat Raj to answering it.

'Raj Gupta Khan's phone, Edward Burlington speaking, how may I help you?'

He grinned while he listened to the voice on the other end. They had been assisting the police with their enquiries, on Porter Williams' behalf, in a bizarre investigation into thefts of upmarket jewellery from a warehouse. Even for these two somewhat unusual Porter Williams' employees this was much more fun than your usual bog standard audit work. It wasn't like checking the payroll or accounting ledgers were all in order.

The firm, Gemstore Limited, was a run of the mill Porter Williams' audit client until the large scale pilfering started. It stored its valuables near Heathrow Airport. They estimated that about a million pounds worth of gold and diamonds had been stolen. The police didn't have a clue how the thieves were getting the stuff past the laser alarms. So Edward volunteered to prove his theory to them comme ci comme ça.

Earlier he bought some small mirrors and inserted them, one by one, as close to the source of the beams as possible. By setting them so, the transmitting laser alarms were deceived into locking on to the mirrors instead of the receivers. Once the experiment proved viable the mirrors could be more easily positioned by sliding them along wooden blocks. The police soon cottoned on and no alarms rang when Edward and Raj walked past the transmitters which were being fooled into logging onto their new receivers, the mirrors.

Chapter 10 - Friday 12th April

The security system was reconfigured and Porter Williams was paid ten percent of the insurance company's payout to its client; a cool hundred grand for an afternoon's work.

'Gemstore want to treat Tom, you and me to a slap up meal tonight. Tom's done nothing, doesn't deserve it. You go. I'll have to decline.'

'A woman perchance?'

'How did you know that? I only met her this morning.'

'She'll be gone by tomorrow then. I'll check with Tom but go it alone as long as it's a Goa.'

The banter was typical. They took the piss out of anything and anyone including themselves. Raj called Tom Anderson, the junior audit partner responsible for Gemstore, to see if he could make it to a celebratory curry at such short notice. Tom had left for the weekend so he would miss out. It was four thirty when Raj rang to confirm the where and when of his dinner and Edward left the office to go home.

When he thought back on the day's events, auditing wasn't all that different to spying or was it? He had been trained like every other member of Porter Williams' auditing staff to check everything he was told with some piece of paper or other. So he always checked what he was told was true and dug around all over the place looking for anything out of the ordinary or suspicious.

No matter what he'd always find oddities such as unfolded invoices that were meant to have come in the post. His favourites were large credit notes that referred to customer complaints that were never made. When he had the time he always looked for details of ongoing litigation that had been accidentally misfiled. It was getting easier given the increasing use of computers by clients. You just searched by name or topic. Most clients didn't even know that facility was available. Edward's track record for flushing out fraudsters and uncovering hidden profits or deep sunk liabilities was second to none.

Montagu Square Marylebone, London England

Suzie was outside the flat when Edward arrived home from work; it had taken him less than half an hour by tube from St Paul's to Marble Arch which was a rare pleasure. They went inside and he popped open a bottle of Bollinger and a can of lager to kick start the weekend. Suzie wanted him there and then but Edward said later. He was expecting a visit from Tessa and he didn't want her walking in on any naked manoeuvres. So they sat and talked. Her closeness gave him goose bumps.

They were getting to know each other, the way a man and a woman do when they first probe each other's beliefs. That time of exploration, when everything is interesting and they liked everything about each other. He liked her: there was no doubt about it. There was something different about her.

She wasn't stereotypically beautiful, like most girls who worked the casinos. Her beauty was more recherché, it crept up on him gradually, when he was least expecting it. He hadn't studied her as a work of art to begin with, when he saw her first, but now he couldn't take his eyes off her. She was one of those women who were fascinating to look at, once you looked closely as you were drawn in by their magnetism. When she smiled that loving look was for him, no one else. The loveliness was there to behold at once and in detail.

She was wearing a fitted Max Mara dress and she looked fabulous as she sipped her champagne. Suzie was trying not to fall for Edward. She knew she had to steal from him and she was sorry now she'd agreed to it. However, she had taken the money, been paid up front, stupidly insisted on it in fact and there was no way out. The people who paid her wouldn't allow it.

So she had to like him but not too much and she was finding that difficult and yet they had only been together a matter of hours. Edward told her he'd be going to the Caribbean for a holiday in the summer and asked if she'd like to come with him. Nobody told him outright his holiday as he put it was a secret.

Tessa turned up at five thirty. Mac had briefed her after his lunchtime meeting and explained Edward was bound for a long stay in Nassau to lie low and relax. She was surprised and annoyed to find Suzie in the flat. This was yet another woman in Edward's life she would have to get checked out. More damn work and all because of another woman. She proceeded to extract as much information from the girl as she could; in that casual MI5 way of her's that made those she was ensnaring so at ease.

Tessa just sat there fiddling with a cigarette packet and listening politely. Suzie was soon fed up with the threesome and decided to make her way to the Golden Palace to get ready for her evening shift. It was obvious to her this Tessa woman had a crush on Edward and was behaving as if she was his agony aunt. As she left Edward said his goodbyes.

'Ok, ma cherie, I'll meet you later.'

'What will you two do until then?'

'My brother's coming round soon. I'll have a few pints with him, and then pick you up. Tessa will be leaving shortly anyway.'

'C'est parfait, formidable.'

Suzie left but Tessa hung around for another hour or so while Edward took a shower and had a drink. Tessa and Suzie were not dissimilar in height and build although Tessa carried a few extra pounds around her hips that she always wanted to lose but never did: that was where the physical similarities ended. Both were a year or two older than Edward.

Suzie was a quadroon with almost black eyes, long jet black naturally curly hair, a soft face with soft features and a small nose combined with a curvaceous body Barbara Windsor would have envied. When Suzie walked into a pub or club heads

Chapter 10 - Friday 12th April

always turned. Unlike Tessa, Suzie overdid the make-up which she didn't need but that was typical of croupiers. They were expected to look that way.

In contrast, Tessa was an unadorned English brown eyed girl with straight short brown hair. She was attractive, sexy too, when she made the effort to dress less like a frumpy middle aged school teacher as she invariably did for day time intelligence work. The idea was she had to be forgettable and when in plain Jane mode she was certainly that.

When working with Edward at night she always changed into her more informal mode, adding a seductive dash of mascara and red lipstick. Of course, it was the nocturnal softer more feminine Tessa that Hugh usually saw although she paid him scant attention.

She frowned on Edward drinking too often because she believed it made him vulnerable and she didn't like him zipping off to the Bahamas either. It would've been ok if Mac was sending her with him but he wasn't. She looked at herself in the mirror. She looked like a rusty old train being driven to the scrap yard; today was an empty cup day.

Tessa recently finished a loose relationship with another MI6 officer called George Francis. There had never been much to it as he spent much of the time in the back of a plane but it had lasted over a year. Francis was eccentric and unpredictable and still a bit of a playboy even though now thirty. He was one of those types who might settle down when he was in a wheelchair, if strapped to it. As a closet impulsive herself, George's flamboyant lifestyle had initially excited Tessa but he went too far on too many fronts for her.

He had been a tech savvy young officer in NATO signals intelligence before becoming an MI6 trouble shooter in Central Africa operating out of Kampala in Uganda. In fact he had become a close friend of Idi Amin Dada since 1970 and helped him clinch the coup d'état that saw Milton Obote leave and Idi Amin take over Uganda. Francis was much too close to Amin for MI6's liking, which was one of the reasons his career in MI6 came to a grinding halt along with one or two of his underlings.

In his heyday he was on close terms with every tyrant in Africa even when at war with one another! His front was simple: he was an arms dealer and flogged obsolete British equipment to the highest bidder. What was obsolete in the UK was cutting edge in much of Africa. He was the man familiar with all the hot spots from Timbuktu to Bulawayo and back, anyway you defined them.

His playboy lifestyle combined with his impulsive nature ended in shame when he was caught on film with Idi Amin testing out new rifles on some innocent villagers. That brought their relationship to an abrupt end so far as Tessa was concerned.

It took some weeks but reluctantly and begrudgingly he agreed to stop pestering Tessa once she made it clear the lady was not for bedding. George didn't like losing at anything and still harboured a grudge against Tessa and Her Majesty's Government yet longed for Tessa's return much as Castle had for Sara's favours back in the forties. It was odd because as characters they were in many ways opposites and Francis had the looks to pull the more flamboyant attractive extroverts you would have thought suited him better, maybe a classy croupier or femme fatale.

George and MI6 parted company in 1973 but MI6 kept a beady eye on him. He remained in the arms trade still operating mainly in Africa but now as a freelancer. Anyway, it wasn't as if Tessa was in love with him. She didn't miss George as a lover but she'd miss Edward as a friend.

Working with Edward had been good fun and she'd grown to like him, maybe much more than like him. It went without saying that any liaison between them was out of the question, more than her job was worth. In any case, Edward hadn't shown any sexual interest in her. Their relationship was as if she was his big sister or surrogate mother, a real agony aunt armed with a knuckle rapping tongue.

Tessa was an administrative genius and well educated as long as you didn't believe there were only two universities in England. She attended Warwick University and left with a first class degree in social sciences of some sort. It may have been a soft touch degree then but she was as hard as nails when she wanted to be and stubborn to an extent that annoyed Edward sometimes. That stubborn side was made all the more impenetrable because she hid her femininity, kept her desires under wraps.

Her brusque Birmingham accent accentuated her austere MI whatever number it was persona when she wanted to turn up the volume. She held inflexible views on most issues including religion and was a confirmed non-believer. Despite all that, Edward and she were close friends; she cared for him and covered for him on more than one occasion.

'Did you tell that girl where you're going?'
'Sure thing.'
'I don't think that was a good idea.'
'Why not? I asked her to come with me.'
'You what?'
'She didn't answer.'

Tessa was relieved. Mac and his superiors would hit the roof if they found out Edward was taking a croupier with him to Nassau. Particularly one whose background hadn't even been checked yet and she would be sure to get the blame.

She was still at the flat when Hugh came round after closing the shop and sorting Scamp out for the night. Hugh was twenty one months older than Ed, as Hugh called him, but the brothers looked and behaved more like twins when they were kids in the fifties. The very early sixties were when many of the similarities ended.

Since leaving Oxford and opening the antiquarian bookshop, as Hugh always liked to call it, he seemingly passed his time in the slow lane. That contrasted greatly with his younger brother's high flying lifestyle. In some ways they were distinctly different. Hugh would shave when the stubble was noticeable or he was going to meet his parents. He didn't bother about the odd hole in a sweater or if the sweater was dirty or smelled of cigar smoke whereas Ed was clean shaven, smartly presentable, a perfectionist in many ways.

Hugh rarely smoked cigarettes but liked the occasional fat cigar. Any make would do. He only smoked cigars when reading or imbibing and then he often just wasted them, leaving them smouldering as his mind was lost in the pages of time or an alcoholic blur. Apart from his wealth of books and meagre threadbare wardrobe Hugh had few possessions and even used Edward's car when he could rather than buy one which he could have easily afforded but for his book buying addiction.

Unlike Ed he wore glasses all the time and much to his parents' annoyance they had to remind their elder son that to see you needed to clean the damn things once in a while. Like Ed he was a loner apart from when with his brother or girlfriend of the year and most of Hugh's few friends were leftovers from his Keble days. That is why he joined in on Porter Williams social gatherings when he could. Hugh was a few inches shorter than Ed and had darker curlier hair. Facially, once the thick glasses were removed Hugh looked a slightly gaunter version of Ed.

Hugh had an insatiable appetite for learning languages and was fluent in most eastern and oriental tongues including Cantonese and Arabic. He drew the line at studying Japanese as the history of Burma was a pet subject of his. Languages were to Hugh what women were to Ed: a source of never ending pleasure. Sometimes serving customers was an irritating distraction from reading the rare books or manuscripts he bought overseas.

More often than not, he'd be found behind the counter with his feet up and an ancient volume in Punjabi or Hindi in one hand. The other was designed to hold a glass of Taylor's Tawny while his cigar smouldered away in a pub ashtray. Hugh didn't even display some of his favourite sixteenth and seventeenth century volumes. They were never listed in the monthly catalogue sent to regular clients. If his Dad queried this, Hugh just said he bought the books and manuscripts as an investment and they could only increase in value.

When he held a tattered old manuscript, he imagined the same book being held by someone several hundred years ago. Hugh wanted to know what those people thought when they read the exact words as he was reading now but unlike they had probably been he was devoid of religious beliefs. To get a proper understanding for this, he went round all the auctions, buying original critiques of his favourite scripts. This wealth of historical interpretation was stored at the back of the shop.

Where Hugh made real money was in the sale of upmarket and egregiously expensive antique trinkets. The tourists couldn't get enough of them. A jewel purported to be from Henry VIII's cousin's hat, a quill pen rumoured to be Cyril Tourneur's or a garter that may have belonged to Marie Antoinette's housemaid.

The words chosen to advertise the wares were never precise or definitive. They merely hinted at some possible obscure unique quality. The higher the price, the quicker the rarity sold to both American and Japanese connoisseurs. The local Chinese were regular buyers too. They liked antique truncheons that might have been used on Jack the Ripper or other notorious London criminals.

Every week Hugh would send one of the shop assistants round to antique fairs and auctions in Portobello Road or Kensington High Street. They would be armed with a few hundred quid in cash. He told them to bring back anything small that might look good in the shop window.

Each rare object d'art was then lovingly adorned with a small tag, briefly outlining a highly dubious possible history no one could disprove. Another tag with the outrageous price on would be added. When compared to cost these adorable antiquities generated gross profits in thousands of percentage points. The business strategy worked well and meant he didn't have to sell his most precious books or manuscripts. It was a con but set against a backdrop of expensive leather bound antique books Hugh thought it fair and reasonable. It was only just and fair that customers should contribute towards the cost of the ambience these days.

If challenged about authenticity he simply responded with "please read the description carefully". His two female assistants treasured their shopping days and he had an unnecessary and unnecessarily complicated bonus scheme to reward them for their enjoyment. Business was not Hugh's forte.

Hugh had girlfriends at college and quite a few since then. While not as prolific as Ed, like his brother his affaires de coeur didn't last that long. His admirers mainly complained he paid more attention to his books than he did to them. Mind you, they also now had Scamp to contend and compete with!

Hugh knew Tessa peripherally. She was often at the flat when he came round, sometimes there alone. He found her enormously attractive, in a classical, sophisticated way. Hugh would have asked her out but he was never totally sure of what lay behind her relationship with his brother. The last thing he wanted was to step on any metaphorical toes or upset any clichéd applecarts. He was sure they had no sexual relationship but couldn't pin down what the relationship was and left it at that.

Hugh could easily have asked Edward what the odds were but was fearful of the reply. What was the point? It was not like she had ever given him any signal the way women do when they're interested. So he reckoned it was better to dream than be spurned. Even when he stumbled across her by herself in the flat she'd just ask him if he wanted a cup of coffee and then leave. She did just that now. Tessa touched his brother's cheek on the way out with her standard parting message which Hugh was almost tempted to say in sardonic unison with her.

'Be careful Edward.'

Chapter 10 - Friday 12th April

Outside, Tessa switched off her surveillance equipment after checking she had all the stuff Suzie told her about herself and her photos were intact. The cigarette packet she was fiddling with was a camera and tape recorder. She'd taken several snaps of the girl when she wasn't looking. Tessa had also slipped a tracking device into Edward's briefcase, just to be on the safe side.

'Why does she always say that?'

'Maybe she knows things you don't, like say I'm off to the Bahamas.'

'You're joking. No you're not. When?'

'Don't know for sure. Soon, I expect.'

'Lucky sod.'

The clock chimed seven as they left. Ed donned his one and only leather jacket and grabbed his keys. Hugh had called a mini-cab which was pulling up outside.

'Let's paint the town downtown.'

Rupert Street Soho, London England

'I have to meet someone in Shaftesbury Avenue later. Let's start at the White Horse and hit the Speakeasy or Whisky-a-Go-Go after that and have a laugh?'

'Who're you meeting?'

'A girl.'

'Do I know her?'

'Good God, not yet. It seems like ages ago but I met her this morning. I'll tell you about her on the way. You can meet her later.'

Hugh knew his brother in many ways more than anyone. The only grey area was precisely how Tessa fitted in, but then Hugh and Ed didn't talk about the basement beneath the shop that much either. Neither did their father who controlled its use for all covert operational purposes. The meetings ranged from those MI6 didn't want anybody to know took place to those caring for lost children of murdered illegal immigrants.

Neither brother knew that their father and not a Triad gang based in China Town was funding the clandestine rescue operations Edward had courageously led during Operation Standpipe. In fact, the only person apart from Roger who knew what that basement was used for was Sir Peter Stafford. He had originally created a criminal front with Roger when he bought the premises so as to use it for more focused covert activities such as infiltration. The first such operation had been to infiltrate a Triad gang in London's China town and remarkably they had remained associates ever since. The Triads were a useful source of information across many fronts.

They were dropped off outside the White Horse in Rupert Street. The pub was less than half a mile from the bookshop and a pub Hugh often frequented on his lunch breaks. Why? It happened to be one of the few pubs that Scamp wasn't banned from drinking milk or water.

At lunchtimes in the White Horse, Hugh would find a quiet corner and settle down with Scamp, a book and a pint of real ale. Scamp had his own name on his own bowl of water and the occasional sausage. Sometimes Hugh lost track of time and came back late to the shop to discover a queue of customers outside when both his assistants were away.

Hugh wasn't big on clubbing, so they normally got slightly pissed in Soho pubs before going on to more vibrant establishments. Friday nights were not for dining out. The pub was fairly full at this time on a Friday evening. The brothers decided to stand at the bar, rather than take an empty table in the private bar upstairs. Ed drank a lager top and Hugh one of his many usuals, a pint of Ruddles real ale, which was six percent strong. After four pints, Hugh was beginning to slur his speech and the conversation had already turned as it often did to reminiscing about earlier days. Ed telling Hugh he needed to get a proper, grownup haircut rather than a DIY job started the reminiscences.

'D'you remember shooting the next door neighbours with a pellet gun when we were playing Cowboys and Indians?'

'They were sunbathing and we decided they were hostile redskins.'

'How old was I?'

'Tennish.'

Hugh mused and then chuckled at the thought of being young again and ordered two more pints.

'They sent you home from boarding school for running a numbers racket.'

'That's where my gambling started. God bless antiquated boarding schools.'

The drinks came. Ed paid for them again.

'If memory serves me, Hugh, I wasn't the only one to get into trouble at school or Oxford.'

'What are you inferring?'

'Not inferring, stating fact. If I mentioned disrupting exams by hiding amplifiers under the floorboards and playing "My generation" by The Who at full volume, would that mean anything to you?'

'Oh, that.'

'Yes, and toothpaste fights.'

'Oh, those.'

'What about ...'

Hugh held his hand in the air, interrupting his younger brother.

'If we're cataloguing each other's delinquencies, then let me ask, who crashed Mum's Mini Cooper when he was fifteen?'

Ed tried to speak but Hugh rumbled on.

'Who caused a thirty vehicle pileup in Aylesbury?'

'Hang on a minute.'

Chapter 10 - Friday 12th April

'Who has been breathalysed over two hundred times outside his favourite clubs?'

'That was to stop them screwing me.'

'One last question then it's your turn. Who crossed the border from Italy to France and back again more than fifty times in one hour?'

'That was you not me, you nit.'

'No, surely not?'

'Hang on a sec, when are you talking about?'

'When you wanted to get into the Guinness book of records but instead ended up in a police cell for underage drinking near Monte Carlo.'

'Ah, you mean the second time because you gave up in the heat on the first try.'

'Only because I was wearing the wrong clothes.'

'You could have changed after the flight.'

So it continued. Ed called the next round of drinks. They still sparred together just as they had when they were youngsters and were known as the terrible twins but now the sparring was more in words than miniature fisticuffs. As characters the brothers were as different as an E-Type was to a Volvo Estate. Yet like those cars they also had so much in common and talk about their younger years was always animated.

'Your trick of stealing exam papers and rolling them round your arm under the sleeve of your jacket tops the bill though Hugh.'

'Maybe but who nicked the paper for me?'

'You always landed me with the shitty jobs.'

They both laughed. By now Hugh wanted to move on to a club but Ed said the clubs would still be empty so they just carried on larking about for a while.

'At least I don't drink two bottles of tawny port a day and ignore my customers.'

'True but you did try to study for a degree in football of all things.'

'Don't go on about that again please.'

Ed switched to more serious matters.

'You remember going into that pub in Portrack with Sam and me when everyone stopped talking?'

'Yes with those bent bloody rozzers leaning on the bar.'

'That's right. I thought I saw one in town last week. He was in a cab near Regents Park. I may be wrong but I doubt it. I tried to follow his cab but it got lost in the traffic.'

'That's weird. I can see their faces now. Do you remember that bent pig Danny O'Leary and what was his big fat mate called?'

'Sands, no Beaches, Tony bloody Beaches.'

They were all of a sudden sober as they could be by now and withdrew from the bar to converse about it further. Sam White was born in Portrack, a slum area between Stockton-on-Tees and Middlesbrough. Edward first met him playing for the other side in a local football match. They became the closest of friends over the years despite falling foul of each other in a far from friendly first encounter.

Sam later inherited a one armed bandit business and in his father's footsteps controlled the expansion of the organisation opening up a new club almost every other month. The Manunta Mob tried to muscle in on his natural business acumen and good fortune. Edward acting as an arbiter at Sam's suggestion arranged a meeting to try to sort out a truce. He wasn't able to make it as he was down south so Sam went himself. After the meeting, Sam was picked up by a couple of coppers and taken to a place where he was tortured and shot through both eyes. His body was dumped on a beach at Seaton Carew.

Edward was framed for Sam's murder by the Manunta Mob backed up by those murdering bastards who used every trick in the book to make Edward's crime sheet look grotesque and interminable. Initially he was accused of trying to muscle in and take over Sam's territory which was undocumented by and large and that was the alleged motive for the killing.

Later the bent cops just went through their copious lists of unsolved crimes and where realistic placed Edward at the scene of many of them and charged him. That was after he was arrested in London for vagrancy, charged with murder and imprisoned for three months before being bailed. The ne'er do wells tried to fix him up retroactively for anything from car theft to drunken driving. Why? To blacken his character and make sure any jury bought the first degree murder charge without a second thought.

Edward lived a nightmare in prison never knowing what was coming next. As an eighteen year old he had to watch his arse in the showers in case any old buggers fancied a shag. After brushing aside unwanted attention and surviving three attempted gang rapes in the first week nothing else untoward happened. He came under the protection of a real gentleman crook, London's most successful fence until caught, one Toby Dias. Toby was straight and reliable. Edward never won any of the many chess games they played and Toby provided helpful insights into how to get at those bent rozzers. Most inside hated that breed more than paedophiles.

Toby was surrounded by powerful friends not just inside but more importantly outside as well. Dias was in for a two year stretch. As he said to Edward that was small beer and low tax for what he had accumulated which was untouchable, rather like him until someone grassed on him. Toby never said what happened to the grass other than that lawns had to be mowed. Others were scared to death of his contacts with good reason. Even the Krays held him in awe.

Like Edward he had a near perfect photographic memory and impressed his fellow inmates by being able to reel off the private numbers of most of gangland UK. Toby Dias was likened to having a telephone directory on hand. Some even called him Bloody Pages, out of earshot. Of course, we know by now Edward had his revenge by

Chapter 10 - Friday 12th April

infiltrating the crooked rozzers and Special Branch finished off the Manunta Mob forever. Still, he always blamed himself for Sam's death.

Hugh was urging Ed to move on to a club. They swallowed the remnants from their pint glasses, left the White Horse and hit the Whisky-a-Go-Go not far away, before ending up at the Golden Palace Casino at midnight. Hugh was quite inebriated and that usually meant something dumb was about to happen. He often acted on the spur of the moment when pissed and did some crazy things in his time. Like helping jettison the Who's drums into the audience at the Roundhouse while Ed and Keith Moon were still bashing away together. On that occasion they had all been introduced to each other at the back stage bar earlier by one of Ed's clients.

Once at the Palace Ed deliberately steered clear of Suzie's table in the posh high stakes area until she finished her shift. Hugh grabbed a couple of pints at the bar and they wandered round the lower staked roulette tables, picking up enough winnings to pay for the evening. This wasn't Hugh's scene and he was already wobbly. The bouncers were watching him and he knew it.

'I'm ready for home now Ed.'

'Ok, let me call my car.'

'How long will it be?'

'Quarter of an hour.'

'I'll wait downstairs.'

That usually meant Hugh might not hold down his drink. On his way towards the door, he accidentally bumped into a rather fat gentleman at a blackjack table knocking the gaming chips he was holding out of his hand. They scattered across the floor.

'Hey, watch it you clumsy bastard.'

'Sorry.'

'Pick them up, now.'

Ed placed himself between the big man and his slightly shorter brother whose glasses were almost opaque with grime and smoke stains.

'Who the hell are you? His girlfriend?'

There was no point in talking. The man was already on his feet with his fists flailing. Ed neatly sidestepped whilst tripping him with his left foot. The man lurched forward head first as Ed's knee slammed into his double chin.

His dead weight hit the floor like a sack of spuds as Ed put a restraining arm on Hugh's shoulder and started walking him steadily to the lift door. Hugh began nervously cleaning his glasses on his coat sleeve. The bouncers came running but, before they could grab hold of the brothers, a loud voice shouted from outside a door marked Private.

'Wait!'

Hakeem Gola came striding across the casino floor.

'I am sorry, Mr Burlington, is there a problem?'

'No, no problem at all.'

The casino manager turned to his bouncers.

'Get him out of here.'

The bouncers lifted the extra large man from the floor and hauled him towards the lift. Gola shouted after him.

'You're banned for good this time.'

The manager looked straight at Ed.

'I apologise. That man is a trouble maker. I should have banned him last time but this time he has lost his bacon. He started the bother. Now, can I get you both a drink?'

'My brother was just leaving.'

'Your brother? Ok then I will get him a car.'

'Mine is on its way.'

'It's no problem.'

Hakeem snapped his fingers and a man in a black evening suit and bow tie came running.

'Have Mr Burlington taken home, and get Mr Burlington a drink.'

Ed saw Hugh safely away, and then went to the bar to wait for Suzie. His knee was throbbing. Not good news for next week's soccer match!

Montagu Square Marylebone, London England

Back at the flat in Montagu Square, Suzie made herself at home while Edward opened a bottle of wine for her and emptied a Carling can into a tankard for himself.

'Pour it please my Édouard.'

She had decided to call him Édouard, in her mysterious French accent. Edward didn't mind. He'd been called worse but not in such a sexy way.

'I'm letting it breathe a minute.'

Edward lit two cigarettes and gave one to her.

'Why were you fighting?'

'There wasn't a fight. He fell onto my knee and I'm not gay.'

Suzie didn't wait for him to pour her wine, she just helped herself and lay back on the sofa opening her legs just enough to let him see she was wearing Fogal fishnet stockings. She put the wine glass down and walked across to where he was standing by the kitchen door. Her face came right up close to his and she blew gently across his eyes and nose as her hand took the tankard from his.

'Are you alright then, no hurt?'

'Yes.'

The bedroom was warm and their bodies blended into a mesmeric milieu of sensuality. As their second day together began she'd developed such tenderness for him. She helped him forget and he explored her in ways she hadn't experienced before, not

Chapter 10 - Friday 12th April

just sexual, more than that. He made her a woman inside, treated her like a woman, not as a croupier, an object.

Edward played music for her, like Stevie Wonder's "Living for the city" that made her want to dance, and Edith Piaf albums that gave her the belief of being special to him. Then there was that je ne sais quoi she couldn't begin to explain when she heard "To know him is to love him" by Phil Spector and the Teddy Bears. Music that gave her so much hope, made her so alive, eternal, part of everything with him.

That morning, after he had gone to work, she had played some of the records back but without him the tunes weren't the same, something essential was missing. Now he was there again the pure beauty of the harmonies returned.

They'd spoken about their hopes and beliefs the night before in soft and sensuous tones. Now her words were like kisses on his ears and her laughter was like the music he was playing. She was surprising and different to him. She laughed at words other people didn't laugh at, didn't think about, words she never thought about until he said them.

Together, he was more than a man and she was more than a woman. He could teach her how to say words she yearned to understand, how to live. She could teach him how to listen, how to laugh. Would they teach each other how to cry? Would that be the last lesson?

Edward lit up another cigarette for her. She snuggled up to him.

'Better?'

'What d'you mean?'

'Not fighting aggressive anymore?'

'I wasn't was I? Some fat jerk picked on my brother.'

'There was more to it than that, wasn't there?'

'Of course not.'

Edward fibbed. In the Golden Palace in a rare flashback he thought he was back in prison. There were three of them who came up behind him in the shower the first time any inmate had shown a licentious interest in his body. The ringleader was fat and obnoxious, just like the man in the casino. That obese pig had been floored by Edward just like the man in the casino had and his two prison mates fled.

The second attempted rape was uglier. He had bruised his foot kicking two of them in the balls and the other two had buggered off out of the shower room. As an aspiring goalkeeper the objects Edward knew how best to kick damn hard were balls. The owners of the two pairs he had kicked both passed out so he heaved their bodies into the cubicle and left them under a cold shower.

The third attempt would have succeeded. There were six of them that time and they dragged Edward face down on the floor into the communal bathroom. Save for the unexpected arrival of one of Pentonville's governors, namely Toby Dias, he would have been fucked every which way. All Dias did was say "leave him". Toby might as well have nuked them.

Suzie was right. He had been fleetingly lost in a belligerent world. She read him like a book. The aggression was gone now. She'd taken it all away. Edward was so close to this woman now, so magically near to her. He could almost touch the pain she had to deal with but couldn't define it. Edward was going to ask her, offer to take it away for her, like she'd just taken his away. He didn't though. He wasn't sure what he would find.

Edward put his arm round her and held her and they fell asleep wrapped in each other's warmth. Two wayward souls who just needed a blanket of companionship to cover them and a pillow on which to rest their heads. A cushion of peaceful dreams to keep at bay the nightmares which were to stalk their days.

Their intimate affair was only in its adolescence but they had bonded fast and inseparably. The affair continued and their relationship strengthened as Edward's lifestyle returned to a normal level of stability he had not known for some years. Once again he took charge of what he did when and where apart from his normal duties at Porter Williams. Mind you, when they thought about it, Raj and even some of the junior partners found Edward guided them more than he followed their lead.

He was like his father in that respect, twisting others' words and instructions round to suit himself. As Edward's diary pages flipped into May he hadn't seen Mac for over a month for the first time in a long time. If only Rear Admiral Putnam hadn't been brutally booted out from the JIC he would have relished May 1974. Putnam would have noted with pleasure that Edward's name hadn't been mentioned at a JIC meeting since 12th April. That was the day when Putnam was booted in the backside as those of that specific rank often are!

The normality and routine that seemed to be somewhat unusually settling down with Edward and Suzie on the sofa of life was not to be long lived. A cacophony of tragedies awaited them in dark foreboding storm clouds queuing up beyond the next few pages in the Burlingtons' diaries.

Chapter 11
Friday 3ʳᵈ May

Duke Street St James's, London England

Friday should have been just another routine normal day, unusual as that might sound, or so it seemed at about seven o'clock when Edward set out for work. The only excitement flickering on the horizon was the FA cup final tomorrow.

He was on an audit at a client's office in Duke Street by seven thirty that morning. The client was a South African based conglomerate, Mines & Minerals International Plc and the audit was due for completion soon. Edward unlocked the audit room door, put his briefcase down and hung his jacket on the back of his chair.

Pieter Reynolds was the temporary finance director at MAMI. Normally he worked in Cape Town. The UK finance supremo had been fired and he was standing in until a permanent replacement could be found. Edward didn't like Reynolds, he was an arrogant Boer who looked like a rugby prop forward and he broke into Afrikaans when he was speaking. His accent was so strong you could hardly work out what he said.

Raj was audit manager on this job in name only. Reynolds, being the racist pig he was, wouldn't have him in the same office. Accordingly, Edward handled all client contact.

After he lit his first cigarette of the day, Edward wandered down the corridor to Reynolds' office. The door was unlocked and the telex machine was spewing out paper all over the floor. Reynolds wasn't in yet, so Edward started gathering up the telexes and had a look through them while he did so. They all seemed to be in Hindi or Punjabi so he wasn't all that interested. He piled them on the desk, picked up the Financial Times and began browsing through it. The machine started spluttering again. This time the telexes were in English and Afrikaans.

Edward put the tray back to catch them but he missed a few so picked them up off the floor and read through them. His first reaction was to read them again despite having memorised them. They were partly encoded but it was obvious what they were about and not one of them indicated who they were for or where they originated.

The telex machine stopped. Edward rolled up the sleeve of his shirt, wrapped all the telexes round his arm and pulled his shirt sleeve back into place. Then he calmly walked back to the audit room, locked the door and started photocopying the telexes.

Edward already remembered the contents of the telexes in English ad verbatim. His photographic mind was in full gear and he could even visualise those not in English and copy them reasonably well from memory.

Once he recalled an entire book on bankruptcy law and if asked for a recital on any topic he'd looked it up in the index in his head. That was the day before one of many accountancy exams. It sounded like a great gift to have been born with but it didn't always work if he tried to digest the reading material down the pub. The aptitude was useless on occasions such as this though. The first thing Raj or Tom Anderson would want would be to see the originals.

Halfway through his copying exercise, the copier ran out of paper. Edward went back to Reynolds' office and borrowed an unopened pack of Xerox paper. He returned to the audit room. This time he was in too much of a hurry to lock the audit room door. The telexes were annoyingly like wide till rolls and difficult to copy. They wouldn't fit on top of the machine, so he was copying them in awkward bits and pieces. That's when Reynolds stuck his head round the door.

'Morning Edward.'

Edward tried not to let the South African see that he'd been startled.

'Have you seen anyone come down the corridor?

'No. Why, is anything wrong?'

'My office is unlocked.'

Edward moved away from the machine with his back to Reynolds. He had speedily placed the telexes he was holding on top of the copier glass and closed the lid to hide them. His subterfuge was far from perfect as bits of telexes were still visible.

'Maybe the cleaners forgot to lock it.'

Edward turned to Reynolds, and perched himself awkwardly on the edge of the desk, in front of the machine which looked peculiarly lopsided with so much paper stuffed under the lid.

'Maybe. Anyway, how are you lot doing?'

'So far as I can tell, nothing to be concerned about to date.'

Luckily Reynolds was in a hurry and didn't notice the slanting lid of the copier or pieces of telex rolls hanging out; he left the audit room and Edward breathed a sigh of relief. He hurriedly finished off copying the remaining telexes and wrapped the copies round one arm, affixing them with elastic bands. Next he did the same with the originals, round his other arm. His plan to return the originals had been thwarted by Reynolds' arrival. He put his jacket back on and left for Porter Williams trying to look as cool and collected as he could.

Chapter 11 - Friday 3rd May

Montagu Square Marylebone, London England

By now, Edward was a big part of Suzie Laurent's life and vice versa. She stayed with him most nights except if she was on a shift that finished after two in the morning.

She woke at nine. Edward had already gone to work. Suzie showered and dressed quickly and went outside to the nearest payphone. She was guilt ridden about what she'd agreed to do for Hakeem and was now trying to work out how she could walk away without getting hurt. Maybe she should tell Edward, he'd know what to do. Or maybe he'd throw her out and never want to see her again.

She'd already been paid and spent most of the cash paying off debts and buying clothes. So why fuss about an old address book anyhow? All she had to do was find it and hand it over to Hakeem. If Edward missed it she could say she didn't know what he was talking about, that he must have mislaid or lost it.

Trouble was, after working out which cameras did what, she just couldn't find the bloody thing and three weeks had gone by already. She had searched every cubby hole, every hiding place from under the carpets to the suitcases in the small walk in attic.

'I can't find it anywhere Hakeem.'

'I told you not to call me.'

'It's ok. I'm in a phone booth.'

There was a hush on the other end, as if Hakeem was considering hanging up the phone.

'You have to find it.'

'Tell whoever wants it to come look for it themselves.'

'How can they do that?'

'I have my own keys now.'

Another silence.

'You said there were cameras everywhere.'

'I will handle that if you send them here to look for themselves. There's nothing else I can do. I want out.'

'You are in and you are staying in; you insisted on being paid up front. Now bloody well earn that and find it!'

Hakeem hung up the phone.

Duke Street St James's, London England

Pieter Reynolds sat at his desk in Duke Street and realised the telex machine had run out of paper but there were no telexes in the tray. Reynolds checked the machine. It recorded twelve incoming telexes but where the hell were they? He called security.

'It's Reynolds. What time did the auditor sign in?'

'Seven thirty, but he signed back out a few minutes ago.'

'Did he take anything out with him?'

'I don't think so sir.'

Reynolds walked along the corridor to the audit room. The door was locked. He swore to himself and called security again and made them come and open it. Once inside, he found Edward's briefcase and tried to unlock it but couldn't. He swiftly searched through the audit files but found nothing.

Reynolds went back to his office and called Marc van den Hoven, the South African Military Attaché. Next, he told security two plainclothes South African police officers were on their way. They were to be shown to his office upon arrival.

They were from the Bureau of State Security, aptly named BOSS, South Africa's equivalent to the Gestapo. Relations between South Africa and the UK were frosty, to say the least, because of apartheid and all the boycotts and bans the UK was arranging. The rapport between Edward and Reynolds was equally frostbitten. Reynolds didn't like Edward any more than Edward liked him.

St Paul's Church Yard, The City of London England

Young Burlington arrived at Porter Williams and went straight to the eighth floor. He put the copies of the telexes into his desk drawer and locked it. Then he showed the originals to Raj, who was able to read those in Hindi and Punjabi.

'I couldn't put them back and I didn't want Porter Williams accused of stealing.'

'You mean you being accused, not the firm.'

Raj put on his glasses and studied the telexes. His face lost some of its natural light brown colour as he did so.

'You know what 94PU is, don't you Raj?'

'Plutonium.'

'Look at the prices. Ten times or more than what it sells for to countries on the United Nations Security Council approved list.'

'You must go back to MAMI Edward. Leave this with me.'

'You understand what it means.'

'Yes but I need to study the lot before reporting it up the chain.'

'The South Africans are selling plutonium to make nuclear weapons to India, maybe Pakistan as well.'

Raj didn't answer. He knew full well what the telexes meant. What's more he knew that what Edward stumbled upon was damn important, to Raj in particular. The contents of the telexes were political dynamite.

'You must go back to MAMI.'

'Is it safe for me to go back? I don't trust Reynolds.'

'Ok, just calm down please. Reynolds doesn't know for sure you've seen these.'

Edward also didn't know that the corridor to Reynolds' office was under camera surveillance. Luckily, thanks to what little training Tessa and Mac had instilled into him, he often made two assumptions. If he was on the move, he was being photographed and, if he was stationary, he was being recorded. Raj took his glasses off, the colour was returning to his face.

'We can't let them suspect we know.'

'What should I say if anyone asks why I came back here?'

'Say you had a meeting scheduled with me. Reynolds will never call me. Just play dumb if they ask you anything else.'

Edward shrugged his shoulders, went for a piss and reluctantly left for Duke Street.

Duke Street St James's, London England

When he returned to MAMI, Reynolds and two plainclothes BOSS officers were scrutinising the camera footage of the corridor. The cleaners had arrived early and unlocked the door to Reynolds' office and didn't lock it again when they left. So that explained that. There was nothing suspicious about them as they moved from office to office but they'd be interrogated later and fired all the same.

The video then showed Edward arriving, entering the audit room and, a few minutes later, going into Reynolds' office smoking a cigarette. He came out shortly afterwards. He held no papers in his hands and was looking quite natural, relaxed. Edward next went back to Reynolds' office and left almost at once carrying a pack of Xerox paper. This time he looked as though he was in a hurry. After Reynolds' visit to the audit room, Edward left, locking the room behind him and again carrying nothing. So, where the hell were the missing telexes?

Reynolds and the BOSS officers went back into the auditors' office to inspect the photocopier, barging in as if Edward wasn't even there.

'Anything I can do to help?'

They ignored him. He tried to carry on with his audit work looking as nonchalant as he could, moving the same papers from one file to another and back again without any logic. The record on the machine's log showed it had been used that morning to copy thirty pages but faxed nothing. They then asked Edward to open his briefcase.

'Why? What's going on?'

'Some confidential documents have gone missing.'

'And you think I have them?'

'No, but all the offices on this floor are being searched.'

'What's missing?'

'Some telexes. Are you sure nobody came along the corridor?'

Edward was thinking on his feet. He still didn't know there was camera footage but he knew what it would have shown them if such existed.

'Just me. You weren't there, so I browsed through the Financial Times. I came back later because I ran out of Xerox paper.'

Reynolds had already noticed that the FT on his desk was ruffled and he hadn't touched it. That accounted for the length of time Edward was in the office.

'What were you photocopying?'

'Just audit documents.'

Edward knew Reynolds didn't believe him but the man couldn't prove anything.

'The briefcase if you don't mind.'

'No problem.'

Edward opened the briefcase but there was nothing inside apart from a pack of cigarettes, a pair of sunglasses, two guidebooks to the Bahamas and a few pens.

'What was in the telexes?'

'We won't know that until we see them, will we?'

When Edward left the audit room for lunch, the BOSS officers went in and placed a microphone in the ceiling and another in the phone. By the time Edward came back, he had another auditor from Porter Williams with him, to catch up the time he'd lost during the morning. Joe Ritchie, an articled clerk, and he were silently working away when Edward opened his briefcase to get his cigarettes.

'Nice briefcase.'

'Yes. I have another one like it with a false bottom. That one was made especially for my twenty first birthday.'

The microphones weren't working perfectly and the BOSS officers only caught snatches of the auditors' conversation that afternoon. What they did hear were the words briefcase and false bottom. Pieter Reynolds was informed and he called Marc van den Hoven again.

'I knew the telexes had to be in that room.'

'It's out of your hands now Pieter. We'll deal with him and the briefcase later.'

Official wheels and political stomachs were churning in various governmental departments across South Africa. The realisations of the potential damage to their economy swept from one departmental head to another. They knew what the English and Afrikaans telexes contained because they had been erroneously transmitted from South Africa that morning. Although they were encoded and anonymous, in the wrong hands they reckoned they could go nuclear.

As for the other ten missing ones that also worried them. Until they found out for sure what they were they had no idea if they were potentially harmful or embarrassing.

South Africa was isolated enough already. Were it seen to be actively giving nuclear proliferation a hand then the heavens only knew where that might lead to next. Some were even muttering that war was not out of the question. Once the Security Council backed a resolution to countenance severe measures US bombing raids could be imminent.

After all, this was one of those rare occasions when all the Security Council members would be simultaneously and unanimously furious despite the cold war. If any

Chapter 11 - Friday 3rd May

other countries were closer to nuclear armament than those members reckoned then the situation was unprecedented and their reactions unpredictable.

Not surprisingly, back in South Africa, to put it euphemistically people were in a panic and the head of BOSS was getting agitated. However, the maniac didn't take into account that his men were operating in the centre of London. The chief was thinking in terms of some Zulu outpost where a trail of black bodies a mile long would be of little consequence to anyone.

He called his military attaché in London, Marc van den Hoven. His orders were clear. Initiate Operasie Wederkerigheid. In English it meant Operation Reciprocity. In other words, steal back what was stolen.

Marc van den Hoven had until eight o'clock that evening to get the telexes back along with the thief who stole them. The culprit was to be taken alive and a private jet was on standby to fly him to Cape Town. A diplomatic flight, SAA-001, was being readied to take off from Heathrow. If Marc van den Hoven failed, he was to be on the plane himself. With that, Operation Reciprocity whirred into action.

Two vans were hired and given vanity number plates. Eight BOSS officers with diplomatic passports were briefed and in the field already. No guns were issued but they carried sjamboks, syringes, phials of odourless and powerful anaesthetizing drugs and a small amount of chloroform.

They were shown pictures of their target. They were under orders not to harm Burlington. It was important because he had to be the one to open his briefcase and not on the plane, just in case someone else opened it the wrong way and triggered an explosion. BOSS had lost irreplaceable data and some staff in similar circumstances previously. As their chief said, Reynolds must have been insane to open it even with Burlington present as he knew about those incidents only too well and detonators were not the most reliable of gadgets.

One of the vans was kitted out like an ambulance, with more tranquilisers, sedatives and other drugs together with a doctor on board.

The embassy staff suspected Edward was an underpaid accountant with blackmail on his mind and was acting alone. They used a bent rozzer on their payroll to find out that he possessed a previous somewhat lengthy police record. The bent cop reported that Burlington somehow managed to cover it up using bent rozzers himself to enable him to work in Porter Williams.

He'd be an easy enough target and no one would connect his permanent disappearance with the South African government; that's what BOSS thought anyway.

Edward looked at his watch. It had just turned half five. Time to get the weekend started. He asked Joe if he fancied a drink as Raj was joining them later.

'Why not? You can tell me who'll let in the most goals tomorrow.'

'The Duke's Head suit you? Hang on, are you taking the piss?'

'Last thing I'd do with our own premier team goalie.'

'Just as well. First one there orders the drinks and the other pays for them.'

Joe jumped at the chance. Edward constantly went of his way to teach him the ropes. They always enjoyed a good laugh together particularly if Raj turned up with a trick or treat up his sleeve. The articled clerk was also a member of Porter Williams' elite soccer team which gave him a licence to take the Mickey out of his seniors.

Edward grabbed his briefcase and in the football fever sweeping London town they almost ran to the pub, which was only a few minutes away in Duke Street. The West End of London was swarming with football supporters. This Friday was the eve of the FA cup final. Newcastle would be playing Liverpool at Wembley.

As the auditors left MAMI's offices, two large South Africans followed them at a distance of about a hundred yards, each of them on opposite sides of the street. Edward looked around him several times while heading to the pub. He even made Joe hurriedly criss-cross the street unnecessarily pretending to lose him so that he arrived at the bar first.

Despite an uneasiness creeping through the pit of his stomach, he couldn't pinpoint anything suspicious amongst the football crowds. Edward told himself he was being jumpy for nothing and began to relax in anticipation of spending the weekend with Suzie.

As the Burlingtons' diaries were to show, Edward was wrong.

ॐ

Chapter 12
Friday 3rd May

Duke Street St James's & The West End, London England

Edward ordered a pint of Guinness and a lager with a lemonade top and lit a cigarette. Joe took over at the bar and agreed to pay for them while Edward went seat hunting. It would be Edward's round next so that would make it less expensive for Joe as Raj would be joining them. Normality returned and his unusual bout of paranoia subsided.

He was pissed off with Raj or perhaps more with the system. As soon as you found something juicy, either the managers or partners took it away from you and ran with it themselves. Maybe Tom Anderson had done that to Raj? In Edward's mind that was not the way to encourage your foot soldiers which is why the likes of Joe warmed to him. The chap who risked his neck getting the information rarely picked up even a thank you; just like working with Mac in a way. Who gave a damn? He decided to put MAMI out of his mind and enjoy the evening.

Edward took a small table with two unoccupied seats outside the pub on the pavement in what was left of the early May sunshine. He wiped the remnants of the last shower from their chairs. Joe emerged with the drinks after what seemed like ages. The pub was small, overloaded and heaving in the swell. They were soon debating the outcome of tomorrow's match although Edward kept looking around under the pretence of making sure Raj didn't miss them.

He noted the neighbouring table was already taken by a couple of couch potatoes in T-shirts, jeans and bomber jackets. They looked like a pair of bouncers from Annabel's or some swanky new Jermyn Street club nearby where they never saw any action. Both were obviously just waiting to put their Moss Bros hired dinner jackets on and lounge around for the rest of the night. The most action they might see was holding brollies so their clientele's hair kept its sheen.

He could not have been more mistaken if he tried. These two weren't bouncers and weren't anything to do with clubs. To make matters worse they weren't the only ones who were keeping a beady eye on young Burlington and his briefcase.

Inside, the pub was packed with Scouse and Geordie accents as the football crowds were starting to accumulate round St James's, probably more in error than with intent. Duke Street was in the posh part of London's West End. The soccer tourists from up north were all eager to see the sights, like Piccadilly Circus and Trafalgar Square. Edward doubted St James's would suit them but for those not in the know this vicinity was a natural extension of Soho. Only later would they realise the clubs and sex shows they sought weren't in this part of town.

The South African Military Attaché, Marc van den Hoven, was controlling Operasie Wederkerigheid and all the BOSS operatives were in contact with each other via earpieces and hidden microphones. One of the two vans was parked in Jermyn Street. It had Dulwich Decorators printed on the sides, along with matching phone and fax numbers. The other vehicle had been parked nearby in the secluded Ryder Yard. It displayed vanity number plates and had been labelled South African Embassy Medical Services on both sides.

Two Newcastle supporters staggered across and parked their empty glasses on the table. The smaller of the two spoke.

'Whey aye man, git the beers in for a die o' thorst.'

Their Geordie accents were incomprehensible to anyone within earshot but themselves, other Geordies and Edward who spoke to them.

'Haway the Toon.'

Edward's voice blended in with the singsong dialect from the two men and they grinned over at him as if he was one of their own.

'Ye a Toon lad?'

'A was once, like man.'

The smaller one pushed his mate towards the entrance to the pub.

'Get'm a drink too.'

'Lager top please, top after the lager.'

'Whey aye man, that's a hinny's drink.'

'A nor, but the beer doon sooth is dire man, like brown bog water.'

'Worra boot ya pal?'

They all looked at Joe and it took him a few seconds to realise they'd offered him another pint. Joe declined the offer and finished his Guinness. This company was too rough for him, so he said goodbye wishing the Geordies good luck tomorrow and left. One of the two Geordies went to the bar, while his smaller friend sat in the vacated seat, between Edward and the two men in bomber jackets.

The Geordie and Edward carried on a conversation in Tyneside dialect about the prospects of both teams for Saturday's match. While the Newcastle fan reckoned Bill Shankly was a dinosaur at sixty one, too old-fangled to manage a top club, he still admired the manager. As for Kevin Keegan he apparently couldn't find the goal if he had his bifocals on backwards.

Chapter 12 - Friday 3rd May

His Geordie mate came back with the three drinks after about five minutes of pushing and shoving inside the bar. As a consequence Edward's lager was stained a darker shade of piss with an overspill of Guinness or ale but he drank it anyway. The Newcastle supporters asked him if he knew any good places to go. Edward started listing the names of a few clubs but found his writing was an illegible scribble. He was utterly pissed but that couldn't be. He'd barely had two pints. The bigger of the two Geordies picked up his briefcase and spoke in Queen's English.

'I'll take this thank you.'

Edward thought it a joke. He stood up to take it back from the man but he was swaying all over the place. The other supporter held him from behind as his legs crumbled. Then he passed out.

Edward was now sandwiched between the two football fans as they draped black and white scarves round his neck. The big one slipped the briefcase to the bruisers in bomber jackets and then he and his mate led Edward from the Duke's Head towards Jermyn Street. It looked to the heaving throng of drinkers that he was just another soccer supporter who'd had too much to drink.

The big men with the briefcase followed at a short distance and within seconds of Edward having been hauled up on his feet the back doors of the Dulwich Decorators' van opened and he was pulled inside. The Newcastle supporters climbed in after him shielding him from view not that they could see anyone watching what they were doing. Once inside, they closed the doors softly while Edward's couch potatoes left the scene in a grey Mercedes with tinted windows. The van pulled away, calmly and unhurriedly, manoeuvring its way towards Ryder Yard. The driver tooted his horn gently to nudge through the crowds thronging the narrow streets.

In just under a minute after standing up, Edward was totally unconscious and being strapped down onto a stretcher. Once he was secured, a large dirty dust sheet was thrown over him, while the men swapped their Newcastle clobber for painters' overalls.

Ryder Yard was quiet and deserted, compared to the roads that surrounded it, which were thronged with jostling crowds. Even if anyone was watching, they would have been oblivious to what was happening. Everything was so quick, slick and professional. The decorators' van pulled into the yard and Edward was transferred to the sham ambulance, still under the dust sheet.

Inside the ambulance were a doctor, two BOSS operatives and a driver. It pulled out into Bury Street, and then set off for the A4 dual carriageway, via the Piccadilly underpass. The driver took his time until Marc van den Hoven's black Merc joined them as they drove past Green Park. From then on Marc van den Hoven himself was in contact with the crew in the makeshift ambulance. His Merc overtook the ambulance and both vehicles headed out of town towards Heathrow. The decorators' van and the grey Mercedes had by now been swallowed up in the evening rush hour traffic in the heart of London.

Everything was as planned and on time too. The South African Military Attaché used his car phone to call his ambassador at the embassy.

'We're on our way to the airport.'

'What about the cargo?'

'Secured.'

'Diplomatic passports?'

'All in order.'

'The plane is ready. So is Cape Town.'

St Paul's Church Yard, The City of London England

Back at Porter Williams, Raj was worried. He tried calling Edward at MAMI but he'd left. Next he'd called the Duke's Head but as half expected there was no answer. No call had come through from Edward. Maybe he had started the cup final weekend early and had forgotten to ring. Perhaps he was miffed that Raj took the MAMI telexes off him and sent him back there. Or he could be in trouble. The man from Goa picked up his phone and dialled a number he was only meant to call in an emergency. Alan McKenzie answered.

'Raj Khan here sir, I'm calling about the atlas I lent you.'

'It's in hand. You'd better come into the office, right now.'

Raj went to the loo to wash off the stains on his tie and shirt: vindaloo sauce could cause unexpected damage when consumed in the heat of the moment! He grabbed a cab in Ludgate Hill and asked for Westminster Bridge. He checked to make sure he wasn't being followed and disembarked halfway across the bridge. After walking the last half mile to Century House in Lambeth he was out of breath and sweating when he arrived.

Westminster Bridge Road Lambeth, London England

Mac was spitting fire. Edward Burlington had stumbled into something so enormous Mac could hardly comprehend it himself, while the rest of the intelligence services sat sipping their select teas and munching cucumber sandwiches. The intelligence on enriched plutonium sales that young Burlington brought to Raj Gupta Khan was huge, even if he had tripped over it by accident.

In one hour that morning, young Burlington, an untrained asset, found what the rest of the British and American intelligence services failed to find after hundreds of man years' effort. They'd been searching for years for nuclear weaponry outwith the Security Council's control and he wasn't even looking for it. It made MI6 and the CIA, and come to think of it the KGB, look like a bunch of incompetent amateurs.

Mac had been seconded to MI6 from MI5 in 1973 to defuse the rivalry and improve the cooperation between those two branches of the intelligence services. He still kept a foot in MI6's camp but was technically MI5 for the moment not that

Chapter 12 - Friday 3rd May

it mattered a lot to Mac or the IRA. They had recently ratcheted up their blitz of the mainland several notches and the intelligence agencies suspected the IRA were getting weapons from a number of external sources.

MI6 was on a war footing and, in such situations extreme measures needed to be taken. One of those was to be able at will to tap into the phones of military attachés in London Embassies of countries antagonistic to the UK. That included the South African Embassy. The reason was they were worried about the IRA getting their hands on a nuclear device or a dirty bomb and as Libya was already arming them that was not just paranoia.

Mac listened to calls made to and from the South African Embassy earlier today and knew all about Operasie Wederkerigheid. Still, as usual he needed to let the rope run to the maximum extent possible to see who was involved and catch the bastards red-handed. It also posed the usual problems for him. For starters Mac didn't want anyone to know the line was tapped, so he couldn't show his hand overtly.

As with Standpipe, it meant he had to make sure it looked like it was the police who fouled things up for the bad guys and not MI5 or MI6. What's more it had to be for reasons unconnected to the selling of enriched plutonium to countries not in the Security Council club. Sir Douglas Castle's instructions had been emphatic: this is strictly a need to know operation. He didn't need to tell Mac any more.

The news about the telexes went up the chain of command in two directions both starting with Raj. He had explained what Edward delivered to both Tom Anderson and then later to Mac. Raj and Tom had seen Sir Peter about it. Sir Peter Stafford, instantly on alert when it mattered, had said no one was to mention it further while he worked out what to do about it. Peter had gone round to Century House rather than call Castle. It was that big a deal. Sir Douglas Castle had then briefed Mac before Raj had a chance to contact him.

After being briefed Mac might as well have been sat in the South African Ambassador's office. MI6 had so many bugs in place it was a joke. As BOSS's plans for Operasie Wederkerigheid took shape Castle was kept informed of all developments. Once Mac told him that the kidnap and extradition of Edward looked likely Castle went apoplectic, then hysterical. He told Mac he must get Burlington out of trouble or the boy's mother would be after their balls with a machete.

Momentarily it seemed as if Edward Burlington's rescue was higher priority to Castle than the illicit sale of enriched plutonium. The latter could so easily lead to a nuclear war. India and Pakistan were open enemies and, if one or both of those countries had nuclear weapons, the probability of them being used was high. Mac could hardly tell what concerned Castle most, keeping his extremities attached to the rest of his body or preventing a war. The honcho was losing his grip, if he hadn't already lost it.

The chance discovery of a few telexes revealed a seismic shift in the balance of super-power and India wasn't a member of the Security Council. Another lesser problem had also been spotted following the subtle questioning of Raj Khan and Tom Anderson by Sir Peter. Peter had wanted to establish the facts and a time line. It appeared Mr Khan took two hours before reporting the telexes to Anderson instead of telling Mac about them first. Mac had only learnt of their discovery when Castle yanked him into his office. Khan reported them to Mac thirty minutes after that.

Raj Gupta Khan was recruited in 1973 as part of a drive by Castle to internationalise the London based staff of MI6. He'd picked up his accountancy qualification in the UK and then gone back to India to work in Delhi. Khan was fluent in several languages and after his recruitment he settled down well into the Porter Williams setup. His first assignment of any significance was to aid MI6 with Operation Standpipe and infiltrate the criminals and diplomats involved. He was ideal because of his links to some of the people involved through diplomatic contacts in Africa, India and the Middle East.

Castle was shocked that Mac hadn't reported the issue to him before Sir Peter did. Moreover, as Peter pointed out Khan was Indian having been born in Goa which was why initially they all relied on his translations of the telexes that weren't in English.

Sir Peter and Castle both arrived at the same question mark. Could he be a double agent? Mac thought about it but decided if he had been Khan he probably wouldn't have mentioned the telexes at all. He would have allowed Edward to be shanghaied to Cape Town to be tortured and slaughtered. Sir Douglas Castle only just bought that and they agreed Mac would put Chad Cooper onto Khan's case, to test his loyalty. That would have to wait. Right now, he had to save young Burlington's hide, again.

Castle had two teams of scientific advisors, headed by Roger Burlington and Daniel Luke, analysing the content of each telex from different perspectives. Daniel was in charge of technical and operational research at MI6. Daniel's team soon found the telexes all had much in common. No addressee or sender was mentioned for a start. Further, after a telephone engineer had visited MAMI, on behalf of MI6, the communications experts agreed the telexes could have been sent from anywhere. What's more their sources had been intentionally obfuscated.

Roger meanwhile was working in all the surrounding mayhem on translated copies of the telexes. He was trying to understand what enriched plutonium was going where and when and for how much and to whom.

No matter what his paranoid selfish concerns were about retaliation by Sara, Castle decided he must come clean with Roger and not just about how the telexes were obtained. He had to disclose that Edward had been abducted. Castle made Roger promise he wouldn't tell Sara and assured the scientist that Edward's rescue was simply a matter of routine. Roger wasn't at ease with this at all. He knew from

Chapter 12 - Friday 3rd May

Sara that when the heat was on little went to plan but he had at least one ulterior motive for agreeing.

This would give him another axe to dangle over Castle's head and he or more importantly Sara could dictate how his son's security should be handled in future. Of course, he warned Castle that Edward might let the truth slip to his mother and, if that happened, may their gods help them all. Castle decided that unless Mac thought up a better idea he should debrief Edward after the rescue and make him swear on a stack of Official Secrets Acts to keep his mouth shut.

Roger decided to go back to ICI and leave the pandemonium and pathos behind him. That way he could concentrate on what he was meant to be doing and use the more recent programs he'd developed for commercial use on ICI's computer. Secretly, he wanted to get away from Castle before he said something he might regret later. He possessed a wealth of information and technical expertise relating to plutonium grades and prices. ICI was deeply involved in the market in a consultancy capacity which was another reason for his ongoing JIC presence. That market was a small world because there were so few players.

Through ICI Roger knew the key operational executives at MAMI but he'd only spoken to Reynolds twice before over the years as he was more financial than scientific and based in South Africa. The main players normally met at the biannual nuclear industry conferences held in Cannes of all places. They discussed hot topics such as any production shortfall forecasts or recent scientific developments. Nowadays Roger usually sent an underling to represent ICI unless there was anything interesting on the agenda. He was bored by these sorts of purposeless thrashes and found private meetings with the key experts much more informative.

Roger was angry and had every right to be. His son had been drugged and kidnapped and was on his way to Cape Town to be interrogated by a bunch of thugs. Those thugs could on occasion make the Nazis look like boy scouts. His youngest son was being used as bait again to draw the sharks out so that they could be netted moments before the feeding frenzy started. One mistaken move and Edward would be lost forever. Yet again though, for multifarious reasons, Roger had no alternative other than to play the diplomat and go along with this cloak and dagger stuff he so detested.

He loathed it so much at times that on occasion he wanted to be part of it to show TeaLeaves Castle just how dismally he performed. Now this lacklustre performance underscored precisely what he was getting at but had left his son in a desperately precarious situation. Call it collateral damage or whatever. Edward's life was hanging on a knife edge and if the South Africans were as clever as Roger he knew he'd never see him again.

After trying to be a father first, Roger was the first to admit he wasn't that good at it. In reality he was a scientist first and a JIC member second but clinical and lethal when active in both at once. He also knew how to apply those aptitudes to support his youngest son to compensate for his parental shortcomings. Roger despised all the subterfuge, the lies and the cover-ups and wished he could just get on and do the job he was trained to do.

The telexes took his mind off all the clandestine shenanigans and he began his analysis. His office was told he wasn't to be disturbed, not even by his wife but if Sir Douglas Castle telephoned he would take the call. He just wanted to work calmly in secret without any bother or interruptions far away from all the hullaballoo.

The hullaballoo about his son was of their making and should have been avoided at the outset. Furthermore the hubbub about their abject failure to even have a clue about what seemed so obvious now was also their homemade fault. In any event Castle agreed to call him as soon as Edward was safe, or when he knew of his fate.

By now Castle had stopped worrying about Sara's revenge, for a while at least, and briefed the Prime Minister and the Foreign Secretary, on a scrambled line. They agreed that the South African Ambassador would be summoned when the time was right and instructed to expel all the diplomats involved. Even so, Castle couldn't stop the niggling fear at the back of his mind. What if Mac didn't have the operation fully under control? What if something went wrong?

It almost always did on rushed jobs. What if the ambulance was just a decoy and there was another vehicle travelling another route? Did the South African Ambassador know his office was bugged to the hilt and was Mac being fed disinformation? What if they managed to get young Burlington out of the country and he was never seen again? Sara would skin him alive.

His secretary brought him in his tea tray but even the sight of the buttered scones made him sick. Castle settled for a glass of water to lubricate his dry mouth and headed for the gents for a long respite before going down to listen to Mac managing the trap and rescue operation. If he wasn't there watching Mac in real time he might even muck it all up by incessantly calling him for a live account of what was happening.

The operation to identify which countries had bought the enriched plutonium and, at the same time, save Edward's life was codenamed Lacklustre at the suggestion of Jim Callaghan. Sir Douglas Castle could not refuse because of the lacklustre performance of MI6 and others in missing everything going on under their amassed nostrils. Like him or not, Callaghan was an astute politician.

Raj Gupta Khan was shown into Alan McKenzie's operations centre at Century House.

'Great job Raj. Well done.'

'Thank you sir.'

'Anyone else know about these telexes?'

'I don't understand. What do you mean by anyone else sir?'

'Anybody besides myself, Stafford at Porter Williams and Sir Douglas?'

Chapter 12 - Friday 3rd May

'Sorry, I see. Tom Anderson, Edward ...'

'Of course, Edward. Who's Tom?'

Raj smiled that jovial smile of his.

'Tom Anderson's a junior partner. Sir Peter told him and me to keep our mouths shut. Tom won't say a word. I assume Sir Peter reported it to one of his government contacts sir?'

'We took a call from the Foreign Office and they dragged Sir Peter Stafford in pronto to explain what he knew.'

'Is there anyone you or Sir Peter, Tom or Sir Douglas has told sir?'

'Sorry, you've lost me Raj.'

'I meant those any of you have told will know too sir.'

'Got it. This op is strictly need to know. Those on the rescue operation are not to be told. Do you understand?'

'Of course sir but what's the rescue. Not Edward?'

'Go and join the airport liaison team. They'll explain what's going on, they're over there.'

Mac pointed towards a group of about half a dozen MI5 officers on the floor he could watch over from his office and slapped Khan on the back.

'Good man and well done. Now see if you can help save Edward Burlington's hide.'

There were several dozen people in the operations centre. Khan joined the team liaising with Heathrow Airport Security as Castle took a back seat in Mac's office. Mac had already identified all the BOSS officers and agents involved, from Marc van den Hoven down to his chauffeur. MI6 had video footage from outside the depot where the two vans originated. The bogus decorators and couch potatoes were already in police custody. Mac also had videos taken from the Duke's Head and Jermyn Street and even Ryder Yard. BOSS weren't the only spies in town.

A surveillance squad of twenty MI5 officers was monitoring the progress of the Merc and ambulance as they made their way along the M4 motorway towards the airport. Edward's briefcase had two tracking devices attached, a left over from Standpipe and a more recent insertion with love from Tessa. Whenever Mac and Chad were running an operation they always had a team twice the size many would have considered overkill. That's why Chad was usually so successful.

Mac ordered one other failsafe. The RAF liaison officers working with Air Traffic Control at Heathrow were given strict orders. Under no circumstances, was the special South African diplomatic flight SAA-001 or any other direct flight to South Africa to be allowed to take off without his or Chad's approval.

Apart from flight SAA-001 all other direct flights to South Africa were put on hold as a precaution just in case they were receiving diversionary disinformation. Unusual turbulence over the Bay of Biscay and the Pyrénées were cited as the cause of the delay. There were only two scheduled departures affected so that wasn't a big deal.

If necessary, police vans, airport snow ploughs or whatever was available were to be strategically parked so the plane to be used for flight SAA-001 couldn't be hauled onto the runway. Surveillance teams were also being deployed outside MAMI's offices and the houses of Pieter Reynolds and other senior executives. Where access could be obtained, listening devices were being planted to bug telephones in cars, homes and offices.

Mac just hoped and prayed the IRA didn't decide to launch an attack in the middle of all this. Sir Douglas Castle was lost in his own thoughts and sat silently listening as Mac conducted the orchestra. Couriers carrying the latest news on all fronts were dashing in and out. Mac's secretaries were handling all incoming calls. He didn't need to be interrupted. The only person who could call his red phone was Chad Cooper.

Heathrow Airport Hillingdon, London England

Completely unaware of Operation Lacklustre, a degree of self-satisfaction spread across the beaming face of Marc van den Hoven as his chauffeur followed the slip road off the M4 for Heathrow. He was thinking of the promotion he'd get for this day's work, maybe even a medal. What he didn't know was the convoy of vehicles around him, from motorcycles to vans, constantly switching position, all belonged to MI5.

The Merc took the route to Terminal Two, before turning into the side road reserved for diplomatic traffic. The ambulance pulled up behind it at the security barrier. Two armed policemen walked up to the car. The military attaché lowered the window and handed out passports for himself, the four BOSS passengers in the ambulance and Merc, the doctor and Edward, along with flight authorisation papers.

'Your embassy notified us you'd be coming sir. How many will be on the flight?'

'Can't you count?'

'Beg your pardon sir?'

'Seven passports, seven flying.'

The police checked the passports against the faces in the Merc and the ambulance.

'We'll need to look inside the ambulance sir.'

Marc van den Hoven showed his impatience with this holdup as he opened the car door. He walked to the back of the ambulance, signalling to the doctor and driver as he did so.

'Is this necessary?'

'We just need to check faces against passports sir. Won't take long.'

The ambulance driver opened the back doors and one of the police climbed inside to validate Carl de Varten's identity. The South African Military Attaché, doctor and driver waited alongside the sham ambulance.

'This poor chap must be Carl De Varten. What's wrong with him?'

Chapter 12 - Friday 3rd May

The doctor answered.

'We suspect he may have a rare and possibly contagious tropical disease he picked up back home. That's why we are taking him out of your country. Weren't you told?'

The police beat a hasty retreat from the ambulance. The driver closed the back doors shut.

'Well, that's all we need to see sir. Does your driver know where the diplomatic departure parking area is?'

'Yes.'

'Please proceed there and those travelling will be escorted to the plane. Have a safe journey sir.'

The police opened the gate and the two vehicles drove on to the waiting plane. Once by the runway Marc van den Hoven exited and proudly led the way, followed by the doctor and the four BOSS operatives carrying Edward on a stretcher. They were escorted by what they thought were armed airport police.

Chad Cooper stood at the top of the stairs leading up to the plane, ebullient and confident as ever. Cooper strode purposefully, almost menacingly down the steps as the drivers of the Merc and ambulance were hauled out and made to lie face down on the ground. More armed officers appeared from nowhere and handcuffed the BOSS officers and agents. Edward was taken away and, within seconds, was being examined by an MI5 doctor. The South African Military Attaché tried to protest.

'You people are making a big mistake. We have diplomatic immunity.'

'I know that thank you. That is the only reason you're being allowed to get on the plane.'

The two drivers were brought across and all eight South Africans were forced onto the plane. Chad followed them up the stairs. Marc van den Hoven gasped when he saw his sham decorators, Edward's couch potatoes and their drivers already inside and handcuffed. The pilot, two hostesses and a steward were sitting in first class, guarded by four men in police uniforms with submachine guns.

Chad got the thumbs up from the MI5 doctor that Edward would survive. He went into the cockpit and patched through to Alan McKenzie.

'They're all here. Over ...'

'Burlington? Over ...'

'Sedated but stable, not critical. Over ...'

'Take him to St. Mary's in Paddington as planned. Over ...'

'Do we let them fly out? Over ...'

'Let them fly. Over ...'

'Roger. Over and out.'

A real ambulance had just arrived and Edward was being strapped to the stretcher bed. Chad gave the order. It set off for St Mary's Hospital in central London with two of his men. Had he been in a critical condition he would have gone to a smaller hospital nearby. Chad Cooper went back into first class. He ordered his minders on board to shunt everyone into second class, except for the South African Military Attaché. Cooper came over and sat beside the man.

'You can't just abduct a British citizen off the streets in the middle of London.'

Marc van den Hoven made no comment.

'Haven't you heard of surveillance cameras?'

Still silence.

'Now, we don't need to cause an international incident but we do have everything on video. We can choose a body from the morgue and say we found it in your ambulance. We can say your doctor gave him too many tranquilisers and the poor sod died from a heart attack. Alternatively we can say the police found the body during a routine check. Actually, we can say whatever we want.'

Marc van den Hoven was becoming increasingly uncomfortable. A look of fear was spreading across his face. He knew what to expect from his superiors when he arrived in Cape Town. There would be no promotion, no medal but maybe a bullet.

'Oh, by the way your ambassador will be issuing a statement if necessary, all an unfortunate case of mistaken identity. Obviously he won't want an incident either.'

Cooper placed his hand heavily on Marc van den Hoven's shoulder and leant down so he could speak quietly in his ear.

'We don't know why you tried to kidnap one of our citizens and we don't care. If this plane doesn't start to taxi down the runway in the next fifteen minutes, everyone will be reading about this little escapade in tomorrow's press. We'll also have video footage available for the TV shows. It's up to you.'

Cooper stood up and signalled to his men who began withdrawing from the plane. He threw some keys down by the military attaché's feet.

'You can un-cuff your men when we've gone.'

The keys landed on the floor. As Marc van den Hoven bent down to pick them up Cooper kicked the man in the shin with a steel toe capped boot. A bone cracked. The noise was audible. So was the military attaché who howled in agony.

'Sorry about that old boy.'

Chad Cooper leant over him and retrieved Edward's briefcase from under the seat where the military attaché had tried to hide it.

'I don't think this is your briefcase, do you?'

Cooper backed towards the door, after his men.

'Good job you've got a doctor on board. Have a pleasant flight.'

Flight SAA-001 was cleared for departure by Air Traffic Control. The MI5 team waited until it taxied down the runway and climbed into the sky to be monitored by radar. Chad stood silently watching almost as if lost in prayer, thanking God it had all gone so smoothly. He snapped back into action.

Chapter 12 - Friday 3rd May

'Right lads, back to London as quick as you can. I can hear the roar of the Red Lion.'

Everyone moved at the double. Chad promised to join them to get the post-op celebrations started and then he would have to meet Mac for a debriefing. Sir Douglas Castle had already relayed the good news to Roger who was still studying every punctuation mark on every telex as he prepared his report on what it all meant.

Little did Chad know that this was just the first of many memorable meetings he was to have with Edward Burlington at international airports in years to come. However, what Chad did know was that the youngest Burlington had by hook or by crook stumbled across one of the hottest secrets on the planet. Never to his knowledge had such a secret been put on a plate for the UK and US intelligence services to dissect and devour.

Yet it seemed just too much of a vindaloo delight. Chad never believed in coincidences. After all, Edward's father was the JIC's chief scientific advisor and ex Porton Down governor. Edward's mother had a track record in British intelligence of clout not far off second to none. Everything seemed too good to be truly coincidental or so he thought.

Cooper mused to himself about some of the quotations he learned. Why had Bernard Shaw written "there are no secrets better kept than the secrets that everybody guesses" when Edward Hubbard had stated "a person may be very secretive and yet have no secrets". The frustrating part was they were both right. Sometimes nothing made sense in the twilight world he had chosen for his career.

He decided valour would have it that he kept his thoughts secret for now. Castle and others or even one of the Burlingtons would probably know how to solve this conundrum but he, like the rest of the world, would never be told. If he had the chance he might ask one of his superiors about it later.

As Chad and his men left for London Tessa was readying herself for Edward's arrival at St Mary's. Not long after speaking to Castle Mac had engineered a plan that was far more effective than reading the Riot Act to Edward when he regained consciousness. All Tessa had to do was deliver it.

Talk about mind tunnels, Edward was just about to be driven through tunnel after tunnel only this time the train driver seemed to have gone missing. Many of those who kept diaries were to make entries in them about what they thought had happened today. Within a couple of months they might find that their entries warranted redaction, erasure or amendment.

Chapter 13
Saturday 4th May

Praed Street Paddington, London England

Tessa sat in Edward's hospital room, then the corridor and then back again by his bed side killing time. She'd selected a room right at the end of the isolation ward corridor for security reasons. The time was two o'clock in the morning and one of Chad Cooper's men had just delivered Edward's briefcase. For some reason it hadn't travelled with him in the ambulance. She was worried. Five hours passed since they brought Edward in and he hadn't come round yet.

The doctors put him on a drip and were pumping glucose or some other such energizer into him. They didn't know yet what sedative had been injected into him and whether it would have any after affects. His blood pressure was low and his pulse was slow.

She just prayed he would pull through unscathed. Tessa blamed herself, even though nothing was directly her fault and she couldn't watch him twenty four hours a day. The people at Porter Williams, particularly Raj, should have protected him. She had known nothing about this South African debacle until Mac called, explained all she needed to know for the time being including his plan and told her to go to the hospital at once.

Tessa considered her relationship or lack of one with Edward, as she sat in the corridor, waiting for him to come round, willing him to recover. To him she was just a contact at the Metropolitan police. Otherwise, a part time PA who was helping run his mushrooming tax advisory and consultancy service to people in the music industry. He trusted her. She knew that, because he gave her a set of keys to his flat and she came and went as she pleased.

Once when some of his clients were round he had even shared a joint in front of her. When they lit up they didn't know she was police or even MI6. She just carried on typing as if nothing had happened. Sometimes he asked her advice about guns, which she said she was familiar with because of her work with the police. There was so much trust between them. Did she want the relationship to be more than

Chapter 13 - Saturday 4th May

that? That was a question she'd asked herself many times and still didn't have an answer.

It would be unprofessional, of course and, if anything like that developed, she'd have to report it to Mac, who would instantly relieve her of her handling duties. Anyway, everything was academic because Edward never shown any romantic interest in her and treated her like the sister he never had. If only he wasn't an MI6 asset. If only she wasn't in the intelligence services. Maybe things would be different. Was she dreaming an impossible dream? Who knew? Yet now she had to lie to him again and this time the orders came from on high.

Edward stirred inside the room and made a groaning sound. The attending nurse went to him and Tessa, who was having a spell in the corridor at the time, jumped to her feet and rushed to his side. He was still groggy but coming round for the first time. She breathed a sigh of relief.

'Where am I?'

Tessa motioned for the nurse to move back from the bed.

'You're in a hospital Edward.'

'They tried to steal my briefcase.'

'Who did?'

'The Geordies who were with me, chatting about the match.'

'No, Edward, they didn't.'

Edward looked puzzled. Tessa smiled down at him in her MI5 way.

'You must have misunderstood.'

'Did I?'

'Yes. They called the ambulance that brought you to hospital.'

'Which hospital?'

'St. Mary's, Paddington.'

'From the Duke's Head?'

'They specialise in toxic substances here.'

Edward frowned. His sharp mind wasn't quite with it yet and he was having trouble remembering what happened after trying to stand up outside the pub.

'What happened? Why am I on this drip?'

'You were given a spiked drink. Probably meant for someone else, a woman is my best guess. The pub was packed.'

'I thought that last drink tasted odd.'

'Nothing to worry about now.'

Edward looked for his watch but couldn't find it.

'What's the time? Where's my watch?'

'Just turned two o'clock, in the morning. Here's your watch.'

'I've been out for eight hours?'

'A strong spike. Lucky you're fit.'

Edward lay back in the bed. His head was splitting but he was starting to think straight. Was that spiked drink meant for someone else or had Pieter Reynolds sent someone after him?

'My briefcase?'

'It's here. They put it in the ambulance with you.'

'D'you know about the telexes?'

'What telexes?'

'I'll tell you later.'

The Geordies couldn't have been responsible if they had called an ambulance for him and sent his briefcase along with him. He was getting paranoid. All this bloody undercover stuff. Maybe a quiet spell in the Bahamas would do him good. Edward looked up into Tessa's smiling eyes as if a child. He started rubbing his left eyebrow to comfort himself as he stared into Tessa's big brown sisterly eyes.

'What happens now?'

'The doctors want to keep you in for a few hours longer. You should get some sleep.'

'I've been asleep for eight hours. Can I smoke in here?'

Tessa looked across at the nurse. She nodded. Tessa found an opened packet of cigarettes in one of his pockets and a lighter in another. She lit one up and put a plastic cup with water in it on the bedside table.

'Use this as an ashtray.'

Edward reached out to take the cigarette from Tessa. He noticed the Elastoplast on his arm.

'What's this?'

The nurse came back over to the bed.

'A booster shot administered by the paramedics in case your heart had been affected by the drug you were given.'

The nurse was MI5 and if she'd gone through a modern airport security scanner alarm bells would have rung. She had a Colt 38 strapped to her thigh.

'I'll be looking after you for the rest of the night. If you're good and can eat some food later, we might let you go home.'

Edward looked at Tessa, not too sure if the nurse would be as helpful as Tessa had been. He'd been holding back the burning question.

'Is Suzie ok?'

Tessa assured him she was alright and before saying goodbye suggested that he shouldn't bother any of his family about this trivial incident. It would only worry them unnecessarily, especially his mother. She prayed her bluff worked or she'd probably be in a dole queue by Monday morning. She called Mac and updated him on her success so far.

Chapter 13 - Saturday 4th May

Later that night Edward tried to slip out but the nurse caught him before he had even disconnected one measly drip. Secretly she thought it rather comical but kept a straight face as she checked the one drip Edward interfered with but failed to dismantle. She had been sat right behind him as he set about his escape!

A threatened injection with a large needle brought Edward to his senses. He hated needles and injections. The nurse agreed to hold back and then picked up the phone. This time a threatened call to Mac and Tessa soon had him asleep once they struck a deal. She would say nothing if he went back to sleep. Normally he would have asked her to keep him warm but for his thoughts of Suzie.

Abingdon Street Westminster, London England

At the time young Burlington was misbehaving in hospital, the South African Ambassador was sitting in front of Jim Callaghan, the British Foreign Secretary. Callaghan was wearing an out-of-fashion Marks & Spencer double breasted two piece suit. It looked like it hadn't seen the inside of a dry cleaner since he purchased it in the sixties.

The ambassador, in stark contrast, wore an immaculate Italian bespoke three piece pressed and creased to perfection. Clothes aside though, Callaghan had the upper hand, despite his sartorial disadvantage. The Foreign Secretary was secretly smirking behind the serious frown on his face. Callaghan had a bullet point aide memoire in front of him, prompting him what to say and what not to say. By now he'd read it several times, knew it off by heart and was twiddling with his bulky glasses.

'Your men went way too far, ambassador.'

'I'm so sorry, Foreign Secretary.'

'Lucky the police spotted what was going on at that pub.'

'I'm so sorry.'

'Diplomatic immunity does not cover murdering a British citizen in his own country.'

'I'm so sorry.'

'What if we did the same in your country? It just doesn't bear thinking about, does it?'

The ambassador stopped his parrot fashioned apologies. Callaghan wasn't going to let him stop squirming until he'd had his say.

'We can only assume this was a case of mistaken identity. The young dentist in question never ventured further abroad than Majorca on his holidays.'

Callaghan paused to look at his notes using his glasses like a magnifying glass rather than bothering to put them on properly. The ambassador opened his mouth at this opportunity to try to apologise again but he was too late.

'Your country will have to pay the costs incurred in diverting so many police to deal with this. You do realise most of them were on overtime and drafted into London to control football crowds. It's going to cost a lot of money.'

The ambassador attempted to light a cigarette but Callaghan's ferocious frown put a stop to that. He carefully slid the unlit fag back inside the packet so as not to drop one leaf of tobacco on the cold unwelcoming marble floor.

'Luckily, there were enough men on the ground because of the big match. We expected trouble from hooligans, not blasted diplomats.'

Callaghan went on about the South African government having to pay compensation to the victim's family, through the proper channels, of course. At the moment, they believed he died from a heart attack but they could easily be told the truth, if the ambassador understood what he was driving at. He got it in one.

'I'll do what I can to keep the incident from the media, provided the proper procedures are followed. After all, South Africa has enough bad press to contend with at the moment, without any more.'

The Foreign Secretary hid his amusement as he handed over official expulsion papers for all the diplomats involved in the murder of a British citizen in the heart of the capital. Callaghan concluded that he would not be making any announcement about the expulsions provided the terms in the documents he'd just pushed under the ambassador's nose were accepted without question.

'Can you sign here, ambassador?'

The ambassador speed read the paper and then he finally had a chance to speak.

'Yes, of course, Foreign Secretary.'

'If any of the expelled try to enter British territory again, they will be arrested and tried for murder.'

Callaghan looked at the ambassador, expecting a response.

'Do you understand?'

'Yes Foreign Secretary.'

'Good night, ambassador.'

Apartheid was finally swept away in 1994 and the African National Congress Party came to power under the leadership of Nelson Mandela. Fresh information about Operasie Wederkerigheid was uncovered by the newly installed National Intelligence Agency. The archived records showed the military attaché, Marc van den Hoven, and two others repatriated by MI6 were executed by firing squad on 8th May 1974. The whereabouts of their bodies was never discovered.

In his memoirs Jim Callaghan, alluded to the discovery of the telexes as one of the greatest post-war intelligence coups of MI6.

Montagu Square Marylebone, London England

Edward was allowed home from hospital in the early afternoon of Saturday 4th May. Tessa collected him and drove him to his flat. Suzie was waiting for him when he arrived. Tessa called her earlier to explain where Edward had been according to

Chapter 13 - Saturday 4th May

the gospel of Mac. She wanted to go round but Tessa said she wouldn't be allowed in the isolation unit but he should be back after lunch time.

'Édouard, my poor baby, are you better? Are you ok? I waited after your secretary told me what happened. Such bad luck.'

'Just having a drink with friends that made me forget the time. Fancy someone trying to take me away on a rape date.'

He winked at her as if to say it's your turn now.

The thought of Edward being unfaithful hadn't even crossed her mind. She rushed to him, flung her arms round him and kissed him several times, taking no notice of Tessa's presence. His head was still buzzing but he was glad to be home. Tessa wasn't too pleased to see Suzie and Suzie only had eyes for the one true love of her short life.

Suzie stopped kissing him and there ensued a stony silence between the two women. Tessa decided to go.

'Anyway, Edward, I've got to leave now.'

'Can't you stay for a drink?'

'Sorry, driving.'

'Coffee then?'

'I'll see you later. Take care Edward.'

Tessa didn't say see you later to Suzie. She hoped she wouldn't see the woman later or ever again for that matter.

Edward just had an orange juice for himself and poured a glass of chardonnay for Suzie.

'Who is that woman Édouard?'

'I told you, she's my PA.'

'Shouldn't your PA be in your office, not in your flat?'

'That's a private arrangement and this flat is my office. That is why she comes and goes so much.'

'How private?'

Normally, Edward wouldn't confide about his personal business with any girlfriend but Suzie was different. She was now closer to him than anyone had been in years and he liked it. He cherished every second of being with her. She found it magical being with him too and he could sense she did. They were easy together, like they were made for each other, and he seemed to relax more when she was with him. By now they'd been a couple for a month or so.

They sat on a sofa. Suzie curled up to him, like a furry cat.

'Why do you have so many cameras?'

'Standard security for these flats.'

'Why do some of them point out over the other roofs?'

The security hardware in the flat was monitored by GCHQ. If alarm bells rang or needed ringing MI6 received the first call and took control of whatever needed attention. GCHQ had set up all the systems and some of the cameras covered the adjoining roofs of next door neighbours. As he lived in a penthouse apartment it was safer from gun and bomb attacks. What was more, the area surrounding all sides of the building was monitored by outdoor cameras.

Edward was by no means the only person living in Montagu Square that the intelligence services had reason to protect. Of course, protection rackets can work two ways. So, Mac could both protect and watch him. There were only four other flats in the block and the occupants had all been checked out by Tessa and most working days in working hours the block of flats was empty.

Edward parked his car in a nearby underground garage. It had a normal commercial round the clock security presence. MI5 covertly fitted two different types of tracker to the vehicle, which he rarely used except to drive down to Epsom or up north. It was unusual for Edward to be profligate but safer for him to use cabs. In any event, as he had bought his rare Mark 1 Jag years ago the old car was increasing in value. It was only used for long journeys. His definition of long included an Epsom return, a comparatively short commuter route.

'The cameras are to keep us safe.'

'I'm glad.'

'Why are you glad?'

She didn't reply but he knew by the expression on her face that she was holding back on something important to her.

'Tell me what the trouble is. I can fix it for you.'

'I'm sorry, Édouard, it's just, well I am scared. My old boyfriend, he won't leave me alone.'

'Who is he?'

'A bank robber. He is a sadist and dangerous.'

'So am I. Give me his details later. I'll sort him out.'

Edward kissed her and she responded. His headache was leaving him as she undid the buttons of his trousers and noticed a faint scar across his abdomen.

'I haven't seen this before?'

'You should have tried looking with a torch. You can barely feel it now anyway.'

'Has it always been there?'

'Since I was twelve.'

'How?'

'Appendicitis.'

She ran her finger along the outline of the scar. He shivered. It brought back memories of being abandoned in a strange country until his mother brought him home crossing borders without a passport as if strolling down country lanes.

Chapter 13 - Saturday 4th May

'Now I know something about you.'

Edward didn't mind. They were still getting to know each other gradually, tentatively; the way people do who've lived through more than most and find it hard to trust and get to know others. They took small steps but advanced every time they were alone together. Suzie was glad she mentioned her problem. Now she wouldn't have to worry about Hakeem Gola telling the man where she was if she didn't find the address book for him.

After making love, Edward jumped out of bed and rushed out of the bedroom startling Suzie. He came back and stuck his arm round the door to reach for his dressing gown and chucked Suzie's to her. She could hear the television in the background.

'Quick. I forgot the FA cup final. You get the booze out the fridge. I'll get the glasses.'

Suzie was so happy. Edward was as joyful and exuberant as a child playing on the beach. She loved to watch the football with him. Well, she didn't watch the TV as much as watch him. She could see him as he was all those years ago. An excited ten year old, innocence personified apart from when punctuated with the occasional four-letter word if his team started misbehaving.

Westminster Bridge Road Lambeth, London England

About the same time as Edward was making love to Suzie, Mac called Chad into his office at Century House in Lambeth. The two men didn't shake hands or greet each other in any formal way. Their relationship was too familiar for that.

'Some day yesterday, what do you think Chad.'

'Good fun sir.'

Chad was a professional killer. Born in the backstreets of Middlesbrough, he left school at sixteen to join the marines. After serving in both of the UK's elite special forces, the SBS and SAS, he joined the intelligence services. He started at the bottom and made it through to the equivalent rank of an army captain. His one flaw as he saw it was his Teesside accent. As best as he could, he tried to cover it up but it slipped out when he was under pressure. However, as for accents, Chad was the master. He could mimic almost any dialect or slang or patois to perfection and this rare talent came in handy in places like Northern Ireland.

While Edward might have been described as naively courageous, Chad was cautiously fearless. He'd always look before leaping. In that respect, he was cleverer than most operatives in the field. If there was someone in his sights, he'd make sure he squeezed them for what they were worth before he pulled the trigger. Or if he found a bug in his house, he'd pump it with disinformation until whoever was listening at the other end drooled into complete disarray. Then he'd nail them.

Cooper had been involved in a junior capacity in the exposure of two of the Cambridge Four, Burgess and Maclean, the Soviet double agents who fled their cushy Foreign Office jobs and retired to Moscow. He learnt volumes from that and similar exercises since then. Virtues like being patient and alert when on surveillance or experience like his targets might not think logically or as he did. He learnt to accept that life wasn't always neat and tidy and if there were loose ends or unanswered questions so be it.

Somewhat curiously, his religious convictions allowed him to justify the amount of ruthless killing he had to do. He educated himself by studying classic British writers, Greek mythology and the Latin language while travelling to ops or waiting for the action to begin. Chad was a master of disguise and martial arts and was renowned for getting jobs done quickly and not sticking to the rules. McKenzie normally turned a blind eye to Cooper's shortcuts because he always wangled winning results. He was Mac's equivalent of Jeeves in a bullet proof jacket in sticky situations.

'I just want to bring you up to date on Lacklustre, Chad, strictly need to know.'

'Of course sir.'

Mac lit a cigarette but didn't offer one to Chad Cooper. As Mac knew only too well, Chad was a health and fitness freak and frowned on the habit. Chad had glibly insisted that, one day, smoking cigarettes would be banned from all public places. Everybody laughed at him.

'Ok, where should I start? The South African Ambassador has been hauled in front of the Foreign Secretary and fed a story about how his military attaché kidnapped and tranquilised a dentist to death.'

'Nice one sir.'

'There's nothing to connect the operation to us and it's all been put down to police vigilance.'

Cooper laughed sardonically. As if the plods could have pulled off something like Lacklustre. The irony of his sarcasm escaped both men given the name attributed to the lacklustre assignment on which they were both now engaged.

'The military attaché and his goons are probably being beaten with sjamboks right now. If the head of BOSS is anything like his reputation, they'll be cremated by Monday.'

'Anyone from Mines & Minerals International sir?'

'The link man there has gone for a jog. He's a guy called Pieter Reynolds who was supposedly just a temp. We now know he was high up in the BOSS hierarchy. Anyway, they pulled him out.'

'What about the rest sir?'

'Nobody of interest. I doubt if the telexes would even have been sent there if Reynolds hadn't been in situ.'

Mac stared down into the busy operations centre.

'We have monitoring systems in place, through GCHQ, on all the communications in and out of MAMI, as well as the homes of key personnel.'

Chapter 13 - Saturday 4th May

Chad brushed away the smoke from Mac's cigarette while his superior was watching the turmoil outside his office.

'We haven't alerted our desks in South Africa and India but Sir Douglas Castle has banned any sharing of data with Pakistan.'

'Where do the Americans stand in all this sir?'

'Up to speed.'

'They want to get involved then sir?'

'Definitely. We're in close liaison already. As for BOSS, we have learnt that MAMI advised the telexes were missing. They suspect Burlington and their cleaners and maybe even their own security. In reality they don't know what happened to the telexes, thanks to Burlington using his wits.'

'So they have no idea that we know sir?'

'Correct. They probably think if the thief was Burlington, the motive was extortion because of his fly trap police record. They'll reckon they've scared him off now and my guess is they'll just keep schtum and hope it all goes away.'

Mac came back from the window and sat behind his desk. He was silent for a moment or two. Chad knew that wasn't the end of the meeting, otherwise Mac would've said so. He waited. Something was on Mac's mind.

'Funny thing sir, Burlington's briefcase was still locked when I retrieved it. Why didn't they try to open it?'

'Who knows? Arrogance, maybe or possibly they wanted Burlington there to do it, booby traps and all that shit. You know what these Boers are like, they were sure they had it all worked out right, like they think they are with everything.'

Chad laughed again.

'The tracker was still transmitting when my man dropped it off at St. Mary's sir.'

'Burlington's police records were checked by a bent rozzer with South African connections. They paid him £1,000.'

'Nice money for five minutes sir.'

'Well it certainly proves the fly trap we planted is working.'

'What happened to the bent cop sir?'

'The little shit will be sacked on Monday, for something else, of course.'

'Serves him right.'

Chad was getting impatient. By now he'd been in Mac's office for quite a while, the smoke was nauseous and he wanted to go to home to Carshalton and see his kids. At best he was a restless man, couldn't sit still for long and always liked to be on the move. He just wished Mac would get to the point.

'Where's Burlington now sir?'

'Back at Montagu Square. Sir Douglas is insisting you keep some of your team in place around his flat for a while. That man is getting bloody paranoid.'

Mac poured himself a whisky. He offered one to Chad out of politeness, knowing his junior officer would decline.

'Right, let's focus on the important business.'

At last, Chad thought.

'I want you to look closely at Mr Raj Gupta Khan. Take as long as you need within reason, use half a dozen of your squad if you consider that sufficient.'

'Any particular purpose sir?'

'Just a hunch. Khan may be loosely linked to Indian intelligence or maybe some splinter group, like one of the Nepalese Independence mobs. I might be wrong, of course.'

Chad nodded. Mac wasn't often wrong. If he smelled a rat, there was usually a two legged rodent around somewhere.

'I want you to liaise with Daniel Luke and his SORT team on this. Daniel will organise a cover story for you. Keep things as quiet and simple as possible.'

'No problem sir.'

'Daniel will give you any background material you need on Khan. No need to climb Mount Everest on this one and keep to the rules.'

Cooper smiled cynically. Mac always said that but he'd do this his own way and get a result. Mac never complained about his tactics once a thorny conundrum was sorted.

'Khan and Burlington spend their days at the same place, Porter Williams near St. Paul's. You know the place. So the same team can watch out for both of them.'

Mac finished his whisky. The meeting was finishing too.

'Well, I don't know about you, Chad, but I'm going to watch the FA cup final on television. Should be kicking off round about now. Damn it. I've already missed most of the first half.'

'Is that so sir?'

'Yes. Who do you think will win?'

'I haven't a clue who's even playing sir?'

Liverpool won. A three nil victory, with Keegan claiming a brace of goals. Operation Lacklustre began on 3rd May 1974 and mushroomed into a major joint intelligence initiative between MI6 and the CIA which lasted for several weeks.

India exploded its first nuclear bomb on the morning of Saturday 18th May 1974. It was the first country outside the United Nations Security Council to do so. The event was described by the Indian government as a peaceful nuclear explosion and was called the Smiling Buddha Project.

Most believe the project was speeded up as a result of the missing telexes. For those who believe in Buddhism Buddha would have laughed at the rest of the world for its woeful incompetence but smiled on Edward Burlington.

Chapter 13 - Saturday 4th May

Nobody in Century House would be laughing though once the inquisitions began in earnest. The intelligence services had changed their methods since Britannia ruled the waves. Sara and Boadicea for that matter would have disapproved as interrogations were all psychological nowadays even compared with the Second World War.

Mind you, those responsible for the Spanish Inquisition might also have scoffed at the modus operandi of a modern gentle probing. Nonetheless, once the investigations started they didn't always end up where you expected them to come to a halt.

Several pages in several diaries were written about Operation Lacklustre and old newspaper clippings were found. In South Africa three more bodies had been disposed of but no one in the UK knew that at the time.

Again a quick read of the diaries written in 1974 would have left you understandably confused. They barely seemed to be about the same subject matter. There were only two words entered in Sir Douglas Castle's diary: "holy shit". No wonder he had been nicknamed Tealeaves. Roger Burlington had written a more cryptic cue at the end of his notes: "Who else knows what?"

Chapter 14
Monday 20th May

Westminster Bridge Road Lambeth, London England

The exploding of India's first nuclear bomb dominated the front pages of the world's press. That weekend Sir Douglas Castle spent hours scuttling back and forth between the Foreign Office, the Ministry of Defence and Downing Street. In the UK press though, the main focus was on bombs of a different kind. There had been seventeen killed and over a hundred injured after several IRA car bombs were detonated.

Castle called Alan McKenzie and Daniel Luke to his office. They thought they'd been summoned to report on the terrorist situation. As they entered his office it looked empty until his head appeared rising from below his desk.

'Sorry, just lost my pen.'

He awkwardly clambered back onto his seat looking slightly flushed. Mac was focusing on the only gold pen he forever used already on top of a pile of papers on his desk. Mac had a pretty good idea what Castle was doing and looked at Daniel who clearly hadn't noticed anything awry.

'Well gentlemen, we've all got egg on our faces, haven't we? As for you Daniel, I am beginning to question what your research team does apart from miss the obvious.'

Mac and Daniel glanced at each other but didn't speak.

'The Smiling Buddha wasn't that hard to detect, was it? In hindsight we are a joke. Luckily so are the CIA and so will the KGB be if they haven't already listened in to the telephone chatter between London and Washington DC.'

Sir Douglas Castle was asking questions he didn't expect answering. Mac sat silently and listening intently. He could just hear the whir of the tape recorder less than two feet from him under Castle's desk. Mac was thinking to himself what a bunch of amateurs they all were; Daniel hadn't even spotted it and not one of them had noticed Smiling Buddha.

'Why weren't we stalking the plutonium market to see what was happening? I suppose we weren't the only clueless ones since neither the CIA nor KGB knew anything about Smiling Buddha either. The Prime Minister said we shouldn't be too hard on ourselves.'

Chapter 14 - Monday 20th May

Mac almost fell off his chair. If Castle believed that claptrap he should get a job with the Guardian. "Shouldn't be too hard on ourselves" probably meant they'd all be out of work by Friday. All this was water under the bridge to Mac now. The Indians had exploded an atomic bomb, so the whole world knew their secret, fait accompli. There was little anyone could have done about it anyway. Depending on your point of view, either the loss or the discovery of the telexes probably only speeded up what was already inevitable.

'We are just Crown servants after all aren't we?'

Sir Douglas Castle was asking a question he wanted answering this time.

Mac looked at Daniel who spoke first.

'Yes sir. I am anyway so if I am you are one sir and so is Mac. Is that right Mac?'

Mac ignored Daniel and looked straight at Castle.

'I'm not sure why you're asking sir as the answer is obvious. We all are including you but only if we admit it so what difference does it make?'

Castle ignored Mac as Mac had Daniel.

'Which brings me to young Burlington.'

Here cometh the punch line, Mac thought to himself. He had been on countdown as to how long it would take his boss to get round to his pet paranoia.

'Roger Burlington was shocked we allowed the kidnap scenario to go as far as it did.'

Mac wanted to quash that red snapper rumour there and then.

'That was low risk sir and necessary.'

Castle wasn't listening.

'Thank the Lord that Burlington's mother didn't find out or at least she hasn't yet.'

Mac wasn't all that surprised his paranoid boss was so fearful of Sara. She'd been his mentor during the late war years and he knew how tough she could be. He also knew Castle had a fling with her some years back but there was more to his anxiety than that, surely? The man looked ill at the thought of her finding out about her son's close shave with a bullet in the back of his head. Yet in reality what could she do to Sir Douglas Castle? She couldn't send him to a torture chamber in South Africa.

'BOSS's pride has been dented. What are the chances of them striking back in anger?'

'Unlikely sir. They have no idea Burlington is linked to us.'

'I'm not worried about us Mac; it is young Burlington who concerns me.'

'They're a less disciplined outfit than even the KGB. I suppose they might try to organise a hit sir, who knows?'

Castle nearly choked on his green tea. It dribbled down his chin onto his polka dot tie.

'Well, we can't allow that to happen, can we, Mac?'

'No sir. Like I said, it's unlikely.'

'When is young Burlington off to the Bahamas?'

'Soon sir, six weeks maybe at most.'

'Thank the Lord.'

This seemed to calm Castle, who wiped the tea spatter from his tie with a crumpled tissue he retrieved from the pocket of his brown Fair Isle cardigan.

Mac decided to allow the rant to subside; he knew it would. Castle never carried on carping for long. He'd have his say and soon get distracted by something else and twitter on about that. Daniel Luke said nothing at all as was his wont. Commander Luke was in charge of MI6's Special Operations Research Team, called SORT for short.

As if he had changed into someone else Castle resumed sipping his cup of green tea, after having decorated it with one sugar lump and a zest of lemon. Mac knew his mind was already wandering.

'Anyway, better India has nuclear weapons than Pakistan or Iraq.'

Castle continued slurping from his tea cup.

'Now, about Raj Gupta Khan, am I right in thinking he was involved with getting young Burlington inside the Cyrus Burton organisation?'

'Through his diplomatic contacts sir.'

Daniel Luke spoke up for the first time in a while.

'The MS wanted a gofer without a conscience sir.'

'The MS?'

'Magnificent Seven sir. That's what Burlington called them.'

A hint of a smile broke across Castle's face, and then slowly wiped itself from his face disappearing as if used toilet paper being flushed away.

'Why all these childish acronyms all the bloody time? Can't we just speak English?'

Daniel Luke continued.

'As I was saying sir, once an alias was set up for him, Khan put Burlington in contact through his sources.'

'So now we're looking into him, that's Khan I'm talking about?'

'Yes sir, Operation Bonaparte.'

'Yes I know about Bonaparte. Quite apt given Khan is short and fat.'

So was Castle and a faint flicker of a smile passed between them but still neither Mac nor Daniel knew where Sir Douglas Castle was going with this. He knew everything and sanctioned the surveillance on Khan himself, so why was he playing this remote lion and zebra game? It was as if he was making it look as though they'd decided to investigate Khan themselves and he knew little or nothing about it. Mac became apprehensive. Castle spoke directly to him this time, after taking another sip of his tea.

'Apart from working for us, Khan also works for the ISI.'

Both men were more than surprised.

Chapter 14 - Monday 20th May

'Pakistani intelligence!'

'Hang on though, he's Indian sir.'

'Goan, to be more precise but his name is Khan, don't forget.'

'May we ask how you know this sir?'

'CIA, earlier this morning. I want Operation Bonaparte to stop.'

'What?'

'Why sir?'

'We, and by that I mean MI6 and the CIA, are going to use Mr Khan as a channel of disinformation to the ISI.'

Mac was seething. Chad Cooper and his team had expended several weeks setting up surveillance on Khan and now that looked utterly pointless. Even Daniel sighed at the thought of another instance of incompetency and lack of communications between the international secret agencies. He said nothing. Castle continued.

'Nobody is to know this, including Cooper. Is that clear?'

'What shall I tell him sir?'

'Tell him?'

'About why he's being ordered to step down sir?'

'Quite frankly, Mac, I don't care. You'll think of something. You're better than me at lying and cover-ups.'

Still conscious of the tape recorder Mac had to answer back.

'You mean disinformation sir?'

'Does it matter?'

Castle put on his glasses and perused a file on his desk. The other two men knew the meeting was over and made their way to the door.

'Oh, by the way Mac.'

Both men turned. Castle brusquely waved at Daniel Luke as if to get him out of the room. He left. Mac was still standing just inside the door and waited for Castle to look up from his file. He didn't.

'Roger Burlington wants to see you.'

'When sir?'

'Now Mac. At some law firm's offices in The Strand. My secretary will give you their address. They're called Baggers something, the Lord only knows. Anyway she has the name. Off you go now. At once ... immediately, do you hear me?'

'What's it about sir?'

Castle ignored the question having just spoken in that matter of fact school masterly way he sometimes did that infuriated Mac.

'Tessa Hislop is already on her way. Don't keep Roger waiting. For the record, it's a formal JIC inquiry. He has full JIC authority to ask what he likes and must be answered truthfully! Pray to the Lord you come out unscathed.'

After Mac left, Sir Peter, cigar in hand, stuck his head around the door looking even more pleased with himself than usual.

'I'm off now. Before I go, do you want to hear my take on the results of the last round of independent interviews before you get the transcripts tomorrow?'

Castle summoned him into his office. Naturally all the interviews were recorded not that the interviewees were told so but they'd be dumb not to assume they were. In any event all conversations in Castle's office could be taped at his whim by the silent push of a button under his desk when he could find the button without having to rummage around under his desk!

As for Mac, Castle deliberately forgot to mention his session with him and Luke was part of the official inquiry. What's more he hadn't said what was the subject of the inquiry, or that McKenzie and Hislop weren't the first to be grilled.

Mac didn't have time to check what a formal JIC inquiry was but he could guess. He took a few large swigs from his whisky flask as he thought of his pension going up in smoke. Castle was both furious and relieved. There was no doubt Sara was behind the inquiry, because the Home Secretary ordered it and his wife and Sara were close. At least Mrs Burlington had gone for the infrastructure and not his jugular. He would be exonerated. The Bashir brothers who also featured in his nightmares weren't even mentioned en passant. He felt good about that.

Mac acknowledged to himself anyway that he had let too much rope out on both Standpipe and Lacklustre but he should be safe as he'd done it for the greater good. Perhaps he might say he was following orders but then look what happened at the Nuremburg trials to the Nazi elite. No, surely Mac would never lie to save his own skin or would he?

The Strand Westminster, London England

Chad had just left the offices of Bagstock & Flintwinch via the rear exit in Carting Lane, just off The Strand. Roger and he had enjoyed a good chat. Roger even recommended some books to him on classical subjects which Chad duly noted. As the meeting became so open, Chad asked Roger if he could ask one question. Roger had of course agreed.

Chad's question was about his concerns over coincidences and the Burlingtons. Roger thought about it before simply brushing it aside by replying "Coincidences have occurred for centuries Chad. That is why the word's etymological beginnings are in Latin. As a scholar of the classics I'm surprised you didn't know that. It's a fair question though and understandable from someone living in your isolated and paranoid world."

Chad hadn't seen it quite that way round but understood why Roger saw it from that point of view and he was right. There was too much paranoia and there were too many trying to jump to conclusions across rivers too wide to bridge and too deep to fathom.

Chapter 14 - Monday 20th May

The ashtray was already half full when Mac and Tessa were shown into the consulting room at Bagstock & Flintwinch. Roger was organising the seating.

'Mac, Tessa. Do come in and sit down on these chairs. Can I get you anything?'

They answered in unison.

'No thank you sir.'

'I'm sure we've met before Tessa. Have we?'

'Not formally sir.'

'Well, I'm pleased to do so now. Edward speaks highly of you.'

'Thank you sir.'

'Please call me Roger, not sir. Before I ask a few questions, can you each confirm you are Crown servants and who you report to? I'm told this is procedural in formal JIC inquiries. You have been told this is a formal inquiry I hope.'

They both nodded. Mac answered first.

'Yes, and I report to Sir Douglas Castle for the record.'

Tessa followed his lead. Her voice was faltering.

'Yes and I am also a Crown servant sir, and the senior officer I report to is Alan McKenzie.'

Roger lit another Players Navy Cut cigarette. He wasn't in the habit of interrogating people. It sat uneasily with him but he'd netted most of what he'd been told to catch in less than thirty seconds. It reminded him of the spell he spent in a Russian prison in the sixties, before Douglas Castle and Peter Stafford negotiated his exit. He and Castle were less antagonistic to one another in the fifties and early sixties. It was only since Castle's knighthood that relations had plummeted downhill as fast as a grouse on the glorious twelfth day of August in the grounds of Gleneagles.

In Russia he wasn't just interrogated but tortured as well, hung up like a pheasant. He told them the truth, as he'd been advised to do if ever such an occasion arose. MI6 knew he didn't even know the name of a single active spy behind the iron curtain. There wasn't a war going on then, apart from a cold one, and there was no need to deny anything. In any event the repeated dose of scopolamine he was given made sure every secret he'd ever held was teased from him. They even told him his confessions included a detailed autobiographical account of his sexual activity from puberty.

Memories of being on the other side of the table flooded back to him. They had wanted to know why he was interested in the Soviets remote viewing and psychiatry budget. Well. For a start the budget was larger than that for their nuclear program. They asked again and again why he had the secret dossier they found on him. The papers they found were not secret at all because he had officially been given them.

The only reason Roger was there because he was invited and the Russians gave the information to him themselves, for scientific research purposes. Even so they knew he was on the JIC and he walked right into their open arms. At the time, a hostage or two to exchange for some of Philby's friends would be useful to them but they had to make it look like he was spying. All that was in the past and the past, as LP Hartley said, was a foreign country. He turned his attention back to Tessa.

'You are Edward's handler, aren't you Tessa?'

'I can explain what Tessa does Roger ...'

'Thank you, Mac, but I'd rather hear it from Tessa herself.'

Tessa looked at Mac, he nodded to her. She turned her face back to Roger Burlington and looked straight at him, and she wasn't going to call him by his Christian name.

'That's one of my responsibilities sir.'

'How can that be Tessa?'

'I don't understand sir.'

Mac was about to interject again. Roger held his hand up to stop him.

'How can you be my son's handler when he has no idea who you are or what you do?'

'I follow orders sir.'

'You follow orders. I see. How many others do you handle?'

'Typically two or three sir but I have other duties besides those.'

Roger wasn't interested in the last part of her answer although it probably translated into her seeing his son on average twice a week for a few hours. That was more than he'd managed most of his life outside weekends and a few family holidays. He paused to light up yet another cigarette. Roger was uncomfortable doing this interviewing for many reasons, including hypocrisy, but he considered it his duty. In any case, better they should be facing him than Sara. He lifted a manual from the desk in front of him and held it in the air.

'I have here an MI5 training and personnel manual. Are you familiar with it?'

'I am, reasonably so sir.'

Roger opened a section he'd already marked and read from it.

'A handler or handling officer has to make certain things clear to his or her agents that are required by law.'

Mac wasn't going to sit there and let Tessa take all the flak.

'Tessa was following orders, like she said.'

'Right then Mac. You are also a Crown servant and, unlike Tessa, you were aware of Edward's role in Lacklustre by the time he left work on 3rd May. Is that correct?'

'Yes it is.'

'You knew what was happening but Tessa didn't. So, who was his handler then?'

'Technically, I suppose I was.'

'Good. So, Tessa was handler on Standpipe and you, Mac, were Edward's handler on Lacklustre.'

Both of them said yes almost simultaneously. Roger seemed to assert this to himself and he smiled cordially as he did so.

Chapter 14 - Monday 20th May

'Tessa, how do you think Edward understood his role while you were his handler?'

Tessa looked at Mac once more. Mac nodded again.

'To answer that question sir I'd have to go back before Standpipe.'

'Please do so.'

Tessa began explaining to Roger what he already knew but he allowed her to continue. His mind drifted back to the morning of Friday 3rd May when he had clandestinely sent Pieter Reynolds about ten telexes in Hindi and Punjabi. He obtained the copies of the telexes. It had been his idea, his idea alone. Hugh had nothing to do with it just because he spoke the languages. He translated many documents when conflicts of interest as to what they meant might arise.

So Chad was right in some respects. There was no coincidence. Yet it had all backfired so hideously and now he must continue with the pretence that others not he had endangered his son's life. However, they had done it before so there was logic in it and in Lacklustre. Edward could have been so easily rescued before the BOSS trap was sprung or even as it was being put in motion.

Of course Roger guessed what was going on between India, Pakistan and the Boers months ago. Only an imbecile could have failed to note that in his opinion. All he wanted was proof to publicly undermine Castle as either complicit in a cover up or downright incompetent. Roger still wanted pay back for Castle's final fling with Sara, the unashamed blatant sexual abuse of his fiancé. It didn't matter to him that it happened thirty years or so ago. Castle despicably used his rank to place her in easy reach and under his command. It would have been like a prep school teacher seducing a twelve year old.

As usual there were other angles. To virtually everyone he knew in the industry it was absolutely bloody obvious what was happening. So why did these myopic civil servants supposedly have no idea about it at all? It had to be monumental negligence or a massive cover up and that was why he had set out to expose Castle for whichever he found it to be.

His plan, well it hardly mattered now, was to have enlisted Sara's help over that ensuing weekend to ensnare Reynolds. He created a cunning double edged sword scheme which would have entrapped Reynolds who would have no choice but to grasp the sword blade and seek political asylum here or die back home at the hands of BOSS. Hence, Reynolds would have unwittingly admitted what the South Africans were up to and Roger could have proved a cover up or negligence.

Even so none of his plans mattered anymore because in one important respect Chad was also wrong. There had been a completely unexpected coincidence. An almost unbelievable coincidence as it happens. His son had stolen the telexes because Edward like his father was sometimes too clever for his own good. He knew he was a hypocrite of the highest order but had told no one, not even Sara as things had moved so fast that Friday. Now as each day passed it only made it all the more difficult to share his secret guilt with her.

She would go ballistic now on two fronts: why he cocked up the timing and why he hadn't told her. Why had he rushed out those telexes without checking Reynolds was on site in his office? All it would have taken was just one anonymous call. Maybe that's why he wasn't a spy. Roger realised he was muttering to himself "the path to perdition is packed with promises" as Tessa interrupted his chain of thought.

'Sorry sir, I didn't quite catch that.'

'Never mind. Sorry. I was thousands of miles away. Where were we again?'

Roger was trying to remember where the cliché came from. He couldn't.

'I was instructed to stay close to him because we would be using him in the future sir.'

'That's right. What did you mean by the word "using"? My son didn't have to agree to Standpipe; he could have just carried on as an accountant and led a safe and secure life.'

'You know your son sir.'

'Do I? I'm not sure if I do. Did he appreciate the dangers?'

'I never asked him sir but I suppose he did. He likes living dangerously.'

'There's more to it than that, isn't there Tessa?'

Again, Tessa hesitated before answering. This was getting personal and she didn't want to be talking about Edward behind his back. She didn't know how much his father knew about him and it seemed like a betrayal. Mac nudged her. She tried to be obscure.

'Edward is an active man if you get my meaning sir.'

'I get your meaning thank you Tessa.'

Roger remembered the comments about Edward's sex life at the lunch meeting five weeks earlier. He had a hunch she wasn't admitting to everything.

'Tell me about this new woman in his life?'

'New woman sir?'

'I know about her Tessa.'

The problem was Mac didn't. Mac looked at Tessa and waited for her reply. She was tongue-tied for a moment. Nobody else knew about Suzie Laurent, at least she believed no one else did in MI5. The croupier had checked out, so there was no reason to involve anyone else. Yet now she was speaking to Roger Burlington, a JIC member leading a formal JIC inquiry. It didn't matter one iota if he was Edward's Dad.

Roger smiled benevolently at her only too well aware she was a better person than him in many respects. For a start she wasn't a hypocrite.

'That's alright, Tessa, your reticence says volumes about your loyalty to Edward. Anyway, I know you will have checked the woman out thoroughly by now.'

'Thank you sir.'

'Thank you for being so candid with me Tessa. I've learned more about my son today, and about you.'

Chapter 14 - Monday 20th May

Both Mac and he lit yet more cigarettes. Mac was still looking at her. Why hadn't he been informed? Why this and why that?

'Right, that should be all.'

Both Mac and Tessa stood up as if to leave together.

'Not you, Mac, just Tessa.'

Mac looked disappointed as he sat back down for more. Roger shook Tessa's hand and she moved quickly towards the door. He called after her.

'What do you think of Edward, I mean personally, not professionally?'

'I admire him sir.'

Roger nearly asked if love would be too strong a word but thought better of it. Tessa, as if reading his mind, smiled at Roger and left the interview room.

After she'd gone, Roger poured two glasses of port for himself and Mac. Mac wanted to take a big hit from his hip flask but controlled the urge. He'd already almost matched Roger cigarette for cigarette and his pack was emptying. Normally, Roger would have said that more could be achieved by cordiality than confrontation but this day had to be different.

Yet he did not want to overly antagonise the MI6 man who was admired by both Sara and himself. They didn't admire many of them but he had to confront him today. Of course Sara knew nothing of Roger's secret, which he was struggling to keep buried deep in the recesses of his mind.

'I chatted with Edward before this meeting Mac. You know what that means.'

'You told him nothing and he told you everything?'

'How much of your time does he take up?'

'I would estimate we see each other once a month though Chad Cooper is beginning to see more of him which I have encouraged. In MI6 I have a few dozen agents under my wing as you'd imagine but none report direct to me unless I'm operationally involved. That only happens when it's important as was the case in Standpipe.

When an op comes to a close is when most contact takes place. I may have seen him almost daily in the final weeks of Standpipe. Mind you that was unusual if you compare it to the offshore elements of the Manunta, Maudling and other affairs he and I were both involved in one way or another.'

Both men seemed lost in the labyrinths of their own thoughts. By now Mac was metaphorically in a different room from Roger and unbeknownst to Mac vice versa. Both he and Roger might as well have been in different cities as their concentration ebbed and flowed. Mac was more concerned about himself if the truth be known.

Had Tessa already gone into another interview room with Castle, and was she maligning him to save her own skin? Was that why Roger tacked all over the place, so as to stick to a timetable of final interviews? Why had Castle sent him here after such a drawn out meeting? Who else had Roger and Castle interviewed? Were there other interviewers like Sir Peter involved?

Mac thought of when he'd first met Frederick Burlington. The old man was giving lectures about survival behind enemy lines. Frederick had been a captain in the Ghurkhas and fought in India and Nepal during the First World War. After the war, he became a teacher, despite being paralysed in one arm and blind in one eye. The captain was a war hero from a past era and Mac liked the old dog. At least he was a soldier and he could understand soldiers.

Roger was still talking, almost to himself, as Mac's attention coasted back.

'Edward said he didn't have to go through minefields with you and Tessa behind him, holding loaded pistols to his head.'

'Nice of him to say so Roger.'

'Yes but you and I both know his similitude isn't totally true, is it?'

'How d'you mean?'

'It's not that black and white. Edward may not have the choices he thinks he has.'

'Can't say I understand.'

'Come on, Mac, we've both been round the block a few times.'

Mac didn't answer. His lack of attention in this game of a dangerous cat stalking its naive prey revealed he didn't have a clue about the rules and Roger latched onto that instantly. Mac always thought the Burlingtons had time for him but maybe he'd gone a step too far. Standpipe was a career booster for him. Unlike Daniel Luke, he wasn't directly on the hook for the fundamental failures underpinning Lacklustre. Also, he had saved Edward even if he let the rope out as much as humanly possible again.

'We extracted your son on Lacklustre. There was no real danger Roger.'

'No real danger?'

By now Roger's secret had sunk to the bottom of his mind. It was rare but Roger was incensed and not just with cigarette smoke this time. Who on earth did this civil servant think he was? Roger lit another cigarette, oblivious to the fact that the previous one was still alight in the ashtray.

'That is a blatant lie according to Mr Cooper and others. I've talked to everyone involved and you know who Mr Cooper reported to on Lacklustre, don't you Mac?'

Mac was surprised at the rapid change in Roger's tenor and tone of voice. He knew the man though and as a scientist he would have been fastidious in his investigations. If he had known of Roger's hypocrisy it would have been a different meeting altogether.

Or would it? On proper scrutiny and analysis there had been no hypocrisy. First, the truth about nuclear proliferation had been established. Next, all Burlington did was try to root out negligence or worse. He'd put his son in danger totally unexpectedly. That danger could have been easily and quickly averted by Mac or Castle if they hadn't insisted on leaving him as bait to see what happened.

Chapter 14 - Monday 20th May

'If there was no damn danger, why were there over fifty MI5 and Special Branch officers involved in and around Heathrow alone?'

'Belt and braces, which is how Chad Cooper operates all the time.'

'Do you think I'm stupid, just because I don't have a silly rank in some obscure part of MI5 or MI6? Did you ask Edward if he wanted to be sedated and have a trial run at being abducted?'

'No, no we didn't, I will admit to that.'

'You knew way before then he was just a worm on your fishing line.'

'It didn't happen like that ...'

Roger didn't let him finish.

'That worm was my son. What if Sara treated one of your daughters like that? What if she threw the line too far out to sea?'

Mac sat motionless, as if waiting for a firing squad to finish the interview. He was surprised at Roger's access to his staff but Sir Douglas' last words "must be answered truthfully" became clearer in an instant. Mac decided to change tack and acquiesce to a greater degree. Roger stubbed out his latest cigarette.

'At last we're getting somewhere. You're a colonel who decides what his assets do in the field. As with Standpipe, you left my son in danger on Lacklustre longer than necessary, according to several of those who reported to you.'

'I'm afraid I disagree but can now see their point of view Roger.'

Mac was taken aback. Which of his people questioned his judgement? Who had the Triumvirate talked to? Castle must have arranged all this. Roger Burlington couldn't have been allowed to talk to staff at operational level or could he? What were the bloody rules? Why didn't he know them? Was silky Stafford waiting to slide in and start a broadside from behind? Shit. This was worse than he'd feared.

'I won't ask why but most people in the intelligence services end up wanting to get out, preferably clutching an honour or two. I hope you haven't stooped to think that low, Mac?'

Mac recalled his thoughts before the final push in Standpipe and remained silent. Roger didn't press home the advantage. He'd had enough of pretending to be an inquisitor and he'd hauled in what he was told to get in bucketfuls.

'Just so you know, Mac, I probably wouldn't have acted differently, if I was acting outside the law. Thank you for coming. I suggest you and your team study the handbook in future. You can take this one with you, I don't need it anymore.'

Roger handed the training and personnel manual to Mac, who took it reluctantly.

'If you read Section 17, Paragraphs 4 to 11, you'll see you risk immediate dismissal if you start asking anyone what they said during this formal inquiry. Take my advice and don't grill Tessa or Chad or anyone else and you'll survive this. That's it. From me at least it's all over now.'

Mac breathed a silent sigh of relief. It looked like the interview was over and he wouldn't have to go through another session with Sir Peter Stafford or another JIC member. Why couldn't he recall the details of Castle's interview? Was it an interview? Roger's tone lightened.

'Sara sends her best wishes, by the way.'

Mac was having difficulty understanding where all this led. Sara Burlington had been his mentor and guru in MI5 and he respected and held the woman in high regard. He also respected any man who could live with her as long as Roger had. There was no way they were after him, or he'd have been nailed to the cross by now. What was going on? Little did he know?

'Likewise to her Roger; I'm not sure if I've precisely understood the purpose of either this meeting or my earlier meeting with Sir Douglas.'

'You're one of the few left Mac. Just watch your back. One day in the not too distant future a team of lawyers and computer experts will be of more use to MI6 than anyone with your pedigree.'

Mac drained his glass of port in one gulp. There was nothing left. It tasted sweet in his mouth and he took a chance and produced the hip flask from his breast pocket.

'May I?'

'A chaser? Of course, go ahead.'

Roger smiled his consent. He guessed he knew now why everyone in the intelligence services drank so much. Mac poured what was left of the whisky into the empty port glass and finished it in one mouthful.

Roger stood up and shook Mac's hand. He looked the MI6 man in the eye and nodded, as if apologising for what had transpired. Mac and Burlington were close, like it or not. Roger knew both of them were acting, or had acted, for the greater good in their own way. Nonetheless, Edward's security needed to be stepped up a gear in the light of recent events. The meeting ended. Mac walked away from the desk and held the handle of the door.

'Anyway, he's going abroad soon, so you can stop worrying.'

Roger didn't respond to the remark but his expression was sceptical. Mac departed without saying another word. Roger considered he'd done his duty. He hated confrontation but at least he could tell Sara that a formal inquiry had taken place. The powers that lurked behind unknown departmental doors had spoken with Sir Douglas Castle and admissions had been made that could be stored up for future reference if need be. Castle hadn't even taken the denial route while acknowledging all that was alleged was possible. He was no match for Philby or the Burlingtons.

Yet again, as if to prove it was all too much, Roger lit up another cigarette, inhaled twice and stubbed it out. He sometimes wished his wife was still in the intelligence services and he could leave all this confrontational stuff up to her. She was much better at dealing with all this classified crap than him, or so he'd been led to believe.

Chapter 14 - Monday 20th May

Roger was joined in the consulting room by the legal team's Managing Partner. The lawyer brought Roger's copy of the tape recordings of the meeting with him. He clapped Roger on the back and poured himself a glass of port.

'Well done.'

'Are you sure?'

The Partner smiled.

'We all know that, theoretically, MI6 doesn't exist. There's specific legislation which applies to these secretive governmental departments. The problem as always is proving that their people are Crown servants. You've achieved that beyond reasonable doubt and that's some achievement. If anything happens to your youngest son, not one of them has any wriggle room now.'

'I'm not after minnows like Tessa and Mac. I like them. Anyway it will be too late if anything happens to Edward and there will be little to gain from restricting their wriggles then.'

'We know that. All we're doing is making sure you're on rock solid ground if you ever decide to launch a missile.'

Roger swallowed his port and lit up another cigarette. The last thing he wanted to hear about was launching any more damn missiles while he was erasing the last botched launch from his mind. He emptied the two full ashtrays into the bin. At least procedures would be enforced to try to ensure Edward's safety and that would satisfy Sara. That's why she'd applied her coffee morning clout with the Home Secretary's wife. That's how she'd explained it and Roger had no reason to disbelieve her; not yet, anyway.

The penultimate words of his lawyer were still resonating in his brain "If anything happens to your youngest son, not one of them has any wriggle room now." He must stop blaming himself. Above all else he knew he hadn't put him in peril intentionally. That was the last thing he would have done if he could have foreseen the unforeseeable although he knew Edward was on the MAMI audit.

He'd buried other secrets before so this one would just have to be laid to rest with the others. There was no logic in telling Sara now Lacklustre was dead and he could lock his secret away for good. Well, that is what Roger Burlington thought as he left his lawyers content that he had a success story to relay to Sara later that evening.

Tortuous as the day had been Khan and Burton and more besides were still on the loose. The handling of Khan had already become another operation where the rope had been left to run out too far.

You might have thought those holding onto the rope would have learnt their lesson by now. One day they'd lose their bait or whatever was dangling on the end of the rope. Maybe they were just about to find out the consequences of such high risk strategies?

Many diary notes would be made of what had happened on this seemingly innocuous day from both sides of the inquisitors' tables. It was as if their trains had split and later joined together at the next junction. Perhaps Roger's would be the most telling. He simply wrote "Inquiries over" and erased his previous entry, "Who else knows what?"

At last he knew no one knew or suspected anything thanks to his inquiries although Chad had come mightily close to the truth. Sara's idea of an official inquiry had coincidentally proved to be a good cover for Roger to check his own position and now no one including Sara need ever know how he had indirectly but unintentionally endangered his own son. Mac had written "major head on train crash averted but when's the next one?"

Chapter 15
Saturday 8th June

Montagu Square Marylebone, London England

Edward was asleep after a Friday night out on the town. Suzie lay naked beside him in bed. By now seven weeks had elapsed since they first met in the Golden Palace Casino. Suzie had moved in much to Tessa's disgust but still retained her small flat near Stepney. She took over one spare room for her clothes and Tessa even knew which side of Edward's bed she slept on although only she could guess why. Edward always kept two loaded guns strapped to the underside of the other side of his king-sized bed.

Tessa checked her background, hoping to find something that would make Edward ditch the woman but there was nothing untoward. Her name was Suzanne Martine Laurent and she was Algerian, a fact that Tessa hoped would be her Achilles heel but it proved to be a dead end. She attended a school in Marseilles but had no university degree.

Tessa didn't find out about Suzi's violent criminal boyfriend until Edward told her of their past relationship. She was not surprised to hear he'd been arrested on a tip off from Edward.

The guy was arrested and charged with the murder of a Stepney drinking club manageress and was banged up on remand, pending a trial. Whether he killed the woman wasn't clear but enough evidence was found to charge him and the police were confident of a conviction. So he'd be out of the way for a long time to come. It had been common gossip in Bethnal Green that he did it and several witnesses came forward.

Tessa also found out that the girl had no close family. She was an orphan, just like she told Edward. To all intents and purposes, she was a typical croupier, trying to make a living in a bustling city. Some of the clubs and casinos where she'd worked had been allegedly connected with Maltese mafia but the Golden Palace Casino was clean. There was no evidence to suggest that Suzie was anything more than a normal employee working at a decent casino. She had no known or obvious associations with organised crime either now or in her brief history.

Tessa had not only missed Suzie's connection with her old boyfriend which admittedly would have been hard to spot but she also failed to find out about the job Suzie had taken on for Hakeem Gola. Mind you, in hindsight to have done so would have been equally if not more difficult. This was dead in the water now so far as Suzie was concerned. The fact that she took it on in the first place could be put down to a combination of circumstances. She needed money. She was given no choice and she agreed to do it before she met Edward.

Now she regretted making that decision but she thought Édouard had put things right for her as she assumed her previous boyfriend was behind it all.

The doorbell rang, waking Edward. He looked at the security screen in the bedroom. The faint noise coming from outside was from a massed band of about a dozen hardened Salvation Army soldiers. They had battled their way through the crowds of shoppers and pickpockets between Oxford Circus and Montagu Square just to harass potential donors in this salubrious area! Why didn't they think of people who'd been out on the town the night before?

Edward was only half awake and their old uniforms reminded him of his grandfather and his stories of unimaginable snowstorms in the Himalayas. He shivered and covered himself. Talk about persistence, the Sally Army tried the bell again but he ignored them and drifted back to sleep, carrying the memories of his grandfather back into his dream.

The snow, the Himalayas and Frederick Burlington leading the remains of a platoon of Ghurkhas, eight months without sight or sound of another Englishman. His men were exhausted, apart from the Nepalese guides, who seemed to thrive on sleeplessness and starvation. Camped seven thousand feet up, overlooking the Tariyani marshland where they'd been ambushed last night. Pro-Kaiser Nepalese conscripts led the attack. The Ghurkas suffered casualties, even though they'd won the fire fight. They now had six prisoners roped together, with falling snow covering their blood stained clothes.

Edward tossed and twisted in the bed as he watched his grandfather slot cartridges into his revolver. The Ghurkhas lined up, looking like lepers, covered in torn and filthy blankets that were once white to blend in with the snow. The prisoners must die. There wasn't enough food for everyone.

Edward writhed as his grandfather walked behind the prisoners and shot each of them in the nape of the neck. Then the platoon moved silently away from the bloody barbarism. Within twenty minutes, they had put half a mile between them as vultures were already beginning to hover over the camp of death they'd left behind them.

The platoon positioned itself higher up the mountain that night. Supper was stale bread in tepid goat's milk soup. Frederick Burlington tried to sleep, as his grandson was also trying to do, all those years later. He thought about his home in England and his job before he became a professional killer.

Chapter 15 - Saturday 8th June

In the real world he was a teacher, an educator, not a butcher, not an executioner. Since volunteering he'd become less than human, barbaric, and all in the name of King George. With hands shaking and soiled fingers numb from the cold he removed his glass eye and lay down on his left side, with his good arm loose. He clutched his revolver, trying to reach the welcome oblivion of sleep through exhaustion.

Edward's dream turned surreal and became Frederick's dream, his nightmare. Frederick continued to fight in the Himalayas until a passing herdsman not far from Kathmandu told his guides that the war had finished. They all thought it was a trap. That was almost four months to the day after it ended on the 11th November 1918. It had taken them that time to fight their way back. Only when they reached their headquarters in Kathmandu a few days later did they believe the news.

Frederick's nightmare of executing, on average, three men a day for not far off four years continued long after the war ended. Unknowingly he became a war criminal. The last few hundred were killed after it all ended.

When Edward woke, Suzie was holding his shoulders and trying to calm him. He was all shivery and sweaty. Suzie could feel the heat coming from his body.

'You're boiling Édouard ma cherie.'

Suzie asked him if he had a thermometer and found one in the bathroom. His temperature was 103 degrees. She wanted to call a doctor but he told her not to fuss and just make the coffee. They agreed he should stay in bed, while she went down to the local chemist to get some paracetamol.

The deadline Hakeem gave Suzie to find the address book had come and gone. She hadn't found it and she hadn't been in contact with her boss either. Suzie hadn't been to the casino in over a week and she sent a message saying she was sick. Most of the money they paid her had evaporated. Spent on paying off debts and this and that, it just seemed to flow through her fingers.

She was still apprehensive, even though she originally thought Édouard had dealt with Hakeem's threat. Although she realised there might be someone else involved she couldn't even start to guess who that was if he wasn't her old boyfriend. Anyway, she was safe with Édouard. She trusted him, and his flat was like a fortress, so what could happen?

Suzie had already told Hakeem she wanted out after falling in love with Édouard and she knew she was in love. Her passion was so overwhelmingly different from any emotion she had experienced beforehand. She was worried in case he found out the reason she went with him in the first place, in case Hakeem told him out of spite. Édouard was bound to return to the Golden Palace Casino sooner or later, even though she resolved never to work for Hakeem again. He could just call Édouard or send an anonymous letter: as a casino club member they had all his details.

Maybe she should tell Édouard herself, be absolutely honest with him but no, she couldn't risk that, she might lose everything. Better to leave things as they were and hope they'd forget about her and the address book and go away. Why couldn't they just leave her and Édouard alone, to be happy together?

By the time Suzie returned to the flat, Edward was in a desperate state. He'd had a quick shower and dressed but now he was lying on the couch in the living room. His teeth were chattering and sweat was pouring off him and his whole body was shaking violently. This was no cold or flu. He was seriously ill and starting to go in and out of consciousness as Suzie called for an ambulance. Castle had called off Chad Cooper's surveillance team but GCHQ were alerted by the 999 call.

Tessa was notified and she called Edward's number from the police car she was travelling in which was by now headed towards Montagu Square. The line was busy. The car arrived with lights flashing and siren blaring just seconds after the ambulance crew entered the flat. Tessa told the driver to block off the ambulance so it couldn't leave until they checked to see if it was genuine. Before checking she dashed up the stairs with two Special Branch detectives rather than wait for the lift.

Suzie still suspected food poisoning but couldn't work out how it might have happened. Tessa suspected another BOSS mission was underway. The paramedics asked her if he'd been abroad recently, as they strapped him to a stretcher. Edward was hallucinating and kept struggling against the stretcher and shouting in a strange accent that none of them could understand.

'Git from aboot uz, ye toon bastards.'

'It's alright, Édouard, calm down my love.'

'Doan let em tek uz, Suzie, Suz ...'

Then he passed out. Suzie was almost hysterical when Tessa led the charge through the door. She didn't bother to ask the obvious, how had Tessa arrived at the right time with these men? Tessa checked the paramedics' IDs and allowed them to carry Edward down on the stretcher. She tried to get Suzie to stay in the flat but there was no way she would agree to that. Downstairs, the police driver confirmed the ambulance's credentials as both women climbed into the back of the ambulance with Edward.

Magdala Avenue Islington, London England

On the paramedics' advice, Edward was rushed to Whittington Hospital in north London. They'd guessed what was wrong but said nothing. He was still unconscious on arrival. Tessa reported the situation to Alan McKenzie and told him Edward had been admitted to intensive care and was now in isolation. No visitors would be allowed until a clear diagnosis was made.

They established that Edward hadn't travelled overseas since a visit to Antwerp in February and there were no obvious signs of a tropical disease. The doctors said they suspected food poisoning and asked Suzie what Edward ate recently. She told them he'd had nothing since Thursday night when he ate an Indian meal in a restaurant called the New Delhi in Charlotte Street. They'd been invited there by a colleague of

Chapter 15 - Saturday 8th June

Edward's and his brother Hugh came along with them. Everybody ate the same food. Tessa became suspicious.

'This colleague, what was his name?'

'Raj something, Gupta something, I just don't know anything anymore.'

Tessa rang Raj to see if he was ill. There was no problem with him or any of the Porter Williams staff. She also called Hugh at the Burlington's bookshop.

'Tessa, this is a pleasant surprise.'

'How are you, Hugh?'

'I'm ok thanks. How are you?'

'I'm fine.'

There was a silence between them. Tessa couldn't decide if she ought to tell Hugh about Edward, without Mac's permission, and Hugh was trying to decide if he should ask Tessa out, now that she'd called. They were both closet impulsives, despite being outwardly quite controlled.

'Good. I was going to ask Ed for your number.'

'You were?'

'Yes. I thought we might get together for a drink or a meal or both ...'

'Can I take a rain check, Hugh?'

'Of course. How stupid of me, I haven't asked why you called. Nothing wrong with Ed is there?'

Tessa decided to hang up; it wasn't her style but she was lost, she didn't know how to handle it. She could always say they were cut off if Hugh made a return call or asked about it later which he was bound to do. She called Mac and asked if she should notify Edward's family, just in case.

'As long as it has nothing to do with us.'

'Raj may be involved sir.'

'For Christ's sake, Sir Douglas Castle will have a bloody fit.'

'We have to tell them sir.'

'Ok, I suppose so but we don't want to press the panic button until we know what's wrong.'

'I can handle it sir.'

'Let's hope so.'

The diagnosis came later in the day. Both Suzie and Tessa were still at the hospital, waiting. Suzie said she was family. Tessa said she was a friend.

Edward was now paralysed and in a coma, due to botulism poisoning. There would be no sneaking out of this hospital in the dead of night for Edward. This was serious with a capital S. The doctor said survival was far from a foregone conclusion and that there might be permanent damage to the nervous system.

There were few effective treatments and, even if he didn't die, he would most likely be paralysed for the rest of his life, possibly brain dead too. The fact that he was in a coma made his chances of survival lower than average and the average was only one in five.

They were doing everything they could for him but predictions at this stage were no more than informed guesswork. They said that the paramedics correctly deduced it probably wasn't straightforward food poisoning and that was why they'd come directly to a special unit at Whittington.

Tessa approached the group who were giving Suzie the third degree about where they'd eaten over the last few days. They had to track down the cause in case other people were affected.

'How could this have happened doctor?'

'Botulism intoxication is caused by either contaminated food or an infected wound. As he has no infected wounds, we can only conclude he ingested it by eating. There may be other complications but it's too early to say.'

They carried out a quick check and currently there were no other known cases in London. Edward hadn't eaten anything apart from salted peanuts and crisps on Friday so far as anyone knew. The people with whom he last ate a proper meal on Thursday night consumed the same food as him. None of them were affected.

Tessa had no option but to interrupt Mac again.

'It's serious sir.'

'How serious?'

'They think he's about to die …'

'Shit! Bloody hell, what's the diagnosis?'

'Botulism sir and there may be other complications.'

Mac was silent on the other end of the line. Tessa tried to hold back her tears as she broke into his thoughts.

'We have to tell the family sir.'

'I'll do it.'

'Sir, I said I can handle it.'

'I said I'll do it!'

The phone was slammed down and Tessa was left looking at the dead receiver in her hand as tears streamed down her cheeks. She couldn't remember when she last cried but it was many years ago.

Hugh was at the Whittington Hospital within half an hour. He was angry with Tessa.

'Why didn't you tell me when you called? That is why you called, isn't it?'

'I called to see if you were alright.'

'Oh, so my brother's in a coma and you're worried about me?'

'You don't understand.'

'No, I don't understand.'

Chapter 15 - Saturday 8th June

Hugh tried to get in to see Ed but he wasn't allowed in the room. Nobody was being allowed near him for now at least. He returned and sat next to Tessa. Suzie was asleep in a chair, her tearstained face resting on her joined hands, as if she was silently praying.

'Maybe you had better explain.'

'Let's get a coffee.'

Tessa took Hugh to a nearby waiting room and paid for a couple of coffees from a machine.

Tessa and Hugh had known each other for over a year. Both were frequent visitors to Edward's flat and their visits often overlapped but that was about it. He was not Edward but she found him attractive and endearing, although she never showed it. Now she had blown it as he was still angry with her for not being completely honest with him.

She was genuinely sorry. Tessa knew she should have told him about Edward, she knew the brothers had always been close, ever since they were young boys and as Edward had called them, the "terrible twins". Still, she couldn't tell him without Mac's approval. Now was the time to reconcile herself with Hugh.

'I'm so sorry Hugh.'

'You should be.'

'I follow orders.'

'Look, Tessa, I don't know what you do and I don't want to know even if it's to do with my parents and all that supposedly secret shit but he's my only brother. Never forget that.'

'I know. I said I'm sorry.'

Hugh's attitude softened.

'Suzie is utterly distraught.'

'Yes, the doctors gave her something to calm her.'

'Best to let her sleep.'

'Yes.'

'She and Ed are so close. Does that bother you?'

'Yes, I mean no, of course not. Our relationship is strictly professional.'

Hugh would have smiled but he couldn't bring himself to do it as he thought of Ed. He was so alone now.

'What happened then Tessa?'

'Botulism.'

'Yes, yes I know that but what happened?'

'We're not sure yet.'

'We?'

Tessa didn't answer Hugh's question and her expression told him not to push it. He put his head in his trembling hands.

'I had a premonition. When you rang I was in a lousy state, feverish, no energy. This explains it.'

'Explains it?'

'A type of telepathy between me and Ed. I'll tell you about it some time.'

'You sure it's not because you ate the same Indian food on Thursday night?'

'I doubt that's anything to do with it. This telepathic stuff started when we were kids.'

Tessa had heard of remote viewing and all the furore there'd been about it in the sixties. Her atheistic convictions made her sceptical about such ethereal matters.

'You saying you're psychic?'

'Yes but I don't know for sure. Whatever it is, Ed has it too. When we were kids if we couldn't sleep we went downstairs and played charades with our parents. If they had guests they would join in with us. Like Macmillan, before he was Prime Minister, and the Douglases, er Alex Douglas-Hume.

There was another Douglas but I'm not sure what he did apart from Oxford dinners. Castle was his name. Yes, he was called Castle, a nasty turn of page in my book but anyway, they always gave up sooner than later. We guessed who they were pretending to be before they'd hardly started, as they were thinking who they would be.'

'Fascinating.'

Tessa found it mesmerising in more ways than one.

Hugh didn't want to be alone that night.

'Why don't we have dinner tonight, I'll explain it?'

Tessa turned her eyes on Hugh, in that MI5 way of hers. He looked quite like his brother in stature, just eighteen months older and a bit shorter. From what she knew of him he was a charming gentleman, much quieter than Edward and not so many girlfriends, less to contend. Above all else though he wasn't involved with any of the intelligence services, well so far as she was aware anyway.

'Why not?'

Tessa rarely made impromptu emotion driven decisions, she was trained not to, but sometimes she made spur of the moment decisions, and this was going to be one of them.

'Great, that's my weakness. I never usually bother to question what counts and talking of telepathy I should have seen your answer coming.'

Tessa burst into nervous laughter at Hugh's attempted joke. The joke wasn't even funny. It was pitiable under the circumstances but the way he said it suggested he liked her. Hugh laughed to cover up the nervous emotions swirling uncontrollably around both of them. When they looked at each other both had tears welling in their eyes.

A doctor had ruled that no more than two people at a time could go in and see Edward, family members only. His instructions were ignored. Suzie was already in

Chapter 15 - Saturday 8th June

the room and holding Édouard's unconscious hand when Hugh came in to join them. They hugged each other through tears and then both sat either side of the bed. Hugh looked at his younger brother. They were together again in a way they hadn't been since they were children.

Outside the room, Mac joined Tessa. He brought a small crew of minders with him.

'Didn't expect to see you here sir.'

'Young Burlington's parents are on their way.'

'I could have handled them sir.'

'Have you ever met Sara Burlington?'

'No sir.'

Mac gave her a wry insipid smile. Even Mac was emotional. He had grown fond of Edward, closer than he should have been and admired his courage. As the seconds ticked away until Sara's arrival he tried to organise the security so that the room Edward was in could not be accessed by anyone, unless authorised. Tessa followed him round like a lost puppy. The hospital staff just kept making the imposition of any proper security impossible.

'Sir, has Raj Khan some involvement in all this?'

Mac didn't answer her question, just continued to set up his security team round the area.

'Who's in the room with him?'

'His brother and his girlfriend.'

'What's she doing here?'

'She told them she was family.'

Mac spoke to one of the doctor's and Suzie was removed from the room. She cried and screamed and two of Mac's minders literally carried her out. Hugh protested and asked Mac who the hell he thought he was? Mac simply told him his father and mother were coming and that the armed men were from Special Branch. Hugh asked no more questions: it was all that unnecessarily bloody top secret stuff. His Dad could explain later.

Mac was at the end of the corridor, waiting for the senior Burlingtons, when they arrived. Sara pushed past him leaving him open mouthed as she rushed down the hospital passage to her son's room, brushing aside staff and security alike. Roger looked at Mac and shrugged his shoulders, as if to say what did you expect? As the two men followed her, Roger fired questions at Mac, even though he'd already been briefed by a feverishly worried Castle.

'Is Khan involved?'

'Don't know for certain.'

'Could Burton have something to do with this?'

'Don't know.'

'Where was security?'

'All the security in the world might not have been able to prevent this Roger.'

'What's being done about the restaurant?'

'MI5 are already there. Everyone ate the same food.'

'Means nothing. A specific dish or even a minute morsel of food could have been doctored with botulism toxin, leaving the rest of the meal safe.'

Mac speculated to himself on how clinically these Burlingtons viewed killing. Old man Frederick murdered thousands during and after the Great War and his son indirectly killed tens of thousands of Hitler's finest in the Second World War. Then there was Sara. How many had she garrotted during her days in occupied France and inside Germany in the name of King George? What a family.

Sara dashed through the door of her son's room, hugging Hugh first and then leaning across to kiss Edward on the face and forehead.

'Oh God, my poor boy, what have they done to you?'

Hugh stood behind her for a moment, to make sure she didn't drag Ed up to hug and hold him. Once his mother was relatively becalmed he moved round to the other side of the bed.

'Where's Dad?'

'He's coming. Have you seen his doctor, Hugh? Where's his doctor? Go get his doctor in here at once!'

'Mother.'

'Go find the damn doctor!'

Roger appeared at the doorway and stood watching the scene rather than go in the room. It was crowded enough. He glanced over at Hugh, who shook his head, then at Edward, lying tubed-up in the bed. Roger didn't say a word.

'We need the doctor in here now Roger. Somebody get the bloody doctor!'

'Please be calm Sara.'

'Damn it, I'll find him myself.'

She stormed out of the room brushing Roger aside. He went round the bed and clasped Hugh. The two men looked at each other. Roger turned his attention to Suzie.

'Who's that woman crying hysterically outside? I presume she's the new girlfriend?'

'Her name is Suzie, Dad. She's not what I would call new, at least not in Ed's terms.'

'Was she with him when this happened?'

'Yes. She called the ambulance.'

'I see.'

Hugh studied his father's inscrutable expression.

'I assume you and Mum know Tessa and the other people?'

Roger looked up, almost absently, at his older son.

'Yes, yes we know them.'

Chapter 15 - Saturday 8th June

'Who are they, I mean in reality?'

'I'll explain later. It is not important now.'

Sara returned with a consultant called Cordell. She was giving the man the serious third degree.

'What's your field?'

'I specialise in coma and paralysis cases.'

Despite her questioning, he couldn't tell them anything about botulism intoxication that Roger didn't already know. He had learnt a lot about poison at Porton Down.

'So, all we can do is hope assuming we have someone or something to pray to?'

'That's about it Mrs Burlington.'

The specialist looked somewhat sheepish under Sara's hostile glare.

'Will he die if the ventilator is turned off?'

'Not immediately. We plan to turn it off intermittently to measure his respiratory motion.'

Cordell hadn't thought Sara was worried if another attack could be effected that way. As a doctor he didn't think like that. Cordell explained that Edward might begin to recover normal breathing motions as the paralysis dissipated. If that happened they might even be able to withdraw the ventilator and allow his body to heal itself. There were positive signs. His bodily fluids were moving and his weight loss had stabilised. Cordell steered clear of further complications.

'Will he have brain damage if he lives?'

'We can't speculate on that Mrs Burlington.'

'I'll ask you again. Will my son be a vegetable if he lives?'

'Mrs Burlington, we can't tell anything yet.'

'Answer the bloody question!'

Roger took hold of his wife's arm, in case she took a swing and slashed the consultant across the throat with a rabbit chop motion.

'Sara, please. They're all doing their best.'

She pulled away from her husband's grip and tried to calm herself. The doctor decided it was safe to speak again.

'The police have given us a list of people who are allowed to visit.'

He was wrong.

'There will be no visitors, apart from us three. Is that clear?'

'What about the police? The security ...'

'You call that security? It's a bloody joke.'

Roger took the consultant by the arm and ushered him towards the door, out of the danger area.

'Don't worry. I'll speak to the police.'

Cordell left the room, followed by Hugh, who decided to go see how Suzie was doing.

Roger and Sara were alone with Edward in what seemed like a mortuary. Tears rolled down her cheeks. The hard woman inside her had melted away at the sight of Edward's gaunt face. Roger held her close and whispered softly to her.

'If anyone can make it, he can.'

Roger knew how desperate Edward's plight was but sunk the thought in the mysterious recesses of his brain where his innermost secrets lay. Hugh thought it all hopeless but Sara tried to look at it positively as Roger had tried to put it. Sara and the rest of the family were going to have ample time to diarise what had happened and what was about to ensue. The Burlingtons' train had all but come to a grinding halt.

Roger went to see Cordell who explained the further complications: they agreed to keep them under wraps unless Edward died. It was as though Edward was suffocating under the pressure of some black magic or dark matter before being crushed and swallowed up into a black hole and lost forever.

Meanwhile Burton was still lurking in the shadows seeking revenge and like some rabid scavenging beast had subconsciously smelt death in the air.

Chapter 16
Monday 10th June

De Wallen, Amsterdam Holland

The police investigations into the murder of Atif and Hamid Bashir had all but petered away in the north of England. They knew Burton was responsible because of the engravings on the bodies.

Carl Hanson was disappointed that the deaths were reported as accidental. He had wanted everyone to know he, Cyrus Burton, was behind the killings. It would have been a deterrent to anyone else who might be thinking about making a deal with the authorities and also satisfied his ego.

It wouldn't be safe to revisit the UK again because they'd be on the lookout for him now and who knew what their investigation might have turned up already. Jordan warned him of stray camera shots, unexpected witnesses, some unanticipated advance in forensic sciences. You could never be too careful.

Hanson didn't fancy spending the rest of his lucrative days in Durham's top security prison. So, he arranged to sell all his UK properties: the house in Newcastle, an apartment in Mayfair, his brothels in London plus a block of seafront flats in Brighton. In addition, he decided to stay out of the USA because he never underestimated the expertise of the CIA, despite their intermittent crass cock-ups.

Further additions to the taboo list included Hong Kong, Singapore and Malaysia. His fate would be even worse if he was caught by one of the Asian Triad gangs he'd double-crossed. These additions complicated his travelling to the Philippines which was one of his favourite playgrounds. Even Marcos was a client and they had many shared interests including warped sex, corruption and cash.

Jordan and Hanson had been working hard during the last couple of months, laying the foundations for the new business empire. They visited Thailand, the Philippines and several islands in the Caribbean. Hanson was enjoying the freedom his new life brought him as a globetrotting bon viveur. He bought nightclubs in Bangkok and Manila and these, along with his club in Amsterdam, were being refurbished with no expense spared.

They reckoned spending several million in Sterling on each club should suffice and the clubs would be ready for a grand opening night extravaganza before the end of the year. Each of the clubs would have a gaming licence and areas where wild animals like panthers, pumas and leopards could stalk around in cages or on the end of chains. A special feature would be fish-tanks where fighting fish would duel to the death to entertain gambling clientele and help overload Hanson's offshore bank accounts.

The gladiatorial fish was an idea Hanson picked up from a friend of his called Ian Tomlinson, a notorious lawyer who controlled the Turks and Caicos Islands in the Caribbean. Not only was Tomlinson a barrister but he was also a doctor and, between the two professions, he knew the deepest secrets of most locals and most of them had secrets they wanted hidden.

Tomlinson created a fictitious persona, living in the Dominican Republic and, from there, blackmailed his victims with any embarrassing information he gleaned as a lawyer or a doctor. A bonus of this little money-spinner was being paid as legal counsel of those being blackmailed, to provide advice on what to do. His advice was always to pay up and on time. An alternative solution would be to have the fictitious blackmailer murdered for an extortionate fee. Some clients opted for this, only to find that the sensitive information had fallen into the hands of another blackmailer.

Tomlinson invented a game which involved feeding a goldfish to a baby barracuda. The barracuda would keep eating and eating; even though the goldfish was normally two or three times its size. Then the barracuda would excrete its undigested remains from one end while still chewing away from the other. The supposed game was a grotesque and gruesome spectacle and it appealed to the depraved and dissolute like Tomlinson and Hanson.

Tomlinson soon realised he could make extra money by having his guests bet on how long it would take the barracuda to eat the goldfish. His thinking later multiplied and it was not long before several goldfish were fed to several barracuda at once. It became known as the "eat and excrete" race. Tomlinson always fixed the odds. He'd starve, overfeed or dope the barracuda so as only he knew which would be fast and fighting fit.

Few of his regular guests ever won in the long run but he did regularly, tens of thousands of dollars a time too. The ultimate show was a gladiatorial fight to the death by the barracuda, which would be painted different colours for easy recognition. Hanson always bet on the black barracuda and now he intended to name all the nightclubs in his new chain The Black Barracuda. The gladiatorial fish were to be imported from the Bahamas and distributed throughout the clubs for entertainment and gaming purposes.

Hanson had only recently returned to his penthouse in Amsterdam after a trip to the British Virgin Islands. He had added another couple of layers of complicated

Chapter 16 - Monday 10th June

trusts between him and his previous persona, hiding Cyrus Burton from view forever or so he hoped.

By now he owned companies all over the Caribbean. His choices included the Bahamas, the Dutch Antilles and the Cayman, British Virgin and the Turks and Caicos Islands. The companies were all owned by trusts in other tax havens that were remotely managed separately from yet more remote tax havens like the Marshall and Cook Islands. It would be impossible for any authority to unravel the chain of ownership without Hanson finding out they were snooping into his affairs well before they could see the colour of the currencies he stashed away.

He was served jam croissants and vodka for breakfast, while Jordan drank a coffee and smoked one of his infamous mammoth joints.

'Have the brochures and tickets for the opening nights been sent out yet?'

'Brochures yes but not tickets.'

'All the people in my ring are to be invited.'

'That's over five thousand.'

'We can accommodate the fuckers, can't we?'

'Of course.'

Hanson wiped some jam from the edges of his mouth and took a long swig of vodka.

'You have reminded me of what I was going to say. You remember that fucker JJ don't you?'

'That double crossing bastard.'

'Yes, well it's come to my attention that he must have copied my address book during his time with us at Harley Street.'

'How do you know?'

'Sources my dear Jordan. You should know by now that nothing gets past me.'

Jordan sipped his coffee. He knew what was coming and wasn't happy about it. What exasperated him about Carl was his reckless taste for revenge or simply his recklessness.

'I want that copy.'

Hanson accentuated that so much that it became obvious to Jordan he was on one of his irrational vendettas which would lead to nothing but trouble.

'You might want that copy but it's not worth the bother. We're bound to have most of it on computer now. Anyway JJ was an informant so he would have given it to the fuzz as you call them to get paid. The British have done their worst and failed. Let it lie and you won't give them a second chance.'

'Over my dead body my dear.'

Hanson stood up, knocking his breakfast plate and knife to the floor.

'I want him dead. I want that fucking JJ really fucked badly.'

'What about the address book copy?'

'Oh yes, that too.'

Jordan was silent for a moment or two, allowing Carl Hanson's outburst of temper to subside.

'You do realise the flat he told us he was living at was only a temporary place. He isn't there and his name wasn't JJ.'

'We can track the fucker through his police records and properly this time.'

'Even if we could identify who he was, because he's an informant they will have set fly traps for us Cyrus.'

'Carl, it's Carl, for God's sake! How many times do I have to tell you?'

'Sorry, they'll have set fly traps for us Carl.'

'Fly traps? What the fuck are fly traps?'

'Anyone nosing around will be identified, fed what they are looking for and monitored, followed. It is too dangerous.'

Hanson smiled. If he was told a job was too dangerous it was like issuing him with a challenge he couldn't resist.

'Let's do it then.'

'How?'

'We'll just hire some people. If they get caught, c'est la vie. We don't need to go anywhere near London and they won't know who their paymasters are so they can't squeal on us like JJ did.'

Jordan put down his coffee cup and listened. He was dazed and fazed by his joint which he had overloaded with hash by mistake and could no longer be bothered to pursue his logical arguments. He knew there would be no talking him out of this, so he might as well save himself the trouble. It became easier to go along with whatever plan his boss had in mind and refine it later rather than try to derail it.

'When we succeed, not only do I get my papers back. We get to kill JJ, or whoever he was, and stick two fingers up at the British cops, just like we did with the Bashirs. We'll see if they can cover it up in the press this time.'

Jordan was finally beginning to understand. Hanson didn't want the address book at all, this wasn't even about revenge. This was to do with the British not giving him credit for the killing of the Bashir brothers. He now wanted to kill again and make sure he was credited with the murder.

Jordan had a knack of understanding Hanson's warped mind but increasingly of late he seemed to be more and more as if he were Jack the Ripper's butler. Hanson's mind was becoming far too convoluted. Yet Hanson was still a good bet. He had never seen the inside of a prison, was worth well in excess of £100 million and was no dumb couch slouch.

'I want people to know the killer was Cyrus Burton this time. I want them to know it was me, that I'm still around, but invisible. The press might christen me The Invisible Hand. We could fix that quite easily. Or would The Invisible Assassin sound better?'

Chapter 16 - Monday 10th June

Jordan didn't answer as Hanson lined up some coke and snorted it all in one.

'Have you anyone in mind, to do it in London I mean?'

'I have a British government contact in my pocket. The guy's a member of the ring and knows many high ranking police.'

'If he's in the ring, won't he be in the address book?'

'Yes, but under an alias. Only I know his real identity.'

Hanson was huffing and bluffing. Yes, he'd dealt with the man before but he only knew him as Smith. Smith was the sources he'd mentioned earlier. He wasn't even absolutely sure if Smith was the corrupt brains behind his arrest and subsequent unexpected release in 1972. All Smith told Burton then was he wanted odd jobs to keep his bank account sweet. This wasn't his first job since then but would be his first job involving Jordan.

Jordan stood up and walked to the window that had a view over the De Wallen district of Amsterdam. He watched the tourists below looking in the windows of sexual opportunity and gratification and turned to look at Hanson.

'Ok.'

'You can call him from La Gare du Nord when you're in Paris next week. Use a public phone and speak in Dutch. Smith understands that.'

'What should I say?'

'Just say, the Reaper wants to remind you that a diamond was a fair exchange for a ruby.'

Jordan paused for a moment, trying to think while studying the landscape down below him again. He turned back to face Hanson. That overloaded joint was hampering his usual computer like analytical capabilities.

'What if his phone is tapped Carl?'

'All the better. Smith will call you back from a safe phone. That's how he works. Call him; give him a number and he calls back. He's not that expensive either. Tell him we'll pay £50,000 in cash up front, to be collected from our Dagenham letter box. Make sure we get photos of the collection.'

'What about afterwards?'

'A further £50,000 if they get me a video of JJ's last moments.'

Hanson grinned, not knowing that his prey was already close to death in a hospital in London.

Montagu Square Marylebone, London England

The alarm was on in the flat when Suzie returned there early on Monday 10th June. She entered her personal code and went into the flat as normal. Her memory was fuzzy and she wasn't sure if she'd turned it on when they left with the ambulance two days earlier. She also didn't even notice whether the cameras were live. As both Hugh and Tessa used their own keys and came and went as they pleased, she wasn't all that bothered. What concerned her more was the smell. She couldn't identify what it was but it smelled familiar and the whole flat reeked of it.

The flat was dark. She moved like a robot opening doors and curtains as she passed through and then up the stairs to open the door to the roof garden. After she opened the studio windows she did the ones in the kitchen. Finally she put the contents of the fridge into a bin-bag in case any food was rotting. Her mind wasn't focusing properly. She was moving around as if an automaton.

Tessa had persuaded her to take a break from the hospital as she had been hanging around there sitting in the corridor alone sobbing and virtually ignored by all but Hugh for much of the last two days. After Sara's visit, she wasn't allowed back into Edward's room. Tessa thought it best to get the distraught girl away from there for her own sake. Now she was a tad guilty for distancing herself from the girl so much.

Suzie agreed to go back to the flat with Edward's clothes and collect some bits and pieces for him, for when he woke up, when he recovered. Tessa didn't tell her the true extent of Edward's condition because she had already started asking too many questions about why there was a need for such security measures.

Suzie bought three packets of cigarettes for him. At the flat she picked up his dressing gown, lighter, electric razor, toothbrush and toothpaste and a set of fresh clothes and packed everything into a black leather overnight bag. She showered, changed and was ready to go back to the hospital.

The smell was still lingering. It was unpleasant and annoyed her. She still couldn't identify it but her autopilot brain told her she knew it from somewhere. The disgusting odour wasn't like rotting food or anything, more like smouldering compost. She waved her hand trying to waft the foul stench away and took the bin-bag with the stuff from the fridge down to the basement bins.

While she was down there, the electricity went off and not just in that block of flats. Every building in the vicinity was affected. The sudden darkness in the basement frightened her, rousing her from her melancholy stupor. She made her way back up the five flights of stairs to the flat. The alarm was still off and the cameras were static now. She looked at them but they only showed an empty flat. She closed the door behind her and went into the living room to collect the sports bag. The smell was stronger than ever and that's when she recognised it.

'Hello Suzie.'

Hakeem Gola was sitting on the sofa, smoking one of his stinking Indonesian cigars.

'What are you doing here?'

Gola was wearing gloves, even though today was warm. He pointed to a chair by the window. She sat on it.

'We paid you £25,000. You didn't deliver.'

'You shouldn't be here, the cameras, I told you.'

Chapter 16 - Monday 10th June

'Don't worry about the cameras.'

Raj Gupta Khan walked into the sitting room from the kitchen. He was carrying a Smith & Wesson .45 caliber with a silencer attached. He stood silhouetted in the archway.

'Where's the address book?'

'I don't know. I searched.'

'Where's the money?'

'Gone, sorry, it's gone. I told you. I'm sorry ...'

She started to cry.

Gola walked over and grabbed her by the wrists. He held her down while Khan strode across into the room. He held the lists of names and addresses, the missing address book copy, in his left hand.

'Goodbye Suzie.'

Raj Gupta Khan put the gun to the top right side of her head and pulled the trigger. The bullet went through her brain and out through her left breast. Blood ran down her body and spread across the carpet. Khan pressed the gun, with the silencer still in place, into her hand, wrapping her index finger round the trigger.

He knew from his involvement in Standpipe and reading the files that the address book had been copied by Edward. What was astounding was that he also knew Hislop had forgotten to collect the copies as they were not in the files. God knows why. There was so much going on at that time maybe she was distracted. So, Edward not having been asked for it had either failed to remember to hand it over or was holding onto it for some unknown reason.

That concerned Khan but not enough for him to do anything about it such as steal it earlier. Back then he had no reason to suspect his real name and address would be in it but after Standpipe ended he'd received a video recording addressed to him at home from Burton, showing the shocking drowning of his friends the Bashir brothers. The film was accompanied by a message in Punjabi warning him if he ever double-crossed the Beast, he too would be starring in a box office hit. That meant he almost certainly featured in the copy of Burton's address book in his left hand.

Once Khan knew Burton had his real name and home address the whole picture changed. If MI6 had seen the copy of the address book they would have soon worked everything out. Alan McKenzie would have been onto him like a bat out of a blasted belfry because he'd told McKenzie he'd never had any contact with the syndicate at all. Only his diplomatic connections had. He'd lied.

The Bashirs and he were close-knit. His cover as an ISI double agent would have disintegrated. He had no choice. Suzie knew too much without knowing anything and had to commit suicide. Khan was just being as thorough as he was when on audit, he didn't like loose ends.

As Hakeem Gola was clearing up, Khan skimmed through the lists of names and addresses. He was listed under a pseudonym as a diplomat at the Pakistani Embassy. There was no trace of Raj Gupta Khan or his home address. Burton must have obtained that from one of Raj's ISI connections after this version was printed out. When they were leaving the flat Khan looked at Hakeem.

'What a waste of twenty five grand!'

More to the point, Suzie had died for nothing.

Lambeth Palace Road Lambeth, London England

That same morning, Chad Cooper was with Alan McKenzie in a cafe near Century House.

'We swooped on the New Delhi in Charlotte Street before they opened last night sir.'

'What guise did you use?'

'The police of course sir. We were accompanied by a public health inspector and a poison specialist though.'

MI5 had already done their research. There were no other reported cases of botulism intoxication in the UK of late. They also had the names and addresses of everyone who worked regularly at the restaurant. The New Delhi was owned by an Anglo-Pakistani called Abbas Hussein and the staff were all either Bangladeshi or Bengali.

'Any connections to our Mr Khan?'

'He's the restaurant's accountant sir.'

'Is he indeed?'

'Yes but not through Porter Williams. It seems he is a moonlighter like everyone else we know at that firm. The place has only been open a few weeks sir which is mighty suspicious after what else we found.'

There was one anomaly. They were short staffed on the Friday night and hired two part time waiters. One of them worked as assistant chef that night. The other served Khan's table.

'We took swabs from everywhere, even underneath the tables and chairs ...'

'So?'

'We found a precise match, the same strain of botulism that laid Burlington low. We closed the place down and took formal statements from everyone. Definitely looks like a deliberate poisoning sir.'

Mac finished his coffee and lit a cigarette. Chad Cooper blew the smoke away from his face.

'Can we prove anything against Khan?'

'Not directly to the poisoning sir.'

'Anything against the temps then?'

Chapter 16 - Monday 10th June

'Disappeared. False names and addresses. Recently registered with an agency. This was their first and only job sir.'

'Nationality?'

'Could be Pakistani or the like but we have no real idea sir.'

It seemed to Mac that this whole thing was set up: the restaurant, the owner and the temporary workers, just to poison Burlington. They, Khan included, must have known the place would be closed down and they'd all come under suspicion. Khan wasn't that stupid. Unless they wanted to make it look like an ISI hit. Why do that though? Some of the diplomats expelled after Standpipe were Pakistani. They would have had connections with the ISI. Khan certainly had. Even so it didn't make any sense. Everything was all too easy for Mac's liking. There had to be more to it.

'Any criminal links?'

'Not with the restaurant owner or his regular staff. As I said, we haven't a clue who the two temps were but everything points to them. Be difficult to tie anyone else in to this sir.'

What Mac didn't know was Edward had taken a copy of Burton's address book and Khan thought his name was in there and had to get it at any cost. His murdering the only two people who might have known about the address book was a logical step for him.

Khan had originally intended to plant evidence that Edward was accidentally poisoned instead of Suzie, by her psychopathic old boyfriend, and she had committed suicide. Part of that plot had gone out the window though as the man had been put behind bars. Now, all Khan could hope for was that it would seem Edward was the victim of a fluke poisoning. The other part of his original scheming had still gone ahead. A grief-stricken Suzie took her own life. Result? It was not ideal but Raj Gupta Khan reckoned he was safe, just.

No matter how much scrutiny he came under he could show he had been quite open about his ties to the New Delhi. Why on earth would he treat everyone to a meal at his friend's restaurant if he wanted to hide any connections or commit murder? Maybe he was the intended victim? Who the hell knew what had happened? More to the point, who could prove it now both Edward and Suzie were so tragically unavailable for questioning?

Mac knew that Khan's involvement with the ISI was top secret and Chad therefore shouldn't know anything about it. He decided to check if that was the case.

'Do you think the ISI are involved, Chad?'

'I was trying to tell you earlier sir. We swept the database at Langley and it's obvious that Raj Khan's brother is an active ISI officer.'

'What?'

'His brother is ISI ...'

'His brother? What about Raj Khan though? What have they on him?'

'Nothing on him sir.'

'Shit!'

Cooper looked puzzled. He thought Mac would be pleased to learn they could connect Raj Khan to the ISI. Mac stood up. He was leaving and in a hurry.

'Settle up for the coffee please Chad. I have to get back to the office.'

Mac practically ran from the cafe along Lambeth Bridge Road. He called Castle as soon as he was back in the safety of Century House.

Westminster Bridge Road Lambeth, London England

'Khan's brother is the ISI officer, Sir Douglas, not him.'

'How do you know?'

'I found it on the Langley database sir.'

'Are you sure?'

'Chad Cooper was able to access it, so I'm assuming everyone else can too sir.'

Mac could hear Castle moaning with frustration. Castle thought he'd pulled off a nice little coup over the CIA by having Raj Khan on board and feeding him disinformation. However, if Khan's brother was a known active ISI officer and not him, and everybody and his aunt knew about it, Sir Douglas Castle would have made himself look a right idiot.

Why would the Americans tell him about Khan but not his brother, unless they were playing political games? Maybe there had been a complete misunderstanding as to which of the Khans did what. He'd only had a conversation about it and hadn't seen any reports. In all likelihood if one was ISI the other would be too. Confusion reigned. It had been easier in the old days, when you knew who your enemy was or thought you did. Maybe he was already too old for all this double entendre.

Lately, he always seemed to be last in the queue to find things out. That was another of Castle's pet paranoias: everybody knew everything and he knew nothing. He decided to ditch the idea of using Raj Khan to spread disinformation. The Americans were probably already doing that through his brother and it would make him look like a complete amateur. Better to forget about the plan and they'd think he'd been wise to them all along if it wasn't a true misunderstanding. Yet as he thought more there still could be merit in his original plan but said no more on the subject to Mac.

'Well, he's no use to us now, is he?'

'I suppose not sir but I suggest we leave the drawbridges down and the portcullises up for present.'

'I agree. What about Sara Burlington?'

'How's she involved sir?'

Mac was thinking here cometh the bloody runaway train again.

'Does she believe her son's poisoning had anything to do with us?'

Chapter 16 - Monday 10th June

'I don't think so sir.'

'Good. Keep it like that.'

Castle hung the phone up; there was no more to say. Mac knew what he had to do. He called Chad to his office.

'Ok, Chad, I want this inquiry into Burlington's poisoning put down to a public health matter. The restaurant will be closed down permanently but there will be no criminal charges. Is that understood?'

'Yes sir.'

'Surveillance on Raj Khan is to resume. I want to know why he would want to kill Burlington.'

'How's Edward making out sir?'

'Not good. I'm sorry Chad. It all looks terribly bleak.'

Chad left the room angrier than he'd been for years. He and Edward became quite good friends in the last month or so. They were northerners after all was said and done. Edward didn't deserve this shit. That bastard Khan had no bloody scruples; he was a cold blooded killer and would pay for this.

Chad didn't for one moment liken him to himself though in some respects they were similar. Chad had little doubt Khan would be proven guilty but so often in matters to do with espionage those in the wrong walked scot free. Just like Blunt in the Cambridge Five though that wasn't in the public domain yet. He would get this man though come what may.

Mac lit a cigarette and poured himself a large whisky. He sat back and thought about the last few days. Everyone involved in MI6 was as brutal as the other. He'd put Chad onto Khan because he was the most ruthless and cold blooded killer he had. Why had he done it that way? Khan was a lethal bastard yet Chad was just as lethal but more humanitarianly so. Why was Chad so good? He'd trained him that's why. Mr Cooper might be one of the greatest charm merchants in town but he was still a pitiless killer.

Mac remembered the days he'd been trained by Sara. She was another merciless executioner. He'd grinned the first time he saw his trainer was a woman. She knew he'd smirked even though her back was turned because she had sliced his legs from under him and whipped her heel into his groin. Before he'd even hit the turf squirming in pain she'd turned round so fast the imprint of the smirk on his face was still visible. She'd asked compassionately why he had slipped up but didn't want an answer as he already had sufficient to remember for one day. She was right. He knew what she meant.

She was so damn clever and such an efficient killing machine. Of course, while he had been trained by her, Khan had been trained by him and Chad and now apparently by others in the ISI so he would need to be prepared for any onslaught.

Mac knew a few tricks when it came to fighting. Mushroom management of the enemy was essential. Trap them in a tunnel after dousing the lights. Misinform them about everything else so they couldn't differentiate between shit and caviar in the dining car.

The trouble was he wasn't the only one to have been trained in such niceties.

Details of Suzi's death were reconstructed from entries in diaries after the event. All that mattered was yet another body had been dumped from the ghost train as it sped forward to the next scheduled stop. Suzie's passing was unfair, despicable and to be unforgivable.

It goes without saying that there were plenty of entries in the Burlington family diaries about what had happened to Edward and what the intelligence services told Roger they had found out. Edward's diary was blank.

Chapter 17
Monday 17th June

Abingdon Street Westminster, London England
The IRA bombed the Houses of Parliament early that Monday morning. There were about a dozen casualties and, although nobody died directly from the attack, the iconic footage broadcast by the world's media boosted the IRA's cause and kudos. Alan McKenzie wasn't in a good mood.

All this stuff going on with Burlington and his girlfriend and the bastards picked this most inconvenient time to try to blow up the government. There was no point in Mac trying to talk to Sir Douglas Castle. The man was running round like a headless one legged mouse in case Sara pounced to reconfigure his private parts. The growing terrorist threat seemed to be way down the list of his priorities but not the Prime Minister's.

Sir Peter was on a tour of Canada and the USA on Porter Williams' business not that he would have been much help given his secretive participation in the JIC. Roger Burlington was at his dying son's bedside most of the time. The rest of the JIC were crouching under their wives' kitchen tables or their mistresses' skirts. So, all the decisions on how to handle the IRA were left to the workers, the likes of Tessa and Mac. There was no JIC guidance, no input from the top. As usual he wasn't happy about the situation.

La Gare du Nord, Paris France
Round about the same time as Mac was hyperventilating over the IRA and the never ending Burlington saga, Jordan was telephoning Burton's inside man in London. He passed the message from the Reaper to Smith. The public phone at La Gare du Nord was called back within a matter of minutes.

Jordan knew the man only as Smith and Smith didn't know him at all but he knew of the Reaper and his ruthless reputation. Hanson's gem of a secret code had worked but Smith wanted no more unnecessary cloak and dagger stuff now and he said so. He told Jordan he could recognise his grainy Swedish drawl on a walkie-talkie with a dying battery on a deafening steam train thundering through a tunnel.

Smith operated from a covert government office in Lancaster Place, just off the Strand. From his office he could watch the southern counties' commuters throng across Waterloo Bridge Monday to Friday to and from Waterloo station. He commuted from Friday Street in Surrey so had to come in via Victoria Station. The Reaper's proposition was accepted and it took Smith less than a day to locate the undercover asset known as JJ who was involved in Operation Standpipe.

His real name was Edward Spencer Burlington and he lived at Montagu Square in London's West End. Smith used the passwords and IDs of other officers and agents to circumvent the system and access data on the intelligence services computers. The fly trap may have snapped shut once or twice but there would be no flies on Smith. He hadn't hacked into Burlington's records directly in case they'd been fitted up but his roundabout methods gave him the information he needed and left no figurative footsteps in the snow pointing to Friday Street. That was the easy part.

Smith made no further contact with the Reaper or Jordan to report his findings. He knew superfluous communications were the downfall of most criminals: just get on with it was his motto. He set about organising a raid on Burlington's flat to find the copied document and kill the culprit if the chance arose. Not surprisingly his investigations didn't turn up the fact that Edward was still in a coma at the Whittington Hospital in Islington. He pulled together a team, including a good cameraman, to be in place for Friday 21st June. Whether it should look like a professional hit or an amateur burglary that would go horribly wrong had yet to be determined. He assumed that choice was his.

Jamaica Road Bermondsey, London England

Suzie's Laurent's funeral started late on the same morning the IRA blitzed the Houses of Parliament.

Suzie's body had been found by Tessa the night she'd been murdered. Tessa had gone to Edward's flat to see how the then retired croupier was coping as she hadn't returned to the hospital. Suzie had stayed away too long to just collect a few bits and bobs.

The only fingerprints on the gun that killed her were her own. The police assumed she must have kept it for her own protection. Some of the other croupiers confirmed that her previous boyfriend was particularly violent and threatened to kill her. However, as he was in prison the day she died it all pointed to suicide.

The handgun was unregistered and untraceable and so far as the police were concerned was a cul-de-sac in terms of leads to any meaningful lines of enquiry. No suicide note was found but, given the circumstances, it seemed fairly obvious to the police what had happened. Her current boyfriend's tragic situation, her past boyfriend's recent incarceration and her unstable mental state had proven too much to handle. Even trained nurses and qualified doctors commented on her parlous mental

Chapter 17 - Monday 17th June

state in the hospital. There was no doubt it all overcame her at once and triggered the suicide.

Tessa was more sceptical but kept her thoughts to herself. If suicide had been the cause of death then Tessa had sent Suzie on a suicide mission and that thought gutted her. Suzie was never told the full extent of Edward's condition. What's more she'd gone back to the flat to get everything organised for when he regained consciousness. She hadn't been told they may be unnecessary. There was even an overnight bag containing those items on the living room floor so why would she kill herself if she expected Edward to recover?

Mac told Tessa to leave it to the police. MI5 weren't interested in Suzie and were therefore not bothered by a locked toilet that stank of cigar smoke with butts in the toilet that couldn't be flushed away. All the open windows at the flat were of little concern and the fact that the power had conveniently been lost at the estimated time of death was put down to coincidence. Tessa was concerned though and she knew about guns. This one looked as though it had been hidden in a damp basement for years.

When she checked it she hadn't the strength to open the corroded chamber to see how many bullets were left. It took two of the forensic officers to do that together. How on earth could Suzie have loaded it? Unlike the gun the bullets were all spanking brand new as was the silencer. Again, Tessa couldn't even affix it once forensics removed it or remove it after they affixed it. She was meant to be an expert. What chance had Suzie of doing it?

The police interviewed those few who knew Suzie including Hakeem Gola at the Golden Palace Casino. Gola knew nothing about Suzie's private life but wasn't surprised she had a gun. Part of the package of being a croupier meant you were sometimes blamed when punters lost large sums of money. Hence many croupiers hid weapons at home, just in case. She was an attractive girl and often socialised and drank with men after her shift ended.

Gola had seen Edward Burlington, her current boyfriend, a few times in the club bar, but knew nothing about him. Neither did he know about any threats from boyfriends or punters from the old days. It wasn't his business what the girls did after they finished their work at the casino unless they reported some customer causing trouble and Suzie had never done that.

Hakeem sounded reassuring, reliable and believable because every question he was asked by the police he answered calmly and truthfully even though they could sense he was emotionally upset. His statement was important at her inquest because he was the main witness as to Suzie's lifestyle and had generously offered to organise the funeral knowing she had no close relatives. As one of the policemen noted at the inquest if only there were more like Hakeem Gola their job would be so much easier. The coroner went out of her way to thank Hakeem on all fronts.

Tessa didn't have to explain MI5's interest in any of these matters to the police. She just said they were tangential but gave them her research on Suzie showing she was an only child and orphan so there was no immediate family members to notify. She had some distant impoverished relatives in Algeria but they didn't want to know. They could sense involvement might cost them, so her cremation was organised as soon as the body was released by the police. It was paid for by the casino on condition there was no publicity.

The police did follow up on the power failure in the vicinity of the flat and found that a switch had been pulled. There were many ways it could've been done and impossible to check who'd done it. Many people had both the access and the knowledge, including engineers, residents, local authorities and private service providers.

There were two burglaries in the area while the power was out and they were deemed to be the most likely reason for it, not Suzie's apparent suicide. The burglaries were clever too but never solved and not linked to Suzie's suicide. There was no video coverage, no fingerprints and nothing else gathered from Montagu Square or Suzie's old flat to suggest that her demise was anything other than self-inflicted.

Mac, like Tessa, had more than a hunch that Khan was involved but he kept his suspicions to himself especially as the man was now back under surveillance. Sooner or later he'd give them enough rope to lasso him and string him up. Tessa had been in tears about it all. She sent the poor girl to her death. There was no other way to put it.

She looked at her watch. A week had passed almost to the hour when she'd suggested Suzie should drop by the flat and now Tessa was frogmarching herself to the funeral. Thank God Hugh was to meet her there and bring her back.

She called Hugh but he was not at the bookshop so she assumed he must be on his way. The funeral was to be held at a Roman Catholic Church not far from Jamaica Road in Bermondsey. She had the name in her handbag, which she picked up as she put the phone down and left for the funeral. As she did she realised she hadn't even thought twice before trying to call Hugh for support and solace. Mind you, Mac was giving her none at work as her absence just made dealing with the IRA problems more difficult for him.

Her calling Hugh just seemed so natural. Maybe there was an element of truth in the telepathic powers he mentioned. Like his younger brother Hugh was an instinctively kind and generous man, albeit he could be a tad slow on getting his round of drinks. His first thoughts on having been told of Suzie's death were for her family. Tessa said she had no family.

Hugh was determined to do whatever Ed would have done and pay for the funeral rather than let her have a pauper's funeral. Neither of them was quite sure what a pauper's funeral was nowadays but Tessa assured him proper arrangements were already in hand. Hugh found it hard to talk about Suzie in the past tense but he'd already started talking about Ed like that.

Chapter 17 - Monday 17th June

She didn't know it but Hugh was thinking of her. He was having a fat Cuban cigar to help him concentrate while out taking Scamp for a quick pee before setting off for the funeral. Hugh was trying to work out if he'd enjoy having kids to look after as much as he loved nurturing Scamp in all his innocence. He thought of Ed and Suzie and wished he could have a dog's life. A tear rolled down the side of his face. Hugh didn't know whether to laugh or cry. Big decisions like which lamp post to wee on were far easier to handle.

Besides Hugh and Tessa, four of Suzie's colleagues from the casino including Hakeem Gola turned up at the church. There were a few other people there, the ones who come in off the street and attend any services that happen to be going on at the time. There were less than a dozen true mourners in all. The service was over relatively quickly and Suzie was now just another suicide statistic.

Tessa was aware that everything was arranged by Hakeem Gola and paid for by the Golden Palace Casino. The benefactor had asked to remain anonymous. It barely mattered. Not even a reporter from the Evening Standard bothered to turn up. The desire for anonymity was not unusual as casinos didn't appreciate publicity, good or bad, and this was both.

Hugh wrote a simple message on behalf of Ed. He left it with a huge bouquet of lilies which overshadowed the one foot square plot Suzie's life had been squashed into in the graveyard. The plaque prepared by the casino looked as though their personnel department had arranged it. The wording was as lifeless as the vacuum left behind her. It simply read Suzanne Martine Laurent 1949 -1974.

As they were leaving the crematorium, Raj Gupta Khan turned up in a new dark blue Jaguar. He looked flustered and apologised for being late. Khan joined Tessa and Hugh on their way out through the gate and pretended not to know Hakeem Gola.

Tessa was apprehensive to the point of being fearful. She had let her guard down with Hugh when they first had dinner together. Another way of putting it was Hugh had asked so many difficult questions he had entrapped her, rather like his father had in the JIC inquiry. She hadn't said anything outright, she never would, but he'd subtly engineered their conversation. She ended up intimating that Khan might be involved in Edward's poisoning and even Suzie's death but it was only supposition. Hugh had instantly cottoned on to what she meant. By now she knew how impulsive Hugh could be and wasn't sure how he would react to Khan's unexpected presence.

'What a tragedy, first Edward and now this lovely woman.'

They didn't comment. He spoke directly to Tessa in a low, covert voice.

'Is there anything suspicious in all this Tessa?'

'You tell me Raj.'

'What do you mean?'

'Well, Edward picked up his botulism at a dinner you arranged in a restaurant of your choosing.'

Khan feigned shock.

'You can't believe, surely not, Hugh was there too and me.'

'Not forgetting Suzie as well.'

'I heard she shot herself.'

Khan realised what he just let slip but didn't draw attention to any possible misinterpretations. Tessa said nothing more. She'd been ordered by Mac to avoid him and if they met not to say anything to him. Tessa had already said too much but she was having a hard time keeping her true fury in check. At rare times like this her pent up boiling emotions wanted to explode but she just managed to keep the lid on. She walked with Hugh towards his car. Khan trotted alongside them even though it was plain for all to see he was unwelcome.

'How is Edward? I called the hospital but they wouldn't tell me anything and visitors aren't allowed.'

Tessa bit her tongue and calmly responded in a Birmingham pitch brimming with anger and quivering with rage.

'He's still in a coma. I thought you knew.'

'Yes, how sad.'

Out of fear of Tessa exploding Khan turned to Hugh not realising he too was boiling over. By now the corpulent accountant and murderer was sweating trying to keep up with them.

'Hugh, if there's anything I can do?'

His offer was dismissed with a shake of his head and Hugh opened the car door for Tessa.

'I can't help but think I was responsible.'

Relieved she was back in the car Tessa answered to pre-empt Hugh who was looking daggers at Khan. If Hugh swung into one of his impromptu mad moments who knew what he might do to the man he reckoned might be involved in trying to murder his younger brother.

'Don't worry Raj; it couldn't have been your fault. Drive carefully.'

Once inside the car, Hugh leant out the window and shouted something in Punjabi. Raj Gupta Khan didn't flinch or turn round. He just kept on going in the other direction. Hugh wondered why. If he had been in Khan's shoes ...

'What was that, Hugh?'

'I just told him to watch where he trod. There is a lot of shit around.'

Hugh started talking about Ed and Suzie on the drive back. He knew his brother had been in love. Ed had only once been so smitten before but that was when he was in his teens up north.

That relationship had lasted years contrary to what many would have expected from a real tearaway like Ed. Hugh hadn't been surprised as he had been one of the few who knew both of them. They had just drifted apart as university, or ultimately

Chapter 17 - Monday 17th June

the absence of university in Ed's case, sent them in converse directions. They were like two trains under their own steam leaving a station behind them as they set off in opposite directions.

Tessa listened with interest as Hugh chronicled those aspects of Ed's past she didn't know. They included parts of his life that Edward had chosen to keep private and not share with her. Hugh's seeking consolation in the past was understandable and natural. He said he was having difficulty concentrating on his reading now and even Scamp looked at him through bleary watery eyes.

Tessa explained her observations about Suzie's murder with care so as not to give too much away. Hugh wasn't the least surprised. He was nobody's fool and though Tessa hadn't mentioned the "MI" letters he added that if MI6 didn't avenge Suzie's death he would. For good measure, he told Tessa he was a bloody good shot too.

He stopped the car to wipe his eyes and clean his glasses with an old scarf taken from the glove compartment. She took the glasses from him and wiped them with a clean white tissue. After intentionally avoiding eye contact for most of the short trip Hugh looked sheepishly, almost lovingly into Tessa's large brown eyes. It sent different types of shivers down her spine. She gently put his glasses on for him. They continued their journey in silence now Hugh could see the road ahead.

'Suzie could have been my sister in law you know.'

Tessa just looked at Hugh. Had he given up the ghost on his younger brother? She couldn't read his drained face but she could read between Hugh's lines and the way he looked at her. Tessa hadn't seen his sad dark eyes before other than hidden behind his glasses. Might she have been an "in law" had Suzie lived? Could she be one to Edward in the future?

Hugh dropped Tessa off at Waterloo Station and drove back to Montagu Square to leave Ed's Jag as if in its final resting space too.

Magdala Avenue Islington, London England

Sara was on the warpath again. Her youngest son was in a coma, possibly dying. His girlfriend had been shot in the head and she reckoned her son's girlfriends were unlikely to be the suicidal type. There were hopeless security guards all over the place.

Still after all that and ten days later she had yet to receive a reasoned explanation of what the hell was going on? Now was the time to kick some arse. Roger was being reticent and it was obvious to her he knew more than he was letting on. Him and his damn JIC pals sometimes irked Sara.

'If I find out Castle has anything to do with this, I'll screw the bastard!'

'I hope you mean that metaphorically darling?'

'Don't be facetious Roger. You know what I mean.'

'It'll destroy your reputation as well as his if you go to the press.'

'I don't care.'

Edward's parents were by his bedside in the hospital, where they'd been for the best part of the past ten days. They watched as the nurses changed their son's bed sheets again. Edward was wearing one of those stupid gowns that never quite fit properly. It hurt Sara so profoundly to see him like this, so helpless, like when he was a newborn but now she couldn't help, just watch as if a passenger in a passing train. She held his hand again. She'd been holding it for days and she was beginning to look even thinner than him.

'If you tell me everything you know, Roger, I won't go to the press.'

'What will you do instead?'

'I'll get rid of Castle another way but only if you help me.'

Roger wanted a cigarette. They wouldn't allow him to smoke in the intensive care unit and that was starting to irritate him. He was forced to go out into a corridor which seemed miles away every time he wanted to smoke and, with his addiction, it was bloody inconvenient. However, he didn't want his wife talking about JIC business or anything to do with this drama in range of the hospital staff. So he took her outside the ward, out of earshot of the security team, and they went into an empty waiting room.

'How do you propose to get rid of him?'

'I'll make him resign.'

'Look, I've already said telling all to the press won't do the boys or me any favours, even if you don't care about what happens to you.'

'I don't need to go to the press.'

'I don't understand.'

Roger was already halfway down the cigarette and contemplating lighting another.

'Beyond Enkription, think about it Roger.'

'Good God! Now I see why you involved the Home Secretary and insisted on that inquiry. You created that as a back stop for pinning Castle to the wall more than a formal safeguard for Edward's security didn't you? The enquiry wasn't pointless at all, was it? You meant to use it to oust Castle from the start. We already had security for Edward sorted or so we thought. My God. Payback time is finally in sight after all these years.'

'I can't do it without your help.'

Roger lit the second cigarette from the red hot butt of the first one. He knew he would have to aid Sara otherwise she would go to the press with utter contempt for the consequences. Then the curtain would fall for many including his family. She might even go to prison if that snivelling little mouse of a man TeaLeaves became antagonistic. Roger twisted and turned the logic round in his mind. There was no avoiding it. Castle would have to be red carded.

Chapter 17 - Monday 17th June

Sara looked quizzically at Roger. He was silent for a minute or so, as he continued to think all the strands through to their logical conclusions. Sara sat and watched him pace up and down knowing not to interrupt his thought processes.

The inquiry was so clever, a double edged sword and he had been too close to realise it. Castle had, by agreeing to be part of it, unwittingly nailed himself to his own cross in the process. His absurd dread of Sara made him overlook its dual purpose. Heads or tails, they should now win. Proving Castle's breaches of procedures and recklessness would be undemanding. He'd read the transcripts of all the incriminating tapes including Castle's ridiculous meeting with Mac and Luke. Roger liked probabilities like that.

'We'll have to go see Alice Bailey.'

Sara smiled and kissed him. She'd won the first skirmish. Thank God her husband was clever enough to see it all. The Home Secretary had already put Sir Douglas Castle, now a proven Crown servant, in a butcher's van en route to the abattoir. He had been stripped naked of the legal protections normally afforded to those in the stratospheric offices on the top floor in Century House. Sir Douglas Castle was on his way to the Bloody Tower unless he surrendered unconditionally and peacefully.

'Good. Now tell me what happened to Edward and his girlfriend.'

Roger explained all he knew but kept it strictly to what he thought was relevant without straining the inner recesses of his mind.

When they returned to the room, Edward's bedding had been changed and Sister Maria, who was in charge of the ward, was smiling down at him.

'He moved. His hand moved.'

'What?'

Sara ran to the bed, almost knocking the Sister out of the way. She checked her son's pulse and noticed a twitch in his fingers as she did so.

'Yes, he's moving, Roger, he's moving!'

'Thank God.'

Sister Maria pulled the emergency cord and three heavy duty intensive care nurses appeared in seconds. The ward sister came to life.

'Nurse, call Mr Cordell at once. Mrs Burlington, stay back, please. Stay back now.'

The specialist consultant arrived and took control. He barked orders.

'I want that ventilator off now. Mr and Mrs Burlington, you'll have to wait outside the room.'

Sara barked back at him.

'No!'

'Well, stand back then, in that corner. Now! Time is critical.'

They watched aghast. It was like a scene out of a horror film. Edward's body looked as though it was being pressed and pummelled, manipulated and manhandled by Cordell, Sister Maria and the nurses for what seemed an eternity. They tried to kick-start him back to consciousness. Drips and pipes swayed to and fro and were pulled out by accident and re-inserted and ripped out again in the mayhem. Sara and Roger stood silently in the corner of that manic room, hardly daring to breath, to hope.

Gradually, the symphony of upheaval subsided and a semblance of normality was restored. The nurses replaced the drips for the fifth or sixth time and showed the specialist the blood pressure and pulse readings. Cordell's face beamed over at the parents, affixed like statues in the corner of the room.

'Mr and Mrs Burlington, your son will survive.'

Both parents let out simultaneous gasps of relief.

'He's no longer comatose. You'll only notice slight movements at first, as his body starts to revive itself.'

The rush of relief overcame Sara. She would have sunk to the floor if Roger hadn't held her. He and Cordell helped her to a chair. Pent-up emotion burst from her in sobs and uncontrolled shaking. She joined her hands as if in prayer to a God she now believed in for once.

'Nurse, please get Mrs Burlington something to calm her.'

Sara took paracetamol and sipped on a cup of lukewarm hospital tea as Cordell spoke to her and Roger.

'It could take just a few hours or up to several days for Edward to regain full consciousness. He will probably be extremely weak and he may not be able to speak. Our next concern is to what extent the paralysis dissipates.'

Roger asked what Sara couldn't bring herself to ask.

'Brain damage?'

'Could be. We can't tell now.'

Sara's euphoria relapsed into a state of uncertainty.

'It's a significant step in the right direction. The vital thing is he's left the comatose phase. There were only two exit doors he could have taken, the one his subconscious and body fought for, or death.'

Around mid-afternoon on Monday 17th June Edward's fingers first twitched back into life. By nine o'clock that evening, he was sitting up in bed and talking hazily about his grandfather, Frederick. He'd dreamt about the old man shooting prisoners in the Himalayas. Edward recalled showering and sweating and Suzie going out to get medicine from the chemist for his flu. After that some Newcastle supporters tried to take him away on a stretcher after he attacked a fat naked man raping some Chinese girls before everything went blank.

They told him his memory was playing tricks on him but this was to be expected and his brain would clear soon. Cordell's best guess now was no permanent brain damage. Edward had a crooked neck left over from the paralysis but that was diminishing, would soon be unnoticeable and eventually it should be almost imperceptible.

Chapter 17 - Monday 17th June

His vision was blurry but would also get back to normal although he had to skew his head if he wanted to make eye contact.

Mr Cordell had only read about but never witnessed such a rapid recovery and conjectured that Edward might be able to leave the hospital in a few days. Sara called Hugh as soon as she'd recovered from the incredulity of Edward's first signs of healing. Hugh had called Tessa and they both came round straightaway. Edward asked where Suzie was as he fidgeted with his left eyebrow. Everyone avoided giving him a direct answer. The consultant concluded that the shock of her suicide could have a detrimental effect on his recuperation and might even cause an unpredictable reaction, either physical or emotional or both at this early a stage in his recovery.

Roger was explaining to Edward what botulism intoxication was, how it attacked the body and how he'd picked it up from something he ate. It had been one of those tales of the unexpected. It could have been Hugh, or Raj, or anyone.

'Or Suzie.'

They smiled benignly at Edward when he said this.

'I'm glad it missed Suzie and I had it. I'd have hated for her to go through this. She may not have survived.'

Such a gathering was a rare occasion. The Burlingtons were all together except this time Tessa was there for the first time and she held each of the brothers' hands but in different ways. She held Edward's hand in a reassuring sisterly way and Hugh's as a lover would.

The relief and euphoria subsided as Edward was sedated at about nine thirty. At least they could leave and even go home happier than when they woke that morning.

Sara stayed though.

Maybe there was something she'd picked up between the lines of what Roger insinuated was going on or some loose thread that still kept her on high alert.

No matter what, her maternal instincts told her this episode in Edward's life was far from over despite the finality of Suzie's cremation that day. She knew he wasn't out of the tunnel yet and it had more twists and turns to take before daylight was discernible. She wrote page after page in her diary that night as her relief poured out like grief. She was also feeling quite sick, having barely eaten much since she had first arrived at the hospital.

What made her feel truly sick was that she had ignored that beautiful girl who Edward was obviously and understandably in love with: how could she have been so pitiless? Roger was in no doubt the ever so lonely girl had been murdered. Mac had affirmed that was his private view and that was good enough for Sara. Both Roger and Sara understood the need to let this Khan bastard walk unhindered towards his own execution chamber. It might well save her son's life and the lives of others. She just wished she had talked to Suzie, got to know her more to understand Edward's love for her. She also wished she could be the executioner of that sad girl's murderer. Whoever had murdered her had wanted to harm her son.

She scribbled away in her diary until way after midnight. Mac had hinted to Roger that this train wreck in slow motion was not yet over. She had no idea why he always talked in metaphors about British Rail of all organisations. Maybe his Dad had been a train driver not that it mattered. Her intuition told her that until Edward was out of harm's way he was still in harm's way big time. At present without her by his side he was weak. He might as well be a sleeper on the mainline between Kings Cross and Darlington: at least death would be quick albeit vicious. The sooner he got on a plane to Nassau the safer he would be.

Nurses came and went but the activity gradually petered out. Finally Sara settled down for the night moving her chair closer to Edward's bed facing the door. She drifted off and actually fell asleep for a few hours.

That was only after taking the safety catch off her Beretta and putting it back in the shoulder holster hidden under the cashmere coat folded on her lap, just as she had been taught all those years ago. Yet she didn't dream of the horrors of war. She dreamt of family seaside holidays at Runswick Bay, before the boys went to school. Building sandcastles and watching them crumble as the tide came in: cameos of all their lives.

Edward and his Mum were woken at three in the morning by the rattling of a trolley full of medicines being wheeled into the room. It was time for Edward to take more medicine.

For a fleeting moment on waking he thought he was back in Innsbruck after his appendicitis operation when Sara had arrived unannounced to save him and take him home. They stayed awake talking for the rest of the night and Edward told his Mum all about Suzie and what he had read about the Bahamas. For his own good she had been told not to tell him Suzie was no more.

Sara's diary for the day read "Innsbruck revisited but where to next before Nassau?" It was as if she knew the slow motion train wreck was only just gathering steam.

Chapter 18
Thursday 20th & Friday 21st June

Kings Cross Camden & Albany Street Regents Park, London England
Early in the morning five bulky police officers boarded a train from Newcastle Central Station, via Darlington to Kings Cross in London. On arrival, they went to the plush five star White House Hotel in Albany Street off Marylebone Road and checked into their rooms. They lunched quietly in the Dorset suite. Barely a word was spoken. No alcohol was served.

They were all large beefy rozzers: one superintendent, two inspectors and two sergeants. After lunch, they were joined in a meeting room by four other men. An operations manager, an electrician, a burglar alarm expert and a security camera specialist, all of whom had worked as a team for Smith beforehand. They were accustomed to his fastidious ways.

The attendees had been told not to introduce themselves to one another. They didn't. They sat silently until a middle aged man wearing thick glasses was pushed into the room in a wheelchair. The man in the wheelchair was sweating profusely and balancing boxes full of clothes, papers and diagrams on his knees. The woman pushing the chair was well over six feet tall and wearing a wedding ring with a stone like a boulder. They were accompanied by a smaller woman of similar age who removed the boxes from the man's lap, then sat down and sorted the diagrams and papers into piles. The giant woman shunted her husband in the wheelchair over to the side of the room. She took up a position behind a slide projector.

The man in the wheelchair was the first to speak. Smith, using some kind of muzzle to disguise his voice, sounded like a Dalek. He was the only one of his group of three to say a word throughout the entire briefing.

'Good afternoon gentlemen. My name is Smith and that's all you need to know about me. This lady is my wife and won't answer your questions so don't bother asking anything of her or her assistant.'

Smith pointed to the large woman, who looked like a heavyweight wrestler. The other shorter frumpy looking woman continued sorting out the boxes meticulously and walked round handing out white envelopes to each of the nine men.

'The envelopes contain the agreed advance. The rest will follow once the operation is complete. As we go through the presentation Mrs Jones will hand out walkie-talkies, clothes and other equipment and instructions that you'll need. Do not talk to her.'

Mrs Jones distributed the first round of bags to each of the men. Smith continued.

'All the documentation, including any notes you make, will be collected at the end of the briefing and destroyed.'

One of the policemen opened his envelope and started counting the money.

'You, yes you, please pay attention.'

Smith's polite but firm tone stopped the superintendent in his tracks and he looked round at the others sheepishly.

'As you can see, I'm disabled, so I won't be there. I will be controlling the operation from a nearby location.'

He waited until he commanded their full attention.

'Right, let's get on with the slide show. If you have any questions, I'll take them at the end.'

Smith gestured with his hand. Mrs Jones switched out the lights and started closing the blinds. Smith's wife operated the projector to show the assembled men Slide 1, which displayed a somewhat crude drawing of Cyrus Burton's address book.

'Our mission is to search an apartment for a copied address book. We don't know the exact form of the copy but it may well be just loose or stapled A4 sized sheets. However, it will contain lists of names and contact details that will mean nothing to you. You are not to read them. Is that clear?'

The assembly collectively nodded their heads.

'As soon as the address lists are found, in whatever form, they must be handed over to the operations manager immediately. Bill, can you stand up so they may identify you.'

Bill stood up then sat back down again. They couldn't see him properly as the blinds were nearly all shut by now so that the slide show received their undivided attention. His six foot seven thin hunchbacked silhouette was unforgettable. There could be no mistaking him day or night.

'Bill and I will be in radio contact all the time. By the way, all names used during the operation are false. Slide 2, please.'

The man in the wheelchair carried on for almost three hours, detailing the area around Burlington's flat in Montagu Square. His wife showed slides of the block of flats itself, including the inside, and Smith attested to the fact that Edward's was at the top.

Smith also outlined the timings, communications arrangements and failsafe plans for a power cut. He detailed the particulars of Edward's roof garden and the positions of alarms and cameras that must be knocked out, even though the power would be cut. The slides showed what vehicles would be used when and by whom, who would be wearing what and cover stories to be given to anyone who might enquire what was happening. By the time he'd finished, his wife was on Slide 193 and every imaginable contingency had been covered.

'Anyone want a call of nature?'

Most of them did. They were allowed out one at a time.

Once everyone returned to the meeting room the blinds were pulled back up, the lights switched on and the briefing continued. Each person was asked to go through his specific role, assuming everything went to plan. The police were given canisters of chloroform and shown how to use them. They were also handed new truncheons and handcuffs that were untraceable. The operations manager would be the only one carrying a gun.

'Your second payment will be made in cash by me back here, after the operation is complete.'

This produced a rumble of agreeing voices round the room.

'All of you are also eligible for a bonus.'

They rapidly quietened down to hear more.

'Lights off now. Next slide, please.'

Edward Burlington's image came up on the slide projector screen.

'We want this man taken alive if he's on the premises, or if he shows up while you're there. You can put him out with chloroform or whatever but he must be alive and handed over to Bill and our camera expert. Then the rest of you can leave the flat.'

Mrs Smith rolled some slides of Edward from different angles comprising close-ups and full length shots.

'You'll only get the bonus if he's taken alive.'

The slides came to an end. Before all the lights came on again Smith didn't notice that some of the assembled police started looking at each other as if to say we recognise that bastard.

'That about wraps it up unless you have any more questions. You kick off at ten in the morning from the hotel reception. We meet back here at sixteen hundred hours tomorrow, after what had better be a successful operation.'

Mrs Jones went round and collected all the paperwork.

'The people from up north should leave now and go to your rooms, one by one, please. Use room service for whatever you need and do not go to the bar or outside the hotel or make any calls. Do not sign for your rooms when you leave tomorrow. We have taken care of all that.'

The northern rozzers began trooping out of the meeting room, each giving the previous man a minute or so before exiting. Smith waited until they'd all left.

'The rest of you can go now. Leave one at a time and go home. Do not attempt to communicate with each other.'

After all the men were gone and the room was cleared, Mr Smith was wheeled out and taken to his suite by Mrs Smith and Mrs Jones. In the privacy of the suite, he stood up and removed his glasses and wig and the padding that had made him sweat so profusely during the briefing. Smith showered and changed into a smart suit, while the tall woman miraculously morphed into a man and the frumpy Mrs Jones transformed into a young, sexy looking redhead.

Within twenty minutes the three people who entered the suite looked nothing like the threesome who left for dinner at the White House Hotel's upmarket restaurant. Had any of the police disobeyed their orders and eaten there the threesome would not have been recognised. Contrarily, they wouldn't have had a clue who these three were by sex, age, sound or shape.

Mind you, the shape of the hotel was most unusual too. The hotel's outline was so remarkable that when seen from the air the Luftwaffe used it as a guiding compass for German planes during the blitz. It was then the safest place in London. The Luftwaffe was ordered never to bomb it because of its usefulness as a landmark. Mr Smith and his companions were confident it would be just as safe now, some thirty or so years later.

Magdala Avenue Islington, London England

As the corrupt rozzers were preparing for their heist on the morning of Friday 21st June Hugh and his brother were laughing together in the Whittington Hospital. They were reminiscing about the pranks they played and the stunts they pulled off when they were back in boarding school. Hugh was lying across the bed and Edward was standing at the window, fully dressed.

'That master was a real bastard to you.'

'I wouldn't go that far Hugh.'

'How often were you caned by him?'

'Only once or twice a week for four years, excluding holidays of course.'

'You were gated most of the time too.'

'True but that was only to improve my forgery of masters' signatures to prove I was at lessons or on the premises every ten minutes.'

Ed didn't have a monopoly on misbehaviour when they were younger. Hugh closed his eyes.

'Wake up you lazy sod. Do you remember Bony Hands' speech after you won outright at Bisley?'

'About the rice pudding battles?'

'No, not those you twit. When he cited you as one of the greatest marksman in the school's history but far too trigger happy to be allowed near a gun in public.'

They laughed again. Hugh tried to keep it going but Ed was getting restless. He was on the mend and wanted to get out of the hospital.

'Where the hell is Suzie?'

Chapter 18 - Thursday 20th & Friday 21st June

Hugh stopped laughing. It was difficult for him not to tell Ed about Suzie. He was betraying his brother but he too had been told to keep quiet so as not to jeopardise his recovery. Hugh manoeuvred the conversation back to the good old days.

'Did you ever see that draft book written by Bony?'

'No.'

'The draft I saw was his first go at a history of the school. I can quote that Master Edwardo Burlington was originally mentioned by name as the most gated and beaten boy since they opened the drawbridge in 627 anno domini.'

'That's libel.'

'It's true.'

Hugh smiled ruefully. While glad his brother was getting better, he knew what was to come. Ed would blame himself for Suzie's death and be angry and hurt that he hadn't been told earlier.

'Well, at least they didn't get me for blowing up the boat house or nicking the lead off the roofs.'

'Maybe not, but they drummed you out of the cadets for selling ammo.'

'Yes, and you just reminded me again that I was the finest marksman in their glorious history.'

'I know, Hugh, I heard you. Bulls-eye Burlington they called you amongst other pleasantries. Do you want me to give you a medal too?'

Hugh made a shooting gesture with his hand and index finger, closing one eye as he did so.

'Which reminds me, do you remember when we were in the library with the megaphone you borrowed and wrecked the parade?'

Hugh laughed out loud. The memories flooded back.

'Three hundred of them, and they didn't know who was giving the orders.'

'Quick march!'

'Squad halt!'

'Total chaos ruled, right in front of all those old boys with their Boer War uniforms and rows of medals and decorations.'

The brothers were once again reliving the wild antics of their reckless youth.

'Not everything was down to me you know Hugh. Who crashed that cruiser in the river Trent? Who set fire to the flat in London?'

'Come on, Ed, they were mistakes and you distracted me.'

'I tried to stop you, not distract you.'

'Stop you drowning us on one occasion and burning us to death on another.'

The brothers bantered back and forth, each trying to imply that the other was the biggest blackguard.

'What was the name of Dad's driver, the one with the beard who drove the old black Rover and pretended not to be a bodyguard?'

'Blackbeard was his name. He caught you taking his revolver out of the glove compartment and nearly crashed the car killing all three of us.'

Hugh laughed again. This was good; this was as it had been when the good times rolled but Suzie was still at the back of his mind.

'What about that French mistress, Ed, the one you tried to touch up in sixth form. What was her name?'

'Madame Fitzsomethingorother. That wasn't my fault, she fancied me.'

'Got you chucked out of the scouts.'

'Yeah, they cut off my lapels and badges. Why didn't you do something?'

Hugh was about to respond when one of the nurses entered the room with a beef and tomato sandwich for Edward. He gave half of it to his brother and asked the nurse if it would be alright to go for a stroll.

'Your mother is coming back this afternoon Mr Burlington.'

'I know, but she won't get here until after three. I'll be back by then.'

'Mr Cordell will be doing his rounds, so make sure you are please.'

Edward bluffed his way past Mac's security saying they'd be sitting in the sunshine at the entrance so there was nothing to fear. At the hospital reception, Edward asked the receptionist to get a cab. Hugh knew where he wanted to go; to the flat to find Suzie.

Montagu Square Marylebone, London England

Smith's operation was going to plan, except for one small detail. They couldn't find anything that even remotely resembled an address book. The flat had been turned inside out and upside down several times. Floorboards were ripped up; cavity walls torn open and plant pots turned over: the place was a complete wreck. They'd been inside for over an hour. Time was short. The power would be restored soon. Even though they'd deactivated every camera and alarm in the building, there were some in the street that would soon go back on automatically. Smith was in a van parked nearby to the block of flats and saw Edward and Hugh getting out of the cab.

'Bill, you have two visitors and one of them is your bonus. Move to the visitor contingency plan. Over ...'

'Leave it to me, boss. Over ...'

'Any problems, call me. Over and out.'

Hugh still hadn't told Ed about Suzie and he was running out of time. When his brother found out the girl wasn't in the flat, he'd want to know why. The truth would have to come out of the bag; no more covering it up with sweet nothings. The electric locks weren't working in the entrance door but Ed's key worked.

'Lift's out too.'

'I don't think you should climb the stairs in your condition Ed. Let's go back.'

'Race you to the top.'

Chapter 18 - Thursday 20th & Friday 21st June

Edward was off up the stairs. Hugh had no choice but to follow, as fast as he could. Hugh stopped to grab the post so Ed reached the top first and was met by a broad shouldered police sergeant. The man smiled cynically.

'What's the reason for your hurry sir?'

'This is my flat. What's going on?'

'There's been a break in here. Do you have any ID?'

'Not on me personally but inside the flat.'

The sergeant didn't move aside to let Edward pass through to the flat. Hugh reached the top, almost out of breath.

'Look, I'm Edward Burlington and this is my brother.'

A police inspector and another sergeant stuck their heads round the entrance way and their flatulent heavyset bodies followed. Confrontation was looming ...

'Hello Danny.'

One of the sergeants looked at Hugh, in response to his greeting.

'Ed, get out. It's a bloody trap!'

The police inspector's truncheon came into violent contact with the side of Hugh's face. He crashed to the floor, blood and teeth spilling from his jaw. The sergeant called Danny lunged at Ed. Edward grabbed his arm and he surged past, tripping over Hugh's body. Edward yanked the arm, using the man's huge frame to gain momentum. Danny thudded into the banister, which gave way. The sickening sound of bone and marrow meeting the marble floor below could be heard from the top floor.

Another two men appeared from nowhere. Everything was moving in slow motion, as the fatigue from Edward's running up the stairs took its toll.

Hugh regained his senses on the floor and grabbed hold of the inspector hovering above him. He stumbled into the other sergeant, knocking the man off balance and sending him down after Danny to the marble reception area. He was dead before the sound of his scream reached the ears of those on the top floor.

Hugh tried to get to his feet but a pad of chloroform was clamped over his face. Edward was dragged into the flat and pinned down, while his ankles were handcuffed to a heavy oak chair. Bill stood over him menacingly.

'The address book you copied. Where is it?'

'What address book?'

'One more answer like that and your brother takes the shortcut to the lobby.'

'Well, if you put it that way, look inside my briefcase.'

'We've searched your briefcase.'

'It has a false bottom.'

Bill forced open the hidden compartment inside the metal briefcase with a knife. There was nothing. He lashed out with his fist. Edward passed out from the force of the blow. Bill spoke into his walkie-talkie.

'How much time have we got? Over ...'

'Two minutes. Over ...'

'It's not here. We have two dead. Over ...'

'Where are the bodies? Over ...'

'In the lobby. Over ...'

'We're coming in. You get out of there. Over and out.'

Bill told everyone to leave the block of flats, except for Kevin, the cameraman. Smith's contingency team backed their removal van up to the entrance. They quickly stuffed the bloody remains of their two comrades into black body bags and threw them into the van.

Back at the flat, Kevin videoed Edward, while Bill decided how they should kill him. He pointed to the exit.

'Let's just chuck him over here from the landing.'

They dragged him to the door but his legs were still cuffed to the heavy wooden chair. The keys to the handcuffs were in the pocket of one of the policemen who'd already left.

'Shit!'

'Just sling him over, chair and all.'

They pulled Edward through the door and threw him towards the landing. The chair jammed in what was left of the banister, leaving Edward hanging upside down with blood running from his face and dripping down off his hair. His body twitched convulsively as Kevin turned the video camera on again. Bill's walkie-talkie crackled into life.

'You have sixty seconds. Over and out.'

Bill ran down the stairs, followed by Kevin, still pointing his video camera at the swaying Edward. Outside, they jumped into the escape vehicle and were long gone in a matter of minutes. Kevin smiled across at Bill, waving the camera above his head.

'They'll have to pay us our bonus when they see this.'

'Yeah, not our fault if there was no address book.'

Hugh was regaining consciousness. It took him a moment or two to realise where he was. Then he saw Ed. He grabbed his brother's feet and looked down at his blood covered head, pointing towards the lobby floor. Ed's body swayed. The banister or what was left of it creaked.

Hugh carefully manoeuvred his brother back towards the landing, managing to grasp his legs, up to the knees. Hugh's whole bodyweight was by now on Ed's lower legs so he couldn't slip back. This was knife edge stuff. Edward could so easily take the chair and the broken banister with him and Hugh would follow.

Lastly he gripped Ed's belt and, with every ounce of strength left in him, pulled the rest of his brother's body to safety. He tugged him, still handcuffed to the chair, back from the brink. Hugh gradually dragged him and the chair inside the flat and

Chapter 18 - Thursday 20th & Friday 21st June

slammed the door. He checked to see if Ed was still breathing. The power came back on at last. Hugh dialled 999.

'All services please.'

The effort took its toll and everything went hazy. Hugh was on the verge of passing out again when an axe head came slicing through the flat door. He heaved Ed further back into the apartment, just as the door caved in completely. Two police officers came through first, followed by others. Hugh hoped these people were the cavalry otherwise they were dead meat. He looked up and saw the paramedics and knew they were safe.

The police searched every room in the flat, while the medics attended to Ed. Hugh made it to a chair on his hands and knees. He sat heavily into it, nervously moving his fingers around his jaw and inside his mouth. Several teeth were missing from his mouth and his jaw ached as if it was hanging off his face. One of the paramedics leant over him to take a look.

'Chloroform, I can smell it.'

'My brother ...'

The paramedic's mouth moved but Hugh couldn't hear the words as he passed out again.

Sara expected trouble. She had even predicted it again in her diary. Now her intuition was unpleasantly rewarded with both her sons being on the brink. Edward's train had crashed again, this time with Hugh on board, and it had collided into the tunnel walls.

Chapter 19
Friday 21ˢᵗ June

Magdala Avenue Islington, London England

When Hugh came round, he had no clue as to where he was, what the day or time was, where his brother was or even if Ed was still alive. He pulled a cord hanging down by the side of his bed. All above his neck was numb, as if someone had given him a serious overdose of novocaine. A nurse appeared, followed by a doctor he didn't know. Cordell came into the room just behind them and approached Hugh's bed.

'Don't try to speak. Raise you left hand for no and your right hand for yes.'

Cordell paused, as if waiting for Hugh's approval, then realised he'd told him not to speak.

'Can you hear me?'

Hugh raised his right hand.

'Do you recognise me?'

Hugh again raised his right hand.

Cordell introduced the other man as Dr Carlton. He told Hugh his jaw had been broken in two places and Carlton had operated and inserted metal joints. It would take several weeks for his face to completely heal. Cordell added that Carlton would be looking after him. He'd just popped in to reassure him he was in safe hands and that his brother Edward was in the next room recovering. Edward had been concussed and several of his ribs were fractured.

'Do you understand?'

Hugh raised his right hand.

'Your parents are with him and he's starting to gain consciousness.'

Carlton told Hugh he would inject some more morphine for the pain and Hugh would be asleep in seconds. His parents would come see him later that night. Hugh indicated that he wanted to write a message. The nurse fetched a pen and paper. Hugh wrote a brief message and handed it to Dr Carlton.

'Ta. Goodnight.'

Then he closed his eyes. The hatred of needles and injections ran in the family.

Chapter 19 - Friday 21st June

Four armed police officers were in the corridor outside and Tessa was in Cordell's office, on the phone to Mac. She was definitely in the wrong place at the worst time. Sara strode in, closed the door behind her, took the phone from Tessa's hand and pressed down on the cradle to cut off the call. She then purposefully dropped the phone onto the floor. Tessa looked at the woman: she meant business. Sara was standing between her and the door and, even though she was over fifty, Tessa didn't fancy trying to get out. She'd just have to take it on the chin and try to keep her composure. Sara's voice was measured, masking her anger.

'My eldest son works in a bookshop. He's a harmless librarian. Now he's in a hospital bed with his jaw wired up so tight he can't talk.'

'Mrs Burlington ...'

'Don't interrupt!'

Tessa clammed her mouth shut. She glanced down towards the phone but knew if she tried to pick it up she ran the risk of coming away with several broken fingers. Mrs Burlington had already spotted Tessa's eyelid movement. There wasn't a hope in Hades of escape or contact with the outside world.

'My youngest son was nearly killed for the fourth time in as many months. Why? How the hell did he get out in the first place past what you dare call security?'

Tessa knew Sara didn't need her to answer that. It was as if she was responsible for a dangerous beast escaping from a zoo. The trouble was Sara was undeniably right to be furious.

'I'll tell you why, Miss Hislop, because he does things for the government that people like you are afraid to do.'

Sara stepped within smelling distance of Tessa, as if she was sizing her up, daring her to do something, so she could vent her anger in a physical way.

'You were on the phone to Alan McKenzie, weren't you?'

Again, Tessa knew no answer was required.

'Mac was a cheeky spotty brat before I trained him. He's probably shitting himself right now, as he scrambles for a car to get him and his umbrella over here to save the day.'

Tessa suppressed a smile. That would be precisely what he was doing as they confronted one another.

'Do you know what I did, Miss Hislop?'

'Did?'

'In MI6.'

'You ...'

'I was the security chief when your boss, Sir Douglas Castle, wet his trousers every time he heard the name Adolf Hitler. So there's no use fibbing to me, I know when people are lying.'

'Why should I lie to you?'

'You wouldn't work for MI5 unless you were a liar. Are you in charge of security here?'

Tessa hesitated. The last time she was asked a seemingly innocent question this woman's husband had asked it. She still didn't know what the consequences of her answer then might be let alone now.

'Well, are you?'

'I suppose so.'

'You suppose so? Come with me.'

Sara turned towards the door. Tessa was about to pick the phone up from the floor but Sara seemed to have eyes in the back of her head.

'Leave it!'

Tessa obediently followed her out of the room. She approached a directional map of the floor, hanging on the wall in the corridor.

'Look at this floor map.'

Tessa looked.

'You have four overweight men with heavyweight water pistols and you think that's security?'

'They're well trained, Mrs Burlington.'

'Are they now? Then why are they all sitting together in a waiting area with no visibility of the approaches?'

Tessa opened her mouth to reply but Sara didn't wait for the words. Sara pointed at the map.

'What if an assassin came from that corridor? Or that one up there? What if the assassin came through this toilet, which can be accessed from that public ward? Or from the other side of the building over here through any one of these windows?'

Tessa could see the vulnerability of the rooms occupied by the Burlington brothers. She looked sheepishly at their mother.

'So Miss Hislop, let me give you the benefit of my experience.'

Sara roused the bodyguards from their comfortable chairs and instructed each of them where they should stand guard. The officers looked at Tessa, who told them to do as she said.

'Now, Miss Hislop, we have what was called a starfish defensive system in my day. If anyone intrudes on any one prong, all the other prongs will know at once provided these living corpses keep awake.'

Tessa could see the logic of the deployment.

'They have the area inside the star covered and can see all the approaches.'

Sara started walking away. As she did, she spoke back to Tessa over her shoulder, without turning to face her.

'If you sit where they were lounging, instead of whimpering on the phone, you can survey those under your command and kick their arses if they have a nap.'

Chapter 19 - Friday 21st June

Sara entered Hugh's room, and Tessa couldn't help thinking to herself how unfortunate it would be if a window cleaner tried to come in through the window just then. Roger emerged from Edward's room as Sara returned to see Hugh. Roger had a sympathetic expression on his face as he smiled in Tessa's direction.

'Don't take it too much to heart, Sara is more upset than I've seen her in years.'

Tessa was glad to hear the softer tones in Roger's voice. She could understand Sara's fury. Four near death experiences in less than four months: it was appalling. Roger seemed to read her mind. The issue of Edward's security wasn't rapidly descending into a farce; it had become one.

'She controls her anger at times like this by reverting to what she knows well, like protection. That way she can pretend nothing's getting to her.'

Tessa knew that her lack of experience had been exposed. Indeed she had been humiliated but then her jaw wasn't wired together. Roger offered her some advice.

'Were I in your position I'd check who the night nurses are meant to be.'

He smiled at her again, this time with a hint of sarcasm. Tessa was glad Mac was on his way to take control. The older Burlingtons were far too Machiavellian and experienced a team for her.

Sir Douglas Castle was thinking along the same lines as he brooded over the events of the day. Just when he thought he was safe from Sara, he was probably going to be turned into fish food again. Castle was sure she'd go to the press this time. That's what he would have contemplated in her position. Nothing could save him now. If push came to shove, he might be able to do a deal with the Prime Minister. Maybe put a gag on the newspapers by invoking a D-Notice under the pretext of the Official Secrets Act. He knew that if he made any pacts he would have to fall on a Burlington cutlass.

Castle sipped at his cup of green tea seeking shelter and comfort but found he had no appetite for the plate full of biscuits in front of him.

Mac arrived at the hospital twenty minutes after Tessa's interrupted phone call. He tried to ring back but the line was engaged. Fearing for the worst, he brought Chad and his team with him to try to minimise any fallout. The Burlingtons had the intelligence services by the short and curlies and Mac knew his balls were within their grasp too. If it had been one of his daughters who'd gone through what Edward had to go through he'd be incandescent with fury too.

Mac held two cards up his sleeve: one was called Chad; the other was a plan called divide and rule. Chad Cooper was introduced to the Burlingtons. Cooper shook Roger's hand and spoke directly to Sara.

'An honour to meet you, Mrs Burlington, Your reputation is legendary in our line of business.'

'You don't say.'

'You taught MI6 the meaning of security during the Second World War.'

Sara's sarcasm was tempered by the fact that somebody, at least, appreciated her in this comedy of errors. Chad broke away from her to bellow at his men.

'What are you standing there for? Establish a perimeter and tell those other idiots where to go downstairs. Jock, I want radio contact in forty five seconds. Hop to it!'

Four of the team went into Hugh's room. They were loaded with equipment and carrying an assortment of weapons. Sara shuddered.

'Where the hell are they going?'

'Don't worry, Mrs Burlington, they'll close the window quietly once they're on the roof.'

Mac took Roger to one side and explained that the team were all either SAS or MI5 and they'd been assigned to guard the Burlingtons, including him and Sara. They'd stay at the hospital until Edward and Hugh were well enough to travel, then they'd be escorted down to the Burlington home in Epsom. In the meantime, if he or Sara needed to go anywhere, they'd be discreetly accompanied wherever that might be.

Unarmed police officers were now stationed outside the house in Epsom, along with Edward's flat and the bookshop in Charing Cross Road. All the other patients on this section of the hospital's second floor had been moved so, if he and Sara were staying overnight, they could have rooms to themselves.

Meanwhile as planned Chad was showing Sara his security arrangements, by means of the directional floor map on the wall.

'As you can see we have set up two perimeters and everyone is now in radio contact with each other.'

Sara was impressed, even if she still thought he was locking the stable door after the wild horses, her boys, had gone and done a runner. Cooper emphasised to her that no one, including her and Roger, could enter or exit the inner perimeter without going through a security check point. The check points were on two floors as organised with the hospital's general manager. Only vetted staff like Carlton and Cordell would be allowed into the restricted area. Sara looked into Hugh's room.

'Did they close the window?'

'They even managed to draw the curtains.'

Tessa was with Mac and Roger by now. Sara and Chad joined them. Mac hesitated before speaking.

'Tessa and I need to speak privately to Edward.'

Sara went on the defensive.

'Why? What for? He won't be cautioned, will he?'

'No, nothing like that.'

'What then?'

Mac faltered again.

Chapter 19 - Friday 21st June

'We need to find out what happened and tell him about Suzie. Edward may know more than we do.'

'Does he need to know about her right now?'

'He's going to ask.'

'Alright, talk to him but do it gently. We don't want to hear any trouble from here or I am joining you.'

'Do you think Hugh will have any objections to signing the Official Secrets Act?' Roger was on the defensive this time.

'Why on earth would he need to do that?'

'Certain, er secrets may have to be explained to him.'

Roger and Sara looked at each other, and then nodded their approval in unison. Mac looked relieved. Little did he know what either of them was thinking?

'Look, why don't you two walk round the defences with Chad and kick arse if there's anything that's not to your liking?'

Cooper was only too happy to have the Burlingtons as company while he did the rounds making sure all was watertight in case it rained tonight. After all, in Chad's eyes Roger was an enigma worthy of emulation, perhaps the ultimate spy, the spy that never was.

Chad knew Roger had been on first name terms with more than a couple of British Prime Ministers since Churchill. It had been rumoured he was the hand that lifted the veil off the Profumo affair. John Profumo, the Secretary of State for War under Prime Minister Harold Macmillan, Super Mac, was discovered to be passing secrets to the KGB. The press had a field day because he passed information via prostitutes like Christine Keeler and Mandy Rice Davies. Profumo and Macmillan resigned, both of whom confided in Roger and yet respected him afterwards.

Rumours abounded at the time as to just what Burlington's role had been in it all but whatever secrets there were between Profumo, Macmillan and him remained untold. Had old Super Mac been too close to Keeler or was it a member of the royal family who had been lured by her sexuality? Many documents that might say so from Lord Denning's 1963 inquiry have unusually not been released and some speculate they were so sensitive they might not be released until 2064.

Even in 1964 Lord Denning apparently ruled that certain documents were too sensitive for Roger Hollis to see: he was only the head of MI5 at the time. Mind you, Hollis and Ward were allegedly friends with Blunt of the Cambridge Five and Lord Astor.

Let's face it, you would have to live in a lunatic asylum to believe there was ever any truth in the absurd allegations that Hollis was the fifth man, Super Mac the sixth and Prince Philip the seventh. Of course, that was the order they finished in one of the Astor's infamous donkey ride races at one of their merry go round parties, nothing to do with Cambridge University or Profumo! No wonder rumours and hearsay blurred the truth.

Ward was an amateur artist of some distinction apart from being an osteopath. He had even been commissioned to do portraits of Prince Philip, the Duke of Edinburgh, and many others in the royal family. Ward had connections, not just with royalty in the UK, but also with a rather famous dynasty in the USA. It was all so incestuous that those few including Lord Denning who unravelled it all never wanted it to enter the public domain. Super Mac, Roger Burlington and the CIA certainly didn't.

There were so many obvious unanswered questions. Some said Anthony Blunt anonymously bought all nine of Ward's royal portraits at auction in his capacity as curator of the royal art collection. Some said Burlington was a double agent and Blunt worked for him. Was the fifth man a triple agent, a Burlington?

Most did say Roger Burlington had been so clever that Stephen Ward, the handler of Keeler and the other working girls thought Roger controlled at the very least Ward's handler, Yevgeny or Eugene Ivanov, a naval intelligence officer from the KGB based in the USSR's London Embassy. It was rumoured, as if fact, that Burlington had Yevgeny Ivanov murder Ward and make it look like a suicide.

Other rumours abounded. Some were linked to the Astors and the royal family where allegedly Prince Philip, the Queen's husband, was involved in an affair with Keeler or another hooker. The FBI and CIA even linked Keeler to a high class hooker ring in Manhattan allegedly with clientele from the Kennedy family. Whatever went on was secret but even donkeys and horses featured in the lurid sexual undertones. All the rumours that spread like hot pants at the time had one fad in common though, Christine Keeler's pussy.

When the smoke cleared in the wake of recriminations and dismissals throughout MI5 and MI6, a relatively junior officer called Douglas Castle became a star. Overnight he shot to stardom becoming one of the deputy chiefs as Peter Stafford ripped through the ranks of MI5 as fast as an express train. Yet everyone knew where the real power lay and that was with this calm and evasive man, Roger Burlington. The undeniable fact that Roger Hollis et al were all stonewalled by Macmillan, Burlington and Profumo at the time spoke volumes about Roger Burlington's power in the sixties starting with the Cuban missile crisis. Whatever the truth Chad knew an enigmatic legend when he met one.

Chad was a raw recruit when the Philby scandal broke and specifically remembered Roger because he looked a bit like Philby. Anyhow, he doubted Roger would remember him so kept quiet. Still, he never understood why everyone failed to prevent Philby defecting from Beirut in a Russian freighter after supposedly signing a confession. Chad conjectured there were many more than five spies and the whole scandal was probably all down to MI5 and MI6 having better relations with the KGB at that time than with each other.

Chapter 19 - Friday 21st June

He proudly led the Burlingtons away as Mac and Tessa began to try to understand what was happening. Edward was conscious but everything was hazy inside his head. Mac and Tessa sat either side of his bed. Tessa held his hand. He'd been told that Hugh was recovering in the room next to his, just as Hugh had been told about him before being sedated.

'Mac and I need to cover some ground with you Edward.'

'Where's Suzie? Was she at the flat? They won't tell me Tessa.'

Mac and Tessa were silent for a moment.

'Where is she? What's going on?'

'Suzie's dead Edward.'

'No, no way. Did they kill her? The bastards, leave them to me.'

Tessa held onto his hand as he struggled to get out of the bed but he couldn't. Tears rolled down his face.

'Suzie's been dead for eleven days Edward.'

'What? That's a lie. How can she be?'

'She shot herself on the 10th June.'

'No, she wouldn't, she can't have. There's been some mistake. She wouldn't shoot herself. Hugh would've told me. This is a set up surely?'

This time, it took both Mac and Tessa to hold him in the bed.

'Hugh will confirm it when you're able to talk to him.'

'Hugh, where's Hugh?'

Brother Hugh was under sedation, in the next room. He couldn't hear his younger brother, even though he probably knew, despite his induced slumber, that his brother was in anguish and the torment would turn to fury.

Edward tried to regain his composure, tried to think. The last time he saw Suzie was that morning, when she went to the chemist, then called someone, an ambulance when she came back home. She wouldn't shoot herself, Hugh would have told him.

'Are you saying my brother lied to me?'

'Nobody has told you a lie. We didn't tell you in case it affected your recovery from the poisoning.'

'What do you mean by poisoning?'

Alan McKenzie told Edward everything that happened from the time he woke on that Saturday morning when he was rushed to hospital up to today. He deliberately left out any mention of Raj Gupta Khan.

Tessa added that, while they held no evidence, they suspected Suzie may have originally been up to no good. She may have been hired to get information from him or report on what he was doing. Then she fell in love and reneged on her arrangement with whoever hired her. Mac wasn't at all happy with Tessa being so forthright and even speculative. He reiterated that all the evidence available pointed towards suicide.

'It wasn't suicide.'

'Nobody can know for sure.'

'It wasn't suicide, I know her, and I am sure.'

'She thought you were about to die.'

'In point of fact she didn't sir.'

Mac shot Tessa a savagely hostile look. He'd already ordered her not to stray into that taboo zone. Edward looked him straight in the eye.

'So, whoever hired her to betray me obviously killed her.'

'We can't say that.'

'I can say that damn you and damn everyone. I can say what I bloody well want to.'

Mac ignored hospital protocol and lit up two cigarettes. He handed one to Edward. This was more difficult than he thought it might be.

'Special Branch isn't concerned.'

'Well, I'm fucking concerned!'

Mac was by now on his feet again and walked round the room. He decided to let Tessa handle the youngest Burlington for a while. Tessa squeezed Edward's hand. As if in response, another tear rolled down his cheek.

'Listen Edward, we can talk about Suzie when you're better. Right now, we need to know what happened at the flat.'

Edward took a deep drag on the cigarette, held the soothing smoke inside him for as long as he could, and then exhaled heavily. Mac returned to the bed, this time on the same side as Tessa. He stood behind her as he spoke.

'As Mr Cordell's explained to you already, Hugh can't talk yet, so we'd like you to tell us what happened when you arrived at your flat.'

'I went there to see Suzie.'

Mac didn't push it. He waited until Edward was ready.

'They were ransacking the flat. Two of them stopped us outside my front door. Then Danny O'Leary came out. Hugh recognised him first from Sam White's clubs, years ago. That's when it all started.'

Edward went on to outline everything he could remember. How the power was off, running up the stairs, the northern scumbags, how two of them fell through the banisters and how they gassed Hugh.

'Hang on, back up a second. Did you say two of them died?'

'Fell to the ground floor, didn't you see the bodies? They were going to throw Hugh after them, if I didn't give them Burton's address book.'

Mac nearly swallowed the butt of his second cigarette. He turned and took a quick hit from his hip flask. Then he turned back to look at Edward.

'Burton's address book?'

'Yes, but that had already gone.'

Mac bent down and whispered into Tessa's ear. She could smell the whisky.

Chapter 19 - Friday 21st June

'Suzie?'

He returned his attention to Edward.

'Are you saying a professional raid on your flat was organised to retrieve an address book that belonged to Cyrus Burton?'

'A copy of it ... I'd forgotten about the address book until they asked for it.'

'Why didn't you tell us about it?'

'I did. I told Tessa.'

'Yes you did. You gave me the contact lists with the manifests.'

'That is right but I don't think I gave you the copy of the address book. It was in the secret compartment in my briefcase. I forgot to open it to give you the papers but that wasn't my fault either. It didn't matter at the time because the copies were the same as the contact lists, well almost the same as I recall.'

Mac wanted to punch someone, even himself if he could, but he held his temper in check as Tessa explained to Mac what had transpired. It happened on the night Edward had almost been caught by Black Rod. No one was to blame. She had mistakenly thought the contact lists were what Edward called the address book. Edward hadn't remembered he had it or wasn't bothered about it as it appeared virtually identical to what he'd given her.

'That's right and I nearly fell out with Raj over it because he'd introduced me to the pigs through one of his diplomatic pals. You remember, Mac. When I told you Burton wanted me to supply him with young girls and boys and I'd told him to fuck off, that I was not returning. It must have been in February. You said I must play along with it and see it through to the end.

Well because Raj handled the intros I gave him stick for not warning me what perverts they all were. I told him I had a long list at home if he wanted to see it. Raj apologised. He said if they were as perverted as I'd said they were he'd have no more to do with any of them. It didn't upset our friendship though. Raj is a good guy anyway.'

'So Raj knew you had the address book or a list of the syndicate's contacts then?'

'That's what I have just said isn't it? So what? Raj never mentioned it again.'

Mac and Tessa kept asking questions but more and more gently and subtly, noting details about this and that. Mac concluded this was a classic misunderstanding. "Send reinforcements we're going to advance" became "send three and fourpence we're going to a dance"!

As for Khan being aware of the address book God could only guess what the ramifications of that might be? Khan and Burton might be linked in some way and that went right to the heart of Operation Standpipe and when Raj Khan was first recruited. The subtle interrogation was helping clear the fog from Edward's mind and he was putting two and three together and coming up with ten as was his habit.

'Tessa, can I ask you a question?'

'Of course.'

'When was the last time you saw Suzie?'

'On the morning of Monday 10th June.'

'What was she doing?'

Tessa explained how she'd persuaded Suzie to go back to the flat to freshen up, having been at the hospital since Saturday.

'I asked her to pack some stuff for you. We didn't agree on a time she'd come back but later I was concerned and went to find her.'

'Who found the body?'

'I did, that evening. I was concerned because she hadn't come back to the hospital.'

'Was there a bag?'

'Yes.'

'Was it packed?'

Tessa lowered her head and looked at the floor. Edward didn't need to be told anything else.

Mac was still going on about the raid.

'So, we can assume whoever raided the flat worked for Burton. They didn't get what they were after because someone was there ahead of them.'

Mac paused, as if he was considering what to say next. He went back round to the other side of the bed and sat down again. Mac realised because Edward still held Raj Gupta Khan in high regard he could put himself at risk again by asking Khan too many questions. What's more, with no Suzie about Edward was bound to contact him sooner than later.

'I have to remind you, Edward, that you've signed the Official Secrets Act.'

'I know.'

Edward remembered he had but then he had only signed it in a pseudonym he had been awarded at the time. He'd even spelt that name wrong accidentally on purpose when putting biro to paper.

'Ok. We've found out that Raj has some murky associates in Pakistan and both the British and US governments are interested in what he and they were doing. So, we're watching good guy Mr Raj Gupta Khan closely but we're prepared to give him some rope. You may not like that now but justice will eventually be meted out and Chad and I'll make sure it's severe. Above all else you're not to contact him. This is how it'll work from now until Nassau.'

Mac explained what security arrangements would be in place until Edward left for Nassau but Edward's mind was elsewhere. He was thinking about Raj being given more rope. Edward knew they would let him get away with murder, for the time being anyway, but he said nothing. He'd almost forgotten about the Bahamas though. Mac was more concerned that Cyrus Burton had linked up with the remnants of the north eastern corruption case that young Burlington and to an extent he had infiltrated.

Chapter 19 - Friday 21st June

Edward had already sussed that one out at the flat hours ago. It made Nassau all the more appealing.

They chatted on for half an hour or so in hushed tones about deception, duplicity and death until Mr Cordell came into the room with a nurse. The time came for Edward's medication. Any further conversation would have to wait for tomorrow.

The nurse wore a bandage round her right wrist. Sara and Chad had agreed on one extra method of making doubly sure only vetted nurses were allowed through the perimeter. With Burton back with known links to Khan and the rotten rozzers no one could be assumed to be who they appeared to be. On the way out, Mac reminded Tessa to get Hugh to sign the Official Secrets Act before they interviewed him.

Tessa was relieved that Raj Khan's possible involvement was out in the open. Although she'd discussed it with Hugh carefully she still knew she shouldn't have. While Mac revealed some secret truths to Edward, he hadn't told him the truth as he said he would.

Edward still didn't know Khan worked for MI6, let alone that he was a double agent. Also he still assumed Mac and Tessa were Special Branch, or police, or something like that. He'd guessed there was more to them than met the eye some months ago but hadn't cared that much as long as Burton's empire was crushed.

What they all agreed on was Mr Khan was bad news for now; guilty until proven innocent. Somehow he was probably allied with Burton and Burton was aligned with bent coppers from up north who'd escaped the purge of corruption in the late sixties.

As for Suzie, the pain of her death cut deep into Edward's heart, but it would help him to recover quicker. He had a new incentive. To make sure no matter what it took that the fat deceitful bastard Khan got what he merited. He'd taken him for almost as close a friend as Sam White. He and everyone who knew him had been so deceived. Khan was a polished operator having fooled all and sundry. He deserved to suffer a fate no less gory than Sam and Suzie had together.

That night he jotted down a few notes which would later be transposed into his 1974 diary. For once, rays of sunlight at the end of Edward's tunnel were flashing on the horizon. His diary was later recovered from his flat to be dutifully updated. Mac's diary or note book as he preferred to call it was choc a bloc that evening. The slow motion train wreck was grinding to a halt and an express train was speeding along in the right direction with its final destination in sight, Heathrow Airport. Both sets of diarised notes were now focused on a plane to Nassau.

Chapter 20
Friday 21ˢᵗ to Sunday 30ᵗʰ June

Albany Street Regents Park, London England
The meeting at the Dorset suite in the White House Hotel in Marylebone Road was more turbulent than Smith expected and started three hours later than scheduled. His contingency plans had been stretched to breaking point.

Later that day the Evening Standard contained a report that two respectable policemen visiting London for a trip to the theatre died in a tragic accident. They leant on a railing that was never meant to take their combined weight of thirty five stone. Hence they plunged forty feet to their deaths in a remote derelict area near Moorgate Station. The Standard went on to report that three of their colleagues who witnessed the accident were unhurt and foul play was not suspected.

The widows of the dead officers had been informed and would receive generous pensions. However, the dead men's families did not get any of Smith's cash they had been paid or were due. It had either been removed from their hotel rooms or withheld.

Smith studied the video recording supplied by his cameraman, Kevin. He knew full well that Kevin had an extensive knowledge of editing in the horror movie genre; that's why he'd picked him. Kevin could make ordinary men commuting to work look like zombies with his special effects. Anyone looking at the state of Edward Burlington in the video would have concluded by the end of it that he was lifeless.

Smith wasn't that easily fooled but it would suffice for Burton. He had the flat watched as soon as the northern scum left. All the subsequent morass of activity had been duly reported to him. Smith was astonished at the level of attention afforded to Burlington. The young man must have been a high grade asset. By now Smith even knew Burlington and his brother were in Whittington Hospital, how many guards were on duty and the room numbers they were guarding.

No more risks were going to be taken by him knowing all that. The film would have to make do as it now stood. Burton had more than his money's worth considering two policemen died. That would do and he'd make sure Burton was irrevocably fucked up if he welshed on this deal. The job he'd organised had been cheap at the price for anyone with that high level of protection.

Meanwhile the three remaining police officers were happy with their bonuses, especially as they knew they'd failed to retrieve the address book. That JJ had been killed in such a fashion seemed to be more important to his client than the retrieval of the document. So, everybody was happy apart from the dead men. Smith was annoyed when their colleagues tried to claim entitlement to the dead men's share of the contract fee and bonus. He made the point that this wasn't a tontine. Also it had cost him a small fortune to cover up what happened to the two who died so tragically.

Beachy Head, East Sussex England

On Saturday 22nd June Smith delivered the video personally to Jordan at the pre-arranged rendezvous. Beachy Head was a notorious place for suicides in southern England and Smith was taking a huge personal risk going there alone without the address book. If his broken body was found at the bottom of the cliffs, nobody would give it a second thought. He knew this before he went there and was relieved to find the Reaper's representative waiting for him and not the Reaper himself.

If necessary, Smith was fully prepared to murder Burton at the rendezvous but hadn't wanted to kill him just yet if at all possible.

He reported to Jordan that he was nearly one hundred percent certain that the document wasn't in JJ's flat. Jordan didn't seem too disappointed, especially when Smith gave him the video of JJ's death. Jordan assured Smith his trust account in the Marshall Islands would be duly credited with £50,000 on Monday morning.

A successful operation all round ignoring the scum who'd died. Jordan also assured him he'd be used again and paid handsomely. Smith had longer term plans in mind but kept those secret. His trust account was topped up as promised. Smith was satisfied that the risks he'd taken in getting closer to these perverts and their empire were justified. They considered themselves to be predators and used him to bait their traps. Smith was the ultimate predator and was biding his time. Normally his victims never saw him but the Reaper was a challenge that required tactics out of the ordinary.

He was manoeuvring Cyrus Burton to where he wanted him. Smith already held a ton of information on him, after a subversive deal in 1972 when Burton was cornered and captured importing cocaine by Smith's men from Customs. Smith kept a low profile while dealing with Burton then but made the name Smith and his voice known to the Reaper. The Reaper had only seen Smith in disguise and would never recognise him again. In some ways Burton had modelled himself on Smith after the great Harley Street escape.

Anyway, there was nothing abnormal in Smith's life for the Reaper to take advantage of, so he was in a strong position even if Burton thought differently. Well, abnormal didn't exclude bent Customs officials: after all, there were thousands of them around the world.

So that was how Smith planned to keep things ticking along, by being the Reaper's odd job man until he was in a position to implode Burton's empire. This meeting was only a small step in that direction. He'd finally met Jordan and gained his trust. Patience was peculiarly a virtue in gangland Britain.

For Smith it had been an important phase of his journey. If he wanted he could later use the fact that Burlington was still alive to destroy Burton's trust of Jordan or to coerce Jordan into killing Burton for fear of the Reaper misinterpreting that Jordan had intentionally misled him. Smith liked to think most criminals were amateurs compared with him. He was right.

The Downs Epsom, Surrey England

As soon as the Burlington brothers recovered enough, Chad Cooper's team escorted them to their parent's house in Surrey on Thursday 27th June. Cooper was in charge of security at their home and he worked out detailed rotas with Sara. There was a team of four during the day and six at night.

When Chad wasn't around, Sara was in charge. She liked this, it took her back to the old days and she and Chad had clicked from the first mention of the word security. In reality, she wasn't in charge at all because, if anything happened, she had to contact a senior officer who would then have taken control. Even so it kept her contented and Chad learned a few old tricks from her that were new to him.

Most of the team took up positions outside, either visibly patrolling the grounds, or out of sight in the building surrounding the main house. If Edward or Hugh went anywhere, they were accompanied by two armed bodyguards and a driver. All four of the Burlingtons wore medallions around there necks which were constantly tracked via GCHQ.

Once Edward left for Nassau, this high security would be taken down quite a few notches. Hugh's flat had been fitted with new cameras and alarms linked to GCHQ and Scotland Yard. The shop and the family home were already wired up with alarms. Hugh signed the Official Secrets Act for Tessa. It had been farcical for Hugh albeit a seriously formal and regimented event for Tessa. After that their conversations became more intimate, as did their relationship. Hugh managed to keep one secret from her which nearly slipped out when he commented on the length of the Official Secrets Act. He had signed it before but in a different language.

Private family tête-à-têtes were also more open. Both Edward and Hugh were given confirmation of matters about their parents that they'd only guessed at or suspected previously. Some topics still remained off limits such as Roger's detention in Russia in 1963 and their mother's relationship with Douglas Castle in the war years.

Chapter 20 - Friday 21ˢᵗ to Sunday 30ᵗʰ June

Sir Peter Stafford's precise roles across a myriad of fronts were never mentioned either and Roger's deep sunk secrets stayed unfathomed.

The brothers also had a regimented formal meeting with Miss Tessa Hislop. She admitted that Alan McKenzie was an acting deputy chief of MI5, on secondment from MI6. She explained that she was similarly seconded and reported directly to Mac. To Tessa's surprise neither of them batted an eyebrow or eyelid at her special announcement. The only part of her proclamation that surprised them was that she made such a meal of her announcement. After all, they were both Burlingtons having been brought up in their family's cloak and dagger world.

That duplicitous tricky world manifested itself in KGB reports and files secured in Lubyanka Square Moscow. That deceitful world was evident in the fact that Roger spoke fluent Russian and why his trips to Russia weren't recorded on his old passports. For those unlucky enough to see, it was also visible in his carvings on the wall of a Russian prison cell. It manifested itself in the deep scars within Sara which revealed themselves to her in recurring nightmares.

Sara would fall into a restless sleep. She would find herself in 1944 in pre D-Day France with a group of MI6 agents and SOE novices dropped behind enemy lines. Their mission is to make contact with a female French resistance fighter codenamed Zola, disrupt German communications and intercept SS couriers.

It's dark and foggy in the dream and the group are moving cautiously through a wooded area in the outskirts of Maisons-Laffitte, a small town not far from Paris. They're using subdued torchlight to pick their way through the blackness, to a prearranged rendezvous point. They can see the pinpoints of light from the town in the distance. The group consists of six SOE and secret service assets. It had been decided to use assets not SOE or MI6 officers. The operation commander, Douglas Castle who was noticeable by his absence, wasn't willing to risk any regular officers getting captured by the Gestapo.

They move in single file, with Sara leading except she's not Sara Burlington in the dream, she's Isobel Wright, and she's twenty one years old. The rest of the group are also young, some only eighteen or nineteen. They've had a short course of six weeks' training. Great Britain's SOE has lost so many assets they're throwing inexperienced people into the firing line like a child throws pebbles into a pool.

The equipment they carry is light, sten guns and backpacks containing radio transmitters and interceptors. There's no moon, no light, except for that coming faintly from the dimmed torches and the faraway town. No words are spoken and communication is by silent signalling. They're like ghosts, moving through a surreal graveyard heading home towards their local crematorium.

Their progress is tedious and it seems as if they're moving in slow motion. The trek is an exhausting business of meticulous attention to detail. Great care is called for as the Germans use schrapnellmines, nicknamed silent soldiers, and trip wires attached to flares. The slightest carelessness could lead to disaster. Now the lights of the town are coming gradually closer as their contact in the resistance should be. Isobel is afraid but also excited. It's her first mission and she wants it to be a success to prove to her older sister Sara that she can be a good spy. Sara objected to her going on this mission but Castle insisted saying there was no real danger.

As if by lightning the area of woodland is lit up like the Ritz. Bright searchlights penetrate the trees and the group stand motionless, transfixed, like rabbits caught in the twin headlights of a jeep. They can't see beyond the searchlight beams, they can't identify who's behind them. Some of them un-sling their sten guns and hold them at the ready. A harsh voice comes crashing out of a megaphone.

'Lassen sie ihre waffen fallen.'

Its authoritarianism is to no avail. The British agents begin shooting at the searchlights, trying to blast away their glare. Isobel shouts an order.

'Run!'

High velocity bullets are zipping through the fog, whizzing and whining and ripping splinters out of the trees. Isobel rushes into the surrounding woodland in a crouched position, the rest of the group follow her. Beforehand they were carefully checking for booby traps and mines. Now they run for their lives, covering the ground at great speed, crashing into branches and getting entangled in clinging undergrowth.

They use a sequence of withdrawal-in-contact, with two of them laying down blasts of fire then leapfrogging in fire-and-manoeuvre tactics. It's as if in training but for real. They're soon surrounded. Isobel can hear the screaming and cries of pain of her comrades as they are mown down in the bedlam of bullets. She keeps on running and dodging through the trees but she's going in circles and soon she can run no longer. Isobel sinks to the ground, exhausted, breathing heavily and spitting saliva. When she looks up, she sees a jackboot in front of her face.

After the war, Sara visited several of the Gestapo kitchens in Paris, where captured resistance fighters and enemy spies were taken to be interrogated. The body of her sister, Isobel, was exhumed and identified once Sara tracked down her whereabouts.

What was left of her naked body displayed evidence of water damage to the lungs, the wrist bones had been dislocated and had puncture marks, as if hung up with a barbaric ligature. Several other bones were broken, including vertebrae which seemed to have been violently struck with a spiked ball. The throat had obviously been severed. The bones to the neck suggested a hanging with piano wire, a favoured mode of execution for the Nazis.

Edward was so lucky to have missed that war. Now he was supposedly leaving the duplicitous world of espionage behind for the sea and sunshine of the Caribbean. He was to fly to the Bahamas from Heathrow on Sunday 30th June. A man called Rupert Fanshaw, who worked at the British Commonwealth Office in Nassau, would contact him within twenty four hours of his arrival. Fanshaw could be trusted as much as

Mac or Tessa; he was a safe old hand who had been in MI6 for thirty years. Edward smiled wryly to himself when he was told that.

He'd had enough of being exploited. If this Fanshaw thought he could push Edward around or manipulate him as others had he was in for a rude awakening. From now on he was to choose his own destiny, if he could. The only problem was he had no real idea of the depth of the manipulation he had succumbed to so far since leaving Pentonville Prison behind him.

Sir Peter hadn't enough time to have Edward's work permit arranged by then or so he claimed. His excuse was that given everything that had gone on, it had only just become apparent that Edward would be fit and ready to go. As Edward said on the phone to him, surely they should have applied for it before he had been poisoned? Were they too in on his attempted murder? Peter laughed it off, on the phone anyway, but he made a note that this level of incompetence was unacceptable and was not to happen again.

All Edward thought was so what? The permit would now probably take four weeks or so to come through and as Peter put it he could have a well deserved break at Porter Williams' expense while he was waiting. He was scheduled to stay at the Nassau Beach Hotel, off West Bay Street, about three miles outside town, in the posh end of New Providence Island. Being a luxurious upper crust hotel it boasted several bars, a discothèque and a casino. Sir Peter reckoned Edward should be right at home there, in the unlikely event of him deciding to stay in for a night or two.

Edward had almost completely recovered from the fight at the flat, but as for the botulism poisoning, he still had slight dystonia in his neck. That made it difficult for him to look anyone in the eye without tilting his head slightly. He was no longer on any powerful medication, although his rib cage still hurt when he bent down or stretched. Hugh was going back to work on Monday, despite experiencing difficulty speaking normally and some of his missing teeth were yet to be replaced. His jaw was healing well and there would be no permanent visible scars on his face.

Jamaica Road Bermondsey, London England

Edward wanted to visit Suzie's grave, a one square foot bland granite plaque, before leaving the country. In contrast to her beautiful femininity and his love for her it was as if there was no marker, nothing to show that she'd ever lived or died. A statue in Trafalgar Square would have made no difference. They might as well have scattered her ashes over London Bridge when the tide was going out. Even so he still wanted to go, to find some essence of her somewhere. He knew the disparity between her tombstone and his memories of her would be stark and cold.

Even the flat where his memories of Suzie lingered had been destroyed by the bastards who raided and trashed it. His pad was being completely gutted for renovation so there was nothing of her left there. There might be some invisible token in the calm of the graveyard where her ashes lay. Maybe a whisper in the wind, the scent of her perfume, just a small sign to remind him of her being, her humanity and her love.

Hugh went with him. They both knew it was to be their last full day together for some time. They had a ton to say to each other but Hugh could only just open his mouth properly and talking was still painful. The bodyguards kept a discreet distance while the brothers walked together through the copper birch and lilac trees.

Edward lit a cigarette. Suzie wasn't here; her spirit and she had gone.

'Can you do something for me while I'm in the Bahamas?'

Hugh nodded.

'Let me know anything you hear about Khan?'

'Yeah but, but ...'

'Tessa will tell you if you ask nicely, now you've signed the Act.'

'Er yeah.'

'If they don't get him before Xmas we will.'

'Yeah.'

They knew what each other meant despite Hugh hardly being able to talk. Edward stared blankly at Suzie's grave in disbelief. He had so many questions speeding haphazardly through his mind like trains rushing through a busy junction but he feared he knew the answers to most of them.

Hugh turned and walked quickly towards the car to leave them alone together for the last time. Edward followed five long minutes later. Chad's men kept a respectful distance. No one spoke during the journey back to Epsom. Hugh's whole mouth was still aching and throbbing despite taking pain killers as fast as he would normally munch through a packet of crisps in the pub. Each brother quietly speculated just how much he now knew about his other brother.

Westminster Bridge Road Lambeth, London England

MI6 made little immediate progress on researching the two Geordie rozzers who'd died raiding the flat. They had been officially reported as having an unfortunate accident on a pleasure trip to London. In the hope that one day Danny O'Leary and Anthony Beaches might lead MI5 to Cyrus Burton the case was taken out of Scotland Yard's hands and a special team assigned to it.

Khan was fed some duff information, just to see if it made its way back to the ISI. The trail led first to the Pakistani Military Attaché in London, and then to his brother, now in Islamabad. Khan still thought he was the rising star in the east and the west but he was soon to explode like a supernova.

In the meantime, Roger spent an increasing amount of time in Century House going through their archives. Sara and he continued to play a dangerous political game for a variety of personal reasons, not least of which was ensuring the ongoing security of their youngest son. To win that game, two specific changes in the top echelons of the intelligence services would be needed.

Their manipulative plans were audacious but achievable. Castle was no longer a safe chauffeur for Edward, if he had ever been. He had to be replaced in a way that made it impracticable for him to stay in his job, impossible to use his Machiavellian skills to save his hide.

The Burlingtons only had one choice for his logical replacement and persuading him to take over from Castle might prove difficult, if it wasn't handled diplomatically and sensitively. The preparations were imperfect but final solutions were rarely perfection personified and often improvised. No press headlines or enquiries or special committees were called for, just a simple and discreet coup d'état, a quiet act of hara-kiri.

Heathrow Airport Hillingdon, London England

Edward sat with his back to a wall in the British Airways lounge. The day was Sunday 30th June. He lit up his third cigarette as he reflected on the events of the past few weeks. Edward had niggling doubts about this move to the Bahamas while Suzie was alive but now he was glad to be getting out of England for a while. Few people knew where he was going and that suited him.

Sir Peter let it be known to everyone in the London office that Edward had suffered an unusually severe bout of food poisoning and was on indefinite sick leave. The audits Edward was involved with had no Caribbean ties. He wasn't due to start work there for a month. So his move would be of little interest to anyone in the rapidly growing Porter Williams international empire until August at the earliest.

Edward, now tired and lonely, hoped he'd be able to sleep on the plane. His flight was called and he stood up and headed for Gate 25. He'd been booked into second class on Peter's recommendation based on his experience of long haul flights. His seat was in the middle and the seats either side of him had also been booked by Porter Williams, and then cancelled a few hours before takeoff. You could pull out the arm rests when flying second class and lie down horizontally to get some sleep. Ironically it wasn't possible in first or business class. After a few Carlsberg cans, Edward's eyes closed and he was back in prep school with Hugh.

As prep schools went, Norton House wasn't the worst but as pupils went, Edward was. He was constantly in trouble for one misdemeanour or another and had to write thousands of punishment lines during his time there. Innocence personified, the first one hundred lines he had been given, he wrote out "I must not be naughty" and with Hugh's help underlined it a hundred times using a pencil and ruler. Well, he had been told to do a hundred lines. He was forced to redo them the way they should have been explained to him.

His misbehaviour included swearing in the Latin class: he had no idea that "fucko, fuckis, fuckit" should have been pronounced "fui, fuis, fuit" or whatever. As for breaking a master's bicycle pump over another pupil's head that was self defence and flicking spoonfuls of jam onto the ceiling wasn't his idea. Why? You waited with glee for them to drip down on the masters' heads and then they would think it to be their own blood! Hugh taught him that one.

Some of his real naughtiness was serious enough to warrant the threat of expulsion. A nearby school was surrounded in a military style operation he led with such a ferocious snowball attack that the school went into lockdown mode. He organised a systematic assault on a visiting soccer team. Their sole escape route was via the public park which was only accessible from a steamed up frosted window. The trouble was they were escaping from the visitors' changing rooms after all their clothes and towels had gone missing.

Even at home, young Edward was the bane of his mother's life. She tried her best to instil discipline into both boys during their father's frequent absences but it only lasted as long as she was in earshot. Then they would revert to their wild ways even before Edward started school. Like jumping out of upstairs windows using sheets as parachutes, or dodging recklessly between traffic on a dual carriageway in rush hour pretending to be Hugh's favourite lollipop woman.

The only person who had any real control over them was their grandfather, Frederick Burlington. The boys' granddad used to show them his service revolver and his collection of kukri knives. He taught them the survival techniques he'd learned over the years. How to follow without being seen; how to set an ambush; how to live off the land and use camouflage to make themselves disappear.

They respected the grand man and absorbed everything he taught them. Frederick never needed to repeat his instructions, never needed to admonish the boys. They re-enacted the lessons they learnt from him in the scrubland surrounding the graveyard near Billingham Bottoms. When dusk fell was the best time to strike. That is when they practised perfecting their ambush tactics on their long suffering unsuspecting neighbours. Who needed training by MI6 after all that!

Edward's drowsy reminiscences were disturbed by a flight announcement advising passengers to fasten their seatbelts in anticipation of a period of turbulence. The "no smoking" sign didn't turn on so he sat up, lit a cigarette and opened another can of lager. It had been stored away in the gap where his left arm rest had been. Edward's watch showed just less than two hours to landing.

He could touch the excitement preventing him from sleeping just as Christopher Columbus must have on seeing the coastline. Edward was nearing a fresh beginning. In hindsight the tunnels he struggled through to reach the horizon of opportunity appeared less daunting than they had been.

Chapter 20 - Friday 21st to Sunday 30th June

What lay ahead were known unknowns and unknown unknowns. Edward had not the benefit of hindsight as to what was about to ensue but he was no longer manacled by manipulation or so he thought to prevent him from dealing with it. His diary entry for the day was short and to the point: he referred to the British Airways trip as his "freedom flight".

Chapter 21
Sunday 30th June to Monday 1st July

West Bay Street Nassau, New Providence Island Bahamas

The plane landed at Nassau mid-afternoon local time to the sound of clapping and shouting by overly zealous passengers. A few were returning home, others starting a holiday. The religious clappers were just glad to have arrived safely and presumed that their prayers, rather than the skill of the pilot, had delivered them there.

The heat was stifling, with not a cloud in the sky, as Edward crossed the tarmac towards immigration. When he made it through to arrivals, he saw an overly suntanned expat waving a sign with his name on it. He walked across to the man who looked a good few years older than Edward.

'I'm Edward Burlington.'

'Pleased to meet you Edward. I'm Jonty Granville-Clifton. Let me take your suitcase.'

Granville-Clifton was a chirpy character who talked all the way to the hotel but Edward couldn't remember a single word. Maybe he had jet lag or maybe he was absorbing so much fresh data. American cars he'd not seen before, unusual sign posts, palm trees and more black people than he'd seen in his entire life. Near white beaches set to the backdrop of an azure ocean and then the ultimate. Gorgeous local women always smiling were sashaying about with hips swaying as they made their way down the narrow pathways alongside the beach. His first impressions were distinctly positive and first impressions count.

There was a small reception committee of junior accountants and auditors in the bar to welcome him. Much to Edward's chagrin they were all white British males in their mid to late twenties. He hadn't flown all this way to meet Brits. As the day was a Sunday, none of the partners turned up to say hello. The Porter Williams expats were all as suntanned as Jonty. They all waffled with equal alacrity about scuba diving, snorkelling and close encounters with killer sharks. They also offered advice on where and when to play tennis, drink cocktails and meet eligible white ladies. It seemed as if they were on a different planet.

Edward asked if they had a soccer team which was treated more as a joke than a serious question. Soccer in this heat, only for the locals, next question please. They

Chapter 21 – Sunday 30th June to Monday 1st July

were all pleasant enough or seemed so. He could tell they weren't racists like Reynolds and most of his MAMI team but they saw themselves as somewhat apart, aloof from the locals. Soon he feigned jetlag and they left as one leaving him to retire to his room.

After unpacking his suitcase, he walked barefoot along the beach for a few hundred yards. A salubrious gated residential plot signposted as Governor's Beach caught his eye. Another sign with a picture of a friendly looking guard dog told him to keep out. He ventured in and saw that the entrance way leading from West Bay Street into the private road was patrolled by police coming out of a nearby pillbox. Edward reckoned an apartment there would suit him well but it was probably out of his price range.

He went back to the hotel and sat in the bar with his back to the wall and ordered two draught beers as they called them. They took so long to be served that he ordered another two when he finished the first. They tasted good. Edward stayed close to the hotel that night.

Before his last bout at the bar he called home and spoke to his parents and Hugh; he'd arrived without incident, had met Porter Williams' finest and was settling in nicely. Everywhere he turned there were stunning attractive coloured girls of every shade and hue under the sun. Some even looked Algerian but he knew they weren't.

A coach load of noisy Canadian tourists entered the bar to intrude on his solitude, so he went to bed. The bedroom was close and clammy despite the cooling fans and the occasional breeze coming off the ocean through the open window. His ribs ached from sleeping on the airplane seats but it wasn't long before the soft little paws of sleep came a creeping.

Bay Street Nassau, New Providence Island Bahamas

Early in the morning of Monday 1st July Graham Sidney-Smith, the senior partner of Porter Williams in the Bahamas was reading Edward's Curriculum Vitae. The CV was accompanied by a fax from Sir Peter Stafford. Sir Peter instructed that Edward rest and shouldn't start work until August, no matter when his work permit was processed. There could be no doubt that Sir Peter held Edward in high regard and Sidney-Smith was ordered to keep in personal contact if any issues arose. Sir Peter Stafford's home telephone and fax numbers were included.

It was also clear from his CV that Burlington was a gifted fellow. It showed he recorded the highest marks in many of his exams, from his eleven plus which he sat when he was ten right through to qualifying as a Chartered Accountant. Not only had he won the top scholarship at boarding school but also a scholarship offer to Oxford University. He had turned that down for personal reasons. Sidney-Smith queried what that meant and made a mental note to find out.

In the British Commonwealth Office, about two hundred yards from Porter Williams, Rupert Fanshaw was also studying Edward's CV. Rupert was not only an ex-army captain but even looked like Bulldog Drummond with his swept back dyed and lubricated black hair and whispery moustache which he constantly stroked or twiddled with. However, the CV he was peering at and turning pages back and forth as he cross referenced incidents in his mind was totally different to the one Sidney-Smith was reading and was well over thirty pages long.

Fanshaw ran MI6 in the Caribbean and he was reading about Edward's role as an asset to the British government to date and how it all started. There was a covering note written by none other than Sir Douglas Castle, stating that any use of this asset by MI6 would require his personal approval. There could be no clearer "keep your hands off" message than that.

Fanshaw had been instructed to meet with Edward, keep a watchful ear and listening eye out on whatever he was up to and to introduce him socially to those that mattered but preferably not any Americans. The list of those not to introduce him to was long: not the CIA, not the FBI, not the NSA, not the NIS or anybody with known links to any of their dozens of covert ops regimes. After studying the paperwork for some time, Fanshaw, the stalwart Bulldog Drummond of the Bahamas, called Graham Sidney-Smith at Porter Williams. In the purest of pure Queen's English he barked out his requirements as if ordering a platoon of hapless recruits around on their inaugural parade ground practice.

'Graham, I understand you're meeting a new chap called Burlington who is coming in today?'

'You're up to date before your time Rupert. What can I do for you?'

'I know his father. Old boy network and all that malarkey, you know the drill. He asked me if I'd help the boy get his feet on the ground, show him where the parade grounds and minefields lay.'

'Anything in particular in mind?'

'Pindling is throwing a reception this evening at Government House and I thought, why not throw the lad in at the deep end, sink or swim and all that jazz. Collette will keep an eye on him too so he should be safe from putting his feet in any muddy patches, no embarrassments if you understand me.'

'I'll ask him and get back to you.'

To Graham it sounded as though Edward Burlington needed not only a life jacket but a few lifeguards too. Fanshaw was about to hang up until he heard Sidney-Smith clearing his throat rather pointedly at the other end of the line.

'Yes, Graham?'

'So where's my invitation?'

'You're far too commercial for this sort of political partying. Chin up though, there's always hope.'

Sidney-Smith threw the phone back onto its cradle. Why hadn't he ever been invited to one of these parties? The chief of MI6 in the Caribbean was taking one of

Chapter 21 - Sunday 30th June to Monday 1st July

his firm's staff, who he hadn't met, to a piss-up with the Prime Minister. Surely this fell into the category of an issue? Graham decided to inform Sir Peter, but only after he'd met Edward.

Meanwhile Rupert was already on his first shaken not stirred iceless gin and ginger of the day while planning his next tax free stock market coup based on insider knowledge. The knowledge or insider tip had just arrived in the form of a coded fax from Manhattan addressed to one of his staff who died in the sixties but was still on Her Majesty's Government's approved payroll just to confuse the CIA. He wondered if Pindling would be interested and then thought better of it. Tell him at the party: it would have more impact.

Graham was concerned by Rupert's plan to get Collette involved. The poor boy could die from sexual exhaustion before his damn work permit turned up. Her reputation sucked. She was only about thirty and everyone knew why she and the bulldog had a twenty plus year age gap between them: money and boatloads of the stuff apparently.

She was one of the few in Nassau who could truthfully refer to Harrods as her local and say she was a regular shopper there. As for her sexual prowess, of the dozens she seduced few could fail to forget that even the most modern vacuum cleaners were no match for what she could get out of them. Indeed on one occasion an ambulance was called by none other than Rupert himself to assist an unfit aged warrior whose pace maker had packed up when climaxing. The ambulance arrived late and the man died. Hearsay had it that Rupert the bulldog got his rocks off as a secret voyeur.

So these three puritans were meant to be the bedrock of stability chosen by the great and good to safeguard young Burlington. At least Sir Peter's choice, Graham Sidney-Smith went to church every now and again in between exercising on the tennis courts. That was more than could be said of Rupert or in specie Collette unless perchance she was attending an expatriate wedding and vying for a photo shoot of a threesome with the newlyweds naked on a four poster bed before they left for their honeymoon. Even weddings and funerals ran as late as the emergency services after a 919 call in the Bahamas.

In fact half an hour late was punctual in Nassau business circles but Edward turned up at Porter Williams on time. The office was on Bay Street where most places that counted were in downtown Nassau and only a few hundred yards from the old British Colonial Hotel, one of Nassau's landmark luxury hotels for decades. Jonty introduced him to Graham and they shook hands quite formally.

'Pleased to meet you Edward.'

'Likewise Graham.'

'We're a small office, compared to London, and you won't be starting until 1st August but I'll introduce you to everyone now while we have the opportunity.'

Graham Sidney-Smith was in his late forties and already flaunted a mop of silvery hair, usually immaculately combed. He was wearing a light blue silk suit that looked like it had been tailored to match his mane and it shone in the sunlight that streamed through the window. Graham was of upper class British stock, a heavy smoker too, who moved to Nassau in the early sixties to escape high taxes and the financial consequences of a messy divorce.

He was almost as tall as Edward but with just a sign or two of tubbiness wallowing in on the tide of life. He kept himself fit swimming before lunch time albeit mostly somewhat pointlessly as the exercise was usually pursued by long liquid lunches. As a single man, he used his dapper good looks and suave mannerisms to the full. There were few lady members of the Bahamian Lawn Tennis Club he hadn't served after dark on the courts.

In some ways, he was an older and wiser version of Edward and, as they chatted, they both found that affinity. Graham was also like Sir Peter Stafford in many respects: the messy divorce, not remarrying and so on except he was as straight and randy as they come no matter where he laid his prey: on the grass court under the floodlights, in bed or a boat hammock at night, on his plush office carpet in mid-afternoon or at sunset on the beach.

'So, Edward, what went wrong at Oxford?'

'You mean what went right, if you're referring to my turning down the scholarship.'

'How so?'

'Hugh, my elder brother, and I had been to two schools together and I wanted to break away from the follow my leader way I'd been educated. I wanted something fresh not like Oxford so chose the University of East Anglia in Norwich? Have you heard of it?'

'I saw the riots on TV back in the sixties if that's what you mean.'

Sidney-Smith was not completely convinced. Edward hadn't realised the riots and sit-ins would have been heard of in these far flung edges of the empire but kept a poker face instead of explaining how he participated in some of them.

'So what happened to your degree?'

Edward thought of Pentonville but decided that wasn't a good idea now either.

'Good question. Peter Stafford won me over to go straight to Porter Williams.'

At the time graduates like Hugh's friends, even with firsts from Oxford, were just queuing up in the ever lengthening lines of redundant and frustrated unemployed. Edward hadn't been that convincing but he knew if he brought Sir Peter into the decision making process Graham would no longer pursue the issue. He did as expected rather than question Sir Peter's judgement.

'I see. It all makes good sense now.'

Graham decided to change the subject slightly and probe just how deep the Stafford and Burlington relationship was. He already ruled out any funny stuff going on as Edward was like him, an obvious target for the ladies.

Chapter 21 - Sunday 30th June to Monday 1st July

'Sir Peter Stafford thinks highly of you.'

'He's a close friend of my father. He's a director at ICI, my father that is.'

Graham sat up in his chair and offered Edward one of his cigarettes.

'I see. Your father would appear to know Rupert Fanshaw?'

'He's in the Commonwealth Office, isn't he?'

'Yes. He asked if you'd like to go to a party with him and his wife tonight.'

'Sounds great. What kind of party?'

'It's a formal do at Lynden Pindling's home in Government House. He's the Prime Minister.'

'Yes, I know.'

Graham noticed how Edward took it all in his stride, not haughtily but modestly, as if all was normal, to be expected. How many from Porter Williams had even attended such a function. He hadn't, not since the day he arrived and that was years ago. Yet this young man had been invited as if royalty within twenty four hours of arriving by no less than MI6 Fanshaw as Graham often called him behind his back.

'M ... sorry, Rupert Fanshaw will pick you up from your hotel at five. His wife is called Collette, quite a charming young lady.'

They continued to get acquainted for a while longer. Graham outlined the musts and must nots of life in the Bahamas for someone who was new to the islands. Discretion being the better part of survival he made no mention of the risks of the vortex known as Collette: anyway Edward would no doubt spot those instantly.

Treat the locals as equals. Never go south of the hill at night; the hill divided posh white Nassau in the north from the black ghettos on the south side. Don't swim in the sea after dusk or near any harbour. Be careful bedding black girls, few are on the pill, stick to US and Canadian tourists. Don't break any bank secrecy laws. There is no law against drunk driving but don't do it. Drivers in Nassau are some of the worst in the world and often doped out of their minds. Don't gamble in Paradise Island. It is rigged. Open a bank account, with Barclays. That is if he wanted paying on time. Don't arrive early for anything; even punctuality is pointless. Bribe the police if you get into trouble.

Graham ended with his most important piece of advice.

'Above all, remember this is a small island and everybody and I mean everybody, knows everybody else's business or they think they do which can be worse. Always keep that in mind.'

In truth, the Bahamas was a string of seven hundred islands tied tightly together by gossip and rumour mongering. It was a microcosm of the small overlapping global diplomatic and intelligence worlds.

Sidney-Smith then took Edward round and introduced him to the rest of the staff at Porter Williams. The office atmosphere was casual, relaxed, and almost comatose in places but Graham commanded instant respect from those behind every door he opened. That done Graham cancelled his pool reservation. The fact that one could reserve a whole pool let alone cancel it amazed Edward. They went for an early lunch at The Smuggler's Inn, near the quay side.

Over lunch Graham explained how the office fitted into the greater scheme of Porter Williams International as it now called itself globally although most ignored the self-aggrandisement. Afterwards, Graham dropped Edward at Barclays Bank to open an account and then went back to the office and sent a fax to Sir Peter Stafford at his home.

It read "Met Edward. He's a great fellow. Rupert Fanshaw, a friend of his father, is taking him to a cocktail party tonight at Government House, given by Lynden Pindling." Sir Peter replied within five minutes. "Well done."

Edward was picked up by Rupert Fanshaw and his wife, precisely on time. Collette resembled Mrs Robinson from the 1967 film The Graduate. Edward guessed she'd seduced more than a few young men in her time. She was a sexy sparkler and knew it.

Her knee was forever rubbing up against Edward's in the short ride to Government House in which Collette's even shorter dress rose higher and higher as she slid back and forth on the back seat pointing out the sights to him. Edward was left in no doubt that her fish net tights pointed to her having forgotten to wear any knickers. She knew he knew as she glanced at his trousers as the mutual sightseeing tour headed down town.

He couldn't help but notice her pearl and black coral jewellery despite her low cut top and suntanned boobs that had a little bounce with every pot hole Rupert drove over. The necklace looked like the stuff the Queen might have worn at a Commonwealth summit. The Fanshaws looked as though they had been born with golden cutlery sets in their cots. Never having been in a spanking new Cadillac or even an old one for that matter Edward was impressed by the car's modern gadgetry. He made himself a promise to drive one as soon as he had the opportunity.

There was only champagne and orange juice to drink at the reception, which was in honour of a new trade treaty between the Bahamas and Honduras. Honduras was the banana republic of the century, with dictators coming and going. Edward was introduced to the latest head of state, one Oswaldo López. Oswaldo had only recently taken over the country in a coup d'état in 1972.

Rupert Fanshaw, who knew everybody and everything about them, pointed out López was a private client of Porter Williams and stinking rich for such a humanitarian head of state. Edward wasn't sure if he was being sarcastic or comparing López's wealth to that of the Fanshaws.

Rupert was politeness personified and an impeccable chaperone throughout the proceedings, always taking just enough time to unearth some fascinating titbit but never lingering too long such that boredom set in. He eventually introduced Edward to Lynden Pindling.

Chapter 21 - Sunday 30th June to Monday 1st July

Edward asked the Prime Minister why Nassau was still split in two by the hill now the Bay Street Boys had gone. They were joined by a big cigar-smoking and overweight policeman who overheard the question and jumped at the chance of joining in the conversation as a bull frog might have rushed forward for sexual favours. His name was Winston, a deputy commissioner of police with more medals on his chest than a seventeen star general. Winston set to giving Edward a well rehearsed history lesson.

'The Bay Street Boys were once a group of influential foreign merchants who controlled the Bahamas for a good slug of this century. The bother boys have gone now but in the old days they dominated the economy, the legislature, us, they disenfranchised us, the black majority. They only quit a year or so ago, when we were made independent. That right Lynden?'

'You nailed it in one. Right on Winston.'

'Yes sir. A good synopsis though I say so myself.'

Edward chipped in.

'Worthy of self-adulation too, if I might say so.'

Rupert gave him a furious stainless steel glance which was ignored. Edward wasn't fazed by being in such company. He'd done his homework too. Anyhow, the Bahamas land mass was probably about the same as all of Yorkshire at most. He was more accustomed to the likes of Harold Macmillan, Alec Douglas-Home or Dr Beeching dropping in for afternoon teas. Young Prime Ministers of smaller islands or banana republic dictators didn't faze him one iota although they were much more interesting in less conventional ways.

Edward was even more tightly chaperoned from person to person by Rupert after that encounter. Rupert had left Collette to fend for herself. Every time Edward glanced at her she looked divine but was inevitably surrounded by different men, usually old enough to be her father.

She was so beautiful that her magnetism was only to be expected. Rupert occasionally flicked his Bulldog Drummond eyes in her direction and twiddled with his moustache but never saw any need to rescue her although he did spot her eyeing up Edward more than once.

What went unsaid at these cocktail parties was that the CIA and MI6 suspected Pindling and his lackeys of being heavily involved in the cocaine and heroin industry. They all turned a blind eye or even encouraged drug smuggling into the USA using the Bahamian islands as marshalling yards.

There was little doubt that since independence the Bahamas had become an important stepping stone for Columbian drug barons. They were shunting tons of drugs through Florida into the USA and even Europe. The rumour mills had it that Pindling plus his cronies had millions salted away in private bank accounts protected by Bahamian bank secrecy laws but nobody seemed to care.

Rupert overheard Edward mention the forbidden "D" word in a conversation with one of the Honduran delegates. Drugs were a forbidden topic at Government House even if they did pay for the never ending receptions.

Fanshaw interrupted the conversation at once as it was getting too risqué and took Edward over to meet Leo Sanchez. Even though such an introduction had been specifically prohibited by Sir Douglas Castle, Rupert decided there and then it must be safer than risking a war in Central America! Anyway Rupert was only really there to chaperone him or so he thought.

The Sanchez family, better known as the CIA in espionage circles, owned as proxies for the USA large tracts of real estate in the West Indies, including Governor's Beach. Leo was a lawyer in his late twenties and worked in Washington DC and Langley. His cousin, Marco, was head of the CIA in the Bahamas.

Both of the Sanchez cousins had been briefed about Edward Burlington by the CIA's London Station. Through the JIC the CIA had access to most of MI6's data. Unbeknownst to MI6 they had secured clandestine access to MI6's most secret data, including Sir Douglas Castle's personal computer files.

The cousins were impressed by what Edward had done gratis for the CIA courtesy of Operation Lacklustre, even if by accident, and Standpipe. They were also aware of his other contributions to western intelligence and his being partly the reason why Operation Tufty had come about.

Both of them had been dying to meet him because he sounded like their brand of drinking buddy; and because they wanted to exploit him as an asset. They already had a job lined up for him, something easy where he could have some fun, before they involved him in bigger and more dangerous operations.

Pindling had just unexpectedly collared Rupert so Leo had the floor to himself.

'Hey Edward, or is it Ed, I hear you're looking for an apartment?'

'I don't mind either but you've a good source of data, Leo or is it Leonard?'

'Let's leave here and I'll take you to the best bar in the Bahamas. You can meet my reprobate young cousin Marco there and if you love the bar you will love Holly. Are you enjoying this?'

'Don't ask me, I'm British. Just get me out of here!'

'One of Graham Greene's comedians too, let's go before Collette swallows you whole.'

Edward knew he was CIA in a fraction of a second because of the way Leo responded to the word data and mentioned Greene who Edward had heard was MI6 from his father.

Ed was glad to get away from the reception. The party was starting to get claustrophobic and stuffy particularly with Rupert's metaphorical hand cuffs. In some ways Rupert was more stifling than his mother on a New Year's Day cocktail party back home. Shame he hadn't been chaperoned by Collette but then who was this Holly?

Chapter 21 - Sunday 30th June to Monday 1st July

Rupert looked as though his team had just lost the FA cup final as Ed and Leo set off for the Pink Pussycat on the edge of the hill. As a consolation prize Ed said he'd call Rupert in a day or so once he'd found an apartment.

Rupert planned to have used Collette to help him but Leo was on the scene first using Holly as bait. By now the Bulldog Drummond of the Bahamas was nearly tearing at his moustache and Collette could do nothing having attracted too many Central American admirers as Leo and Edward said their formal farewells.

It was as if Edward had found paradise but still not set foot on Paradise Island. For the ensuing weeks anyone reading his diary would have thought it was now being written by a different person, not the hostage to fate from the preceding months. The fearful forebodings and sinister references to slow motion train wrecks in others' diaries had disappeared ... for the moment anyway.

Chapter 22
Monday 1ˢᵗ to Wednesday 17ᵗʰ July

Delancey Street Nassau, New Providence Island Bahamas

Edward was in charge of his own destiny now, just as he wanted. There was to be no more checking in with Tessa or Mac or the newly found Fanshaws whom MI6 tried to foist onto him as a substitute for them. He was free. Well, he thought so but no doubt the CIA would have different manacles for him. No matter what it would be a change and MI6 had told him to have a rest and both were proverbially speaking the same.

Marco joined them soon after they arrived at the club. The Pink Pussy Cat was one of the most chic and exclusive venues on the island. The men, particularly Marco and Edward, discovered they had lots in common, like smoking, drinking, gambling and womanising when not in a relationship and they all liked living dangerously.

Marco agreed to take Edward on a tour of the island the next day, show him some apartments he might like and introduce him to some useful people. Edward wondered if it was as obvious to others as it was to him that they were both CIA even though they never said as much. When they left the club later that night, Edward noticed that nobody paid the bill.

Holly Goodman, the manageress who'd been sitting on Marco's lap, kissed them all as they left but only Edward was kissed on the lips and had seductive suggestions whispered in his ear. It made him feel good after the disappointment of not having been escorted round the Pindling party by Collette in the flesh.

Bulldog Rupert might have been immaculately dressed in his dinner suit but he was a bit of a bore, too old and set in his ways even if his heart seemed to be in the right place. He was quite clever though and a charmer: like Hugh he studied languages and was fluent in many but unlike Hugh he couldn't suppress his Queen's English when talking native.

Leo and Marco looked more like brothers than cousins, in fact more like the Everly Brothers as Leo was not far off that era having been born in 1934 and was clearly still instructing his barber to remain firmly old fashioned. They were your typical clean shaven bright American boys from upmarket neighbourhoods.

Chapter 22 - Monday 1st to Wednesday 17th July

Marco moved with the times but still sported a small quiff that mirrored his cousin's appearance. Both lawyers by training, they were CIA career cats and though Marco at thirty was way junior to Leo, he would probably be the high flyer given time. Nonetheless Leo was in the senior ranks and already accustomed to attending meetings at executive office level.

Leo was a family man and far more conservative in all respects compared to his cousin. Flash man Marco looked set to be an eternal expat Bahamian bachelor except that he would no doubt be promoted soon. Leo lived and slept on planes in a suit whereas Marco lived in a pair of jeans or swimming trunks.

Both were tall and marginally gangly looking but Marco somehow had sex appeal by the bucketful and exploited it but with greater care than Ed. As Ed was to find out, work wise the cousins were both smooth and precision perfect operators in their own fields although Marco being that much younger still had a lot to learn but then so did Ed.

Marco was unlike your average expat in Nassau as he didn't have time for fishing, snorkelling or sunbathing although he swam a mile every morning as Holly explained rather intimately. Apart from liking swimming Marco was about the nearest Edward had ever been to meeting his male counterpart or soul mate, even more so than Sam White. The cousins' assessment of Ed had been spot on.

New Providence & Paradise Islands Bahamas

As promised, the next day Marco took Edward on a tour of New Providence Island and Paradise Island, including south of the hill. The islands were linked by a bridge so they left Marco's speedboat behind and went by car.

Marco told Edward to keep his door locked as they drove through the shanty town streets, comprising rows of huts with corrugated iron roofs. Sanchez drove carefully, making sure he avoided the kids who ran alongside and in front of his red Camaro. Now and then, Edward saw a dead cat or dog lying beside the kerb. The ones that were alive looked half starved and mangy. This was a part of Nassau that Pindling didn't want the heads of state at his champagne receptions to see.

'Who owns those flash cars parked in some of the cul-de-sacs?'

'Drug runners, probably. These islands are stepping stones to the US of A.'

'Where's Bobby Vesco now?'

Marco shot Edward a surprised look, as if to say you know your stuff as Vesco's mansion was just coming into sight.

Bobby Vesco was the man responsible for the world's largest securities fraud in the US and was a friend of Richard Nixon. Vesco was also involved in Watergate and was island hopping round the Caribbean, trying to avoid extradition.

'That's his pad over there.'

Vesco's pad had gold coloured gates. The guards looked like they'd stepped out of a black and white Al Capone movie.

'Pindling won't let him come back here but hasn't confiscated his assets. Vesco's into drugs now.'

Marco Sanchez drove back north and stopped for lunch in Paradise Island. They sat outside in a hotel bar overlooking a dark blue swimming pool and drank American beers, which kept coming without either of them having to call a waiter.

'You're not starting work until August, I hear.'

'That's right. Work permit delays.'

'Fancy moonlighting in New York while you're waiting?'

'Sounds interesting. I've never been there yet. What would I have to do?'

Edward took a drink from his glass and smiled at Sanchez.

'Fall in love.'

'What's she like?'

Marco pushed some photographs across the table. The woman was beautiful and about nineteen years old.

'Nice. Why me?'

'She likes men with a British accent. Seriously though, have a look at this file while I make a call from our office in paradise. I'll only be a minute or two. Just look at the numbers of families' lives he probably wrecked.'

Marco had done his homework and knew what motivated Ed from his psychological profiling reports which MI6 had helpfully placed on computers now for all their staff and agents. He handed Edward the fat file he'd taken from his uncharacteristically old fashioned doubly strapped brown leather briefcase and left on foot. They used an expensive hotel suite for operations on the island. Ed learnt later they changed it every week or so.

The report in the file was a long affidavit prepared by Berner & Collins, a well known US law firm with offices in Nassau. It had been lodged at a Bahamian Court as the date stamp showed. The report was an original as it had been initialled in purple ink. Berner & Collins didn't hold back any punches. Edward was staggered by the sheer effrontery of the main crook, Donald King, originally from New Orleans.

He guessed much about this man in the file had been redacted or removed even though the file was fat. The CIA didn't hunt down bank robbers. He was right. Marco had redacted all the data relating to Watergate. What Marco didn't know was that before Leo sent him the file he removed information relating to an entirely different matter as instructed by no less than Jimmy Butler Junior, his boss at the top of the CIA.

This was going to be a complex operation run at several levels for several years to come.

Mr King had been dumped by the CIA for larceny in the late sixties. After that, with nothing better to do, he set about ripping off thousands of US pensioners by advertising that his Bahamian bank would pay one percent more on deposits than the

Chapter 22 - Monday 1st to Wednesday 17th July

highest rate advertised by any other bank. He hammered his message home in each month's issue of Time Magazine for most of 1973. Edward speed read the report even absorbing the footnotes, the last of which noted Porter Williams were the liquidators.

Like all con tricks it looked too good to be true but thousands of unwitting US veterans and elderly citizens fell for it. Then King ran off with their life savings. To Edward there was no other way to describe it. Cowardly daylight robbery: no better than mugging grandmothers hobbling to the corner shop and then running off with their frayed handbags.

It reminded Edward of all those supposedly hard buggers he'd put up with in Pentonville Prison who'd boasted about their bank robberies. They were just as despicable but maybe more foolhardy. He'd heard all the bravado about the guns they used and their heroic getaways.

A proper translation of their escapades might not have read as they would have liked it. "We shot a few disabled pensioners today even though some of them were crippled war heroes and then ran away scared to death." Lamentably that wasn't the way these criminals interpreted their résumés assuming they knew what a résumé was. Given they were mostly illiterate, not that it was their fault, their appreciation of anything artistic was as limited as the Nazi crosses of hatred tattooed on their arms.

Sanchez returned.

'Got the picture. This turd has done much worse than the report implies which is why we're on the chase. We don't normally concern ourselves with bank robberies.'

Edward nodded with mixed emotions as he handed back the file. This King guy deserved to have his flash Harry lifestyle and luxury marina ripped apart but as for his daughter, what had she done wrong? Marco read Edward like a book.

'Don't worry. If King behaves he'll be able to carve out a modest life. We won't wreck his kid's life by wrecking his so you won't be laying her to put the knife in him. Provided he's sensible she won't be the collateral damage.'

Marco was staggered at just how much Edward absorbed in the few minutes he'd been away. He hardly had to explain anything before Burlington asked if he could go to Rio way before he reached that part of what Edward had to do.

The background was King had set up a dodgy bank in Nassau that went broke after a con job involving US$30 million. On his way to Brazil, conman King stopped off in Las Vegas and gambled US$10 million in bankers' drafts. The casinos believed bankers' drafts couldn't bounce. Normally they would have been right, but they bounced because the bank went bust and that made the Polano Mob, who owned the casinos, livid.

Marco was just wrapping up what was required of Ed when he abruptly seemed to change the subject.

'Look behind you Ed.'

Edward turned.

'The yacht. The large black one.'

There were many yachts moored off Paradise Island. Marco pointed towards one in particular.

'Beautiful, ain't it?'

Edward took a collapsible monocular from his pocket, pulled it open to its full length and looked at the yacht.

'Look at the upper deck, in a hammock under the first mast.'

'Worth closer surveillance I reckon.'

Edward took out a Minox camera, zoomed in on the yacht and clicked. Marco's voice gave away his surprise.

'Jesus, does that matchbox work over such a distance?'

'It's meant for documents but this one's good for other objects d'art too.'

'Ok, the broad in the hammock is Vesco's mistress, Linda, if you label the photos in your albums, and that's one of Vesco's yachts. Donald King is a pal of Vesco.'

'That's not the woman in the photographs.'

'The woman in the photographs is King's daughter, Kate, and before you ask she hasn't a second name like Kay. They're not connected to the Klu Klux Klan and we've checked. She hasn't presently any lovers, yet, but you'll have to be quick about it.'

Edward grinned. This looked more like fun than sitting next to the ugly Borges sisters on a basement sofa with a panoramic view of permanently drawn curtains. He put the miniature surveillance equipment back into his pocket.

'You working for the Mafia Marco?'

'Funny you should ask. We must get to King before the mob does. The Polanos are understandably annoyed as you might be if you'd lost that much.'

Two more beers were served up by the waiter, along with medium rare steaks, with side orders of fries and salad.

'You still want in, Ed?'

'When do I start?'

'We'll fly you to New York the day after tomorrow and you can take it from there but first we need to talk about money right?'

'You pay my expenses and I'll go.'

Marco's research told him he was going down the wrong alley. Offer Burlington cash and Ed would doubtless accuse him of bribery. All the reports he read said Ed had never been motivated by money. He changed tack.

'Ok but we have one other rule.'

'Yes?'

'You must stay in a safe apartment if you're helping us out. We're getting three new ones this month so you can move into one of those. Better still we can choose one today or tomorrow. Don't worry. You'll pay the rent so we ain't holding you by the balls. All we'll do is take care of security.'

Chapter 22 - Monday 1st to Wednesday 17th July

All Edward was thinking about was here comes another goldfish bowl the only difference being that unlike in London he didn't own it. What the hell? It would mean he was safer and they would pay for any security he needed. If it wasn't them it would be MI6 and Fanshaw. Much as he liked Collette he wanted to escape from them.

'Does that suit you?'

'Is that an offer I can't refuse?'

'That's my final offer.'

Marco winked. They shook hands.

'I liked the look of Governor's Beach. Is that in the right area?'

'That's near to where I live and the new block of apartments is cool. Let's go take a look after lunch.'

Marco didn't sign the check or even call for it. They set off from Paradise Island through downtown Nassau to West Bay Street, just past the Nassau Beach Hotel. There had been no need to even mention the CIA. Marco had done what Leo asked. Get Burlington out of the clutches of Fanshaw pronto and set him up for a test run to see if he lived up to the fables on his files.

So far as Marco was concerned so far was better than expected. The files didn't do Ed justice.

Central Park Manhattan, New York USA

Edward was given a more in-depth briefing by Marco before he set off for New York City. The plan was simple but subtle. His cover was that he was a Brit touring the Americas, looking to expand his real estate interests. Donald King's daughter, Kate, worked in a real estate office and Edward would be introduced to her as Edward Jameson by a colleague, who was a CIA plant.

Edward's job was to seduce her, make sure they had lots of photographs taken together and get her to send the photos to her father in Rio de Janeiro. Edward would then be invited down to Donald King's marina and this would open the door for Marco and his friends to follow.

Kate was adventurous and liked to spend her weekends camping and mountain climbing. Edward's cover persona would have that in common with her. In reality, one of the side effects of Edward's poisoning was that he now suffered from severe vertigo and couldn't stand heights. This meant that mountain climbing was totally out of the question: odd for a man who, as a school kid, climbed into the rafters of York Cathedral for a quick fag and used to clamber across roofs in the snow to get to the pub.

The first part of the plan went well and Edward's British accent and charm had the desired effect on Kate. She was under the sheets at his hotel on the southern edge of Central Park in 5th Avenue without too much effort on his part. Despite his initial negative surprise at just how humid and sweaty Manhattan was, Edward soon discovered a positive.

After the working day many of the smaller Manhattan offices turned into makeshift nightclubs. Kate's was one of those. With booze and joints and the piped muzak from the elevators, dull workplaces were soon transformed into wild discos. He was told it could all be blamed on the traffic. If you delayed a car trip home it meant you still arrived about the same time as you would have if you'd set out earlier.

Within a week including one all night party with Kate, there were lots of photos for her to send down to her Dad in Brazil. She called him almost daily and Edward even managed to have a few words with the man and confirmed he'd be in Rio soon, looking at real estate. Donald was happy to meet him. Any friend of Kate's, especially such a close friend, was also a friend of his.

Kate took time off work to be with Edward and show him the sights, mainly from the water much to Edward's amazement. He'd never thought of what he wrongly termed New York as an island. What staggered him was there was only one Indian restaurant in Manhattan. He took Kate there to introduce her to Indian cuisine. She loved it and he had another surprise for her as they sat there sweating through Edward's selection of vindaloos.

'I have a small present for you.'

'Oh do let me see.'

'Take a look at this. It's a ten day camping and mountaineering holiday for two in Hawaii. You get to visit all five islands.'

'Jesus, it must have cost a fortune Eddy.'

She kissed him several times and her face was beaming.

'Cost nothing, I won it in a prize draw.'

'Are you sure?'

'There's a condition. You have to fly out Friday. Can you make it?'

Kate's smile faded. She took a closer look at the brochure.

'Sounds like a hoax to me Eddy. Is that a Hawaiian number at the bottom?'

'Don't ask me, I'm British. What's the time difference?'

'Five hours. They'll still be open.'

'Why not call them?'

'When?'

'Now.'

Edward called the restaurant manager over and he agreed to let Kate phone Honolulu for an extra ten dollars on the check.

'What should I say?'

'Ask them how you know it's for real.'

Kate made the call and read out the draw number. They confirmed she held the winning ticket.

'How do I know it's not a hoax?'

Chapter 22 - Monday 1st to Wednesday 17th July

They told her she could check with Pan Am within an hour of confirming the names of the two people who would be travelling. Their seats would be booked on flight 331 from Newark via Los Angeles and then on another flight of their choosing to Honolulu. She could also call the Holiday Inn Hotel at Honolulu Airport for confirmation of the rooms. Kate was ecstatic.

'You'll be coming with me, won't you Eddy?'

'I'm afraid not. I just can't alter my schedule for ten whole days, it'd bankrupt me. One of your climbing friends, surely?'

Kate called another mountaineering enthusiast and, within an hour, everything was confirmed for the holiday of a lifetime with her friend Sharon. She also called her father and left a garbled message about her trip and ordering him to take care of Eddy in Rio, because he was the most wonderful man in the whole world.

West Bay Street Nassau, New Providence Island Bahamas

Edward returned to Nassau mid-morning on Wednesday 17th July after saying a long and lingering goodbye to Kate King. They promised to stay in touch when he returned to England and maybe she'd come visit him in London sometime. Marco Sanchez met him at the airport. Unlike when he had first flown in to Nassau, the ambience was refreshing after the heavy humidity of New York City.

'Looks like the plan worked a treat Ed or should I call you Eddy?'

'Certainly does so far.'

'Now for the hard part: we've chartered a plane to Rio for Friday morning. You'll be briefed on the flight.'

As Edward and Marco left the terminal building, a tall blonde man was getting into a chauffeur driven limousine. The gentleman was Jordan. He didn't notice Edward and Edward didn't see him.

As Carl Hanson's empire was expanding, Jordan was travelling more and more in the Caribbean. On this occasion, he'd been to Grand Turk for a meeting with one Dr Ian Tomlinson. Jordan also had meetings to attend with several of Hanson's bankers in Nassau, then a flight back to Amsterdam via Miami and Heathrow.

There was no problem with Jordan flying anywhere in the world. His Swedish passport was clean and he had no criminal record. Before each trip, he created a new handwritten list of code words. Hanson and he would use them whenever they spoke to each other from public telephones at hotels or in airports. The list was usually made using words from a paperback novel. Jordan would leave Hanson the list and bring the book with him.

Hanson was of course still on many wanted lists under the name Cyrus Burton with all the out of date mug shots. As a result of the unreliability of Caribbean airlines, there was always the danger of being diverted to Miami. That became too big a risk for him as his drug taking led him increasingly into paranoia.

As well as that, British Airways dominated flights to the Caribbean islands and to get there via a direct flight, you invariably had to go through Heathrow but the greatest nuisance was hiring private planes in the West Indies. It became a bureaucratic nightmare.

Travellers were subjected to rigorous checks including finger printing as a gesture to the US, indicating that these small countries were taking a proactive stance against drug trafficking. So, Hanson spent most of his time in Amsterdam and Jordan did all the travelling. Unlike many of his victims, Hanson was not going to have his fingers chopped off to remove traces of his identity.

True to his word, Marco had started to sort out the apartment Edward liked at Governor's Beach while "Eddy" was in New York and the place was being renovated in readiness for him to move into soon. They took a detour round there before going to the Nassau Beach Hotel where Porter Williams were putting him up for about a month.

Edward celebrated having passed Part 1 of his CIA Asset Assessment Exam by the beach bar in the Nassau Beach Hotel lying in the sun with an uninterrupted supply of lagers. Meanwhile intriguing developments were afoot precisely 4,321 miles away, as most birds fly when sober, back in the UK!

Edward may have been in celebratory mood when he wrote in his diary that day but his mother's diary was unusually blank apart from one name, Alice.

Chapter 23
Wednesday 17th July

The Burlington Bunker Corsham, Wiltshire England

Alice Bailey was an old colleague of Sara. She was like a mother to her during the Second World War and was a secretary in the Cabinet Office. She handled much of the JIC's dealings in the 1960s, including the turmoil caused by the Profumo affair. In those days, people knew how to keep secrets, so that they were completely beyond encryption. Alice was retired now. She was getting on too and lived in the small town of Corsham in Wiltshire.

At half past two in the afternoon that Wednesday the Tower of London was packed with tourists from all over the world. Five minutes later, the place was in turmoil after the IRA detonated a bomb in the basement of the White Tower, in what was coincidentally called the Mortar Room. One person was killed and forty one injured, some of them seriously.

Castle had been one of those notified of a threatened IRA attack on the Tower of London itself the Sunday before and this had been noted in JIC minutes. There was a warning but the normal code wasn't used. Even so, the UK's top bomb experts claimed to have searched the Tower before the explosion and found nothing.

Roger and Sara were on their way to Wiltshire when they heard the bombing reported in a news flash on their car radio.

'I don't believe it. Castle was warned about this.'

'My God, Roger, if he can't protect the Tower, what chance has Edward got?'

'We should go back.'

'No! This makes our mission all the more urgent.'

'There will be an emergency meeting though Sara.'

'I'm sure there will be. The usual locking of the proverbial gate after the horse is long gone. They can do without you for a few hours.'

Roger lit a cigarette and sulked the rest of the way to Corsham. Sara took no notice and drove on westward bound, away from London. Their meeting planned for later today was more important than any "after the event" emergency meeting. It was a "before the event" meeting.

They collected Alice Bailey from her cottage in Monks Park. She was delighted to see them again and they her. Her presence soon lifted Roger's spirits. Roger now drove which allowed the two women to natter away in the back about the old days, as they headed to their final destination. Her going out for tea was a big event as she rarely saw anyone these days. She'd already heard on her 1955 radio about the London bombing.

'Many in MI5 will have a sleepless night tonight, I expect.'

'You're right, Alice, all trying to blame each other. Trouble is, there are so many MI5 infiltrators in the IRA, one of them probably ordered the damn attack in the first place. If you took away the infiltrators along with Gaddafi's henchmen the IRA might collapse. I could suggest that.'

A few minutes later, the car pulled into a place few people knew anything about: the secret bunker near Corsham. The bunker was where the British government would operate from during a nuclear war. It had many names, like Site 3, but more often than not it was called the Burlington bunker. Roger sat on the Site 3 Committee as its technical advisor on and off since the war. The meetings were invariably chaired by the Prime Minister of the day.

So far as Roger knew it was a complete coincidence it bore the Burlington name. Alice always took the Mickey out of Roger about it in private referring to it as the family cottage. Of course, she knew it was pure coincidence too. Burlington had been added to the already burgeoning list of code names it had been given and was not the first name it was christened.

The bunker in Corsham would be the alternative seat of power if there was ever a nuclear strike on the UK. It had been built to house the Prime Minister, Cabinet Office, local and national government agencies and intelligence and security advisors. Even the royal family were rumoured to have suites prepared but that was never referred to even in conversation.

The bunker was designed to safely house about four thousand government employees, ministers and civil servants. It had been designed to be a totally self-sufficient, radiation proof fortification which covered an area of thirty five acres. The complex was so large that all the main corridors were sign posted using American style street names, such as First Avenue.

It remained one of the MoD's best kept classified secrets. No member of the public had ever been inside the crypt like place. No details or photos of the bunker ever leaked out through its blast proof walls. The site contained all the facilities the occupants needed to survive for three months or so, maybe more.

There was a medical centre with an infirmary, radioactivity contamination examination rooms, operating theatre, wards and even a dental surgery. In addition there was a bakery, a laundry, a couple of vast kitchens, a map room, a library and a

Chapter 23 - Wednesday 17th July

broadcasting centre for the BBC. It housed one of the largest telephone exchanges in the UK. There were living areas, including washrooms with showers.

Travel round the bunker was by battery operated vehicles, which were charged up in an underground depot equipped with maintenance areas and workshops. Storerooms had everything from cigars and beer to ashtrays and toilet brushes. The stores were packed with tinned food, loo paper, office equipment and enough fuel to run the generators for many months.

After getting past security, they descended the hundred feet to the bunker vehicle depot. From there they took a battery car to the dining room at the top of Area 5. Roger smiled at Alice.

'When we asked where you'd like to meet for afternoon tea, we never thought you'd suggest here.'

'Why not? It's extremely apposite Roger and it reminds me of old times.'

'Apposite is the right word, or maybe ironic. I have a special present for you, my dear.'

Roger handed her a large gift-wrapped parcel which she looked at from every angle. After they arrived at the serving area, ordered tea with scones and clotted cream, she opened the package at the table Sara had chosen in the corner. No one was in hearing distance anyway: they were alone in the canteen apart from the waitresses. Alice's present was a signed first edition of Nat King Cole's autobiography.

'Oh Roger, how thoughtful and you too, Sara my darling. I always knew your bookshop was more than just a safe-house.'

'We knew you listened to his music.'

'I listen to him for hours on end on my old gramophone.'

Alice produced a small brown envelope from her handbag, along with a pair of lace gloves.

'I have two presents for you as well.'

She slipped the gloves onto her thin, frail fingers.

'They are original too, you know, and still valuable, to some people, I dare say.'

Alice opened the envelope and took out several faded documents.

'Who should I give them to, Sara?'

'Roger will look after them.'

Sara used a napkin to take the documents from Alice. She placed them in a small plastic folder which she'd taken from Roger's briefcase.

'You know where that was filed in the ministry, don't you Roger?'

Alice was pointing at the largest document.

'I do my dear.'

Sara put the folder back into the briefcase.

'Sounds intriguing?'

'We had a filing cabinet bottom drawer where we temporarily dumped anything the team couldn't decipher.'

Sara watched as Alice returned her gloves and the envelope to her handbag. Roger laughed, remembering the cabinet.

'Yes, the cabinet drawer was labelled Beyond Enkription, misspelt with a "k" and an "i".'

'Roger was the only one to spot the spelling mistake, Sara, because he was forever asking to look at that one document.'

'Yes, I always brought them a present, chocs or flowers, when I wanted to take a look at it.'

'I've read it, but I have no idea who wrote it or who was meant to receive it. Nowadays I suppose with all these modern computer gadgets, deciphering anything is possible.'

Sara listened intently, while Roger cut a scone for Alice. She took it and applied a liberal amount of cream and strawberry jam before eating it.

'Before he was detained in Russia, Roger told me never to let it out of my sight. He was still in prison over there when I retired, so I took it with me.'

'What else was in that drawer Alice?'

'Absolutely nothing Sara ... apart from Nat King Cole records. We would play them if we worked late which we did night after night as Roger knows only too well.'

Alice took another bite of her scone. Jam stuck to the corners of her mouth, which she wiped away with a serviette and took a sip of her milky tea.

'The other paper is a letter in German from Douglas to Zola. It's not terribly pleasant to read. I hid it at home. I know I shouldn't have done that but much as I loathed the man I didn't want Douglas executed. No need to read it now Sara but my intuition was right. It must have been filed in the wrong cabinet or something but wasn't referred to when Douglas was nearly hung drawn and quartered. If they'd read it properly when he was investigated he'd have probably been shot. It leaves no room for doubt. Haven't you killed him yet Sara?'

'Not yet Alice.'

'I'm surprised you've allowed him to live so long, after what he did to your sister.'

Alice Bailey was the only one apart from Castle who knew the whole truth about the doomed operation behind enemy lines during which Isobel Wright was captured and killed. Douglas Castle persuaded Sara Wright as she was then that her sister's sacrifice had been for the greater good. Unfortunately he was relying on information supplied to him by a supposedly trustworthy source to ensure the success of the mission. It was disinformation and the trusted source was a female German spy. To save his own skin and cover up the fatal mistake, Castle flew to Paris the day after its liberation in August 1944 and helped the spy escape.

Chapter 23 - Wednesday 17th July

In early December 1944, Alice Bailey let something slip to Sara, not knowing the importance of what she was saying. That slip of the tongue informed Sara that Douglas Castle had put a Parisienne spy up in a Zurich hotel the day after the liberation. The plan was she would stay there until the war ended. Sara and he were still an item then and she smelled a rat. Upon further investigation she discovered Douglas Castle had stayed at the same hotel and signed for meals and drinks for himself and the French woman, codenamed Zola.

With Alice's help, Sara now had evidence that proved the woman was a double agent. Zola had been responsible for the deaths of dozens of resistance fighters, SIS or MI6 officers and SOE agents. They included Sara's sister Isobel. It became clear Castle must have known this Zola woman was also on the side of the Nazis long before he helped her escape, and he was her lover.

Sara was enraged and went after him. She wasn't going to give him the chance to slither his way out of a secret military trial and disappear. She shot the French woman dead in front of Douglas Castle on Christmas Day 1944, in their hotel bedroom. Castle stood by his story that he didn't know she was a double agent and all he was guilty of was infidelity. Sara's finger trembled on the trigger while he begged for his life on his knees. In the end, she couldn't bring herself to kill him, but she kept the evidence provided by Alice at the time and held on to it.

The trouble was Zola was murdered on neutral territory. If Sara released her evidence, that would crucify her too. Alice had just now handed over fresh evidence she told Roger wouldn't incriminate Sara but for the first time would prove beyond doubt that Castle and Zola were traitors to England and France. Neither Sara nor Roger knew of its existence until Roger called Alice about the filing cabinet letter and they still hadn't read it yet. Sara touched Alice's wrinkled hand.

'I have plans for Castle, Alice, don't you worry. I'm dying to read this letter too. It may help.'

'Please don't say "dying" Sara, but it will and I hope I live to see the day, my darlings.'

'You will Alice. You will.'

'He's as slippery as a bag of live eels. You'll both need to have your wits about you.'

'We have several contingencies my dear. Castle might be able to dodge one bullet but not three or even four now with your letter.'

Alice smiled broadly. This little meeting made her year. She had never known which way to turn with the letter from Castle to Zola so she had just sat on it. Since capital punishment was improbable now she had decided it was fair that Douglas should answer the questions the letter posed. As it was in his own handwriting he must have been guilty of treason. At least there would be no blood on her delicate hands: she had always hated the sight of the stuff.

Alice soon tired after the excitement and intrigue of her outing. They left the Burlington bunker and took her back to her cottage, her sanctuary in Monks Park. They both hugged her closely before leaving for Epsom.

When they were indoors back home, Sara quietly and carefully made several copies of the documents before hiding the originals in a place known only to her and Roger. They both sat on one of the settees in the living room and read the copies of Castle's letter to Zola. Roger finished reading it first and put a comforting arm round Sara as she too reached the end and stared at him. For once she was lost for words.

'Alice was right. It's not pleasant but it's a damn solid silver bullet.'

Roger could see Sara wanted to do something drastic and held her close until the tension subsided.

They never talked espionage at home. There had been so many visitors over the years. Sara estimated there might be as many as twenty or more bugs in the house alone ignoring those rusting around the grounds. Who knew how many were still operational?

She could have found them and destroyed them but she had more fun in her mind thinking she could mislead whoever might be listening in to them. In any event, she knew sweeps for bugs were more often than not pointless. Whoever undertook the sweeps could never be sure they identified all the bugs, so why bother looking in the first place?

Parliament Street Westminster, London England

Later that evening, Roger attended a series of meetings in Whitehall, where allegations, insinuations and recriminations were bandied about, beaten against the walls and thrown to and fro. The IRA bombing was blamed on MI5 by MI6 and on MI6 by MI5 and on the Royal Ulster Constabulary by Special Branch and vice versa.

Castle, as usual, managed to slide out from under the guillotine. He and others shifted responsibility squarely onto the shoulders of someone lower down in the pecking order, claiming their lofty positions prevented them from access to detail. After all, his job and those of his confederates, was to be concerned with overall strategy and the larger picture. If warnings went unheeded, they didn't go unheeded by him or his most senior peers and colleagues.

Afterwards, Roger met with Sir Peter Stafford at the Carlton, a private gentleman's club in St. James's. The meeting had been arranged earlier that day, under the pretext of chatting about Edward's sojourn in the Bahamas.

Peter ordered a bottle of Sangiovese, which wasn't ideal under the circumstances, but it was better than the club's Cabernet. He was puffing away for his life on a ten inch Brazilian cigar. Roger lit a cigarette and sipped the dry red wine: he was biding his time.

Chapter 23 - Wednesday 17th July

'Yes, Edward's settling in nicely. I gather Rupert Fanshaw took him to a reception at Government House after his first visit to the office, introduced him to a few people.'

'Not throwing him down any mineshafts, are you Peter?'

'Of course not. Your son doesn't even start work at the office until next month.'

'Sara will be pleased.'

'Tell her to relax. Edward's probably lying on the beach, sipping a cold beer and eyeing up the ladies.'

Peter filled the glasses again from the bottle. Roger lit another cigarette as Peter puffed on his cigar.

'To be completely honest, Peter, that wasn't the real reason I wanted us to meet.'

'Oh, so what was the real reason?'

'Douglas.'

Peter shifted uneasily in his chair. Tape recordings sprung to his mind but that was not all. He didn't like talking to Roger about Sir Douglas without him present even though Roger and he had many secrets they kept well away from Castle's in-tray.

They were after all the Oxford Triumvirate but there was always that element of contention between Roger and Douglas, that dissension called Sara. Peter was careful to avoid being in the middle of any sandwich someone might pick up and bite into one day.

'What's he not done now? If you're about to mention this latest IRA outrage, I must say I concur.'

'In what way Peter?'

'It's a complete fiasco.'

This was what Roger wanted to hear. His plan with Sara was to remove Castle from his lofty position in MI6 but he needed to have a replacement ready. Sir Peter Stafford was the obvious candidate. As well as that, TrumPeter Stafford was closer to Edward than Castle and would be more likely to protect him.

'Douglas has passed his sell by day Peter.'

'Do you realise what you're saying Roger?'

'Couldn't be clearer.'

Peter took a big swallow from his wine glass; he no longer cared whether it tasted perfect. He stubbed out the remnants of his cigar, embers scattering all over the table. Pausing intentionally, he lit another with one match before he spoke.

'This is bordering on treason.'

Unlike Castle, Peter was not paranoid but as an ex-head of MI5 he knew a lot about hidden tape recorders.

'Don't be ridiculous, I'm just voicing an opinion and, may I say, an opinion held by many. You saw the vultures circling earlier. If we do it my way at least it will be humane.'

'Douglas will never resign.'

'He might, given the right set of circumstances.'

'What precisely would that set of circumstances be?'

'Nothing you would have to concern yourself with Peter.'

'So why are we having this discussion?'

Roger lit his third cigarette in succession, having only smoked half of the previous two. He knew Peter was anticipating, on the verge of realising, what was coming but he let him wait.

'There would be the matter of Douglas' successor.'

Peter waved his hand in the air. A waiter came running.

'Two large brandies, your Armenian vintage, there's a good man.'

Peter turned his attention back to Roger.

'Who might that be, strictly in your opinion, of course?'

'Why, you Peter. There is no one else.'

The brandies came. Peter drank his down in one go and ordered two more.

'I couldn't be part of any coup d'état. You must know that Roger?'

'Of course not and nor could I.'

Roger's ambivalent response passed over Peter's head. He was getting too pissed to pick up that level of innuendo. Peter watched the smoke spiralling from his outlandish cigar. Roger sipped his brandy.

'Let me pose a hypothetical situation Peter.'

'Go ahead.'

'Say, for instance, Douglas decided the job had become too stressful for him and he took the decision to voluntarily step down from office. Suppose, for instance, you had the backing of the Home Secretary and the Prime Minister as the man to succeed him.

I know they aren't Tories but they are in power. All sides of the house hailed you as a success at MI5; they would back you. They'll have to pick a trusted proven person. No matter which side of the house they're on none of them can outlive many more IRA successes. Mind, they probably won't serve a full term in office anyway so when they go Ted Heath ...'

'Yes. I see the logic.'

'Would you be amenable to the idea, hypothetically speaking, of course?'

'Hmm.'

'As you already have a knighthood I assume it would be a peerage after a couple of years elapsed, you understand.'

'Hmm?'

Sir Peter was on the verge, he could see his name shining with honours, he could see the glory, smell it, taste it. Roger knew he was close.

'This country needs you Peter. Douglas is making us look like a sick joke. We're becoming a laughingstock around the world.'

Chapter 23 - Wednesday 17th July

'Hmm.'

'You're the only man with the flair for the job. We both know that.'

'Hypothetically speaking, Roger, if Douglas were to step down voluntarily and without any bad smell, I would hypothetically be prepared to step into the breach.'

'Good man.'

'On one condition though Roger. We bring the operations run through your basement in Charing Cross Road back into the fold. With Douglas gone, there will be no further need for you to run MI99.5z or whatever number it is underneath our nostril hairs and behind our spines if you get my twisted drift.

It's now far too complicated remembering who knows what. It has become as convoluted as a snake committing suicide and we don't want any dead snakes in any wardrobes do we now?'

'Simplicity is best Peter and neither of us is getting younger. I agree. By the way you did authorise me to use any numbers I chose and there are only about six in use currently. I'll send you the details once all this tedious political business is out of our way.'

Peter placed his cigar on the ashtray. They clinked brandy glasses, and shook hands.

That night, a trifle tipsy from the wine and brandy, Roger visited his office at ICI. He ran the text of the document from the Beyond Enkription filing cabinet given to him by Alice Bailey through the deciphering programmes he had installed on computer there. Roger believed that this one letter was the key to deciphering dozens of other documents already in transit to him from the British Embassy in Moscow.

Many of those documents originated in the USSR. If they proved his theory, unless handled with extreme diplomacy the consequences for the UK could be as damaging as the Profumo affair. Roger knew how damaging that could be too. On balance he still had as much to fear from the wrong fallout from that as Sara had from her Zurich hotel visit.

It would take several weeks or longer to come to a definitive conclusion but there was much at stake so the effort would be worth it. Sara and he had their other bullets with which to try to assassinate Sir Douglas Castle but those bullets could cause immense collateral damage if everyone started shooting at once. This one would be silent and unstoppable.

Roger ordered a black cab back to Epsom. He was well on the road for the revenge he'd been seeking for decades now. As the black cab headed for Surrey, he watched as the Thames flowed past him and trains criss-crossed over darkened bridges. His thoughts flitted from topic to topic.

He kept wishing he and Sara could push the clock back so that he could devote the time he should have to bringing up his sons. At least he had sired sons unlike Peter and Castle so he guessed they might see him as the one with luck on his side.

He tried to imagine how Edward was getting on in Nassau. Roger had never been there or to Rio de Janeiro either. Little did he know that was where his youngest descendant was heading on Friday to take Part 2 of the CIA Asset Assessment Exam. This exam was as different to the earlier one he passed as getting a PhD was to passing your eleven plus exam. When he returned home to Epsom, Sara asked of Edward.

'He's fine, still having a holiday until the end of the month.'

'Not out of the shade and into the mid-day sun?'

'Not according to Peter.'

'So where is Peter in all this?'

'He's in, dei gracia.'

Roger went to bed. Sara sat up late by herself. She finished reading Graham Greene's novel, The Comedians, for the third asking. She put it down and made a note in her diary to remind her to invite Sir Peter and not Sir Douglas to their New Year's Day cocktail party in 1975.

Chapter 24
Friday 19th to Saturday 27th July

Copacabana Beach, Rio de Janeiro Brazil

Leo Sanchez was on board the chartered plane that flew down from Washington DC. His plane was now taxiing towards a hanger at Nassau International Airport to be refuelled before take off to Rio.

He was anxious. What appeared to be a simple op had to be completed without a hitch. Yes, it looked simple on paper but King was as slippery and dangerous as they came. Leo locked King's file away in his briefcase. The fact that they were out to trick an ex-CIA head of station didn't help matters.

At least they had the Brit up front and his daughter was ecstatic about him. If he had been US trained King would have spotted him on arrival. Leo tried to becalm himself but his gut kept churning even though his life wasn't on the line. Only his career was but Burlington's life would be.

The flight had diplomatic status. On board with him were a doctor, a nurse and four Navy Seals who were familiar with Rio and spoke Portuguese. Seals only started working with the CIA from 1963. They were created in 1961, when John F Kennedy was US President. Marco and Edward boarded the plane at Nassau and it took off for Rio shortly afterwards.

Leo had a slide show rigged up to brief Edward, as they headed down south. He tried his best to hide his jitters as he kicked off with the first slide.

'Ok, Edward Jameson, your job is to get us in or King out through the front door, so we can bring him home to justice without a bullet being fired.'

Leo smiled somewhat awkwardly and placed a document on a thick leather folder in front of Edward, along with a pen. Edward couldn't help but notice Leo's fingers were trembling and tried to avoid looking at the man but that only made the embarrassment worse.

'Can you sign this please Ed?'

The document was full of legal jargon. Edward assumed it to be their equivalent of the Official Secrets Act, so he signed it as Leo watched him. He handed back the folder which he had closed with the document inside. Leo did not even open it to look. All he would have seen was the signature of Edward Jameson. Edward's antennae had already picked up Leo's anxiety but he said nothing as he conned his way past providing a proper signature. He wondered why the usually steady Leo was so on edge. Perhaps he wasn't used to being on the front line. More to the point, maybe he hadn't said just how dangerous this mission was.

'We don't want King for his frauds in Nassau or Vegas, it's much bigger than that.'
'Like what?'
'Let's say it's to do with illegal fundraising and leave it there.'

Leo set about reasserting his authority to help calm his nerves but Edward had realised by now that was precisely what he was doing.

'Then we won't have to talk about why you were gated in your first term at boarding school!'

'My, you have done some homework but there are no points for closing the gate after the horses have zipped off, are there? Anyway I was falsely accused, charged and arrested as was my wont so to speak. They even planted empty lager cans on me.'

Edward shrugged his shoulders as if to laugh it off but he had got it in one or thought he had: Watergate. Leo was obviously shit scared if anything went wrong but couldn't explain all. It was obvious now since he had given away just how much research they had undertaken on him. It was too much unless this mission was big and the only way Edward could see it as being big was as that this mission was a hangover from Watergate.

How the hell did they find out about his leaving the taps running? It wasn't his idea in 1963 but the assistant housemaster who was soaked while sleeping below didn't buy it because he thought Edward was drunk at the time.

The plan for Rio was for Edward to book into a hotel, then go to meet King. King was expected to ask him to stay at the marina and send some of his men to the hotel to pick up Edward's luggage. They would check his stuff to make sure he was clean and that he was who he had told Kate he was. Edward would persuade King to come quietly back to the USA with him. Failing that he would try and find a way the Seals could effect an entry and kidnap King without firing a shot.

Once back in the United States, King would know he was facing a long prison sentence, but the CIA would offer him immunity if he joined the right team. Kate and he would be given new identities and everyone would live happily ever after, apart from the bad guys. Easy? Only if you believed in fairy tales. For a start, King was a crook running from the law and the mafia. What's more his marina was in fact more of a fort surrounded by untrained trigger happy armed guards.

Leo ordered that the operation was to be closed down at once if anyone fired a shot. He also explained his non-existent contingency planning. If Ed happened to be inside the King compound, his men would seal it off but for complex diplomatic reasons there could be no gung ho rescue attempt. They could call the local cops in an

Chapter 24 - Friday 19th to Saturday 27th July

emergency but as they were probably on King's payroll Ed wouldn't be able to escape using that route.

For the first time, Edward realised the implications of what he was involved in and, unlike Harley Street, there would be no pre-planned exit if things went awry. He also sensed from Leo's mood that, if he tried to back out now, he ran the risk of a high altitude exit into shark infested waters.

As predictable as ever, Edward had jumped at the chance to visit New York and Rio but was now having major second thoughts but they were all too late. What was it with him? He needed to learn more, like only committing himself or giving his word after asking all the pertinent questions.

Kate may have been beautiful but then so was Holly. When she was kissing him goodnight at the Pink Pussycat her soft words in his ear left him in no doubt where to keep cosy in Nassau on a rainy night. So it definitely wasn't sex that motivated him. Holly was a certainty; Kate might not have even fancied him.

Edward still believed in western democracies trying to do good and being morally honest. Why not? He wasn't old or worldly enough to even know where to start to question that. His real motive was that this man King had been not far off as dissolute as the buggers Edward dealt with during his stopover in prison. King, just as they had, stole what he'd accumulated from weaker mortals. Altruism still kept Edward's heart beating and it had started pounding on this particular mission but there was a difference.

The main driver this time was that he was showing to himself he was back in the driving seat where he belonged. Yes, he still took orders and now they were from Leo Sanchez and not Alan McKenzie. Even so there was a big difference. On this occasion he and no one else decided who gave him his orders. That was the first big step he'd made in the direction of freedom in a long time and it wouldn't be the last.

His manipulators and managers were losing their grip. Mac, Tessa, his parents, Peter and now Graham along with Rupert the bulldog and Collette Fanshaw hadn't a clue he was just about to land in Rio de Janeiro. That knowledge was refreshing for him.

Apart from his altruistic tendencies, one fad hadn't changed. He still relished living dangerously, on the edge, doing things that you only saw in films. As he peered down on the Statue of Christ overlooking the sprawling metropolis beneath him the adrenalin flow was back as he buckled up his seat belt as if to contain his addiction for excitement.

Edward checked into a hotel overlooking Copacabana Beach but intentionally didn't unpack. Late on Saturday morning, he parked his spanking new hired Cadillac outside the entrance to Donald King's marina in the gorgeous sunshine. He was wired up but didn't have a gun. Within a matter of seconds, he was confronted by armed bodyguards with a pack of muzzled Dobermans and asked what he wanted.

'Mr King might be expecting me.'

'Might be?'

'His daughter Kate said I'd be coming.'

He gave them a business card and one of them patted him down while one of the others disappeared. The incompetent bodyguard didn't find any weapons, or the wire, which wasn't on his search list. Edward breathed easier until he realised Donald King was standing a yard behind him.

'You must be Edward, Eddy, Mr Burlington. Glad to meet you after all this time.'

Young Burlington swallowed saliva as he turned round, trying not to show any nervousness. The address he was given was just a front or rather a back to front to confuse anyone looking for King.

'Why didn't you call?'

'You won't believe this but Kate didn't give me your number.'

'I would believe it, I know my daughter.'

'Now she's halfway up some Honolulu mountain.'

King laughed at the Englishman's naivety.

'You mean Hawaiian mountain, there ain't any in downtown Honolulu apart from the Diamond Head crater.'

Next Edward was inside the heavily guarded compound. King's feeble effort at a joke wasn't that funny. Inside was just dark, eerily dark. The shutters were down and the lights were dimmed almost as if to spite the cacophony of light exploding outside in the hot Brazilian sunshine.

'You look just like your photos. Kate tells me you like a beer or two?'

'Just three or four.'

'I bought a couple of crates of Bud in case you called. Hope that's ok with you?'

One of the three men now with King opened two bottles using a large stiletto flick knife to remove the bottle tops. Each had a gun inside identical leather shoulder holsters and one of them was playing with the flick knife: not exactly a welcoming committee. Edward asked for a glass. King and he drank a toast to Kate and the mountains in Honolulu.

'Where you staying?'

'The Dominion.'

Once he imparted this information, Edward caught King nodding to one of his men who disappeared into the hallway. Moments later Edward heard a car driving out of the compound. He could still hear the menacing click of that stiletto flick knife as the blade snapped back in and out every few seconds.

'Why not stay here?'

'That's most kind of you, Mr King.'

'Not at all.'

Edward's luggage and Jameson's passport had been meticulously prepared and checked by Marco and his team. He was carrying all that any normal business traveller required for a three week tour of Nassau, New York and Rio.

Chapter 24 - Friday 19th to Saturday 27th July

King was outlining his plans for the marina and Edward was making small talk about planning permissions. He knew zilch about planning permissions and not much more about the real estate business. Luckily his luggage arrived before his cover could be probed. King was no fool. In the USA if you said you were into real estate in some states it meant you were a pimp or a hooker and was a flimsy cover.

Edward feigned surprise on seeing his bags arrive but King just put it down to his own natural generosity, and efficiency. A minute later Edward could just about get the gist of the end of a conversation in broken Portuguese between King and one of his bodyguards. They'd checked his passport and he had the remaining half of a return ticket to London via Miami in his briefcase. There was nothing to cause concern.

They were making serious inroads into the crate of Bud when King suggested they should go out to eat, obviously accompanied by an armed escort. Edward knew it would be easier to act now than later.

'Mr King.'

'Call me Donald.'

'Donald, do you think I might talk to you in private?'

King gave Edward a suspicious look for a moment, then a broad smile broke across his face and he waved his minders and gofers out of the room. The incessant clicking of that damn flick knife was still audible from the room next door. Beads of sweat were forming on Edward's forehead but not because of the heat. He wiped them aside striving to look less nervous than he was. He tried not to think of why Leo had been trembling on the plane or just how dangerous or important this man King was to the CIA.

'Hey Edward, sorry, Eddy I know how polite you British guys are but that's no sweat, there's no need to be embarrassed.'

'Embarrassed?'

'Sure. You want to ask for my daughter's hand in marriage, ain't that how you Brits put it?'

'Not quite.'

'Look, Eddy, you don't mind if I call you Eddy? I got no objection to you marrying Kate. It's time she settled down and you seem like a man who's doing ok for himself.'

Edward drained the Bud in his glass. He looked at King, who was smiling at him like a Cheshire cat pleased his daughter had brought this mouse home.

'Donald, I sincerely wish that was all I needed to ask you.'

King's smile faded to a puzzled expression.

'What is it then?'

'There's no easy way to say it. Kate's been kidnapped by the Polano Mob. Neither of us will ever see her alive again unless we do precisely what I'm being forced to tell you.'

'Are you kidding me Eddy?'

'I wouldn't joke about matters as serious as this sir.'

King was about to call some of his men. Edward grabbed his arm.

'Please, I love Kate. I don't want her to get killed.'

King hesitated. This was it, the moment of truth. Edward's mouth went dry. Chad Cooper wasn't outside waiting to blast through the window.

'The holiday in Hawaii?'

'That was a charade, a con, a trick and we all fell for it. I am a victim too. If you are thinking I am in on this somehow you have it all wrong.'

'I spoke to Kate when she arrived.'

'Call the Holiday Inn Hotel. Use a number from directory enquiries.'

Edward could tell from Donald King's expression that the man didn't know whether to believe him. Yet the stakes were too high for him to take a chance.

King found the number and called the hotel. They'd never had a reservation for Kate, Katie, Kath or Katherine King, Miss K King or her companion, a woman called Sharon Davide. Nothing no matter how you spelt their names. King asked them to check all the Holiday Inns in Hawaii. Nothing. Donald King hung up the phone.

'I am lost Eddy. If the flights were genuine ...'

'Of course they were. Think about it, they had to be to get her where they wanted her. Look, you said she called you to say she arrived, does your phone record incoming numbers?'

'Sure.'

'Call that number back.'

King did. The number was dead. He called directory enquiries in Honolulu. No such number ever existed. Edward realised that proved little but as Leo had said, we need you to pull every anxiety chord you can real hard.

'What do they want?'

'Your money, I suppose. Mine too although I'm not rich like you. You're to ring this number in Rio. You'll get put through to a lawyer called Gomez. They said he'll prove they have Kate and tell us what to do next.'

King was going to call the number, and then he thought better of it. Alarm bells in his mind weren't chiming in tune. He stopped dialling and put the phone down. Mr King was not buying it as Edward had packaged and tried to sell it.

'Why lure her to Hawaii, Eddy? Surely they could have simply kidnapped her in New York? You ain't working for the NSA are you?'

'Who the hell are they?'

'The US National Security Agency.'

Edward knew alright. He thought his game was over. At the very mention of the NSA the minders were instantly back in the room and that clicking noise was right behind his left ear lobe. He could smell the putrid garlic on the minder's breath.

Chapter 24 - Friday 19th to Saturday 27th July

'The CIA then?'

Edward didn't bat an eyelid but batted back with sarcasm.

'Now I have heard of them. Are you mad? What would they kidnap Kate for? Why the hell would they demand money from me, a Brit God damn it? Why don't you tell that twitchy fucker behind me to stop breathing down my neck and let's look at this rationally?'

King signalled to the minder and he backed off but not much. Edward went on the offensive.

'I'm in this fucking mess too you know. They don't just want your bloody money. Let's concentrate. Why weren't you worried about her working in New York?'

'I have people watching over her.'

'So you were fucking well watching over us while we partied and slept together. Did your minders enjoy the videos? Did they watch Kate naked? If it wasn't for Kate I'd walk out now in disgust.'

'I'm sorry Eddy. I didn't mean it. No one photographed Kate in bed or anything like that. I wouldn't allow it. I'm just so fucking mixed up I don't know what the hell is going down. I thought she was protected in New York.'

'There's your answer then. That's why they wanted her as far away as possible in Honolulu.'

'How would the Polanos know that?'

'Don't ask me, I'm British. Why don't you ask your men what they know? How should I be expected to know everything? I'm no expert on kidnapping. I'm just a real estate guy trying to make a good living.'

Edward's plan was working as King glowered at his minders. By now he could trust no one.

'I didn't want to get caught up in all this shit. Maybe they used private eyes to watch her every move. Who knows? The Polanos could have bribed anybody, even the bodyguards you had to protect Kate. The cost would be small beer for them or anyone compared to a double bloody ransom ... one from you and one from me.'

King told his minders to get out in no uncertain terms.

'... and close both the fucking doors behind you.'

Edward's cunning plant in the mind of this paranoid man that his bodyguards might know something had hit him slap bang on the chin, just as expected. It was clear he now suspected his own men of some involvement in the kidnap rather than Edward.

The CIA weren't as fastidious and nit picking as the British intelligence services when it came to planning. There were holes in Edward's cover story. He had talked fast trying to cover all the bases and, luckily for him, just like most Dads in these circumstances Donald King wasn't thinking straight. That was until the word Polano finally sank into his thick skinned skull.

'Yeah, I guess you could be right. God dam shit it. Those money grabbing wops! They kill people for fun, not money.'

Edward was trying to work out in his mind whether killing for fun was much worse than murdering for money. Meanwhile King reluctantly called Gomez and after a minute or so of fencing around asked him how the last banker's draft he bounced in the Diamond Casino in Las Vegas differed from the rest. Gomez, or whoever was talking to King, had the answer.

'It was the only one for US$1.2 million.'

Donald King was frantic by now. He knew what the Polano family was capable of doing. He spoke to the man on the phone.

'What d'you want me to do?'

'The pair of you go back to Jameson's hotel with the damn luggage your men just collected. Take no weapons, no minders or your daughter is going to start looking less beautiful than when you last saw her. Call me again when you get there. You have one hour.'

'How do I know Kate's alive?'

'Take down this number.'

King wrote it down and tried to speak but Gomez hung up on him. Donald King realised he wasn't in control for once.

He dialled the number. That was Hawaiian too.

'Yeah?'

'Gomez said I could speak to my daughter, Kate.'

The phone went quiet at the other end. Then ...

'Dad, Dad please help me ...'

Edward couldn't hear the words but he could hear the scream. A rough voice came back on the other end of the line.

'That's the last time you'll hear from her unless you and Jameson both stop fucking about and do as you're both fucking told. You tell that fucker Jameson he's had it too if he tries any fucking fancy stuff.'

Donald King dropped the phone. Edward knew he was a beaten man. King picked up his half empty Bud bottle. While King had been writing down the number in Hawaii to call, Edward had slipped a sedative into the bottle that King was now finishing off.

Edward and Donald King left for the Dominion Hotel overlooking Copacabana Beach. Edward drove in his hired Cadillac and King was unarmed. None of his bodyguards went with them.

After about a mile, King passed out from the sedative and Edward pulled over to the side of the road. King was transferred to a van that had been tailing him at a discrete distance. Edward also climbed into the van with his luggage. The van was full of audio equipment. A man Edward hadn't seen before got into his hire car and drove it away. Marco Sanchez shook his hand.

Chapter 24 - Friday 19th to Saturday 27th July

'You're one cool dude, Edward the Eddy Jameson. What was that line again, "Don't ask me, I'm British"? Is that what you say every time you're cornered? We thought you were just about to get punched or shot. Even the Dobermans were getting restless. What was that constant clicking noise we could hear?'

'A stiletto flick knife. It freaked me out too.'

The van headed for the airport. Leo was still tense and insisted on one of the Seals gagging King for some unknown reason. It was noticeable because Mr King was unconscious and couldn't speak if he tried. On the flight Edward asked Marco why. Marco hadn't any idea and Leo pretended not to have heard the question. Otherwise the flight was uneventful.

Until he was entrapped by the CIA in Rio de Janeiro, Donald King had been a close friend and business associate of Bobby Vesco. Just like Vesco, King was peripherally involved with Richard Nixon and the Watergate fiasco. Unlike Vesco, King became a key witness for the prosecution and was given a fresh start by the FBI or to be precise the US Department of Justice under their Witness Protection Program. King was one of the first to be enrolled under the Program, introduced into the USA by the Organised Crime Control Act of 1970.

However, King was more important to the CIA than simply that. What Leo did not tell Marco was King used to be a CIA asset and an important one too. He had operated in Rio for many years but in his latter days as an agent he got to know his way around places like Tegucigalpa, Managua, Santa Ana and Bogota like a native. His missions were known only to Jimmy Butler Junior who had leaked that he'd been fired for falsifying his expenses in Rio.

If Marco or Ed thought this was the last time they were to encounter Donald King they were mistaken. This Mr King was more intriguing than Vesco, more dangerous than Jordan and as Machiavellian as Smith. In a similar vein to Burton he was that rubber ball you could never throw away but in contrast to Burton he was relatively civilised.

Leo knew all that even if Marco and Ed didn't and praised Ed for his cool handling of a potentially dangerous, complex and volatile situation. Unlike your typical film in this genre made from standard prison issue bog paper, in real life and here not all our operations end with the US cavalry or Chad Cooper arriving ten seconds before Armageddon!

This operation could have turned distinctly disagreeable with Edward being taken hostage. Luckily for him it hadn't but it had only been a trial run in one respect although it wasn't a dummy one by any measurement. In terms of Leo's priorities this op had been top of the pile and given King's experience its outcome had been comprehensively unpredictable. The CIA weren't finished with Ed. They had only just started. At least Edward could now choose who he did what for and when. He was well on the way to being more in charge of his own destiny.

New Providence & Paradise Islands Bahamas

It took until late July for Edward's apartment to be made ready. The work would've been done in half the time back in the UK but this was Nassau. The deal Marco pushed on the apartment was that the CIA paid for the security. That included the phones and calls, parking and all service charges. Intentionally not much but a gesture now Ed had helped deliver Donald King.

Leo knew from his research too that if they were overly generous or just paid Ed normally it might backfire and that was the last problem he wanted to handle. Ed knew full well that as a safe-house the apartment would be bugged from under the floor boards to above the ceiling but he didn't give a damn. He'd been living in one goldfish bowl or another much of his life. Anyway, the bugs might even save his life one day.

He thought he knew how to outwit the CIA whenever he wanted, just as he outwitted his prefects at school and those in the intelligence services who monitored him in London. There were hidden cameras outside the apartment block and in the elevator. No doubt there would be more inside the apartment itself once it had been fully refurbished.

The lack of privacy was a small price for Ed to pay for the level of security it provided. The flat was in a fabulous location, a few yards from the beach, a stroll from the Nassau Beach Hotel and a small shopping mall as well as being equidistant between downtown Nassau and the international airport.

You could easily fly from the Bahamas to almost anywhere in the USA and back again in one day, as long as there was a direct flight to a nearby city. Miami Beach and Fort Lauderdale were both about half an hour away from downtown Nassau by seaplane.

Edward bought a second hand hard topped black Camaro which he loved, but there weren't many roads where he could take off, see what it could do. It had a high-tech radio and the first song he heard in his car was George McRae's "Rock your baby", which was number one in the US.

He couldn't park the car in a secure area, as he did with the Jag in London. There was no secure area so it could be tagged by anyone. He didn't care one iota about that either. If you thought about why you shouldn't do something for long enough, you'd never do anything. So why not just get on with it and live life to the full? That was his philosophy but he knew his mother and father would have a fit if they heard him advocate it.

So far as women were concerned, until recently, Edward's single man lifestyle meant that the one night affairs of the past were no longer regular occurrences. His intense relationship with Suzie took the gloss off that disposition for him although his brief encounter with Kate King had reminded him of what he was missing.

Chapter 24 - Friday 19th to Saturday 27th July

Suzie had left a huge psychological imprint on him and he longed for what they had together to reincarnate but it didn't. There wasn't anybody in Nassau in his sights yet to take her place even though he was tempted by Holly and dreamt about many others including Collette and even Linda whom he had only viewed through his monocular's lens.

Before the sun set that Saturday evening Edward met Marco Sanchez by a swimming pool outside a discothèque on Paradise Island. They had left Rio early that afternoon thanks to everything with King having passed so smoothly. The pool and disco bar belonged to the hotel where Jordan stayed but he was long gone by now.

'I doubt they have a clue about what you're doing, Ed?'

'Who?'

'Your guys at Porter Williams.'

'Not their business.'

Marco laughed.

'I reckon you must find them pretty boring?'

'Harmless might be a better word but I don't know them yet so never judge a library by its librarians. It's refreshing to be with normal people but you might have forgotten that mate.'

In the USA, Richard Nixon was on his way out and America was in civil turmoil as the world's media focused the spotlight on Watergate.

'Was Donald King mixed up in all that Nixon stuff or more besides?'

'No comment.'

The Supreme Court Chief Justice rejected Nixon's claims of executive privilege and ordered him to surrender all the tape recordings of White House conversations. The scandal was getting messy and embarrassing for the USA. Marco changed the subject.

'What d'you know about Bahamian bank secrecy laws?'

'Only that I've been told never to break them.'

'Good advice. The government here takes these laws seriously. If you were caught, you'd probably die in prison.'

Marco waved to one of the waiters.

'They're sloppy here tonight.'

The waiter came, and so did the drinks.

'People use these Bahamian banks for hot money, to avoid paying their taxes. They are mainly US citizens. I get paid a third of what the IRS recovers in tax, interest and penalties if I report someone. You know who the IRS are?'

Edward knew who the IRS were: who didn't?

'Well, it's getting difficult to get through bank security nowadays. They even encrypt stuff now and then put it on the computers. That's unfair.'

Edward wasn't stupid. He knew where this conversation was leading. Marco went on to spell out the dangers involved which was more than they'd ever done in London. The CIA man said if Ed ended up in a Bahamian prison he'd probably be buggered to death by the black inmates after the guards had taken their toll.

'Before you came here two Dutch accountants were caught stealing information from the Bank of Nova Scotia. The police really buggered them and their bodies were dumped in the sea.'

'Ok, Marco, I get the point. It is dangerous to steal bank information.'

'You got it.'

'So you're asking me to do just that.'

'You don't need stuff spelled out for you, do you, Ed?'

Edward lit up a cigarette and took a drink from his glass while he worked out the pros and cons of doing this menial stuff for the Americans. He'd already seen how they operated down in Rio, when it could've gone either way like the flip of a coin, heads or tails, dead or alive. They took less care in catering for contingencies than the likes of Alan McKenzie. They didn't try to plan for every conceivable outcome, like their British counterparts. They gave their assets much more leeway instead.

It became clear to Edward that, if he did agree to this, he'd have to think on his feet as opposed to going by the handbook. He'd have to do what came naturally rather than play by the rules. It all added up to his being free to do what he was good at: being in charge of his own destiny.

Edward had already decided what he would and would not do. Given time he knew he would get bored doing nothing but accountancy and auditing. No one would get hurt except greedy bastards who didn't want to pay their taxes on money that was probably stolen anyway. It would serve them right. Marco reckoned he knew by the glint in his eye that the Englishman was up for it.

'Look, Ed, I should be safe enough because I have diplomatic immunity. Anything I have on me can't be searched. Even so, that fat cigar-smoking over promoted constable Winston Bridges don't give a goddamn about diplomatic protocol.'

'What's he got to do with it?'

'Winston's in charge of financial and economic crime every which way you want to interpret it.'

Edward remembered Winston from the Government House reception. He looked like a tough corrupt bastard and he was in with all the wrong people. No doubt Bridges could probably get away with murder. In fact he no doubt had already. Better to stay out of his clutches.

'You wouldn't believe what people get up to so as to hide their identities. They used dental x-rays at one bank with instructions that a qualified dentist had to confirm who they belonged to before cash could be withdrawn.'

Chapter 24 - Friday 19th to Saturday 27th July

Edward wasn't concentrating on Marco now. There were so many beautiful women round the pool and instead of trying to score with one of them he was listening to Marco going on and on about the IRS and tax evasion. Surely he hadn't changed that much in the last six months?

'Some use thumb and finger prints as the only link to their accounts, others use false names and codes. It gets real complex when computers are used with encrypted messages.'

'Ok, Marco, enough. As an auditor, this is what I can do. You tell me what you need. I get the information. We meet for lunch and one of your men takes the stuff from the boot of my car, that's the trunk to you. Your gofer gets it copied and returns the originals. We finish lunch and nothing happened.'

'Sounds perfect.'

'To be on the safe side, I'll make sure there are plenty of other documents in the car, the old snowflake in a snow storm routine. If anyone checks, they won't be able to pinpoint papers on your depositors as the sole purpose of the meet and all I'm doing is taking the paperwork to Porter Williams to work on it. I can't help it if the CIA nicks the contents of my trunk.'

Marco Sanchez was impressed. Two more beers came, without him having to call the waiter this time.

'Just one small detail Marco ...'

'What's that?'

'I'm not going to do it for the IRS. If you have a specific target and can prove why you want him, like you did with King, that is a different matter. I don't want to be a vacuum cleaner for the IRS.

MI6 may have much more interesting jobs lined up for me, I'll bet. It has nothing to do with damn money. I have enough to live comfortably but I am no millionaire. You should know that by now if you've done your homework properly. Thanks but no thanks as we say in London village.'

'Ok. Why don't we wait for something more exciting to come along?'

'I'll drink to that. Otherwise don't ask me, remember I'm British!'

Marco didn't laugh as he swilled back his beer. He wasn't looking particularly self-satisfied. After today's lesson Marco learned Ed was no pushover but he didn't give up. Just like Ed, he wasn't that type.

'Of course, it doesn't stop with the IRS. We help the FBI on drug trafficking and money laundering and do our own things too.'

'I'm still listening even if I'm not looking.'

'You could help us out hunting down specific names every now and again or on some assignments.'

'I get the specific route. I said I would consider each job on its own merits.'

'You'd be a CIA asset ...'

People passing by said hi to Marco and he waved a greeting back to them. Everyone in this town seemed to know him. How many in town knew who he was? Edward was getting exasperated by Marco's persistence.

'As I said Marco, if I am told all, all any normal person would need to know to make a sensible, the right decision, then I'm available. To repeat though, just so you don't forget or ask more questions why, money isn't my Cadillac driver.'

'Don't ask me, I'm from Washington DC!'

They both laughed this time.

'I understand you Ed. I'll run anything specific past you but we'll dump the vacuum cleaning jobs. You know, you're just a simple guy who drinks too much beer and seems to be too interested in American or are they Canadian tourists?'

Marco winked at Ed as if that was it and they could start having some fun. There were many fresh faces in town since Edward left for New York.

'Who else knows I'm helping the US government?'

'Me and Leo, that's all.'

'No problem, no problem at all except for those two chicks dancing over there. I prefer the brunette. My spies with their little eyes say she's looking for a Brit and the dumb blonde with the boobs likes Virginians!'

Edward winked as Marco had. That was like a hand shake, there was no more to say and Marco called the waiter over again.

'Joseph, get those two whatever they're drinking and tell them we're the really good guys they've been searching for all day.'

'Yes sir.'

'Hang on Joseph, four more draught Buds here too.'

They toasted Rio and more to come and started focusing on something else they were both accomplished at doing.

The drinks were delivered. Both the girls looked over and giggled to themselves, then brought their drinks over to join Marco and Ed. The brunette's name was Mandy and she came from Toronto with her buxom blond friend. Today was the last day of Mandy's vacation and the first time Edward had been free from any chains for years. Mandy was a bundle of laughter and merriment until she snuggled up warm to Edward and transformed into a bundle of ecstatic delight.

When they all met that evening Edward would have bet a million bucks he'd wake up in the morning somewhere in the Bahamas. We know had he done so he would have lost and if he had written it down in his diary he would have had to erase it the next day!

Chapter 25
Sunday 28th July to Thursday 1st August

Oakville, Toronto Canada

Edward woke up in a huge bed in the luxurious Park Plaza Hotel in downtown Toronto. He was reasonably sure he was in Toronto. The naked body of Mandy, asleep beside him was reassuring. He went to the window and peered out over a deserted courtyard and the streets beyond it. Not having done any normal work for weeks, he was unsure what day it was.

It couldn't be a working day or there would be traffic and people milling about in the streets. He turned on the TV and just caught the beginning of the six o'clock morning news. It was Toronto alright and today was Sunday 28th July. The weather man forecast a clear day, with a high of 86 degrees. As the sound of the television woke Mandy she opened her eyes and smiled when she saw his naked body.

'Edward.'

'Good morning sunshine.'

'How long have I slept?'

'There's still time for Mandy's first of the day.'

Edward turned the TV off and was back in bed before she could sit up straight.

'How did I ...'

'Superbly. You performed so well I need reminding.'

They spent the next hour wrapped together until they both decided the sunshine outside was too good to miss.

Edward called room service. Breakfast arrived promptly as ordered, with a couple of bottles of Bud for him and a spritzer for Mandy. The waffles, strawberries and cream with maple syrup were lifesavers and they were soon as right as a randy rabbits once more.

They took a shower together which slowed progress. Mandy had to dispose of his erection thrice and then Edward dressed in the same jeans and shirt he was wearing on Saturday night. His wallet and passport were luckily still in his back pockets. Now he was in Canada, there was only one trip he'd always wanted to make, that is before he met Mandy.

Niagara Falls, Canada & USA

Edward hired a Cadillac convertible and drove down along the eastern edge of Lake Ontario to Niagara Falls. Mandy came with him after he insisted she put on some clothes and they laughed together as the wind on his face cleared his mind and he knew something had changed, a fresh era was upon him. He had told Mandy what happened to Suzie and Mandy had helped carry the burden, take it away never to be forgotten but not to smother his every breath.

That lingering melancholy had left him and he was back, back to his old self. He'd forcefully placed the memory of Suzie Laurent behind him for the first time since her violent ending. Even though it had been only just over a month ago he was ready to move forward again. As Mandy had said, she would have wanted, demanded no less of him. He was healthy again. The dark remorse enveloping her murder was bad for him and he knew it. Only now had he been able to shake it off with Mandy's help. His thoughts of Suzie had turned into positive memories.

The pair of them viewed the Horseshoe Falls and the American Falls from the Canadian side first. Mandy was so natural. An emotional open door, childlike but womanly: it was as if they had been married for years. Next they crossed the border into the US to view the Bridal Veil Falls and follow along all the usual well trodden tourist paths. No one asked to see their passports. That reminded Edward of some of his earlier border crossings with his mother.

Niagara Falls was a memorable experience for him and it made him happy being with Mandy watching its splendour together. He was glad not just for seeing the majestic Falls themselves but also for Mandy's zeal and determination to help emancipate him from the ghoulish trance surrounding Suzie's death. Suzie seemed to be there standing shoulder to shoulder with Mandy willing him to return to being the man she loved, not the man that mourned her. It was a watershed, an exorcism. There was still a score to settle, of course but that had to wait until the time was right and he held the upper ground.

They drove back to Toronto that evening. Mandy washed Edward's clothes and left them to dry overnight. They were still damp in the morning but they soon dried out in the heat. Edward had lost track of time during their ceaseless love making which had sapped every last drop of energy out of them both. Later, exhausted, the couple parted.

Paradoxically their parting had more the air of a reunion about it. They both knew deep down inside they'd never forget each other but never see each other again as well. He promised to call her, if ever he woke up and found himself in Toronto again and she reciprocated the promise.

There was one other place Edward wanted to see, as long as he was this far north, and that was the downtown towers in Chicago. That's where he decided to go despite all the deadlines looming for his starting work, leaving the Nassau Beach Hotel and

Chapter 25 - Sunday 28th July to Thursday 1st August

moving into his new apartment. He didn't know if his apartment was ready to move into yet as the electricity wasn't working last time he'd spoken to the decorators. This was Edward of old, always living on the brink, and he relished in it because it was of his making.

The South Side & Downtown Chicago, Illinois USA

On Monday 29th July Edward picked up another Cadillac convertible at O'Hare Airport and headed downtown. Before leaving Toronto, Mandy gave him some sound advice.

'Never hit the south side, day or night, or you might come back in a box.'

Edward was so overwhelmed by the freeway when the lanes started changing direction that he went with the flow and ended up lost. He kept on driving around, taking a left here and a right there until he noticed that he hadn't seen a white person for at least three miles. He pulled up at a gas station to get directions and, when he came back outside five young black guys were all over the Cadillac. There was no debate. He was in the south side.

They looked threatening as he walked at a measured pace towards them showing no fear. The taller of them held what looked like a crowbar in his left hand half hidden under an oily old rag; whatever was there Edward smelt the danger. He stretched out his arms as wide as he could as if a goalkeeper awaiting a penalty and trying to put off his adversary and then put on his biggest smile. He was praying they would read his t-shirt.

'Hey chaps, what's going on downtown tonight?'

His English accent and Bahamian t-shirt threw them into confusion. The t-shirt read Black is Black in the Bahamas. Holly gave it to him saying it would definitely attract all the black pussy cats in town. Now his clothing was being used for an entirely different purpose, defence. They looked at Edward for what seemed a long moment, and then smiled back. The taller of them jettisoned his crowbar.

'Hey, man, you from Bahama? Cool dude man.'

They all started lining up, as if for communion and shook his hand patting him on the back and talking to him in a patois he could only barely understand. He kept smiling trying to look like a cool dude and the danger passed. Edward reckoned they hadn't seen the inside of a church since they were christened if they ever had been.

'Hey guys, where's the action in this town?'

'We can show this white dude some action.'

'Climb aboard guys.'

The blacks had never travelled in a brand new Cadillac convertible before. Edward followed their directions downtown.

'You want some real action man?'

'Sure.'

They pulled up outside a small cinema. Edward could see signs to the Central Station so knew he was downtown.

'I don't want to go to the movies.'

The black guys all laughed loudly and clapped him on the back, as if he'd just told them a hilarious joke.

'Just go man.'

'Where will I leave the car?'

'We'll take care of the parking lot.'

Edward handed over the keys. They were all smoking hash and he joined in with them. One of them took his car off to park it.

'Are you guys sure this is safe for a white guy?'

They all laughed again.

'Just hit inside dude. You be ok with us.'

Inside the cinema there was a house party going on. Edward had never been in or even heard of a den of iniquity like this. It made the clubs in the north of England seem like nursery schools. The stench of dope, sweat and sex filled the theatre. The relentless beat of the music filled his head. The party people were having it off all over the place no positions barred. From the stalls to the balcony, no one was bashful. There were unclothed couples on stage performing Kama Sutra exhibitions with style and zest in time to the incessant music. The scene was theatrical, as if it had been choreographed.

Two of his new friends were chaperoning him and had by now become his bodyguards. He was the only white person in the cinema. They told him to stay close to them. The other two had been absorbed into the melee by friends they passed before reaching the main bar. The fifth was kindly parking Edward's hire car but not downtown.

Just after three in the morning Edward finally left the theatre come cinema and returned to his hotel. He flopped onto the bed and his lights went out.

Next morning, with guidance from a charming receptionist he did some quick shopping for new clothes. Luckily he brought some bathroom necessities including his electric razor from Nassau but alas no clothes. Unlike Hugh, Edward always felt uncomfortable if he hadn't shaved and brushed his teeth in the morning.

He reported to the car hire company his Cadillac had gone walkabouts. Edward guessed it might be in a thousand pieces by now or had its appearance changed beyond recognition. Once armed with fresh clothes and a new holdall he showered, dressed and devoured yet more glorious waffles and a few pints of milk. At least he hadn't woken up to find two or three black girls in his bed.

Edward spent the rest of Tuesday 30th July sightseeing round Chicago. The weather was perfection personified, a beautiful hot summer's day, with visibility of seventeen miles, according to the TV, so he went up the Sears Tower, then the tallest

Chapter 25 - Sunday 28th July to Thursday 1st August

building in the world. He wanted to see if the vertigo he'd been left with after the botulism poisoning was still there. That wasn't a particularly good idea because he was still marginally stoned from the previous night and stepped into a high speed goods elevator by mistake.

He had to be scraped off the floor when it arrived at the level below the Skydeck. Once in the observation tower he kept a respectful distance from the glass as the vertigo broke loose. Come what may he wasn't going to let anything bother him now he was carefree again. Next he hit the Hancock Tower. He enjoyed his own company in the clearness of the day, with downtown Chicago at his feet and a new life waiting for him back in the Bahamas.

Edward left Chicago that evening. He only had one day left to prepare for starting work at Porter Williams, Nassau.

West Bay Street Nassau, New Providence Island Bahamas

Finally Edward's holiday ended on 31st July. When he returned to the Nassau Beach Hotel there were a few messages for him. The Fanshaws had tried to call him again and again. Graham Sidney-Smith left a message saying Edward's work permit was in place. The decorators reported his apartment at Governor's Beach was now ready.

Moving out of the Nassau Beach Hotel was a sorrowful experience. Although he'd hardly spent any time there during the past month, he had grown attached to it. The beach bar was still his favourite watering hole on the island, apart from the Pink Pussycat of course. At least the hotel was within walking distance of his new home.

After unpacking his meagre belongings, which still only filled one suitcase, Edward spent much of Wednesday 31st July calling England. He told his mother and father he'd been sunbathing and was looking forward to starting work in the morning. He also had a long chat with Tessa, who revealed that she was seeing Hugh regularly and the two of them were growing ever closer. Hugh had even had a rare taste of Brummie life and met Tessa's family in Edgbaston or Idgbastin as Tessa's oldest brother called it.

Ed's main call was to his brother. Hugh's face had finally healed and he could talk normally. He even tried out his Brummie accent which failed to impress Ed to such a degree that he answered back in Geordie. They agreed that if Edward couldn't get home for Christmas, Hugh would come out to Nassau instead. Hugh said Tessa might come too depending on all sorts of ifs and buts to do with her work and if they had enough cash.

'How are we doing in the league?'

'You won't believe it. Porter Williams are second. They would be first but for the goal difference.'

'Good God! That's the most incredible news I've heard this year.'

'You know what they put it down to?'

'I'm listening.'

'Joe Ritchie in goal.'

'Since when?'

'When did you last play?'

'Piss off Hugh.'

Hugh was in different sorts of stitches than medical ones, stitches of sardonic laughter, until they talked about Raj Gupta Khan without mentioning his name. Edward could hear Scamp in the background along with the occasional siren of some passing emergency.

'He's left Porter Williams, of course.'

'How do you know that?'

'T told me. He's set up in his own accountancy practice.'

'How?'

'Well, that could be a long story.'

Both Edward and Hugh knew better than to say too much over the phone in an unrehearsed conversation. You never knew who was listening. In this case, Edward did: the CIA. Not that it mattered much given their ability to help themselves to most electronic data and information they weren't provided with gratis courtesy of their seat on the JIC.

'So, he's being monitored?'

'Yes, but they're getting impatient.'

'Is T keeping an ear to the ground?'

'Of course. There have been developments, to do with diamonds.'

Edward decided they'd best curtail the conversation. He told Hugh to keep clear of any trouble and take good care of Scamp. He even had a word with Scamp before hanging up: the woof indicated recognition of one of his masters' voices and that he liked watching David Attenborough wildlife videos.

Edward had bought them for Scamp before leaving for Nassau. He had read that it really was a dog's life for dogs left at home alone but that leaving a video or the TV on helped prevent them getting lonely, anxious and depressed. Hugh always played them for Scamp when he had to leave him alone for more than a couple of hours.

Edward's diary that night was full of hope without fear as he jotted down his expectations of the day ahead: they were to be surpassed.

Chapter 26
Thursday 1st August to Monday 23rd September

Bay Street Nassau, New Providence Island Bahamas

Edward turned up for work at nine o'clock on the dot on 1st August. Apart from the cleaners he was the only one there. When the others finally arrived, he was told his first job was to work on an audit of the Bahamian Royal Bank. The partner in charge was Graham Sidney-Smith and the manager, Paul Rutherford.

Rutherford was a long term expatriate in his mid-thirties who'd worked his way around the Caribbean. Paul had already decided to retire in Nassau as soon as possible. He held no aspirations in becoming a partner and was only interested in buying a bigger and better boat to go fishing.

The abysmal quality of his audit files defined his professional pride. Albeit he was pretty observant and knowledgeable so far as local banking laws and practices went, he was strictly a ten to four man. His audit team were anything but enthusiastic and wouldn't even have been considered for a job in London.

There was only one black qualified accountant in the firm although the trainees were increasing in number. His name was Christopher Albury and he was on a fast track to becoming a partner. Under the ever changing employment laws, all companies had to have a Bahamian citizen as a director and now that was soon to apply to partners in partnerships.

Chris was far more intelligent and dedicated than any of the sun, sea and shark seeking Brits in the office, apart from Graham. Edward and Chris were pals from the start. It had helped that Mr Albury was able to instantly resolve Edward's biggest dilemma since arriving: where to show off his goalkeeping skills.

Even so, it still meant if there was anyone to watch out for regarding non-adherence to bank security laws, it would be Chris. The partners considered him to be a government spy and he considered them to be overpaid crooks.

Chris had two basic contentions. The lack of training and opportunity for local kids came first. Second was the corrupt and needless spinning out of liquidations to make more fees for accountancy firms. He was a moral and churchgoing man but considered taxation to be a sin so evading it couldn't be wrong.

There was no taxation of any kind in the Bahamas and telling Bahamians like Chris that the banks' customers were crooks and tax dodgers didn't work. The Bahamas had no equivalent to the IRS or the British Inland Revenue and it took Edward some time to get his head round that from all sorts of dimensions. The ramifications of a country having no tax affected every walk of life from the gutters full of dead kittens over the hill to the marinas choc a bloc with sparkling yachts moored outside the mansions in Lyford Cay.

Most of the time in the seventies firms of accountants and lawyers as well as banks in tax havens had to be up to no good just to stay in business. The problem was how to define good or bad and that depended on which side of whose laws you backed. The expatriates spent hours debating these issues just as Porter Williams' partners did to justify their heavy duty tax free charge out rates.

Even Chris Albury supported egregiously high fees, but only for overseas clients of course. Why? Simple, it was because they got tax relief on them. Although his arguments differed from those of the Bahamian Brits, as one might have expected the size of their net worth was their common choice of chauffeur. Morality was normally firmly in the boot or trunk and rarely even in a back seat to comment on the driver.

Where these businesses' profits came from was of little interest to any of the pros involved as long as it didn't look bad. If a dictator used their services to hide his syphoning off charitable aid from his starving impoverished citizens, who even noticed? Were they to help disguise profits from the heroin trade as foreign exchange dealing gains, who cared? If they advised on the indirect financing of ethnic cleansing, who gave a shit? Any services were totally acceptable as long as bank secrecy laws prevented the accountants, lawyers and bankers implicated from telling anyone.

Edward steered away from the many debates about the consequences of doing business in a tax haven. For him, mass murderers and drug barons deserved what they got as did those who parasitically profited from them so fuck the ridged client confidentiality rules and phoney bank secrecy laws.

Why was secrecy about crime not secondary to basic morality as enshrined in most civilised countries' laws? No wonder the gap twixt rich and poor throughout the world was always widening. Mind you it had been worse in the Bahamas before independence when its waves were ruled by Britannia. In Edward's mind crime shouldn't pay and if it harmed the weak and innocent the perpetrators should pay, dearly and not just in cash.

He didn't like to thrash out these sorts of issues with those holding opposing views at social gatherings. It was as pointless as telling a starving African kid not to eat a poisoned banana. The accountants, lawyers and bankers weren't starving kids though. They were fat cats and like so many so called professionals should have looked more closely at who filled up their pay packets.

Chapter 26 - Thursday 1st August to Monday 23rd September

What made it worse was many of the expats smoked more dope in a week than he did in months and in some lesser known firms they snorted cocaine or injected heroin in the loos at work. He never released the pent up anger he held back listening to that particularly nasty breed of expats he met at social events opine on the core moral issues as they, the hypocrites, saw them.

They had never seen the evil that ultimately paid for most of their tax free salaries and their fat cat partners' profits. They never acknowledged evil was the driving force behind all the hot money that flowed like lava wreaking havoc and horror in its trail. To think these professionals were being rewarded for assisting tax avoidance was naive. As naive as thinking Papa Doc Duvalier, the father of modern Haiti was kind and gentle and his Tonton Macoute were recruited from monasteries.

Edward wasn't going to sit back idly and watch dictators' looting humanitarian aid programmes or the mafia laundering their drug monies through Nassau. If he could nail any of the players the consequences were entirely their fault. That had been his offer to Marco. To help if called upon in that specific arena but so far he hadn't been called.

No one forced Central American dictators to starve their citizens to death while they filled their offshore bank accounts with diverted aid funds. Normal people didn't have to become heroin addicts just so that the mafia could lounge about in luxurious yachts. Of course the yachts were paid for by laundered money through tailor made offshore trusts and companies housed in expensive prime real estate, all organised by their offshore professional advisers.

Perhaps Edward didn't belong in the Bahamas after all. He could argue until the owls dozed off how morally justified he was in determining by himself his perfidious path as some misguided souls might have described it. Yet they had probably never been confronted by the likes of Oswaldo López, Cyrus Burton or the Manunta Mob or had dealings with the Polanos or even Poulson and co.

He knew it had to be a lonely and most likely a dangerous trail to take but this was his decision. As a result Edward started to steer well clear of any office politics. He opted out of office or coke parties or boat and hemp trips. Apart from earning himself the reputation of being a loner, prima facie he had an uneventful seemingly inauspicious start at Porter Williams in Nassau.

As was the way of the Burlingtons nothing was as it seemed. The lack of security in the office suited Edward down to the bottom of every filing cabinet. It gave him time to plan before deciding which of Marco's targets he would take on board if asked.

There was one small cupboard for keys to the offices of the banks Porter Williams were auditing and it was rarely locked. Computers weren't password protected and sensitive documents were openly on display all over the place. So Edward volunteered to work overtime at Porter Williams, to help get uniform tests and filing systems used on all audits, in line with London.

A blitz approach was needed and he didn't want any extra pay, he just wanted to work in an orderly environment or that's what he told Graham. Under the current system, looking for anything on any file was a nightmare. All the expats used their own methods that they'd learned from other firms and there was no uniformity.

Edward's biggest task was doing the unheard of, namely convincing the partners he needed to work at weekends. This was unprecedented in Nassau. Graham said it could spread, as if he was talking about a virulent virus. A realistic estimate that it might save the annual cost of two expat accountants and Edward's persistence won the day in the end and he was given a set of keys to the office.

Marco then made copies of all the other keys Edward borrowed from the cupboard so as to be able to go anywhere he wanted when or if ever called upon to do so. What's more he could raid files in storage, he could access bank records and he could do it when no one else was there. Marco was well pleased especially as many of the keys were to the offices of Porter Williams' clients.

Several uneventful weeks passed before Marco offered Edward his first target. In the interim, the work at Porter Williams interested Edward as he was learning all the intriguing tricks of those professionals he despised so much. He soon learnt how the cess pit of dictators' and drug barons' wealth kept on earning exponentially larger tax free profits for all and sundry behind the locked doors of bank secrecy.

Socially speaking Edward was having a ball but it didn't satisfy him even though he was sleeping with a different Canadian or American chick every week. It had all become too blasé. The Fanshaws took him out or asked him over for dinner every other week but Edward steered clear of Collette's Mrs Robinson moves. He was sorely tempted though; he reckoned she'd be a strict disciplinarian if he came and joined in her nature classes. No doubt she was an instructive teacher.

Chris Albury kept his promise and Edward played soccer south of the hill once a week either on Saturday mornings or mid-week in the evenings. The evenings were preferable to professional Edward! They were much cooler even if all he did was stand in front of goal.

Edward was the only white in the team but that didn't bother him or the team. He considered his skills weren't being used to their full though. Chris's attacking team, of which Chris was captain, invariably won. Most of every match saw the ball in the opposition's half of the pitch about seventy percent of the time so the quality of Edward's goalkeeping was rarely tested.

Edward saw little of Marco or Leo in the first few weeks of August. They were too busy saying goodbye to Richard Nixon and hello to Gerald Ford's classmates. He made the acquaintance of his neighbours at Governor's Beach. None of them were British and most were connected to the casino or shipping industries.

He also touched base with the police in the pillbox at the gate, just so they'd know who he was at night. Edward didn't want to be shot if he came back late one evening

Chapter 26 - Thursday 1st August to Monday 23rd September

smelling of alcohol. Marco told him they had guns hidden there even though they were in theory unarmed like British police.

Life continued in the slow lane, from Edward's perspective anyway, until about mid-September, when he was invited to yet another expat party. Mind you, he was getting inured to the leisurely pace and liked it in some ways. Normally he avoided these get-togethers and rarely went to them.

This time Paul Rutherford persuaded him saying they were mainly from a different crowd from the usual conch crunchers who even bored him. Paul introduced Edward to Jasmine Moreau, a tall, well stacked sexy and she knew it seductive quadroon from Guadeloupe. She wore glasses but not much else and once the glasses were off most men would have wanted their hands on her hot pants. Ed certainly did and wasn't slow in putting his hands where nature intended them to be!

He was attracted to her and vice versa from the outset. Who wouldn't have been attracted to her? Had Whitney Houston been famous by then Ed could not have been reprimanded for thinking either Whitney or her lookalike had just been introduced.

She said she answered to Jazz but not Jasmine so he said he'd answer only to her. At first she said she was a student but it seemed that she had once led an itinerant lifestyle, working in Miami, New York and Washington DC. Edward took her home that night. She liked sex and she liked cannabis. They combined the two and established a strong affinity for each other. Within a week, Jazz and Edward were living together at Governor's Beach but to be on the safe side, Edward asked Marco to check her history.

'She worked for US embassies in various Caribbean islands.'

'What did she do?'

'She was thrown out, too many drugs.'

'I mean, what was her job?'

'The French would call her a femme fatale. We'd call her a high class hooker. She was rumoured to have had a connection with the Fanshaws. My bet is she had a fling with Collette. I think she's only about twenty you know, no college education, barely two dimes to bang about in her hot pants.

She is studying at present but as the surfers say God only knows what a course in sociology in Nassau actually translates into: how to be a mistress or a hooker again? Not a good bet for you Ed is my take.'

If Marco had said she had syphilis Edward would have still stood by his decision. The fact that Jazz was once a courtesan didn't bother him, it excited him. The youthful cavalier was falling in love again.

Maybe it was the unusual mix of French and American accents this time or her sense of fun; her perfectly balanced body; her sexual experience even compared to his; perhaps it was because she usually wore nothing or a bikini at home or for formal occasions satin hot pants and a bikini top. He didn't care.

Whether Edward was able to distinguish between love and sex was a moot point in Jazz's case but after a few drinks and a shared joint who knew? Still, he was lonely in Nassau, despite all the girls, and he wanted some real company. He already spent enough time with spooks, fatuous expatriates and frivolous female tourists.

Marco told him Jazz had a lover in the agency but he was killed on a job, something to do with black coral smuggling. Good quality black corals were as valuable as diamonds. Jazz said she was a student, but never went to college.

She was a walking disaster. Had two young children she never saw and a family she never contacted. Already suffered from a liver problem from drinking too much and partial blindness but refused to wear glasses all the time, particularly when driving. Smoked too many joints and had a criminal record. Was she a good match? Probably not, certainly not, but Edward was restless.

None of this mattered to him. By Saturday 21st September they were celebrating their first month of living together. She was a kindred spirit, a woman with whom he could relax with and lower his guard. Edward never even considered that it might all end in tears and tragedy.

She might have initially appeared to be a close relative of danger woman but that had largely been because she had been lured into the supposed excitement of living on the edge with the CIA. At home, other than in bed, she was quite a different person. For a start she was a good cook when not too stoned. She was reasonably hushed when Ed worked from his flat and would just quietly listen to music they both liked while forever manicuring her nails and trying out new hair styles. Who could complain at that?

When would he learn his ABCs? The trouble was he had never been taught them and probably thought ABC stood for Avoid Being Caught or more to the point, Always Be Careful!

Jazz might have been a fine specimen of a gold medallist in sexual athletics which she described as her hobby but even compared to a duplicitous croupier she was the personification of "danger". It was as though the word was metaphorically brazenly embroidered on her firm bum and other parts of her anatomy.

According to Edward's diary the week that kicked off on Monday 23rd September 1974 was to be nothing out of the ordinary, just another week in paradise with his Whitney Houston lookalike.

For his parents though this was to be a watershed moment. It was to be the crescendo and culmination of a sometimes horrifying often harrowing always unpredictable train ride that started in 1939 when Hitler invaded Poland.

Chapter 27
Wednesday 25th September

London Road Royal Tunbridge Wells, Kent England

Sara arranged to meet Castle at a quiet luxurious hotel not far from Royal Tunbridge Wells. Unusually, she did this through an intermediary, the Home Secretary's wife. Castle was chary about meeting her and had the hotel suite she booked swept for bugs by a technical team. They found nothing.

While wary, Sir Douglas Castle was also excited at the prospect of meeting Sara again, alone. Even though their relationship ended in acrimony and violence he'd never lost what he originally felt for her.

Castle knew he could never get that back but he could always hope. He decided not to bug the suite himself. Sara had an eye for such things and if she checked and found something, only hell knew what she'd do. In any event, he didn't know what she wanted to discuss this time. It could be something personal that he wouldn't want officially recorded. Those organising the bugging usually had a brief listen in supposedly to check that all the equipment was working or had done its job.

He still regretted what he did to Sara all those years ago and he never married after what happened in that hotel room in Zurich on Christmas Day 1944. Since then, and until his appointment as one of MI6's top honchos, he had sexual relations about once or twice a year with an old admirer who lived in Petersfield. The arrangement suited him because there were no complications down in London. They were both past it now and he'd lost interest in sex long ago, until he thought about Sara.

He wore a dark suit for the meeting, with a white shirt and his college tie with the silly white manuscripts in the crests of arms. His hair had been cut, or had a trim round the edges: this year, as every day passed, he could see less on top than the day before. He had even splashed out some cash and splashed on some cologne. He wanted to look as best he could, under the circumstances.

As for what she wanted, he still hadn't a clue. His last telephone contact with her had been hostile but her son Edward was out of the country at last and so far as he was concerned, no longer his responsibility. If anything happened to her younger son now, it would be down to the TrumPeter and his accountants in Nassau. In any case, she always telephoned when she wanted to talk about the boy so this had to be something else. What though? Would she be wired up or even armed? Castle peered outside but couldn't see much. He made a mental note to get some new specs.

The only equipment Sara came armed with was a low-cut black dress that complimented her natural red hair, so it shone like gold in the late afternoon sun. Naturally she had bugged the suite beforehand but only after Castle's morons left. She was armed in other ways though.

Sara was carrying copies of Alice Bailey's letter from the Beyond Enkription filing cabinet, in English and Russian, and Douglas Castle's letter to Zola in German. In addition, she had arranged some other treats for her former treacherous lover. Roger had been able to decipher enough of the documents sent over from the British Embassy in Moscow to provide Sara with more ammunition.

Castle was already in the suite when she arrived. He tried to stand on his gammy leg as she came through the door.

'Don't stand on ceremony Douglas, it doesn't suit you.'

She took a window seat opposite him, casually threw her mink beret and scarf onto a chair and assumed a provocative pose. Her slim figure, silhouetted against the glass, made her look fifteen years younger. She tossed her head back so that the shining strands of her hair caught the fading rays of autumnal light. Even though overwhelmed, he decided to go on the offensive, just in case.

'Is this about your youngest son again?'

Sara remained demur, evasive and distant.

'He could have been your son Douglas.'

'I know that, but he wasn't was he.'

'True but he helped you, didn't he, as if you were his father.'

'How so?'

'Well, the Poulson enquiry for a start. Then all the northern corruption before Reginald was hung out to dry. Oh, and not to mention infiltrating those perverted diplomats who's expulsion was all your doing according to the false gospel of Sir Douglas Castle. Finally let's not forget exposing nuclear proliferation if you have your calculator out and are totting up all this.'

'Yes, he did well. Is that what you want me to say?'

Castle lit a cigarette. Sara knew that meant he was nervous and sniffed disapprovingly at the smoke but said nothing just to disturb his composure further. It would have been hypocritical to comment, considering Roger's habit. She waited for him to compose himself after he hastily stubbed out the cigarette.

'I suppose all those good results, the diplomatic expulsions and the Buddha exposures all helped distract the Cabinet Office's attention. How are the IRA doing today? Lost count of the moles you have in Derry or Dublin? Presumably we're safer here than in London. Is Buckingham Palace next on their hit list?'

Chapter 27 - Wednesday 25th September

'There were dozens of other people involved in operations your son worked on, not just him. As for dealing with the IRA these operations are damned complicated and have to be painstakingly planned and controlled.'

'I'm sure you're right as usual, my dear Douglas. What a pity they weren't. So many bombs with so many warnings must be terribly confusing and painful for those on the receiving end.'

'We've been through all this, several times.'

'You're right. There have been too many damn bombs. As for Edward we have tried to discuss his treatment when you haven't ducked the questions. Anyway, that's not why I'm here.'

The relief was evident on Castle's face. He relaxed in his chair.

'Although indirectly, that is why I'm here.'

He sat up straight again.

'I don't follow?'

'Well, if you'd treated Edward better, cared more for him like the son you never had I might not be here now. You do know your assets are human beings don't you?'

From Castle's viewpoint Sara was talking in riddles. Maybe she just came here to taunt him, to show him what he could have had but lost. He wouldn't play that game. If she came up with nothing original to say, he'd leave.

'Can you get to the point Sara? I've travelled a long way down here. Why couldn't we meet in London?'

'Too many spies in London: anyway people bloody well commute from here every day. It's not as though we are meeting in Cornwall.'

She rose to her feet and walked to the phone. Castle recoiled as she passed him, in case she wrapped a cord round his neck or sliced his throat wide open with a knife.

'I'm forgetting my manners. You're my guest, can I offer you something?'

'Do they have green tea here?'

'I'm sure they do. Some biscuits as well?'

'No thank you.'

'Oh dear, lost your appetite?'

She called room service and ordered a pot of their best green tea and half a bottle of claret. She went to the bathroom while they waited. Not because she needed to go, but because Castle would assume she was checking her recording device. She flushed the cistern quicker than she would have normally, just to unsettle him.

A maid brought the refreshments and Sara ushered her away. They both sat in silence while Sara poured the wine and Castle dispensed his tea.

'Alright Douglas, let's not talk about Edward. He's in the Bahamas now and, as I understand it, having a much quieter life than he did in London.'

'Good.'

'Let's talk about you instead shall we?'

'If you wish.'

'I wish.'

Sara drained her glass and poured herself the remainder of the wine. Castle sipped at his green tea trying to put on a poker playing face as his mind spun around in turmoil trying to guess which one of all the nasty topics she could choose from she might select for discussion.

'You, Douglas, have reduced the moral fibre of MI5 and MI6 to a level Sir Stuart Menzies would have had you shot for during the war.'

'Who says so?'

'We will get round to that. They are no more than bungling bureaucracies now. You stay behind locked doors manipulating good men and women who you dispose of at will.'

'This is about you son again.'

'No, Douglas, it's about much more than my son or any one man, including you.'

Castle stood as best he could on his leg. He was in two minds whether to stay or walk out the door. Sara wasn't finished, she had hardly begun ...

'It's about all the people who are dying needlessly now and died needlessly in the war.'

'Your sister?'

'Yes! My poor sister included.'

Sara was no longer demur. She was shouting now.

'Do you know what they did to her Douglas?'

'I can guess.'

'Can you? I'm surprised you have to guess. Didn't that Zola woman tell you? Well, I'll tell you. They stripped her naked and threw her into a tub of freezing water.'

Castle turned his face away from her.

'They tied her legs to a bar across the tub and every time a chain attached to that bar was pulled, her head went under the water and she drowned.'

Castle put his hands up to his ears. Sara stood up and pulled them away. Sara wanted him to hear. She'd wanted him to hear for so many years.

'My beautiful sister was drowned, Douglas, over and over, again and again.'

'Please, Sara ...'

'Then they slung her up, using handcuffs with spikes inside them. Did you guess that too?'

Sara gulped down the rest of her wine. Castle tried to get to the door but he couldn't move fast enough on his gammy leg. He looked so undignified. Sara got there first and stood against it, preventing his escape.

'Did you know they beat my sister with a spiked ball until she was broken in pieces, and then they hung up what was left of her with piano wire?'

Chapter 27 - Wednesday 25th September

Castle staggered back to his chair and collapsed into it. He held his head in his quivering hands and sobbed.

Sara composed herself. She walked towards him and symbolically kissed him on the top of his balding head. Then step by step full of purpose she backed away from him to an adjoining door, between the room and another suite. Castle looked up at her, tears streaming down his face.

'It's all in the past now Sara.'

'I wish it were but it isn't. It's still happening and I can't allow it to go on anymore. I want you to know that. I want you to know why I'm doing this.'

Sara opened the door. Roger Burlington came into the room from the adjoining suite. Castle sat up in his chair and mopped at his face with a handkerchief.

'Roger, good God, what the hell are you doing here?'

'I could ask that of you. Sara invited me.'

'What's all this about?'

'You haven't been listening, Douglas, have you? That is why we're here and not in Lambeth.'

Sara took a back seat and allowed Roger to speak directly to Castle. Roger explained that before he was detained in Russia he removed some papers from the briefcase of Professor Sokolov who ran the KGB's science farms. The papers were sent to London via a diplomatic pouch but they never arrived. Sokolov committed suicide the same day Roger was imprisoned and he had assumed the Russians intercepted the documents. At the time he was particularly interested in those papers because they related to remote viewing which was a big ticket back in the sixties for a few years.

'Do you know what remote viewing means Douglas?'

'I guess so.'

'Do you know the CIA still has a department devoted solely to that operating out of Fort Meade?'

'Do they?'

'Yes, Douglas, they do.'

To ensure there were no misunderstandings in the event the tape recordings being made of the meeting had to be used as evidence Roger explained that remote viewing was a psychic phenomena like telepathy and extra sensory perception. In the sixties the USSR took it so seriously that the running of what they charitably described as "psychic hospitals" was included in their defence budget and huge resources were allocated to it. The British and Americans followed the fad but on a smaller scale. They used the Stanford Research Institute extensively for remote viewing experiments.

'The CIA still uses the facilities at Stanford.'

Castle had obviously heard of and understood the concept. In a nutshell, they were trying to read people's minds, but where was Roger heading? Both the British and Americans all but dismissed the theorising as rubbish or so he'd been led to believe; and what did any of this have to do with him?

'Sokolov claimed to have perfected remote viewing techniques.'

Castle laughed cynically, surely Roger couldn't be serious?

'You remember Alice Bailey, Douglas? She was a JIC secretary and worked in the Cabinet Office.'

'I can't be expected to recall every secretary Roger.'

Roger paused to light up a Players Navy Cut cigarette. He knew from Castle's deceptive remark he remembered Alice. How could the bastard forget what he did to her? Roger ignored his anger, put it to one side for later if needed, and went on to explain the letter that he'd given to Alice to look after while he was in Russia. Sara handed Castle a copy of the letter which had been translated into English.

'The original, with fingerprints, including Sokolov's, is in a safe place just in case you rip it up in one of your fits of bad temper.'

The letter was from Professor Sokolov to someone in the Russian Embassy in London. In it, he referred to a British intelligence officer as the thinker. Sokolov believed his people in Moscow were reading the mind of this person and he intended to get someone at the embassy to prove it. The letter asked for a covert system to be put in place to check if what was in the thinker's head was the same as what his remote viewers were recording. Naturally it had to be executed without the thinker knowing he was being monitored in such a way.

'It sounds like science fiction, doesn't it Douglas?'

'Thank the Lord at least you see it for what it is.'

Castle hoped his prayers would be answered and said no more. This was becoming more sinister by the minute. Castle thought of trying to get out again but Sara had repositioned herself between him and the door. He would have had no chance thirty years ago let alone now.

Roger carried on unrelentingly explaining that when he was in Russia Sokolov boasted to him that he now had the proof he wanted. Roger stole that proof from Sokolov's briefcase before being arrested but it disappeared en route to London from the British Embassy in Moscow.

After he was released from the Russian prison Roger had to get out of the country as quick as he could so it was not possible to try and find the papers. Anyway, Sokolov was dead by then and Roger believed the papers had been intercepted by the Russians. The KGB claimed it was suicide. Everyone knew he was murdered because the KGB thought he had given Roger the stolen papers.

'Well it is not as fictitious as you would like to think. I was talking to someone from our Moscow Station a few months ago who said, en passant, that the papers

Chapter 27 - Wednesday 25th September

were still in our embassy there. No one could read them because they were encoded and they just lay there, gathering dust. I had them sent over here.'

All Roger had to do was work out who the thinker was from what the Russians recorded as being in his head. An encrypted multidimensional crossword puzzle would have been easier to do.

The documents were in Russian and German and it took a long time to break the codes, even with the help of MI6's new computer models. Roger didn't want to bring in anyone else because he didn't know what he'd find. It could have been a set up or disinformation to destabilise the intelligence services again after the Cambridge Five. Roger rounded off by saying Sara gave him the answer, after he'd been working on it for weeks.

'Sara?'

'Let me read this for you Douglas. Hang on, got it. I quote "and the thinker is besotted by frequent thoughts of a woman chauffeur wearing a mink beret and, unlike his other thoughts, these are in German".'

'My Lord, good God, Roger ...'

'Quite.'

Sara came back across the room. She looked down at Castle cringing in his chair.

'How far have they penetrated into your mind Douglas?'

'This could easily be a set up as you well know. You and I were common knowledge.'

'Not the chauffeur and mink beret bit.'

'We've been fed crap from Moscow for decades.'

'It doesn't matter. They'll say there's no smoke without a fire. It will cause mayhem along with everything else; it may even bring down the government, maybe several governments. This briefcase is full of similar papers taken from Sokolov which I've decrypted and translated. They are copies but you can read them now if you want. They do show what you have always been so good at: deceit. That is why you are where you are today. I must admit even I was astounded by your duplicity.'

'Duplicity? Bring governments down? Have you both lost your senses? Thank the Lord I am in charge still.'

Roger and Sara both stood over Sir Douglas Castle. His mind was racing. How did they do all this telepathic stuff? Were they bluffing? What if the Americans found out? What if it hit the press? He'd be the joke of military intelligence for centuries. Thank the Lord he'd stopped writing his silly memoirs. Castle was beginning to crack but he was still defiant.

'I won't resign. This remote viewing crap has been discredited for years.'

'Were I you I would read the contents of this briefcase before jumping to irrational conclusions. The perfidy, the double standards, your contempt for me and your jealousy of me, a lifelong supporter and colleague of your's is bad enough. It's all there, including your disdain for Prime Ministers, particularly Macmillan and worst of all Churchill especially during the war. What on earth would the world's media make of it?'

'I said I won't resign. Let me see those papers?'

'So be it Douglas, you'll force my hand. Roger, let him read the damn documents while I call my man in the News of The World and we'll start with the war crimes evidence.'

'Roger, please. Talk sense into her. She'll destroy us all. Anyway as the Lord knows I was investigated and exonerated.'

'It has gone beyond that now Douglas. The investigators didn't have this letter you wrote to Zola.'

Roger threw a copy on his lap. Castle took one look and gasped. He didn't need to read it just like he knew perfectly well who Alice Bailey was. Sara stared at him in disgust. Castle writhed on the chair as if having an angina attack. He looked as if he was waiting for the hangman's noose to be tightened.

'We also have recordings of not just senior MI6 personnel confirming they are Crown servants under your command. We have the tapes we asked you to make to cover your arse in the JIC enquiry. You know what all that means in the eyes of the law of course. The tapes show beyond reasonable doubt not just admissions of incompetence but genuine and intentional breaches of the Geneva Convention. They are in your own words and those of others stating unequivocally they were acting under your orders.'

'What about the evidence a propos my sister and all the other agents you sent to the gallows in the war?'

'Then there's all the tawdry details of your affair with that Nazi spy Zola. Alice Bailey hasn't forgotten you. She's itching to tell a jury about what she discovered about that affair after you did what you needed to keep her quiet. Are you that callous you can forget what you did to Alice? Then there's your raping my fiancé to take into account before all this Zola business. How did you say it? After you were exonerated; I would call it cheated the damn hangman.'

'In case you forgot now there's all this too.'

Roger emptied the contents of his briefcase onto the table next to Castle.

'Read them if you don't believe me. They're but a small part of the package Sara can give to the press.'

Castle haphazardly rummaged through the papers trying not to show his shaking hands and focused on one which he read. His hand began to tremble more noticeably and shake. Sara just stared at his hand. He jettisoned the paper trying to hide his trembling hand but his gammy leg jerked uncontrollably knocking the tea table over and the bone china teapot shattered symbolically. Sir Douglas Castle looked down at his wet trouser leg. He was quivering as Sara tossed back her hair scenting victory was her's.

Chapter 27 - Wednesday 25th September

Castle was stuck in a corner. He could kick and scream and protest as much as he liked but it would all be to no avail in the end. They held too much awful evidence. His disdain for Churchill and his letter to Zola were the killers.

The media would crucify him. Better to die at the hands of the Gestapo than live in ignominy forever. How on earth did this Sokolov know all this? Where, how had the Zola letter been found? She'd destroyed it. It meant she too never loved or trusted him. His only salvation from his nightmares, his belief in her love for him, had been cruelly torn from his heart.

Roger might bluff but he wouldn't lie. Was Sir Peter Stafford involved? Peter was too clever to go along with anything that would even come close to tarnishing his own reputation.

Castle was beaten and he knew it. If he escaped from any one of the four corners, he'd be done for in the next. Had he been a younger and braver man, he might have tried to call their bluff but he wasn't and they weren't bluffing. He had never told Sara of his misgivings about Churchill. Even so, he would have one more Houdini like attempt to escape the consequences of all his crimes.

'Suppose I go. Who'll take my place?'

'Peter Stafford has already agreed to step in to your shoes.'

'He knows?'

'Not everything. It can be kept that way. That is up to you.'

'You can do this the easy way or the hard way. It's your choice Douglas.'

Sir Peter's involvement sealed it. Sir Douglas Castle telephoned Downing Street from the hotel. Once he was put through to the Prime Minister's secretary he offered his resignation. The IRA campaign was getting him down and, as a result, his health was deteriorating fast. He couldn't cope any longer and his doctors had suggested he step down for his own good.

As for his replacement, he advocated that Sir Peter Stafford take his position. At a time like this the country needed someone with proven experience, someone who could be trusted.

Sir Douglas Castle left a broken man. The dart that pierced his heart was his letter to Zola. Its existence meant she never loved him. She had sworn on their undying love and her father's life she had destroyed it. She had betrayed him, rendered his whole life pointless.

Roger let Sara collect all the eavesdropping equipment before they left. They didn't speak. On the way back home Roger promised that next year they would visit Isobel's tomb, by the Holy Trinity Church in Maisons-Laffitte near where she was captured on that fateful night in 1944. After that there was no need for conversation.

Castle's resignation was formally accepted the next day once Sir Peter told the Cabinet Office he would stand in for him. However, given the potential propaganda value it would have for the terrorists, an agreement was reached that Sir Douglas Castle would remain in situ, but only nominally.

An announcement would be made in due course about his deteriorating health. He need no longer attend JIC meetings or continue in MI6. Sir Peter would take over his position and Castle was to be given gardening leave until 1st January.

One tangential and nonetheless important spin off from all this was having Peter manoeuvred into a position to protect Edward better than Sir Douglas Castle ever did. Roger believed in Peter but had misgivings. As an egotist Sir Peter knew what his number one priority was.

Peacocks liked to preen their feathers and were the first to strut away at any hint of danger. However, he would blow his trumpet if he did so, if only to warn others so that he could say he had warned them. TrumPeter Stafford was a better option and unlike Castle he would never slide off unnoticed and deny any wrongdoing the next day once his alibi was organised.

Peter was clever in some ways like that and on many occasions had shown he was quite capable of making himself look as though he was sinking in dire straits, stuck at the nadir. Then he'd rise Phoenix like from the morass he fashioned to create a greater contrast but only when he was ready. Ready to trumpet his successes much to the applause of those he had assembled to praise him.

The Burlington's long train journey was near to an end. Castle had been thrown off at the last scheduled stop before it reached its destination. Roger and Sara could look to the future now.

Since 1944 their lives had been blighted, put on hold in so many ways with one foot chained to Isobel's lifeless body. She had been avenged in a civilised way, not the way she had departed but it was a form of closure for Sara. As she wrote in her diary that night "Castle's gone now my darling Isobel." Sara had only waited patiently some thirty years for that moment.

Chapter 28
Thursday 3rd October to Monday 4th November

Bay Street Nassau, New Providence Island Bahamas
Marco had plans for Ed. He wanted his CIA asset to target Graham Sidney-Smith at Porter Williams. Sidney-Smith was on a list of people who were of interest to Leo Sanchez and his team in Langley. Leo was after any document, no matter how seemingly insignificant, that linked Graham or anyone else in Porter Williams to Oswaldo López the Head of State of Honduras.

Marco said it might be connected to Vesco and King and their involvement in Watergate but he hadn't been told specifics. They were trawling for any dirt on the majestic el Presidente of Honduras.

Edward knew López was a client and he'd read about the atrocities that occurred in Honduras under his command. He had no qualms about spying on anyone in particular, Graham included and the firm at large, if they were involved in anything underhand with that brute. Mind you, at the time Edward did say to Marco that he would be shocked and surprised if Graham was up to no good.

Marco told him Graham effectively spied on Ed all the time. He partially proved it by playing back calls between Graham, bulldog Rupert and Sir Peter that the CIA had covertly taped. Apart from Edward's indirect links with Jimi Hendrix, Jazz was the main subject of the more recent calls.

Fanshaw had details of her background which he passed on to Graham who then divulged the information to Sir Peter leaving the impression he uncovered the stuff himself. What was pathetic was that each man's reports were sometimes contradictory, blatantly inaccurate and embellished specifically about Jazz's nocturnal activities. Even Peter picked that up and asked questions why.

Ed and Marco laughed their way through the recordings especially the one where Rupert and Graham were chatting about whether Collette might be able to maintain a closer position vis a vis their target. Rupert even remarked on her "oral skills which could come in handy". Ed remarked that he was looking forward to a demonstration!

Seriously though, the annoying issue was that half of what Fanshaw and then Graham reported was totally inaccurate. There was nothing Ed could do about it though as it would expose both Marco and him. Marco assumed Ed knew about Sir Peter's pending role so made no mention of it.

This was an easy assignment for Edward. He knew where the López files were kept and he could access them. All he did was take six files from the office at five thirty one morning for Marco to copy. They were returned to their homely filing cabinet in less than three hours. To get data from the firm's computer should have been just as easy. It still wasn't password protected and all the expats were going on a deep sea fishing trip that Sunday, the 6th October.

Edward went into Porter Williams at about eleven o'clock and started copying the López contents from the hard drive onto discs supplied by Marco. As he was doing so, he heard the front door being opened. He yanked the computer plug from its socket and opened the windows. The office door swung open.

'Edward, what are you doing here?'

Chris Albury had incredulously turned up at the office on a weekend. Albury never went on the firm's fishing trips. Was there a major crisis or had he mistakenly thought it was Monday? To arrive at work around eleven on Mondays was not that unusual for Chris but to give him his due he worked later than everyone else.

'I'm admiring the view. What a surprise seeing you on a Sunday. I heard a noise. These windows were open, must have been the blinds flapping in the breeze.'

Albury walked across the office towards the open windows. Edward pointed to the balcony of a nearby building.

'Take a look at that pair.'

Two perfectly formed blonde women drizzling with suntan oil were sunbathing topless on the balcony. Albury laughed.

'Which pair? Now I know why you like to work weekends.'

Albury assumed the cleaners must have left the windows open. They both returned to their offices after Edward closed and locked the window. Albury stuck his head round Edward's office door and suggested he report it to Graham.

Edward nodded, pretending to be editing the training material that was so close to Chris' heart. Albury stayed for half an hour and made several long distance calls. Once Chris left, Edward rebooted the computer and finished copying the López data.

As he had nothing more interesting to do he read some of the correspondence. A firm of lawyers were advising members of the Honduran government on how to establish a trust in their own names to invest charitable donations. The gifts were meant for sick, homeless and dying kids after Hurricane Fifi slammed into Honduras in September. This sounded about as generous and morally upright as the Great Train Robbery. Was it?

Edward didn't bother to read why the banks in question were asking their lawyers for advice or even if Porter Williams was involved and if so in what capacity. These sorts of trivial issues were not what interested the CIA.

Chapter 28 - Thursday 3rd October to Monday 4th November

Yet why would anyone invest such donations in a trust in their own names rather than spend them on what they were intended for? Speed was of the utmost importance. The donations were for urgent humanitarian relief. After all, Hurricane Fifi hadn't waited before killing over eight thousand Hondurans.

Maybe as one would have expected Porter Williams were acting for the charities to put a halt to the apparent abuse. Nevertheless at least one firm of lawyers and several bankers weren't. As for Porter Williams, López was a client or so Edward had been told by Rupert Fanshaw. All these files seemed to suggest there was some connection.

After the López and Graham Sidney-Smith links, Marco's next target was Joseph Cohen, a wealthy Bahamian banker. Marco was interested in one of Cohen's banks in particular, a small bank with less than two hundred customers, López included.

Marco suggested that Jazz would be able to help them with this one as she'd already met the banker socially before Ed came to Nassau. He assured Ed she wouldn't need to get sexually involved to do a good job so they agreed to act. Cohen liked the high life, he made frequent visits to Las Vegas and Florida and he stayed at the Jockey Club in Miami and a hotel in Los Olas in Fort Lauderdale. He was easy prey.

Again, as promised, Marco explained and proved, to Edward's satisfaction anyway, the rationale for asking for his pro bono help. Cohen was laundering money for the mob including of course the Polanos. He was providing drug traffickers with a bureau de change as cover for their doing business in Florida. The trouble was as usual everything was political because various heads of state, in other words gangsters running banana republics, were major investors in Cohen's bank.

After some talk over a few beers Marco and Edward decided to organise some entertaining. Much to Edward's amazement he had even managed to get Marco to accept that Jazz could be reinstated as a CIA asset if she did a good job. Initially though her involvement was to be on a retrial basis provided she didn't have to proffer any sexual services and steered clear of drugs when operational.

Las Olas Fort Lauderdale, Florida USA

On his next flight to Fort Lauderdale, Cohen bumped into Jazz with a couple of distinctly sexy looking girlfriends. They were travelling back to Florida after a weekend on Paradise Island. They accepted his invitation to dinner and, afterwards, while Cohen was having sex with her two companions, Jazz photographed the contents of his briefcase.

Marco and Edward were in the suite next door and didn't even bother to video the dirty games Cohen liked to play. It really was that simple and wasn't the stuff you could write much more about unless you wanted to read about Cohen's shady sexual preferences.

While on the subject of explicit sexual imagery, as it's all available on the web we haven't bothered to go into it in graphic detail. Why bother when if that's your favourite beverage there's more than enough in cyberspace to watch live?

Be that as it may, Jazz took about two hundred pictures of the entire contents of Cohen's briefcase, using six different cameras. Cohen woke late next morning with the pair of femme fatales either side of him.

Jazz met the girls later at Fort Lauderdale-Hollywood International Airport of Bermuda Triangle infamy and paid them $5,000 each. They then flew home to San Francisco. It was the first time Jazz had been in the field for a while.

As a femme fatale for the CIA, this was all in a day's work for her. She was paid $10,000 and went back to Guadeloupe to visit her family to give them the money. That was her story anyway: a family that Ed had never seen or heard her communicate with in any way. He returned to Nassau. Marco went straight to Washington DC with the photographs. They were worth tens of millions to the US Treasury.

Bay Street Nassau, New Providence Island Bahamas

Leo Sanchez started visiting Nassau more frequently. The CIA lawyer was getting agitated about drug trafficking and illegal Haitian immigrants. He was also worried about looming civil wars in Central America, the gateway to the USA. Castro was still rapier rattling in Cuba and influencing liberals in Nicaragua and Honduras. Vesco now owned Costa Rica and Duvalier was increasingly becoming a puppet for Colombian drug barons. In other words, all wasn't well on America's southern front.

Everyone in the US was twitchy, especially after Watergate. In many ways albeit more public, for the CIA Watergate was like the Philby moment for the British intelligence services. Watergate was the harbinger of many lustra of mistrust and inquisitions to add to those ongoing since John F Kennedy's assassination.

Graham Sidney-Smith was fiddling with the air-conditioning in his office early that afternoon. Unusually for Graham, other than after a good fuck on the tennis court, he looked sweaty, with perspiration beads on his forehead and neck.

'Edward, do come in and take a seat.'

Graham sat behind his mock Victorian desk and gestured for Edward to sit down while trying to mend the air-conditioning unit.

'Bloody air-con's packed up just when I needed it.'

Edward waited for him to get to the point.

'Sir Peter Stafford's coming for dinner to my house in Lyford Cay.'

'When?'

'Why, tonight of course.'

Edward didn't know Peter was even in the country.

'Would you like to come too?'

Chapter 28 - Thursday 3rd October to Monday 4th November

Lyford Cay, New Providence Island Bahamas

Graham lived in affluent splendour in the middle of a community of international film and pop stars in one of the world's most expensive private beach and harbour complexes. Edward had been there a few weeks earlier with Chas Chandler of The Animals rock group whom Edward knew from his Newcastle days.

Apart from being in The Animals Chas managed Jimi Hendrix before Jimi's untimely death just over four years earlier. Chas was staying at the Nassau Beach Hotel. Other clients of Edward's equally well-heeled music industry associates stayed there too from time to time. Chas took Edward and Jazz to a party in Lyford Cay.

Peter was already at Sidney-Smith's house when Edward arrived. Sir Peter's chauffeur was lounging against a brand new crimson Cadillac outside Graham's palatial home. After the usual pleasantries, Peter took Edward to one side.

'We'd like you to volunteer for something.'

'We?'

'Porter Williams. However, in this case, you won't be officially one of our staff. You may be aware that Porter Williams is the auditor for Haiti Air, the national Haitian airline.'

Edward wasn't aware. Sir Peter didn't stop.

'The US Federal Aviation Authority is concerned that they have insufficient working capital to service their planes. They need evidence to be able to ground them. We don't normally set about forcing our clients out of business but this is different.'

It sounded more like an operation than an audit to Edward but he let Peter keep talking.

'The political consequences could be huge, it might even stifle what little tourism or trade they have and topple the Duvalier regime forever.'

This was definitely an operation.

'We need you to go to Grand Turk first and then maybe to Haiti.'

'What if there's trouble?'

'Hmm, trouble? No, no there won't be any trouble. If any problems arise, the US authorities over there will sort it all out.'

That was a vague answer, to say the least. Peter's voice was shaky, full of trepidation, about as confident as a punter putting his last five dollar bill on a two hundred to one shot. He was chain smoking his damn cigars too which was never a good sign. Edward lit a cigarette and poured himself another Bud.

'What if I get stuck there?'

'You won't. I promise.'

Another wobbly answer.

Why had Peter come all the way out here to ask him to do something Graham could have asked on his behalf? Or was there another agenda? Of course, he still had no idea that Peter was once the head of MI5 and was about to be a bigwig in MI6. Was there something bigger than an audit of Haiti Air going on?

Sir Peter himself seemed preoccupied. He was remembering the JIC meeting earlier that year when Rear Admiral Putnam was put in his place. An official minute came out of that meeting, deploring the abuse of agents' human rights. It stated categorically that disposing of and denying them was as reprehensible as any war crime, act of torture or political murder, and certainly a breach of the Geneva Convention. However, Sir Peter was also looking ahead to his appointment in MI6.

To upstage his US counterparts would be a dramatic way to make his entrance to the job and this little operation could do just that. He eased his conscience by promising himself to initiate a total overhaul of the employment criteria for agents. He would get Fanshaw to have it typed out tomorrow.

'I'll go then Peter.'

Sir Peter didn't hear Edward's reply. He was still busy justifying his actions to himself.

'I said I'll go then Peter.'

'What? Good man. Hmm, Graham will brief you and you can sort out your tourist visa. You do realise that if, as we expect, you have to prove they have no proper records you can't just do it in a day. You'll have to stay a good two weeks.

We must be able to report truthfully that we spent that much time there trying to get proper manifests, bank statements you name it. Look upon it as a well earned all expenses paid holiday for all the overtime you've worked. Graham keeps me informed, don't you Graham?'

Sir Peter didn't want an answer from either of them. That was an order to Edward and a rhetorical question to Graham. He smiled awkwardly at Edward. It was an uncomfortable embarrassed smile of betrayal, like that of a traitor watching his long time friend being arrested ahead of his certain execution.

'Now, Edward, what have you been up to out here apart from overworking? All I hear about are the praiseworthy bits. Tell me about the stuff Graham never reports to me. I hear there are some good jazz clubs here.'

Peter glanced at Graham who nearly fell off his bar stool at that last remark. After dinner, Peter was the first person to leave. He shook hands with his host and walked with Edward to his car. Sir Peter tried to light yet another cigar but the wind wouldn't let him so he gave up trying.

'Apparently, the most dangerous objects you're likely to encounter in Haiti are beautiful women. Good to see you looking so fit after that terrible food poisoning. Do take care and enjoy your trip, put your feet up and relax for once. Let the client do the work, that's what I always say.'

Peter climbed into the back of the limo and was able to light his cigar. Edward pitied his chauffeur if he hadn't an oxygen mask with him. He was confused by all the incongruous body language. Sir Peter's parting smile was even more forced, more of pretence than earlier. Before tonight Edward hadn't seen that guilt-ridden look and as he left it was laced with emotion.

The Cadillac set off back to the other end of the island. He was staying with the Fanshaws but told Edward he was billeted at a hotel in Paradise Island whose name he'd forgotten. As the car moved off he quipped that as long as the driver could remember which one that was all that mattered.

Bay Street Area Nassau, New Providence Island Bahamas

Edward visited the Haitian Consulate in downtown Nassau the next day. It comprised two ramshackle rooms in a rotting shack. There was no air-conditioning, just two sweaty officials wearing shades who looked like Mafia hit men.

They kept asking stupid questions. Yes, he was going on a holiday. No, he hadn't been previously. Yes, he'd had all his injections. No, he hadn't decided where to stay yet. It took two humid hours to process the visa. By the time all the formalities were finished, Edward surmised no one in their right mind would visit Haiti as a tourist. Did they even have tourists?

François Duvalier, euphemistically known as Papa Doc to his long suffering subjects, had died in 1971. Haiti was now ruled by his feckless son Jean-Claude or Baby Doc as he was called. Baby Doc was nineteen when he inherited the dictatorship. Simone, his mother, was left to run the country while her son spent his time living the lavish life of a playboy.

Baby Doc paid for his pleasures through fraud and corruption and, consequently, Haiti was one of the poorest countries on earth. A dollar a day was executive pay in those days.

Duvalier managed to hold onto power with the help of a brutal paramilitary force called the Tonton Macoute. When translated, it meant Uncle Gunnysack, a mythological creature who kidnapped children and ate them. The myth wasn't that far from the truth as Edward was to find out.

Marco Sanchez knew Sir Peter Stafford was in town and he was interested in why Ed was going to Haiti. He offered to help Ed in any way he could, as a friend and as a means of covertly finding out what was going down. Ed was given a list of names and numbers which he memorised and gave back to Marco.

They included a guy called Fed and the name and address of a casino near Port-au-Prince where he could be found. Marco also gave Ed another US passport under the name of Edward Alexander Racter Junior, quite an ear load of a name! Ed was to take the passport with him to the casino if he stumbled into any trouble.

'How much are they paying you for this Ed?'

'Nothing extra, just my salary but they said it would be more of an all expenses paid holiday.'

'You must be nuts.'

'I suppose so but I have to see the world so if Porter Williams agree to pay my way who am I to argue?'

'If you get into trouble, just go to the casino. Fed will get you out the country. If I call you ... on second thoughts forget it. I was going to say take that Caribbean guide book I gave you so we could talk in code but you probably know it off by heart now anyway.'

Ed made a mental note to take it just in case. Jazz was still away, so they went on a booze up at the Nassau Beach Hotel, hit the Pink Pussycat late and ended up south of the hill with Holly. When he woke next morning at Governor's Beach, Edward played back a message on the answer phone from Jazz. She hoped all was ok and said she was still staying with her family but they had no phone. Edward checked the origin of the call but the number had been withheld. He didn't believe her.

As the days passed by Edward still hadn't the green light from Graham to go to Grand Turk, the stepping stone to Haiti. The trip kept being postponed for the flimsiest of reasons. It must have been connected with MI6 because Graham clearly hadn't a clue why. Oddly though if it had MI6 origins neither Marco nor Leo had any bright ideas as to what was going on. That was all the more peculiar given that Leo had access to JIC minutes and more besides through the CIA's representative in London.

At eleven o'clock on the morning of Sunday 3rd November Jazz called from the airport and Edward drove out to collect her and her luggage. When he arrived, she was completely stoned and carrying two ounces of hash in one of her bags. Jazz must have been mental to bring that much dope through customs particularly as she'd come from Guadeloupe via Tampa but she had smuggled it through somehow.

Apart from being higher than an eagle, she was acting weird and she told Edward that two friends of hers from the FBI would be arriving later. They were chasing black coral smugglers across the Caribbean.

They'd been on the move for over two days and would need to borrow his car and a change of clothes, if that was alright. She kept asking the time, even though she was wearing a watch. Her friends were coming to Nassau from the USA because the drop-off point for the black coral was Paradise Island.

The two men arrived by taxi from the airport at four in the afternoon. They didn't look like FBI officers, agents or whatever to Edward and he was going to tell them where to piss off to, but Jazz persuaded him to help them. They said they'd been refused permission to carry firearms into the country. It didn't ring true but Edward was trying to be patient for Jazz's sake.

To his astonishment she gave each of them a jiffy bag containing a Smith & Wesson .38 handgun and ammunition. After showering they dressed in Edward's clothes which weren't a perfect fit for either of them. Edward was getting less and less happy about their presence and pacing round the apartment, in two minds about what to do. Jazz suggested he should go and get a drink, so he walked over to Marco's place.

Chapter 28 - Thursday 3rd October to Monday 4th November

Marco did not like the smell of things one jot. As head of station, he should have been told about any FBI activity on the island. Edward didn't trust Jazz much, not like he had trusted Suzie. Marco didn't trust her at all.

Two armed men wearing Ed's clothes and driving around in his car was testing Marco's concept of common sense to the limit. He told Ed he should have said no. It could so easily be a potential set up just like the Sam White business. After making a few quick calls to Washington DC, Marco decided to contact Winston Bridges, the deputy commissioner of police in Nassau. Just in case Ed was being framed Marco made sure he was with him every step of the way.

Edward's Camaro pulled out of Governor's Beach without him, past the police pillbox, and headed for the north of the island. Jazz was sat on the lap of one of her FBI friends. As they left dusk was settling. Marco was driving behind them, two cars back. Edward was beside him in the passenger seat.

The car in front had three men in it; they were plainclothes policemen. Edward's car pulled into the British Colonial Hotel, about two or three miles short of Paradise Island. Everyone in front of them went into the lobby in the order they had left Governor's Beach. Edward and Marco watched from a distance.

The two men with Jazz checked into a reserved room on the first floor overlooking the harbour. The police booked into a neighbouring suite on the same floor. Shortly afterwards, Jazz departed for an unknown destination driving Edward's car. She was tailed by another unmarked police car.

Meanwhile Marco and Edward met Bridges in the bar. Winston told them the room next to the one taken by Jazz's friends was occupied by a man with a Jamaican passport. The Jamaican had checked in two hours earlier.

The police backup squad which had been hanging out at Paradise Island arrived an hour later and those inside waited for Bridges' instructions. Marco was getting impatient. He wanted Bridges' men to go in but Bridges kept stalling. Finally, after a shouting match between the two of them, six police forced their way into the two adjacent hotel rooms.

They found an unconscious, semi-naked waiter in the room where Jazz's friends should have been and most of Edward's clothes scattered over the floor. Next door, a neatly tied up and gagged sergeant from the Bahamian police was lying on the floor, also out for the count and virtually naked. The two supposed FBI men were gone and there was no Jamaican either. Marco was as inquisitive as ever. Winston smiled knowingly at him.

'We were one step ahead of you Marco.'
'How so?'
'We kept the Jamaican under surveillance. We knew he had stolen some black coral, so we arrested him and put one of our men in his place, to catch anyone who was buying the stuff.'

Marco was angry because Bridges had deceived him.

'So where's the black coral now?'

'My men have recovered it.'

'How much?'

'Ten thousand dollars worth.'

Marco knew this was all false. He went to the wash room and signalled for Edward to follow him. Marco explained to Edward that his earlier calls to the USA confirmed that the two FBI officers were imposters and well known smugglers of coral. The FBI also confirmed to him that two million dollars worth of black coral had been stolen from an authorised jeweller in Guadeloupe the previous Friday.

It all became obvious to Marco. The phoney FBI agents meant to either steal the black coral from the Jamaican thief or they were in on the heist in some way. Unfortunately Bridges got there first and confiscated most of the coral to boost his personal pension fund.

'Say that again Marco. They left only ten grand's worth with his undercover guy.'

'That is correct. The two supposed FBI guys would've known there should have been much more, realised they'd walked into a sting operation and fled.'

'Yes, by dealing with the room service waiter and the undercover policeman and taking their clothes.'

Edward could understand that Bridges knew about the Jamaican and had kept him under surveillance but how would he have known that Jazz was bringing the other two with her? He asked Marco.

'He has spies everywhere Ed. They probably knew long before these fakes landed at the airport. He may have let them through so he could make his arrest later. More likely still is that at that time he may not have known how much coral the Jamaican had on him. We only have Winston's word about the timings and you can bet your missing shirts on it that he's lied to us.'

So that was how Jazz smuggled the hash through so easily. Edward didn't mention it to Marco. He realised it would have been easy enough for the two FBI imposters to get into the hotel grounds from a first floor balcony. With one dressed as a waiter and the other carrying police ID they could have passed any challenge.

They were only a few minutes' walk from the waiting seaplanes which were usually moored outside the hotel. They could be anywhere in the Caribbean by now. Marco zipped up his pants and headed for the door. Edward followed him.

'Why won't the Jamaican say he stole two million's worth of coral and not just ten grand's worth? It is obvious he stole the lot.'

'Would you? By playing along he'll get only two years instead of ten. In any case, he'll probably end up as a shark's dinner before it gets to trial. Let's ask Bridges shall we.'

When they returned to the bar, Bridges concluded that it had been a successful day for the police.

Chapter 28 - Thursday 3rd October to Monday 4th November

'The other two are obviously long gone by now, so we won't bother chasing them.'
Edward asked if there would be any other repercussions.
'What about Jazz?'
'Ah yes, the young woman. I have been told most authoritatively that she clearly had little idea what they were doing.'

It suited Bridges to let her go. One less to make any noise about the amount of coral confiscated. He carried on lying.

'The Jamaican has confessed to stealing the ten thousand dollars worth of coral and we need no further evidence. So, you can take your clothes with you Mr Burlington. I gather your car is back in the parking lot in Governor's Beach.'

Marco couldn't resist taking a pot shot at Winston. He wanted him to know that he knew how much coral was stolen, in case he needed a favour at some time in the future.

'My sources have confirmed that two million dollars in black coral was taken in Guadeloupe, Winston.'

'So I understand, Mr Sanchez. So I understand. In truth I was told that too. However, our Jamaican turned up at the jewellers after the original thieves left. What with the front door open, he couldn't resist the temptation to take the small amount they overlooked.'

Marco smiled wryly at Edward. He hadn't expected such a slick cover story but Bridges had all the bases covered. There was nothing anyone could do. Bridges knocked back his glass of brandy and left the hotel. A vapour trail of cheap Brazilian cigar smoke followed him.

West Bay Street Nassau, New Providence Island Bahamas

Marco dropped Edward off with all the clothes he'd recovered at Governor's Beach and headed back downtown. He had more work to do on this as he feared it might not be as simple as it first appeared to be. Edward hadn't decided what to do about Jazz but he knew he could never trust her again.

It saddened him because he was foolishly hoping she'd bring back that emotional closeness he lost when Suzie was murdered. Maybe he was just destined to be alone, to go from one short term relationship to another. Perhaps he wasn't meant to get too close to any woman. Perchance being alone was for the best?

Edward noticed his car was back as Bridges advised but the lights were out in the apartment. He took the elevator up to his floor. Apart from the light of the moon it was still dark when he opened the front door so he assumed Jazz was asleep. He dumped the clothes he'd retrieved from the British Colonial Hotel onto the sofa and headed to the fridge for a Budweiser. That's when Jazz lunged at him from behind the door. Her voice was high-pitched, shrieking, screeching like a banshee.

'You bastard, you rotten bastard, that's my fortune lost you jerk!'

She was wielding a carving knife in her hand and Edward just managed to evade the slashing. He flicked the light switch off knowing her poor sight would limit her choices. It also meant the cameras wouldn't work. He backed away from her witch-like stance, silhouetted in the gloom of the apartment by the moonlight reflecting off the blade of the long knife.

'You're gonna pay for this you shit!'

Edward weighed up his chances of getting past her without being slashed by the knife or the odds of disarming her before she could do any serious damage to him. She'd been trained to kill by the CIA so either alternative was risky. She moved towards him, crouching like an animal ready to spring. He decided that attack was the best form of defence.

Before she could lunge at him again, he flew at her, feet first, booting her in the face. Her reactions were lightening quick. The knife jab into his thigh was agonising. As she fell, he removed the knife from her hand. She caught her head against the edge of the table. Edward landed on top of her on the floor. There was blood everywhere.

Jazz was unconscious but still breathing. Edward wiped the blood away from her head and realised all the blood was his. Blood was gushing from his thigh but somehow his right hand was unscathed. He ripped up a shirt from the pile of clothes on the sofa and tied it as tightly as he could round his thigh, above the knife wound, to stem the flow of blood. Then he poured rum over the cut to disinfect and cauterise it. After a minute or two, the bleeding stopped. He looked at his hand in sheer disbelief. How he took the knife from her by the blade without cutting himself was not far short of a miracle.

Edward quickly emptied a storage cupboard of suitcases. He checked her breathing again, then dragged her across the floor by the legs and bundled her in and locked the door. It was all he could think of at the time.

Edward gulped down a Bud and tried to work out what to do next but he was in too much pain to think straight. One of his neighbours was a doctor and Edward was on nodding acquaintance with the man. He decided to ask for help. He went to the apartment and knocked on the door. The man opened the door and looked shocked when he saw the state of Edward.

'My God, what has happened?'

'I'm afraid I've been in an accident.'

'How? Come in to the kitchen. Should I call 919?'

'No. The police won't be necessary.'

Edward explained to the doctor that he'd been drinking earlier and slipped while using a kitchen knife. There was nothing suspicious about it and no need for the police to be involved, especially those loitering around the pillbox.

Chapter 28 - Thursday 3rd October to Monday 4th November

'You should go to the hospital.'

'Can't you take a look? I have to leave in the morning and I don't want to be stuck in hospital.'

'I don't think I should.'

'Please. I can pay.'

The sight of Edward's wallet opening convinced the doctor to examine the wound. Fortunately the wound wasn't as bad as it looked and the doctor cleaned it properly with pure alcohol. He then applied cyanoacrylate, otherwise known as superglue, to keep it closed and avoid scarring.

After bandaging Edward's thigh tight he gave him a bottle of pure alcohol to clean the wound with later and showed Edward what to do. He recommended Edward go to the hospital if there were any complications. Edward thanked him and paid him five hundred bucks.

Back at the apartment, Edward removed the still unconscious Jazz from the cupboard and laid her on the bed in one of the spare rooms. He locked the door, and then packed up all her stuff. In the turmoil Edward had almost forgotten Monday was upon him so he readied himself for work even though he would arrive hours too early.

On the way out he unlocked the spare room door. Jazz was beginning to move. He had already placed her packed bags beside the bed, along with some money and a note simply saying Goodbye. As he closed the front door of the apartment and walked painfully and gingerly towards his car, he didn't know that Jazz was pregnant. She didn't know it herself.

As he headed for work, his mind played tricks on him. He wasn't sure if he had known Rutherford or possibly a twin brother of his from his Newcastle days. Rutherford had of course gone out of his way to introduce Jazz to him.

Edward dismissed any conspiracy as being paranoid since Rutherford had been in situ in Nassau for many years or so he said but he would check if he had a brother of similar age. Meanwhile Sir Peter was still planning in secret his own Caribbean coup. First though, he had to deal with another matter. That dear old chestnut Raj Gupta Khan was back on the agenda.

Khan had been playing with pretend submarines in the Indian Ocean, not Mac's model railway near Surbiton which now had replicas of all London's major Monopoly Game stations. Talking of which, as noted in Mac's diary, there had been far less hoax calls from the IRA warning of bombs planted at train stations in London since the bombing of the Tower of London. Perhaps they were saving them up for Xmas.

Chapter 29
Thursday 7th to Tuesday 12th November

Westminster Bridge Road Lambeth, London England
Alan McKenzie and Daniel Luke met in one of the redecorated meeting rooms in Century House. There was only one item on the agenda, Raj Gupta Khan. Later that same evening, Thursday 7th November 1974, Lord Lucan was to murder his wife's nanny and then disappear off the face of the earth.

The Lucan case was to intrigue Mac, purely out of personal interest. As the case developed Mac reckoned unlucky Lucan was murdered having become a liability as opposed to an asset to his gambling acquaintances. No matter how much Mac probed he could sense doors closing in front of him whenever he asked George Simpson of Special Branch questions.

Was it true Lucan's children were forced to watch the puppies Lord Lucan gave them being drowned? Was the same fate as Lucan suffered to await Khan or like Lucan would we never know for certain?

Metaphorically, while Lucan played the gaming tables, Khan had been playing with his yellow submarines in the Indian Ocean but that little game was getting Operation Tufty nowhere. Tufty stood for "Two fingers to you" and had been set up by the CIA after Standpipe to establish Raj and his brother as double agents in the ISI. As operations go it had gone backwards like a train failing to go uphill while running out of steam.

So far as MI6 could tell, the ISI did not know Raj Khan was being fed a load of crap about purported Indian nuclear submarine research. Sadly, however, when they set him up in his new accountancy practice, they hadn't realised how rarely accountants spoke to their clients. The bugs they placed before he moved in were all working but they were getting no useful feedback. Khan seemed to spend most of his time putting on weight in Indian restaurants; and so were Chad Cooper and his merry team. However, it was one of those rare occasions when Daniel Luke had noticed some peculiarities.

'Remember the Geordie cops who died in the raid on Burlington's flat?'
'Not by name Daniel.'

Chapter 29 - Thursday 7th to Tuesday 12th November

'Daniel O'Leary and Anthony Beaches. We've been digging and found they were loosely connected to Atif and Hamid Bashir.'

'Cyrus Burton's accountants.'

'That's right, who in turn are connected to Khan.'

Daniel Luke reminded Mac that the Bashir twins were reported as having drowned at sea but had chlorinated water in their lungs. O'Leary, Beaches and several other seemingly honest members of the Tyne and Wear Constabulary invested in a company that built and serviced swimming pools. It owned outlets in Newcastle, as well as Brighton and London.

'Guess who's a major investor?'

'Burton?'

'No, Abbas Hussein, Khan's mate who we now know is in the ISI who owned the New Delhi restaurant where Edward Burlington was poisoned.'

'That is interesting.'

'All the voting shares are owned by Hussein but held by a nominee company in Willemstad, Curaçao. That's in the Dutch Antilles.'

Mac was indignant.

'I know where Willemstad is thank you Daniel. Are you saying the ISI are connected to Burton?'

That's precisely what Daniel Luke was saying. What's more, all seven of the diplomats expelled from the Pakistani Embassy in March were ISI. Of course, it was purportedly through them that Khan introduced Burlington, alias JJ, to the syndicate and Cyrus Burton.

'What I'm saying is our research suggests Raj Khan is one way or another closer to Burton than we suspected.'

'You think he could lead us to the Beast?'

'With the right plan, through intermediaries, yes.'

'Why don't we drag him out of his bath full of toy submarines and get him to do just that?'

'Will Sir Peter play?'

'He thinks Tufty is dead in the bathwater too. Do you have a plan?'

Daniel Luke had a plan alright. It involved Cyrus Burton's other great passion, apart from corruption, blackmail and depraved sex: collecting diamonds. However, they would need the help of the Americans.

The CIA had recently confiscated an uncut diamond that was bigger than the Koh-i-Noor in the crown jewels. Their gem was 130 carats and worth a few million on the black market, right up Burton's street. It had been picked up near Kinshasa on the Congo and Angola border and was still there, still in the hands of the CIA.

'If we can get Khan to whet Burton's appetite, he might turn up to view it in person.'

Mac smiled cynically.

'Not if he knows about the curse of the Koh-i-Noor.'

Koh-i-Noor, Persian for "Mountain of light", refers to a cut diamond owned by the British royal family which was probably mined in India in the thirteenth century. It became part of the crown jewels in 1877 when Queen Victoria was proclaimed Empress of India.

The curse originated in 1306. When translated from Hindi it read "he who owns this diamond will own the world, but will also know all its misfortunes. Only God, or a woman, can wear it with impunity". In Great Britain, both Victoria and Elizabeth II enjoyed long reigns as queens, but the kings in between them didn't.

'Maybe that curse will add to the excitement for Burton.'

'We'd need to have everything in place to see how Khan contacts him.'

'Already done Mac.'

'Good man.'

Normally when Mac said "Good man" it meant you were in deep trouble, never to be seen again. A few days later, Raj Gupta Khan was called into a meeting with Sir Peter. Khan didn't know he was carrying a brand new prototype: an experimental harmonica bug, later to be known as an infinity transmitter. It had been planted in his briefcase on Tessa Hislop's unofficial orders.

When Hugh was told by Tessa what these devices might be able to do one day he reckoned George Orwell wasn't as dumb as he first thought. He'd never liked Nineteen Eighty Four. The novel was just too much science fiction for his traditional literary tastes.

All that changed once Tessa showed him what these modern bugs could do. Hugh surmised that the technology would one day be pre-built into every phone including these new fangled ones in posh cars. That way you could track them, know who had called or was called and eavesdrop.

With her MI6 cap on Tessa sighed at the thought of it. Who on earth would have the resources to squander listening in to everyone else nattering away about their health? What about all the other chatter about personal trivia like where to dine out or every business call? How many millions of calls were there a day across the world like "I'm running late dear, I'll be home in half an hour or don't wait up for me"?

She wondered what she would be doing in 1984, thought of Hugh and hoped for some little Hughs. If Mac or Chad had been asked what they thought they might be doing would they have guessed they could be working alongside Edward Burlington hunting down villains from Cyprus to Panama? Unlikely. They probably would have said there was more chance of them being dead by then.

Tessa and Hugh were an item now. Hugh persuaded her to plant the device so he could keep tabs on Khan for his brother. She didn't want to, this was an impromptu maverick operation and she could lose her job over it, maybe even go to prison but

Chapter 29 - Thursday 7th to Tuesday 12th November

Hugh could be a persuasive bloke, when he wanted to be. As he commented, who could prove which agency planted it? The adrenalin of making a spontaneous and rash decision together bonded them as a couple in every sense of the word.

Tessa took advantage of the opportunity when Raj Khan's briefcase needed a new lock and his regular repair man couldn't fit the job in for a few days. She said she could get it done quicker and turn it into a virtually bullet proof shield by having the interior reinforced with metal. The technology was futuristic and needed an expert friend of hers to install. All it consisted of basically was a telephone receiver and microphone welded into a hollow metal sheet about half an inch thick.

After discussing it with Hugh, she cautiously contacted her old boyfriend George Francis telling him not to rekindle any ideas he might have about a relationship revival. He had a large house in Rosslyn Hill in Hampstead and by all accounts his arms dealing business was raking it in. Somewhat to Tessa's surprise he not only knew instantly what to do and how to do it but added some frills that she hadn't heard of. She told him the briefcase belonged to a "friend", he asked no further questions, she was to pay him when she collected it and that was it or so Tessa thought when she went to pick up the briefcase.

Francis had been overjoyed to see Tessa again and, after doing the job for her, asked her to join him for dinner. She had to remind him she had contacted him on condition it was a strictly business only arrangement but he persisted. His exhilaration evaporated in a flash when Tessa told him she was now living with Hugh at the Burlington's bookshop.

Tessa had never seen him so bad tempered before, even when they had broken up last year, but she grinned to herself as she left: he had torn up the large cheque she gave him in his fit of fury. As she now had the briefcase she was damned if she was going to write out another cheque.

Once installed, Tessa simply called the number of the concealed phone and, instead of the hidden phone ringing, the call activated a microphone. All Tessa needed to do then was put her phone on a loudspeaker and she could record everything within earshot of the microphone in the briefcase.

The bug worked well no matter where Khan was and, as she expected, he took the briefcase everywhere with him to show off his importance. Of course, neither Khan nor the people he communicated with always spoke English but that didn't bother Hugh. He could understand Hindi, Punjabi and Urdu and probably every other language that Khan and co were likely to speak.

The deception of Khan made Tessa uneasy. She normally played it straight but Raj Khan had murdered Suzie and nearly succeeded in murdering Edward. She wasn't convinced that Alan McKenzie and Sir Peter were genuinely planning to bring him to justice. They would just use him forever to squeeze value from him. Furthermore, there was no name or number for the Khan operation Mac had promised. What's more Mac hadn't made any pronouncements about progress on the Khan front in his daily briefings for ages.

So it had been left to Tessa and the Burlington brothers to volunteer as privateers to make sure that Khan paid for his crimes. The slightly convoluted way her mind had worked to reach and enjoin in that conclusion was new to her. It was as if she were already a Burlington: in any event she was by then most assuredly under the influence of one or two of them.

Sir Peter dispensed with operational names like Standpipe and Lacklustre. From next year they were to use six digit codes instead, three numbers and three letters. Tufty, being a CIA creation, was unaffected but that op was dead anyway.

Strangely, it was the least popular of the changes he was ushering in ahead of his formal appointment. What's more, in his haste to announce his arrival by issuing decrees he forgot to put any interim arrangements in place. Consequently, new projects had no identifying label and, as such, were quite facetiously top secret.

Talking of top secret matters, Sir Peter's involvement in the JIC since leaving MI5 had been a well kept secret and his pending appointment was meant to be secret too but as with any issue to do with personnel, leaks can occur. They did. So within both MI5 and MI6 a secret, not top secret, notice was issued explaining what was happening with Castle, Sir Peter and the JIC.

It didn't bother the likes of Khan that much although he was shocked that a senior partner in Porter Williams he had reported to on some audits had been a JIC member without his knowledge. He decided not to mention anything when called to see Sir Peter in his new role as it might have unintended results or cause unexpected collateral damage. Despite knowing Peter, Khan was nervous of his impending meeting.

'Raj, long time since we had the pleasure of a chat. Do come in and have a seat.'

'Thank you sir.'

'Hmm, do call me Peter. The formalities of Sir Douglas Castle are cobwebs I'm sweeping away. Anyway, we know each other from the good old days at Porter Williams on MAMI, Gemstore and the rest of them. They were good fun weren't they?'

'Yes Sir Peter.'

'Now, back to MI6 matters which are usually more interesting. We seem to have plumbed the depths of the Indian Ocean and haven't found evidence of any Indian nuclear submarines.'

'Well, I ...'

'Good, because I have a more interesting assignment for you.'

Sir Peter reminded Khan about Operation Standpipe and the part he played in opening doors for his colleague the younger Burlington.

'Where is Edward these days?' I keep calling but get no reply.'

'He's still with Porter Williams but working overseas now.'

Chapter 29 - Thursday 7th to Tuesday 12th November

'Overseas?'

'Not what you think. He's on a tour of offices, starting at Singapore from memory, getting them to use the same audit programmes as London.'

'Not an agent anymore?'

'No. Given what happened to young Burlington, we won't be using him again in that capacity. As a matter of fact, we've stopped using assets on dangerous assignments and are trying to use properly trained officers instead.'

Raj Khan pursed his lips as if to indicate he didn't know if this was a good idea or not.

'All part of my new policy to make us more human.'

Sir Peter also reminded Khan about the food poisoning incident and how young Burlington miraculously survived.

'Hmm, you were with him as I remember.'

'I was sir, sorry, Peter.'

'You were lucky not to be affected too.'

'It appears so.'

Sir Peter poured himself some coffee from a pot on his desk. Intentionally he didn't offer a cup to Khan.

'Burlington's been through a rough few months, what with his flat being ransacked and then his girlfriend's suicide.'

Sir Peter intentionally mucked up the chronological order to see if Khan fell into the beginnings of his trap and tried to correct him.

'Yes ... you are right. It must have been horrible for him.'

Sir Peter tried again from another angle.

'We know who was behind that by the way.'

He purposefully left this throwaway remark hanging in the air. Khan waited, trying not to show panic or even undue interest. Sir Peter preoccupied himself with cream and sugar for his coffee and stirred the cup languidly, relishing every second of disquiet he had created out of thin air. He took out a large Brazilian cigar from his desk drawer and lit it intermittently, without any hurry so that he could draw out the suspense he'd left Khan hanging in, with much sadistic pleasure. Raj Gupta Khan could bear it no longer.

'Who?'

'Hmm, I beg your pardon?'

'Who turned over Edward's flat?'

'Why, Cyrus Burton's men of course.'

Raj Khan's poor attempt to disguise his relief was visible.

'That man is pure evil.'

'I'm glad to hear you say that. Sadly we are the ones who have to tolerate and deal with evil.'

Sir Peter gave up playing mind games and went on to explain, in the nicest possible way, how he wanted Khan to entrap Cyrus Burton via the same contacts he used in Standpipe using a rare diamond as bait. He emphasised this was a high profile operation. That's why Khan had been chosen. Not only for his knowledge that had put Standpipe into orbit but also because of the skilful, sagacious judgement that he had displayed in Lacklustre.

Peter was struggling to keep a straight face but persevered. Raj Khan would report directly to Alan McKenzie on the ground and Daniel Luke's SORT team would help with logistics.

The next day, Khan set about locating Burton. First though, being the wary sod he was, he called Porter Williams' Singapore office and asked for Edward Burlington. Daniel Luke heard the receptionist say that Burlington was there, but had left two weeks ago. When asked where he'd gone, she replied that she couldn't say, company policy and all that but she could take a message. That satisfied Khan. For once Daniel had all the expected corners covered.

Within a day or so Khan worked out how to contact Cyrus Burton but had no idea where Burton was. Khan contacted a colleague of one of the expelled Congolese diplomats in Burton's address book. A senior Congolese civil servant called Sadiq Solomon whom he'd known for some time. Solomon said, as Khan expected, that he had a line into Burton but it was always through an intermediary. Khan said that would do and arranged for Solomon to view the diamond at a secret rendezvous in Kinshasa.

Sadiq photographed the stone from every angle. He then contacted Burton through his normal channels, intermediaries on payphones at major railway stations like La Gare du Nord in Paris. They always used phone booths at train stations because in all respects security was usually slacker at those compared with airports.

The photos were sent to a Caracas post office box. Khan told Solomon that the gem could be purchased for two million dollars cash, in small denominations. Burton wanted to collect it in person, as he didn't trust intermediaries. Solomon reported back that Burton had agreed terms but wanted to inspect the diamond in the flesh before parting with his money. Many were listening in or interested.

All the arrangements and conditions made by Khan were translated by Hugh for Tessa. Tessa reckoned someone like Hugh, with such multiple language skills, would do well working in MI6. Then she thought to herself maybe he was.

When she looked back at what had happened this year it was as if he had almost taken the Mickey out of her on "MI" related matters, particularly when she had him sign the Official Secrets Act. He'd even said over their first dinner together "I'm not taking the MI key out of you". That was long before she had told him she was with MI6.

She recalled her first ever training session, the ABC of survival on which MI6 claimed copyright saying it had been nicked by MI5 and the police. Conceptually applying the ABC rules to all the Burlingtons made sense.

Chapter 29 – Thursday 7th to Tuesday 12th November

Jordan had been the go between twixt Burton and Solomon. He didn't like the idea of Carl Hanson travelling in person to Kinshasa. He wanted to make the trade himself but Hanson said Jordan didn't know enough about diamonds which he was the first to admit.

In any case, Carl trusted Sadiq Solomon who was being paid a fortune in Congolese terms to make sure everything went to plan. If it didn't, not only would he lose the money, but his life as well. Solomon was one of the many who'd been sent a copy of the video of the Bashir twins in the swimming pool.

The plan was that Burton was to tell Solomon where to meet him on the morning of his arrival in Kinshasa. Sadiq was to follow Burton's instructions to the letter, in case he was followed or bugged. If Burton's men encountered anything suspicious, Solomon and his entire family would experience a great deal of pain before they were consigned to hell.

Khan reported everything back to Mac who, in turn, reported it to Sir Peter. Much to Mac's dismay, Sir Peter said the Americans would take care of Burton, dead or alive. Mac wanted to be there when they finally caught the Beast. Peter insisted that as the Americans already had a strong presence on the ground close by, they should be involved.

Also to Mac's regret, Sir Peter preferred to keep Khan as a living double agent rather than a dead one. Mac pointed out Khan was not a double agent as he didn't know he was being used de facto as a robot for disinformation purposes but all Mac's arguments were to no avail. Khan was given details of whom to liaise with in Langley, Kinshasa and Luanda, the capital of Angola which neighboured the Congo. Daniel Luke guessed that if Burton was going to turn up then Luanda might be the safest airport to use.

Jordan was thinking along similar lines, so concluded anyone setting a trap would be too. Hanson and he therefore decided that Cabinda Airport in the Congo would be best; they could use a seaplane or fast boat as backup. What's more they could drop in on Lagos on the way as no one would be expecting Burton to go there on the way. They had rich corrupt clients there and Hanson wanted to be present as Burton's emissary when the late payers were shown the follies of not paying Cyrus Burton on time.

All the planes were soon to leave their respective airports as the excited passengers made their final preparations. How many would land safely and, more importantly, return from whence they came?

Looking at the abnormal hurried scribbling in Tessa's diary that day, a handwriting expert would have correctly concluded her hand was trembling. Whether that was with fear or excitement or out of sheer revenge had yet to be determined.

Chapter 30
Wednesday 13ᵗʰ to Saturday 16ᵗʰ November

Charing Cross Road Westminster & The West End, London

Raj Gupta Khan's every move was being monitored, not just by Mac and Daniel, but also by Tessa and Hugh. She'd taken the rest of her annual leave that was due to her: goodbye Xmas. Hugh closed the bookshop for minor renovations as they geared up for Khan's trip to Kinshasa. Scamp had been despatched to Epsom despite Sara's fictional protestations: she had even offered to collect him and his belongings which were burgeoning anyway you wanted to measure them.

Despite Scamp spending an exponentially increasing amount of time on the Downs Sara's protestations were also ever increasingly becoming more of pretence than real. She now looked forward to Scamp's stays. She was not alone. Scamp did too.

By now when Hugh dropped him off with all his precious belongings or Sara collected him, his bones and videos, it was more of a "hello Sara" than "goodbye Hugh" event from Scamp's perspective. Sara loved running with him on the downs. Scamp loved it too particularly if there was a fox or two around to chase. He never caught one but they exhausted him and afterwards he could curl up next to Sara and watch his favourite films calmly and quietly on the couch.

He could really concentrate without interruption. At Hugh's he had to watch alone from his rickety basket and he was often interrupted. The racket caused by passing traffic, police or ambulance sirens and even noisy customers downstairs were constant distractions in central London but unheard of in sleepy Surrey.

The closer Tessa and Hugh became the greater the mystery of the shop had become for Tessa. The comings and goings in the basement and the adjacent buildings were more akin to those at the single entrance way to Marble Arch tube.

Tessa was beyond caring now even though Mac warned her that the Burlingtons were probably into everything and more than was imaginable. He even mentioned rumours of MI24, MI34 and other departmental numbers being housed in Charing Cross. Tessa thought there was an element of jealousy in the tenor of Mac's remarks because he wasn't in the know and was worried she might be. Situations like that

Chapter 30 - Wednesday 13th to Saturday 16th November

arose on a daily basis around the River Thames. To Mac it was as if someone had built a station on his railway network without obtaining his permission.

Tessa had already begun to share Hugh's love of antique books. Every time she passed under the archway at the shop's entrance she looked up at the crest of arms' mottos Nil Desperandum and Dei Gratia Burlington. It seemed as if she were Alice entering wonderland. What was in that wonderful land she wasn't sure but it never failed to intrigue her.

Khan recruited Abbas Hussein to go with him. Hussein was a close friend of Sadiq Solomon and they were members of the same club in Amsterdam, The Black Barracuda. The club was licensed in the name of a Dutch playboy called Carl Hanson but that wasn't of any interest to MI6 or the CIA. Abbas insisted on bringing two bodyguards with him because Africa was such a dangerous place.

Sir Peter Stafford sanctioned the inclusion of Hussein and his bodyguards in the operation, knowing full well that all three were ISI. It became obvious Khan had his own agenda and MI6 would let the rope hang out and play along, just to see where it would lead. The CIA were putting a combat team in theatre and it was already within striking distance having been moved nearer to Luanda.

Khan insisted that he should be in overall charge of the unnamed unnumbered operation. That meant he personally could make the exchange with Cyrus Burton. Hugh thought the whole thing was like something out of the movies, too farcical for his liking, but Tessa assured him this was not only real but dangerous.

Hugh had already told his brother what was happening and that Tessa intended to follow Khan to Kinshasa and report back to him what Raj Khan hid up his sleeve. Ed gave Hugh the name and number of an experienced minder from the old days, who he recommended should go with Tessa to protect her. Marco was enlisted and informally arranged for two unmarked old all purpose Berettas to be available to them when they arrived there.

Normally, Ed would've been totally against anyone going anywhere near Africa. This time though such concerns were inconsequential. He wanted to know what Khan's secret agenda was and, anyway, Tessa had promised Hugh she'd stay well back from any threat of serious action.

In the meantime Tessa was gearing up to go. She checked every detail as if her life depended on it and made sure any clues as to what she had been up to with Hugh were wiped off the face of the world. She even erased her diary note about meeting George Francis and threw out the cheque book she had used to try and pay him.

Ngaliema, Kinshasa Congo

The American combat team was to assemble at a private house inside a high walled two acre compound covertly owned by the CIA on the outskirts of Kinshasa. They hired a Congolese army helicopter for three days. The hit squad consisted of

Raj Gupta Khan and his three ISI companions, six Seals and their commander. In addition, the military attaché from the British Embassy in Kenya and two colonels from the Congolese army were seconded to the team.

Everyone was armed and wired. To the extent practical all communications were being monitored from a locked room in another part of the compound. From there data was relayed to the US National Security Agency, NSA at Fort Meade, Maryland, as well as to SORT at Century House, Lambeth. In London Mac and Daniel were on the lookout for anything unexpected as were their counterparts in Maryland and Langley.

The plan was simple, wait for Sadiq Solomon's call. The combat team would then get to the meeting point by helicopter and take cover, while Khan and the ISI agents would travel there by Jeep. As soon as Cyrus Burton showed up, he and everyone with him would be taken alive if possible, but dead if necessary.

If there was a fire fight and people died on either side, the bodies were to be buried at sea which when translated meant dumped from the chopper into international waters, with weights tied to their legs. The American SEAL commander had the diamond which he handed over to Khan.

Cabinda Airport, Cabinda Congo

Carl Hanson's boat was anchored off the Congolese coast outside the national jurisdiction, about fifteen miles from Cabinda Airport. Jordan went ashore by a fast dinghy and called Sadiq Solomon.

'Mr Solomon, I represent the import business you've been in contact with recently. We'd like to arrange a meeting.'

'I will only deal with the Chairman.'

'My chairman anticipated that. Please listen carefully to his taped message.'

Jordan played a specially recorded tape into the phone.

'Hello Sadiq my dear. Please do as you are told by my associate, no more and no less. Do not stay on the phone too long with him: I hate unnecessary telephone bills. Hope to see you later.'

Jordan pushed the stop button on the recorder.

'Are you satisfied that was him, Mr Solomon?'

'Yes.'

'Ok, now listen to my instructions.'

Jordan's voice was low as he relayed Cyrus Burton's orders to Solomon. At ten o'clock precisely, he was to start walking from the Hotel Grande, down the Boulevard Triomphal, heading west. Someone would give him a business card with a number to call for further instructions. He was to go to any payphone in the area to make the call.

'Assume you are being watched all the time, by us and by them. Is that understood?'

Chapter 30 - Wednesday 13th to Saturday 16th November

'Yes.'

Jordan hung up the payphone.

Lingwala & Centre Ville, Kinshasa Congo

Tessa and Hugh checked into the Hotel Grande in Kinshasa two hours earlier. It was one of the best hotels in Kinshasa. Hugh had insisted on coming with Tessa in place of the minder Ed recommended. He didn't tell Ed because he knew he would have found a way to stop him.

Tessa stood on the loo seat in the en-suite bathroom and found the two Berettas with bags of ammo wrapped in a cloth wedged behind the cistern. Courtesy of Marco's rogue CIA element there was already a listening device, hidden in a portable radio, which was connected to the surveillance room at the CIA compound in the suburbs of Kinshasa. When Sadiq Solomon called Raj Gupta Khan to relay the instructions he'd received from Cyrus Burton via Jordan, Tessa and Hugh heard every syllable and Hugh understood it all no matter what the language.

'Edward will strangle me with his bare hands for getting involved in all this Hugh.'

'What he doesn't know won't hurt him.'

'You didn't need to come. You shouldn't have.'

'What, and let you gallivant off with some muscle bound minder. You're far too precious for that.'

He kissed her and she responded but she was still worried about what Edward would say if, when he found out. She was more worried than if Mac discovered what she was doing on holiday. It was not anywhere as bad as say Sir Douglas Castle's fear of Sara Burlington: real but irrational, which translated into paranoia.

Everyone in the intelligence services needed a psychological outlet. This sort of fabricated fear replaced what those in this field should have been shitting themselves about but didn't because they had imprisoned the shitty stuff at the back of their minds. The paranoia then escaped in other forms often through the least logical routes such as Tessa's and Castle's irrational fears.

That is why Roger Burlington was, as Chad had sussed out, the spy that never was: he didn't have to think about compartmentalising emotions such as fear and guilt or about imprisoning them in the recesses of his mind. Roger, just like his sons, did it on auto-pilot, subconsciously. Hence at the very moments when the Burlingtons should have recognised danger they saw no fear. Whether it was when facing torture in Russia, a gun in the hand of a psycho in Harley Street or arrest in the Congo that was when they kept their collective cool.

Meanwhile, Jordan was with Kinshasa's chief of police, Pierre Mahad, who liked to be called Madi, the name of an old African warlord. Pierre was a big man, the same colour as shining black coral and he made all six foot four inches of Jordan look small. Madi had been useful so far, monitoring who was new in town for Jordan. Hanson was paying him handsomely for his services. Surveillance in the Congo was usually done by children. They were cheaper and much more reliable than their parents.

Pierre reported to Jordan that an odd English couple called Mr and Mrs White had registered at the Hotel Grande. He also showed him copies of Khan's passport and the passports of his ISI companions whom he'd put under close watch. Khan and his Pakistani cohort entered the Congo on a private jet that landed unscheduled at one of Kinshasa's smaller airports. This didn't escape the attention of one of Madi's lookouts. The visitors were all carrying Pakistani passports and Jordan guessed they must be ISI.

Carl Hanson's seaplane arrived and Madi escorted him to the roofless hut where Jordan was waiting. Two police officers followed Hanson. They carried four large suitcases full of US dollar bills in mixed denominations. The suitcases were carefully placed in the hut while Madi stood guard outside until Hanson leaned through the glassless window frame and asked him to move out of earshot.

'What else have you for me?'

'Take a look at these.'

'That one's Raj Gupta Khan, the one with the diamond.'

'What about the other three?'

'Abbas Hussein and wait a minute, I know these other two chicken fuckers.'

Hanson was looking at the copied passports of Hussein's bodyguards.

'They tried to murder me the last time I was in Bangkok. They're fucking ISI too.'

Jordan slammed his fist on the table. It just survived the assault.

'That's it. I knew it, a damn trap. We should go right now.'

'No, the diamond's here, I can sense it and I want it.'

'That's too dangerous Carl.'

'Who else has come to the party?'

Jordan laid out more photos on the rickety table.

'Madi's people followed this lot to a CIA compound on the outskirts of town. An American team also arrived there in a chopper from the south, probably Luanda. The helicopter is old so it must be local military hardware. It could be Angolan or from here. I don't know nor does Madi and we decided it best not to get inside their compound even with the kids we're using. The Americans will know all those tricks and maybe pull out. I would in their shoes.'

Carl Hanson paced around the roofless hut. He was thinking and Jordan didn't interrupt him. He guessed the reason Hanson was still a free man was just about to be proven again. At his best Hanson was brilliant.

'Alright. Change of plan.'

Hanson called back Madi to join them and asked for a map of Kinshasa. The chief of police was then paid an extra US $25,000 up front, with a promise of more if the new plan succeeded. His face was shining even more brightly than black coral as a convoy of police vans left for downtown Kinshasa.

Chapter 30 - Wednesday 13th to Saturday 16th November

Carl Hanson returned to the seaplane and flew back out to his boat. First on Jordan's to do list was to have Madi organise a surprise visit to the English couple in the Hotel Grande. Hanson was to return as Burton to meet Solomon once all was in shipshape array ready for his inspection.

The Scandinavian sat outside in a police car while Madi sent six of his men into the hotel to find out just who these two people were. The receptionist was reluctant to hand over the spare room key. After a sustained bout of shouting threats and banging the desk by the sergeant in charge, she handed it over to him.

Tessa heard the commotion and left the bedroom to look. She saw the Congolese police starting to come up the stairs. She ran back to the room. They had three floors to climb.

'We're leaving right now. The radio, quick!'

Hugh picked up the radio as Tessa grabbed the two handguns and ammo. They hurried out of the room and closed the door behind them.

'Which way?'

Tessa could hear the heavy footsteps of the police approaching the third floor of the atrium. She signalled to Hugh to run the other way. It was no use. The corridor was too long and they'd be seen before they reached the end of it.

A few doors down, a young curvaceous maid was taking out blankets from a storage cupboard. Tessa clamped her hand over the girl's mouth and forced her back inside the cupboard. Hugh followed, just as the police turned the corner. He closed the door quietly. The girl was struggling so Tessa pointed one of the guns at her. That quietened her down and she stared at the floor, motionless.

They could hear the police banging on their room door down the corridor. When there was no answer, they unlocked it and entered. After a few minutes, they came back out sounding agitated. They started advancing down the corridor, knocking on room doors as they came closer.

Frightened hotel guests answered their brusque questions and were allowed to go back inside their rooms. Tessa silently signalled for the hotel maid to lock the cupboard, quietly. She did so, just before the handle turned. When the policemen outside couldn't open the door, they banged on it.

'Ouvrir.'

'Qui est là?'

Then the voice of the sergeant could be heard.

'Allons-y, il n'y a personne.'

He wasn't interested in linen storage cupboards. The police moved away from the cupboard, further down the corridor. After checking all the rooms, they came back. Tessa and Hugh could hear them outside their room, then they left and everything went hushed. Hugh took out five twenty dollar bills from his wallet and showed them to the maid. She was young, cute and frightened.

Hugh tucked the money into her overall pocket and put a finger up to his lips. Tessa removed her hand from the girl's mouth with the gun raised. The maid stayed quiet. Tessa unlocked the cupboard door and opened it slightly; just enough to peer down the corridor. One of the Congolese policemen was stationed outside their bedroom door. They wouldn't be able to emerge without him seeing them. Hugh turned to the young girl and whispered.

'You speak English?'

She shook her head, with a puzzled expression on her face.

'Parlez vous le Français?'

'Oui.'

Hugh pointed in the direction of the policeman.

'Distraire le gendarme?'

He made gestures to suggest removing her bra might help. He took two fifty dollar bills from his pocket and waved them in front of the girl's face. She smiled even more than before.

'Cinq minutes.'

The girl nodded eagerly and prodded Tessa's breasts with her elbows while undoing her bra. Hugh gave her the money.

They were taking a risk. There was nothing to stop her taking the money and then shopping them to the policeman but there wasn't another option. The girl slipped quickly out of the cupboard.

Tessa held her Beretta at the ready. She'd never been in a situation like this and realised what it must have been like for Edward when in a hapless situation. Just like him she was now an unpaid volunteer. Was she mad or had she finally become a Burlington? Did she share Edward's no-nonsense beliefs in what was right and wrong?

She looked at Hugh. He was as calm as if reading a book back home. That reassured her but she didn't know if she could do this. If she could shoot a policeman should it come to that. Her hands were shaking.

The young maid sashayed down the corridor in her uniform which she loosened at every step. The policeman on guard turned at the sound of her approaching. A broad smile broke across his face as her firm nipples appeared then disappeared again and again as she sidled up to him. Her small breasts were gently bouncing up then down inside her half open shirt with every step she took.

She was close to him now and tousled his hair with her fingers, then manoeuvred him round so his back was turned towards the cupboard and slid the palm of her other hand inside his trousers. The lucky policeman opened the door and shut it behind them as the new lovers started undressing one another.

Tessa and Hugh moved quickly down the corridor and round the corner, out of sight. They knew there would be more policemen in the lobby, so they found a back way out and emerged into the sunlight on the Avenue de Batetela.

Chapter 30 - Wednesday 13th to Saturday 16th November

'We can't go back there.'

'I know.'

'Passports?'

Hugh put a hand into his jacket pocket and pulled out the two passports.

'Got them on the way out.'

'Good thinking.'

'Ok, we've passports and money, weapons and the radio. All they took were our clothes and tickets.'

'We wouldn't be able to use the tickets Hugh. They'll be watching the scheduled flights like hawks.'

'Just have to find another way out of here then won't we?'

Hugh smiled at Tessa's worried frown and put his arm round her. They hailed a taxi. Hugh asked the driver to take them to a cheap hotel anywhere in the vicinity. He guessed the cab driver must have thought they were off to emulate the seductive scene they had just witnessed. Why not? Hugh was beginning to enjoy this: he too could be Hugh, not James Bond, listening to the secret radio in bed with his dream girl. He told the taxi driver to hurry.

Sadiq Solomon had been walking down the Boulevard Triomphal for about five or so minutes when a group of children barged into him. One of them stuck a piece of paper in his hand and shouted Joyeux Noël, then ran off after his friends. Sadiq headed to a hotel a hundred yards away to call the number he'd been given.

Solomon waited for a police van to pass before crossing the road but it didn't pass. It stopped. He was told to clamber on board. He didn't argue or ask questions: that was the way to stay alive in the Congo. The van driver drove to a nondescript house without any windows about a mile away and he was shown into a room where two other men were already present. Solomon only recognised Pierre Mahad, Kinshasa's chief of police. The other was a white man who he didn't know, until he spoke.

'Sadiq, my old mate, my dear, I'm so glad you could drop by to see me.'

'Cyrus? Is it you, it is you Master Cyrus Burton?'

'Who else?'

Solomon quizzically, almost adoringly sized up the Burton he had never seen before.

'Cyrus, you look so formidable and so excitingly different. Yes, truly magnificent, wonderful, formidable as we say.'

'All the better to fool you with my dear.'

Sadiq clutched Cyrus Burton's hand and pumped it excessively, almost genuflecting at the same time. After a few moments, Burton extricated his fingers from Solomon's grasp.

'Now Sadiq, we have to go get this diamond, don't we?'

'Yes, of course Master.'

'I need you to make a call first.'

Solomon called Khan and told him that he'd received further instructions from Cyrus Burton. Raj Khan was to bring the diamond to the entrance of Kinshasa's Zoo on Avenue Ruakadingi in two hours, precisely. If it was a green light, Sadiq would be seated on one of the park benches at the entrance. If he wasn't there, then it was a red light and Khan should keep driving and return to await fresh instructions. Khan asked if Burton was in Kinshasa and Sadiq confirmed that he was and was armed with the money.

'Have you seen him yourself Sadiq?'

'I'm pleased to say I am with him right now.'

Khan was excited when he hung up. The plan was working. The American Seals escorted by the two Congolese Colonels set off in the helicopter. Khan and his ISI friends had a celebratory drink when the others left. Khan proposed a toast. They spoke in Hindi.

'Here's to the demise of Cyrus Burton.'

'Yes and the rise of his successor.'

'A backwater like the Congo is the perfect place to kill the Beast. Burton's vulnerable here.'

'Then we can take over his empire worldwide.'

'With you, Raj, at the head of it.'

'The king is dead.'

'Long live king Khan!'

The surveillance team in the locked room were listening in and relaying what they heard to SORT and the NSA. The ISI men were speaking in Hindi and nobody in the room knew what they were saying.

No one had thought of taking along an independent interpreter: after all, they had Raj and his team with them. Everyone assumed they were just happy that all was going to plan. Tessa and Hugh were also listening, in bed together. Hugh knew exactly what they were saying and it was not just a good natured celebration. He explained all to Tessa and hatched a plan.

Meanwhile Raj Khan, along with Abbas Hussein and the two ISI bodyguards gave the Americans an hour's head start to take up their positions. They were to stay about a mile back so as not to be seen and give the game away. Everyone had assumed that Cyrus Burton would have his own observers on the ground, watching. It all suited Khan.

Once he and his ISI team were alone with Burton and whoever he brought with him they could open fire and claim self defence afterwards. They checked their weapons and the walkie-talkie they would need to call in the Seal team. Then one of the bodyguards drove them out of the compound. Adrenalin was flowing round the Jeep. If they managed this simple murder they'd be rich beyond their most feral dreams and hailed as heroes into the bargain.

Chapter 30 - Wednesday 13th to Saturday 16th November

Sadiq Solomon was sitting on the park bench by the entrance to the Zoo. Everything was quiet as the Jeep drove past him and turned round to return and park outside the zoo entrance. The only other vehicle around was a caged truck, waiting to make a delivery of about thirty spotted hyenas. A uniformed Zoo attendant came out to handle the paper work and was talking to the driver.

The Jeep pulled up next to the delivery truck. Khan and Hussein stepped out and approached Sadiq. The two ISI bodyguards also stepped out of the Jeep and stood either side of it, looking round for anything suspicious.

'Sadiq, it's terrific to see you.'

Abbas Hussein held out his hand to shake Sadiq's. Sadiq looked towards Raj Khan.

'The diamond if you please?'

Khan took the diamond from his pocket, showed it to Sadiq but kept it clenched in his hand.

'Good.'

'Where's Cyrus?'

'Cyrus will be here.'

Nobody noticed that the Zoo attendant had unlocked the gate to the hyena cage and opened it. The hyenas started streaming out into the street. As they escaped the attendant sprinted round and jumped into the passenger seat. The driver reversed the delivery lorry into the Jeep and crushed it.

The truck sped away, leaving nearly three dozen hyenas prowling around Sadiq and the ISI men, whooping and yelping and screeching. Khan drew his gun but Sadiq grabbed his arm before he could get off a shot.

'Nobody move! They're not dangerous, they are only spotted hyenas. They never attack humans unless provoked. Do not shoot, the smell of blood will excite them.'

What Sadiq didn't know was that these hyenas hadn't been fed properly for a while and they were in an excitable state. All of a sudden, Raj Gupta Khan's kneecap exploded in an eruption of blood and shattered bone. He screamed and fell to the ground. The hyenas were provoked. Now they attacked.

About fifty yards away, under cover of some bushes, Hugh looked down the barrel of his Beretta. He smiled wryly to himself. That was why he was called bulls-eye Burlington in the cadets after he started wearing and cleaning his glasses.

As Hugh watched the bloodshed begin the ISI bodyguards were shooting at the hyenas but it only made the mayhem and slaughter worse. A feeding frenzy began. Sadiq and Abbas tried to run but they were overtaken and brought to the ground by a splinter pack from the main cackle of hyenas. The animals tore them to pieces. Raj Khan was right in the heart of the core cackle, being eaten alive. Hugh was straining his neck as he looked disdainfully at the scene of carnage.

'That's for Suzie and Ed.'

Tessa grabbed his arm and pulled him away. They needed to get out of Kinshasa right now. Hugh stooped down, turned and left holding onto Tessa. He took the lead and steered her out through the bushes and shrub. By now her whole body was shaking and she was vomiting. She tried to come to terms with what she had just witnessed. She hadn't even seen a film like it.

The bodyguards were being devoured and the walkie-talkies lay lifeless on the road. All five men were dead. What was left of their limbs and carcasses was being dragged about and fought over by the frenzied pack of hyenas.

A traffic jam formed, with onlookers rubbernecking to see as much as they could while keeping well back out of danger. Most of them thought the scene unfolding in front of them was a movie shoot and they were scanning the faces for a glimpse of any movie stars. Hugh and Tessa were soon back to the safety of their dingy lodgings. Once there it was Hugh's turn to be sick.

Jordan and the Congolese police managed to shunt their way through the gridlock in an armoured vehicle. Jordan was videotaping everything but he was too late to catch who'd started the chaos by shooting Khan. He panned the camera round but the sniper was long gone.

The police were using their rifles and handguns to systematically kill the remaining hyenas. Jordan walked through the blood and gore, armed with gun and camera, shooting hyenas in both senses of the word as he went.

He reached the body of Raj Khan, barely recognisable as human by now. Khan's right arm had almost been severed but his right hand was still intact and the fist tightly clenched.

Jordan prised open the fingers and retrieved the diamond. He wiped some blood off it using the remnants of Khan's jacket and then made his way through the crowds to a waiting car with Madi at the wheel. The car drove away while the police continued their target practice and mopped up what was left of the beasts.

The Seals heard the shooting from their position some distance away. They arrived on the scene far too late to be of any use to anyone. By then the area was gridlocked and swarming with armed police. They decided not to get involved as it would be messy and could provoke an international incident.

Two others had witnessed it all unfold. Amazingly, despite his early training amongst the overgrown weed ridden tombstones in Billingham, Hugh hadn't noticed two little boys in camouflage pretending to be soldiers lying in the undergrowth about five yards from where he had fired his one shot. They had been taught well by their grandfather. They lay motionless until all was over. Then they made their getaway.

They moved in a sequence of withdrawal-in-contact, with one of them laying down pretending to shoot then leapfrogging one another in fire-and-manoeuvre tactics. It was as if in training but make-believe, a scene from neverland, until they

Chapter 30 - Wednesday 13th to Saturday 16th November

looked up and saw the Congolese army jackboots in front of their frightened little faces. They were taken away for interrogation.

Had Frederick Burlington seen them he would have been a proud man were they his grandchildren. He would have also boxed Hugh's ears after lecturing him in a way he'd never forget.

The Seal team had by now returned to the helicopter and headed straight back to the compound on the outskirts of Kinshasa. They reported that Khan and his companions were all dead and the diamond had in all likelihood been swallowed by a hyena. As all the hyenas were most likely dead by now too, it was implausible that the stone would be passed through the animal that ate it. As far as the CIA were concerned, this mission was a write-off and had been a cock-up in all respects.

Jordan took a speedboat out to the cruiser where Carl Hanson was casually and triumphantly drinking champagne. Once again he had lived up to if not surpassed his reputation as the Beast.

Tessa and Hugh surreptitiously hired a Land Rover and made their way over the border into Angola long before a livid President Mobutu had been briefed by his generals on what had happened: at times like these he trusted his army more than the police. His loyal right hand man Solomon was dead and he wanted his murderers to face Congolese justice.

He ordered a news blackout, not that any newspaper correspondent had heard the news. Mobutu also commanded his head of intelligence to bring the killers back to the Congo no matter where they were, no matter what the cost. The zoo had animals that were more likely natural born killers than spotted hyenas: the culprits could face those.

The chief of intelligence, Francois Solomon who was Sadiq's son, took on the task with tearful eyes. He soon had a slow head start: the boys had identified about a hundred couples who could have been involved in the murders. They included Mr and Mrs White from Preston in England after the boys had studied copies of white foreigners' passports collected later that day from hotels in downtown Kinshasa.

The first problem was most of the photographs were so grainy the portraits were far from clear. The second was they spanned some thirty nationalities. This was all getting beyond the Congo's forensic capabilities and would stretch its intelligence resources.

The couple the boys saw might not have stayed at a hotel anyway and to put all the photos in the press of each relevant country and offer rewards would look amateur at best and foolish in reality. It might also result in some very expensive lawsuits for defamation.

Even if they narrowed it down it could develop into a major international incident with only the statements of two illiterate kids against those of the accused and no doubt many others. Furthermore, the chances of obtaining an extradition were slim at best. Those accused would be facing the death penalty and in terms of evidence all they had was one bullet which hadn't even hit Sadiq Solomon. A clever international law firm could easily brush off any accusations of murder relating to Francois' father.

Even after their experts had tried to enhance the photos, the boys could not narrow down the list of suspects. As Francois had noticed, the boys' final list simply comprised the photos of every white couple less than fifty years of age whose passports had been copied. Reluctantly he advised against further pursuit of the murderers. As for the two men who organised the delivery of the hyenas, they and their truck would never be traced now.

Francois knew there was more to it than the Congolese army surmised but then they hadn't a clue that most of the dead men had been ISI agents. Mobutu also agreed it best to close this chapter in the Congo's history knowing that if there had been a realistic chance of success Sadiq's son would have followed it through to his dying breath.

Mobutu left it in Francois' hands and if he perchance had a bright idea they could always follow it through later. There was no statutory time limit on bringing charges of murder in the Congo, or even conspiracy to murder in conjunction with a cackle of spotted hyenas.

The two little boys who between them added up to a whole ten years' worth of experience were rewarded with a trip in an army helicopter over Kinshasa, as they had requested. In the meantime the erstwhile Mr and Mrs White had to spend a few dollars here and there in bribes but within two days they were on board a scheduled flight to Cairo from Luanda and back on their way to London.

During the trip back Tessa started feverishly biting her nails. Hugh had to restrain her reverting to what she explained was a childhood habit. She was the first to admit that being on unofficial active service was a trifle too much for her. By Xmas she would kick the habit thanks to Hugh buying her some foul tasting nail polish for her birthday which was the day they landed safely at Heathrow.

Westminster Bridge Road Lambeth, London England

Sir Peter Stafford hardly raised an eyebrow when Mac reported Khan's death. Mac was sat opposite him and Chad Cooper was waiting in the corridor. He was trying not to focus on what happened. Shit like Khan got what they deserved, usually.

Of course, Peter had been involved with entrapping agents before not just with Vassall and Profumo but others connected to the Cambridge Four as he preferred to call them. Sir Peter understood the golden rule for success was the fewer who knew the better but Khan's end had been savage to put it mildly and would be much talked about.

'I need a job done and Cooper will be ideal.'

'Certainly, should I bring him in and you can brief us.'

'Not just yet Mac. Cooper has a signals man in his team. Jock something or other?'

'Jock McGrath is his point man Peter. We met him at that demonstration we attended weeks ago. Damn good too, even built his own TV set. Jock's an experienced

Chapter 30 - Wednesday 13th to Saturday 16th November

all rounder and ex SBS. Like Chad Cooper he joined them after the Signals Corp or whatever they were called then and ...'

'I remember him. His Scottish accent needed translation but he clearly lived by anything with a wire hanging from it be it a bomb or a bug. Hmm. That's reassuring. I want them to report to me for the next few weeks. Your sole job is to give them covering fire so no one knows that and nobody noses around asking questions. I don't want Daniel Luke or SORT to know either but I need to know if anyone starts asking too many questions.'

Sir Peter liked playing the disinformation card. No doubt Mac's brain was in overdrive working out what Luke had to do with Khan. Then his mind would go into reverse and conjecture if what he had just said was flak to throw him off the scent. That was precisely what Mac had thought and he was now about to try probing in a roundabout way to see where that landed him.

'Of course. Do you want an assignment number for the job?'

'This job as you so eloquently put it will have no number.'

'Maybe if you briefed me on any of the more sensitive issues we could then call Cooper in?'

'Mac, no offence but this is strictly need to know. Your job is to make sure no one and I mean no one asks any questions. No one is to know where Cooper and McGrath are or what they are doing and that includes you.'

Mac got the gist. He'd seen these ultra secret jobs years ago. Even worked on some and they usually involved mole hunts.

'Yes Sir Peter.'

'Hmm, I was thinking about Khan playing with his toys in the bath tub.'

Mac looked at him. Was he taking the piss?

'Both having been SBS, I thought a month's special undercover training on one of our nuclear submarines would be an impenetrable cover. You know, learning all about handling nuclear weapons and all that malarkey. What do you think?'

'Clever Peter, that's extremely clever indeed.'

'Good. Glad you like it. Can you create chatter and noise about it? Call Admiral Parrington. The admiral's been told to make all the necessary arrangements so that they get nowhere near any Polaris missiles. Remember, if anyone tries to contact them they're uncontactable on HMS Resolution until Xmas.'

'Anything else?'

'Hmm, both men have plenty of fake identities at the ready I assume?'

'Yes Sir Peter.'

'Good. Get me about thirty thousand in Sterling, used notes. That should do them for a month or so. I'll approve it and they can account for it once it's all done.'

'When do you want it?'

'In about an hour. I should have briefed Cooper by then.'

'Right away Sir Peter. Should I get Cooper in?'

'Yes and thank you Mac. Not many I can trust yet, and not a word to a soul about this.'

Mac left. His roundabout probing had landed him nowhere. Chad entered somewhat bemused by Mac's departure despite his body language which indicated nothing untoward. Mac liked working for Peter so much more than that paranoid Castle man. The informality Peter introduced added to camaraderie even for the ex-military like Mac, and Peter liked to understand the detail.

A few weeks ago Sir Peter had spent nearly half a day with Mac learning about the technological advances they were making with the Americans. Peter had been especially interested in telephones without any wires and what had now been officially called infinity bugs. He'd insisted on trying them out and Jock taught him how to install the devices. Even Mac hadn't a clue how until then. Jock quipped that they were better than guns so he should pay attention. Peter certainly had.

'Come in Chad and sit yourself down on the couch. Please call me Peter. I have a job lined up for you and that, hmm, Jock chap who works for you.'

Sir Peter had nearly used the word jock-strap but luckily he averted the error of his ways. His mind had momentarily flitted elsewhere again. This time he was thinking of the young man of his same persuasion he'd met on the plane coming back from Nassau. The pleasure and surprise at the silken perfumed underwear he found inside his trousers once they started getting properly acquainted had literally overcome him.

It was fascinating the details some like Sir Peter put in their diaries while the less extrovert were far more cryptic, more evasive about the truth. In Peter's, if his admirer had satin underwear you knew about it. Perhaps he read them late at night to his lovers before they got their kicks on route sixty nine.

When MI5 searched the homes and offices of Khan and co in the UK they only found one diary with any meaningful information in it. That belonged to Hussein. There was no doubt according to that who had killed Suzie. Why he had put pen to paper about Khan in that way no one knew but mistrust was a common virus in those disloyal circles.

For Edward the nightmare train ride he had endured before his arrival in Nassau had now seen off most of those passengers from his past who might do him harm with the principal exception of his nemesis and his loyal servant Jordan whom he didn't even know. As Mac had noted in his diary the bloody train hadn't stopped, there were just fewer passengers and Burton had yet again outfoxed them all. Not bad for a beast, even better for a junkie and somewhat naively no one had thought through the repercussions of the last few days.

Chapter 31
Monday 18th to Friday 22nd November

Shirley Street Nassau, New Providence Island Bahamas

Winston Bridges was promoted not long after the black coral incident. The press painted him out to be a nature lover. He managed to worm his way into glowing editorial articles in the Nassau Guardian and Tribune about the two hundred plus types of black coral living in the tropics and why coral was classified as an endangered species.

Even the US picked up on the story as black coral was the official state gem of Hawaii. Winston was a hero, a national treasure or glow worm who'd saved the delicate ecosystems of the oceans.

Hugh was the one to tell his brother that Khan had been torn to shreds by a cackle of hyenas while still alive. He truthfully outlined the circumstances of Khan's death in picturesque detail from their arrival in the Congo to their homecoming. He had no option.

Hugh knew from the irate messages left that Ed had discovered his suggestion about a minder had not been followed up. They agreed to disagree about the risks taken. Maybe Edward was maturing: earlier in the year risk wasn't a word in his vocabulary! However, they unanimously agreed that all's well that ends well and this was one of those occasions when it had ended perfectly. Given the risks Ed reckoned it was a miracle both Hugh and Tessa were now back safely in London and life was progressing as usual so why make a big deal out of that. He had other more depressing matters to deal with.

Jazz had a miscarriage about ten days after trying to kill Edward in the apartment at Governor's Beach. He was distraught when he heard the news. Not only had she lost the baby but she was now seriously ill. He decided to go see how she was, see if he could help her somehow. Wishing someone well who'd tried to kill you not so long ago wasn't an easy decision to make. Edward bought some flowers and was met at the hospital by a nun called Sister Monica.

'Jasmine will be so happy to have a visitor.'

'Has anyone else come to see her?'

'No one.'

Somehow, Edward found an inner strength in the presence of Sister Monica and he asked her if she'd come with him to see Jazz.

'Of course I will my child but you have nothing to fear.'

She said this as if she knew what had happened between them but she couldn't have, unless Jazz told her. Edward started rubbing his left eyebrow for comfort, to reassure himself his efforts would not pass unnoticed.

They entered the hospital ward together. It was as if Monica was holding both their hands. Jazz was in bed. She looked so frail and helpless, like a starving African girl. The violent would be killer that she was when Edward last saw her was gone, replaced by this vulnerable feeble woman, now a skeleton of her former being.

That vibrant sexual athlete had been destroyed by her miscarriage and cold turkey. A tear rolled down her cheek when she saw Edward. He held back his own tears because he knew they could never be together again and he was sorry it had to be that way.

'Edward I'm so ...'

'How are you?'

'Not well. How are you?'

'I'm ok.'

The atmosphere was strained between them and conversation came hard. Edward stayed as long as she wanted him to but she was so weak that even speaking was a chore for her. Sister Monica called time. He had to say goodbye to Jazz. They knew it was forever.

She held his hand as if she didn't want to let it go. He pulled gently away from her and left the ward, followed by Sister Monica. He couldn't look back. It was far too emotional for that and he wanted to remember the good times, not what had been in front of him today.

Outside the room, he shook Sister Monica's hand. She stared directly into his watery eyes.

'There's a strange sensation inside me young man.'

Edward could sense it too.

'Some being is telling me we will meet again.'

'I know.'

'Do you? Well, until then take great care. You may not know it but God has smiled on Jasmine and you will look back with pride on having come here today.'

'I hope so and thank you so much Sister.'

Edward left the hospital and the strange sensation went with him. His thoughts were with Jazz. Could she pick up the pieces? Edward had heard her tales of her escapades. She believed she was a heroine working with the CIA yet she was in the gutters of life.

Chapter 31 - Monday 18th to Friday 22nd November

Her reminiscences weren't tales of heroism. They were tales of depraved sex and prostitution involving scumbags. The tales were evidence of just how gullible and innocent she had been to allow herself to be recruited and abused. Her life was the simple story of how to catch a villain: create one. That is precisely what the CIA did with her.

Like so many untold heroes she started adulthood with good intentions. Clean up the world with the CIA. Help the great USA remove the communist bacteria from the earth especially if they were in their back garden. No doubt some narrators would wrongly say such a person was best forgotten, tossed onto the pile of books never to be remembered, rendered to the scrapheap or ashtray of history. Let them rest in peace there, not her.

Most of us never hear of the likes of Jazz. She was a toxic by-product of the US intelligence services' factory, its industrial production machine tailored for humans. She was one of millions who suffered in the cold war, US citizens or not. They were killed or maimed, scarred physically or mentally, in the name of America's long proxy fight for freedom and democracy in far flung lands.

In such fights proxy meant you hid cowardly behind others. Just as the British taught the Americans to do having learnt the trick while controlling their empire for centuries or as Stalin did in Vietnam, Korea and elsewhere. The USA wasn't the only villain in the long history of that town called Earth.

As the cold war gradually became the war that never was these recruits were abandoned, forgotten. These hypnotised or drugged robots didn't just wear US standard issue uniforms. Some answered the call of duty just as Jazz had, sometimes naked in order to do their duty.

Her only problem at first had been she couldn't take the pressure, the stress and fears that go with working in such a polluted environment. In that world everyday missions included being fucked by the pits of human kind like Cohen to lure them in for rendition. She volunteered to make the world a better place but had been easily duped. She was too naive to understand how easy it would be for her to be industrialised, to become a vacuum cleaner.

Then the drugs followed to prop her up to face each new mission she was ordered to enact. Those missions involved tasks that often disgusted her. As if on a runaway train, a crash was inevitable as she strived to pay for her drug addiction. She was the victim. Jazz was just one of many raw recruits wrecked and left to rot in that phony war. She would have done better as a nun. Maybe that was her destiny.

Other than the departure of Castle, irrespective of Jasmine's or Jazz's destiny her affair with Edward was tangentially to have the most profound impact on MI6 compared with any other single event in 1974. Edward and Marco missed the obvious.

Edward had even explained the issues to Marco but both failed to understand the implications. Luckily, someone more experienced than them had not let the issues pass undetected. Talking of which, it goes without saying that you obviously spotted it too. If you didn't, don't worry: you can say you did once all is explained later!

Jazz was truly an unsung heroine but not of her own volition but as an accident of history, waiting to be unveiled.

Grand Turk, Turks & Caicos Islands

Graham Sidney-Smith got the green light for Edward to leave for Grand Turk to start his investigation into the finances of Haiti Air. He was to get together with a lawyer called Curt Walter who would arrange a meeting between Edward and the Haitian airline's directors so that he could go through the accounts with them.

Edward flew out in a four seater plane from Nassau. He was the only passenger. Franco, the pilot, looked like an archetypal First World War fighter ace straight out of a comic book with a handlebar moustache almost the width of his shoulders. He even wore an antiquated helmet and a light blue scarf round his neck. Franco somewhat irritatingly kept turning the engine off and gliding to save fuel.

He boasted that he'd once taken off in this same plane from a standing start in the sea. Edward didn't quite believe him but wasn't certain whether he was exaggerating. The lack of certainty meant he didn't want Franco to give him a demonstration. He told the man he was a magnificent pilot to have survived such a challenging situation in such a magnificent flying machine and changed the subject.

They reached their destination early in the evening. In the water, Grand Turk was a beautiful place, on the edge of the ocean wall, with a sheer drop only a few dozen yards off the beach. The waters surrounding the islands were paradise for divers and snorkelers.

On land, the island looked like a rubbish tip, full of half built houses, empty beer cans and lacerated whisky bottles. Other than sea, sand, surf and sex the locals had little else to do but drink. They'd work on the cruise lines that toured the Caribbean, then come home and work on their homes. Once home they'd quickly run out of money because most of it would go on booze, so they'd go back cruising again. A pleasant little vicious circle of time watching if you liked that laid back approach to life.

Ian Tomlinson, the island's doctor, hosted a gathering of local dignitaries to meet Edward. In the seventies there were no tourists to speak of and given Edward's reception visitors were a rarity too!

The doc looked like a black and white photograph of Abraham Lincoln. Indeed, everyone there including colourless Curt looked like refugees from an old nineteen thirties movie. Curt told Edward to enjoy himself and he'd come and collect him at his hotel the next day. Grand Turk's one hotel had less than ten rooms. Curt seemed rude ignoring Edward from then on but drunk was probably more apt a description.

The local dignitaries were a motley crew of pirates. Gambling and alcohol were their pastimes. Most had enjoyed sex for the last time long ago. Tomlinson spent most

Chapter 31 - Monday 18th to Friday 22nd November

of his time trying to stop one fifty something woman from drinking. She'd clearly been quite a starlet once upon a time but the years of boozing had done their damage. Her patience went walkabouts and she grabbed a bottle of white rum. Tomlinson tried to get it back, without much success. He held one end and she would not let go of the other.

'Please let go, you're worse than an alcoholic Betty.'

'Just like everybody else here Doc.'

Tomlinson gave up trying to wrest the bottle from her grasp and Edward gave her a glass to use. It looked more dignified than her drinking from the bottle.

As the night wore on, the booze flowed faster and Edward caught a whiff of cannabis in the air but couldn't place its source. Excitement in the main reception area heightened as more and more money was piled onto two tables, one black and one red. Edward estimated there was well over $10,000 in one pile alone. Heavy duty gambling was in progress but Edward couldn't understand the slurred rules that Betty was trying to explain to him. Tomlinson came to his rescue.

'The barracuda that eats its prey quickest will win.'

'How do you choose?'

He explained all the rules leading up to the finale.

'Simple, if you think it's in the fish-tank with a black cross, bet on the black table. If you think it's in the fish-tank marked in red, bet on the red table. Each fish will de daubed in black or red paint just before the finale. I will cover all winning bets.'

Edward decided to bet on neither.

The barracuda show was the start of the evening's entertainment. Some of the baby fish were only about an inch and a half long and they were fed goldfish more than twice their size. The one inside the black fish-tank took the goldfish head first, spewing out excrement from its tail as it gorged itself. Meanwhile the barracuda basking inside the red fish-tank took its prey from behind and the eyes of the struggling goldfish said it all.

The fish inside the black fish-tank won the finale after snapping its opponent in half. It was too full to eat the residue which sank to the bottom of the fish tank. Tomlinson made a net profit of about $5,000.

Nausea flowed through Edward after such a display of wanton bestiality so he smoked a couple of fags in the garden. He inhaled the fresh air more deeply than his cigarette smoke. He returned to the savagery of the cocktail party and sat watching the silent black waiters delivering an endless supply of baby barracuda and goldfish. Tomlinson kept winning as those gathered kept topping up his bank account.

An hour or so before midnight, the fifties style black telephone rang for about two minutes until a waiter picked it up and tapped Tomlinson on the shoulder. The doctor listened to the caller, then hung up and turned to his guests.

'I'm afraid there's an emergency at the hospital. I have to go.'

Edward watched as he left in his Land Rover, without turning on the lights. It was pitch black out there. He hoped the doc wouldn't need to operate on anyone if he actually arrived there. He'd consumed at least one bottle of Bacardi. After Tomlinson left, the party lost its zap and others started to drift away. Edward walked back alone to the only hotel on the island.

That night, he slept in a bamboo chair. His bed was infested with insects of all shapes and sizes. When he woke, he tried to have a shower, but there was no water. Edward consumed a breakfast of fruit on the patio. He preferred not to risk eating anything he couldn't recognise like the bacon which might have come from an iguana. He was accompanied at breakfast by an emaciated cat that caught and unashamedly ate a live lizard on his table.

Half an hour later Curt Walter arrived. The lawyer was still wearing his evening suit and bow tie and drank three double martinis in less than fifteen minutes. Edward drank from a large plastic bottle of coke so as to avoid the soiled ice cubes in his glass. Walter told him that the Haitian airline directors were flying in with the accounts and the meeting would be at his office.

His office happened to be the study in his house, full of antique books and black and white nude photographs from floor to ceiling. The contrast was surreal, even artistic in its own unique perverse way. Walter consumed several large scotches while they waited for the Haitian directors who never arrived.

'Can't you ring and find out what's happened to them?'

He did and then told Edward that their plane had broken down, so the meeting would have to be postponed.

'For how long?'

'Who knows?'

Edward didn't want to be stuck in this dump indefinitely so he suggested that he could fly to Haiti and have the meeting there. Never having been there Edward didn't realise he was simply swapping a small trash can for a much larger one.

'I'll see what can be arranged.'

After half an hour of calling around Walter said a plane would be available at a nearby landing strip. He gave Edward a piece of paper with an address on it and said a reservation had been made at a hotel in Haiti by Porter Williams. Walter then drove to the airstrip himself even though he was so drunk his car veered all over the road on the way there.

That wasn't the gravest problem. When they arrived at the airstrip Edward discovered that Franco was the pilot again and dusk was falling. The combo was not that appealing! This time the plane had a few other passengers, a dozen chickens cooped up in the back behind cases of empty coca-cola bottles. By the time they were airborne darkness had descended both inside and outside the plane. Franco turned

Chapter 31 - Monday 18ᵗʰ to Friday 22ⁿᵈ November

the lights off and only occasionally flicked them back on for a second or two to check the dashboard readings.

The flight was bumpy and turbulent and the chickens clucked and squawked as if they knew they were about to crash into the side of a mountain at any moment. Edward was glad they weren't flying in one of the area's frequent storms like Hurricane Fifi, back in September. It killed thousands living near the northern coastline of Honduras before losing strength inland.

Arcahaie, Ouest Haiti

They finally bumped and bounced their way back onto terra firma on a runway in a field that was lit by burning piles of brushwood. The traumatised chickens and cracked coca-cola bottles were taken away by an army of women. Two men loaded small sacks of what Franco called cement onto the plane for his return trip. As far as Edward could tell from his pre-holiday research they had landed somewhere between Gonaives and Port-au-Prince but he couldn't be sure.

'How far to Port-au-Prince?'

'Maybe two hours.'

'Where are we?'

'In the countryside not far off the coast road.'

'How do I get to Port-au-Prince?'

Franco pointed towards a car that was barely visible in the darkness beyond the brushwood fires. He swung himself back into the cockpit of his ramshackle plane and took off again. Edward didn't think he'd make it over the tree line on the horizon but he did with what from that distance looked like inches to spare.

It brought to mind Edward's escape from Innsbruck with his mother when he was in the Scouts, and how they had made it back to England without a passport between them. Unluckily he didn't have the legendary spy with him now and Franco had gone. He was totally alone in a strange, unpredictable environment.

His limited French was of little use. The local patois differed from the French he'd picked up at school and on family visits to Brittany, Avignon and Monte Carlo et al. Edward could have done with Hugh right then. His brother's grasp of languages was far superior to his. The cab driver shoved Edward into what resembled a car that had been rescued from a scrap-yard crusher after it had its first bite. He gave the driver the piece of paper Curt Walter had given him. Edward hoped he could read.

They waited for hours, not enough gas. It came about four in the morning in half litre cans carried on the heads of some local women. Naturally Edward had to pay for it. They moved off once the gas-tank had been half filled. At the end of the dirt track that took them away from the improvised airstrip, the makeshift cab stopped. Two burly Haitians jumped in either side of Edward in the back.

The car set off again, with the driver repeating the words mes amis as if in prayer. After an uncomfortable long and painstakingly slow back jarring drive avoiding pot holes and negotiating broken down bridges, as dawn was breaking they passed a signpost. Edward was relieved that Port-au-Prince was ahead, until the car turned right.

Alarm bells rang in his head. He was so tightly wedged in between the other bulky passengers that even if he was carrying a weapon he wouldn't have been able to move his arms to use it.

As the sun rose the driver was now constantly looking at Edward in his mirror. So much so that they nearly careered off the road at every corner and every pothole they hit. The driver could see Edward was pinned between the two hulks and started repeating the word bientôt instead of mes amis. Edward resigned to his fate and pondered if the driver had ever seen a white man that close up beforehand. Perhaps that was why all three were staring at him when he wasn't looking at them for different reasons.

Menetas, Ouest Haiti

After another half hour the car reached its destination and pulled up outside a detached building with pale green shutters over the windows. A woman in her early thirties came out and started shouting at the driver and hitting him on the head with a bamboo brush. The two heavyweights in the back jumped out of the car and bolted. She came round to the window and spoke to Edward in a mixture of pigeon English and patois.

'Pardon Mister, je suis désolé.'
'I don't speak good French.'
'Mon frère he comes, look for way to where you go.'
'The address I gave him?'
'Oui.'
Edward pointed towards the fleeing backseat passengers.
'Those men, hommes?'
'Son amis, his friends. My brother gives them ride.'

Edward breathed a sigh of relief. He hadn't been abducted after all. The cabbie was simply giving his mates a lift. The woman sat down in the car, still shouting at her brother. She directed him to the hotel address that was written on the piece of paper. The fare from the remote airfield came to five dollars. Edward gave the woman twenty dollars and told her she could keep the change.

Yet again his diary was to show he was heading into the unknown. He might have matured in some ways but he just couldn't kick this habit of jumping before checking out his parachute.

Chapter 32
Friday 22ⁿᵈ November to Wednesday 11ᵗʰ December

Rue de Chilli Saint Gerard, Port-au-Prince Haiti

By noon he had checked into the suite Porter Williams booked at the old converted mansion called Hotel Oloffson, the source of inspiration for Graham Greene when he wrote The Comedians. The mansion was set high up in the amphitheatre layout of Port-au-Prince, overlooking the bay. The hotel was opulent and the rooms he had were luxurious with magnificent views across the city and bay beyond. The hotel has retained its magnificence and, of course, is no longer infested by the Tonton Macoute.

Edward only had a small overnight bag with him. He hadn't expected to travel on to Haiti immediately after Grand Turk. He bought a pair of swimming trunks in the hotel foyer and after a shave and shower he made for the outdoor Jacuzzi.

The pool was located above a row of gleaming Rolls Royces, with a doorless hut about a hundred yards below them outside the hotel compound. Edward watched as people came and squatted in the hut. It was a public toilet.

The proximity of the extremities of wealth and poverty was distressing and far more noticeable than in Nassau. Edward knew how the system worked by now, run by offshore bankers for tyrants who made Hitler look positively philanthropic. It made him fucking furious but now was not the time to upset the regime's status quo.

He looked with sadness as the waitress approached. Why had she been born into this hell? Another yellow bird cocktail arrived unordered and Edward's eyes were drooping as he sipped the smooth mixture of rum, orange and grenadine. It had been an exhausting, clammy, anxious day and night.

That was the same as every night for the locals except they could only dream of staying at the Hotel Oloffson drinking cocktails. He decided to go back to his suite, rather than risk falling asleep in the Jacuzzi or more likely waking in a dream about throttling a few Tontons only to discover they were for real.

There was a gift-wrapped parcel on the table containing six thin wooden hand-carved plates. There was no message or card. Edward checked each plate in turn as if they were made of semtex but there was nothing suspicious about any of them. He lay down on the bed and soon fell asleep dreaming about being at Raj Khan's funeral with Hugh, Tessa and Suzie until a cackle of hyenas burst into the church. It wasn't the hyenas that woke him. It was the telephone. Marco was calling.

'How did you know I was here?'

'Checked with the bulldog as you call him, good old Rupert.'

'How did he know?

'Search me, probably Sidney-Smith. There are no secrets in Nassau.'

Ed and Marco began a coded conversation, not just in case anyone was listening but because someone was listening. Marco loved calls like that. He'd either pass across the disinformation professionally or as in this case take the piss and start talking to those eavesdropping.

It turned out Marco wanted Ed to meet a young lady called Vivienne while he was in Haiti. She'd come to the hotel and have dinner with him. Marco was still interested in the real reason Edward was there and Vivienne could hopefully help find out. She was going to have been based at the Oloffson anyway for a week or two.

'What does this Vivienne look like?'

'Think of a white suntanned version of Diana Ross with Caucasian hair and pray she likes you.'

'Why?'

'One way or another you'll either be dead or eaten alive!'

'What colour hair has she got?'

'That depends on the day of the week. I can't imagine all the Supremes are accompanying her or there are that many Diana Ross whitewash lookalikes staying there. If so let me know and I'll fly in for the weekend.'

After the call Edward dressed and went down to the dining room. He had learnt one minor point. Marco was as ever helpfully diligent and he'd checked out Edward's work colleague Paul Rutherford who had no living siblings. What was odd was that he was the survivor of triplets born in Newcastle upon Tyne not that it mattered now.

Edward was the only guest there. It had been disconcerting to be alone in a restaurant with sixty or so empty tables and being outnumbered ten to one by the waiters. He waited for Vivienne but she didn't show up so he ordered a medium rare fillet steak with mashed potatoes. Edward was surprised how good the food tasted. Unsurprisingly he forgot he hadn't eaten anything since the fruit he'd had for breakfast in Grand Turk.

He tried the local Haitian lager. The four waiters who attended him nearly made him spew out the lager in uncontrollable laughter when he tasted it as he wondered what Hugh would have done in the restaurant. It was a nervous reaction. Edward mused whether the lager was poisoned as it tasted like a foul home brew he and Hugh once concocted.

Of the four waiters, one brought the bottle, another brandished the glass, one more wielded the bottle opener and there was a supervisor with a coaster in his hand.

Chapter 32 - Friday 22nd November to Wednesday 11th December

The lager was undeniably disgusting and Edward quickly changed back to yellow birds. After dinner he checked for messages at reception but there weren't any. When he returned to his suite he found the door wide open. Two white leather suitcases were on the floor inside and more were being delivered by the porters.

'This isn't my luggage. There must be some mistake.'

The seemingly deaf porters took no notice and deposited the cases inside the entrance way.

That's when a woman in her mid-twenties breezed into his bedroom. She was fit, naturally tanned but lighter than Jazz and extremely good-looking. She wore a flimsy body-hugging white dress and her dark nipples looked swollen with anticipation. She kicked off her high heels and quickly diminished in stature to not many inches above five feet. She tousled her light brown blond hair and her gentle brown eyes twinkled angelically from deep within her soft featured face. Marco was right. She was drop everything gorgeous.

'Edward my darling, so sorry about dinner, but you know what it's like at the airport with no porters.'

She spoke with a slight Cuban accent and on her tip toes kissed Edward on the lips before he could ask who she was. Then she tipped the hotel porters and closed the door behind them.

'You must be Vivienne.'

'That is so perceptive of you my darling.'

She let the white dress slip to the floor and Edward wasn't surprised to see that she was wearing nothing underneath. Her body glistened with splendour as she turned full frontal to Edward. A large silver crucifix lay between her pouting breasts.

He started to rub his eyebrow not knowing what to do, as if in a childlike trance. She slipped past him to retrieve a bikini from one of her bags intentionally bending over to display her firm body from yet another angle. Once dressed, her bikini, as if made to measure, hid the almost invisible appendix scar Edward had noticed.

'Let's go explore the Jacuzzi together.'

Vivienne was already in total command as she started to undress Edward and feel his body.

'You are so tense Edward. I'll have to deal with that properly once we start our exploration.'

Vivienne was not just drop dress gorgeous but intellectual too. She had been to Harvard on a scholarship. She started studying medicine to become a doctor but dropped out and became an air hostess solely because she wanted to see the world while she was young. She worked for a temp agency that provided hostesses at short notice to major airlines that used Miami International Airport.

Her father was a Ranger killed in the Vietnam War and her mother, who started her career as an African missionary until falling in love with her father, died of cancer shortly afterwards. Above all else Vivienne was a believer and do-gooder like her mother. Next she was a patriot like her father. So, she supplemented her income by acting as a courier for the CIA and planned to return to medicine before she reached thirty.

All this Edward found out while they sat in the Jacuzzi together and talked in whispered tones and drank yellow birds. They touched each other gently at first but more feverishly and intrepidly as the night wore on.

'I see you received the plates.'

'Yes. What are they for?'

'I'll show you how to open them and more besides but we will talk little in the bedroom my darling. The Tontons have earlobes in the wardrobes.'

She grinned as that ceremony was for later. Right now Vivienne's interest was in opening the strings of Edward's swimming trunks to caress what was bulging inside there. She slipped out of sight under the surface of the bubbling spa.

What began in the Jacuzzi continued in the bedroom well into the night. Vivienne was quite versatile and if the Tonton Macoute were listening they would have counted Vivienne's rolling orgasms with ease. She might have said little but she forgot discretion was the better part of eavesdropped sex each time she came. Edward was glad he'd had that sleep during the day; otherwise he never would have been able to keep up what was required of him.

At midnight she sat bolt upright in the bed and held onto Edward's shoulder with one hand and Gideon's bible with the other. She prayed for about five minutes, softly murmuring to God in Latin much to Edward's amazement. She lay straight back down and fell asleep in Edward's arms.

After showering together the next morning Vivienne showed Edward how to open the plates in total silence. She used her nail scissors to prise the two halves of one of the plates apart, just like opening an oyster. Inside the hollow area was a film from a Minox camera. To close it up again she slid the plate halves round until the grooves met and then snapped them back together.

After giving Edward this demonstration with the first plate she asked him to open the next one. One by one, Edward opened the plates and took out the hidden films. Vivienne meanwhile was snapping them shut one after the other.

She hid all the films in a secret compartment in her handbag and, while the bag was open, Edward noticed the butt of a small caliber handgun. As she put on her dark blue air hostess uniform Edward mused to himself. He hoped he wouldn't have to defend himself against her gun the way he had to deal with Jazz's knife. It said much about the women with whom he associated.

Vivienne told Edward that more presents would be delivered later and she'd be back at four o'clock. He was about to ask a question but she put a finger up to his lips and then wrote "I'll explain all tonight" on a piece of paper. As soon as Edward read

Chapter 32 - Friday 22nd November to Wednesday 11th December

it she tore the paper up into little fragments and flushed them down the toilet. Then she left the suite after hugging him as if she were never to return.

Edward did not know when Haiti Air would make contact. He didn't want to hang around Port-au-Prince any more than he wanted to loiter about in Grand Turk, despite Vivienne's attentions. Now they were acquainted they could easily see each other either in Fort Lauderdale, Miami or Nassau any time.

With nothing better to do, he wandered round the hotel grounds and down to the high wrought-iron gates. He decided to go for a stroll. The attendant reluctantly opened the gates for him and took out his revolver as Edward walked down the hill towards what he thought were empty abandoned derelict houses. He discovered they weren't deserted at all.

Soon he was surrounded by a large crowd of people trying to sell him stuff. Straight sex with one man's daughter, oral or anal sex with another man's wife, or at least that's how Edward's limited French interpreted their offers. He didn't want any of it, nor with anyone's mother or grandmother for that matter. Nor did he want pornographic pictures or anything to eat or a taxi or a haircut. He tried to turn round, to get back up the hill to the hotel but the crowd had him surrounded. Edward held up a ten dollar bill.

'Hôtel!'

He pointed in the direction of Hotel Oloffson. The biggest man in the multitude cleared a path through the throng and escorted him back to the solid iron gates in exchange for the ten dollar bill. The children followed all the way and stuck their outstretched hands through the railings. With his revolver back in its holster the attendant now pulled out a cosh and was about to strike them but Edward shouted at him in his best French.

'Arrêtez vous, fuck off you bastard!'

Edward wasn't sure if the guard understood the detail but he definitely got the message. He put away his cosh and started fiddling with his revolver again as if to warn Edward off rather than the cheeky little kids.

Edward ignored the guard and went straight to the railings and gave each child a dollar and returned the big smiles they flashed at him through the bars. Sadly that was probably all they'd get this Christmas and for many Xmases to come. He was beginning to despise the Tontons' dictatorial way of life.

Avenue Lamartiniere Nazon, Port-au-Prince Haiti

Back at reception, a message was waiting for him from Curt Walter saying the directors of Haiti Air would be unable to meet him. That was it. No reason or indication of when they would be available was given. Edward decided he'd come too far to turn back so he hired a car at the hotel and drove downtown to the airline's office on the Avenue Lamartiniere. It wasn't a long trip but by the end of it he had no idea on which side of the road you were meant to drive in Haiti. When he parked up there, the office was closed. Through the window he could see a spiral of steam rising from a beaker of coffee.

Edward rang the bell several times but, by now, he was again surrounded by people repeating the offers he'd received outside the hotel earlier. Only now there were extras such as voodoo exorcisms and hexes. He was on the verge of pulling his ten dollar trick to get back to the car. The crowd around him was getting too large and pressed closer and closer until the office door opened. A woman emerged waving a wooden broomstick and the crowd moved back enough to allow Edward to slip inside the office.

The woman was once beautiful but her skin had peeled away in places, leaving short scars all over the parts of her body that weren't covered by her dress. It looked like scurvy to Edward and was probably the result of a life of malnutrition.

'Vous êtes Monsieur Burlington.'

'Oui.'

'Moi Madame Louise Fournier.'

'Do you speak Anglais?'

'Oui, yes, little.'

Louise was apparently Haiti Air's administration, accounting, marketing, sales and logistics departments, all rolled into one. Edward explained in a mixture of Franglais that he was expecting to meet with the airline's directors. She said there must be some mistake. Both of them had gone to Grand Turk and wouldn't be back for two days. After a largely haphazard conversation, they agreed that Edward should come back then. He asked if he could make a call to Nassau and Louise dialled the number he gave her. Edward explained the situation to Graham.

'Only to be expected.'

'What should I do?'

'You'll just have to stay as we agreed for about two weeks. Remember what Sir Peter told you. Try to get as much paperwork as you can from their staff and work on that while you're waiting. Call me at least every other day at home in the evening to let me know how you are getting on, even if you're getting nowhere. That way when we report we can honestly say we tried. Don't call on Thursdays or Fridays though because I'll be at the tennis club.'

Just as he was handing the phone back, a thunderclap went off directly overhead. The bang was so loud that Edward ducked. Neither he nor Louise could hear each other speak for the next five minutes. Their words were drowned out by the noise of the thunder and the rain hammering down on the corrugated iron roof. They watched as the street filled waist-deep with water and the locals rushed out to wash themselves. The rainwater flowed away down the gradient, into downtown Port-au-Prince and the bay beyond it.

Chapter 32 - Friday 22nd November to Wednesday 11th December

Louise Fournier explained that there wasn't much paperwork but what there was she'd have copied and sent to the hotel in batches when she could do it. She would despatch one batch in the morning and one in the afternoon if she could.

'We could copy it now.'

'No copier. I will have to go à traverse la ville.'

'Ok, but only financial documents, papers, accounts, balance sheets, stuff like that.'

'Stuff?'

'Bank statements, passenger and cargo manifests.'

She nodded but he wasn't sure if she understood or not.

'Tickets, airport bills, stuff like that.'

'Oh, stuff. Papers. Oui.'

She nodded again and they drank more coffee in relative silence until she said the roads would be dry enough to use. She directed him where to go to buy some clothes and he set off quickly in his hire car, an old Cadillac, before he attracted another crowd.

Edward lost his way once or twice because the streets were impassable and detours were not that memorable. There were few buildings that looked even remotely like shops but he finally made it and bought enough to last him a fortnight. What's more he even managed to sneak in a bit of Xmas shopping.

His car was followed all the way to the shop and from there back to the hotel. He was going to stop and ask the goon in the car for directions every now and again but thought better of it. The thug might not appreciate his sarcasm because the way he drove indicated he thought he was tailing Edward incognito. He was wearing the uniform of the Tonton Macoute: dark glasses, black trousers, blue shirt and straw hat. The minder watched Edward all the way until the heavy gates at his hotel were chained and closed behind him. It reminded him of entering Pentonville Prison.

Rue de Chilli Saint Gerard, Port-au-Prince Haiti

Two days turned into two weeks as December came and there was still no sign of the Haiti Air directors. Every time Edward called Graham to report no progress he repeatedly insisted he must wait.

More plates arrived at the hotel for Vivienne and she extracted more film from them and snapped them back together. Paperwork was also delivered from Louise Fournier; customs stamped manifests and bank statements but nothing much else. Vivienne photographed all the papers with a Minox camera and it became clear to Edward that the plates were also coming from Madame Fournier.

By now, Edward and Vivienne were growing quite close. Maybe in love wasn't the right phrase but they certainly had more to offer each other than pure lust. Although that was always there: morning, noon and night. Edward would never have stayed this long in Port-au-Prince if she hadn't been there. Neither of them wanted to say goodbye or so long or sayonara either. It wouldn't be over until it was over and they were both stringing it out for as long as possible. There was a rare essence about the woman that appealed to Edward, apart from the sex. Some je ne sais quoi quality that women like her had. Women like Suzie and Jazz and now Vivienne were powerful magnets for Edward. But the magnetism was a two way street.

There was that something about him she loved: an indefinable quality, more than charisma and style or decisiveness and all the obvious physical stuff. She couldn't put her finger on what that was but he had it and she wanted it. Sometimes she sensed he was reluctant to get too close, as if he'd been hurt in the past by getting too close. That was when the magnetism worked its magic. The more he relaxed the more the bond grew and the more inseparable they became.

They spent much time at the pool and one night as they passed the small black and white TV in reception he asked who the news presenter was. She laughed.

'That's Duvalier, Baby Doc. They only have one or two regular shows at night so they play his speeches the rest of the time.'

Edward thought that must be exciting to rush home to after work. Later, at the poolside Vivienne took half a dozen photos from her bag.

'These are the best of the films delivered yesterday my darling.'

The pictures were all taken aboard Haitian aircraft. You could tell from the faded seat covers.

'Who are they?'

'They're mostly Columbian drug barons.'

'Who's that friendly looking thug?'

'Luckner Cambronne. They call him the Vampire of the Caribbean.'

'Nice.'

'The bastard mainly lives in Miami now but he was Papa Doc's right hand man and head of the Tonton Macoute.'

Vivienne told Edward that Cambronne was a vicious killer and responsible for thousands of murders. He owned a company in Haiti called Hemo Caribbean that exported blood plasma and bodies to the USA for experimentation in universities and hospitals. The blood and corpses were sourced by the Tonton Macoute from Haiti and Africa. If they didn't have enough for export they just roamed the streets collecting live ones until they filled their quota. It reminded him of Burton.

'Tonton Macoute brutality makes the Gestapo look benign at times.'

'What's the CIA's interest?'

'They think Cambronne is planning a coup in Columbia. We must be careful my darling.'

She said she photographed the manifests supplied by Louise Fournier because all these drug lords were frequent flyers. The CIA wanted to keep tabs on their

Chapter 32 - Friday 22ⁿᵈ November to Wednesday 11ᵗʰ December

movements and see who was consorting with Cambronne. Edward was curious about Madame Fournier and how she fitted into the CIA scheme of life.

'I am so sorry for her Edward. That pig Cambronne killed her whole family and poisoned her. That's why she looks so pale and sickly.'

'Is that why she helps, for revenge?'

Vivienne didn't answer his question. She kissed him and they decided to go back to their suite. It was the last night they were to spend together in Haiti but by no means the end of the affair.

Edward had plenty of time to keep his diary up to date while staying at the Oloffson. The minutiae noted in some of the entries were fascinating: like that on his last night with Vivienne when she had secretly and somewhat cheekily written underneath a note he made of her address "You'd better come as you made me come so much I lost count darling!"

Despite both of them being experienced agents neither saw anything untoward during their sojourn at the hotel apart from the regular comings and goings of the Tonton Macoute. The calm before the storm had lulled them both into a false sense of security. Extraordinarily enough, Edward noted how tranquil life was with Vivienne in his diary even though his comments were juxtaposed with statements like "what the hell am I really meant to be doing here". It was still a complete mystery, for now anyway.

Chapter 33
Thursday 12th & Friday 13th December

Rue de Chilli Saint Gerard, Port-au-Prince Haiti
Edward did not relish lounging around doing nothing. It wasn't his style. The Haiti Air directors never showed up and now Vivienne had gone, back to Miami. Now was the time to leave. He called Graham Sidney-Smith.

'What have you got?'

'Not much more than since we last spoke.'

'Anything else from their accounts office?'

'Only what I've been told before. Most transactions are in cash and go unrecorded.'

Graham asked for Edward's opinion on Haiti Air more openly and formally than in any preceding conversations which had always been on a no names no details basis. Edward repeated that the directors didn't want to speak to him and he'd had several planned meetings cancelled. There was no evidence of solvency and not enough accounting records to produce even a rough balance sheet so they could never prove insolvency or disprove solvency.

'That's all I need to hear now. I'll call Peter.'

'What should I do?'

'Come back now. Leave any paperwork behind, we won't need it ...'

The phone crackled and Edward couldn't hear what Graham was saying. Graham called back and repeated his comments about not needing the papers and added that all Peter would need was a report.

'I'm due to take the rest of the month on leave.'

'Oh? Yes. Christmas is coming isn't it?'

'Yes, my first leave too.'

'You'll need to write up the report first.'

'Can I go straight to London via Miami and then write it up there?'

'I don't see why not as long as the report's on Peter's desk by Monday but do copy me in by fax.'

Their conversation closed on that note with mutual wishes for a happy Xmas. Edward was pleased. He was leaving Haiti and would pick Vivienne up in Miami and

Chapter 33 - Thursday 12th & Friday 13th December

take her to London with him for the holidays. The day was Thursday 12th December and he was able to book a Pan Am flight out for the next day. He had twenty four hours to kill and he had put up with the nosy Tonton guards and receptionist for long enough.

So he thought he'd switch to the Hotel Carré Noir, which was nearer to the downtown action and the airport for the morning. He hid the manifests in a secret compartment of his latest briefcase and flushed the bank statements in small pieces down the toilet: the nosy Tonton Macoute must have thought he had diarrhoea.

Rue Sans Fil Bel Air, Port-au-Prince Haiti

Edward took a cab downtown and checked into the Carré Noir using his American passport under the name Edward Alexander Racter Junior. After showering and changing he was about to leave his room and go out to Haiti's most exclusive casino when the phone rang. That surprised him. He'd only just checked in and nobody could conceivably know where he was. He hadn't told anyone.

'Hello, Edward can you hear me, this line is awful.'

'Dad? How the hell did you find me?'

'Never mind that. How are you?'

'I'm fine. Should be leaving here tomorrow.'

'Good.'

They talked for a few minutes and Roger confirmed he could stay at Epsom with his new girlfriend over the Christmas holidays.

'That will please your mother.'

'Ok, I'll see you soon Dad.'

'Just remember, Edward, you are never alone. Do take care. We love you.'

Edward went down to the bar with his father's final words swimming round in his head. What did he mean about love? His father had never whispered "We love you" before in his life. The choice of words was so out of character.

His Dad must have known all the phones were bugged. What on earth did he mean? Vivienne was safe. More or less he had kept himself to himself, apart from visiting Louise Fournier, which was why he was there in the first place. Maybe his father meant he was watching his back in some way? Who knew?

The Burlington family always moved in mysterious ways. Edward thought he was secure. That was all that mattered. He was going to a nearby casino where he would meet up with his CIA contact, Ferdinand Garcia, or Fed as Marco called him. He'd find out if anything was brewing that he hadn't spotted, heard or smelt.

The Casino Royale wasn't the same one as that of James Bond fame nor was it a swish Monaco establishment or remotely like Les Ambassadeurs or Crockfords in London.

Water leaked from the flaking ceiling and the lights flickered on and off every ten minutes or so. The wallpaper was peeling in places and the carpet was threadbare and muddied around the tables like the grass along the lines of an overused unkempt tennis court. Apart from that it was swell as the Americans would say, if you liked tacky places.

Edward signed in showing his US passport and a passing waiter brought him a drink while he tried to work out which tables were fixed. After two cans of American beer and an hour's casual walkabout he reached the conclusion that all the tables were rigged.

He moved unhurriedly intentionally, as he looked about him to see if Fed would make himself known. He didn't. Edward sat near the wheel at one end of a roulette table. At the other end was a flash Columbian talking loudly in Spanish, spilling drinks and dropping cigar ash everywhere. The croupier didn't mind. The man was losing money.

His name was Jose and Edward played with the house. Whatever Jose bet on Edward went the other way but only placed a third of what the Columbian bet. His first few bets won so he put fifty dollars on zero and stopped betting against Jose. He won.

Edward doubled the bet and won again. The Columbian was ranting and raving now because he was losing again and heavily. The truly beautiful Haitian hookers were beginning to drift away from him and towards Edward. Edward won again. His bets were getting into the thousands by now and people were gathering round him to join in the excitement.

A thin, grey-haired man slipped into the seat next to him and Edward scented the faint whiff of marijuana. The man was immaculately dressed in a white colonial suit. He looked like a Victorian expatriate from somewhere in middle Africa but had a peculiar French accent with an American twang.

'I normally sit where you are.'

'I'm sorry. Should we swap?'

The wheel stopped spinning. Edward won again.

'It's the best seat in the house. You can see everything going on, except right behind you.'

Edward rotated his seat. Four of the broadest men he'd ever seen were standing right up behind him, their dark glasses reflecting the flashing lights of the slot machines. Edward swung his seat back, leant over the table and started stacking his winnings.

'If I were you Edward I'd bet to lose.'

'Like hell I will and you're not me, are you, Fed.'

Edward placed ten thousand dollars spread over black, even and the first dozen. Black two came up. He won on all bets again.

'You need to lose Edward.'

Two came up again. He couldn't lose even if he tried. The men behind him were so close now. Edward could smell the garlic and Gauloise cigarette smoke on their

Chapter 33 - Thursday 12th & Friday 13th December

breath. Their shadows fell menacingly across the roulette table. Edward decided to take Fed's advice. He restructured his bets and soon lost over half of what he'd won. The air cleared and light filtered back onto the roulette table as the hulks withdrew. Nevertheless he still had a good stack of chips.

Ferdinand Garcia took Edward to the bar. They both needed a drink.

'That was close.'

'What's the point of coming to a casino if you can't win?'

'You have to get permission to win here.'

Fed advised Edward not to go back to the Hotel Carré Noir that night.

'You can spend the night at Les Girls. My driver will wait for you until you are ready to head out to the airport.'

'I have all my clothes in my room.'

'Henri will take care of all that too but you had best both wait for daylight.'

Fed and Edward headed for the restrooms. Edward had left several stacks of chips on the table by his seat and Fed told the croupier to keep a damn good eye on them.

The Tontons must have guessed they were only going out for a reefer, not leaving, but one still followed them. The thug could see their hunched silhouettes as if in animated conversation through the rear exit door by the restrooms and returned. Fed was watching him through the corner of his eye and shook his hand.

'It's time to go. Good luck and have fun. Les Girls are magnifique. Here's Henri, he shall take care of you. I'll get your chips changed for the airport.'

Edward handed over the high value chips from his jacket pocket and jumped into Fed's car which had just pulled up. They were off in seconds as Fed nonchalantly returned to play with Edward's chips. Fed sat on his favourite seat again. He was already up well over ten thousand bucks without even betting.

Route Soleil Cite Soleil & Downtown, Port-au-Prince Haiti

Henri spoke about as good Franglais as Edward. Les Girls was on the outskirts of Port-au-Prince and was supposedly one of the premier bordellos in Haiti. The bordello was a wooden motel on three stilts with a ladder at each end leading to a long row of about forty bedrooms.

The bar was in the car park under the stilts. It comprised a few tables and chairs with several fridges lined up together and wired into a street lamp. It didn't have walls, fences might have been a better description and the roof was the bordello above it. Scruffy as it was, les girls themselves made London's top hostesses look like cattle walk models: they would be unemployable in Port-au-Prince.

The bordello staff and les girls were all gathered round a small fire, chatting away, drinking and smoking hash. As for the girls themselves they were beautiful and each one looked like a film starlet or model.

All Edward wanted was a room to sleep in and he was prepared to pay whatever it took. On arrival he was told he must have two girls. He was told that's why the bordello was called Les Girls and not La Girl.

He didn't want to argue and draw too much attention to himself so he selected two of the healthiest looking women. Everybody noticed the hundred dollar bills wrapped round the wad he had used to pay for them. Edward was thinking of Vivienne. He wanted to remain faithful to her and the last thing on his Xmas wish list was to give her the clap.

The girls were called Camille and Sabine and he chatted to them in the room he had been given. Their English was better than his French and they drank and smoked and didn't believe him when he said he wasn't interested in sex. They tried to get him going by touching up and kissing each other but they gave up when they realised he was already asleep.

Edward was woken at five in the morning by a hand inside his pocket. He instinctively lashed out and swiped the side of Camille's face before he even clocked on who it was. A trickle of blood ran down from the corner of her mouth and his wad of notes fell from her hand. She ran from the room, screaming, followed by Sabine. Edward knew enough about these places to know precisely what would happen next. He wasn't to be disappointed.

He put the wad of money back into his pocket, unplugged the bedside lamp and removed its shade. He gripped the heavy lamp stand and wound the electric flex round his arm to stop it being knocked out of his hand. As sure as dusk follows day the manager arrived with two bouncers but these were Tontons and the three of them were carrying machetes.

Edward was told he had to pay extra for assaulting the girls and he knew straightaway that even if he paid them they'd still kill him. Henri's car wasn't visible from the window. By his reckoning the odds of him getting out alive might increase if he could get past them and onto the balcony. He stalled for time trying to think of a ruse to escape.

'How much?'

'Quoi?'

'Argent, combien d'argent?'

'Two hundred dollar.'

Edward threw two one hundred dollar bills onto the floor. The men didn't pick them up and advanced towards him with machetes raised menacingly. They wanted the wad of notes. Edward was about to swing the lamp when the whole building structure shook violently.

The men tripped and fell across the room as Edward made it past them like a bolt of lightning. He made it onto the balcony. Henri had rammed his limo into the central wooden stilt holding the bedrooms in place. Again Henri rammed the car into

Chapter 33 - Thursday 12th & Friday 13th December

another pillar. The bordello started shaking once more and began to sway. Then it started to collapse, slowly at first but predictably, like dominoes.

Edward could hear the screams of the other occupants. It was as if the structure was a flimsy matchstick ship in the grip of a huge ocean wave. One of the Tonton Macoute came onto the balcony behind Edward and aimed a blow with his machete. The moving edifice threw the big bastard off balance again and the weapon embedded itself in the balcony handrail.

Henri moved the car back from the crumbling building and shouted at Edward to jump. He did, but the Tonton Macoute jumped too. Henri shot the man through the stomach in mid-air. A stream of blood and guts went skywards. He chucked one of several handguns on the front passenger seat to Edward.

'You must shoot others.'

The manager was already dead, crushed under tons of timber. Meanwhile another Tonton Macoute was rushing towards Edward, machete raised, as Edward was picking up the gun Henri had thrown. Before Edward could unload one shot the man's head exploded and Edward's face was blanketed in his membranes and blood. The remnants of the man fell backwards as if in slow motion and his torso thumped onto the concrete.

Edward looked round as Henri fired volley after volley of shots from different guns as a warning to the others to stay back. As Henri backed up Edward jumped into the passenger seat.

'We should leave here Mister Edward.'

'You're damn right. Let's get out of here. These bullets make a mess Henri.'

'Mister Fed makes special dumdums.'

'What'll happen to the girls?'

'They will not talk. They never talk.'

Edward latched onto "They never talk". How many times had Henri done this? He looked back as the car rattled away. The bordello was on fire. Clients and hookers were rushing from it clothed or not. Some were making for their cars and others were standing a safe distance away watching the pandemonium.

The staff were pointlessly trying to put out the flames as they spread through the rotting timbers. Edward wondered what he was doing at this godforsaken brothel. Surely he would have been safer staying at the Carré Noir rather than taking Ferdinand Garcia's advice to stay at Les Girls.

Henri drove them to a place called Cloche. He got out and inspected the damage to Fed's ageing limo. The damage was extensive. He hotwired and stole a jalopy for Edward to drive behind him until they reached the coast. Then they shunted the old limo over a small cliff into the sea. Henri drove to a deserted beach. Edward dumped his ripped jacket in the ocean and washed the blood off his face and clothes and they waited for his shirt and trousers to dry as the sun rose.

'How much money you have Mister Edward?'

Edward counted the notes left in his wad.

'About fifteen thousand dollars.'

'Mister Fed will like his new car.'

Edward thought this was a cheek considering it was Mister Fed's advice that had landed him in this ridiculous situation in the first place. What's more Fed had Edward's gaming chips. Yet Henri did save his life so he had to do something for the man in return.

Henri drove back to town and left the jalopy where it was before he stole it. They then walked to a second hand car depot. Henri stopped Edward from going anywhere near it with him.

'You will only put the price higher. You are Gringo, yes? Give me the money.'

Edward handed over the wad of cash and waited a safe distance away. After a short while Henri returned driving a dark blue convertible Cadillac. It certainly was an improvement.

'Mister Fed will like this.'

'How much?'

'They ask twenty thousand but I get it for twelve. Here is the rest.'

Henri held out the remaining three thousand dollars to Edward. Edward took the wad, removed a few hundred dollar bills and stuck the wad back in Henri's shirt pocket.

'You keep it for services rendered.'

Henri's expression looked puzzled for a moment until he smiled broadly and transferred the wad from his shirt to trouser pocket. He drove Edward up to the back of the hotel, asked him what room number he had checked into and ten minutes later reappeared descending from a fire escape in a hurry with all Edward's meagre belongings. Within less than half an hour they were at the airport.

Duvalier International Airport Delmas, Port-au-Prince Haiti

'I will wait until you go Mister Edward. I do not know where Mr Fed is with your money. He may have trouble at casino.'

'We can't risk waiting. Marco can recover what Fed didn't lose, if there's any money left. You've done enough for me Henri. I'll never forget your driving skills.'

'Yes and memory my shooting skills.'

'Those too.'

'Tontons kill my family so now I kill them when I can. That is why I shoot good and practice lots.'

'Tell Mister Fed I think he's lucky to have a man like you.'

Henri left and Edward made his way to what resembled a check in desk. He was amazed to find there were some American tourists boarding the plane for Miami. The plane was already waiting on the tarmac.

Chapter 33 - Thursday 12th & Friday 13th December

Edward joined the line that was worming gradually towards a row of trestle tables and passport control if you could call the men that. Everyone was carrying their luggage. There were no porters or trolleys and heavily armed police prowled all over the place. Edward chatted to the Americans in the slow moving line. They were even more surprised to see an Englishman than he was to see them.

They were nature lovers on safari as they put it and the trip was organised by their local church and veterans' organisations. Some of the older ones had been at Omaha and spent time in England before D-Day. Others fought in Korea and had memories of the British Commonwealth troops out there.

They laughed and joked with Edward until one of the Haitian police shouted at them to keep moving. They all placed their luggage in turn on the trestle tables. Some of the tables collapsed under the weight. The heat of the sun made it stifling hot and the procedures for departure were chaotic and primitive but this was Haiti.

Edward sensed the rifle butt coming for the side of his head. That was the last he remembered as it hammered into him before he had time to duck.

The captain of the Pam-Am jet saw what happened and ran forward but was met by a wall of police rifles. The American veterans were also held back. Edward was dragged unconscious across the tarmac by one of his legs. He was booted in the stomach from time to time as he went.

They were dragging him to a hut about a hundred yards from the plane. A police officer goose stepped behind carrying Edward's bag and briefcase. Three Tonton Macoute outside the hut took custody of Edward and dragged him inside. The officer followed and shut the door. Four armed policemen stood outside on guard duty.

Meanwhile the passengers were being herded onto the plane by more police who were using their rifles in a threatening manner. Captain Schwartzman contacted Miami to report what was happening. The air hostesses checked the manifest and told him the abducted passenger's name was Edward Racter and that he was a US citizen.

Schwartzman waited for a response. It seemed like an eternity as he could hear phones ringing and people talking on the end of the line.

'I'm passing you across to an FBI agent. Please bear with me sir.'

'This is Agent Collier, FBI. You can't leave without him. We are aware of this man. He is a serving US officer. We don't leave our own behind no matter what.'

'What can I do?'

'I don't know. You are on the ground. Tell me what's happening.'

They assessed the scene. There was now a line of police between the plane and the hut which was still guarded and Racter remained inside the tiny hut. Collier reached a decision.

'First tell the control tower you've been ordered not to leave without him.'

'Then what?'

'Just do it. Say you have checked it with the US Secretary of State's office or whatever. We'll think of something after that.'

Schwartzman called the control tower and relayed the message saying it was directly from the US government. The response was derisively non-committal and Schwartzman told Collier just that.

'You have about 80 passengers and crew. Is that right?'

'Yes.'

'Surround the hut then.'

'Are you serious?'

'Use the hostesses, the passengers, everybody but leave your co-pilot on the line. Say if they want to talk about it with Duvalier we'll call him direct and they can fucking answer to him when they see the bombers overhead.'

Schwartzman confirmed there were some veterans on board who might be prepared to take a risk. Collier just told him to move it and get his co-pilot to give a running commentary. The FBI agent needed to know what was happening in case the State Department had to call Duvalier's office. They were now on standby and were already in touch with the US Ambassador's office in downtown Port-au-Prince.

Collier could hear Schwartzman address the passengers and crew over the tannoy.

'This is your captain speaking. As you've just seen a fellow passenger has been abducted.'

The captain chose his words carefully, hoping they would connect with the fighting spirit of the veterans on board.

'I've been told by the FBI in Miami that I cannot leave without him. If I do, he's as good as dead.'

An angry growl of voices rumbled round the plane.

'I'm going down to that hut to demand his release. I'd welcome support from anyone who's brave enough to come with me. We are not leaving one of our own behind in this godforsaken place.'

The captain set off down the staircase with one of his crew. His co-pilot stayed on the line to Collier giving him a blow by blow account of what he could see. Over sixty of the passengers followed him, including all the veterans who could walk unaided. They made it across the tarmac and marched almost in formation barging through the first line of police who moved back without so much as a scuffle.

The passengers had by now surrounded the hut and the police guarding it. The captain shouted to the officer inside demanding to see him at once. The Tonton Macoute in charge opened the hut door to be challenged by Schwartzman.

'Do you speak American?'

'Oui.'

'Ok, we're not leaving without Mr Racter.'

Chapter 33 - Thursday 12th & Friday 13th December

The Tonton Macoute smiled cynically, as if to say piss off or I don't give a shit. This riled Schwartzman.

'I can get the White House to call President Duvalier if you want.'

The man's smile disappeared.

'Watch my lips and listen to my words. I will say this slowly. We can have an international incident if that's what you want. If one more American citizen, one more Gringo is hurt, touched by your Tonton Macoute or police I would not want to see President Duvalier about it if I were you. Would you? Do you understand? You'll be responsible when the American warplanes, the B-52s come over Haiti. You know what B-52s are don't you? They drop bombs that kill people.'

Schwartzman's tone was menacing, every syllable was clear and laced with sarcasm to inculcate fear. The Tonton officer in charge had got it in one. He looked round at all the American citizens and thought it over for a moment. The thug decided starting a war with the USA was unwise and facing the fury of Baby Doc might have even more horrific consequences for him and his family.

'You take him away now.'

The officer scowled, then turned and went back inside the hut followed by Schwartzman. Edward was tied face down on a trestle table, still unconscious and bleeding badly. His clothes had been ripped off and they lay in a heap on the ground. Schwartzman covered Edward's naked body with the clothes he purposefully picked up off the floor staring threateningly at each of the Tontons in turn.

Satan could only guess what the slimy buggers were about to do with him. Four veterans were inside by now. Without a moment's hesitation they picked up the whole table with Edward still on it and marched back to the plane.

Captain Schwartzman followed with Edward's bags. Edward was laid carefully on the floor in first class with cushions under his shoulders and head. The passengers were urged to get back on board quickly before the Tontons changed their minds. The staircase was removed from the side of the plane and the doors locked tight.

Schwartzman and his co-pilot started taxiing for takeoff less than a minute later. Two of the veterans tried to bandage Edward and stem any further bleeding but they weren't good at it.

One of the hostesses, Jenny, asked over the tannoy if there was a doctor on board. There was: a Dr Henderson who worked on the pleasure cruise lines. Henderson had never seen a man so badly beaten up as Edward. The doctor managed to stop the haemorrhaging but it hadn't been easy. The injury to his head was worst of all but his arms, legs and stomach had also sustained wounds. By now Edward was regaining consciousness.

'Where am I?'

'You're safe on an aeroplane flying away from Haiti.'

'Who are you?'

'I'm Dr Henderson. Just rest, you'll be in a hospital soon.'

The doctor went to the cockpit so he could converse with the captain out of Edward's earshot.

'How long before we reach Miami?'

'Two and a half hours.'

'He may not survive that long. Is there anywhere we can stop off earlier?'

'Havana maybe but I've just been told only if it's a matter of life or death.'

Edward was persona non grata in Cuba because of his involvement with Marco and the CIA. The Sanchez family had been involved in the Bay of Pigs debacle in 1961 and Castro's spies in Nassau would know Edward worked with Marco.

'Is he going to make Miami or not doctor?'

'I honestly don't know.'

The captain left the cockpit and went into the cabin. Edward was sitting up with a helping arm from Jenny. She had a bottle of champagne in her other hand and smiled at Schwartzman.

'As he's travelling first class he asked for champagne.'

Schwartzman gave Dr Henderson a rather irritated stare.

'Let's forget about Havana shall we?'

Edward drank from the bottle Jenny held as Schwartzman returned to the cockpit. At least the doctor stopped the bleeding otherwise who knew what might have happened. As the plane headed for Miami Schwartzman was pondering if anyone in his golf club would believe him when he told the tale of what had happened that day especially as it was Friday the thirteenth.

It would be like saying he saw an unidentified flying object or UFO and it had definitely landed in a place signposted in a passing cloud as Area 51. Yet it had unfolded in front of his eyes and there were dozens of witnesses. Schwartzman took over the controls and told his co-pilot to write up the report. They could both sign it today and have it witnessed by the cabin officer of the day, Jenny, whether drunk or sober: nobody would know she had been drinking with this young man.

In the heavily censored Haitian press in the following few days there was no mention of any incident at Duvalier International Airport. Come to think of it, why on earth should there be? It was their Operation Able Archer moment or Nisha incident so they had every right to issue a D-Notice just as the UK does.

A fire at a motel was reported later the following week with a body bag count of thirteen including four named from the Tonton Macoute, described as heroes. The brave police officers named had gallantly saved dozens of guests and staff from the devastating fire which destroyed the motel but alas they had been consumed in the flames. There was even an eye witness account given by a member of staff: she must have been blind drunk and stoned or more likely her statement was made up by the make-believe journalist who wasn't there.

Chapter 33 - Thursday 12th & Friday 13th December

The Civic Center Miami, Florida USA

With a little help from the champagne and the air hostesses Edward made it to Miami alive. He was taken to the Jackson Memorial Hospital by ambulance at full siren speed and Vivienne was soon at his bedside. The Pan Am hostesses knew her and phoned her with the news about her boyfriend on touchdown.

After examinations and x-rays they established he'd collected three broken ribs, a nasty head wound and multiple other cuts and bruises but had not been gang banged. The x-rays showed the ribs had previously been broken once or twice.

He was confined to the hospital for a minimum of an overnight stay with a further assessment scheduled for the morning. They gave him strong painkillers that put him to sleep but only after Marco and Collier had asked him a few questions and temporarily taken possession of his briefcase.

The CIA went through the documents in the secret compartment to his briefcase while Edward slept. The cargo manifests named the sources and destinations of the cement Haiti Air spent so much time ferrying around the Caribbean. Vivienne's photos of them were useful but to have the originals was far better.

Vivienne lay on the bed beside Edward with her arm gently round his waist making sure she didn't hurt him. She woke at midnight and knelt down next to his bed as he slept and prayed for him. When he woke, she kissed him and he smiled at her and touched her tears.

At the same time Marco was called into the main meeting room in the CIA's Miami office just off North West 36th Street by the airport. There was a conference call with MI6 just beginning. Marco was introduced in whispers to Chad Cooper and Jock McGrath who were sitting next to Collier. There were other CIA officers present as well as some of Collier's FBI colleagues. Marco recognised Sir Peter Stafford's voice on the other end of the call. So he should have. He'd heard enough tapes of that unmistakable voice.

Many diaries of what many thought had happened in 1974 were about to be rewritten.

Chapter 34

Saturday 14ᵗʰ December

Miami International Airport Miami, Florida USA

Sir Peter had just opened the conference call. Marco was handed a list of participants as he entered the meeting room. He realised this must be important as he reckoned the time was around five in the morning in London.

A quick look at the list proved the point. Sam Towers, the head of London Station and their representative on the JIC was with Sir Peter Stafford. There were other celebrities present too. Apart from Leo in Langley Jimmy Butler Junior, his boss, was on the list. Was this an overhang from Watergate? Would he be fired?

Sir Peter was still setting the scene. For those with him in London gas masks were the order of the day as despite the early hour he was already on his second cigar.

'The point is I suspected treachery but couldn't prove it. Some of you who knew only part of this may have thought I was off for a ride on my supermarket trolley when I sent our man, Edward Burlington, to sit in a Jacuzzi. I don't normally let our agents have holidays at our expense living lives of luxury for a fortnight or so in places like that plush Oloffson Hotel. In any event, the longer he was there the more danger he was in and so protecting him was costing a fortune too and not without risk for those brave enough to volunteer.

Nevertheless he had to be there to twiddle about or whatever with your agent Miss Templeton but he didn't come back empty handed and he did make it back. So if anyone here or over the water thought I was bonkers placing one of our best assets at risk they were wrong, absolutely and utterly wrong given what was at stake.

Now we have the proof all I can say is what turned out to be a joint exercise went well. I would like to particularly thank Agent Collier on your side of the Atlantic for his quick thinking. Without that input we might now be debating our plans for invading Haiti tomorrow had those passengers and crew been shot along with young Burlington.

Chad, would you like to explain it all as they say? We can then determine who to arrest when, how to do it, and in what order and in which country. For those of you

Chapter 34 - Saturday 14th December

who don't know, Chad Cooper reports to one of my deputies who is here with me, Alan McKenzie or Mac as we call him when it rains.'

There was some polite laughter. Mac nudged Sir Peter and pointed to a line on his briefing notes.

'I will host this Jimmy if that is alright with you ... and can everyone who speaks please say his, yes his name before speaking. We have no hers here. Over to you Chad.'

'Chad Cooper, MI6. On 16th November Sir Peter tasked me and one of my officers, Jock McGrath, to investigate suspicions that Sir Peter had concerning corruption in MI6. Corruption is the right word but duplicity or treachery applies too as agents' and officers' lives were being put at risk. If Sir Peter's suspicions were proven to be correct it meant that some CIA officers or agents working in the Caribbean were probably also rotten apples.

Apart from me and Jock no one knew what Sir Peter suspected other than Mr Towers and Mr Butler Junior. I was told they both wanted it to be a British only operation for reasons that will become apparent later.

These suspicions first arose when Sir Peter was getting conflicting reports about Edward Burlington's activities in Nassau. The reports centred on a girlfriend living with him called Jasmine Moreau, known locally as Jazz. She was once a CIA asset but her duties were too much for her and she was no longer used. Sadly she became a drug addict but I gather the CIA are footing the cost of her rehabilitation.

Sir Peter was intrigued why the reports about Jazz were confused, contradictory and inaccurate and asked us to investigate. He had her background checked out by SORT. That's our research team in London run by Daniel Luke. Daniel is one of three deputies Sir Peter has. SORT produced the facts on Jazz which confirmed Sir Peter's concerns. Those suspicions were not directly about this Jazz girl but they all started because of fallacious and false reports about her.

As ever though we needed more proof so McGrath and I were despatched covertly to Nassau to install listening devices we could monitor.

We gained access to our targets ...'

'Leo Sanchez speaking. How did you two get in to Nassau Chad?'

'By a sea plane. A private charter using one of your lesser known drug dealers from Fort Lauderdale sir.'

'Leo Sanchez again. Sorry to interrupt again but how did you get into the USA?'

'As tourists sir. We took a flight from Melbourne to Los Angeles. LA was our port of entry sir.'

'Leo Sanchez, finally. Just interested, apologies for interrupting, please ...'

'Yes sir. Once we established the listening posts in Nassau we immediately set off for Haiti. To save questions we flew into Santo Domingo as Australian tourists and entered Haiti covertly by boat at Belle Anse just south of Port-au-Prince. We had two tasks.

One was to establish more secure listening posts to get the evidence we wanted. The other was to try to safeguard Edward Burlington who thought he was there to collect information for the FAA to effectively close down their international airport. We had one hiccup but I'll ignore that as it's detailed in our report ...'

'Jimmy speaking. Hey Chad you tell us about that. We can all learn so much from others' hiccups.'

'Yes sir. The glitch was more an Edward Burlington hiccup sir. He switched hotels unexpectedly on his last night in Port-au-Prince and because he changed passports when checking in to the new hotel alarm bells were ringing in the Tontons' ears. He would have been arrested by them that night had he gone back to the hotel. We tried to warn him. We asked Sir Peter if he could get his father, Roger Burlington, to ...

'Jimmy speaking, you don't actually say you mean Roger Burlington married to Sara, the Brit the Gestapo nicknamed Boadicea do you?'

'Yes sir. His father was an obvious choice as we couldn't trust anyone else to warn him delicately. Mr Butler knows him as they both attend JIC meetings. As I was saying, if we had called he'd have reacted differently. It's all about knowing your asset sir. So his father got through and tried his best but in truth there was not much he or we could do apart from that.'

'Jimmy again, I like that Chad, that's good. Know your asset. That's what this is mainly about for us all. I hope notes are being taken.'

'Thank you sir; to continue, we just prayed the younger Burlington would at least realise it was all a bit odd and keep his wits about him. He would have known his father was wise enough not to say anything incriminating on the phone. If Marco had called the Tontons would have smelt a rat and moved in. If I had called we would have handed the Tontons details of our location nearby the hotel. By then the younger Burlington was using a US passport we believe the CIA gave him under the name of Racter Junior.'

'Leo Sanchez again, that's correct sir.'

'Thank you sir. His every move was watched by over a dozen Tontons by then and his phone was obviously bugged. International calls on all the phones in the better Haitian hotels are either taped or listened in to as a matter of course in any circumstances. If McGrath and I had gone in he would have been killed or captured along with us. There were too many of them and we needed to exit Edward safely. It just was not realistic, achievable.

Anyway, that night young Burlington went to a casino and met your agent as planned if an emergency arose so his father's call seemed to have worked. Burlington didn't ring him though. London did and your man went straight to the casino in minutes. We lost Burlington after that as did the Tontons we believe until as we heard after the event he was arrested at the airport. He definitely didn't go back to the hotel.'

Chapter 34 - Saturday 14th December

'Sir Peter here. Hmm. So what questions had we before all this and what answers did we get after Burlington's trip? Our research pointed to corruption and treachery within MI6. We now have irrefutable proof of both thanks to Chad's and Jock's recordings of his telephone calls. Rupert Fanshaw has been auctioning classified information to the highest bidder and using Garcia and other CIA assets to aid him. He has a ring of over a dozen CIA agents on his damn payroll.

We estimate from what we uncovered that Fanshaw earned in excess of five million US in the last three years. It was his past affair with Jazz and then his wife's spending habits that first alerted us to all this. He not only paid for Jazz's addiction until she left him in September but his wife, Collette, often bought much of the contents of Harrods every time she visited London.

Apart from keeping Harrods in business Fanshaw had also been keeping Jazz in a style she couldn't afford and that's why she turned to crime once their affair ended to pay for her drug addiction. He falsified reports on her so as not to arouse any suspicion that he was living way beyond his means by keeping both women in such luxury. The point was none of the facts we were being provided with about this Jazz woman tallied.

We stopped Pindling's police arresting her for drugs and the theft of some black coral we tipped them off about. It was a quid pro quo for making sure they didn't interfere by mistake or whatever once Chad Cooper started working out there. Pindling was quite malleable as Fanshaw had been giving him useless insider tips that we fed him. Having lost a lot by then, he did not have much time for Fanshaw anymore.

Your Mr Collier from the FBI helped there too by turning a blind eye when this Jasmine woman passed through the USA loaded with drugs. The police out there are a corrupt bunch though. There was one in particular, Bridges ... Sorry. I am digressing.

Hmm. Anyway, as I was about to say, who paid the traitor? Normally the highest bidder has been Fidel Castro, sometimes as a proxy for the Russians. Of late though Fanshaw has been selling information via your agents to various Central American dictators and on this occasion he sold it to Duvalier.

Fanshaw is currently aboard a British Airways flight from Nassau to Heathrow, accompanied by his wife, and knows nothing about his impending arrest. Unless God forbid the plane crashes or he jumps off he will be arrested for breaches of the Official Secrets Act any time we choose after his arrival about six hours from now.

As for the CIA involvement maybe Jimmy would like to explain the background and what's going on. Then we can get a quick update of what has happened in the last twenty four hours. I understand time is now of the essence regarding Garcia.'

'Jimmy speaking Peter; I created a diversion, well that's my job when we think we have rotten apples. I said to myself if Peter as a new broom has reason for concern with MI6 I should heed the sound of the trumpet call. At the time we were looking into Oswaldo López about similar issues but I won't bore you with all those.

So to start the distraction, in October Marco Sanchez was tasked with digging up what he could on López. He persuaded the younger Burlington to help as López was a client of the firm he was working at, Porter Williams in Nassau. Marco was told to tell Burlington we suspected corruption linked to Watergate, although not in the agency but in Porter Williams. Young Burlington bought it and dug up ton after ton of data on López.

In the smallest print in the bottom corner one of the last documents we looked at we found a bank account belonging to Fanshaw's wife. That added fuel to the fire Sir Peter started but while mighty suspicious it proved nothing. After Sam Powers and Peter chatted in early October we decided to leave it up to the Brits.

They then started finding other accounts connected to over a dozen of our agents including Ferdinand Garcia. Garcia is handled by Marco's team. Trouble was the evidence was always circumstantial. As Leo told me, as an attorney he could brush it aside in minutes.

We couldn't get Marco to investigate his own men or have any inkling as to what was happening. It's against our own rules, so Sam agreed with Peter that the Brits' investigation would extend that way too. Young Burlington was used as a trap. His mission was potentially of immense importance to Duvalier and Sir Peter made damn sure Fanshaw knew it by staying with him in Nassau.

We now have recordings which according to Leo, thank you for your legal insights Leo, incriminate Garcia and over a dozen others beyond any doubt. Do correct me if I'm wrong Leo but its larceny and God knows what else bearing in mind their contracts with Uncle Sam.'

'Leo Sanchez speaking, you are correct sir and those of us to be involved can look at the charges in detail during the next conference call. To say they are complicated is an understatement.'

'Jimmy again and thanks Leo: by the way Marco, as Mr Cooper and Mr McGrath were monitoring everyone who moved or spoke we knew you were as clean as a roof slate in a storm. You were trying to protect young Burlington and find out why it seemed he was being fed to the hyenas. I'm told that's the in crowd terminology in MI6!'

No one laughed so Jimmy tried another joke.

'You almost got in the way. The important point is the Brits wouldn't have killed you ... without my say so anyway!'

This did get a few titters of nervous laughter.

'Just before we close, I know Sir Peter has to rush and that it is late here but can Marco shed any light on what else we might get Garcia or any others for? Marco has been debriefing the younger Burlington earlier this evening, sorry I mean last night now.

Before you do Marco I wanted to let you in particular know we have some assets deep sunk in Nicaragua, Panama City and most of the other Central American

Chapter 34 - Saturday 14th December

countries on standby to apprehend these traitors. They have helped Mr Cooper get some documentary evidence and they will be freezing bank accounts all round, over and in the Caribbean on Monday.

No guessing who they report to Marco and don't say any names today but you know him well. He is under the Witness Protection Program and Leo and you met him on holiday with younger Burlington in Rio.'

Marco kept silent for a few long seconds but he looked as though he was sitting on an electric chair.

'Apologies, Marco Sanchez here. Yes sir, thank you. I had no idea about our banker in Rio but as you imply he should know all about freezing orders.

As for Haiti, Garcia should have taken Edward Burlington out through the Dominican Republic. From what Edward has told me he was set up in a cheap suburban motel on the pretext of it being unsafe to return to the downtown hotel he chose. That suited Garcia as he took over Burlington's seat at the casino where there was over ten thousand dollars for the taking.

Later there was quite a fire fight and several Tontons who'd come to arrest him were killed. What's odd is that Garcia's Haitian driver saved Edward's life and then dumped him at the airport after buying Garcia a new car. You guessed it: with another twelve thousand bucks of Edward's cash. I don't think we have enough there in terms of proof or ...'

'May I just add a comment? Sorry, Leo Sanchez speaking again. If there was a fire fight we cannot get involved with this chauffeur. We can have Garcia arrested on various other counts. I understand he's coming to Miami later this morning to see you Marco?'

'Yes Leo ...

Sir Peter interrupted. He sensed this was getting too detailed for him and didn't want to fritter away any more of his time. The point that he had cleaned up the shit in the CIA's backyard had been made and they should be forever in his debt.

'Well Jimmy that clears up the affair from our side. We'll be able to guarantee Fanshaw's crimes are kept under wraps until Monday noon your time. Hopefully that gives you time to decide what to do about this Garcia man and the others before anyone can alert them or they get suspicious.

It's down to legal and banking matters now for your team. Your WPP banking expert has already been given every document we found. Cooper and McGrath will make sure you have affidavits and so on with all the original recordings and transcripts.

From what little I have seen it appears Fanshaw made calls to your agents from every hotel under the sun in Nassau so I'm afraid there's a lot of data to analyse. McGrath must be the most qualified Bahamian telephone engineer around by now!

Mac, have the Fanshaws brought straight from the plane into the office and say it's urgent. Say I want to see him about a rumour we need verifying about Castro.

That should whet his appetite. His wife can go shopping in Harrods later and we'll interview them formally in the evening.

Jimmy, as I said if we hold them both until Monday noon London time is that long enough for you to sort out what you're going to do with your liabilities?'

'More than we deserve Peter. You've been swell and once again thanks for all this. We won't forget it.'

'Any time we can help you know where to come. London is closing down now so over and out.'

'DC too. Leo will call you guys in Miami back from his office in an hour or so to cover the legalese properly. Our WPP banker will be on that call too. Good morning, over and out.'

Marco slumped into his chair. At one point he thought he might be the centre of attention in a night of the long knives. Jock's tapes implicated over a dozen agents in five countries under his remit including Haiti. As Sir Peter pointed out they were now CIA liabilities not assets.

The WPP banker was none other than Donald King, who was listed as Agent Z420 on the sheet for the next conference call. Marco surmised he must have played an extraordinary hand in the Watergate affair to be back on their payroll. As for Jazz she was just lucky not to be in a Bahamian prison and responding well to rehab. Her meeting Ed had been most fortuitous. Marco thought about the subterfuges and different layers of shared knowledge. They were all part of the game they all loved to play and were all par for the greens they chose.

It looked like a long night lay ahead of them so they ordered hamburgers and pizzas and settled down to business. Time wasn't on their side. They were all taken aback by Rupert the bulldog's perfidy. He was the last any of those on the later conference calls would have suspected. Mind you, as Leo sagaciously said that meant he should have been first on everybody's list of suspects.

Rupert Fanshaw had become a part of Nassau, just like the old British Colonial Hotel, and that was his camouflage for many years. He had been incredibly clever and extraordinarily foolish to throw it all away. No doubt Collette would soon inherit a sob story to attract some oil tycoon or even British, French or Italian nobility.

Fed Garcia woke up early to prepare for his trip to Miami. He was quite proud of his replacement Cadillac and had told himself that the day he stopped working for these clowns he would get a brand new Rolls Royce just like Duvalier's.

Rupert Fanshaw was awakened just as Collette brought him to a climax. She licked her lips and pulled the blanket over Rupert's open trousers. He kissed her gently. They were looking forward to a traditional English Christmas with their children. They had no idea the last Christmas they would ever spend together was in 1973. Meanwhile their flight continued uninterrupted as a reception committee assembled at Heathrow.

Chapter 34 - Saturday 14th December

Rupert would have plenty of time on his hands to prepare his memoirs in prison. Sadly for him though, he would have to do it all from memory as his diaries were soon to be the subject of a confiscation order. Similarly, all his and Collette's bank accounts would be frozen too: despite its climate there were frequent freezing orders made in the Bahamas!

While on the subject of tales of the unexpected London had one of its mildest Decembers in history with little freezing fog, frost or snow. That may have lulled many into a false sense of calm as the past was catching up with the Burlingtons and those close to them in more ways than one.

∞

Chapter 35
Saturday 14ᵗʰ to Monday 16ᵗʰ December

The Civic Center Miami, Florida USA

Vivienne waited until the doctors completed their further examinations of Edward in the Jackson Memorial Hospital. They wanted him to undergo more tests to make sure there was no permanent damage to the grey matter inside his skull. He explained he was alright and wanted to leave as Marco arrived. Vivienne stayed.

'You're one lucky guy Ed.'

'Yesterday was Friday the thirteenth mate. Only to be expected. Any news of what happened from Fed? He's still got some of my cash unless he lost it and what was all that bother at the airport?'

'We don't know for sure, it could have been a mistake by the police.'

'A mistake!'

'Maybe, but we think they were after the cargo manifests.'

'Where are they?'

'We have them and they are legible, which is more than I can say of Vivienne's photos.'

She blushed but Marco continued with a grin.

'We've put photocopies in your briefcase so as you can hand them over to Porter Williams.'

Edward wasn't all that interested in the manifests and he told Marco he didn't think the Tontons or Porter Williams were either. Marco pretended to look puzzled and disconcerted, unusually uncomfortable. Edward knew there was bad news on its way.

'What else should I know?'

'Louise Fournier was picked up by the Tonton Macoute. She was tortured and killed.'

Marco had rattled the words out as fast as he could to try and show no emotion but he couldn't hide his distress. Edward punched the pillow but hurt his ribs more than the pillow. Vivienne started to cry and held onto his arm.

'Louise was one hell of a brave woman Ed.'

Chapter 35 - Saturday 14th to Monday 16th December

'You should have taken care of her Marco. Why didn't your man Fed get her out through the Dominican Republic? Why didn't he get me out that way come to think of it?'

'We're looking into it Ed, that's all I can say now but if anyone has loused up for the wrong reason they'll be in deep water, trust me. I'll leave you in Vivienne's safe hands and we can meet up once they have let you out. If you need me just call. I'll update you if I hear of any more developments, maybe early next week.'

Edward was angry at the loss of such a good life. Marco thought it best to leave and did so. Vivienne caressed Edward trying to console him as he tried to do the same for her. She and Louise had worked together for months and she was devastated. Her murder brought it home to her just what a dangerous game she had got mixed up in. Maybe it was time to go back to Harvard?

Outside the hospital Marco had arranged to meet Fed and he was waiting at the main entrance. Marco maintained an air of normality, asking him a few questions and getting nothing but lies back in return. He tried to look pleased after the quick debriefing and they said their goodbyes.

Fed was leaving on Sunday but had some business in town first. Marco knew what business that was by now and a large surveillance team was already on the move before Garcia had time to flag down a cab. The driver was needless to say an FBI employee.

Marco Sanchez phoned his cousin Leo from his car.

'Fed hasn't a clue we are onto him. What a clown?'

'Good. Keep it like that and we'll have him picked up just before he flies back tomorrow. Let's hope in the meantime he leads us to more of his kind. By the way, I've sent the warrants for his arrest to Collier.'

'Are you aware Louise Fournier was tortured and murdered yesterday?'

Leo was not and he was enraged.

'You're not the only one fuming and I haven't told Ed the truth yet. He'll go ape when he learns Garcia sold her out.'

'Will it put him off working for us?'

'No. Vivienne will help him get over it.'

'Ok Marco, catch you later but just make sure Louise's family is properly treated.'

'She has no family. They were all killed by the Gunnysack guys.'

'Nothing we can do then or is there?'

'I'll have a think about that. Maybe Vivienne might have a better idea.'

There was nothing anyone could do for Louise Fournier. Even so, at Vivienne's suggestion the CIA gave enough funds to Save the Children to open a foundation for deprived kids from the village where Louise was born. They called it The Fournier Foundation.

Edward wrote his report for Sir Peter while he was in hospital. Vivienne had it faxed to London with a copy to Graham in Nassau. The report made no mention of what happened in Haiti. After that Edward was officially on holiday. The doctors let him out of the hospital very early on Sunday 15th December. Vivienne was still with him and drove up to her place in Fort Lauderdale where they would stay for a short time.

It was too early for anyone to tell him what the consequences of what went on in Haiti were. Marco had been tasked with working all that out but not until all the corrupt assets had been put in boxes.

Vivienne had a small rented apartment near the beach in Bayview Drive, Fort Lauderdale. As it was the day of worship she took Edward to St Sebastian Church to pray for Madame Fournier.

He found being at church comforting for once. Vivienne never let go of his hand and it gave him an inner strength just as being with Sister Monica had. For Vivienne thoughts of wedding bells sprung to mind. Back at her pad, her greatest pleasure was showing Edward her collection of family crucifixes and Christian crosses explaining the history of each one: quite a task as she had not far off a hundred of them.

Her pad was the best place he could be to recuperate and Vivienne proved to be a very attentive nurse, tenderly caring for his every need. It wasn't long before he regained enough strength to reciprocate.

The Strand Westminster, London England

Francois Solomon had been staying at the Savoy Hotel now for almost a week. The Pakistanis had denied any knowledge of their citizens who had been torn apart by the hyenas. Their ambassador had said all the passports they were carrying must have been faked, even that of a man named Raj Gupta Khan.

As for the two hundred or so passports that had been copied by the Kinshasa hotels all of them checked out as valid apart from two. Francois had followed them up with the British Ambassador to the Congo who had been summoned last month to try and find out literally who on earth Mr and Mrs White were and extradite them on charges of murder. The ambassador only got back to Francois mid-December and had been most unhelpful.

'As I told you before Francois they looked like very good forgeries from the papers you gave me, and that is what they are. We simply have no idea who these photos are of and never will if you ask me. These people could be anybody and do not exist under those names. They are fakes. The passports were never issued by Her Majesty's Government. For all I know they may have been made in China. You have hit a dead end old boy.'

The British Ambassador could have added that if they had been identified as British citizens they wouldn't be extradited to face barbaric justice. However, he didn't. There was no point in rubbing up the Congolese intelligence chief the wrong way particularly about the death of his illustrious father notwithstanding he had lived by the skin of his teeth and died by those of wild animals.

Chapter 35 - Saturday 14th to Monday 16th December

So far as the British Ambassador was concerned he was as likely to be eaten alive by a pride of lions as Francois was to identify the real names behind the passport pictures. The ambassador loathed being in the Congo and never left the city because he was petrified of snakes.

He had told Francois that in any event the couple may not even be British citizens and if in court it boiled down to their word against those of two illiterate little kids it was obvious were there a fair trial what the outcome would be even if it was unfair so far as his father's murder or manslaughter went.

Solomon had passed copies of the passports of Mr and Mrs White around to his counterparts in other countries in Central Africa that might help but drew a blank on each one apart from Uganda. His contact there, who worked for Idi Amin, suggested he try and get in touch with the CEO of an investigations outfit called Deep Drop Security Services Limited, part of a privately owned arms dealership group based in London. The CEO had been in military intelligence and apparently MI6 once and might be able to help. As the Ugandan intelligence chief knew the man personally he set up a meeting for when both Solomon and the CEO were both next in London which was today, Monday 16th December.

That had given Francois Solomon an idea. As most of the investigatory firms in the world were made up of old grey haired boys or wrinkly faced girls from the intelligence world why not see if they recognised Mr or Mrs White or could find someone who did. He had already given up using his normal channels to trace his father's murderers as he called them.

So instead he had come to London and had already appointed seven international investigatory firms to hunt down Mr and Mrs White. All the firms had to work strictly on his terms and all agreed to do so much to his surprise. They would only get paid if they identified the Whites successfully before the Congolese government did. So far they had all suggested there was not much likelihood of success but had all agreed to have a look.

Solomon was a crafty sod though. He never even hinted to those he appointed that more than one firm had been appointed and no one had asked him the somewhat basic question. That way he never had to explain what would happen if more than one firm hit the jackpot at the same time. Deep Drop was just one of the eight firms Francois' own research team had looked into and selected for him to approach and it was the last on his list to be seen.

Given what they had been told, the better quality firms had immediately latched on to the fact that the Whites were unmarried and connected somehow to a state intelligence outfit in a country whose natural tongue was English. They also bought Francois' theory that few "whites" other than highly trained spies would risk operating in Kinshasa under cover using that surname.

One even spotted that Mr White was wearing a regiment, college or club tie from its knot which was barely visible under his jersey. The image was too grainy to identify which one.

Indeed in hindsight the choice of the name "White" was almost insolent, as if taunting the authorities in a country like the Congo: it was Hugh's idea of course. Most of them knew they were chasing a lost cause but were hoping further work might come their way if they showed they had tried. Nevertheless the intelligence world was a small one and as most investigators had been spooks in their former lives, there was a realistic but small chance someone might recognise one of the people in the photographs.

All of them were trying to use their old boy and girl networks around the world to answer one simple question: does anyone in your firm recognise these people? To date no one had and some of those appointed had already approached the other firms Francois had signed up which meant the search was going nowhere.

The meeting with the CEO of Deep Drop was to be at eight in the upstairs bar at Simpsons in the Strand, just round the corner from the Savoy. Each was to carry a copy of today's Financial Times folded back to front with the Lex Column showing. Solomon arrived first and waited. A white man who looked in his thirties approached him.

'Are you Francois Solomon?'

Francois wasn't given a chance to answer or stand up as he looked up. They shook hands and Giles Cartwright handed him his visiting card.

'I'm a close friend of Idi Amin, the black Dada, and you may be surprised to know I met your father with your old boy Mobutu on several occasions. I used to sell them all armaments but now also run this investigations business as part of the DDG, that's the Deep Drop Group. Some just call us the Drop Dead Gorgeous gang!'

Francois remained totally unimpressed and poker faced. He knew his father had met Cartwright to buy armaments. If it hadn't been for that he would have probably left by now: the sales pitch hit all the wrong notes. He instinctively didn't like anything about Giles as he had that Afrikaans' air of superiority about him and deep down was no doubt as racist as they came. Solomon, like his father, was no saintly monk but he wasn't racist or tribal other than when ordered to make ethnic distinctions.

He wondered why the Ugandans had recommended this prat. To avoid looking at the buffoon he studied his visiting card. Eventually he looked up again and forced a smile back at Giles while handing him his own visiting card. All it contained was a telephone number which wasn't even a direct line. The waiter came and took Giles' order for a glass of house white. Giles offered Francois a cigarette but he declined preferring to smoke his own brand.

'Now Francois how can my company help you? I assume you know we already sell arms to several African and Middle Eastern countries. Anything you want really,

Chapter 35 - Saturday 14th to Monday 16th December

from AK47s to tanks, motor torpedo boats to Chinook helicopters, new or used, take your pick.'

It was obvious the commissions generated from armament sales normally dwarfed the rewards for investigatory efforts.

'We don't need any of those. I'm here about an investigation. You just said you did that sort of work ...'

'Oh yes, we do that too.'

Francois asked Cartwright to sign a confidentiality agreement. That was a figurative punch below the belt to the salesman. It was in French and he didn't understand it. He had to trust this callous black henchman, the chief of Congo's intelligence services. To Giles this henchman sounded so damn well educated he probably had a wider vocabulary in any one of several languages than Giles did in English alone.

Mind you Cartwright's company had an unreasonable and vicious confidentiality agreement it usually thrust in front of its unsuspecting clients but not today. As Giles didn't represent a country and Francois did he had no option but to sign if he wanted the work. He did, so he signed blindfold.

That done Francois explained the background to the work as he saw it and how far their investigations had got them. Solomon did not say DDG was the last of eight firms to be appointed and the others had got nowhere. He gave Giles a copy of Mr and Mrs White's photographs. Giles didn't recognise them. Well, he might have recognised Tessa from his MI6 days but didn't.

'So we will only pay your company a success fee.'

'We don't work on success fees Francois.'

Francois leant over the table and picked up the paper he had showed to Giles and the confidentiality agreement they had signed. He didn't give a giraffe's balls which investigatory company did the work.

'No problem; I'll find another firm.'

'Wait a minute. I'll talk to my board and let you know. How much had you in mind?'

'Let's say £25,000 a head and double that if you get both. We'll pay cash too.'

Giles tried not to appear shocked and interested by such a large sum.

'I'm sure my board will agree. Will you still be in London tomorrow?'

Francois decided to show who was in charge. He would give the buffoon another chance solely because DDG had been in his father's contact list so they must be good at something despite this Giles Cartwright whom he couldn't stand.

'You can contact me through our embassy. Let the ambassador or military attaché know by five in the evening tomorrow if DDG can do it otherwise the job goes elsewhere. If you can do it you will be sent a copy of these.'

He brandished the papers he had collected from the table.

'They will handle all contact about this. You are not to try to contact me directly. I am too busy. If you do the deal is off. As I said I need a copy of those two's driving licences or passports from whatever country they live and before you get paid the Democratic Republic of the Congo will check you have got it right.'

Solomon left. He intentionally left the bill for Cartwright to pay and he didn't bother to shake Giles Cartwright's hand. He quite simply didn't like the man. It had never crossed his mind that others might not like him. In fact many more hated him than others did Cartwright but then if they had known Cartwright supplied the ammunition they might have both been equally despised for their involvement over the years in ethnic cleansing.

Solomon returned to the Savoy. He checked with reception to see if he had any messages.

'You've had these calls sir and there are two men in the lounge waiting to see you. They've been here over an hour sir. They gave these names.'

The receptionist handed over two visiting cards. Solomon recognised the firm they worked for and nodded his approval. The receptionist called over a bell boy who took Solomon to meet them.

Unbeknownst to the Burlingtons they were about to have yet another bloody slow motion train wreck on their hands.

Chapter 36
Tuesday 17th to Friday 20th December

De Wallen, Amsterdam Holland
Carl Hanson's new business plans were all falling into place and the money was rolling in like a sea tide night after night. His Black Barracuda brand was going down a storm in Amsterdam, Bangkok and Manila and his drug trafficking and blackmailing enterprises were growing steadily. Despite all this, he'd started locking himself in his bedroom and watching the horrific video of Khan and co being eaten alive by a cackle of hyenas. He invariably turned the volume to full.

Jordan was worried about his state of mind. Hanson's despondency resulted in Jordan traipsing round the world and running everything himself. Since he was already in charge and all the clubs' licences were in his name why did he put up with it? Why not simply eliminate Carl and take over the empire? The thought was just fleeting at first but lately it had become more and more entrenched in his subconscious.

The new club in Amsterdam started doing fast business in early December. An official inaugural opening ceremony was planned for New Year's Eve. Otherwise everything was quiet apart from an unusual contact on Tuesday 17th December. Smith had called and asked Jordan if he could meet privately with Sven Gustafson. Smith's unexpected request took Jordan by surprise. Sven Gustafson was his real name, something which was known to few people in the world. Not even Carl Hanson knew it.

Jordan was intrigued to know how Smith knew this name but he was also cautious. It could be a trap. He considered whether Hanson was reading his mind but dismissed that as paranoia. Obviously Jordan had told no one of his tenuous temptation to grab the reins of power so he wasn't worried on that front.

He decided to tell Hanson about the call, just to be on the safe side, but Carl wasn't interested. All he wanted was more cocaine. He responded by locking himself away with his ear-splitting and nauseating video. Was it all because the blood diamond from Kinshasa was cursed, just like the Koh-i-Noor?

Jordan called Smith back and said Sven Gustafson would be attending the grand opening of the club in Amsterdam on New Year's Eve. Smith asked how he could get in to the party as if he had never been to one. Jordan promised that an invitation would be waiting for him on the door provided he could prove his identity. Smith accepted. Jordan didn't care what identity he would assume. He could recognise him after having met him at Beachy Head.

Rosslyn Hill Camden, London England

Giles Cartwright was trying to close a large arms deal with Rhodesia that Tuesday morning and it was all going wrong. He called George Francis for help. George owned most of DDG and had already started his seasonal holidays in the Alps. Once they had discussed how best to land the deal Giles told him about his meeting with Solomon.

George was already on a long anticipated holiday and wasn't enthused by the length of the interruption. However, the rewards from the Solomon assignment were large enough to hold his attention after discussing the multi-million Rhodesian armaments: the margins on such big deals were small so the Solomon investigation was of interest. Nevertheless he was angry with Cartwright.

'Bloody hell Giles, you had better say yes just to see what you bloody well signed. Solomon's father probably drafted the damn confidentiality agreement so for all I know you might have agreed to donate a thousand AK47s to the Congolese army every month for the next ten years. Get it translated by our lawyers and let me know straightaway if there's a problem. I can hardly believe you could be that dumb.

As for this sort of assignment I don't think we should make a habit of doing business on a success fee basis even for these sums. From your track record to date we wouldn't have made one Swiss Franc. I told you there was no money in investigatory work. Let's hope I'm proved wrong although I really doubt that.'

'We could work on it when we have nothing better to do.'

'Ok then but this is the exception that won't break the rule. If we win that's great but if we don't it's the last job we take on a success fee basis. Agreed?'

'Agreed George. I'll let them know.'

'Ok and just out of interest fax me a copy of the photographs to my hotel when they come through if I'm not back by then. It might just be our lucky day.'

They carried on chatting about the Rhodesian deal as a couple of afterthoughts had come to George's mind and ended wishing each other happy holidays. Giles called the Congolese Embassy and spoke to their military attaché. He said his secretary would send the documents round by courier later that day.

Giles Cartwright didn't wait for them and left the office on a quick trip to Damascus trying to flog more weaponry to the Syrians. Early the next day he returned and was rather proud that he had successfully negotiated a deal without George Francis' input for once. On his return to the office late that Wednesday morning he opened his post which included a package from the Congolese Embassy containing the confidentiality agreement he had signed and the photos of Mr and Mrs White.

Chapter 36 - Tuesday 17th to Friday 20th December

He faxed the agreement to DDG's lawyers who must have thought him stupid to ask them after the event if it was alright to have signed it! He then faxed the photos to Francis at the hotel he was staying at in Switzerland before turning his attentions to the Rhodesian deal which looked as though it might ultimately alleviate some pressure from his ever watchful bank manager.

The City of London & The West End, London England

Wednesday 18th December was Sir Peter Stafford's last day at Porter Williams and he was clearing out his desk. George Franklin, his successor, decided there would be no extravagant farewell party in these austere times. Eighty of the London office staff had been made redundant just coming up to Christmas.

Sir Peter wasn't all that concerned about partying. He was already planning the sweeping reforms he had in mind for MI6 when he officially started in 1975. His coup with the CIA had already brought him greater respect than Sir Douglas Castle had earned in the preceding five years.

As for Castle, he was on his way to enjoy Christmas in Australia. He was looking forward to retirement with a generous pension and the money he'd saved. By now he was quite wealthy as he'd nothing or no one to spend his money on during his long stint in MI6. There would be no more anxiety attacks about the IRA, the Soviets or Sara Burlington.

Tessa had no holidays left having used up her annual leave to go on the African excursion with Hugh. From Wednesday 18th December right through the Christmas period she would be on duty much to Hugh's annoyance. Ed was coming home and would be spending time with the new love in his life down at Epsom and Hugh wanted himself and Tessa to be there too but that was not to be. He had planned to propose to her on Christmas Day but it would now have to wait until the New Year unless she made it to Epsom for New Year's Eve.

In any case, all leave had been cancelled by decree. That diktat was issued by Sir Peter because several authentic warnings had been received from the IRA and a bombing campaign over the busy shopping period was anticipated. As it turned out though Tessa could have New Year's Day off so she might be there to see the New Year in hopefully and definitely to attend the traditional New Year's Day Burlington family cocktail party.

Nothing was going to stop her making that because she wanted to see Edward again, even if her attentions were now firmly fixed on his brother. She also wanted to meet the new love of his life whom she had secretly researched with a little help from Sam Towers who she knew quite well. There was no debating Vivienne's beauty.

Apart from the cameo role he'd played in covering up Chad's activities Alan McKenzie was working almost full time on the ever increasing Irish coded warnings. As Christmas approached he increasingly thought about the conflict to put it in a religious perspective but he knew deep down inside religion didn't feature in the ongoing barbarism. How could it?

Chad and Jock McGrath were the only two officers under Mac's command who were to be allowed off duty at Christmas. Mac was office bound like most of his staff. Mind you, it didn't stop him calling Hamleys secretly twice or more a day to double check that his wife was ordering him the right equipment for Xmas. Last year she bought the wrong gauge of equipment and it had caused him no end of trouble to sort it all out. It was a shame Mac didn't run British Rail!

Daniel Luke's investigations into the activities of Cyrus Burton were progressing painfully at tortoise speed and had been downgraded. Sir Peter's new numbering system had already reached ABF192, so there were many new operations taking precedence.

They hadn't even started on Raj Gupta Khan's computer records because there were now only two part time people on that dead case. The festive season was in sight so who cared? Everyone was thinking about turkey, mince pies and mistletoe even if the firm's annual dinner or bash as most called it was the only Xmas fare most of them would consume.

The Downs Epsom, Surrey England
Sara and Roger Burlington were traditional once a year churchgoers on Christmas Day. By the Thursday before Xmas the house was busy preparing for the homecoming visit of Edward and Vivienne. Hugh would be coming down too. Christmas Day fell on a Wednesday.

Hugh was going to lock the shop shut from close of play on Saturday 21st until Thursday 2nd January. Scamp had already moved to Surrey in anticipation of the festive season and was looking forward to seeing snow on the Downs for the first time, not that he knew that! Sadly for him it was to be too mild for snow this year.

Sara was excited about the cocktail party and the whole shooting match what with Edward coming the weekend before Christmas and Hugh a tad later. Normally her Christmases had been full of mixed emotions, mired with memories of the Zola execution and Castle's abuse of her but this Christmas was different with Douglas Castle out of her life forever.

She'd have her family together if only for a short while and she was glad Peter was taking control. Her intuition told her his reforms would ensure her son's safety in the future. So far so good as she had at least been right about his intent.

TrumPeter Stafford was looking forward to the Burlington's cocktail party too. He was to announce that Roger was being awarded a knighthood in honour of services to his country. Roger didn't know about this. The award was meant to be a surprise for both of them. It was a thank you from Stafford's friends in Parliament where party loyalty was not the most important of allegiances.

Chapter 36 - Tuesday 17th to Friday 20th December

Sara's network of information sources was so well structured that little was kept secret from her or so she thought. Nonetheless, Peter kept Roger's impending knighthood under the wrapping paper. She didn't know about Edward's trip to Haiti or Hugh's visit to Africa either. Nor did she know her husband called the Hotel Carré Noir in Port-au-Prince. Maybe she was losing her touch.

Roger was not as upbeat as his wife. He had more sinister matters on his mind. One of those was that in the coming year Peter wanted to use Hugh's bookshop as part of an elaborate upmarket sting. Sir Peter's aim was to entrap foreign currency dealers who were laundering money for a particularly hostile African dictator called Muammar al-Gaddafi. Hugh didn't know about this yet and neither did Sara.

Ever since Sir Peter was briefed in outline on what Hugh did in the shop, including activities in the basements, he had been looking for an excuse to put it all under his command. As he had said to Roger at the time they agreed his appointment he couldn't allow him to continue to run MI99.5z.

In the coming year Sir Peter was to repatriate all the MI numbered departments Roger had been running with since the days when Peter ran MI5. Now Castle had gone some of them could even be disbanded.

Nassau, New Providence Island Bahamas

The pace of life in Nassau slowed to what a snail might have found frustrating during the crawl up to Christmas. The combination of parties, power cuts, more tourists than usual and the build up to Junkanoo reduced everything to the pace of a funeral march. A tempo that finally came to a complete halt on Friday 20th December when Nassau closed for Christmas and New Year.

Graham Sidney-Smith was notified by London that Sir Peter was stepping down at the end of the year. The new commander-in-chief of Porter Williams would be George Franklin, another longstanding senior partner. Graham was disappointed as he was just beginning to build up a good rapport with Peter and Franklin had already upset everybody by trying to keep the Caribbean offices open over the festive season.

There had been a near mutiny and it took a petition signed by all of Porter Williams' partners in the Caribbean to scotch the plan. All the political comings and goings in London were beyond Graham. He was happy as long as his offices were making money with no taxes to pay.

Edward and Vivienne Templeton flew back to Nassau a few days after he was discharged from hospital. They'd booked a flight to London for Saturday 21st and were doing some last minute shopping for presents.

Marco called Edward to let him know that Jazz had recovered from her miscarriage, her rehab was progressing well and that she had turned to religion. Edward was glad. He bore no animosity towards the woman he once thought he loved, even if she did try to kill him.

Marco also explained all about the Haitian trip. As expected Edward went ballistic on hearing of Louise Fournier's gruesome finale. He understood the law enough to know that Garcia was going away for a long time. Still, it annoyed Edward that he couldn't be charged with being an accessory to her murder and get a longer sentence.

The only piece of good news Marco had was that Graham Sidney-Smith was not involved in anything untoward with López or any of his minions. Indeed, as Edward hoped, Graham was on the other side fighting the trusts to hand back what had been stolen from the charitable organisations involved.

The only flight Vivienne could find to get them to the UK this late in the day was via Miami and Bermuda. At least they wouldn't have to change planes so Edward got Vivienne to use the booking trick he learned from Sir Peter's secretary. That way they'd have enough room for some fun and some sleep. It would be a long, slow-boat to London, but they'd have the pleasure of each other's company and that's all they needed.

They had done their Christmas shopping. Vivienne had already bought most of her presents in Miami including one for the most important member of the Burlington family. She had visited a dog parlour in Miami and bought Scamp some new videos specially made in the USA for pampered dogs to watch rather than get bored and depressed when home alone. After Xmas he could watch well known canine heroes like Tibetan Terrier Tim and Coco the Cocker Spaniel chasing each other through the long grass, learn how to look after puppies and even see snippets of Lassie films in the advertisement slots.

Mind you Scamp now virtually lived with Sara in the countryside. They both loved the outdoors and being together. Whether he had time to fit these new films into his busy schedule or if he would prefer them to watching lions on the Serengeti grasslands of Africa was debatable. Sara had discovered he hid behind the couch when he saw crocodiles on the attack so she had banned that particular video from Scamp's daily "must watch again" list of favourites.

※

Chapter 37
Saturday 21ˢᵗ December

Bermuda International Airport, Hamilton Bermuda

Both Edward and Vivienne drank heavily before resuming the flight from Miami. They slept most of the way to Hamilton until they were woken by the passengers preparing to disembark. The metal staircases were already being moved forward as the plane taxied to a halt.

The captain had been in constant dialogue with Bermuda International Airport for the last half hour or so. He was utterly confused by the seemingly unbelievable clap trap he was hearing from Bermuda. Being more accustomed to taking instructions, from air traffic control, than dishing them out to anyone, especially his crew, he had acquiesced subserviently to the unorthodox orders he had been given. The captain's voice came over the tannoy.

'This is your captain speaking. Can everybody please remain seated? Do not stand up or block the aisles. Thank you.'

As the doors opened, four airport security police wearing balaclavas and carrying submachine guns boarded from the front and stood looking along the rows of seats. Four more carrying handguns boarded via the rear of the plane. One of them walked to the front, looking left and right, until he reached Edward's row.

'Edward Burlington?'

'Who wants to know?'

'Vivienne Templeton?'

Vivienne grabbed hold of Edward's arm.

'You're both under arrest. Stand up and follow me.'

'What if we don't?'

'I'm sure, Mr Burlington, you wouldn't want us to use force on the young lady.'

Edward stood up first, with Vivienne clinging onto his arm. All the other passengers who could see watched as they were led off the plane, down the back staircase. The police took them to an in-transit lounge about a hundred yards away. Edward was indignant. Bermuda was a British Overseas Territory.

'What the hell's going on?'

No one answered him. They were taken into the transit area and told to sit on two seats in front of a dark green curtain that had been hung up in a hurry. Edward leaned across and whispered to Vivienne.

'Let me do the talking.'

The sudden sound of what he thought was submachine gun fire echoed round the empty room. He pulled Vivienne to the floor lying across her to protect her. When he looked up, Commander Mark Burlington was standing over him.

'Welcome to Bermuda Ed.'

Mark smiled broadly and stepped back as Edward jumped up and took a swing at his cousin. The punch didn't land and Mark held up his hands to signal surrender.

'You sod, Mark!'

Edward's cousin helped Vivienne to her feet.

'You haven't introduced me to this gorgeous lady. Where are your manners Ed?'

What Edward thought was gunfire was the sound of half a dozen champagne corks being popped. Edward introduced Vivienne.

'This hulk is my cousin Mark who is a commander of something-or-other, champagne receptions or whatever. I never know what you're in charge of you sod.'

'Maybe it is better you don't. Enchanted to meet you my, well all I can say is angel. Right, let's get these glasses bobbing up and down at once. We have less than an hour.'

Mark Burlington was a practical joker and a lady's man. Six foot four of solid muscle and a pair of light blue eyes that seemed to issue a light hearted warning on a flag which read "watch out, I'm about".

'Is this what you call a training session Mark?'

'That's what it'll go down as officially. Consider it an engagement present.'

'We're not engaged.'

'Alright, a Christmas present then.'

They talked about old times and the family and drank champagne while some passengers disembarked and others boarded for London. Mark took what had historically been the more traditional Burlington career if you went back to the nineteenth century. Mark Burlington started in the Navy where he reached the rank of captain. His maritime friends called him Nelson because the Burlingtons played a paltry role in the Battle of Trafalgar.

On a trip to Bermuda he fell in love, started a family there, got married and stayed put. Mark shifted careers and was now with the Bermudan police in charge of airport security and liaison with the US law enforcement agencies. He knew Leo Sanchez well as the US had a special office in Hamilton dealing with maritime insurance fraud. Mark was a close friend of Leo's or as close a friend as anyone could be to a career CIA officer.

Time zipped past and after an hour they had to re-board the plane in a hurry. Edward shook hands with his cousin and they promised each other to link up if they

Chapter 37 - Saturday 21st December

were ever in the same country at the same time and knew it. Mark hinted that there might be a good chance of that as he wanted to rejoin the Navy and move back to the UK to bring his kids up in what he defined as civilisation. He was looking for a cosy number in the Admiralty, not on board a ship or anything useful like that.

The other passengers looked intimidated as Edward and Vivienne took to their seats. The captain announced that it had all been a misunderstanding which had now been resolved. Even so, once they were back in the air, several passengers asked to be moved away from them. They were not alone in having been shocked by what had happened. The captain made sure, just as Captain Schwartzman had when leaving Duvalier International Airport, that his log of what took place was witnessed by two other members of his crew. He found it unbelievable but then he hadn't been told it was a practical joke dressed up as a training exercise.

It was not long before Edward and Vivienne found they had the whole back of the plane to themselves. It started to get dark so Edward removed the arm rests on their rows. They lay down together completely unaware of what they were carrying with them on the plane that was still several hours flying time away from Heathrow.

Vivienne was tired what with the champagne and the excitement of the stopover. Edward covered her with a blanket and she was soon asleep. He lay back and thought about the extraordinary year he had survived.

Would 1975 be as eventful? What chance had he of reaching George Orwell's nirvana, Nineteen Eighty Four? What on earth or hell lay in store for him and the rest of the Burlington family?

He should have damn well known better than to think that far ahead. There was still over a week to go to get out of 1974 and that might just prove to be difficult. Furthermore, he was on a plane and had no parachute.

But even before then Saturday 21st December was going to be a day all the Burlington family could never forget and not because Mark Burlington had played a practical joke on Edward.

Charing Cross Road & George Street Westminster, London

Hugh had locked up the bookshop. He was on his way to Montagu Square to meet Tessa and collect his brother's Jag in readiness for collecting Ed and Vivienne from Heathrow. He would have to leave at three in the morning but the thought didn't upset his mood that evening.

Ed's flat had been let but Hugh still left Ed's Jag in the nearby underground car park. Ed had paid the rent up front for a full year's parking in early April just before Sir Peter had told him he was bound for the Bahamas.

Before Hugh closed the shop he'd decided to add an extra Xmas bonus for his two assistants. He'd opened their Xmas cards to stuff some more cash in. It was the thought that counted. Their envelopes were now sellotaped shut. They looked about as inviting as some of the more dilapidated old books for sale in the boxes on the floor at the back of the shop.

Hugh was happy: everything was going well. Talk about bumper pre-Xmas sales. A rich American connoisseur, a regular catalogue customer, had dropped by for the first time in the flesh and splashed out over £15,000 on numerous rare first editions including a three hundred year old set of the complete works of Shakespeare.

It had been the best ever day in the shop's history. Sales had doubled the record high set in 1972. Every object d'art in the window had been sold as gifts and Xmas stocking fillers. Hugh had slashed their prices in the sale brazenly announced in purple on the shop window. The price cut had only been five percent but who could resist a Xmas sale. The notice was in purple as Hugh had no other paint and he and his two staff were far too busy gift wrapping their sales to even contemplate a lunch break let alone going out to buy a can of red paint.

Tessa was to meet Hugh in the Aristocrat for a swift supper before he collected the car for a quick getaway to Heathrow in the morning. She was working in that part of town so it was all rather handy. Hugh hardly recognised anyone in the pub which was only just beginning to get busy when he arrived at about seven o'clock that evening.

The Aristocrat had been Ed's local before he went to Nassau. Maybe there were no familiar faces because the brothers rarely drank there on a Saturday night. Not even the bar staff were familiar. He nodded to the landlord who was deep in conversation at the other end of the bar but saw Hugh enter.

He ordered a pint of stout and had drunk most of it before he made it to a table and picked up the left over paper. Hugh started to read about Lord Lucan's disappearance.

Tessa arrived accompanied by a colleague from work whom she introduced. They were both in an ebullient mood despite the long night that lay ahead of them. Her colleague's name was Liz, a raw recruit with just one week's active service under her bra, so to speak.

Tessa and Liz took over the table while Hugh went to get the drinks in. The girls discussed Lucan's vanishing act after Liz speed read the article in the paper. Hugh returned with the drinks, menus and a big kiss for Tessa. She looked up at him as he sat down beaming.

'Do you know I reckon Mac has spent more time studying the Lucan case than any assignment since Lacklustre? He's forever ringing George Simpson to get the latest gossip. You'll doubtless meet George one day Liz. He's a regular visitor from Special Branch. Mind you unlike many from the Yard he's a solid reliable type. I bet you Mac imagines he will solve the Lucan mystery for Scotland Yard and become a national hero, a modern day Sherlock Holmes.'

Liz looked surprised at Tessa's openness in front of Hugh.

'It's alright Liz, Hugh's signed up. Lucan's disappearance is a fascinating story though. I can see why Mac is so captivated by it all. He reckons Lucan went to

Chapter 37 - Saturday 21st December

Africa and was murdered in the deep dark jungle just as Edward might have been in Lacklustre.

It's a joke how many grown up men have so many silly theories about Lucan. George thinks he's in Switzerland. Sir Peter thinks he's in the Scilly Isles. They should have had a raffle on his whereabouts yesterday at the Xmas bash. Anyway, who cares? Here's to a happy Xmas.'

They clinked their glasses in unison.

'What was Lacklustre?'

'I'll tell you more later Liz but to sum it up in a hurried handbag Hugh's younger brother was abducted and saved at the last minute at Heathrow instead of coming to a grisly end in a deep dark African jungle.'

'Talking of Heathrow I have to pick him up with this Vivienne girl before half five tomorrow morning: a very nice start to my Xmas holidays.'

'Now Hugh, lose the self pity. At least you are off work.'

'True but if I am to be there on time I'll have to get up at three o'clock. Will you be back by then?'

Tessa was on the night shift not that she was a shift worker. They had a major operation on that Saturday night. She had to be at Century House by ten o'clock and would be back at their flat above the bookshop by about six in the morning.

Knowing it was their last supper together before Christmas Liz sensed she might be intruding so only stayed for the one drink and grabbed a sandwich on the way out. She left for Century House where Tessa was to join her shortly after supper.

They dined and had a few drinks with the landlord until Tessa told Hugh enough was enough as he was driving, so they left for the car park round the corner after wishing the landlord and his merry crew a very happy Xmas. He knew both of them well, gave Tessa a peck on the cheek and shook Hugh's hand.

They left the pub heading in the direction of the underground car park at about sixteen minutes past nine o'clock as recorded on the Aristocrat's CCTV. No one left soon after them.

According to what was later christened The Burlington Files that was the last sighting of Hugh and Tessa. They never made it to the underground car park. They, like Lucan, had simply vanished from the face of the earth.

Edward and Vivienne were asleep on the plane at the time: their nightmare was to be served up with breakfast later the next day.

Epilogue

Some forty years later on Wednesday 5th March 2014 I was with my son in a casino off Park Lane in London. He had arrived at a business meeting I was holding in what they called the "study". We were to have dinner once my guests had left and then return to Surrey.

We used membership only casinos for meetings because it made it difficult for anyone "uninvited" to follow those attending. Also, if I was meeting someone who wanted to remain anonymous he or she didn't remain anonymous for long.

After checking my guest's ID, security on reception, who knew me well, would email a copy of the person's passport to my office. Within half an hour I would have a reasonably detailed background report on the person on my mobile. Such information often gave me the upper hand in "anonymous" discussions!

My son had just finished reading the final draft of Beyond Enkription and was trying to find out how much of the book was true and what happened to the brothers and their partners after Saturday 21st December 1974. Inadvertently I had left my digital voice recorder on. That enabled me to reproduce a transcript of our chat. The relevant parts are set out ad verbatim below.

'So both those airport scenes were accurate?'

'Yes and they actually happened in the same month too. What's more the captains of the planes were related to each other but I thought if that was in the book no one would believe it.'

'How did you find out?'

'Mark told me. Vivienne couldn't believe it either because she thought she knew all the pilots but Mark showed us the flight log and his name was Schwartzman too. I suppose it was a bit of a mystery.'

'As you always say, coincidences happen, but what actually happened after Hugh and Tessa disappeared? What on earth were you and Vivienne carrying? You must have landed otherwise I wouldn't be here to ask you!'

'That's in the next book and anyway, if you'd read the synopsis properly you would have been able to make a reasonable guess.'

Epilogue

'Oh, well, I didn't have time. So what happened?'

'Read the synopsis on your laptop again. There's no way I am going to tell you here. One of the waitresses might overhear me.'

We both laughed. There wasn't one in sight but I remember he checked for bugs again under the table. It was a bad habit he'd inherited from me.

'I'll tell you in the car on the way back. Now let's order something should we.'

As we were finishing dinner my son's mobile rang. He had to leave urgently so we never had that car ride. Next time we spoke all I had to say to him was "Read on Macduff"! Mind you, he had no option: he was spending the night in a police cell for his own protection.

To Be Or Not To Be Continued, That Is The Question

Printed in Great Britain
by Amazon